Praise for Claire Lorrimer's novels:

Ortolans

'A sweeping saga of powerf[ul] [...]
house full of secrets'   [...] Realm

'A story of three women's passion and turmoil within
the house they love'   *Bookseller*

'A hefty romantic saga of love, mystery and romance'
                                          Bookworld

Last Year's Nightingale

'Matchless storytelling . . . a fine historical saga'
                                          Yorkshire Post

'Unashamedly romantic'   *Evening Telegraph*

'Gripping, vivid . . . a stirring tale'   *Bookseller*

The Silver Link

'Lovers of romantic fiction will love this book'
                                          Bookseller

'Yet another successful historical family saga – perfect
holiday read'   *Yorkshire Post*

Claire Lorrimer wrote her first book at the age of twelve, encouraged by her mother, the bestselling author Denise Robins. After the Second World War, during which Claire served in the WAAF on secret duties, she started her career as a romantic novelist under her maiden name, Patricia Robins. In 1970 she began writing her magnificent family sagas and thrillers under the name Claire Lorrimer. She is currently at work on her seventy-first book. Claire lives in Kent.

Find out more about Claire: www.clairelorrimer.co.uk

Also by Claire Lorrimer and available from Hodder

In ebook and paperback
Georgia
Ortolans
Last Year's Nightingale
The Silver Link

Available in ebook
Second Chance
The Secret of Quarry House
The Shadow Falls
Troubled Waters
A Voice in the Dark
The Woven Thread
Variations
The Garden
You Never Know
Deception

Beneath the Sun
For Always
Relentless Storm
The Spinning Wheel
Dead Centre
An Open Door
The Reunion
Over My Dead Body
Connie's Daughter
Never Say Goodbye
The Search for Love
House of Tomorrow
Truth to Tell
Infatuation
Dead Reckoning
The Faithful Heart
The Reckoning
Emotions

CLAIRE LORRIMER

FROST IN THE SUN

HODDER

First published in Great Britain in 1986
by Century Hutchinson Ltd.
With the title *Give All to Love*.

This edition published in 2015
by Hodder & Stoughton
An Hachette UK company

1

ACKNOWLEDGEMENT

The author and publisher would like to thank Constable and Co. Ltd. for
permission to quote from 'Romance', a poem by Lady Margaret Sackville.

A CIP catalogue record for this title is available from the British Library

Paperback ISBN 978 1 473 61303 4
eBook ISBN 978 1 444 75050 8

Typeset in Sabon LT Std by Palimpsest Book Production Ltd,
Falkirk, Stirlingshire

Printed and bound by Clays Ltd, St Ives plc

Hodder & Stoughton policy is to use papers that are natural, renewable
and recyclable products and made from wood grown in sustainable
forests. The logging and manufacturing processes are expected to conform to
the environmental regulations of the country of origin.

Hodder & Stoughton Ltd
338 Euston Road
London NW1 3BH

www.hodder.co.uk

For my mother who so loved Santa Clara

Family Tree of the
Costains and Monteros

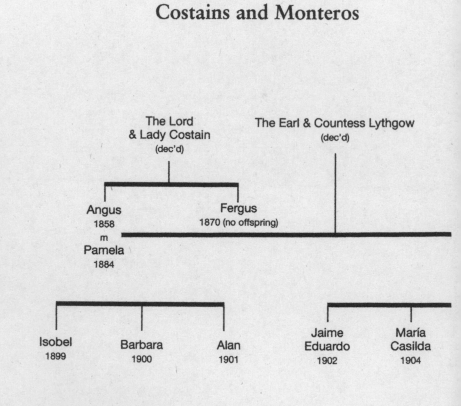

The Lord
& Lady Costain
(dec'd)

The Earl & Countess Lythgow
(dec'd)

Angus
1858
m
Pamela
1884

Fergus
1870 (no offspring)

Isobel
1899

Barbara
1900

Alan
1901

Jaime
Eduardo
1902

María
Casilda
1904

Jaime Enrique Montero
m María Casilda Leca } Marqueses de Fernandez de la Riva

Jaime Montero y Leca
1878
m Ursula
1883

María Concepción
m
Conte Guido del Castiglione

Luisa
m
Albert.Graf von
Lessen

Patricio
1905

Carlota &
Cristobal
1908

Luis
1911

María
del Carmen
1913

Mariano
1914

Amalía
1923

PART ONE

1909–1923

CHILDHOOD

. . . I am the moon, I am the sea;
I am every ship that sails
Trackless waters, knowing not
Where she steers.
I am the light which never fails; . . .

'Romance'
by Lady Margaret Sackville

CHAPTER ONE

September 1909

Don Jaime Montero, son of the Marqués de Fernandez de la Riva, dismounted his Arab stallion and handed the reins to the groom awaiting him in the hot dusty patio adjoining his country house, the Hacienda El Campanario. Both he and the horse were sweating profusely, and with a sigh of relief he removed his sombrero and allowed the cool breeze from the surrounding plains to blow through his thick, dark hair.

'It went well, the *corrida*, señor?' the servant asked as he threw a colourful blanket over the stallion's steaming flanks.

Don Jaime smiled, his handsome face lighting up with pleasure as he recalled the bullfight in Sevilla where two of his best beasts had put up very creditable performances.

'It went very well, José!' he said. 'I regret you could not be there. Vincente Pastor was magnificent – at his best. Francisco will tell you about it when he arrives home.'

It would be another hour at least before his head herdsman returned with the empty carts in which the bulls had been transported to the corral outside the bullring the previous afternoon. Don Jaime's friends had wanted him to remain in Sevilla to celebrate, but with a three-hour ride ahead of him he had declined. He could have stayed overnight at the family's house in the Plaza San Isidoro, but his wife and children were at the Hacienda and since Ursula was pregnant with their sixth child, he felt obliged to return as quickly as possible.

Ursula was English and had never really become accustomed to the isolation of the Spanish countryside. Elder daughter of an earl, she had spent her childhood in the luxury of their big London house. She had never become reconciled to the somewhat primitive conditions of the Hacienda, and the bulls he bred on his ranch terrified her.

Jaime turned now and walked through the archway into the courtyard of his home. Momentarily he was sheltered from the dying rays of the September sun by the arched entrance, on top of which was the belfry – the *campanario* from which the Hacienda had several hundred years ago derived its name. He had always loved the place. Spanish law decreed that on the death of his parents an estate such as this must be divided equally among all the surviving children. Jaime considered himself fortunate that since his two sisters had married foreigners, they had already agreed that he should buy out their shares in the property when that time came.

His arrival had been noted and the courtyard was a bustle of movement. A servant was placing a tray of drinks and a plate of olives and almonds on the table beneath the big bougainvillaea tree where Ursula was seated in a cushioned basket chair, her tapestry by her side. She had made the patio as English as possible. In the centre of a lawn of coarse green grass was a stone goldfish pond. A gardener was watering the grass, as he did every night when the heat of the sun was gone. Carnations, geraniums and roses which Ursula had had planted gave off a pleasant perfume, and Don Jaime greeted her with a feeling of pleasure and well-being.

Ursula looked cool and elegant in a lavender tea-gown that concealed most of her seven months' pregnancy. It was not her fault, he thought as he kissed her hand, that she did not look either passionate or sensual. The excitement of the bullfight had left him with a strong desire to end the day with the rewarding pleasures of a woman's body, but the mistress he kept in Sevilla was away in Madrid and was not, as was usual, at his disposal.

He sat down beside his wife and poured himself a glass of manzanilla. 'I am surprised to see you alone, *cariña*. Where is everyone?'

'Your mother and father are still resting,' Ursula replied in English. 'Nanny Gordon is changing the little ones' clothes. Miss Smart is reading to Eduardo.'

Jaime lent back in his chair with a barely concealed sigh. He could not abide the governess Ursula had recently imported from England; moreover the thought of his eldest son, Jaime Eduardo, pleased him little better. He was invariably irritated by the sight of this delicate, undersized child whose timidity was such that he was always to be found clinging to either his nanny's or his mother's skirts. Born prematurely, the boy had been close to death for the first few months of his life, and as a result Ursula had become obsessively careful of him.

At least he now had two more sons, Jaime reminded himself – Patricio and Cristobal, who had a twin sister. But by the time they had been born, Ursula had already presented him with his eldest daughter who, despite her sex, compensated totally for his disappointment in his first-born son. Casilda, not yet five, now outstripped her eldest brother in every field. Fearless, she could sit her pony without a lead rein where Eduardo would still not go near a horse. She loved nothing better than to ride behind her father when he inspected the vast acreage of his olive and orange plantations or the bull ranch. The child seldom grew tired and was happy chatting animatedly to the olive pickers or herdsmen whilst he stood discussing matters with his administrator.

Ursula had complained to him many times about Casilda. 'You indulge her, Jaime, and the servants follow your example. Nanny tells me the child is incorrigible and it does not surprise me since you forgive her every transgression.'

There was an element of truth in his wife's accusation, but Jaime had not the slightest intention of altering his ways. He adored his pretty, dare-devil child, and now he put down his glass and rose to his feet.

'. . . one or two things to see to . . .' he murmured, unwilling to admit that his intention was to go in search of his small daughter, who he had fully expected to greet him, since their love for one another was perfectly mutual.

It was ten minutes before he found her in one of the many stables where the farm carts were normally housed. Since this was in the middle of the olive-picking season, the carts were out and Casilda, with a young companion, had taken the opportunity to convert the building into a miniature bullring.

The children were too engrossed in their play to notice his approach and he stood in the shadow of the doorway, observing them with considerable amusement. His daughter, barefoot and only just recognizable beneath a coating of dust and grime, was charging round the bullring pushing a little cart on which was mounted a pair of carved wooden horns resembling those of a small bull. He vaguely recognized the boy as being the son of his *mayoral* – the all important overseer of his herd of fighting bulls. The child, a year or so younger than Casilda, was waving a piece of scarlet cloth in perfect imitation of a matador tempting his bull towards him.

Casilda's wild, uncontrolled charge with her little trolley brought a moment's apprehension to the watching man as he realized how easily the small boy could be hit – and hurt – were he not quick enough to avoid the charge. But the child stepped aside with remarkable skill, and involuntarily Jaime called out:

'*Olé, matador, olé!*'

The children ceased their play instantly at the sound of his voice and Casilda, dropping her cart handles, rushed into his open arms.

'Papá, Papá!' she cried, her big, dark eyes sparkling with pleasure. 'We are playing *corridas* and Benito is Vincente Pastor and now it is his turn to be the bull and I shall be Pedro Romero because once you told me he was the most magnificent matador of all! You must watch me. I have been practising all day. Jorge says I perform very well – *muy, muy bien*! . . .' She broke off to draw a long, painful sigh before adding reluctantly: 'But Benito is nearly as good as me. He says he is going to be the best matador in Spain, which I cannot be since I am a girl. Why am I a girl, Papá? I want to be a boy. Can you not ask our priest to pray for a *milagro* to change me to a boy? Don Alfonso says if we have faith in God, He can even move mountains. Will you ask him, Papá, *please?*'

Amused, and yet sensitive to his daughter's earnest hopes, he said gently: 'I do not think I will, *mi amor*, even to please you. You see, I love you as you are. You are a very pretty girl and it would be a terrible waste, would it not? Come now, show me quickly how you perform, my little matador.'

Diverted, the child leaped from his arms and ran to snatch the red cloth from the boy's hands. He had been watching motionless, silent, but with a grin on his brown face which deepened as Don Jaime winked at him. He had no fear of his father's employer who, everyone said, was a stern man but kindly and fair. Don Jaime became angry only if his horses or his magnificent herd of fighting bulls were mishandled, never blaming a man for a mishap that was not of his making.

'*Dáte prisa*, Benito, hurry yourself!' Casilda commanded both in Spanish and English, confusing the two languages as she often did when she was excited. 'I want to show Papá how good I am! You must be a strong, fierce bull. You are to forget I am a girl!'

Don Jaime leaned against the cool stone wall and watched silently as the children played, their movements perfect imitations of adult man and beast. This was no girl's game, and he knew his wife would object most strongly were she to know of it. But he had played such a game many times as a child and he knew the pleasure of it. Moreover, it pleased him to know of his daughter's interest, young though she was, in this particular hobby of his. It was his obsession to breed the best fighting bulls in the country.

His thoughts returned to the small girl who seemed to him to have few of his wife's characteristics. Casilda was all fire, passion and laughter where Ursula was cool, dignified and rigidly self-disciplined. His wife had borne him five children, but from a liaison which had never been more than dutiful on her part, and he wondered now how between them they had fashioned so exotic and wild an offspring as his elder daughter. Even Ursula, who disapproved of the child as forcibly as he himself loved her, admitted that one day Casilda would grow into a beautiful girl.

She would have to be found a rich and indulgent husband, Jaime thought with a smile as he carried her on his shoulders back to the Hacienda. But meanwhile, he wished her to enjoy the freedom of childhood a little longer. Soon enough, she would be constrained by the restrictions that must inevitably be imposed on her as she grew up. Listening to her bright, happy chatter, he could not now envisage her cooped up in the English convent Ursula was determined she should attend. A convert to Roman Catholicism upon her marriage to him, his wife was deeply concerned with their daughter's religious education and, since boarding schools were not *de rigueur* in Spain, she had made up her mind that Casilda should go to England – a proposal Jaime did not support.

Fortunately, he told himself as he handed the excited girl over to her governess, he need not worry about Casilda's education for several years yet.

'The child is quite filthy, Milady!' Miss Smart said disapprovingly to Ursula. 'And she has torn her dress. Really, Casilda, you look like a gipsy!'

Jaime grinned as he saw the brief play of emotions on his wife's face. She clearly supported the governess's opinion but knew from past experience that her husband would champion the child. Casilda knew it, too – the little minx! – and was clinging to his hand, gazing up at him appealingly.

'*Anda, niña!*' he said, giving her a playful tap on her bottom. 'Off you go and put on your prettiest dress for Papá to see at dinner. We will show Mama and Miss Smart that you are no *gitana!*'

With a laugh the little girl ran off, her stiff-backed governess in pursuit.

Jaime seated himself beside his wife and said placatingly: 'She is very young, *cariña*. Youth is too fleeting, is it not? Although when I look at you, my dear, I find it hard to believe that you are the mother of five!'

Ursula's thin mouth relaxed momentarily into a softer expression, although she was well accustomed to such facile compliments from her handsome husband, aware that they could slide from his lips as easily as did the harsh recriminations when his temper flared. Her sister, Pamela, had once asked her if she loved her husband.

'*I* would be quite mad about him if I were you, Ursula,' she had said with her disturbing candour. Ursula preferred not to talk about such things, but her younger sister's temperament was the very opposite to her own. She herself did not care to think about love – far less about sex. She was reasonably certain that Jaime kept a mistress in Sevilla, but welcomed the fact since it meant he came to her bed less frequently. Her husband's attentions never failed to sicken her and inevitably culminated in another pregnancy – a state that she felt reduced her to a level little better than one of Jaime's cows.

Pamela, however, envied Ursula, saying that she would willingly change places with her sister. 'Jaime is so romantic!' she proclaimed. 'And your life is so exciting, Ursula! You should try being married to Angus!'

Angus, Lord Costain, a full generation older than Pamela, was a dour, crotchety Scot who refused to participate in the social whirl of London society that his wife enjoyed. He spent a great deal of his time on his estate in Scotland, and it was many years since he had claimed his marital rights. This was not a subject Ursula cared to discuss, but her aversion to what Pamela called 'girlish gossip' did not halt her sister from talking quite shamelessly about her married life.

Sisters they might be, Ursula thought, but they resembled one another in looks only. Pamela, she considered, was a 'libertine'. Ursula had tried to persuade her younger sister to convert to Roman Catholicism, but soon realized that

Pamela had little or no interest in religion, whereas for her
it had become the mainstay of her life in this foreign country.
The family priest was not only her confidant but her constant
companion whenever Jaime was away. If her husband were
not attending bullfights in Sevilla or Madrid or Barcelona,
he was at the Coto Doñana where he hunted with the young
King Alfonso. Ursula had met the Queen, a pretty girl,
granddaughter of the late Queen Victoria, who had already
given the Spanish monarch an heir – a child now two and
a half years old and rumoured to be a haemophiliac. As a
consequence, Ursula and the priest had increased their daily
prayers of thanksgiving that her first-born, Eduardo, had
grown into a healthy, if delicate, child. He was a quiet little
boy who gave no trouble – unlike Casilda who was thoroughly disobedient.

Ursula was unaware that part of her aversion to her elder
daughter lay rooted in jealousy. She had to compete with
Casilda for Jaime's approval, knowing that from his affection
for her sprang his willingness to indulge her – a state of affairs
by no means common in Spanish husbands, who were very
much a law unto themselves. His parents, both elderly and in
poor health, lived with them. Ursula was disgusted by the old
Marqués's habit of falling asleep at table, but Jaime refused
to agree to her request that the old people should be kept
apart in their own rooms. He was a family man and at his
happiest with his entire family gathered around him.

That night, Ursula regarded his flushed, smiling face with
well-concealed resentment. She still found the late hour of ten
o'clock for dining did not suit her digestion. Whilst her husband
could eat with hearty enjoyment, she could only toy with her
food. Casilda, she noted, piled her plate as indecently full as
Jaime's. Without regard to her mother's oft-repeated adage
that children should be seen and not heard, she was chatting
between mouthfuls alternately to her grandmother and to her
father, monopolizing his attention as usual. Nanny was trying
to feed the twins, Cristobal and Carlota, who, at the age of

two, still chose to use their fingers in preference to their cutlery. Miss Smart, her little finger outstretched in the manner she considered to be refined, was chasing a quail's leg around her plate in rapt concentration. Only Eduardo and Patricio were free of Doña Ursula's resentment as she contemplated her family.

But the comparative calm of the meal was suddenly shattered by the arrival of Jaime's head groom. Clutching his sombrero against his chest, the man bent to whisper in his employer's ear. His face was indicative of his apprehension, as was the nervous twisting of his hands.

Ursula's head turned sharply as her husband sprang to his feet and stood glowering at his servant.

'What do you mean, lame!' he shouted in Spanish. 'The animal was perfectly all right when I rode him home.'

The groom's mutterings seemed only to increase Jaime's anger. He grabbed the man's arm and strode out of the room, his raised voice audible to the silent group at the dining table.

Casilda appeared to be the only one not affected by her father's furious outburst. In a high, excited voice, she said to her grandfather: 'José has just told Papá that Ramón, Papá's white stallion, has been found with a knife buried in his foot. José said it was not his fault because it is always Jorge who looks after Ramón.'

Ursula sighed as she signalled to the servants to clear away the dishes. The uneasiness affected them all, and her sensitive Eduardo more than most, Ursula thought as she saw him refuse the apricot tart which she had ordered especially to please him. It was almost a relief when Jaime came storming back into the room.

'*Maldito! Estúpido!*' he exclaimed as he paced the floor. '*Imbécil!*'

For once Casilda sat still, not daring to go to her father to ply him with questions.

He needed no prompting, however. His handsome face was distorted by fury.

'It's more than probable that I shall lose Ramón as a result of this idiotic piece of negligence,' he raged. 'Jorge swears that he replaced the compactum knife in the tack room the last time he used it, but you could see by his face that he was lying. He probably dropped it in the straw and didn't see it! How could it have got from the tack room to Ramón's stable by itself, I asked him? Knives don't walk! The bistoury was exposed and my poor Ramón must have put his weight fully on it. José found the confounded scalpel wedged beneath the shoe, and the point had pierced right through the frog. It makes me sick to think about it. It's out now, of course, and José has poured disinfectant into the wound, but blood poisoning will probably result!'

Now at last Casilda left her chair and ran to throw her arms about her father's legs. 'Poor Papá! Poor Ramón!' she said with genuine concern. 'Did it hurt him very much? Don't worry, Papá. I will pray for him.'

Jaime's face softened as he lifted his daughter into his arms. 'We must pray for his recovery,' he said, sitting down once more, Casilda on his lap. 'In the meantime, I have fined Jorge a week's wages and dismissed him.'

'But Papá . . .' Casilda's voice was filled with astonishment. 'You have always said Jorge was so good with the horses – and that one day you would make him head groom.'

Jaime's voice was stern as he replied. 'No doubt my praise of him went to his head,' he said coldly, 'and has resulted in him becoming complacent – and at the very least, criminally careless. I consider his punishment perfectly just. It is his misfortune that he has a young wife and family to support. He will get no reference from me if Ramón dies.'

Suddenly, the old Marqués spoke. 'There have been many people in the yard today, my boy. How can you be certain that one of them did not take the knife to the stable?'

'Who would do such a thing? And for what purpose?' Jaime said. 'Of course I am certain it was Jorge.'

'Why, Papá, *I* was in the yard with Benito and we . . .'

Casilda fell suddenly silent as her glance went to the bowed head of her brother, Eduardo. *He* had gone to the yard with her and Benito. He had not wanted to play bullfights and seemed content to remain on his own with the tin train he had been given for his birthday. He was going to mend it, he had told them, for it had a big stone wedged in its wheels.

Casilda's face turned a fiery red as she recalled perfectly clearly that she and Benito had seen Eduardo, a short while later, leaving the tack room and disappearing into Ramón's stall. She had thought nothing of it at the time, but now she knew that her brother, not Jorge, must have been the culprit.

She felt a thrill of fear as she realized how furious Papá would be if he were to learn the truth. He might beat Eduardo; he might even be angry enough to kill him! She felt Eduardo's fear as if it were her own. But at the same time she liked Jorge, who had taught her to ride her first pony, and it was not fair that he should be dismissed because of her brother's carelessness. Confusion was causing her to shift restlessly on her father's lap and he lifted her down. For a moment she lingered at his side, wanting him to know the truth and yet not wanting poor Eduardo to become the butt of his wrath.

Suddenly, the boy was sick. Nanny Gordon and the younger children jumped to their feet as the evil-smelling, undigested food spread slowly over the table.

'Poor Eduardo, poor darling!' Doña Ursula said.

Jaime drew a deep sigh of exasperation.

'Take the boy to his room, Nanny,' he ordered, as he beckoned to a servant to fill his glass. His anger and fear for his beloved Ramón were abating and now he felt only depressed. Not only was he in danger of losing his favourite stallion but he had lost his best groom. Not that he regretted dismissing the man. A man not to be trusted was not worth employing. No, he was well rid of him, even if he was the most intelligent groom he'd ever had. The fellow was head and shoulders brighter than most of the peasants from the nearby village and the men looked to him to solve their problems.

He sighed again as his wife instructed Nanny to put the little ones to bed. He informed her that he would finish his drink in the *salón*. Casilda could stay up a little longer, he added, smiling at his daughter. She would distract him from his unwelcome thoughts.

Don Jaime might have found it a great deal more difficult to dismiss his anxieties had he realized that the day would come when his dismissal of Jorge would bring tragedy to him and his family. The future seemed as secure for him, the future Marqués de Fernandez de la Riva, as it was precarious for his groom.

CHAPTER TWO

September 1909

'For heaven's sake, Nanny, he must be somewhere! Surely one of the servants has seen him?'

Lady Costain's voice was only slightly tinged with concern. She adored her only son, Alan, in her vague, detached way, but felt the children's nanny fussed over him far too much. He was, after all, almost eight years old and no longer a baby. Doubtless Alan had sneaked away somewhere where he could amuse himself without Nanny's endless cautions.

'It's getting quite late, Milady – and if Master Alan is out in the garden, he'll catch his death of cold. These autumn nights can be perilous and . . .'

Pamela Costain stopped listening as her thoughts turned to the Scottish climate, which she always found uncongenial. This huge stone mansion was never free of draughts even in summer, and the winds howled in over the moors from the Atlantic Ocean. Angus, her husband, seemed impervious to the cold and to the isolation of his ancestral home, and came to Strathinver Castle as often as he could, mooching around with a gun or a fishing rod or tramping the hills stalking some wretched stag.

Whenever she was able, Pamela remained in London in their large, comfortable house in Rutland Gate. There were endless diversions there to help her forget her growing conviction that she should never have married a man whose upbringing and interests were so totally opposite to her own. She had been very young when Angus had first proposed during her débutante season. Because he was wealthy and titled, her parents had persuaded her that it was a most satisfactory match, and that love would come with marriage. Far from it – her physical aversion to her elderly, ginger-haired husband had alienated her still further from him. Her two daughters, now nine and ten, had inherited their father's colouring, their white skin freckling at the slightest hint of sunshine and their eyes an unbecoming, watery blue fringed with sandy lashes. Alan was the only one of her three children who resembled her – his hair gold, and his eyes a beautiful hazel green.

'Yes, Nanny, I'm sure you're right. Tell Macpherson to send someone to instruct the gardeners to make up a search party. But I'm certain no harm has come to the boy.'

Pamela walked restlessly across the drawing room to stand by the tall, narrow window looking westward towards the sea. At any moment now a servant would come in to draw the curtains, for darkness was falling fast. She would get one of the footmen to light the fire, she thought with a shiver. Nanny was right – the autumn evenings here in Sutherland could be bitingly cold. She seemed always to be cold.

Ursula, she thought enviously, would doubtless be basking in the hot summer sun of southern Spain – that land of music, colour, excitement – with her stunningly attractive husband to fuss over her.

As she expected, one of the maids came in to draw the heavy velvet curtains across the windows, breaking her train of thought.

'Has Master Alan been found, Jean?' Pamela asked, the first real tinge of fear causing her to shiver as she realized how quickly darkness had fallen.

'No, Milady,' the girl replied. 'The bootboy said he thought he'd seen him down by the stables, but that was at three o'clock, Milady, and no one's seen the wee lad since.'

Pamela frowned. 'Tell Macpherson I want the house searched again, Jean,' she said. 'And I'll have this fire lit . . . the nursery fire, too. If Master Alan has been outside, he may be cold. Where are Miss Barbara and Miss Isobel?'

'With Nanny in the schoolroom, Milady,' Jean told her. 'Nanny said they were to have their tea at the usual time, no matter what.'

'Very well, Jean. That will be all!' Pamela dismissed the maid. For the time being, she thought, she would not report Alan's disappearance to his father. Angus would simply be irritated, for he hated being drawn into discussions about the children's upbringing, which he considered his wife's responsibility. If only he would show more affection for his children, she thought, as one of the footmen came in to light the fire – a vain wish when she knew very well that he was quite incapable of showing any affection to *her*. She doubted sometimes if Angus knew what it meant to be fond of another human being.

Although Pamela was correct in supposing that there was no love lost between Alan and his father, at this particular moment the boy wanted his father more than anyone else in the world. Alone, somewhere in the depths of a vast pine forest, Alan knew that he was lost. His legs were scratched by brambles and there was a painful weal across one cheek where a branch had hit him. But it was not physical discomforts which brought tears to his eyes – it was the realization that he would almost certainly have to spend the night alone in this alien place where, for all he knew, wolves would be lurking to attack him; or, worse still, the witches and ogres of his storybooks might at any moment appear in terrifying guise.

Crouching with his back against one of the large pines, the boy shivered. His jersey was not keeping out the cold. There were terrible noises everywhere around him, as if the whole forest had suddenly come alive. He tried calling for help but his voice sounded feeble, echoing forlornly around him and causing him further fright as birds flew up in alarm from their branches. If *only* his father – or someone – would come! Surely by now the household would have missed him and started looking for him? But commonsense warned him that no one had the slightest idea where he might be . . .

Rubbing his eyes, Alan thought back to the start of this disagreeable adventure. It had begun so excitingly when he had seen a fox in broad daylight steal one of the chickens raised by the lodgekeeper's wife and sneak off with it.

He decided at once that it must be a vixen taking the fowl home to feed her cubs. For as long as he could remember, he had wanted a fox cub to raise as a pet. Now he might find an earth, were he to follow the vixen. Quickly and stealthily, just as Willie, the head gardener, had taught him, he followed the animal across the field. He had been able to keep it well in sight until it disappeared into the outer perimeter of the pine forest. Certain that he would soon catch sight of it again, he hurried into the wood, looking eagerly about him. This was forbidden territory – a rule Alan thought unduly restrictive and quite frequently had disobeyed this summer.

Spurred on by excitement, he had gone deeper into the forest. It had been warm, soaked in afternoon sunshine and smelling of hot pine needles. He had heard the soft cooing of wood pigeons and occasionally he had glimpsed a red squirrel. Of his thieving vixen, however, there was no sign.

The discovery of a burn, silvery bright and filled with crystal-clear water, had proved yet another distraction. He had taken off his shoes and socks and paddled for a while, until he became aware that the bright floor of the forest was no longer visible beyond the tree trunks and that he was hungry. It was time he found his way home . . .

Only then had he appreciated the frightening fact that he was lost and might well not be found until daylight.

Now his fear increased as he heard the sudden snapping of a branch. His legs turned to jelly and his body froze into stillness. A second later, he heard another noise that could have been a bear growling or – far worse – an ogre coughing. Frantically he tried to recall the words of his bedtime prayers, but his mind was numb. Closing his eyes, he waited for the Evil Thing to strike him.

But there was no blow on his head, no vice-like grip

around his neck. Instead he felt himself scooped up by a pair of human arms and clasped against a warm chest smelling of pipe tobacco, wood smoke and fish. The next moment, a flask was held to his lips and a stream of fiery liquid ran down his throat, making him choke. He both heard and felt the rumble of laughter in the man's chest and at last found courage to look up.

Just for a fleeting second, he thought it was his father – the man had the same gingery red hair; but then Alan noticed that the stranger had a long, ragged red beard and that his face was tanned – like those of the gardeners and labourers at home. The clothes too, were those of a crofter and the eyes, although blue, were quite unlike his father's. They were twinkling as if the man was finding the situation funny. His fear now quite gone, Alan smiled back.

'I'm Alan Costain,' he said, 'and I'm lost. Can you help me find my way home, please?'

The man did not reply, but set Alan back on his feet. Only then did the boy notice how tall he was – much taller than his father, he thought as he gazed upwards. For the first time his rescuer spoke.

'Home tomorrow!' he said slowly. 'Come, boy!'

Once again, the man stooped and lifted Alan effortlessly, this time onto his shoulders.

'Are you one of my father's foresters?' he asked curiously as the man strode sure-footed through the trees. Alan heard him chuckle and felt him shake his head. Obviously he *could* talk, the boy thought, but did not do so unless he had to. The steady jolting of the man's body was rhythmical, and the rocking, combined with the tot of whisky, was helping to increase the child's fatigue. He allowed himself to relax, and for a little while he dozed.

When he woke, his companion was tucking him into a small truckle bed. A storm lantern on a rough-hewn, wooden table was casting a golden glow around the small room whose whitewashed stone walls looked primitive but clean. A peat fire burned cheerfully in an open hearth and a sooty black kettle was singing merrily on its trivet.

Alan's eye was caught by a shadowy movement beneath the table. A pair of brilliant green eyes stared into his, and for a moment he wondered if he could be dreaming. It was a fox – the one he had been following, he wondered?

With a thrill of excitement, Alan realized that here was his own dream come true – a fox tamed, as he hoped to tame a cub. He wanted to question his rescuer but there was no sign of him, and whilst waiting for his reappearance exhaustion overtook Alan and he fell into a deep sleep.

It was several moments after his eyes opened next morning before he could recall where he was. He lay listening drowsily to the strange noises around him. He remembered the fox but it was not to be seen. A big stew-pot was simmering on the edge of the fire, reminding him that he was intensely hungry.

He was about to jump out of bed to inspect the contents when he heard a voice that was instantly familiar. Astonished, he recognized the clear, high tones of his mother.

'Of course I'm tremendously grateful to you, Fergus, but I do wish you'd let us know sooner that Alan was safe. The whole household has been up all night; we were worried out of our wits.' Her voice trailed away as if suddenly uncertain. Then the door opened and, followed by his rescuer, his mother came in.

Alan allowed her to hug and kiss him, looking shyly over his shoulder at the tall man whom he now knew was called Fergus.

'Really, Mummy, I'm perfectly all right,' he said. 'Mr Fergus found me and brought me here.'

'I know, dear, but we *were* terrified something awful had happened. And it isn't Mr Fergus, darling. This is your uncle. He's Uncle Fergus.'

Alan's face must have revealed his bewilderment for she added: 'I'll explain on the way home, darling. Have you any idea, you naughty boy, how far you wandered from the house? It must be all of seven miles.'

But there was no reproof in her tone – only an immense relief – and Alan was instinctively aware that, if he said the wrong thing now, she might embarrass him by bursting into tears.

He climbed out of bed and did his best to smooth his tangled hair. He allowed his mother to take his hand, holding the other out politely to the man she had said was his uncle.

'Thank you very much for looking after me, sir,' he said. 'I . . . I hope I shall see you again . . .' But his mother was hurrying him through the door, saying: 'Come along, Alan. I promised your father I'd bring you straight home . . .'

Alan felt the man's hand lying briefly on his head, like a benediction; then the waiting groom lifted him into the trap and his mother was gathering up her skirts to climb in beside him.

Angus, Lady Costain thought uneasily, would not approve of her telling Alan about his uncle. But for once she was not prepared to consider her husband's wishes. Fergus may have saved Alan's life, and someone must explain to the child why his uncle was a family outcast. She did not want her son to hear Angus's version of past events.

'Your Uncle Fergus is your father's brother,' she said in a low voice, aware of the servant sitting on the driving seat in front of them. 'He was a young man, only twenty-five years of age, when he went to the Sudan to fight the Dervishes. No one is quite sure what dreadful things he witnessed, but he was sent home more or less in disgrace. There were those who called him a coward, but the truth was he was out of his mind. For two years he lived at Strathinver, in the east wing, spending most of the time under his bed. He never spoke to anyone and the doctors could do nothing to help him. The only person who could go near him was his batman, Hamish, who fed him and washed him and gradually nursed him back to some semblance of normality.'

She glanced down at the face of the small boy, wondering if indeed he could comprehend what she was telling him. He was silent, and after a brief pause she continued: 'Whilst your father was prepared to keep poor Fergus under his roof so long as he considered him a lunatic, his attitude changed as his brother began to recover his senses. It was not, you see, as if the young man had been wounded in battle. The damage was in his head – in his mind – and your father saw this as a weakness unbecoming to a Costain.'

'Father says our clan has been famous throughout history for the bravery of its warriors,' Alan said, frowning.

'Yes, dear, but Fergus wasn't being cowardly. He was ill. Anyway, he lived at Strathinver Castle for four years. By then, your father behaved as if he were dead. No one was permitted to mention Fergus's name and your father confined him to his room. Then one day Fergus disappeared. It was the night you were born, Alan. The house was in somewhat of an uproar and Hamish, your uncle's "guardian", had been sent to the village to fetch the doctor for me. Fergus took advantage of the lack of supervision and disappeared. Of course there was a huge search party sent out to find him. No one believed he could survive, and when after three months he had still not been found, your father was convinced he must be dead.'

Aware of the boy's rapt attention, she continued her story. 'Then your uncle was discovered . . . in the forest, Alan, where he found you. He had made a shelter – a kind of hut – and had somehow managed to survive – like a gipsy. I wanted him to come home but your father would not hear of it, and anyway Fergus did not want to come back. He was perfectly happy where he was. He had been such a terribly tormented soul, poor man, and was now at peace. But that winter he caught pneumonia, and when he recovered he was given the crofter's cottage on the cliff. He's been there ever since, living a hermit's life, although he does sometimes go fishing with the local Lochinver fishermen, and Hamish very occasionally goes fishing with him in the loch. He can talk now – although Hamish says he seldom does. The local people have accepted him – partly, I think, because whatever his mode of living, he is still the Laird's brother, a Costain. Fergus upsets them sometimes because he breaks up their rabbit and fox snares; he can't stand killing, you see. I think it's to do with whatever atrocities he saw in the Sudan. He seems to have an affinity with animals, and now, if anyone has a sick beast, they take it to him and, often as not, he's able to cure it. It's said he has no fear of animals, nor they of him.'

'I know, and it's true!' Alan burst out, his eyes bright with excitement. 'He has a tame fox and . . .'

'Alan, I know you are only seven years old and it may be hard for you to understand,' Lady Costain broke in quickly, 'but you simply *must* promise me not to talk about Fergus to your father when you get home. As far as Father is concerned, he's grateful to Fergus for finding you last night, but you won't be allowed to see your uncle ever again. You must promise me, Alan. Father would not permit you ever to . . . to become friends with your uncle – no matter how kind he was to you or how much you may have liked him.'

It was a long moment before the boy spoke . . . a moment in which he left the innocence of babyhood behind him and thought very carefully what he would say. It was not that he wanted to deceive his mother, whom he loved very much, but that he knew he could never keep a promise not to try to see his uncle again.

'I promise not to talk to Father about Uncle Fergus when I get home,' he said solemnly. 'Not then or ever after.'

Pamela gave a sigh of relief and smiled down at her son. The boy would very soon forget the odd-looking, silent stranger who had 'rescued' him. Besides, a letter with a Spanish postage stamp had been delivered to the house during her absence. It was from Ursula, saying that Jaime would shortly be coming to London for a few weeks and, if it was convenient, would bring the three eldest children with him. It was high time, Ursula had written, that Eduardo, Patricio and Casilda met

their English cousins. Since she herself was still suffering
complications following the birth of a stillborn child, she
needed to rest quietly at home.

'It will be very pleasant for Alan and the girls to enjoy
the company of their cousins,' Pamela said to her husband
after dinner that evening, omitting to add how pleased she
herself would be to return to the amusements and diversions
of London. 'You have no objections, Angus?'

He grunted his assent, secretly relieved that his wife did
not require his presence back in England. Impatiently, he picked
up his *Times*, and forgot his Spanish relatives as he gave his
full attention to the news. Lloyd George was a confounded,
rabble-rousing Liberal, he thought irritably. By the look of it,
he himself would almost certainly have to go down to the
House to vote against the Finance Bill.

He put down his paper with a sigh of exasperation. At least
Parliament was closed for the summer recess. He still had two
more months to enjoy some good shooting.

The prospect cheered him enormously. The unsatisfactory
state of the country's politics drifted from his thoughts, as did
last night's unnecessary fuss over his boy Alan, and the
disturbing reminder of the existence of his lunatic brother,
Fergus. As for his wife – he had already dismissed her from
his mind.

CHAPTER THREE

September 1909

'It's ever so good of you to let me bring Joscelin, Your Ladyship. What with it being Doris's day off and Cook gone to her sister's funeral, there wasn't anyone I could leave her with. Of course, my neighbour would . . .'

Lady Costain gently interrupted the flow of words that was threatening to overwhelm her and the little girl standing by her mother's side.

'Please don't concern yourself, Mrs Howard. Nanny can look after her, and she can play with my children in the nursery whilst we tackle the task in front of us.'

As the dressmaker spread out the pattern books she said hesitantly: 'Perhaps I ought to tell you, Your Ladyship – Joscelin's no trouble – no trouble at all but . . . well, she's not quite normal. I mean, your Nanny might think my little girl is being disobedient, but it's just that she doesn't hear what's said to her, and of course, being deaf, she can't talk. But you've only got to show her . . .'

Once again, Lady Costain cut short the flow of chatter, turning her attention to the solemn child who was gazing at her from large, grey eyes. Her hair, looped back from her forehead, was a pale, natural gold, unlike the brassy yellow of her mother's which was heavily waved and obviously peroxided. Again, unlike her bright, rosy-cheeked parent, the little girl was pale with high cheekbones and a delicate jawline. Though not pretty, there was something arresting in that trusting little face and, although not by nature very maternal, Pamela reached out and patted the child's head.

'Don't worry about her, Mrs Howard. Nanny will manage.'
She rang the bell and instructed the maid to take Mrs
Howard's daughter up to the nursery, and to tell the children
they were to be especially nice to the little visitor since she
was deaf.

With a sigh, she gave her attention once more to the dressmaker. 'As you know, Mrs Howard, I expected to be in Scotland
until Christmas, but now my relatives are visiting me in a few
weeks' time I shall need at least three new outfits for the
autumn. I am so pleased you could come at such short notice.'

Peggy Howard smiled. 'I promised, didn't I, that I'd always
come if I could,' she said as she leafed through one the swatches
of material patterns she had brought with her. 'I was thinking
on the bus coming here that it's all of ten years since I stitched
your first dress, Your Ladyship. Of course, neither of us was
married then . . .'

Lady Costain wondered if she would have to listen to this
story each time the voluble but efficient dressmaker came to
the house. The woman always talked incessantly whilst she
measured and jotted down figures – at least saving Pamela
herself the necessity to make conversation. There was little
she did not now know about the Howards, although she had
never met the quiet, hard-working bank clerk who, from all
accounts, adored his pretty, rather common little wife. He had,
so it seemed, married beneath him – which was to say that
Peggy Howard believed herself very fortunate to have married
'above her station'. Pamela wondered now if the little girl
resembled her father – she certainly bore no likeness to her
mother. How sad they should have a handicapped child, she
thought. But there was no need to worry about her today –
Nanny would be well able to cope.

On the third floor of the big London house, Elsie, the
nurserymaid, had arrived with the tea and Isobel and Barbara,
who had been sent to wash their hands, came back into the
schoolroom, whispering and giggling.

'That's enough of that, young ladies!' Nanny said sharply.

'You're quite old enough to know it's rude to whisper in front
of a guest. Now sit down and behave yourselves!'

She turned to Alan, who was already sitting at the table,
his attention riveted on the four-year-old girl.

'Stop staring!' Nanny said. 'How would you like someone
staring at you as if you were an animal in the zoo?'

Alan's mouth tightened. 'I wasn't staring at her. I was
trying to make her smile.' He tucked two fingers into the
corners of his mouth, stretching it sideways into a wide
grimace and, as the little girl's face was suddenly transformed
into laughter, he said triumphantly: 'There you are – she *can*
smile!'

'Her name is Joscelin and kindly remember it!'

'What a silly name!' Barbara said, grinning at her sister.
'I'd just hate to be called Joscelin!'

'It's not as silly as Barbara!' Alan shouted.

'There'll be no tea for any of you if you don't stop quar-
relling – this instant!' Nanny ordered. 'Now, bread and butter
first!' she reminded them unnecessarily. '*Then* cake and
biscuits!'

Hurriedly, the plate of bread and butter was handed round.
With the barest concession to good manners, the girls wolfed
down their obligatory bread and Isobel reached out for the
plate of biscuits. There were only three chocolate ones.

'One for me, one for you and one for Alan,' Isobel said,
adding spitefully, '*she'll* have to go without!'

'She can have mine, Greedy-guts!' Alan retorted through a
mouthful of bread.

Nanny stood up, her bosom heaving beneath her starched
white apron. 'I just don't know what's got into you two girls,'
she said. 'You've done nothing but quarrel ever since we
came back from Scotland. Anyone would think the three of
you had been brought up in a pig-sty. Put that biscuit down,
Isobel! Go to your bedroom, both of you, and stay there
until I say you can come out. Now pass the biscuits to
Joscelin, Alan.'

After tea, Alan felt obliged to 'entertain' the small, silent visitor since his sisters were not there to take on the responsibility. At least she could *see*, he thought, taking her by the hand and leading her over to the window where his pet canary was hopping from perch to perch, waiting for its customary sugar lump.

Suddenly, the little bird burst into song. Alan looked down at the child's upturned face. Her head was tilted sideways and it was perfectly clear to him as he stared at the entranced delight in her big grey eyes that she could hear the high, pretty trilling of the bird's song.

'Look, Nanny!' he shouted. 'She's not deaf at all. Joscelin's listening to my bird. She can hear him. Nanny, *look*!'

With a sigh, Nanny looked across the room. Her mind was on the domestic upheaval that faced her with the imminent arrival of the Costains' three small cousins, and she nodded her head, saying vaguely: 'Yes, dear, I can see!'

'But, Nanny, *look*!' Alan insisted.

By now the bird had stopped singing and the child's eyes were regarding him. There was a different expression in them and he was convinced she wanted him to make the canary sing again. But the bird could never be made to sing to order and Alan's elation evaporated. He knew Nanny had not taken in the extraordinary discovery he had made, but he was quite convinced that he had not been mistaken. Slowly, a grin spread over his face. He reached into the pocket of his grey flannel shorts and found his whistle.

'There now, Joscelin, just listen to this!' he said triumphantly, and blew a shrill blast which brought an instant rebuke from Nanny and Elsie, who had come in to collect the tea things. Alan ignored them, a look of elation on his face as he saw the little girl flinch and, when he blew a second blast, clasp her two small hands to her ears.

'I told you, I told you!' he shouted. 'She's no more deaf than you are, Nanny. You must go and tell Mummy. You must tell *her* mother. *I'll* go and tell them.'

'You'll do no such thing, Master Alan,' Elsie said as she piled the crockery onto her big wooden tray. 'Your mama has sent for Paget to drive Mrs Howard and the little girl home. She's to go downstairs at once, Nanny. Her Ladyship said to hurry 'cos Paget's got to be back in time to take her to the theatre. So she won't want no delays now, Master Alan.'

Disappointed but undaunted, Alan waited until it was time to go down to the drawing room to bid his mother goodnight. As she enveloped him in a scented embrace, he drew back and held out the whistle.

'I was blowing it, Mummy, and the deaf girl heard it. I know she did! Nanny wouldn't let me come and tell you. But I know the girl liked it. Can we send it to her? I wanted to give it to her, but Nanny wouldn't let me. Please, Mummy, can she have it?'

His mother patted his head affectionately. 'I'm afraid Joscelin is completely deaf, darling, and that's why Nanny . . .'

'But she *did* hear it, I know she did,' he interrupted. '*Please* let her have it, Mummy!'

With a little sigh, his mother took the whistle and laid it beside her cocktail glass on the sofa table. 'Very well, darling, if it's so important to you. I'll post it tomorrow.'

As Alan went upstairs to bed, he was only partly reassured by his mother's promise. He hoped desperately that she would remember. He just knew by the way the Joscelin girl had stared at the whistle and at him that she had heard it. No one seemed to believe him, but if *she* learned how to blow it, they would all know, like he did, that she was certainly not deaf.

Clifford Howard neatly folded the sheet of crested paper and put it down on the table. The contents of Lady Costain's letter had greatly disturbed him, and for the moment he did not wish to relate to his wife what news it contained. The bright golden glitter of Peggy's head was bent over her desk where she was writing out the week's menus for their daily cook. His daughter sat curled up on the window seat, and Clifford stared uneasily at his child's thin, straight back. He sighed, wondering if there was any point in reading the letter again. 'My son insists your little girl could hear his whistle and, although Alan was probably mistaken, I promised him I would send this letter and his whistle to you . . .'

What does a little boy know about such things? Clifford Howard asked himself. He must be out of his mind allowing his hopes to rise on so slender and unlikely a reason. Yet just for a moment, he had hoped. There *had* been a time, after all, when little Joscelin was no different from other babies of her age. At one she had spoken her first few words; at two she had been stringing a few words together. But then she had tumbled down a flight of stairs and had seriously damaged her eardrums. There was nothing at all they could do, the doctor had informed them. Perhaps in time nature would repair whatever damage had been done . . . but they should not entertain any false hopes.

His beloved, cheerful Peggy had adapted to the circumstances, but he had found it less easy to accept the fact that his child was handicapped. He loved his baby girl almost as much as he adored his wife. He had so looked forward to the years when Joscelin was growing up and they could discuss things together, for real conversation was the one thing lacking in his otherwise happily married life.

But his little daughter, though deaf and consequently mute, seemed happy enough, finding a quite extraordinary pleasure in drawing and colouring. Even at the age of three, she had been able to reproduce recognizable objects with her pencil.

With the whistle in his hand, Clifford stood up and went across to the window seat. The child cuddled up to him as he sat down and put his arm around her.

Two wide grey eyes stared into his as if trying to read his thoughts. He attempted a smile but knew that he had failed. As if seeking for something to divert him, Joscelin reached for the whistle he was holding in one hand and put it to his lips.

Clifford's heart jolted. 'You want me to blow it, do you, Poppet?' he said, his excitement intense as he blew a short blast. Joscelin bounced up and down on the padded cushion and urged him with hand movements to repeat the action. When he did so, small gurgles of pleasure came from her mouth.

It can't be! he told himself, trying to keep his emotions under control. It's just coincidence! Miracles don't happen to ordinary people like us . . .

But by the fifth blast of the whistle, he was in no doubt that Joscelin could hear, and when his wife came over to ask what on earth he thought he was doing, he was unable to answer her for the lump that had gathered in his throat.

'Peggy, she can hear! She really can hear!' he whispered huskily, and whilst Joscelin laughed and clapped her hands, he blew the whistle again.

Two weeks later, he sat down and wrote to Lady Costain in his neat, precise script.

My wife and I will be indebted to you for the rest of our lives. We took Joscelin to an ear specialist yesterday and he has confirmed that she can hear – at least the sounds on high register. He believes that when she fell downstairs eighteen months ago she probably burst her eardrums, and that now they are beginning to heal. In time she may well be able to hear sounds at lower registers, and he has given us every reason to hope that, with elocution lessons, Joscelin will eventually learn to talk normally. He called it a stroke of fortune that we had discovered these first signs of recovery so soon, since at this young age the child can still be taught words and sounds, whereas had a few more years passed, she would have found it far harder to achieve normal speech.

Mrs Howard and I both know that it was no 'stroke of good fortune' but your little boy who brought this about, and we are hard put to find words to thank you.

Joscelin will not part with the whistle your son so kindly

gave her, but I have this morning posted a new one to him together with a little gift I trust you will permit him to accept.

Yours very respectfully,
Clifford Howard

'Now isn't that nice!' Lady Costain said as she regarded her son's delighted face. 'You've always wanted a real penknife – though goodness knows what your father will say! It looks quite lethal. You must write and thank Mr Howard, Alan. I suppose I'd better write too. I can mention that convent school where your aunt is going to send her girls. I'm sure Ursula said something about them being able to have elocution lessons with the nuns. Anyway, dear, run along and write your letter. It can go in the envelope with mine. Are you listening to me, Alan, or are you only interested in that fearsome-looking knife?'

Alan snapped in the blade and slipped the knife into his pocket. He was whistling cheerfully and swaggering a little with secret pride as he dug his hands into his snake belt and went out of the room.

CHAPTER FOUR

1913–1914

There was nothing to suggest that the two little girls in their clean white pinafores squatting on the nursery floor were sisters. The elder child, Casilda, had her father's dark Spanish colouring and, at the age of eight, bore an uncanny resemblance to him. Six-year-old Carlota was in marked contrast, her pale, delicate face framed by soft, silky hair so fair that it was almost white. She was staring at her sister with solemn blue eyes made larger than ever by her expression of fascinated horror.

Carlota's reluctance to part with the precious musical box Papá had brought her from Paris had just been severely undermined by Casilda's threat . . . 'If you won't give it to me, I shall tell the *bruja* to come and get you!' Despite their governess's firm insistence that there were no such things as witches, neither Casilda nor Lota doubted their existence. The servants, too, feared them and even Papá, who was the bravest, strongest man she could think of, was not prepared to concede that witches and warlocks were only Andaluz superstitions.

Silently, Lota handed over the little gilt box. From past experience she knew better than to run to her mother or their governess, for although they would undoubtedly have punished her sister for frightening her, Casilda would threaten once more to send the witches to get her when she lay in bed at night. As Casilda pointed out, they would whisk her out of the bedroom window with no one any the wiser until the morning when they found her bed empty, and by then it would be too late.

Casilda, now playing with the coveted musical box, was happily ignorant of the fact that her victory over her younger sister was this time to be short-lived. That night Carlota's nightmares began. So violent were they that she woke soaked through with perspiration, her hysterical screams continuing long after the older members of the household had come to her room in an attempt to quieten her.

Carlota was put to sleep with the governess, who quickly discovered the cause of the child's nightmares.

Although Don Jaime did not approve of Casilda's methods of obtaining what she wanted, he was none the less secretly amused by his daughter's tenacity. But there was little amusement in Doña Ursula's eyes as she surveyed her husband.

'Casilda cannot be allowed to disrupt our lives any longer, Jaime,' she said in a cold, hard tone with which he was more than familiar.

'Casilda is only eight years old, *cariña*,' he said now, hoping to placate his wife: 'She is high-spirited and . . .'

'And thoroughly spoilt as well as disobedient. Miss Smart tells me she is quite unable to control her.' Ursula's mouth tightened as she said emphatically: 'I have made up my mind, Jaime, I am sending her to the convent in England where Pamela's girls are doing so well. The child will get a good Catholic upbringing, a sound education, and she'll learn a much purer English than she would here at the Convent of the Irlandesas.'

Don Jaime frowned. 'To send a little girl abroad . . .' He broke off, unable to express the deep feeling of distress his wife's proposition had aroused in him. He had but to enter the house for Casilda's small, vibrant figure to come rushing towards him; and probably the only time she sat quietly was when she curled up on his lap, her arms around his neck, her glowing little face pressed against his cheek. To lose his eldest daughter would be to lose a lot of the sunshine in his life.

But with the birth of yet another child not eight weeks distant, he decided not to argue the matter of Casilda's banishment for the time being. However, after the baby's birth early the following spring Ursula was far from well, and became so hysterical in her determination to be rid of Casilda that Don Jaime saw no alternative and arranged for his beloved daughter to be escorted to her aunt's London house by the triumphant Miss Smart. She was to commence her education at the Convent of the Sacred Cross in the Lent term.

On the morning of Casilda's arrival in London, Lady Costain received an unexpected letter from Peggy Howard saying that she and her husband had decided to board their little girl at the Convent.

'I must remember to ask Barbara and Isobel to keep an eye on the poor little thing, Nanny,' she said. 'It will be quite a step for the child. Perhaps I should offer them some of the girls' cast-offs, though I don't want to offend the Howards.'

Far from taking offence, Peggy Howard was impressed by her former employer's thoughtfulness.

'Now isn't that nice of Her Ladyship,' she said as she sorted through the blazers and gym slips with a practised eye. Her smile faded as she saw the look of apprehension on her daughter's face. The child's lack of enthusiasm at the prospect of boarding at the Convent brought back all her own misgivings.

'Run upstairs and tidy your room, dear,' she said firmly, and as soon as Joscelin had left, she turned to her husband, her eyes full of tears.

'Oh, Clifford, do we *have* to send her away?' she asked. 'Are you *sure* we're doing the right thing?'

Clifford put down his newspaper and laid a comforting arm around his wife's shoulders. As he had done so often recently, he recalled his meeting with the ear, nose and throat specialist who, in the past four years, had helped his little daughter back to normality. Her progress had been quite astonishing. Her hearing, according to Mr Sargent, was now eighty per cent normal. Following this good news, Clifford had wondered why the specialist had asked to see him so specifically on his own. In the nicest possible way, Mr Sargent had explained that Joscelin was unlikely to make further progress unless she was removed from the protected environment in which Peggy, in an excess of maternalism, was imprisoning her, nor, indeed, would her speech improve whilst her mother did all the talking for her. At boarding school, Mr Sargent had pointed out, Joscelin would be obliged to stand on her own feet.

Clifford looked now at his wife's unhappy face and said gently: 'Joscelin has been attending lessons at the Convent for the past two years, and academically she is only a year behind her contemporaries. She will soon make friends, and before we know where we are she will be home again for the Easter holidays.'

'That's not for three whole months, Clifford,' Peggy wept against his shoulder. 'Whatever will I do without her?'

Three whole months seemed an eternity to Joscelin too, as she completed her first day as a boarder – a day of confusion with a never-ending stream of girls, nearly all older and bigger than herself, talking, laughing, staring. And the nuns, few of whom she had met before, giving her instructions: 'You're in cubicle four in St Catherine dormitory . . . Evelyn will show you where to put your things . . . You may not be excused during class, so make sure you go before the bell rings . . . If you disobey the rules, you'll be given an order mark. Three bad marks and you will be punished by the Mother Superior . . .'

Joscelin was hopelessly confused and desperately homesick, a lump coming into her throat each time she thought of her mother's tearful face and drooping shoulders as the huge convent door had clanged to, shutting her parents away from her.

She cried herself to sleep, a state of oblivion which came mercifully quickly as a result of nervous exhaustion. But sleep did not come so easily the second night. It was forbidden to talk once the dormitory nun, Sister Agnes, had turned down the gaslights above the ten cubicles that filled the room. Feverishly Joscelin tried to go over in her mind all the rules she had been taught in the last two days. She was on the point of tears when suddenly she became aware of a head appearing over the partition dividing her cubicle from the one beyond.

'You're new, aren't you? I also am the new girl. Wait there!' the voice commanded, as if Joscelin had been contemplating leaving the comparative security of her bed. A moment later, a small dark figure in a warm dressing-gown came through the curtains and snuggled down under the eiderdown at the foot of Joscelin's bed.

'You're Joscelin, no? I'm the Spanish girl who sits beside you in class, yes?' Despite the dimness of the room, Joscelin had a vivid picture of the dark-haired girl of about her own age who that morning had daringly drawn everyone's attention to herself when the pencils and exercise books were being distributed.

'You have given me a green pencil and I want a red one,' the foreign girl had complained to the Sister in charge in a strange accent. 'I would like also a pencil with a rubber on the end.'

The class had held its breath while Sister had admonished the new girl, not only for speaking without permission but for daring to raise an objection. Terrified, Joscelin had heard the nun's cold voice demanding the new girl's name.

'María Casilda Francisca Ursula Montero y Lythgow.'

The confident, imperious little voice had brought forth a titter from the other girls and a tightening of Sister's mouth. Only the fact that the Spanish girl was new had saved her from an order mark.

'I don't like this school, do you?' Joscelin's visitor said now. 'Can you imagine that they send us to bed at nine o'clock! Why, in my home we are preparing for the evening meal at this time. It is *absurdo, ridículo*! You do not wish to sleep, do you? We shall talk and become friends.'

It was the beginning of a lifelong friendship between the two little girls.

Both were by way of being 'oddities', Casilda because she was Spanish and spoke with a foreign accent, Joscelin because those early years of her deafness had left her speech impaired. Whilst the other girls readily accepted one of their own kind, they were suspicious of anyone who did not appear to be the same. Nor was it long before it was noticed that Joscelin came from a different background. Nearly all of them were from wealthy homes and many had titled parents; all were accustomed to large households of servants and had the self-confidence that Joscelin lacked. Moreover, they were for the most part Roman Catholics, looking down on her always as if her Protestant faith made her a 'pagan'.

Casilda seemed not to care whether the other girls accepted them or not. '*Me importa un bledo!*' she said, shrugging her shoulders. 'Why should we care about them? They are *estúpidas* . . . stupid! and I certainly do not mind that you are poor.'

Although Joscelin longed to acquire Casilda's indifference to the opinions of their classmates, she remained embarrassed by her social inadequacies. Painfully she learned not to say 'Pardon' as her mother had taught her; she learned not to start eating before everyone else at table had been served – so contrary to her mother's admonition to eat her food quickly before it became cold. She discovered that she was the only one who did not have a pony; whose home did not have a tennis court, a big car, a chauffeur, maids to wait on them. Casilda's English relations, too, appeared to have all these advantages. In her extrovert way, Casilda chattered about them incessantly.

'My aunt is very nice but I do not like my mamá at all. She is almost as – how do you say? – ghastly as Tío Angus. Tía Pamela is very beautiful and kind and I love her very much. Maybe I shall go to Scotland with my cousins in the summer holidays. Tío Angus has a castle there where he goes shooting like Papá. We do not have a castle. We have a *casa palacio* in Sevilla and an old *palacete* in Madrid and of course the Hacienda where my father breeds fighting bulls. You must come and stay with me. It will be warm and sunny there now. If we were at home now we would go to the Hacienda and I could show you the bulls. I could teach you to ride, too.'

It never ceased to surprise Joscelin that this astonishing Spanish girl had chosen her to be her Best Friend. They called each other Joss and Cassy, and invented a sign language which only they understood.

As the weeks passed, Joscelin gained enough confidence to join in her friend's never-ending pranks. She even dared to visit Cassy's cubicle, which was strictly against the rules and if one were discovered, meant instant dispatch to the Mother Superior – even a chance of being expelled.

'I don't care if she does expel me!' Cassy declared with a hint of bravado. 'She cannot send us to Hell, only God can do that. Anyway . . .' she added more cheerfully, 'I shall confess all my sins on Friday and I shall be absolved.'

It was all very well for Cassy, Joscelin thought. As a Protestant, she herself could not seek the comfort of the Confession nor receive the easy forgiveness of a vengeful God by the repetition of a few Hail Marys. Yet this awesome Being whose All-Seeing Eye was aware of every misdeed was far less important to Cassy than her father, whom she adored.

'If Mamá dies, I shall marry him,' she declared. 'I don't wish to be a Bride of Christ like Sister Agnes.'

Joscelin would not have believed at the start of her first term that it would ever be possible to long for the start of the next. She had wanted then only to be home again in the cosy intimacy of their suburban house; and yet, by the middle of the Easter holidays, she was fretting for Cassy's company. Her mother's pleasure in having her home, the shopping expeditions and the treats such as the Mary Pickford film and tea in the big Lyons Tea Shop at Marble Arch, somehow lacked the excitement of sharing things with her Best Friend. Cassy so often made her laugh, and she herself seemed to amuse the Spanish girl with the little caricatures she found so easy to do – the one of Mother Superior looking like a big black crow;

another of the haughty Barbara Costain looking like a carrot.
But surprisingly quickly, the Easter holidays came to an end.
Although Joscelin had little to report, there was no lack of
fascinating news from Cassy. Her beloved papá had taken her
to her first bullfight.

'Mamá was very angry. She doesn't approve of girls going
to bullfights, but Papá knew how much I wanted to go. The
corrida was *estupenda, magnífica*,' she cried forgetting to lower
her voice. 'I cannot describe it to you, Joss. I tried to tell my
brother, Eduardo, but he is so silly – like a stupid girl. Once
when one of the *peones* cut his leg, Eduardo fainted because
of the blood. Papá says that perhaps English school will make
a man of him, but I doubt it. He is going to Downside soon.
Now he goes to what we call a preparation school with my
Cousin Alan. He is also eleven like Eduardo, and when my
brother Patri is old enough, he will come to England to school
too.'

Cassy, Joss discovered, had four brothers and a sister, and
as well her three English cousins, the Costain children, she
had aunts and uncles dotted all over Europe. Joscelin, whose
grandparents were dead and whose only aunt had married a
Canadian and lived in Toronto, envied the Spanish girl her
varied and exciting relations. Perhaps most of all she envied
her her sister, Carlota. But for Cassy, Carlota seemed to hold
little importance.

'We aren't in the least alike,' she dismissed Lota casually.
'She's too serious about everything, and I never have fun with
her the way I do with you. I think she should come to the
Convent with us, but she says she won't leave home. She's
quite soppy about the new baby, Luis, and cuddles him for
hours.'

She told stories of the exciting life she led, taking its exotic
fascinations quite for granted as she prattled on about fiestas
and bullfights; of parties with family friends and relations,
many of them dukes and marquises. As if it were of complete
indifference to her, she would refer to the King of Spain as

one of her father's friends, important only because he had sent her a beautiful lace fan for her birthday.

The long summer term cemented their friendship. Both girls were now accepted by their contemporaries and even looked up to as natural leaders by the younger ones. Joscelin was no longer derided for being odd man out. The credit for this she gave entirely to Cassy. Since the day Cassy had physically attacked a classmate who was imitating Joscelin's halting speech, the girls had ceased to make fun of her.

Cassy, Joscelin thought, was the bravest person she knew. She would never forget how appalled she had felt, how embarrassed, when one of the seven-year-olds had been refused permission to leave the classroom. A puddle had formed beneath the girl's chair and she had sobbed as the nun berated her for her 'disgusting' lack of control and given her an order mark. Cassy had jumped to her feet and shouted:

'That's not fair. She couldn't help it. She held up her hand twice but you wouldn't let her be excused.' She lapsed into Spanish: 'Qué injusticia!' The nun had withdrawn the order mark from the offending girl and given it to Cassy instead.

Joscelin feared that she would never be able to match her friend's courage, but shortly after the half-term break Cassy invented a new game. To relieve their boredom one night when they were unable to sleep, she rolled up her vest and tossed it over the dividing partition for Joscelin to catch. It was a good game since it could be carried out in silence.

Inevitably, a high throw from Cassy resulted in the rolled-up vest becoming entangled with the gas mantle. Horrified, Joscelin looked up at the smouldering garment. Not even if she stood on her bedside locker could she hope to reach it. It was only a matter of minutes before Sister Agnes became aware of the smell of singed wool and came sailing down to investigate.

At the very least they could expect order marks, but it would be Cassy's ninth that term. Cassy might declare that she did not mind one jot if she were expelled, but Joscelin could not bear the thought.

She jumped out of bed, her courage almost failing her as she confronted Sister Agnes. Her heart thumping furiously, she stammered out the lie – it was *her* vest; she had been trying to throw it into Cassy's cubicle in order to wake her; it was all her fault . . .

'BE SURE YOUR SINS WILL FIND YOU OUT' was the text on the sampler Joscelin had been given in sewing class this term; but for once, she said later to Cassy, God's All-Seeing Eye must have been looking elsewhere, for no obvious sign of damnation was forthcoming. She received an order mark and a severe dressing-down from Sister Agnes – both punishments a million times worthwhile, Joscelin thought, as Cassy applauded her bravery.

'Let's make a pact that as long as we live we'll help each other when we're in trouble,' Cassy enthused. 'My brother Patri says people can become blood brothers if they mix their two bloods together. Let's do it tomorrow at lunchtime. No one will see us if we do it under the table. I'll dare if you dare and we'll make ourselves blood sisters for ever and ever.'

From then on, Joscelin allowed her natural sense of fun to override caution and became as much an instigator as Cassy of any mischief that was afoot. But at the end of the summer term both girls were told to report to the Mother Superior. She looked at them through her steel-rimmed spectacles – a piercing gaze that was more than sufficient to strike terror into the hearts of even the most senior girls.

'It has been decided by your teachers that your examination results justify you being moved up two forms so that you are with your own age group,' she announced. 'I have agreed to this against my better judgement. You, Casilda, have the highest number of order marks ever held in any term – a most shameful record which will cause deep distress to your parents when they read your report. As for you, Joscelin, you appear to have ignored the opportunity Our Lord has given you to hear and to speak His good words and have chosen instead to express yourself in the most malicious, wicked manner by your pen.'

She withdrew three sheets of paper from the drawer of her desk – papers which Joscelin recognized instantly as coming from her sketchbook. Why hadn't she torn them up, she asked herself as the caricatures were thrust in front of her. Mother Superior's voice was heavy with sarcasm as she said: 'These cruel distortions of the nuns who have done so much to help you may have earned you a certain popularity with your classmates. But your hand has been guided by the Devil, and I shall have no hesitation in expelling you if one of these disgusting abuses of your talent is ever again brought to my notice. I have no alternative but to tell your parents of my deep concern that you are corrupting the minds of the Catholic girls in my charge.'

Slowly, methodically, she tore the drawings into tiny pieces and dropped them into the waste paper basket. Straightening her wimple, she added: 'It is to be hoped that next term you will behave in a manner more befitting your age. I shall leave it to your parents to punish you adequately when they receive your reports.'

Don Jaime Montero regarded his favourite daughter with approval. Each year she seemed to grow prettier and more vivacious, and with a shrug he tore up Casilda's report before his wife could see it. All nuns, he thought, were bigoted, dried-up spinsters which, thank God, his daughter would never be.

Clifford Howard also forbore to show his wife the Mother Superior's comments about their daughter's conduct. But he did ask Joscelin for an explanation.

'Honestly, Daddy, my drawings weren't meant to be cruel – only funny!' Joscelin said with genuine concern.

Clifford looked at his daughter's innocent little face. He resented the nun's implication that a child as young as Joscelin could possibly corrupt anyone's mind. He himself was delighted that she had settled down so well at boarding school, and most of all that her diction had improved beyond all recognition. She now talked freely and easily and was making excellent progress academically.

Nevertheless he felt obliged to say: 'School rules are made to be obeyed, Poppet, so kindly confine this type of drawing to your holidays. Meanwhile, I am anxious not to upset your mother, so we will say no more about your report. She will be delighted to hear that you and Casilda have been moved into a class with your peers.'

He gave the matter no further consideration, for his thoughts were elsewhere. A month ago the Archduke Franz Ferdinand and his wife had been assassinated and Austria was accusing Serbia of complicity in the crime. The repercussions had been disastrous, with Vienna sending an ultimatum to the capital, Belgrade, demanding that Serbia surrender her freedom. Now Russia was mobilizing to defend Serbia and the Slav minorities in the Austro-Hungarian Empire. Three days ago his newspaper had reported that Austria had declared war on Serbia and shelled Belgrade. This morning, *The Sunday Times* announced that Germany had declared war on Russia.

His fears that England might be drawn into the conflict were confirmed the following week. On Monday morning the British Fleet was mobilized and England was in readiness for war. Germany was demanding free passage for her troops through neutral Belgium, and by Tuesday her troops had crossed the frontier, violating Belgium's neutrality. He attempted to explain the situation to his wife and daughter.

'None of us wants war, but we cannot allow Germany to remain in Belgium. We have a treaty by which we are morally bound to support the Belgians. We have delivered an ultimatum to Germany to withdraw her army. She has until midnight to do so.'

But no answer was forthcoming, and on 4 August Britain was at war.

Clifford Howard did not believe that this ill-conceived,

irrational war would last more than a few weeks. Nevertheless, its advent was sufficient to divert his thoughts completely from the nagging worry that Joscelin's Spanish friend might be proving a bad influence on his precious child.

He need not have worried, for the outbreak of war in Europe gave Don Jaime every excuse to keep his mischievous young daughter at home for the next four years.

CHAPTER FIVE

January 1919

'You're the only reason I persuaded Papá to let me come back to this ghastly place, Joss darling. It seems so much smaller than I remember! But *you* haven't changed. You're exactly as I remember you.'

Joss took the bundle of neatly folded clothes Cassy had lifted from her school trunk and put them into the chest of drawers. She couldn't recall when she had last felt so happy. After four lonely years, Cassy had come back to the Convent, bringing with her that aura of excitement and fun that was so essential a part of her. She smiled.

'Of course I've changed! I've grown like a weed, so Mummy says – up, and not out. I must be at least three inches taller than you, Cassy.'

'Who cares!' Cassy said, holding up another armful of clothes. 'We're together again and that's all that matters.'

Joscelin felt an overwhelming sense of relief. She and Cassy had exchanged countless letters throughout the long years of war during which the Spanish girl had not been allowed to risk the journey to England. But despite these communications she had been afraid that, after such a separation, they might not be able to re-establish that same close friendship.

'I've wonderful news, Joss,' Cassy was saying, her dark eyes sparkling with excitement. 'Tía Pamela says you can come and stay at Rutland Gate next holidays. Papá and Mamá are coming over for Easter and staying for Isobel's and Barbara's presentation in May, so I won't be going back to Spain for the holidays. Tía Pamela said you can come and keep me company. You'll be able to meet my cousin Alan. He's seventeen and terribly handsome, and I'm going to marry him when I'm old enough. Have you fallen in love yet, Joss? But of course, you said in your letters you don't meet any boys. I met lots of them in Sevilla, but none of them are like Alan. Look, here's his photograph.'

Joscelin studied the snapshot of the good-looking young man in white cricket flannels and blazer and felt a twinge of misgiving. The war years had changed Cassy, if not herself. Cassy, at fourteen, had a retinue of girlfriends with whom she was permitted to go for walks – provided, of course, that one or other of them had a chaperon in attendance. Families such as Cassy's also met at dancing classes and went riding together.

Still more exciting, Cassy told her, were the parties at the houses of her friends who had elder brothers. *Their* friends would be present and the girls would secretly choose a special boyfriend for themselves or pair off a girl who was not yet romantically attached. She could attract any boy she fancied, Cassy told Joscelin proudly, and she had been practising how to look up from beneath her lashes which, she had noticed, always seemed to arouse a boy's interest.

How different had been the last four years of *her* life! Joscelin thought. She had lacked the society of other young people since her holidays were spent quietly with her parents at Surbiton, and now she found herself envying Cassy this handsome cousin who, Cassy told her, despite being almost a grown-up, appeared to enjoy her company.

'I just know he likes being with me,' Cassy said, giving that spontaneous, almost breathless laugh Joss had all but forgotten. 'Of course, he thinks I'm much too young to be taken seriously. All the same, he promised to write even though he'll be pretty busy now he's Head of House and Captain of Games. You're just bound to like him, Joss.'

Love, marriage, boys and babies were Cassy's main topics of conversation that term. Joscelin listened, made not a little uneasy by the realization of her ignorance of all Cassy's favourite subjects. Contrary to Mrs Howard's explanations, babies, Cassy told her, were not delivered by storks or found under gooseberry bushes. Doña Ursula's eighth child had been born not long after the outbreak of the war and Cassy had been well aware of her mother's bulk before the midwife and doctor had been called to the house to deliver it.

'I still don't see how the baby got into Mamá's stomach,' Cassy confided one afternoon when they were permitted to go for a walk round the games field. 'My brother, Patri, says people mate – just like bulls and cows.'

Joscelin's cheeks burned. At her home, such subjects were never raised except in the vaguest terms. 'You'll understand when you're older' was her mother's answer to any question her daughter had found the courage to ask.

Casilda appeared quite unembarrassed by the topic she had raised. 'Of course, Patri doesn't really know much about women yet. He's only thirteen, younger than you, Joss, and he hasn't mated with a female yet. But he's going to the *Kursaal* as soon as he's old enough to mate with one of the *tanguistas* who will do it for money.' Seeing the look of incomprehension on Joscelin's face, she explained: 'It's a large hall in the Calle Sierpes where the boys can dance with the *tanguistas*. They are the girls who entertain with their flamenco dancing. Patri says that Eduardo has been there but *he's* hopelessly stuffy and never tells me anything.'

She then launched into a graphic description of life on her father's *ganadería*. 'The seed bulls are brought down from the pastures in January and allowed to mate with the cows until June. Nine months later, the calves arrive. Mamá has forbidden us girls to talk about such things, but Papá has always taken me to the Hacienda with him ever since I was little, and once he let me watch a calf being born. I think it was partly because Mamá did not want me to spend so much time with Papá that she sent me to school here in England. She wanted my sister to come too, but Lota is dreadfully shy because of her limp.'

Joscelin recalled the letter from Cassy, describing how her sister had fallen from her pony and broken her ankle. Poor Cassy had been blamed for the accident by her mother because she had dared the younger girl to jump a gate that was beyond the capability of her mount. But it had not been her fault that the doctor who had set Carlota's ankle had made a mess of it, leaving the ten-year-old girl with a pronounced limp.

'It's not anything like as bad as Lota seems to think,' Cassy said, 'but Papá has allowed her to stay at home and continue her education with silly old Miss Smart.'

Cassy's return to school seemed to delight Mrs Howard almost as much as herself, Joscelin thought, when her mother wrote the following week suggesting she invite her friend home for half-term. It was several days before she mentioned the invitation to Cassy who, Joscelin was certain, would be not only bored but shocked by the simplicity of Whitegates. She was well aware of Mrs Howard's reasons for approving her friendship with the Spanish girl. She was old enough to appreciate that her mother was obsessively class-conscious, and that the convent education was of little importance to her compared with the opportunity it provided for Joscelin to mix with girls from the upper classes. Realizing that Cassy could not fail to notice the vast difference in their backgrounds, Joscelin hesitated before passing on the invitation.

She need not have worried. By the end of Cassy's first day at Whitegates, she declared herself enchanted.

'It's like a little dolls' house, Joss. And you are so lucky to have a mamá like yours – always so anxious that we are happy and amusing ourselves. Do you think she will allow us to make toffee again? I am not allowed to touch anything in the kitchens at home and my mamá would be quite horrified if she saw me cooking. And your papá – he is so funny the way he looks at us over the top of his newspaper, pretending he is paying no attention. I wish I was an only child. I wish more than anything my mamá spoiled me the way yours does. She makes me feel like a princess!'

Such remarks, made without guile on Cassy's part, brought an intense feeling of relief to Joscelin, who was only too well aware that her mother felt obliged to wait on Cassy hand and foot and was, indeed, treating her like royalty.

'I was once her aunt's dressmaker, dear!' Mrs Howard whispered to Joscelin. 'We don't want your friend telling Her Ladyship that we couldn't look after her niece properly, do we?'

It was one thing to have Cassy staying as her guest, Joscelin thought as the end of term drew near, but it was quite another for *her* to be a guest at Rutland Gate. The prospect of staying in such exalted circles became an ordeal as, for the first week of the holidays, her mother became increasingly agitated. She dragged Joscelin from shop to shop, buying new clothes for her and chattering ceaselessly about the Costain household. There would be a big staff, Mrs Howard informed her daughter. She went on to describe the complicated hierarchy in the Upstairs and Downstairs *ménage* of an aristocratic household. Joscelin must not open doors for herself if there was a footman nearby to perform the task; she must remember which knife and fork to use; she must not treat the servants as equals. If she did not behave correctly, they would all be thought 'common', her mother warned.

Her admonitions were endless. Not only was Joscelin convinced she would never remember everything, but she was worried that she would let her parents down.

Seeing his daughter's nervousness, Clifford Howard tried to counteract the state of near-panic his wife had induced in her.

'Now you've nothing to worry about, Poppet,' he said as he waited with her for the arrival of the Costains' chauffeur. 'You can hold your own with any of these so-called "ladies" your dear mother so much admires. Just be yourself, darling, and they'll all love you. And if you are not happy, then telephone me at the bank and I'll drive straight up to London and fetch you home.'

Not entirely reassured by her father's words, Joscelin kissed her parents goodbye and scrambled into the back of the Daimler. Paget – never *Mr* Paget, Mrs Howard had instructed her – closed the door and climbed into the front seat. His face was impassive and, if he was unused to collecting guests from so humble an environment as Surbiton, his expression gave no sign of it. Nevertheless, glancing from time to time in his rear mirror, Joscelin's white face and obvious anxiety transmitted itself to him.

'Miss Casilda's that impatient for your company, she'd have had me break the speed limits to get you home quicker, miss,' he said, as he guided the big car towards the centre of London.

Uncertain whether it was permitted to speak to a chauffeur or not, Joscelin cleared her throat and tried to smile.

'It's been a bit lonely for Miss Casilda with Mr Alan in Scotland with His Lordship and Miss Barbara and Miss Isobel busy preparing for their presentation.' Paget's voice was conversational. 'Miss Casilda said you'd not yet met Her Ladyship, miss. A very nice lady, if I may say so. It's a pleasure to be in her service. Her Ladyship's loved by everyone. You'll soon feel at home, miss, if *she* has aught to do with it, mark my words!'

But would that ever be possible, Joscelin wondered as a butler opened the big front door and Paget handed her suitcase to a footman. A maid in cap and apron appeared from behind a green baize door and, seeing Joscelin, bobbed a curtsey. No one had ever curtseyed to her in her life before!

Then Cassy came racing down the wide staircase, long dark pigtail flying as she flung herself into Joss's arms.

'I've been waiting for you *all* morning,' she said. 'Come upstairs and I'll show you our room. We're sleeping together in the Blue Room. I've been having German measles but I'm not in the least bit ill. Tía Pamela was going to telephone your mother to tell her, but thank goodness she forgot. And guess what! Mamá has had a miscarriage so she and Papá won't be coming to stay after all.'

As usual, not waiting for Joscelin to reply, she hurried upstairs to the beautiful blue and white guest room where Joscelin was to sleep for the next two weeks. The bootboy carried in her suitcase, and was followed by the Costains' semi-retired governess.

It was old Miss Dawkins who helped Joscelin put away the clothes so neatly packed by Mrs Howard in layers of tissue paper. The governess's muttered exclamations as she fussed over the new purchases brought back Joscelin's misgivings.

'I suppose this will do, dear, but so much lace! I believe in plain Chilprufe combs and liberty bodices for girls of your age. Aren't you a little too young yet for a bust bodice?'

It was the same argument Joscelin had attempted to use with her mother, but Mrs Howard had been determined that she would not be found wanting.

'I read in my magazine that lots of young girls are now wearing bust bodices in place of a camisole.'

'But, Mummy, I haven't got a bust and . . .'

'Nevertheless, dear, you never know when you'll suddenly blossom out.'

'I'm only going for two weeks!'

Her all but flat chest had concerned her for some time. Although the girls of her age at school who had 'blossomed out' did their utmost to hide this outward sign of femininity, Joscelin had begun to wonder if there were something wrong with her. The extroverted Cassy had proudly displayed two jutting protuberances and announced that she had started 'the curse'. Since Mrs Howard had told Joscelin nothing about this coming ordeal, Cassy's explanations had added a further worry, for no such sign of developing womanhood had shown itself to her.

'I shouldn't think you need bother too much, Joss,' Cassy had tried to console her. 'It's probably because you've been growing upwards instead!'

Cassy was waiting impatiently for the governess to complete Joscelin's unpacking. As soon as it was accomplished, she took her to the schoolroom. Every wall was lined with book and toy shelves, like the toy department at Harrods store at Christmas time, Joscelin thought, as her eyes roved from a giant black and white rocking horse to a fully furnished dolls' house. There were rows of tin soldiers, arranged neatly in regiments; musical boxes, clockwork trains and carriages, and dolls in every conceivable costume.

'Oh, Cassy!' she breathed, round-eyed. 'No one could ever get bored in a nursery like this!'

Cassy pouted. 'You can't play with toys at *our* age!' she said. 'It's different when Alan's here. We play cards and draughts and put on the gramophone.' She sighed. 'I'm dreadfully disappointed – Alan's staying for the whole holidays in Scotland, salmon fishing or something silly like that. Look, I had a letter from him!' She withdrew from the safe confines of her knicker elastic a single dog-eared page.

Sorry about the measles, Spotty-face, but at least I shan't catch them as I'm up here for the hols with a friend of mine, Monty Piermont. He saw the snapshot you sent me of you and Carlota in your Spanish fiesta costumes and thinks you're stunning! I've warned him you're only a school kid but he wants to meet you.

Kindest regards to your chum, Joss, and love to you, Spotty-face.

Cassy's eyes sparkled. 'I take it to bed every night and keep it under my pillow,' she said confidentially. 'It's not exactly a love letter and I wish he wouldn't keep calling me "Spotty-face", but he *did* send his love. I wrote pages and pages back to him this morning whilst I was waiting for you to arrive. Tía Pamela's gone off shopping with the girls and they're going out to luncheon and then on to tea with some other débutantes, so we're going to be on our own. That means we'll have our meals up here with Miss Dawkins!'

Joscelin breathed an inward sigh of relief. At least she

would have today to grow more accustomed to this palatial establishment before she was obliged to present herself to Lady Costain.

'It's hard to believe you've never met Tía Pamela,' Cassy commented as they seated themselves at the big wooden table. 'I know you're going to like her, Joss. Everyone does. She's frightfully pretty and fashionable. I expect that's why she's so popular. She's out nearly every night dancing.'

The morning passed quickly enough, with Cassy taking Joscelin on a guided tour of the house.

Tía Pamela's bedroom had huge wardrobes filled with frocks and coats, gloves and shoes, hats and scarves. Each item of apparel was graded in colour, so that her maid would have no difficulty in matching the outfits at a moment's notice.

Although Barbara's and Isobel's rooms on the floor above were sparse in comparison, they were filled with luxuries – quilted satin bedspreads, broderie anglaise nightdress cases, silver-backed hairbrushes and manicure sets. Their wardrobes, too, were filled with lovely clothes.

'They'll have to look decent for their Season,' Cassy said vaguely in reply to Joss's exclamation at so much extravagance. 'I wish we were being presented this year, Joss.'

Joscelin, whose father had agreed to send her to art school after she left the Convent, was as impatient as Cassy to acquire that 'grown-up' status which seemed to loom so far off in their future.

That night, her first in Rutland Gate, she discovered that at least one further step in her development was achieved. She woke in an agony of embarrassment to find that she had not only stained her nightdress a bright red, but the beautiful linen undersheet, too.

'For goodness' sake, Joss, whatever are you crying about? How were you to know it would begin the night you came to stay with me?' Cassy said as she rummaged through her chest of drawers to find a towel to lend her. 'Have you got a pain? Do you feel sick?'

'No!' Joscelin wept. 'But whatever will the maid say?'

'The maids are paid to clear up after us!' Cassy said. 'Don't be such a goof, Joss darling. I suppose we'll have to tell Miss Dawkins. That means we won't be allowed to go to Regent's Park Zoo.'

When Joscelin returned from the bathroom, Cassy put her arm round her shoulders and hugged her.

'It's an awful bore, isn't it?' she said kindly. 'No wonder they call it "the curse"! I'm not allowed to ride or go dancing or do anything at home, and at school it means no games. Maybe Tía Pamela will let us go for a walk in the gardens. Sure you feel all right?'

Joscelin nodded. She did feel a little strange – an odd inclination to cry and a very mild ache between her legs. But it was quickly forgotten as she and Cassy tucked into the breakfast one of the maids brought in to them.

'Usually we have to go down to breakfast,' Cassy explained. 'But because of the measles, Tía Pamela lets me have it here in bed. There's more to choose from if you go downstairs, but this is more fun – like a picnic!'

The big silver tray laden with food, the dainty linen napkins and thin, flowered china seemed very far from a picnic to Joscelin. Taking care not to spill anything on the pale blue eiderdown, she found she was after all extremely hungry, her appetite quite a match for Cassy's.

The meal over, Cassy suggested that, as soon as they were dressed, they find some playing cards and tell fortunes. But she quickly became bored. Momentarily, she stared out of one of the windows, her eyes gazing down into the fenced-in gardens in the square below. She could see the distant figures of several uniformed nannies walking along the gravelled paths between the dusty, drab shrubs, proudly pushing smart, glossy baby carriages or dragging toddlers beside them.

'London is so frightfully boring,' Cassy sighed.

Joscelin was silent, for once in complete disagreement with her friend.

But despite the minor indisposition of her measles, Cassy was full of restless energy. Unlike Joscelin, who could have sat for hours with a book, with pencil and sketchpad or paintbox, Cassy needed physical activity. Her face suddenly brightened.'

'I know, Joss, let's put on the gramophone in the school-room! Alan has a whole lot of records. We'll teach ourselves the tango!'

Joscelin grinned. 'I'm the tallest – I'll be the man,' she said, happy as always to fall in with Casilda's plans.

'I'll be Tía Pamela,' Cassy said, hurrying across the room to wind up the gramophone and put in a new needle. 'Alan says she's a frightfully good dancer. That's why she goes to so many tea dances. She told Alan the best band of all is at the Savoy with a dashing new bandleader from New York. Look, here's one – "Alexander's Ragtime Band". It's Tía Pamela's favourite.'

As they glided and stumbled around the schoolroom floor, their giggles becoming increasingly noisy, and lost in their game of pretend, both girls were entirely happy as they played at being 'grown up'.

Gradually, Joscelin began to feel at home, although she was never entirely relaxed in the company of the older members of the Costain family, or in the presence of the servants. Perhaps fortunately, she developed German measles during her third day at Rutland Gate, and although both Barbara and Isobel had had the childish ailment, Lady Costain thought it best to confine the two younger girls to the nursery floor. She herself put in an occasional visit to the schoolroom, usually with her arms laden with 'something to keep you amused, my darlings!' There was even a huge, expensive box of the very best Reeves' paints for Joscelin. Whilst Cassy sprawled on the window seat, diverted by the latest romantic novels she had borrowed from one of the maids, Joscelin was content to sit at the schoolroom table drawing and painting. To amuse Cassy, she did a cari-cature of Lord Costain, inspired by the big oil painting hanging in the dining room. She made him look like a big fat walrus and Cassy was enchanted.

'He's the grumpiest, crossest old man that ever lived,' she grinned. 'I just can't think how darling Tía Pamela can stick being married to him!'

The remark was made with Casilda's customary surface view of other people's feelings or motives, yet her words were prophetic. Six months later, Pamela Costain decided to abandon her sterile marriage and elope with the first man with whom she had ever fallen in love. She chose to do so in the middle of the autumn term.

It was a bright, cold October afternoon and Cassy and Joscelin were looking forward to releasing their energies on the netball court. The first inkling they had of the upheaval at Rutland Gate was when Cassy was summoned to the Mother Superior's study.

Cassy raced to the cloakroom where Joscelin was changing her shoes. 'It's Mamá!' she gasped as she tried to rebraid her hair into a more ruly plait. 'I just can't believe it. She's here in England, Joss, so something awful must have happened. Perhaps one of my grandparents has died! Perhaps Papá is ill!'

'Here, let me do that for you,' Joscelin said, taking the comb from Cassy's wayward hands. 'And calm down. Maybe your mother just wants to surprise you!' She tied a neat bow at the end of the plait and added: 'There, that looks fine. You'd better go, Cassy. I'll see you after evening prayers.'

As the afternoon wore on, Joscelin considered the implications of Lady Ursula's unexpected arrival. She'd never met Cassy's mother, for, at the end of every term, the Costains' chauffeur and governess collected Cassy and her brothers and drove them to Southampton where they boarded the ship for Spain. She found herself praying silently that whatever crisis had brought Lady Ursula to England, it would not necessitate Cassy's return home.

That evening, when prayers were over, she was joined by Cassy in the common room.

'I just don't understand it, Joss,' she whispered, looking more puzzled than worried. 'Mamá said Tía Pamela had been ill and is now in a sanatorium in Switzerland. Tío Angus has gone to Scotland and the house in London has been closed. Barbara and Isobel have been sent abroad and Alan is to come with me and the boys to Spain for the Christmas holidays. It's jolly bad luck for Barbara and Isobel in the middle of their deb year. They'll miss all the hunt balls and Christmas house parties. But Mamá said it was "all for the best", though she wouldn't say why!'

She paused for breath.

'Of course, it'll be absolutely wonderful having Alan with us in Spain, but what I can't understand is why Tío Angus has gone to Scotland. Miss Dawkins could have managed Rutland Gate and chaperoned Barbara and Isobel to their parties. Honestly, Joss, I smell a rat.'

Their discussion came to an end with the arrival of the nun who was to read to them, and could only be continued later that night in whispers in the dormitory.

'Alan did not say a word about his mother being ill when he wrote to me a fortnight ago,' Casilda told Joscelin. 'He just said everyone was enjoying the Season, and the girls were exhausted with so many parties, and all of them were out nearly every night, including Tía Pamela. It didn't sound one bit as if she was *ill.*'

'Perhaps she is just exhausted,' Joscelin whispered back, 'and she needed a rest.'

'But why has Mamá come to London? And why has she closed up the house and sent the girls abroad? Isobel is to go to Papá's sister, Tía Luisa, to a place called Württemberg in Germany – she married a German count, my Uncle Albert, but I've never met him because of the war.' She gave a sudden giggle. 'Imagine Tío Angus letting his eldest daughter go to stay with a "bloody Hun"! Barbara's being sent to Papá's eldest sister, Tía María. She's married to an Italian duke. He came to visit us one summer and was always trying to make me sit on his knee!'

Joscelin was accustomed to Casilda's habit of referring casually to her many foreign relatives, but she doubted if she would ever comprehend clearly how all these glamorous and exciting people related to one another. Only the Costains were known to her personally, and even Cassy's brothers, Eduardo and Patricio, who were at school in England, were merely familiar names.

She heard Cassy give a long, deep sigh as she said sleepily: 'I dare say I'll be able to worm the truth out of Eduardo at Christmas. Mamá tells him everything.'

It was halfway through the Christmas holidays when Joscelin received a long letter from Casilda written in her large sprawling hand explaining the astonishing facts behind Lady Costain's sudden departure abroad.

I have finally heard The Truth. Honestly, Joss, I wasn't eavesdropping. I simply couldn't help overhearing my parents rowing about Tía Pamela, so of course I just *had* to listen. Now hold on to something because you are never going to believe this. Apparently Tía Pamela fell madly in love with Aubrey Roche – he's the jazz bandleader who played at lots of those tea dances she used to go do. Anyway, when the Season ended, he went off to Paris and Tía Pamela followed him.

Someone saw them together in a hotel and wrote to Mamá. (Don't you think it was absolutely rotten of them to sneak?) So Mamá dashed to the rescue to keep it all hushed up because if it was known Tía Pamela was having a love affair, you can just imagine the scandal!

Anyway, Tía Pamela was so much in love with this Aubrey chap she was even prepared to let Tío Angus divorce her so she could marry him. But when Mamá said Tío Angus would certainly cut her off without a penny, the chap decided he didn't want to marry her after all, the cad! So then Tía

Pamela really did go to Switzerland because she was broken-hearted and wanted time to get over it all before she goes home.

I told Eduardo, who made me swear on my oath I would never tell anyone else – but you don't count, being my Best Friend. Eduardo thinks it's quite shocking and refuses to tell Alan.

Now to the rest of the gossip. Alan has promised to come and take us both out to tea next term. When you do meet him, you must never, *ever* let him know I told you about his mother. It's been super having him here . . .

Joscelin reread the letter several times, but still could not reach any conclusions about Lady Costain's shocking behaviour. Try as she might, she could not imagine her own mother eloping to Paris with a bandleader, leaving her husband and child to face the inevitable scandal! It was too improbable a situation for Joscelin even to imagine her own reactions. She felt a rush of affection for the fussy, frilled, conventional little woman who could be depended upon so totally never to defy convention.

There was an uncertain smile on Joscelin's face as she tore Cassy's letter into tiny strips and set fire to them in her bedroom grate. Whilst her initial reaction was of relief that Cassy might continue to spend some of her holidays with her aunt, and therefore that she also might be invited there again, she was left with a distinct feeling of unease. Eduardo had expected his sister to keep the secret; Cassy had given her *oath* – but she had broken it. Cassy was her dearest and Best Friend, but could she ever quite trust her again?

CHAPTER SIX

May 1920

'Can I get you something, Miss Howard?'

Joscelin glanced shyly up into the bespectacled face of Casilda's seventeen-year-old brother Eduardo, and saw to her dismay that he was blushing, the colour obvious despite his olive skin.

Nervously, she swallowed the mouthful of Post Toasties she had just taken, but they refused to go down her throat and she was obliged to gulp twice before she could reply to him.

'I don't mind . . . whatever you like . . .'

She broke off, aware of the blush now rising in her cheeks, and wondered why she made such stupid remarks – 'whatever *you* like . . .' she had replied when he had asked her what *she* wanted.

'I'll get you a little of everything,' he murmured as he went over to the long sideboard on which stood numerous silver chafing dishes.

Toying with the large damask napkin on her lap, Joscelin thought longingly of the simple breakfasts at Whitegates, her mother placing eggs and bacon in front of her father and herself with the daily admonition to 'Eat up now before it gets cold.' Here, at Rutland Gate, servants hurried in and out with racks of hot toast or fresh pots of tea or coffee. Despite this being an informal meal, the long table was immaculately laid with beautiful china and silver and, although the family helped themselves from the sideboard, there was always a servant within call should anything more be needed.

Joscelin studied the various members of the family seated

at the table. Lady Costain was absent, following her long-established custom of having breakfast in bed, but Lord Costain, his face hidden behind a beautifully ironed copy of *The Times*, insisted that everyone else report for breakfast by half past eight, regardless of how late they had gone to bed the night before. On his right sat Cassy, who between mouthfuls was chatting animatedly to her younger brother, Patricio. Joscelin had met him briefly at Isobel's wedding the previous afternoon, but had seen him only fleetingly at the reception, and now he glanced across the table and gave her a friendly grin. Eduardo returned with a plate so heaped with food that Joscelin was overcome by an embarrassed certainty that she would never be able to eat it. She was all too well aware that Lord Costain objected vociferously to food being left on plates.

Joscelin put a forkful of scrambled eggs into her mouth – too hurriedly – for at that moment Cassy's cousin Alan, seated beside her, said:

'I'm awfully glad you are staying for the weekend. There was such a scrum at the wedding that I didn't get a chance to talk to the famous Joss I've been hearing about from Cassy for years.'

Joscelin swallowed, coughed, and hoped desperately that for once in her life she was not going to blush again. Her mother had sworn that this was an adolescent phase which she would soon grow out of, but Joscelin had almost despaired of that day ever coming.

'Casilda had shown me your photograph, so of course I recognized *you*, Mr Costain,' she said, glad that at least her voice sounded calm and under control.

The young man laughed. 'You'll have to call me Alan,' he said easily, 'because I shall certainly never be able to think of you as anything but Joss – Cassy's *very* Best Friend – and the second naughtiest girl at the Convent of the Sacred Cross.'

Despite her shyness, Joscelin smiled.

'I don't know if that's quite true. I suppose we *have* been in quite a lot of trouble one way or another, but we're both seniors now, so we have to set a good example.'

Alan raised his eyebrows sceptically. 'Cassy – a good example! I just don't believe it!' he said, but his tone of voice was humorous as well as affectionate. 'Come to that, now that I have met you, I find it difficult to imagine that you were ever half as naughty as Cassy. I think she must have bullied you into those escapades.'

'No one can make me do anything I don't want to do,' Joscelin said truthfully.

Alan gave her a long, searching look. 'Ah, well, I'm not altogether sure I believe that. For instance, my mother said she had to coax you into being Isobel's bridesmaid yesterday. It was rotten luck that Carlota was too ill to come at the last moment, and I think it was jolly sporting of you to step in at such short notice. My mother told me how nervous you were – and, I can only say, quite without reason. You carried it off magnificently, and I thought you and Cassy looked ripping.'

'You're very kind,' Joscelin said, blushing furiously. 'Your mother is, too. She is always so sweet to me . . . indeed, to everyone.'

Alan nodded. 'We all love her – and Isobel owes a lot to her.' He lowered his voice. 'I expect you know my father was dead against her marriage to a German. He's very prejudiced, although Rupert von Lessen was no more involved in the war than I. Poor fellow, he was packed off to a sanatorium the year before war broke out. He had a collapsed lung, or something. Anyway, it kept him out of the fighting and he never saw active service.'

Joscelin became aware that, whilst he had been speaking, Alan Costain had been staring at her – not rudely but with a quizzical glance.

'I know this will sound like a cliché,' he said with a smile, 'but I keep thinking I've seen you somewhere before. It's your eyes . . . I mean, that's what I seem to recall – your eyes. Do I sound as if I'm talking absolute rubbish?'

Again, that charming smile and Joscelin felt herself relaxing. 'As a matter of fact we *have* met once before,' she said. 'I was only four years old at the time, so I don't remember anything about it, but you were older – I think my mother said you were about seven or eight . . .'

Briefly, she recounted Mrs Howard's version of that fateful day in the Costains' nursery when her hearing had returned – and the part Alan had played in discovering it. 'I owe you a big thank you,' she ended shyly. 'My father said that the early sign of recovery from my deafness was enormously beneficial.'

Alan Costain was regarding her with intense interest. 'I remember that afternoon quite clearly. Whyever didn't Cassy tell me that you were that solemn-eyed infant? I remember how frightfully pleased I was to be proved right. I think that meant almost as much to me as the penknife your father sent me. It was the first I'd ever had!' He laughed. 'This has made the day for me – knowing that you, Cassy's famous Joss, are that same little girl and that you have made such a splendid recovery. Were you *really* deaf before that? It's hard to believe! You speak so clearly. We must tell Cassy!' He glanced across the table at his young cousin, who was chattering to his sister Barbara. He could guess the subject of their conversation, for Barbara talked of little else but her newly acquired Italian fiancé. It seemed odd, he thought irrelevantly, that both his sisters had chosen to marry foreigners; odder still that his father had consented. Perhaps his mother's persuasions had been valid. Neither of his sisters, with their carroty-coloured hair and freckles, could be termed pretty, and so many of the young men who might have proposed marriage were dead on the battlefields of France – a whole generation of them.

No such misfortune would face Cassy, he thought. His generation had been just too young for the holocaust, and apart from that Cassy, at fifteen, was one of the prettiest girls he knew.

'She really is quite stunning, isn't she?' he remarked impulsively to Joscelin. 'And one of the nicest things about her is that she's quite unaware of it.'

Joscelin nodded as if in agreement, although she knew this young man was mistaken – Cassy talked endlessly about her looks. 'My eyes are quite big, aren't they, Joss, though not as big as yours. But I can make them sparkle if I want!' or: 'Tell me what I look like with my hair up, Joss. It shows my neck, doesn't it, and that's one of my best features – long and graceful, like a swan's.'

With a loud 'hurrumph' that interrupted her thoughts, Lord Costain laid down his *Times* and cleared his throat.

'Haven't you anything better to do than sit here gossiping like a lot of old maids? Fresh air! That's what you all need – fresh air and exercise.'

'As it's such a nice day, Pater, I've planned a picnic,' Alan said. 'I've asked Cook to put up a hamper. I saw Monty Piermont at the wedding and he said we could borrow their punt and spend the day on their stretch of water.'

'Good, good!' Lord Costain muttered as he stood up to leave the room. 'Need a bit of peace and quiet after yesterday's rumpus.'

Barbara informed Alan that she had a great many letters to write and would not be accompanying them on their picnic.

'So there'll just be the five of us!' Cassy said brightly. 'You and me, Joss, and Eduardo, Patri and Alan. What a stunning idea, Alan!' She put down her napkin and came round the table to stand behind Joss's chair.

'It's going to be great fun, Joss! We shan't have to take Miss Dawkins as a chaperon since Eduardo's coming with us. Now you two can get to know each other properly.'

As Alan jumped to his feet to offer her his chair, she chattered on inconsequentially: 'Barbara's fiancé sounds quite nice. I think she may have done much better for herself than poor old Isobel. But I suppose even Rupert von Lessen is better than no one. Even now, I can't believe Tío Angus has let Isobel marry "one of the enemy", can you, Alan?'

He gave an uncertain shrug of his shoulders. 'You can see Pater's point of view. Although it's two years since the Armistice, he can't forget that some ten million men died in the war and that the Huns have still not paid their war reparations. I believe it's pretty awful in Germany – a vast number of people are starving, although von Lessen tells me things aren't so bad in Württemberg. The von Lessens live on Lake Constance, near the Bavarian border. I warned Isobel that she may find a great many of their relatives and friends as deeply prejudiced against the British as Pater is against the Huns.'

Cassy shrugged. 'Let's not talk about the war,' she said. 'Tell me about Oxford, Alan. Will you like going to university? Tía Pamela says you'll have a marvellous time there – lots of parties, punting on the river and . . .'

'Hey, steady on!' Alan interrupted laughing. 'I'm going there to study, unlike lots of chaps. I'm really looking forward to it. If I work hard, I should get my degree in three years' time.'

'It sounds frightfully dull to me. But I suppose if it will help you with your book . . . Alan's going to write a book one day, Joss. About wild animals, isn't it, Alan?'

'No, not exactly.' Alan turned to Joscelin and said hesitantly: 'I don't suppose you're particularly interested – most people aren't – but that's the whole point . . .' His eyes suddenly glowed as if with some inner excitement, transforming his rather lazy good looks into something quite else, Joscelin thought as her interest quickened.

'I want to write a book that will make people as concerned as I am about what our so-called civilization is doing to nature. People just aren't aware how many of the world's birds and animals are becoming extinct – and not through natural causes. We slaughter animals wholesale and destroy their environment for no better reasons than to make money or for what is called "progress" . . .'

He broke off, glancing at Cassy's impassive face. 'I'm afraid

I'm boring you,' he said apologetically. 'Once I get on my hobby horse, I'm apt to forget that the subject doesn't interest other people as much as it does me.'

'Of course we're interested, Alan,' Cassy said untruthfully, but belied her words almost instantly as her younger brother came over to join them. 'Patri!' she said affectionately. 'Come and talk to us!'

Patricio Montero nodded, smiling at Joscelin as he sat down beside Cassy. He was as relaxed and amusing as his elder brother Eduardo was stiff and shy. He was tall, like his mother and Lady Costain, and so self-assured that he seemed far more mature than Eduardo. He had the Costains' fair hair and hazel-green eyes and bore a greater resemblance to his cousin, Alan, than to his Spanish-looking brother and sister. Cassy, Joscelin knew, was devoted to him.

As brother and sister began an animated conversation about the absent Carlota, Alan turned back to Joscelin. 'It's strange that you've known Cassy so long and yet never met the Montero family until yesterday,' he said. 'It must be quite difficult sorting us all out.'

'Well, not really,' Joscelin said. 'You see, Cassy's talked about you all so much . . .'

Alan laughed. 'Cassy never stops talking – but you are very quiet. I thought you might be finding us a bit overwhelming en masse.'

Joscelin blushed: 'Perhaps I should try harder to be sociable, but . . . well, it's stupid, I know, but I'm hopelessly shy. I'm not used to this . . . this kind of life. We live very simply at home and my parents don't have big parties or anything, so I'm somewhat out of my depth . . .'

She broke off, aware that for the first time in her life she had discussed her private thoughts quite openly with someone other than her father.

'No one would know you were not quite at home in these surroundings,' Alan said in a quiet, kindly tone. 'You'll soon get used to us all. Cassy tells me she has persuaded my mother to present you both when you're old enough. By then, you'll have forgotten what it is to be shy!'

He stood up as one of the footmen came over to tell him that their picnic hamper was now ready. 'Tell Paget to bring the Armstrong Siddeley round to the front,' he said. 'I won't need him, I'll drive myself. Come on, chaps, we leave in a quarter of an hour.'

It was the most beautiful day and, at Cassy's request, Alan folded back the hood of the car. As they drove through the outskirts of London and into the countryside, the May sunshine was warm on their faces. Cassy sat beside Alan in the front and Joscelin was tucked snugly between Eduardo and Patricio, a warm travelling rug over their knees.

In little over an hour they reached the turning to Shamley Green and were bumping down the rutted cart track leading to the Piermonts' boathouse. The river came into sight, a gleaming silver ribbon sparkling in the sunshine.

Cassy jumped out of the car and ran down to the water's edge. Poised on the bank, she called excitedly to Joss: 'Come and look!' She pointed to a family of swans sailing regally downstream. 'Aren't they *majestuosos*?'

'Majestic or not, they can be very fierce when protecting their young,' Alan cautioned, as he lifted the hamper out of the dicky. 'Give us a hand, Eduardo. Good old Gibson has put in a bottle of Veuve Cliquot for us and there's lemonade for you girls. You can stick the bottles in the water, Patri, to keep them chilled.'

He spread a groundsheet against the side of the boathouse and laid the two car rugs over it.

'Let's go and look at the punt!' Cassy called out. 'Come on, Patri. Is the boathouse locked?'

'Shouldn't be!' Alan replied. 'Monty said he'd get one of the gardeners to come down and unlock it.'

'I'll go and see,' Eduardo offered as Alan stretched his arms above his head to relieve the stiffness brought on by the drive. He sat down on the rug and patted the space beside him.

'Take a pew, Joss. There'll be lots of time for boating after lunch.'

Joscelin sat down obediently, leaning slightly forward as she clutched her arms around her hunched knees. It really was stupid, she told herself angrily, to feel so shy, sitting here in the sunshine talking to Alan who was himself so perfectly relaxed and quite content to talk to her – a schoolgirl of fifteen! Why should she worry about it if *he* did not?

'Decent sort of chap, Monty!' he was saying with a lazy smile. 'Known him since prep school. Plays cricket, as a matter of fact . . .'

How languidly graceful he looked, Joscelin thought, wishing she had her pencil and sketchpad there so that she could draw him just as he lay, his head turned slightly towards her, one slim hand holding a stalk of grass which he was chewing absent-mindedly. In his Fair Isle pullover and grey flannels he looked absurdly handsome, romantic. No wonder Cassy was determined to marry him when she was old enough! They would make a beautiful couple – Cassy so petite and dark and glowing, Alan so fair and tall!

'Cassy told me you were reading zoology,' she said, wishing very much that she sounded less mundane. Why could she never think of anything witty, the way Cassy did? But Alan's face lit up as if she had touched on exactly the right topic.

'Zoology's the best subject to study if you want to write about animals,' he said earnestly. 'It's something I've wanted to do since I was a kid. It was really my Uncle Fergus who put the idea into my head.' He gave her a considering look. Then, as if making up his mind that he could trust her with a confidence, he related his first encounter with his uncle.

'I didn't meet him again for ages,' he said finally. 'I came south, you see, for my first term at prep school. That must have been when I first saw you – a silent, skinny little kid, all golden hair and huge grey eyes.'

As he saw the colour flare in Joscelin's cheeks, he added gently: 'You mustn't be embarrassed when somebody pays you a compliment. You'll be getting a great deal more when you're a bit older. You'll have to take a leaf from Cassy's book and accept them as your right . . . I was telling you about my Uncle Fergus, wasn't I? I suppose I was ten or eleven before I discovered one summer holiday at Strathinver that I could slip off undetected and spend an hour or two with the eccentric old man. He was supposed to be almost dumb but he would talk to me, a child, for hours on end – about the red deer and the walrus, the great buzzards and the natterjack toad.' He leaned forward, his voice deepening as he said eagerly: 'He couldn't bear to see anything killed without good reason and, young though I was, I think I knew instinctively that his hatred of wanton destruction of life had to do with his experiences in the war. Of course, my mother found out I was visiting him, but she turned a blind eye. And now, of course, I don't have to pretend when I go to see him.'

'Oh, Alan, you're not on about your Wild Man of the Woods, are you?' Cassy broke in as she flung herself down on the rug beside him. Her voice was teasing but, Joscelin sensed, with an edge of criticism. 'Don't encourage Alan, Joss darling, or he'll go on for hours and hours.'

For a split second, Joscelin thought she saw a look of disquiet in Alan's eyes. But then he gave his good-natured laugh and said: 'Cassy and the boys came up to Scotland for the holidays one summer. She was still very young and poor Uncle Fergus scared her out of her wits – although there was absolutely no reason for you to be frightened of him, Cassy. To tell you the truth, I think he was far more frightened of the two of you.'

Cassy pouted. 'But he looked so wild and unkempt . . . and dirty!' she said. 'He had a great mane of red hair and a beard, Joss, and looked like a giant.'

'There is no gentler person in the world than my Uncle Fergus, Cassy,' Alan said defensively. He turned back to Joscelin. 'He's wonderful with all animals but especially with the tiny and helpless. I've seen him putting a minute splint on

the leg of a kingfisher – and when he had finished, the bird
didn't attempt to fly away. The fishermen believe the birds
destroy the salmon spawn in the rivers and that they poach
the fish; so they kill them when they can. But Uncle Fergus
maintains that they prefer the larvae of dragonflies and water
beetles which do far more damage to the spawning beds. Now
the little dippers – as the local people call them – are becoming
extinct and . . .'

He broke off as Eduardo and Patricio came out of the
boathouse to join them. Alan looked apologetically from
Joscelin to Cassy, who had picked one of the wild kingcups
growing on the bank and was gently pulling off the petals
murmuring: 'He loves me, he loves me not . . .'

He said stiffly: 'Cassy's quite right – I bore everyone when
I get on my hobby horse!'

Patricio grinned as he squatted on his heels beside Joscelin.
'You ought to know by now, Alan, that my vain little sister
is always bored if the conversation does not revolve around
her!'

'Patri, you *brute*!' Casilda laughed, aiming the remains of
the kingcup at her brother's teasing face. 'It isn't true, is it,
Joss?'

'Of course it's not true!' Joscelin said quickly, loyally.

'Long may you remain in your sweet innocence,' Patri
retorted with a friendly smile at Joscelin. 'Now tell me, Alan,
because I really want to know, how do you reconcile your
"Save-the-animals-lives" obsession with all that hunting and
shooting you enjoy. I know you're a crack shot – almost as
good as I am, in fact!'

Alan laughed. 'Modesty is clearly not one of your virtues,
Patri. At the ripe old age of fourteen I suppose you are too
big for me to give you a good hiding. I seem to remember
walloping you one Christmas when you were still in a romper
suit.'

Patricio lifted his hands and clenched his fists like a boxer.
'Times have changed, Cousin Alan. I am now Downside's

middleweight boxing champion and you might regret an attack upon my person.'

'Stop squabbling, you two!' Cassy interposed, for she was indeed disliking her own exclusion from the conversation. She glanced towards Eduardo. 'What time is it, big brother? I'm starving. Can't we have lunch?' She turned to Alan and looked at him appealingly from beneath her lashes. 'You *are* going to let us have some champagne, aren't you, Alan? I had two glasses yesterday and, despite what Tía Pamela said, I haven't come out in spots!'

Alan allowed both girls a glass of champagne with the elaborate picnic Cook had provided.

'Leftovers from the reception,' Patri said mischievously as he took his third helping of caviar. 'I wonder if there'll be anything left to take back to school tomorrow night. For heaven's sake, Eduardo, why don't you pick that drumstick up in your fingers? Half the fun of a picnic is eating without a knife and fork.'

Eduardo was now blushing furiously as he continued to struggle ineffectually to cut the meat off his drumstick. His plate was perched precariously on his knee, and without warning his knife slipped and the half-eaten portion of chicken shot sideways, knocking over Joscelin's glass of champagne in its flight. She tried to keep a straight face as Cassy and Patri burst into uncontrollable giggles.

Alan, too, tried manfully to make light of Eduardo's clumsiness: 'For goodness' sake, will you kids stop fooling about! Let's get this meal over – that is if you do want to go punting.'

Unable to rid herself of a sneaking sympathy for the unfortunate Eduardo, Joscelin elected to sit beside him in the back of the punt. Alan poled whilst Cassy and Patri quarrelled over who should hold the dinghy paddle he had found in the boathouse.

'There's no point in our going upstream,' Alan said as he guided the punt skilfully away from the bank and into the main current. 'We'll go downriver for half an hour and allow ourselves double the time to get back.'

The punt rocked gently as it glided over the shining water. On either side, the meadows were green with new spring grass, the buttercups bright splashes of yellow against the emerald carpet. Occasionally they saw moorhens and ducks scampering into the reeds, disliking the disturbance of their afternoon peace; and once Alan stopped poling to point out the brilliant blue flash of a kingfisher. Apart from a distant figure walking beside a horse and cart, there was not a person to be seen.

It was not just the tranquillity nor even the fresh beauty of the countryside which was affecting her so strangely, Joscelin thought, watching the steady, rhythmic movement of Alan's arms and shoulders as he dipped the pole in and out of the water; it was simply being there, an accepted member of the family. No one seemed to notice her failure to make amusing conversation. They had accepted her as she was – Cassy's friend – and she wished the afternoon would go on for ever.

But it was not in Cassy's or Patri's natures to remain quiet for long. Within half an hour the drowsiness induced by their lunch and the afternoon sun had worn off and they began battling with one another for the right to hold the paddle.

'It's my turn, you little beast!' Cassy insisted, as she tried to wrench it from her brother's grasp. 'Don't be so mean. You know it's my turn. Give it to me!'

Patri responded by holding it even further from her grasp. 'Try and take it, then,' he said, fending off her hands with his other arm. 'Possession is nine-tenths of the law, you know.'

Cassy jumped to her feet, her eyes flashing.

Alan called out a warning: 'Sit down! I can see the weir. For heaven's sake, Cassy, *sit down this minute*. Can't you see I'm trying to turn the punt round?'

They now heard quite clearly the roar of tumbling water and, with a stab of fear, Joscelin saw a sign on the river bank – the bright scarlet letters saying: DANGER DO NOT PASS THIS POINT. The current seemed to have quickened and, although Alan managed to turn the head of the punt slightly, it was now broadside on and carrying them with ever-increasing speed towards the weir. Now they could all see the white flash of broken water not a hundred yards beyond a curve in the river.

Suddenly they were all shouting, Alan's voice the loudest, as he beseeched Patri to paddle harder. Eduardo, too, was trying to make his voice heard.

'We'll never get it round in time, Alan! Backwards, Patri, towards the bank!'

Cassy's voice was shrill with undisguised terror as over and over again she screamed: 'I can't swim. I can't swim. *Dios nos tenga de su mano.*' She was still standing, her arms flailing wildly as the punt lurched heavily against the force of the current, pushing them nearer and nearer the weir.

'For God's sake sit down, Cassy, or we'll all be drowned!' Alan said violently.

Eduardo leaned forward and pulled Cassy downwards. The terrifying fall of water was now all too apparent as it rushed over the weir, exploding in a cloud of spray fifteen feet below. Joscelin could see the sweat pouring from Alan's forehead, his face as white as Patri's as the two of them struggled to edge the punt towards the bank. Glancing sideways, Joscelin saw the point they were making for – a large willow, its branches dipping down into the water. But Cassy too had caught sight of it, and only feet away from the outermost branch she stood up and leaned forward to grab at this obvious lifeline.

'Oh, my God!' Alan cried as the punt, almost in slow motion, tipped sideways, flinging them all into the river. Joscelin felt the ice-cold tug of her grey flannel skirt pulling her down, down until her mouth and nostrils filled with water. It was the same sensation she had felt once in the sea at Bexhill when a wave had knocked her off balance and she thought she was going to drown. As if in a dream, she recalled her father's voice shouting: '*Kick, Poppet, as hard as you can!*'

She began to kick now, and rose slowly to the surface.

She heard Eduardo shouting: 'Hold on. I'm coming.'

'I'm all right!' she gasped. 'I can swim!' As she struggled towards the bank, she saw Eduardo hesitate, then turn and make for the punt, now some twenty yards distant. It was being carried towards the weir, and clinging to it was Cassy. Her bright pink dress formed a pool of colour around her. Not far away were two heads and four arms threshing the water as Alan and Patri fought to catch up with the boat.

Joscelin crawled up the side of the muddy bank and, turning her head, saw with horrifying clarity that Alan and Patri were trying, apparently unsuccessfully, to pull Cassy away from the punt. Too terrified to release her hold, Cassy was refusing to let go. Joscelin was afraid all three of them would drown if the punt went over the weir. Their only chance was to swim with Cassy to the bank.

Now Eduardo, too, had reached them, and with a great sigh of relief Joscelin saw a gap between the punt and the four heads bobbing in the water. Moments later, the punt went racing over the top of the weir like so much driftwood. There was nothing Joscelin could do but wait, as slowly they battled their way towards her against the current. Now she could hear Alan's shout to Cassy: 'Hang on a little longer, we're nearly there. *Keep still!* You're going to be all right.'

Patri was the first to scramble out of the water. Somehow he managed to grin at Joss. 'You all right?' he asked as he turned to assist Alan and Eduardo who were dragging Cassy up the bank. '*Qué horror!* Thank God *you* could swim, Joscelin!'

It was a comment echoed by Alan as Joscelin bent over Cassy's bedraggled body and tried ineffectually to wring some of the water out of her clothes.

'It needed all of us to make her let go,' Alan said as he bent down to brush the soaking tangle of black hair from Cassy's forehead. 'Poor girl! She was terrified! For one ghastly minute I thought I was going to have to knock her out . . .'

'I was on the point of doing it myself,' Patri said, his voice lacking the sympathy that coloured Alan's. 'It was all her fault anyway. She could have drowned the lot of us. Thank goodness you kept your head, Joscelin. Jolly good show.'

Guiltily, Alan looked at Joss. 'You *are* all right?' he asked, and as she nodded he turned quickly back to Cassy. 'Ought we to give her first aid, or something? Thank God she's breathing . . .'

At that moment, Cassy opened her eyes. 'I feel sick,' she murmured, 'and I'm cold.'

It was the first time Joscelin became aware of the cold. She shivered as she watched Alan help Cassy into a sitting position.

'Nothing dry to put round her!' Alan muttered. 'We must get help. We can't possibly carry her back to the boathouse. It's miles away.'

But help was on its way. A man fishing a quarter of a mile beyond the weir had seen the accident and alerted the nearby village constable. With surprising foresight the bobby had abandoned his bicycle and commandeered a motorcycle with a sidecar.

'Just what we need!' Alan said thankfully as the constable arrived. 'I can get the car and be back in a jiffy. There'll be staff at the Piermonts' who will fix us up with dry clothes and a hot bath.'

The water dripped slowly from their clothes and hair as they waited silently for Alan's return. He reappeared ten minutes later, sounding his motor horn encouragingly as he drove the big car bumping and skidding over the grass.

They looked an ill-assorted group when finally they gathered in their borrowed attire round a blazing fire in the Piermonts' drawing room. Cassy had entirely recovered her good spirits and laughed happily as she pirouetted in the fashionable tweed suit that Lady Piermont's maid had found for her. Her hair had dried in front of the gas fire in the bedroom and now curled in tendrils round her flushed cheeks. As they drank hot tea and ate buttered toast and scones she complimented Alan and her brothers on their bravery.

'Miss Howard – Joscelin, I mean, was the brave one,' Eduardo said, peering short-sightedly at his sister. He had lost his spectacles, and as a consequence was the only one to suffer any lasting inconvenience. 'If she'd panicked and lost her head, you might have drowned.'

Cassy put down her teacup and hurried over to Joss, hugging her. 'Eduardo's quite right, you were terribly brave. I was terrified! I've always been frightened of water. You really were wonderful, Joss.'

Aware of all the eyes focused on her, Joscelin blushed. 'I wasn't brave. It was just lucky that I learned to swim.' She was painfully conscious of how ridiculous she looked. Where Cassy's borrowed clothes somehow served to make her seem sophisticated and elegant, she herself appeared painfully frumpish in a mustard-coloured knitted jumper and skirt. But Cassy had been so anxious to wear the tweed costume that Joscelin had not liked to insist. After all, it was Cassy who had had the most terrifying experience.

The sun was still shining when, after tea, they drove back to London. They left an explanatory letter for Lady Piermont, apologizing for the trouble they had caused.

As they neared Rutland Gate, Alan said thoughtfully: 'I shall have to replace the Piermonts' punt, so it's all bound to come out sooner or later, and we'll have to admit to the parents that we had an accident. But the Mater will have hysterics if she hears how dangerous it really was, so I think we'd better tone the facts down a bit.'

Unaware, therefore, that not only her beloved son but her niece and nephews had come perilously near to drowning, Lady Costain's main concern was that they had not returned home in time for tea.

'You knew the von Lessens were coming, Alan,' she said reproachfully, 'and your father's patience is exhausted.' She waved her arms vaguely in the air and whispered: 'They simply won't go until they've seen you all. Now go and get into some respectable clothes and hurry down.' She patted Alan's cheek, adding softly: 'We really must do our best, darling, for poor Isobel's sake.'

For Joscelin, the next half hour was almost as much of an ordeal as the punting catastrophe. It was the first time she had met Cassy's mother, the formidable Doña Ursula. A gaunt, angular woman, dressed entirely in black, she looked years older than Alan's mother. Her manner was cold and forbidding as she dismissed Joscelin with no more than a critical glance. Mercifully, Isobel's in-laws showed even less interest in her when they realized she was not a relation, and she was able to remove herself to the far end of the room where Eduardo stood glowering at the assembled company. The object of Eduardo's derisory glance was his aunt, Lady Costain. She was gazing up into his father's face in a shameless way, he was thinking. Her youthful looks and unconventional behaviour had always made him feel uneasy. Her gaiety and flamboyant way of dressing bordered on the immodest, he considered, comparing her with his mother.

He had the greatest respect for his mother and was totally devoted to her, and although he knew that most married men had mistresses, he deeply resented the fact that his father had two. He noted with disgust that at this moment his father was flirting quite openly with his aunt. But then Tía Pamela was totally without morals. Her shameful affair with the bandleader was known to his father, who had been more shocked by the fact that she had been found out than by the fact that she had taken a lover. His aunt was behaving now as if nothing whatever had transpired, although it was only a few months since she had returned from the so-called sanatorium.

Eduardo wondered how Alan felt about his mother's disgraceful behaviour – if indeed he knew! He envied Alan his easy self-assurance, his casual good looks, his maturity and, most of all, that indefinable asset – sex appeal. It had not escaped his notice how all the girls looked at his cousin. As for Casilda – she was as shameless as his aunt, declaring to anyone who would listen that she was 'madly in love' with Alan and wanted to marry him! He agreed with his mother that Tía Pamela was not a suitable guardian for her after what had happened, but his father had laughed at their fears.

'Casilda is just an innocent little girl, far too young to bother her pretty head about men.' Even if poor Pamela wished to corrupt her niece, he had reiterated, his Casilda was not yet of an age to be corrupted. He would hear no more of such nonsense!

His father might have changed his tune, Eduardo thought bitterly, if he could see Casilda now, smiling provocatively at Alan. She had linked one arm through his, the other through Patricio's, and was crossing the room towards him.

'Are you two as bored as we are, Joss darling?' she asked brightly. 'Alan says he thinks we ought to stay a bit longer, but I don't see why. The von Lessens are Tía Pamela's guests, not ours.' She smiled up at Alan. 'Let's just slip away to the school-room. If we leave one by one they'll never notice. We can put on the gramophone and dance. Come on, Alan. We can play those new records of yours.'

Alan glanced questioningly at Joscelin. 'Would you like to?' he asked, as if her opinion mattered. With a teasing look at Cassy, he added: 'We all seem to end up doing what Milady wants, whatever our preferences – so we may as well give in without a fuss.'

Cassy was laughing, her beautiful face flushed with excitement. No one could resist her, Joscelin thought, least of all Alan, who was staring at her with a strange expression in his eyes.

As Eduardo looked on the point of protest, Patricio said quickly: 'Now don't be a spoilsport, old chap. It'll be fun!'

Cassy linked her arm in Joss's. 'Come on, we'll go first!' She slipped out of the room, dragging Joscelin with her. Joscelin half expected that they would be called back, but Cassy's plan seemed to work, for ten minutes later they were joined in the schoolroom by the boys. Cassy wound the handle of the gramophone and Alan stood beside her, sorting through the pile of records.

'Can any of you tango?' he asked.

'Of course we can, can't we, Joss!' Cassy replied, putting the record on the turntable and adjusting the speed. 'Come on, Alan. I bet we know more steps than you do!'

As she drifted into Alan's arms, Eduardo bowed formally to Joscelin. 'I'm afraid I'm not a very good dancer,' he said, his whole face darkening with embarrassment. 'If you'd rather not . . .'

His shyness increased Joscelin's own and she felt the familiar blush colour her cheeks as she said brightly: 'No, of course I'd like to dance.'

A moment later, she wished very much that she had not spoken so impulsively. Eduardo's hand was hot and sticky against her back, the dampness seeming to burn through the material of her dress. He trod frequently on her toes, whilst their bodies came even more frequently into collision. Their hurried apologies, uttered simultaneously, only increased their nervousness.

'Good grief, Eduardo, can't you do better than that?' Patri called out from his chair by the gramophone. 'The poor girl won't have a foot to stand on soon!'

Joscelin's embarrassment was forgotten in her sudden pity for Eduardo. No one knew better than she how dreadful it was to be shy.

'It's partly my fault, Patricio,' she said in a rush of sympathy. She forced a smile to her face. 'I'm only learning, too. Come on, Eduardo, we're doing splendidly!'

His dark eyes glowed with gratitude, and momentarily he straightened his back, held up his head and managed a passable imitation of Alan's flamboyant postures as he and Cassy sailed past them. But within moments he and Joscelin were once more stumbling over each other's feet, and with a sigh of relief he came to a halt as the record ended.

Patricio grinned at Joscelin as they sat down. 'Now it's my turn. I've found a *pasodoble*.'

With one arm firmly about her waist, he pulled her to the centre of the room. Grasping her hand, he clicked his heels

and struck the exaggerated *pasodoble* pose. Suddenly Joscelin's
shyness slipped away. What did it matter if she was uncertain
of the steps! She was having fun. In the background Cassy,
Alan and Eduardo were clapping their hands and calling out:
'*Olé, olé!*'

'You dance as well as any Spanish girl!' Patricio told her
as the music ended with a flourish.

'You looked really professional,' Alan said. 'It is my turn
now to claim a dance. A waltz, Joss? That I can accomplish
reasonably well.'

Joscelin's heart missed a beat. Dancing with Patricio was
one thing, but the thought of being in Alan's arms brought
on renewed shyness. She felt her body stiffen as his arm went
round her, and for the first few turns her feet stumbled and
she heard her voice murmuring stupid apologies.

'Just relax,' Alan said in his quiet, kind voice. 'I know from
watching you that you are a good dancer.'

Cassy swirled past them in Patricio's arms and called out
to Joscelin: 'This is much more fun than dancing by ourselves!'

It was more than 'fun', Joscelin thought. The music was
soft, romantic, the voice of A1 Bowlly singing 'Alice Blue
Gown' both soothing and seductive. Despite the unexpected
trembling of her limbs, she knew she was moving effortlessly,
her feet perfectly in time with Alan's. She closed her eyes,
imagining herself as the beautiful, petite, golden-haired film
star Mary Pickford, whose much-publicized arrival in London
for her honeymoon had absorbed both Joscelin and her
mother as well as the thousands of her fans who mobbed
the 'World's Sweetheart' at the Ritz Hotel. And Alan was no
longer Cassy's cousin but the handsome, romantic Douglas
Fairbanks, Mary Pickford's new young husband and co-star.
They were magically, wonderfully, perfectly in love as they
whirled around the dance floor; there existed no one else in
the world but the two of them . . .

Joscelin's dream came to an abrupt end as the gramophone,
which Patricio had forgotten to wind up fully, lost momentum

and the high tones groaned down the scale to a deep growl. Alan's laughter, joining with that of the others, was like a dash of icy water bringing her back to reality. Embarrassment added to her confusion as she realized how perfectly ridiculous had been her thoughts. Joscelin wished herself a thousand miles away, and was greatly relieved when Lady Costain sent one of the maids to tell them that it was time for Alan and Eduardo to change for dinner and for Casilda, Joscelin and Patricio to go downstairs to say their goodnights before returning to the nursery schoolroom for supper.

'If we'd been at home, Papá would have allowed me to eat with the grown-ups,' Cassy said bitterly when she and Joscelin finally retired to bed. But she cheered up almost immediately, convinced that the dinner table conversation would certainly have been very dull and now she and Joscelin could go to their bedroom and catch up on their own gossip.

Joscelin would have preferred to switch off the light and lie in the darkness mulling over every detail of the exciting day. But Cassy was wide awake and, in her usual exuberant manner, wanted to talk, fortunately not just about Alan.

'Do you not think Papá handsome, Joss? I knew you would like him. He told me he thought you looked "a most sensible girl" and would be a "steadying influence" on me!' She giggled. 'I warned you about Eduardo, of course. He's old-fashioned! You can imagine how shocked he was when Tía Pamela ran off with that awful bandleader!' Her voice rippled with laughter, then sobered as she added: '*I think Alan knows*. He went all quiet when I asked him when his mother had returned from Switzerland. I should think he'd have fifty fits if he thought Eduardo and I knew what had happened!'

Joscelin's cheeks burned. 'You would never tell him . . . that you'd told me . . .?' she faltered.

'Of course not,' Cassy said brightly. 'After all, I did promise Eduardo not to let anyone into the secret. Joss, do you think Tía Pamela was in love with that man – really in love, I mean

– the way I am with Alan? She looked tremendously pretty today – and years younger than Mamá. I wish Mamá would smile more often and not look so stern and disapproving.'

She gave a deep sigh, and a moment later was laughing as she jumped out of bed and struck a theatrical pose in front of the cheval mirror, putting one hand on her hip.

'You should have seen Tía Pamela the night she went to the Duchess of Albany's charity ball. She looked absolutely stunning. She outshone even Lady Diana Cooper, who everyone says is considered to be one of the most beautiful women in society. Lady Cynthia Curzon, who came to tea the next day, said Tía Pamela had stolen Lady Diana's thunder and wanted to know who made the dress she was wearing. It was a dream, Joss, floating pale blue georgette with masses of embroidery in silver thread. Lady Curzon said she looked absolutely divine.'

Pausing briefly to glance at Joscelin's rapt face, she added thoughtfully: 'Mamá would never wear a dress like that – she'd say it was indecent! She's only two years older than Tía Pamela but I think she looks lots more. Last holidays she cross-questioned me about your family, Joss. "Where does her father have his country seat, Casilda?"' Cassy's voice was a perfect imitation of her mother's. "What year was her mother presented?" She laughed softly. 'But you mustn't let that worry you, dearest Joss. Papá won't mind in the least about your English connections, and as for Eduardo, you're the first girl he's ever shown the slightest interest in. Wouldn't it be ripping if he ended up marrying you? You'd be my sister-in-law and one day you'd be a Spanish *marquesa* and head of the Montero family!'

She gave another giggle. This time, Joscelin joined in.

'Not that it could ever happen,' Cassy went on, 'what with you being a Protestant as well as socially too far down the ladder to suit poor Mamá. Still, you could become a convert like she did to marry Papá. Of course, Alan's not a Roman Catholic either. Do you think he'd be willing to be converted,

Joss? My parents would never allow me to marry him if he was not.'

'I don't know,' Joscelin said doubtfully. 'I should think that the fact of you and Alan being first cousins might be more of a bar to your marriage. My father said first cousins sometimes have mad babies.'

Casilda sat up and hugged her knees, her interest kindled. 'Did he? It sounds like an old wives' tale to me. Oh, I wish I were twenty-one and could do whatever I want. If they don't let me marry Alan, I shall run away with him. Joss . . . you do think he'll want to marry me, don't you? I mean, he hasn't *said* anything yet. He still treats me as if I were a child. But I just know he does like me . . . really likes me, I mean!'

Joscelin smiled. 'By the way he looks at you, I should think it's a good deal more than that,' she said bluntly. 'But how can he possibly say so, when you're only fifteen?'

'*You* like him, don't you, Joss?' Casilda's voice sounded confident again as she climbed back into bed. 'I know Papá does. He told Alan at Christmas that, whenever he feels like going to Spain, he's to treat our house as his second home, just as I do this house. Joss – Alan's going to ask his friend, Monty Piermont, to invite us both down to Shamley Green for the annual cricket match they always play against the village. Miss Dawkins could chaperon us if Tía Pamela doesn't want to go.' Her voice became husky with happiness as she added: 'Alan said he wanted to show this Monty chap what a pretty cousin he has. You'll come, won't you, Joss? It'll be fun!'

Joscelin was in no doubt that she would accept. It was oddly comforting to think that Alan had even considered including her at all.

She fell asleep, thinking of a bright summer's afternoon, sitting in a deckchair on Shamley village green, watching Alan Costain batting for his friend's team. It was little enough to long for so passionately, and yet she felt entirely happy knowing that soon she would be seeing Cassy's handsome cousin again.

CHAPTER SEVEN

August–September 1920

The remainder of that summer holiday was, for Joscelin, a painful anti-climax. The Costains and the Monteros went en masse to Strathinver Castle, and Joscelin went to Bexhill-on-Sea with her parents. The weather was cold, windy and wet, so there was little opportunity to bathe. Her father spent most of his time in the small hotel lounge doing the crossword or reading. Sometimes he tried to interest her in the political articles in the newspapers. Once he showed her a picture of Lady Astor in the *Illustrated London News*, explaining how important a step it was for women actually to have one of their sex accepted as a Member of Parliament.

'The war has changed people's outlook a great deal,' he told her. 'We men have been forced to appreciate the enormous contribution women made to victory. Despite her brilliance Lady Astor could never have achieved such recognition before the war. Your horizons are widening, my Poppet,' he added, smiling.

Normally Joscelin enjoyed such conversations with her father, but she was missing Cassy. She missed their long talks and envied her the 'fun' (Cassy's favourite word) that she must be having with Alan, Eduardo and Patricio in Scotland.

Mrs Howard fussed about Joscelin's health, unaware how irritating her motherly fretting was to her daughter. Joscelin was too pale; too thin; too quiet. In her bustling, kindly way, Mrs Howard attempted to find distractions for Joscelin as the summer rain poured down, leaving the promenade and beach deserted.

She ought to be grateful for her mother's unselfish attempts to divert her, Joscelin thought, but somehow their relationship had changed quite drastically recently in a way that confused her. It was as if Joscelin were now the older of the two and had joined forces with her father in an unspoken desire to protect Mrs Howard from ridicule. Joscelin, who would have died rather than admit it, had come to see her mother as slightly absurd. With her peroxide yellow hair carefully dressed each week in tight marcel waves, her rouged cheeks and Clara Bow painted lips, she looked rather like an ageing chorus girl. She chattered interminably on the most frivolous of subjects, happily ignorant of the fact that for most of the time neither her husband nor daughter was listening to her. Joscelin found equally absurd Peggy Howard's sense of inferiority regarding her class, although she herself was aware of the difference between her mother and Lady Costain. Joscelin's good taste, derived from her artistic talents, evoked her admiration of the chic that was so natural to Lady Costain. Similarly, the garishness and fussiness that surrounded Mrs Howard was as tiresome to Joscelin's eye as the beauty of the furnishings at Rutland Gate was pleasing.

But most worrying of all to Joscelin in this newly awakened awareness was the realization that Mrs Howard could never fit into the Costains' circle of friends. Lady Costain would undoubtedly receive her kindly, but women like those rich, bejewelled intimates of Lady Costain's who floated in and out of Rutland Gate would in all probability laugh at her mother behind her back. Joscelin would never allow her to be so humiliated, and for this reason had not followed up Lady Costain's vague suggestion that she bring her parents to tea.

Growing up, Joscelin decided that long, wet summer holiday, was far from being a pleasant state of affairs, and their return to Surbiton was a welcome relief to both her and her father. She found a postcard from Lochinver, from Eduardo Montero, waiting for her.

It would be nice if you could have been here. The weather has not been good but the shooting is excellent. Casilda has asked me to say she is missing you and to remind you of Alan's cricket match in September. I hope to see you before I return to Downside. Eduardo.

'Goodness me, Clifford, Joscelin's blushing!' Mrs Howard cried. 'So now we know why you've been so down in the dumps, don't we, Clifford? All the time she's been worrying whether her young man had written to her!'

Joscelin's blush deepened as she protested. 'Honestly, Mummy, I've hardly given Eduardo a single thought, and you'd understand if you'd ever met him. He's short and wears thick-lensed spectacles and his hands are sweaty! If you really want to know, I much preferred his brother, Patricio, and since *he*'s only fourteen, I'm hardly likely to have been mooning about a schoolboy, am I?'

'Time we had some tea, my dear,' Mr Howard interrupted tactfully. 'I haven't had a decent cuppa since we left home, Peggy. Go and have a word with Cook, eh? See if she's made one of her nice fruit cakes.'

With his wife safely disposed of, Clifford Howard put his arm around his daughter, his blue eyes kindly behind his spectacles.

'Don't pay any attention to your mother's teasing, Poppet,' he said gently. 'She's a born romantic. I know you're still fancy-free . . . and quite right too, at your age.'

He was by no means as sure as he made himself out to be. Astute in all his dealings with customers and staff at the bank, he was even more so where his beloved daughter was concerned. Odd snatches of conversation came back to him. 'Cassy's cousin Alan is going to be a writer one day . . .' 'Patricio is almost as handsome as Alan Costain but miles younger – Alan's grown up . . . he's at Oxford.' Clifford Howard was certain that Joscelin herself was unaware how often Alan Costain's name cropped up in her account of her brief stay at Rutland Gate.

He felt a sudden pang of anxiety. Joscelin's nature was particularly sensitive – and he could not bear the thought of her being hurt. He was seriously wondering now whether he should have been more firm with Peggy when she encouraged Joscelin's friendship with the Spanish girl. If his daughter had been a ravishingly pretty child, then perhaps she might find her feet even in those unfamiliar and exalted circles, since beauty was so often a key that opened all doors. But Joscelin was thin and over-tall for her age, with a pale, creamy skin which could at times look almost sallow. Her mouth was no rosebud like her mother's, but wide and generous.

Unhappily Clifford recalled how often, in the privacy of their bedroom, Peggy had referred to their daughter as 'a plain Jane'; but Joscelin's eyes, a deep grey-blue fringed with dark, curling lashes, redeemed what would otherwise have been a genuinely plain face. Those who cared to look deeper – at the perfect bone structure, the delicate but firm jawline, the wide, deep forehead – might see the underlying loveliness of his daughter's face. But even he had to admit it was not a 'fashionable' one and found himself praying that she would not, in these precious days of her girlhood, find her affections misplaced.

However, it was far too soon, he told himself now, to warn his daughter what the future might have in store were she to lose her heart to one of the Costain family. For the time being, he would keep his counsel in the hope that Joscelin herself was too intelligent to set her sights so high.

His hopes that she had not already had her head turned by Alan were diminished when he witnessed her reaction to a telegram from Casilda announcing that the young man's cricket match had had to be postponed because of the bad weather.

'We'll be back at school before the match is played!' his daughter informed him, her disappointment too great to conceal, for she had thought of little else these past weeks and the day at Shamley Green was to have been the highlight of the summer holidays. But a subsequent telephone call to Cassy from a kiosk changed her mood instantly to one of nervous happiness.

'I've thought it all out, Joss darling, and my plan is foolproof . . .' Cassy's voice was full of excitement. 'The match is to be on Saturday – the day we go back to school – and I know Tía Pamela won't want to take me to the Convent – she always gets Miss Dawkins to go with me. But if I say I've promised to collect you, then I'm sure she'll let the chauffeur drive me as far as Surbiton *without* a chaperon. So . . . when we leave your house, we'll tell Paget that he's to take us to Shamley Green before we go to school, and if he says those were not his instructions I'll remind him how vague Tía Pamela always is and say she probably forgot to inform him.'

'But what about school?' Joscelin asked. 'Mother Superior will be certain to notice if we're late . . . hours late, I imagine, and . . .'

'That's easy,' Cassy interrupted. 'I'll tell her we had a breakdown. What luck we're seniors now and don't have to go back in uniform!'

Apart from the lies involved, Joscelin could see no flaw in Cassy's plan. It was not even as if they would miss anything important on the afternoon of a new term.

It did not cross Mrs Howard's mind that her daughter's muttered lie was other than the truth. If Lady Costain approved of the girls going to a cricket match at a friend's house, Mrs Howard was not going to argue against it – although, she told her daughter, it would be the first time she and Daddy had not driven Joscelin to school.

'Will your Eduardo be there?' she asked with a coy smile.

Joscelin explained that he and Patricio, who had been joined by the younger Montero brother, Cristobal, had all returned to Downside, but that Alan Costain was not due back at university for another fortnight.

'Fancy him wanting two schoolgirls to go and watch him play cricket!' Mrs Howard exclaimed vaguely. But even if

Joscelin looked very much a schoolgirl in her neat striped cotton frock, white stockings and panama hat, Casilda Montero did not. Unaware of Mrs Howard's astonishment, she sailed into Whitegates totally self-confident and looking at least seventeen in a flimsy, rose pink dress with a fashionable low waistline, and a hat swathed with chiffon.

Half an hour later, as Paget drove them in the Daimler through the countryside towards Shamley Green, Cassy confessed that she had 'borrowed' some of Tía Pamela's face powder and a pair of her pink silk stockings.

'I've also borrowed this for you,' she said mischievously as she produced from the window ledge behind them a large straw hat decorated with multicoloured flowers.

Casilda seemed quite impervious to the dangers of her daring plan and strode confidently down to the scene of the cricket match, chatting to the butler who was accompanying them.

'We must not leave a moment later than five o'clock,' she instructed him. 'So please make sure that Paget is ready. And please remind me if I forget the time.'

The players were already on the field, their cricket flannels an immaculate white against the green turf. Joscelin, in Cassy's wake, approached the group of people seated in deckchairs outside the wooden pavilion. She was painfully aware that all eyes were momentarily diverted from the batting as their hostess rose to greet them.

'You must be Alan's cousin!' Lady Piermont said as someone brought out two deckchairs. 'Monty said you might come . . . and you, dear . . .?' Her voice sounded questioning as she gazed at Joscelin curiously.

'This is Joscelin Howard,' Cassy said, settling herself happily into one of the chairs. 'She is my friend and Alan said you wouldn't mind if I brought her along since my governess fell ill at the last minute and couldn't accompany me.'

'But of course you are most welcome, Miss Howard. Do you enjoy cricket? Alan is batting and I would not be in the

least surprised if he doesn't make his century. No wonder dear
Monty always insists upon having him in his team!'

Whilst Lady Piermont chattered on, Joscelin's eyes strayed
to the players. She could recognize Alan now, and at the end
of an over he turned to wave. Her heart jolted and then
quietened as she realized that he had been waving not at her
but at Cassy, who was frantically waving back.

Suddenly she shivered, wondering how she could possibly
have allowed Cassy to persuade her into this escapade. The
lies and deceit must be worth it to Cassy, who would shortly
have the admiring Alan at her side. But she herself was amongst
strangers in an unfamiliar environment and was on tenterhooks
lest she make some social gaffe. She did not know what to
talk about, and at the break for tea, she knew she would
be obliged to be a participant rather than a silent observer at
the gathering.

With the scoreboard standing at one hundred and five, Alan,
looking hot and flushed but extremely happy, came over to
greet them. His friend, Monty, immediately demanded an
introduction to 'your charming young cousins, Costain. Where
have you been hiding them?'

Shorter than Alan by six inches, and as stocky as Alan was
slender, Monty was an amusing, extrovert young man. Shyly
holding a bone china teacup in one hand and a cucumber
sandwich in the other, Joscelin listened quietly to their spar-
ring. Cassy's repartee was flirtatious, she thought, envying her
nonchalance. Alan, however, looked more amused than
impressed.

'I see you are pretending to be grown-ups!' he whispered
to Joscelin. 'But don't worry, I won't tell anyone. I must
congratulate you on your hat. It's very becoming. Mother has
one very like it!'

If he noticed Joscelin's fierce blush, he pretended not to,
and lounged on the grass beside her chair, idly watching the
group of young men encircling Cassy. Cassy glanced up and,
catching his eye, gave him a brilliant smile.

'She's going to be such a stunner!' Alan said. 'I fully expect she'll be Deb of the Year.' He had no need to name Cassy, Joscelin thought, since his eyes seldom seemed to leave her, although he talked for a while about his sisters.

Did Joscelin know that Barbara's marriage to her Italian count had been arranged for the following Easter? 'His name is del Valbo and he seems a nice enough fellow, although the Pater is muttering about "foreigners" – you know what he's like! He's still sulking about Isobel and von Lessen, but they'll be producing his first grandchild next year and it's to be hoped that will reconcile him to having a German son-in-law.'

Joscelin relaxed, suddenly perfectly content to be who she was, on this glorious September afternoon; to be here with Alan who seemed to want nothing better than to talk to her, plain Joscelin Howard.

All too soon, the tea interval was over. Alan scored only five more runs before he was caught and rejoined the group outside the pavilion, but this time it was at Cassy's feet he sat, absorbed by her chatter and bright laughter.

Suddenly it was five o'clock and a servant came across the lawn to inform them that Paget was waiting. Regretfully, Cassy rose to her feet and thanked Lady Piermont. She linked her arm through Joscelin's as Alan accompanied them to the waiting Daimler.

'Awfully glad you could both come!' he said as Paget opened the car door for them. 'The Mater was obviously confused – she said you'd both be back at school and I'd told Monty you couldn't make it.'

'We had a reprieve, thank goodness!' Cassy said smoothly as she climbed into the back seat beside Joscelin. 'Now you *will* write to me, won't you, and don't forget to sign *ALL* your letters from your loving COUSIN – otherwise Reverend Mother will confiscate them.'

Alan stood smiling and waving as they drove away.

'We're a bit late,' Cassy said leaning forward to speak to the chauffeur. 'Go as fast as you can, Paget.'

But the traffic was unusually heavy on the road back to Kingston, and Cassy looked continually at her wristwatch. 'If we are later than six, there's bound to be a rumpus,' she said anxiously.

But even had they arrived a half hour sooner, it would not have forestalled the impending disaster. As the car drew up, a nun stood awaiting them at the entrance of the Convent.

'You are to go straight to Mother Superior,' she said, no smile of welcome on her face. 'Both of you, immediately!'

'*Demonios!*' Cassy swore softly in Spanish as she stared at Joscelin's white face. 'Looks as if we've been rumbled, Joss. Oh, well, it was worth it. And try not to look as if Madame Guillotine is about to chop off your head. It was all my idea, and it's probably best anyway if I take the blame.'

The Reverend Mother was standing in front of the unlit fire in her private room, a tall, forbidding figure in a heavy black habit. The tone of her voice was icy.

'Come in, both of you. Joscelin Howard, I am deeply shocked that you – for whom I had such high hopes – could behave in such a wicked manner. You have lied, deceived your parents and were doubtless hoping to deceive me with more lies. But perhaps I should not be so surprised since you have not had the benefit of a good Catholic upbringing . . . You, Casilda, should have known better even if Joscelin was unaware of the sin of deceit. I suppose you thought that no one would discover your wickedness.'

She glanced briefly at the crucified figure of Christ on the ebony cross hanging on the wall above her desk. 'Well, our Heavenly Father obviously did not intend either of you to go unpunished. Your poor mother, Joscelin, decided to telephone me to inquire if you had arrived safely and to send you her love. When I informed her that you were already three hours late, she told me an extraordinary story of a cricket match to which you had both been invited. I therefore telephoned your aunt, Casilda, and after speaking to Lady Costain I was at last able to put two and two together.' Her mouth tightened ominously. 'I do not wish to retain in my school two girls who have so little – if indeed *any* – sense of right and wrong,' she said sternly. 'Your trunks can remain packed. You are to go now to the sanatorium and remain there until your parents collect you. You are both expelled!'

CHAPTER EIGHT

March 1921

'Where are you going, Carlota?' Her governess's voice stopped Lota halfway down the staircase.

'To find Cristobal, Miss Smart,' she replied. 'Patricio says he has gone to the stables with the visitors to see Papá's new stallion.'

That Lota became her twin's shadow the moment he returned from school for the holidays was a fact known to everyone, and the governess raised no objection to her leaving the house.

It was not *exactly* a lie she had just told Miss Smart, Lota thought uneasily. She *was* going to find Cristobal – so there would be no real need to confess the falsehood to Padre Alfonso on Friday. Nevertheless the prime reason for her sortie was to see Benito. Her papá had arranged for there to be a *tienta* tomorrow – an occasion when the bull calves were tested for bravery – and tonight there would be a party. Meanwhile there was a possibility that Benito would have left his precious bulls to help the grooms prepare the horses for tomorrow's event.

The opportunities for her to see him nowadays were all too infrequent. The wonderfully happy childhood days spent at the Hacienda had come to an end after her tenth birthday, when Mamá and her governess had ordained that she must stop behaving like a child. It was no longer 'proper' for her to treat Benito as an equal; to sit with the other children of the ranch hands, perched on the *burladero* of the Hacienda bullring admiring Benito as he practised his passes; clapping their hands as they shouted '*Olé*' like true aficionados.

Instead, as soon as her broken ankle had healed sufficiently for her to be able to walk, she had been obliged to go visiting with Mamá or be taken on educational outings by her governess to churches and museums. As a result of her accident, she now had a pronounced limp and her right foot turned slightly outwards. This had made it impossible for her to join in the dancing classes enjoyed by her friends and she was painfully aware of their pity. Mamá became quite angry at her reluctance to appear in public. Even Casilda seemed unable to understand how self-conscious she felt, reiterating constantly: 'Don't be such an idiot, Lota! You're so pretty the boys are never going to notice your foot and you can still go to parties even if you can't dance.'

But she was not like her sister. Even with strangers, Casilda could talk and laugh as if she had known them all her life. Lota could only be her true self with the two people nearest and dearest to her – Benito and her twin, Cristobal. They were the only people she trusted not to pity her and to whom she believed her deformity made no difference.

But the occasions when the family went out to the Hacienda and she could see Benito were all too few. Before Cristobal had gone to England to school last year, he had always been eager to spend time with his childhood friend; but since he had been at Downside his interest in bulls, and indeed in Benito, had declined. It was the first rift between her and her twin, and one which Lota felt deeply.

'Well, dear, you *must* see that Cristobal has much more in common with his school friends than with an illiterate peasant boy,' Nanny Gordon had tried to comfort Lota at Christmas.

But Benito was not illiterate, Lota thought, even if he hadn't had the good fortune to be well born. Her papá agreed that one day Benito was destined to become a famous matador and had promised to find him a manager when Benito was old enough.

As she turned into the yard she could feel the warmth of the spring sunshine like a caress on her head. The sound of her father's genial laughter was distinguishable over the voices of his guests as they stood grouped around the new stallion. Cassy stood by their father's side pleading with him to permit her to try out his new purchase. Nearby stood their English cousin, Alan, who had travelled out with Cassy and her brothers to spend the Easter holidays with them. As Lota took a step towards them, she caught sight of Benito disappearing into the tack room.

Her mouth curved into a mischievous smile. For once there was no Miss Smart or Mamá to stop her talking to Benito on her own. Here was a chance for her to explain that it was not by choice she had been avoiding him but that she had been forbidden to seek him out when she came to the Hacienda.

Although one side of the big yard was bathed in sunshine, the other was in shadow, and despite her limp Lota moved swiftly into the shade and made her way to the tack room unobserved.

Benito Lopez was polishing one of many ornate leather saddles. At fifteen he was nearly as tall as Eduardo. His hair was jet-black, as were his eyes, and his high cheekbones and straight nose lent his young face a slightly imperious look. Don Jaime had once remarked that the boy had inherited a lot of the physical characteristics of his Moorish ancestors.

Lota called his name in a whisper. 'I want to talk to you,' she said softly. 'Meet me in *los soberados*. You know, Benito, the granary where we used to play hide-and-seek.'

There was no answering smile on the boy's face. 'I have much work to do, Señorita Carlota. I have no time for childish games . . .' he said stiffly.

Lota laughed. 'Oh, Benito, how silly you are being! I'm not asking you to play hide-and-seek. I want to talk to you – *privately* – and do not call me Señorita Carlota. You are my friend and should call me "Lota" as you always have.'

The boy refused to meet her gaze, and resumed his polishing with exaggerated concentration. Lota took a step towards him and laid a hand on his arm. Irrelevantly, she noted how white it looked against the dark bronze of his skin. Her tone became one of appeal. 'Please don't be cross with me, Benito. I'm still your friend – as much as I ever was. That's what I want to talk to you about. It isn't my fault they won't allow me to see you very often or talk to you when we meet.'

Now he raised his head and stared directly into her large blue eyes. There was a hint of defiance in the lift of his chin, but his voice was gentle as he said: 'Very well then . . . but we must be careful not to be seen. You go first and I'll follow in a few minutes.'

Lota breathed a sigh of relief, tinged with excitement, as she slipped unnoticed towards the ramp leading up to the granary. It needed only Cristobal's presence to make this seem like one of those magical days when the three of them had played together.

It seemed a long time before she heard Benito's soft footfall. He came into the room and knelt a little apart from her on the pinewood floor. A dust-laden sunbeam slanted through a crack in the shutters, linking them by its bright shaft as it fell across their shoulders.

'There will be much trouble if we are found here,' he said. 'We should not stay long.'

In a sudden rush of words, Lota tried to describe the distress she felt that the circumstances of their birth were proving so effectual in separating them. 'It is not a situation of my choosing, Benito,' she ended sadly. 'I've not changed in my affection for you and I still believe that one day the whole world will admire you. You will become a legend like the great matadors, Romero and Guerrita, and you will be welcome in every home – most of all in Papá's, because he will be so proud of his protégé.'

For the first time, she saw Benito's face soften.

'I thank you for your faith in me and I shall carry it with me, as always, when I face the bulls . . .' In a low fierce tone, he added: 'Yes, I shall be famous and people like your father will be proud to entertain me – the best matador in

Spain – in the world. But that cannot be for many years yet. You forget that I must wait until I am sixteen before I become a *novillero* and then two more years before I can take my *alternativa*.'

Lota frowned. 'But that is something we have always known, Benito,' she said. She gave a soft laugh as he looked away from her. 'You are not thinking that *I* shall cease my affection for you over those years?' she asked, gently teasing.

When he did not reply, she leaned forward and touched his hand.

He turned swiftly back towards her and she saw the muscles tighten in his cheeks, saw the gleam of white teeth as his jaw clenched. Even in the dim light of the granary, the hot colour suffusing his face was obvious to the young girl. She withdrew her hand instinctively as if she had touched a burning brand. She was trembling, partly with anxiety because she did not understand the strange feelings that were coursing through her; partly with bewilderment at the change in her childhood companion. She was certain of one thing only – that she could not bear the look of sadness in Benito's eyes.

'You must not doubt me – *you must not!*' she cried childishly.

She saw the sudden sag of his shoulders. His look of resignation frightened her. 'Please, Benito, *please* . . .,' she murmured, without knowing what it was she was asking of him.

He drew a deep breath and, as if now in control of himself, he said in a small, hard voice: 'It is not your fault, Carlota . . .' His unexpected use of her name, spoken in a tone that sounded like a caress, brought tears of relief to her eyes. 'It is the way of things – we cannot change them. Your parents will find for you a rich aristocrat – perhaps someone like that tall Englishman who is your papá's guest – and you will marry and obey your husband's wishes. He would not approve of your friendship with one of your father's *peones* – a mere herdsman, *por Dios!*'

'Then I should not marry such a man!' Lota cried fiercely. 'And anyway, Benito, that Englishman you speak of is our cousin, and if he marries anyone, he will marry Casilda.'

Her voice trailed into silence as she stared at the boy who occupied her thoughts so insistently. This was still Benito, her childhood friend – yet he had changed. She saw him now no longer as a boy, but as a young man, far more handsome than any other she had known; someone who mattered so much to her that she dared this secret meeting. There was no one else – not even Cristobal – who was so important to her happiness. Instinct told her that she was as important to Benito as he to her, yet she had to be certain. She waited in a frozen silence for him to speak.

It was some moments before he did so. Then he said: 'It is not the same now that we are grown up.'

Confused, Lota asked: 'Why is it not the same? It's you who have changed, not I. You no longer care about me. It is because I am not so pretty as Casilda; because you think me ugly now with my horrible foot . . .'

Lota's small, tragic voice undermined the boy's guard. He leaned forward and grasped her hands. 'Look at me, Carlota. Can you not see in my face that I find you beautiful? I did not notice your silly foot. I do not care about it except that I am sad for you. And no, I have not changed! You are as important to me as my dream of becoming a matador. You are part of that dream.'

Benito's face was a mask of despair. Did this young girl really believe that there could be any kind of future for them? She had spoken of a far-off day when he would become a legend, but even then he would not be welcomed as a possible suitor for Carlota's hand. Was she still so innocent that she did not realize it? But what could this young girl know of life outside the protected circle of her family? Carlota, he thought bitterly, took for granted the beautiful clothes she wore; the food she ate; the soft beds; the water that a servant had drawn from the well and heated for her on fuel some other servant had gathered. She was totally protected from the squalor of the poor; the crying need by so many for employment; the relentless fear of starvation and sickness if such employment were suddenly to cease. Could such a girl ever understand that if one day he became rich – as he truly believed he would – his first duty would be to secure his family?

Even to *think* of loving Carlota was madness; but her pale, unhappy face, her declaration of her feelings and her belief in him, had weakened him. He felt ashamed of his weakness, knowing full well that he must discourage any romantic dreams she might have – for her sake as well as his own.

Knowing nothing of his thoughts, Lota sat in happy silence, content that Benito really thought her beautiful; that she was important to him. He had released her hands and she wished very much that he would hold them again. With a shyness she had never before felt in his company, she dared not reach out and touch him, although she longed to do so.

She felt his sadness as if it were a tangible barrier between them, and longing to comfort him, she said: 'No matter what happens from now on, even if we are forbidden to see or talk to each other, I shall think about you every day, Benito. I shall never marry anyone else. I'll wait as many years as necessary for the time when everyone, including my mamá and papá, will make you welcome. I shan't mind how long it takes.'

It was as if she had injected a powerful drug into his veins. The look in his dark eyes changed. He jumped to his feet, his head lifting proudly, and stood as a matador might stand facing the crowd after a perfect killing of the bull. In that moment, he was no longer in the dusty, dim granary; he was standing in the brilliant sunlight, feet planted firmly in the sand, a big, brave bull like Don Jaime's Gregorio facing him.

Lota, too, had risen to her feet. Unconsciously, each had moved nearer to the other and now their arms touched. As they stared into each other's eyes, both were trembling. Tentatively, Lota lifted her hand and touched Benito's parted lips with her finger. The tender little gesture came dangerously close to breaking the tight control the boy was struggling to keep over his longing to take her in his arms, to kiss her with all the fierce passion of youth. He caught her wrist and forced her arm back to her side, stepping away from her as he did so.

'You must go, *mi alma*. *We must both go*. If we are caught . . .'

Lota nodded, a faint, rapt smile curling the edges of her mouth as she stood unmoving, savouring the moment of perfect happiness. Benito had called her 'my soul'. It was like a benediction. She did not care now if they were caught. No matter what anyone did to her, they could not take away her joy.

'*We must go!*' Benito said more urgently. 'I will leave first. When you hear me whistle, you will know it is safe for you to leave.'

Again Lota nodded. 'I will see you tomorrow – at the *tienta*,' she said.

But he was too concerned for her present safety to rejoice in 'tomorrow'. He allowed himself one last look at her face before hurrying down the ramp.

As Carlota waited for his whistle, she realized that for the first time in her life she had lost all trace of the timidity that had affected her in her childhood. So overwhelmed was she by the strange new emotions engulfing her that she forgot even the need for caution as she made her way down to the courtyard. She did not feel guilty of any wrongdoing and her head was held high, her step was jaunty and there was an innocent smile on her face which allayed any suspicions Cristobal might have had as he came hurrying across the yard to her.

'Where on earth have you been? Miss Smart said you were looking for me.'

Lota laughed. 'Don't look so angry, Cris! I have been talking to Benito. He . . .'

Cristobal's face – like her own in feature, but lacking her gentle expression – remained tight-lipped as he interrupted: 'I can't think what you have to discuss with someone like

Lopez. Mamá would be furious if she knew you'd been talking to him without a chaperon . . .'

It was Lota's turn to interrupt. 'If you tell her, Cris, I shall never speak to you again as long as I live. I mean it. And anyway . . .' she added, tears suddenly filling her eyes '. . . how can you of all people be so beastly about Benito? You used to tell me he knew much more about *everything* than you did. You're turning into a horrible snob!'

Her brother's pace quickened and his grasp on her arm tightened as they came to the big wooden gates of the Hacienda. 'That's all in the past – what we *used* to do!' he said fiercely. 'In those days I didn't know much. Now I'm being properly educated; my friends are intelligent and we talk about important things like politics and cricket and we discuss world events and . . . and so on.' He broke off momentarily to draw breath and then, in a gentler tone, he said: 'I know it probably seems unfair to you, Lota, but you must see for yourself that you can't keep up a friendship with a . . . a simple peasant. I like Lopez. I admit that he's quite outstanding with the bulls and he may even make the grade as a matador . . . but you've got your reputation to consider; the family's reputation. Whatever would people think if they saw you mooning around with one of Papá's herdsmen?'

'I don't care what they think!' Carlota said miserably. 'It isn't Benito's fault he was born poor. I shall go on seeing him whenever I can; and I mean it, Cris, if you tell anyone – even so much as a hint – I shan't talk to you ever again.'

By now they were within earshot of their father's friends, who were standing near the open doorway of the Hacienda. Cristobal shrugged. 'You're being a silly little fool,' he said in an undertone. 'But I'm not a sneak. I won't tell anyone. But don't say I haven't warned you. If they catch you meeting secretly, they'll probably shove you into a convent where you can't *ever* see him. It'll be too late then to come crying to me to help you, because I shan't.'

It was the nearest they had ever come to a serious quarrel,

Lota thought as she hurried up to the bedroom she was sharing with Casilda and the English girl who was staying with them for the Easter holidays. But, hurtful as it was to know that Cris and she were at odds, her feelings of happiness and excitement rose quickly back to the surface. She knew now that she was as important to Benito as he was to her. Although nothing concrete had been said and the future only alluded to in the vaguest of terms, she felt committed now in a way she had never done before.

Next morning, Lota awoke at dawn, her feeling of happiness intensifying as she remembered that this was the day of the *tienta*. Not only would she be in the company of Casilda and her three brothers as well as the nice English girl, Joscelin, but she would certainly see Benito.

She jumped out of bed and ran to the window. Opening the shutters, she stared down into the patio below. Her heart leaped as she caught sight of Benito. He was helping to bring the horses round from the stables. She wondered if she dared call out to him, but before she could do so he turned his head and looked up at her window. His white teeth flashed in a smile and she waved back at him, unaware that the English girl had woken and was standing behind her.

A faint flush stained Lota's pale cheeks. 'That's Benito – Benito Lopez!' she said shyly. 'He's the son of Papá's *mayoral*. He and Cris will be testing the bull calves today and you will see what a magnificent horseman Benito is.'

The arrival of one of the maids with a jug of hot water interrupted them and awakened Cassy, who sprang out of bed and struggled into her underwear.

'What time is it? Are we late? Is Alan down there, Lota? Goodness only knows what time Papá and his friends went to bed last night. All that laughing and singing kept me awake for hours!' She began hurriedly to put on her riding habit. 'Oh, do get a move on, you two! They'll all have left before we've had breakfast.'

Lota needed no chivying. She was as anxious as her sister not to miss a moment of this day. As she followed Casilda and the English girl into the dining room, she informed Joscelin proudly that one day Benito was destined to become a famous matador.

'He shows great skill at the *tientas* when they test the bravery of the cows in the little bullring we have here. But today you will see him out on the pasture overturning the bull calves to test their courage.'

Cassy scowled. 'I do think Alan should try his hand as a picador. I suppose he's afraid! Really, he's no better than Eduardo. They're both cowards.'

But Joscelin and Lota looked shocked.

'You shouldn't say that, Casilda!' Lota protested. 'Cousin Alan explained to Papá he was unused to a Spanish saddle and that his horsemanship might not be good enough.'

Cassy tossed her head. 'Even so, Alan is a wonderful horseman and since *I* shall be helping to test the bulls, he should be able to match the skill of a mere girl.'

'You, a mere girl!'

Patricio, who had sauntered into the dining room, ruffled his sister's hair and grinned at Joscelin. 'Casilda's utterly fearless on a horse – that's why Papá loves to show her off to his chums at these *tientas*. But even *she* can't match Cristobal or Benito. I expect I shall make a fool of myself as always.'

But he put up a surprisingly good performance when an hour later the large party gathered on the flowery plains stretching for miles around the Hacienda.

'The young bulls graze happily out here,' Lota explained to Joscelin. 'They have no fear of man, for they are left unmolested until they are two years old.' She pointed to the mounted *peones* separating one of the calves from the distant herd. Cristobal and Benito, holding blunt-tipped lances, were waiting for the animal to escape from its pursuers.

'Their lances are called *garrochas*,' Carlota said. 'See, the bull has left the herd and is running now!'

Cristobal and Benito galloped off in pursuit, and as they drew near to the young bull, they competed with one another to thrust their lances at the animal's flank in an attempt to overthrow it.

'Look!' Lota called out, her eyes bright with excitement. As Joscelin watched, she saw Don Jaime place himself between the bull and the herd to prevent its return. The animal fell but quickly regained his feet.

'He will try to rush back to his companions,' Lota said. 'Papá must knock him to the ground again with his *garrocha*.'

She clapped her hands as the animal fell a second time.

'Do you see that man with the *pica*?' she asked. 'Now it is *his* turn . . .'

Joscelin watched, fascinated by the spectacle as indeed she was by everything she had seen in this exotic country during the past two days. The young bull was standing his ground defiantly, and as the picador approached he charged.

She saw the man's arm lift and then thrust downwards, placing the point of his lance in the animal's neck. Three times the bull charged and nausea overcame her. She felt the young beast's pain as if it were her own and covered her eyes.

Lota put a comforting hand on her shoulder. 'It is not the same *pica* as is used in the bullfight,' she said. 'The point is much smaller and the bull is not badly hurt. Look, Joscelin, he is free now to go back to the herd. He has done well and shown himself brave enough for the ring.'

Joscelin felt it wrong that the only way to test the animals' courage was to torment and hurt them.

'What happens to the bulls who are not brave enough to charge again?' she inquired.

'Oh, they are condemned to death,' Lota said calmly. 'A fighting bull *must* have courage. So too must the *garrochistas*. Quite often one of the bulls will charge the nearest person, and since they have no protection there are many accidents. Benito once saved Papá from a charge by waving his jacket in front of the bull and fending him off long enough for one of the herdsmen to distract him.'

'Deuced dangerous sport!' Alan commented. 'I'm surprised that females take part. Is that usual, Lota?'

Lota nodded. 'Not many of the ladies wish to participate,' she explained. 'But the ability to turn a bull is considered an accomplishment. Once Grandfather entertained the Infantas and each overthrew a bull. Benito's father can remember it.'

Alan frowned. 'Somehow it seems quite wrong to allow a young girl like Cassy to take such risks. If she fell . . .'

By now a second bull had been separated from the herd and Alan turned anxiously in its direction as he recognized Cassy, with her father beside her, galloping towards it.

With no such concern for her sister, Lota's gaze was concentrated on her twin who was now walking towards her with Benito. She hurried to greet them, her cheeks colouring with pleasure as she smiled shyly at Benito. He stood silent, a little apart from Cristobal. His liquid black eyes with their sweeping dark lashes were regarding Lota intensely, his expression unfathomable.

With a defiant glance at her twin, Lota went to stand at Benito's side. 'I present Benito Lopez,' she said in Spanish, her chin lifting fractionally as she spoke. 'Benito, this is our English friend, Joscelin, and I think you may already have met Cousin Alan when he was here at Christmas a year ago.'

As Benito gave Joscelin a formal little bow, Alan stepped forward, holding out his hand. 'I remember you very well, and how much I admired your performance with the cape at the *tienta*.'

Alan's Spanish was halting, but Benito understood enough to appreciate a compliment. He acknowledged it with another slight bow.

'Benito and Casilda used to play with a pretend bull in the stables when they were only three or four,' Lota said to Joscelin. 'Do you remember, Cris?'

'Every child in Spain plays at bullfighting!' Cristobal's voice was edged with scorn. 'Come, Alan, I will take you to meet the Condesa de Figueroa, a cousin of my father's.'

Alan looked apologetically at Benito as Cristobal led him away. In a small, angry voice, Lota said to Joscelin: 'I do not think Cris's school has improved his manners!'

She turned to speak to Benito but the snub had not escaped him either, and without a word he gave a stiff bow and walked off to join a group of ranch hands.

Cassy's sister was quite unable to hide her feelings, Joscelin thought uneasily. The expressions on Lota's face were transparent, and anyone interested in her must be able to see that she cared a great deal for the Spanish boy. Her twin knew it, and that was why he had snubbed the young ranch hand.

In the few days since Joscelin's arrival at the Monteros' home, she had noted the younger girl's sensitivity and felt an instant affinity. She, too, found it hard to conceal her feelings; she, too, had failed as yet to control those betraying blushes. But it was not for her, a comparative stranger, to invite Lota's confidences.

That night, the dining room in the house in Sevilla was ablaze with light; servants hurried in and out carrying heaped platters of food to the sixteen people gathered round the table. The March nights were still surprisingly cold and the *copa* had been lit, a welcome warmth emanating from the glowing charcoal in the brass tray underneath the table.

There was a hubbub of noise, mostly caused by *los chicos*, Carlota decided as she glanced at the youngest children. Luis, the eldest boy, was still only ten; her little sister, Carmen, nine and her youngest brother, Mariano, not yet eight. Nanny Gordon and their governess were not proving very successful in keeping them quiet! But that was Papá's fault. He was in the most jovial of moods, as was usually the case at Easter, and *los chicos* were over-excited.

If only she could be certain when she would see Benito again, she would feel happy too, she thought. There was little doubt that he would accompany Papá's bulls when they travelled from the Hacienda to the city. But Cristobal had refused to take her down to the bullring before the fights, so Joscelin, with sympathetic understanding, had promised to ask Eduardo to take them all. Surely Eduardo would not refuse their visitor's request!

The rift between Lota and Cristobal had deepened since the *tienta*. She toyed with the plateful of squid in front of her, hating this feeling of alienation from her twin. Cris had changed in so many ways, she thought as she looked across the table. He was engaged in animated conversation with their father, disputing heatedly the rights and wrongs of the war still raging in the Spanish Protectorate in Morocco.

'The fighting has been going on ever since I can remember – and for what, Papá?' he was demanding. 'We pour millions of pesetas into supporting an army which can only be supplied from the mainland and whose casualties are appalling – and for what purpose?'

'The purpose is quite clear,' Don Jaime replied patiently, 'and there is no need to raise your voice, Cristobal. I am not deaf. We need to keep this North African coastline out of the hands of the French. The Franco–Moroccan Treaty gave France Tangier – a rich port, I will remind you. The eastern and western zones of the Protectorate are all *we* have and they *must* be retained.'

Cristobal was not to be silenced. 'It all seems so uncivilized, Papá! Why are we so backward? The British can afford guns and tanks and decent roads, yet here in Andalucía we have no mechanized armaments and scarcely one road worthy of the name.'

'That's a bit steep, Cris!' Patri intervened.

'He's not so wide of the mark,' Don Jaime said thoughtfully. 'The wealth of our nation remains very much in the hands of people like ourselves, and not enough has been done to develop the country as a whole. These terrorist uprisings in Barcelona, dreadful as they are, are just the tip of the iceberg.'

As if regretting the serious turn the conversation had taken, he smiled. 'But come, let us enjoy our meal. I would not wish our little English visitor to think that we cannot find more interesting topics to discuss. Tell me, Joscelin, are you always so quiet? I never did believe that it was you who led my wicked Casilda into trouble, and now, having met you, I am even more convinced!'

Unexpectedly, Doña Ursula joined in the conversation. 'If you want my opinion, Jaime, Casilda should have suffered the punishment meted out to her by the Reverend Mother. I am sorry to say that, so far, Casilda has shown little sign of remorse for her regrettable behaviour.'

'Come now, my dear,' Don Jaime said placatingly, 'no harm came of their escapade. The Reverend Mother made too much of it.'

Glad to have the attention diverted from her, Joscelin bent low over her plate, hoping that she might once again be overlooked. In a way she agreed with Doña Ursula – she and Cassy ought to have been punished for playing truant that day at the Piermonts, instead of which she had been invited to spend the Easter holidays here in Spain, which seemed very like a reward for her misdeed!

Her father had questioned the ethics of the whole affair. Don Jaime, on hearing that his beloved daughter had been expelled, had immediately telephoned the Mother Superior and persuaded her to rescind her verdict. Mr Howard echoed Cassy's belief that it had been Don Jaime's large donation to the convent that had brought about this change of heart. 'I suspect that I, too, am being bribed into setting aside my principles,' her father had said when Don Jaime's invitation to Joscelin arrived.

Joscelin preferred not to question too deeply the ethics of the matter, since the threatened expulsion had ended miraculously with this wonderful holiday in Spain.

Nevertheless, she still felt very much an outsider, sitting here at this huge table in the company of fifteen members of the Montero household – or was it sixteen? She glanced at Cassy, looking surprisingly grown up out of school uniform, who was laughing and joking with her father and Patri. Patri was already a head taller than Eduardo, who to Joscelin's embarrassment was staring at her across the table through his thick-lensed glasses. His ill-concealed interest in her might be considered flattering but she did not welcome it, and looked hurriedly away from his gaze to the face of his mother. Her artist's eye could discern the marked likeness between Doña Ursula and Lady Costain, not only in their colouring, but in the bone structure of their faces. But where Lady Costain's blue eyes were gentle and smiling, Doña Ursula's were piercing, narrowed, as if she had no wish to conceal from Joscelin her obvious disapproval of the fact that her favourite son, Eduardo, 'had a crush' on her – which was hardly her fault, Joscelin thought. With Doña Ursula's critical eye upon her, Joscelin was painfully aware that she looked dowdy and old-fashioned.

The maids were now clearing away the empty plates and Mariano took the opportunity to get down from his chair and go round to Patricio to show him some private treasure. He was talking excitedly, as indeed were all the children.

Beside her, Alan said: 'A bit different from home, eh, Joscelin?' He gave his charming smile as he added: 'Just imagine the Pater's face if he were in Uncle Jaime's chair!'

'I'm afraid I don't know your father very well,' Joscelin said. 'I saw very little of him last May when I came to your house for the wedding. Cassy and I were too young to be allowed down to dinner. As a matter of fact, this is the first time I have ever dined at night with grown-ups!'

'How silly of me!' Alan commented. 'Everything's so different here in Spain, isn't it? In England, the children are supposed to be seen and not heard! Here they are all frightfully spoilt – at least, when Uncle Jaime is at home. Of course, when he's away Aunt Ursula rules the roost with a very English rod of iron!'

Whilst Alan was talking, Joscelin noticed that his glance

went frequently to the far end of the table where Cassy was sitting. She looked astonishingly pretty in a pink organdie dress tied loosely just below her waist with a satin sash. At the age of sixteen, she had the softly rounded figure of a mature woman. Joscelin, who worried endlessly about her flat chest and lanky, angular shape, envied Cassy and drew little comfort from her attempts to sympathize.

Alan turned to talk to Carlota, and Joscelin looked round the table. If there were time, she thought, she would like to sketch this scene – to draw all the faces of this huge family. The contrasts were remarkable – Eduardo, Cassy and the little ones so very Spanish-looking with their dark hair, dark eyes and olive skins; Cristobal and Lota so closely resembling their unmistakably English mother.

Lota, noticing Joscelin's glance, smiled at her shyly. Although Joscelin had been their guest for only three days, the younger girl knew that they could become friends and that she could trust her. She wished now she could join in the air of excitement that pervaded the room. It was the same every Easter. In a few days' time it would be Palm Sunday, the start of Holy Week; then there would be the important Easter Sunday bullfight followed by the Sevilla fair, with three more bullfights traditionally part of the six days of festivities.

If she could be certain of seeing Benito, she would be as excited as everyone else at the thought of the feasting and fireworks, the parades that would go on till dawn. Before the big bullfight on Sunday there would be drinking and dancing in the family *caseta* – one of the tented booths in the fairground where Papá would entertain his friends in two little furnished rooms gaily decorated with paper flowers, lampions and pictures. At such times, Mamá had many preparations to make and became even more irritable than she looked tonight, Lota thought as she glanced anxiously at the severe, upright figure of her mother. It was Mamá's wrath far more than Papá's she would fear if ever she were caught meeting Benito secretly.

It was long past eleven o'clock when at last the meal ended

and Miss Smart and Nanny took the little ones off to bed. Don Jaime suggested that Patri should entertain them for a while with his guitar.

'Shall I dance for you, Papá?' Cassy asked eagerly. Since she could first stand on her chubby legs, she had loved to move in time to music. With Miss Smart or one of the other governesses to chaperon them, they were taught by one of the fashionable teachers in Sevilla how to perform the *bulerías* or the *Sevillanas*.

'You will do no such thing, Casilda,' her mother said sharply from her armchair by the fireside in the *salón*. 'You have clearly forgotten that it is Lent.'

Cassy's mouth turned down in a grimace. She was more anxious to perform tonight, not just for her admiring papá but because Alan, too, would be watching. She turned instinctively to Don Jaime and gazed up at him appealingly.

'Just one dance, Papá – a *bulerías*, perhaps? After all, we're quite private here in our own house and who is there to object?'

'Don Alfonso, for one,' her mother said bitingly, 'and I for another.'

Don Jaime had been on the point of supporting his wife's religious objections but the mention of the priest's name had much the same effect upon him as a cape upon one of his bulls.

'Your priest, my dear, does not rule this household,' he said firmly. '*I* decide what is best and I can see no objection to a little quiet dancing. Sit yourself down, Alan . . . and you, Joscelin. If you've not seen a *bulerías* before, it will interest you. And stop fidgeting, Carlota. Find some embroidery to occupy you like your mother.'

'It is a pity that my friend, Benito Lopez, cannot be here to dance with Casilda,' Lota whispered to Joscelin as a space was cleared for Cassy in the centre of the room. 'Once I saw him dancing flamenco in the courtyard of the Hacienda. It was almost as if I was watching him in the bullring, perhaps because the movements of a matador are in a way a kind of dance.'

Joscelin's eyes were on Cassy. Straight-backed, her arms raised, her bright pink dress swirling about her knees, her posture was dignified, her expression demure; and yet with her black hair flying and her dark eyes shining so brilliantly she was astonishingly sensual. This was a woman dancing. There was nothing child-like in the glances she gave Alan as she passed by him, and Joscelin could well understand why his gaze was riveted upon her friend.

Joscelin's first introduction to Spanish dancing awoke in her a confusion of strange new emotions. She could, she thought, become caught up in the music; could rise to her feet and join Cassy – as, indeed, Cristobal was doing now that Patri was playing a *Sevillanas*. It would be so easy to lose herself in the wild, haunting tempo of the guitar, forget her self-consciousness, her shyness, and become someone else – one of the Spanish gipsies, perhaps, who, according to Patri, claimed flamenco music as their own.

But Joscelin's mood was shattered abruptly when, as the dance ended, Doña Ursula rose suddenly to her feet, folded her tapestry and said icily: 'That's quite enough! It's getting late and it's high time the girls were in bed!'

Don Jaime drained his brandy glass and smiled benevolently as he, too, rose from his chair and put an arm affectionately round Cassy's shoulders.

'Mamá is quite right, it is late – *es tarde*,' he repeated in Spanish, with a jovial laugh. 'You girls need your beauty sleep and we men shall be out shooting tomorrow and will have to make an early start.'

No amount of pleading from Cassy would make him change his mind.

In the few days remaining before Holy Week, Don Jaime, Alan and the boys were often absent from dawn to dusk, hunting and shooting with friends. As a consequence, the three girls were thrown together in a companionable female society. Cassy kept both Joscelin and Lota entertained as she expounded her wild theories about life and love.

'If only I knew whether Alan was in love with me! What do you think, Joss? I just know he finds me attractive, but he talks to me as if I was still a child! He knows it makes me absolutely livid when he teases me, and I think he does it because he likes to see me lose my temper. He says I look stunning when I'm angry! When he says nice things like that to me, I could positively swoon!'

Although she was half in earnest, she joined in Joscelin's and Lota's laughter as she play-acted the part of a damsel swooning with love.

'You know Mamá will never agree to your marrying Alan,' Lota said practically. 'He's a Protestant – and even if he becomes a Catholic, he's our first cousin!'

'Lots of first cousins marry,' Cassy announced. 'Just look at all the royal families. They are all intermarried.'

'And look at the Spanish royal children,' Carlota reminded her sister. 'Two of the *infantes* are haemophiliacs and the middle one is a deaf mute!'

Cassy was only momentarily put out. 'Then I may not have any children,' she announced, and, dropping her voice to a whisper, she added: 'I'll tell you both a secret if you swear not to tell anyone. One of the girls at the Convent told me that someone called Marie Stopes has opened a clinic in London where women are instructed how to prevent having babies. She said hundreds of women go there. Well, I shall too. I want to get married when I'm very young, but I certainly don't want hordes of babies like Mamá! The girl who told me about this clinic is going to go there if her mother won't tell her how to stop having a baby. She doesn't think her mother *will* tell her because the Church would look on it as a dreadful sin.'

'If it is a sin, then *you* can't do whatever-it-is either,' Lota said thoughtfully.

Cassy shrugged. 'Oh, I don't care about committing a sin

if it's really necessary,' she said blandly. 'After all, no one goes through life without breaking the rules, do they? Look at Papá – he commits adultery every time he goes to see that woman in Madrid. And don't look so shocked, Joss – I know he has a mistress there because Patri told me. He says it's quite normal for men in Papá's position to have a mistress, and Patri thinks Eduardo is silly to make such a fuss about it. Not that Eduardo would dare say anything to Papá!'

'But what if you do marry Alan and *he* wants babies?' Joscelin asked suddenly.

'Then he'll just have to wait until I'm ready to settle down!' Cassy replied with a shrug. 'Anyway, he wouldn't want to miss all the fun. Just think, Joss, he could take me to Ascot and Henley and to all the London shows and parties, and we could travel all over the world, just the two of us enjoying ourselves.'

'I thought Alan wanted to be a writer,' Carlota said doubtfully.

Cassy frowned. 'Why must you think of dull things, Lota! I dare say, when Tío Angus dies, Alan will have to spend a lot more time up in Scotland seeing to the estate, and he can write his silly old book then, can't he?'

After breakfast next morning she raised a new topic as she stretched herself full length on the sofa in the drawing room. The maids had not yet closed the windows or lowered the thick esparto blinds, and the early morning sunshine was streaming into the room onto Cassy's excited face.

'I could hardly believe it when Mamá read Tía Pamela's letter to us at table. Can you imagine dumpy old Isobel becoming a mother! I'm sure Tía Pamela can't really want to be a grandmother. What a Christmas present for her! Now Isobel can't be matron-of-honour at Barbara's wedding in May.' She jumped up and sailed down an imaginary aisle humming the opening bars of the Wedding March. 'Barbara's so dull,' she added wickedly, 'and she'll hate all the fuss and socializing on her wedding day. Oh, I wish it was me getting married!'

She walked over to the window and stared restlessly down

into the little square below. The orange trees were in blossom and the scent from their fragrant white flowers was intensified by the growing heat of the sun. She gave a deep sigh. 'I'm so bored with being a child. Mamá won't permit me to come out until next year and Tía Pamela says *she* won't present me in England until the year after that.' She tugged at her pigtail despairingly. 'The first thing I shall do is have this cut off. All the really chic women have their hair bobbed or shingled, don't they, Joss? And in London now, Lota, they have their skirts and dresses yards shorter than Mamá, almost showing their knees. And lots of them smoke cigarettes. Just imagine Mamá allowing us to smoke!'

All three girls dissolved in a heap, giggling uncontrollably. The noise soon brought Doña Ursula to the room. She stood in the doorway, surveying them disapprovingly. 'Have you forgotten that it is still Lent? You are behaving like hooligans!' she said in a cold voice. 'You, Casilda, and you, Carlota, should know better. Any more noise and you will none of you leave this house.'

As she sailed out of the room, her displeasure evident in the ramrod stiffness of her back, Cassy caught Joscelin's eye and grinned. Despite herself, Joscelin's mouth twitched. Glancing at Lota, she saw that the younger girl, too, was smiling. So the reprimand from the awesome Doña Ursula was worth it, she thought, just to see Cassy's little sister at least momentarily happy again.

CHAPTER NINE

April 1921

For as long as she lived, Joscelin thought, she would never forget Holy Week in Sevilla. The spring air was filled with the smells of incense, wax and orange blossom, and her artist's eye was almost blinded by the colourful spectacle of the processions passing through the streets on their way to the beautiful Gothic cathedral to be blessed. They converged on the cathedral from all quarters of Sevilla throughout the days and nights preceding Easter Sunday. The huge floats, called *pasos*, were enormously heavy, each one bearing statues of Christ or the Virgin, or a group representing a scene from the Passion.

Some of these Joscelin thought macabre – Christ falling to the ground unable to bear the weight of the crown of thorns on His head, or having His side pierced by a soldier mounted on horseback. She did not care for these colourful scourgings, crucifixions and portrayals of agonized sufferings. But the Virgins were for the most part indescribably beautiful, sumptuously dressed in priceless robes. One she noticed in particular – 'la Virgen de la Concepción' – whose weeping face was framed in delicate ivory lace beneath a crown of gold.

The effigies were mounted on *pasos* decorated with silver and flowers. From them hung long velvet draperies to conceal the sweating porters who supported the heavy tableaux on their shoulders. Sometimes as many as forty men were needed to carry one *paso*; and since it could take a single procession as long as twelve hours to travel along the processional route many of the porters returned with deep wounds in the back of their necks, despite the protective pads they placed beneath the wooden bars.

Unlike Joscelin and Alan, Cassy became quickly restless at her point of vantage in the red velvet box outside the Casa del Ayuntamiento – the City Hall.

'There are so many *pasos*,' she complained, 'one cannot admire them *all!*'

'At least allow your guests to enjoy this unique spectacle in peace,' Doña Ursula said sharply. 'There is nowhere else in the world where Alan and Joscelin can see this historic gathering of the brotherhoods commemorating the progression of Christ to Calvary.'

The brotherhoods, she explained carefully, called *hermandades*, had first been formed in the thirteenth century. Some had as few as a hundred members, another five thousand, of whom only eighty or so took part in the procession. King Alfonso was head of one ancient *hermandad* called Holy Mary of Victory, and would almost certainly be taking part, as was Casilda's father. In all there would be over a hundred floats.

The streets were crammed with people. Some had climbed trees and lamp-posts for a better view, others were standing on rooftops. The air was filled with the solemn beating of drums, and fanfares of bugles and trumpets from the bands accompanying each brotherhood as it passed. Once in a while, a solitary singer would render a *saeta* – a flamenco song expressing hope, desire, remorse, faith, repentance and love. In the same way as the crowds cheered the floats of which they approved, so they received these impromptu solos.

Every so often the procession halted as a brotherhood was held up by the one before it. The exhausted bearers of the heavy floats would grab the opportunity to rest and be given a drink by a water carrier. If one was overcome by the heat and exhaustion, his place was taken by another.

On one of the days of Holy Week, Don Jaime took Alan and Joscelin to see the most unique of all the floats, 'La Muerte', in the chapel of the Convent of San Gregorio. A statue of Death, in the form of a skeleton, sat on a globe of the world which was encircled by a serpent with an apple in its mouth – the symbol of Original Sin. Death sat in a pose of despair and misery, his bowed head supported by a skeletal hand.

'It is interesting, isn't it, Joss, how both beauty and death go hand in hand in Spain,' Alan remarked as they walked slowly back through the crowds to the Monteros' house. 'No wonder Lota warned us we should find the statue macabre.'

Thinking of Lota reminded Joscelin that she had promised the younger girl to use such influence as she had to persuade Eduardo to take them to see the bulls on the morning before the big bullfight. Lota had made no secret of the fact that she wanted to go because Benito would certainly be there.

When they reached home Alan went off to find Cassy, and at once Eduardo appeared at Joscelin's side. He had, he told her, been watching for her return. Joscelin blushed as she attempted a welcoming smile, although she was longing to go to her room to wash and change her clothes. For Lota's sake, she raised the topic of the bulls.

'I gather they're on public view in the open-air corrals before the fight on Easter Sunday,' she said tentatively. 'Lota said it is a fashionable event and that your father is providing the bulls.'

Eduardo nodded, his dark, bushy eyebrows rising slightly in surprise above his spectacles. 'Yes, indeed they will be at the Venta de Antequera on the outskirts of the city. I shall be very happy to escort you, if you'd like to go, although I thought that you shared Alan's disapproval of bullfights.'

'Oh, I wouldn't want to watch the fights,' Joscelin said quickly. 'But I've only seen the bulls at a distance and . . . and I thought I might make some sketches . . .' she added lamely.

'Then of course I shall take you – Lota, too, if she wishes. You might also like to see the *sorteo* on Sunday morning when the selected bulls are paired. The Easter Sunday fight is a very important one and so the bulls will be almost identical in age

and every other way – to make the contest keener, you understand. The three matadors will draw lots to see which pairs
they will fight.'

Joscelin did not really want to hear the details, but listened
politely. Her patience was more than rewarded when later, she
told Lota that her brother had promised to take them to the
sorteo on Sunday.

Lota did her best to conceal from her family her happiness
at the prospect of seeing Benito. But after their morning at
the Venta de Antequera, she was unable to hide her joy. 'Thanks
to you, Benito and I had plenty of time to talk. He is going
on the Rocío pilgrimage again this June,' she announced with
shining eyes as she, Cassy and Joscelin were changing their
clothes in preparation for the evening meal. 'Just think, I shall
be seeing Benito for seven whole days in a row! Aren't I lucky!
It's everything I've prayed for.'

Cassy splashed water into the china bowl on the washstand
and turned to face her sister, scowling.

'Honestly, Lota, you're behaving as if Benito was your suitor.
Surely your girlfriends can find someone more suitable for
you? What about that good-looking brother of Pilar's? Or
that cousin of Sofia's who's such a marvellous rider? If I were
your age, I'd be hoping to be paired off with one of them.
There's nothing special about Benito, *por Dios*! And what's
more, he's nothing but a peasant even if he *is* going to be a
matador!'

Joscelin's heart went out to the younger girl, whose eyes
were now brimming with tears. Hurriedly she intervened.
'Won't one of you tell me about this pilgrimage? Rocío is a
town, isn't it?'

Cassy was instantly diverted. As she dried her face with a
soft hand towel, she said: 'No, it's a tiny little place right in the
middle of the *marismas* – the marshes. Hundreds and thousands
of people go there every year. Lota can tell you about it, since
I shall be back at school and she's the one who's going,' she
added tartly as she pulled on her dress and tidied her hair.

'I'm going downstairs. I expect Alan and the boys will be down already, having a drink with Papá.'

Lota, Joscelin thought, was always more voluble when her sister wasn't there, and now she launched into the story of Nuestra Señora del Rocío.

'That's Spanish for "Our Lady of the Dew",' she explained. She went on to relate the legend of the shepherd whose dog had discovered a carving of *la Virgen* in a hollow tree growing in a swamp, her lovely face covered with dew. According to the legend, the shepherd had decided to carry *la Virgen* back to his home in Almonte; but he had paused to rest and fallen asleep, and when he awoke it was to find the statue gone. On the following day the villagers of Almonte, to whom he had related the story, decided to go back with him to see the place where the shepherd had found *la Virgen*. Unbelievably, it was back in its original position.

'Of course, it was a miracle,' Lota said, 'but the villagers did not realize it then. They too decided to carry the statue back to Almonte. Once again, it vanished whilst they were resting, and each time they tried to remove *la Virgen* from the swamp, the same thing happened. It was finally decided that Our Lady wished to remain where She had been found, and the thicket was declared a shrine.'

According to Lota, the Virgin – sometimes known as the White Dove – had over the years been credited with many miracles. The little shrine in the centre of the wastes of marshland was given the name of the Rocío – the Spanish word for dew. In winter, the cold winds swept through the village which grew up around the shrine. In summer, it was a ghost town, drowsy in the heat; and for one week in the year it burst into life, with hundreds of pilgrims converging there to pay homage to the Señora de las Rocinas, sometimes travelling for as long as four days on horseback or in wagons.

But June was a long way off, and meanwhile the entire family had the prospect of the spring fair in ten days' time to occupy their thoughts. The general air of excitement intensified

Cassy's feelings, reaching fever pitch when the morning finally arrived and she could don her brightly coloured flamenco dress. She fidgeted restlessly whilst the maid dressed each of them in turn.

'Oh, do hurry up, Purita!' she complained as the girl fastened the back of her scarlet dress; then, with a typical change of mood, she smiled happily at Joscelin. 'You look divine in blue!' she commented approvingly. 'No one will recognize it as my last year's effort. The colour has made your eyes blue-grey. You look nice too, Lota.'

Joscelin was far from sharing Cassy's ebullience. The previous night Don Jaime had been in a particularly jovial mood after the Sunday bullfight, and when Cassy had announced that she was riding side-saddle behind Alan next day, he had insisted that Joscelin ride behind him. Her repeated declarations that she had never learned to ride were swept aside. 'Here in Spain we take care of our ladies. We have a special pad behind the saddle for *caballeros* to use when they take up their ladies behind them – *a la grupa*,' he had explained. 'It has a grip near the horse's tail which you can hold with your left hand . . .' he added with a twinkle, '. . . with your right, you shall hold tightly around my waist. I will not allow you to fall off, I promise!'

It seemed to Joscelin, as she rode behind Don Jaime, that everyone in Sevilla who was not on horseback must be jostling one another in the packed streets, shouting, singing, cheering as the horses paraded to a cacophony of noise. But although Don Jaime's beautiful, high-stepping horse shied nervously from time to time, Joscelin's fears slowly vanished. She even enjoyed her vantage point, although the occasional compliments shouted at her by the young men in the crowds made her blush.

Behind her rode Alan with Cassy clinging to his waist. Once, when the crowd surged inward towards them, Patri rode up beside her and, grinning cheerfully, suggested she should ride behind him if she preferred his company to his father's! He did not stay long, however, having espied a particularly pretty girl across the street.

It was not until they reached the *caseta* in the Real – the main street running through the fairground – that Joseclin realized how privileged such families as the Monteros were. Each of the little booths provided a refuge in the bustling fairground where people could entertain their friends. Fanciful arches with palm fronds and lampions decorated the main entrances to the streets where the *casetas* were installed. The pavements in front of them, liberally sanded with bright yellow *albero* earth, were broad enough to allow passage for both pedestrians and the horses bringing the numerous visitors.

There was, Joscelin soon saw, a great deal of 'showing off', but somehow here in this festive atmosphere it seemed quite appropriate to do so. Cassy moved easily among her father's guests, laughing and flirting with any unattached young man. To Joscelin's chagrin, Eduardo remained firmly at her elbow, becoming increasingly pink and silent as he drank endless glasses of manzanilla and gazed into her eyes.

Wickedly, Patri whispered to Joss: 'Don't discourage him. He will fall asleep before we go to the fairground this evening and then I shall be able to escort you!'

Later that day Eduardo did indeed excuse himself on the grounds of tiredness from accompanying them to the Calle del Infierno. Having changed into their ordinary clothes, they travelled through the streets in cars, Miss Smart and Nanny Gordon in charge of *los chicos*.

By now the town was alive with people from every quarter making their way to the fair. Many of the Monteros' friends and acquaintances were in their carriages or cars but the poorer people travelled on foot, groups of girls singing and snapping their castanets as they passed the freshly whitewashed houses; young men clapping out the rhythm of a *Sevillanas* as they eyed the girls. Everywhere was the heady scent of orange and acacia blossom.

The fairground was dazzling, the noise deafening. Music

blared and children screamed as they whirled skywards in the Ferris wheel or rode on the merry-go-round. Alan and Patri took turns to accompany the younger Montero boys, Luis and Mariano, whilst Cassy and Joscelin took care of the eight-year-old Carmen – much to the children's delight – for neither the old nanny nor the governess was prepared to risk her life on moving pleasures. Afterwards the boys won prizes at the shooting gallery and *los chicos* took turns at the lucky dip. They wandered round the sideshows and the little ones watched their older brother and cousin try their hands with the heavy iron mallet, driving long steel nails into a large wooden plank.

But at ten o'clock Nanny Gordon was beyond being cajoled into staying longer and returned home in one of the cars with the excited children. Miss Smart remained to ensure that Casilda and Joscelin left the fair no later than eleven.

'It's ridiculous,' Cassy complained. 'She treats us as if we were children!'

'Which you are!' Patri rejoined. 'A couple of schoolgirls, no more!'

Alan put an end to the threatening squabble by suggesting they go for a ride on the ghost train. Cassy's mood changed instantly, for she knew that part of the little track ran through improvised tunnels where a girl could cling to her companion on the pretext of being afraid of the skeletons, fluttering bats and cobwebs with which they were festooned.

Patri put a protective arm around Joscelin's shoulders as they climbed into their carriage. 'Be not afraid!' he grinned. 'Neither witch nor wolf-man shall get you!'

It was frightening all the same, Joscelin discovered, not so much inside the tunnel, but as the little train emerged into the starlight, a fearsome wolf-man leaped out of hiding and ran along the carriage, uttering piercing yells and threatening the occupants with a large stick.

Cassy was still clinging to Alan's arm as they climbed out of the carriage. Her cheeks were bright pink and her dark eyes huge with excitement as she turned to Joscelin.

'Were you frightened, Joss? I'd have died if I hadn't had Alan beside me!' She glanced up at him, her lashes fluttering. 'I'd never be scared of anything if *you* were with me,' she said provocatively.

Although Alan looked pleased enough at the compliment, Patri would have none of it. 'You've never been scared of anything in the whole of your life,' he said with brotherly bluntness. 'You weren't even scared that night when we found Jorge skulking in the road outside the Hacienda!'

'He was only drunk!' Cassy said frowning.

'And drunk enough to carry out some of those threats he was shouting at us!' Patri rejoined, explaining to Alan and Joscelin that Jorge had once been his father's groom and still bore a grudge against the family because he believed he had been unfairly dismissed.

'And it probably was unfairly,' Cassy said tossing her head. 'I just know Eduardo was the one who left the knife where Papá's stallion trod on it!'

'You can never believe a word Casilda says,' Patri said dismissively. 'Come on, let's go and look at the lion-man in his cage. Ever since I was a kid I've wondered if he was real. Now I'm going to find out!'

Later that night, as they were undressing to go to bed, Cassy whispered to Joscelin: 'There are times I positively hate my young brother. Alan was just beginning to get really keen on me – I know he was. He squeezed my hand in a special way when we went into the tunnel the first time and might have kissed me the second time, only we weren't in the dark long enough.'

She climbed into bed, stretched her arms above her head and yawned. 'Never mind!' she consoled herself. 'There are more days still to come and I'll make Alan take me on the ghost train again. Did you enjoy it, Joss? Don't you think it's marvellous fun – all of it I mean? There's nowhere else in the whole world where I'd rather spend the Easter holidays – especially with Alan here too. I just love being in love, don't you?'

Cassy's mood of euphoria continued next day and was matched by her father's as they sat down to dinner the following night. Don Jaime was at his most jovial, having enjoyed an excellent bullfight earlier in the evening at which one of his home-bred bulls had won great admiration from the aficionados.

'It seems I can be justifiably proud of my ability to breed well!' he commented, winking at Alan and Patri to ensure they appreciated his double entendre. But aware of his wife's disapproving frown, he turned politely to Joscelin and asked how she had spent her day.

'Far more rewardingly than the rest of us, Papá!' Cassy answered for her. 'She has painted the most beautiful picture of "la Virgen de Regla". I will fetch it for you to see.'

To Joscelin's intense embarrassment, she did so. Don Jaime examined it critically. 'This is remarkably good, Joscelin,' he said with genuine admiration. '*Muy bien!*' He smiled at her kindly.

Joscelin blushed as Alan took the watercolour from his uncle and added his own congratulations.

'There are many more of Joscelin's pictures in our room,' Lota said to her father. 'But she is far too modest to show them to you, am I not right, Joscelin?'

'Oh, but they are only rough sketches!' Joscelin protested quickly. 'Most of them were done in a hurry.'

Cassy sighed. 'Lucky old Joss went sightseeing with Miss Smart each time we've been cooped up in church.'

'Miss Smart took me to the Cathedral,' Joscelin said, 'and to the Church of El Salvador at the beginning of the holidays and to the palace of the Condesa de Lebrija and to see the Roman columns, but I've not yet seen the view from the Giralda. Miss Smart said she couldn't manage the climb to the top of the tower.'

Almost immediately she regretted her words, for Alan said kindly: 'Then I shall take you there tomorrow, Joscelin, while the family are at Mass. I haven't climbed the Giralda myself. If we set off early, there'll be nobody about.'

'No honestly, it doesn't matter . . .' Joscelin began, but Alan would not allow her to continue.

'I've nothing else to do – and I'd enjoy it,' he said firmly.

Joscelin's sleep that night was restless. The thought of spending a whole morning alone with Alan held much the same excitement as the last day of term; only this feeling was somehow different. It was tinged with nervousness and an acute anxiety lest Alan might regret his generous offer and find some excuse to get out of his commitment. He, Eduardo, Patri and Cristobal had not come home until the early hours the previous night. Suppose he stayed out late again and overslept tomorrow morning?

But she need not have worried. He came down to eat breakfast with her. As soon as the household had departed for morning Mass, he turned to her with a friendly smile and said: 'I've been thinking, Joscelin. You're going to be shown a great many of the glories of which the people of Sevilla are justifiably proud, but this is a perfect opportunity to see how and where some of the poor people live.' He was looking at her speculatively as he added: 'Would it bore you, Joscelin? I have an idea that when you sit so quietly, apparently daydreaming, you are in fact observing a great deal more than the rest of us; and if you really are going to be an artist, maybe you should see both sides of the picture.'

Joscelin turned quickly to pick up her coat and hat so that Alan would not see the flush of pleasure on her cheeks. Since his attention was more often than not directed at Cassy, she was surprised – and pleased – to know that he thought her perceptive.

As they left the house, Alan tucked his arm through hers in a friendly manner. The sunshine was dazzling as they made their way along narrow, twisting streets. He walked her up long avenues, past statues and beautiful golden and grey stone buildings. Everywhere she seemed to see a tower.

'I believe there are sixty-six in all,' Alan informed her. 'Now look, Joss, there is the river – the Guadalquivir. Some call it "the River of Gold", for a flood of treasure from all over the world once sailed into this port.' Joscelin tried to imagine the slow-moving water in the days when it was alive with sailing vessels. It was up this very river that Columbus had returned from his epic journey, joyful no doubt to see land once again as he sailed those last fifty long miles from the sea.

'This iron bridge,' Alan said pointing, 'is the old Puente de Triana. Triana is on the far side. It is a gipsy ghetto and I think you'll find it very interesting.'

As they crossed the bridge into Triana, Joscelin understood why Alan had brought her here. Staring around, she was almost overcome by the reek of fat and charcoal wafting through the open doorways of the whitewashed, ramshackle houses. The women gossiping outside stared at the two fair-haired strangers with smiling curiosity. Grubby children, some half-clothed, surrounded them, holding out dirty little hands and chattering like starlings as they begged for money.

'Don't give them anything, Joss,' Alan said quietly, 'or word will get round and we'll be mobbed. Every one of them is in need and we can't possibly help them all.'

But despite Alan's warning, Joscelin dropped some coins onto the dirty sack on which sat a half-blind beggar, his arms two ugly stumps.

Seeing the look of pity and horror on Joscelin's face, Alan quickly redirected her attention to the flowers hanging from pots on the walls. Geraniums and pelargoniums trailed from every window and splashed the narrow, dark passages with colour. Poor as these people clearly were, Joscelin thought, they were still determined to have *some* beauty in their lives.

Triana, she thought, was in total contrast with the Sevilla Miss Smart had shown her. Here were no handsomely attired noblemen like Don Jaime: no beautiful, richly dressed ladies riding to church in carriages. Here, men and children were scrabbling for scraps of food in the market; and the gutters and doorways in which beggars sat were blocked with filth. Yet astonishingly, these poor people did not seem miserable.

Many were singing as they swept out their doorways and the ragged children were laughing as they played in the narrow, dirty streets. Over a hundred of them were now following Alan and her, back towards the bridge, the older ones carrying bare-bottomed babies or holding toddlers by the hand. They seemed cheerfully unresentful that their continued demands for pesetas were ignored.

'It's partly the Andalusian temperament,' Alan explained. 'They are proud to be *Trianeros* and you must remember, Joss, that life has always been like this for them. They know nothing else, nor . . .' he added with a smile, '. . . should we forget that here in Spain the sun is shining nearly every day, and at least for a large part of the year these people aren't cold as well as hungry.'

Alan lost the way only once as he led her back through the streets to the Patio de los Naranjos, the Orange Courtyard, from where they could see the magnificent Gothic Cathedral basking in the sunlight. He pointed up to the belltower.

'Do you see the weathervane at the very top?' he asked Joscelin. 'The tower has been named after it. The Giralda is two hundred and fifty feet high and the view from up there must be magnificent. We'd better get a move on, as I'm sure you'll want to sketch the tower itself as well as the view. It's beautifully carved and its lace-like designs are unique.' Joscelin was silent as she followed Alan into the tower. Together they walked up the steep ramps. 'These were built instead of stairs and legend has it that King Ferdinand I rode to the top on his horse.'

Overcome by the breathtaking views, it was not until Joscelin was seated, her sketchpad on her knee, that she found her voice. 'Oh, it *is* kind of you to bring me up here!' she exclaimed.

'What rot!' Alan replied, smiling down at her. 'I've nothing else to do and besides, I want to see which of the views most inspires you. Over there to the east, beyond the Ronda de Capuchinos, you can see the plains of Carmona; and to the south, the plain towards Alcalá and Dos Hermanas. There, over the top of the Plaza de Toros, is the river and Triana. You can see the movement in the docks from here. Look! Down there is the Real and the Montero booth, and there is the fair-ground!'

Joscelin took out a pencil and began to sketch. Her mind was partly occupied with the surprising fact that here she was in what must be one of the most beautiful cities in the world, a plain, sixteen-year-old schoolgirl escorted by a divinely handsome young man of nineteen who seemed not in the least bored by her company.

Alan had been leaning casually against the parapet absorbed in the view, but now he came to stand behind her. 'How's it going?' he asked, and suddenly she felt his hands on her shoulders as he leaned forward to look at her sketchpad. His unexpected touch was like an electric shock. His warm hands, lying lightly on her shoulders, were the focal point of an extraordinary maelstrom of sensation that spread insidiously down through her body to the pit of her stomach. Uncontrolled thoughts leaped to her mind. She was aware of that same combination of excitement and fear as had gripped her once as a child, when her father had sent her swing a fraction too high and she had felt herself falling, falling . . . She was aware, too, of an immense sense of relief that Alan was behind her and could not see the betraying colour suffusing her cheeks. She gripped her pencil tighter, trying to control the nervous trembling of her hands.

'That's amazingly good, Joss!' The warmth of admiration in Alan's casual tone added to her confusion. Tongue-tied, she wished despairingly that she had Cassy's ability to chatter so unself-consciously. Cassy would not have been so over-whelmed, so inadequate, in a situation such as this.

As Alan dropped his hands and moved away, the spell was broken. Now, feeling only the need to escape, she sprang to her feet, but in doing so sent her box of pencils flying. Alan laughed as he stooped to help her retrieve them and, apparently indifferent to her clumsiness, he said gently: 'We've got another quarter of an hour at least, so you've plenty of time to finish what you're doing.'

Staring at him stupidly, Joscelin at last found her voice: 'But it must be so dreadfully boring for you . . .' she stammered. 'Wouldn't you rather . . .'

'No, I "wouldn't rather"!' Alan interrupted gently. He handed her back her pencil box. 'I shall smoke my pipe, Joss, if you don't mind. You carry on, and forget I'm here.'

Forgetting Alan's presence was an impossibility, Joscelin found, as she tried to concentrate once more on her drawing. She wished his kindness was directed exclusively towards her, but she knew it wasn't so. He was equally patient and thoughtful with *los chicos*.

'I've been thinking, Joscelin,' Alan said as he leaned against the carved stone parapet beside her. 'If you really are going to art school when you leave the Convent next year, then by the time I'm ready to write my book you'll be a professional artist. How would you like to do the illustrations for it? Come to that, if you learned to type you could be my secretary as well as my illustrator, and come with me on my travels round the world!'

He was speaking light-heartedly, without any real sincerity, Joscelin told herself quickly as her heart leaped at the picture he had painted for her future. If only he meant it! In a thousand years she could not have imagined a way of life she would prefer. Willingly – with all her heart – she would learn to type; she would even learn to do shorthand if that would make the dream come true!

Her hand trembled as she drew a fan-tiled rooftop, and she was obliged to erase it and wait a moment before drawing it again. For Alan to have meant he wanted her help would be a miracle. But miracles, she knew, did not happen to people like herself!

'Tell me more about your book,' she said, hoping her casual tone of voice concealed her see-sawing emotions. 'It's easier for me to listen than to talk when I'm drawing . . .'

Alan needed no encouragement. 'When I came out here last Christmas,' he said, 'my uncle took me to his coto de caza – that's a game reserve in the marshes – so that I could see the wild camels. There are fifty or sixty of them, living and breeding there, but we saw only four. What really made the day for me was seeing a lynx. Uncle Jaime tells me they are getting much rarer . . .' His words were drowned by the sudden boom of the Cathedral clock as it sounded the quarter hour. But as the noise faded, he continued to talk eagerly of his plan to go round the world compiling a list of all the beasts and birds which were in danger of becoming extinct.

'Cassy thinks I'm quite potty! But I really mean to do it, Joscelin. Of course, the Spanish don't feel about animals in quite the same way as we do. One has only to see what happens to the wretched horses in the bullfights! Patri and Cristobal, and of course Uncle Jaime, think nothing of the horrific gorings inflicted on the horses by the bulls – and Cassy won't miss a fight if she can help it. Once was quite enough for me, even if it does make me sound a bit of a funk to say so. It savours of barbarity – a primitive thirst for blood – although I admit that despite the cruelty there was a certain splendour in the spectacle. I was moved by the courage of both man and beast. But I shall never go again.'

'Strange, isn't it', Joscelin replied, 'how violent the contrast is – so much that is indescribably beautiful in Andalucía – just think of those altar carvings in the Cathedral beneath us! – and yet there is a wildness too, an underlying hint of cruelty, as if the extremes of passion and beauty must run hand in hand with pain . . .'

She ceased talking when the town suddenly broke into a confusion of noise as all the surrounding church and convent bells sounded the hour, followed by the deafening echo of the Cathedral clock.

'The family will be coming out of church,' Alan said, putting away his pipe. 'Have you nearly finished, Joscelin? If so, we could go down and meet them. I told Cassy we might do so.'

Joscelin swiftly closed her sketchpad and rose to her feet. Alan's words were like a dash of cold water, bringing her to her senses. For a little while she had forgotten that anyone but the two of them existed. The happiness of a moment ago was gone as she followed him out into the crowded cathedral square. Alan caught sight of Cassy standing with Eduardo and Patri amongst a group of their young friends.

'There they are!' Alan said eagerly and, taking her arm, hurried her towards them. Cassy was talking animatedly to the three youthful Spaniards surrounding her and she did not notice their approach. The young men were clearly competing with one another for her attention. She was laughing, her dark eyes flashing as she made some pert reply to one of her admirers.

'It would seem we are not, after all, required to escort Cassy home!' Alan said wryly, as he slowed his pace. 'Ah well, let's go and join them, shall we? Who knows but Cassy will spare one of those good-looking boys for you, Joscelin!'

He had intended to be kind, his remark a casual throwaway, Joscelin told herself, and quickly bent her head so that he could not see the effect his words had on her. At least he had no inkling of how he had preoccupied her thoughts all morning. Did this preoccupation with Alan mean she was falling in love with him, or was she, like Lota, taking life – and herself – far too seriously? The practical side of her nature told her that she was behaving in the most ridiculous manner. Girls of sixteen talked about love and pretended they were 'madly in love' with a film star or, as Cassy had been for a few weeks, with the good-looking Prince of Wales. She herself had had a crush on Rudolph Valentino for years. Real love was different – as they all knew. Real love came later as a prelude to marriage, and she and Cassy were still schoolgirls, however grown up they liked to think themselves now.

But for once practicality and commonsense would not assert their usual command of her emotions. What she felt for Alan was somehow different from any other feeling she had ever experienced. Perhaps, she thought, it had something to do with the magic of Spain. Everything was so different here . . . the colours, the heat, the singing, the spectacle of Holy Week, the people themselves. Everything seemed to have another dimension; it was as if the gold and crimson sunsets had set her on fire, the conflagration forcing her to acknowledge a part of herself she had not known existed; which she longed for and at the same time feared.

'Pity we're going back to England tomorrow,' Alan said as Eduardo detached himself from the group and started walking towards them. 'It's been a marvellous holiday, don't you agree, Joss? We'll have to get Cassy to invite us again.'

Joscelin had forgotten they were leaving on the following morning. The reminder sent her spirits plunging. But then Alan said: 'I say Joss, would you think it an awful cheek if I asked you to give me that sketch you did of Cassy on her horse out at the Hacienda? It would make a ripping souvenir of this Easter!'

Like a tilting see-saw, Joscelin's happiness returned. Alan thought well enough of her simple little drawing to want to keep it; whenever he looked at it, he would be reminded of her. But as she nodded her agreement, she realized suddenly that Alan's reason for treasuring the memento was that, each time he looked at it, he would be reminded of Cassy, rather than of her.

CHAPTER TEN

June 1921

Weeks before the start of the pilgrimage to the Rocío on 4
June, preparations began at the Hacienda. The administrator,
Pedro Porcel, and Don Jaime consulted for hours regarding
the food and drink to be packed into the mule carts which
would serve as the family's mobile larder. Don Pedro had
suggested one hundred crates of Fino, fifty Tío Pepe and a few
of brandy, but Don Jaime did not consider these sufficient.

'Add another fifty crates of manzanilla,' he ordered. 'And
if the Jabugo hams have still not arrived, send someone to
Sevilla this afternoon to see why not! And there should be
five not four suckling pigs . . .'

His wife stayed aloof from the preparations. Soon after her
marriage to him, he had taken Ursula on the pilgrimage which
for him was the highlight of every year. He had tried to explain
to her the significance of transporting the beautifully adorned
bullock cart carrying his brotherhood's sacred standard with
its image of the Virgin through the marshes to the shrine at
the Rocío; but her unrelenting Englishness limited her understanding. She had complained throughout the three-day
journey about the dust, the noise, the drinking, the primitive
sleeping quarters in one of the wagons, luncheon picnics on
the grass, the informality between the classes – which in
particular she abhorred. She had been frightened by the occasional glimpses of wild boar and lynx and shocked beyond
measure when they drove through Castilleja. Only with difficulty had he been able to explain that the men who congregated
there, the *maricones*, preferred each other's company to that

of women. In England, she had informed him icily, such men would be imprisoned for criminal offences.

In many ways Jaime was delighted by his wife's yearly refusals to accompany him on the pilgrimage, for he could then enjoy to the full the pleasure of his mistress's company. This year, when he was taking Lota and *los chicos* with him, he would of necessity have to be more discreet, although his mistress would be somewhere in the caravan, travelling with the brotherhood from Triana.

His irritation with his administrator's penny-pinching gave way to a familiar feeling of excitement as he anticipated the days and nights to come. As he caught sight of Lota approaching him he beamed at her, delighted suddenly to have such a pretty young daughter to show off to the friends who would visit their camp sites when they stopped overnight or en route. He had been regretting that his beloved Casilda was not here for the pilgrimage, but now as he kissed Lota's cheeks, he noted with surprise how pretty she had grown of late. She looked like a pale, golden-haired Madonna.

'Miss Smart has packed your pretty dresses, *niña?*' he asked Lota. 'You must pay proper respect to *la Virgen!*'

Lota nodded, too full of excitement to speak. She could not wait for the day after tomorrow when she could wear her new frilled dress and riding boots, the coloured ribbon with the medal of the Virgin round her neck, her *sombrero ancho* on her head. Papá had given her a pretty new mare especially for the pilgrimage, a gentle, peach-coloured animal which looked particularly dainty alongside Papá's big black stallion. Papá was taking spare horses, of course, and several of the servants would be riding too. But most important of all, Benito would be riding with the brotherhood on a spirited chestnut gelding loaned to him by Papá . . .

Lota's excitement grew as the last of the preparations for the journey were completed and the day of departure arrived. Dressed in her new finery, she was ready even before Don Jaime appeared with intricately worked leather chaps covering his dark *corto* trousers, and his flat *sombrero ancho* set at a jaunty angle on his head.

Lota was helped into the saddle by a groom whilst Miss Smart and *los chicos* scrambled into one of the wagons. With the mule cart and the other two wagons following they set off in the direction of the village, the little pieces of mirror and the silver and gold embroideries that adorned the horns of the oxen refracting the bright sunlight. In the village, thirty other wagons awaited with four spare pairs of oxen in case of accident. Don Jaime was joined by a further two hundred or so pilgrims with four pairs of civil guards to accompany them. As soon as Mass had been said, the Brotherhood set off to the musical accompaniment of drums and flutes. People were singing, snapping castanets, the dust rising in the morning air churned up by the hooves of the horses and the plodding mules and oxen.

Within a short time, the caravan had linked up with the other brotherhoods from Triana and Sevilla. The police band all but drowned the jubilant cries of farewell and the shouts of '*Viva la Blanca Paloma!*' as the sun beat down upon the departing cavalcade.

Riding at her father's side, Lota watched eagerly for a glimpse of Benito's slim, dark figure. She knew he was riding with their Brotherhood but he remained out of sight. Perhaps, she told herself anxiously, he was trying to find the courage to approach Papá to ask that she should be permitted to ride *a la grupa* with him – a break with convention that was an accepted tradition of the Rocío pilgrimage. She was beginning to tire in the hot sun and joined Miss Smart and *los chicos* in their wagon for the climb up to Castilleja.

Don Jaime came riding up to the wagon and told Miss Smart she might dismount with *los chicos* to buy some of the oil cakes that were a speciality of Castilleja. Fortified by a half bottle of the wine he had shared with one of his friends, he wickedly drew her attention to the group of *maricas* perched on the whitewashed town wall. Lota quickly diverted her governess's gaze from the effeminate-looking men to the garlands of flowers, flamenco shawls and straw hats hung out by way of welcome to their ornate standard. By the time they remounted the wagon, Miss Smart had regained her lost composure.

Leaving Castilleja behind them, the caravan passed through the ancient Moorish farmsteads on the open roadway leading to the marshes. Suddenly Benito appeared alongside the wagon and requested that Carlota might be permitted to ride with him. Don Jaime had encountered a number of his friends in Castilleja and willingly surrendered his daughter to Benito's care. As happened quite often, a group of wagons had halted in the shadows of some pine trees so that the riders could dismount with their ladies to drink some wine and rest a while, and he was anxious to join them.

As Lota was lifted up behind Benito and she wound her right arm around his waist, he smiled at her. 'Don Jaime is a good man,' he said in his soft voice. 'It is not every employer who would allow his daughter to ride with one such as I!'

'You should not speak so humbly, Benito,' Lota protested. 'One day you will be Spain's most famous matador.'

The boy's handsome face flushed with emotion. 'You have faith in me, Carlota, but my mother is fearful for me and does not wish me to risk my life as a matador. She would prefer that I should take my father's place as Don Jaime's *mayoral* when I am older.'

Lota's eyes were shining. 'I understand why your mamá is fearful for you. It is because she loves you. I, too, am afraid when I watch you face the bulls at Papá's *tientas*. It is the way of women . . .'

She was innocently unaware that her words had told the boy he mattered a great deal to her. But *he* had noted it and his throat went dry. This pretty young girl whose arms were encircling his waist had been his beloved since as long as he could remember. To be in her company meant more to him even than fighting her father's bulls. He was nearly the same age as she in years, but in many ways he was far more mature, and certainly far more apprehensive about the yawning gap between their stations in life. What hope had he, a simple *peon*, of bridging that gap between them – even were he to achieve his ambition to become rich and famous?

It was by no means an impossible dream. He had fought his first bull calf at the age of seven, since when Don Jaime had taken an interest in him. He had now found a patron, and next year when he was sixteen, he would become a *novillero*. God willing, if he performed well as a novice, he might be a matador by the time he was eighteen. He knew he was talented and could justify Don Jaime's faith in him; but none of this made possible a relationship with his employer's daughter . . .

A group of wagons ahead of them stopped in a shadowy grove of eucalyptus trees. Their occupants called out a friendly greeting to the youth and his girl, inviting them to share their simple meal. Lota nodded her agreement as Benito looked questioningly at her. A tantalizing smell was coming from a pot stewing over an open fire. The rest of the Andaluz country repast, consisting of asparagus and potato omelettes, chick peas, black pudding and smoked ham, was spread out on the grass in front of the travellers.

No meal had ever tasted quite so good, Lota thought as she picnicked by Benito's side. He was gently teased as their hosts inquired of him if she was his fiancée, and if not, why he was wasting this chance to invite so pretty a young girl to marry him.

'He has first to become a matador,' Lota answered shyly, since Benito himself seemed incapable of words, and told them proudly of his progress towards becoming a bullfighter. But Benito soon hurried her away from their new companions, reminding her of his promise to her father to keep her for no more than an hour, and reluctantly returned her to her governess's care.

That evening, in the very best of spirits, Don Jaime dismounted and helped his children down from the wagon for their first night's stop. This was the moment he most loved. As the pink and mauve sunset slipped behind the clouds, the breeze stirred in the tallest branches of the pines and the Chaplain of the Brotherhood said the rosary. The air filled with the smell of broom and pine cones as the campfires began to glow in the dusk and the cooking pots started to simmer. The servants busied themselves about the encampment, singing to the soft notes of a guitar. The children ran around, clapping their hands in time to the music, laughing, their shadows chasing over the lace curtains and arched covers of the wagons. The oxen, released from their yokes, were given their meal of carob and left to graze the grass near the groups of tethered horses.

A tablecloth was spread on the ground and Josefa produced a mouth-watering *pepitoria* – a type of chicken stew which Don Jaime particularly enjoyed. No sooner was the meal finished than Miss Smart began fussing that it was long past the little ones' bedtime.

Don Jaime waved her aside. 'Have you no feeling for the pilgrimage?' he asked. 'They can sleep in the *carreta* tomorrow if they are tired. Meanwhile, they shall watch the dancing with Carlota and me!'

In the clearing of the encampment, the fires of the various brotherhoods glowing in the darkness, shadowy figures were moving into the circle as the flutes, drums and guitars began playing. Soft, rhythmic clapping accompanied the music. A young woman came over and laughingly invited Don Jaime to dance with her. The guitars thrummed and soon several couples were performing, Don Jaime in the centre of the circle.

Lota sat on the Rondeño rug, her back propped against her father's riding saddle, her limbs aching from the long hours of riding, yet her weariness tinged with a strange excitement. A soft breeze was stirring the lace curtains of the wagon into which Miss Smart had disappeared. Around her swirled the scents of damp earth, rosemary, thyme, wild mint and resin from the mastic trees.

From the shadows of the pines, a figure appeared.

'Benito!' Lota whispered. 'I am so pleased you have come to talk to me. Look, Papá is dancing! I have never seen him so happy before!'

Benito stood staring down at her, his young face serious. 'I came to ask Don Jaime if he will permit you to come with me for a ride tomorrow morning,' he said.

Lota rose quickly to her feet, her face pink with pleasure. 'I would enjoy that!' she said, adding shyly: 'Do you think we might dance, Benito? I would so much like to try!'

His hesitation was only momentary, for there was no one who knew better than he – Lota's closest confidant in those early days she had spent recuperating at the Hacienda after her accident – how self-conscious she was about her twisted foot. He did not care whether she could dance well or not. It was enough that she should want him for her partner. As they joined the group of dancers he stared down into the girl's bright, excited eyes. He knew that Carlota was unaware of the passions that she stirred in him; of his desperate awareness of her young, supple body, the smoothness of her skin, the temptation of her small, laughing mouth.

Next day, Don Jaime gave his permission for Lota to ride with Benito, and as the standard was driven off towards the *marismas* he seemed to take it quite for granted that Benito would ride alongside the family's wagons. When he himself was not conversing with the friends he met at frequent intervals, he talked to the boy of bulls, of bullfights he had seen, of his calves who would soon be old enough for Benito to fight in the *novilladas*. Time passed swiftly, and the sun was going down as the pilgrims finally reached the *marismas*.

That evening, as the music and dancing started once more, Lota thought of her mamá, who would certainly not have been as permissive where Benito was concerned as Papá was proving to be on the pilgrimage. Doña Ursula had made it clear these last few years that she disapproved of her friendship with one of the ranch hands.

Why must there be these stupid rules about people's position in society, Lota asked herself? If growing up meant one must not see those who mattered most, then she wished she need never grow up.

Shortly after Lota had gone to bed, Don Jaime went off in search of his mistress, who was with the Triana Brotherhood encamped nearby. He spent what remained of the night with her in the eucalyptus grove, returning in the early hours of the dawn to sleep beneath the stars, his mistress's words of love echoing in his ears.

A few hours later, he woke slowly as the rhythm of the drums and flutes heralded the dawn. The brotherhoods were preparing for departure. He could smell the smoke of the wood fire where his manservant was heating water for his morning shave. Miss Smart appeared. In her shockingly bad Spanish, she directed one of the maids to bring her more water for *los chicos*. From nearby came the sound of songs, the soft clapping of hands and the calls of the wild birds in the trees above his head.

'You are happy, Señorita Smart?' he called out wickedly and saw the look of embarrassment on the governess's face as she glanced towards him, nodded and dived back through the canvas awning of the wagon. Remembering recent hours of love, Don Jaime grinned, thinking how such a night might change the prim little English spinster who had clearly no idea what passions might lurk beneath her high-buttoned blouse and shapeless grey skirt.

Setting out after breakfast, Lota riding on her pretty little mare beside him, Don Jaime breathed in the salty air blowing across the alluvial delta. Seagulls flew overhead, and far away on the horizon he could see the pinewoods of the Atlantic dunes. Now they were on the plains which were covered with spiny, rosin-scented umbrella pines, and dotted here and there were lakes and inlets. It was a perfect spring day and they rode silently through meadows carpeted with wild flowers and into the iris-flagged marshes bright with tiny, jade-green narcissi and noisy with clouds of wild birds. The sky was a misty blue.

Several times they glimpsed a herd of deer. The animals had been startled from cover by other riders in the growing number of processions converging on their destination. Once Don Jaime's stallion nearly unseated him when a large boar raced past from a thicket. Only Benito's tight hold on the head of Lota's little mare stopped her from bolting in fright.

There was now an increasing air of excitement as the Brotherhood prepared to cross the famous shallows of Quema, the river waters of the Guadalimar. Don Jaime espied his mistress, dressed up for this last day of the journey in a salmon-coloured flamenco dress with its low waistline, and a little three-cornered silk shawl pinned at the base of the V neck. After a day of steady drinking with his friends, he found her more desirable than ever. Knowing that the pilgrimage to the Rocío was the one occasion when the lower orders could mix with their superiors, he was amused to see his administrator flirting with the wife of a wealthy neighbour.

Soon after one o'clock, the journey to the Rocío was over. Clouds of dust raised by the horses and carts which had preceded them covered Don Jaime and his party from head to toe as they rode into the little town. From everywhere around them came cries of '*Viva!*', singing and applause, as they made their way to the little chapel where the Virgin stood resplendent on her silver float before the high altar. Through the open door of the chapel, they could glimpse the mountain of wax candles in the presbytery covering the length of the simple transept. Don Jaime stopped to light three dozen of their own candles which he offered to the Virgin.

Riding between her father on his favourite stallion, and Benito on his chestnut gelding, Lota was aware of the heat of the sun as it reflected off the silver and gold embroideries adorning the horns of the oxen. Handkerchiefs waved, guitars played and there was a continuous pealing of the chapel bells competing with the cries acclaiming the Virgin. Lota was conscious, too, of the scent of heliotrope, fresh-cut pine branches and the sweat of men and animals as slowly, through the singing, jostling crowds, Don Jaime's family eased their way to his little house.

With a sigh of relief, Miss Smart climbed down from the wagon and followed the servants as they carried the family's belongings into the simple whitewashed rooms. Although they were furnished only with truckle beds, a dressing table and a night table, Miss Smart reflected that at least she was in less primitive surroundings than those afforded by the covered wagon in which she had slept for the past three nights.

Lota was enchanted by the little house with its thatching of hay, and the roof of the tiny veranda formed from freshly cut branches of pine and rosemary. Outside in the thronging street, she could see the walnut and chestnut sellers who, her father told her, had stored their wares underground since the winter.

Later in the day the Brotherhood would make its official entry into the Rocío, but for the moment there was lunch to be prepared by the servants, and Miss Smart insisted upon the children washing and changing their dusty clothes before they could go downstairs. Don Jaime took the opportunity to ride round visiting his friends, taking glasses of wine here and there in the shaded booths. From here they could watch the young girls walk by, their skirts frilled to the thigh and tight around their bottoms, the outline of their jutting breasts clear beneath the percale bodices. Their smiles and glances were inviting, and for the moment he forgot even the presence somewhere in the Rocío of his favourite mistress.

Lota found it impossible to sleep after lunch during the siesta demanded by Miss Smart. The noise of the singing and drums and the cries of welcome to the newly arrived pilgrims were too deafening for sleep.

Whilst she rested on her bed, one of the servants was kept busy ironing the frilled dresses she and Carmen would be needing, for it was the custom to wear the very best of their attire for the formal entry and ride past the chapel. No dress or man's shirt must have a single crease, and even the wheels of the wagons must be repainted white for the procession.

The senior Almonte Brotherhood, with the authorities from Sevilla, Cádiz and Huelva, all with their staffs and insignias, were already at the chapel awaiting the arrival of the lesser brotherhoods. At six o'clock, when Don Jaime mounted his freshly groomed horse, the sky was turning from blue to pink. Impeccably dressed, he rode past the chapel to the sound of drums and cornets, and drew applause from the teeming crowds as he swept his hat from his head like a musketeer, making his mount first rear, then kneel on the ground outside the chapel.

From inside the wagon, Lota watched this exhibition with pride, and clapped her hands in delight as the senior driver goaded his oxen to their knees also.

The formalities completed, Don Jaime rode off once more to visit his friends. The ox drivers unyoked their exhausted beasts and took them to graze in the meadows, their empty yokes resting on the ground like ploughshares. An anxious Miss Smart did her best to keep her small charges under control but when they had had dinner that night, they were too excited to sleep. Benito came to the door to ask if he might take Carlota for a walk in the cool night air to see inside the chapel. Looking quite shocked at the mere suggestion, Miss Smart would have sent the boy packing, but for once the most docile and accommodating of her charges argued her decision.

'One of the maids will chaperon us!' Lota pleaded. 'I am sure Papá would not mind. He let me go riding alone with Benito on the *marismas*. Benito will see I come to no harm. Please, Miss Smart! This *is* the Romería del Rocío! I promise to behave myself exactly as you would want. Please, *dear* Miss Smart?'

Too exhausted to argue, the governess gave in. After all, she thought, things *were* very different here – to put it at its mildest

– and if Don Jaime did not object to his daughter keeping company with the son of his *mayoral*, why should she? Carlota was a quiet, well-behaved child and could be trusted.

'But for half an hour only, Carlota!' she said reluctantly. 'And you, boy, make sure no harm comes to her or I shall see you are dismissed.'

Her Spanish was so poor that Benito did not understand and, laughing happily, Lota refused to translate. Proudly, he walked beside her.

'Tomorrow in the daylight you will see the pretty colours of the pink and white and yellow houses,' he told her, 'and the white *palomas* you so much want to see! Nowhere in Spain are there so many doves as here at the Rocío.'

He took her hand and held it tightly in his own, explaining that he must do so in order to ensure that she was not separated from him in the crowds still milling around the streets despite the lateness of the hour. The singing and dancing would continue all night, he added, glancing over his shoulder to make sure that the Monteros' maid, Purita, was following. Plain though she was, at the Rocío all women were desirable to those who had had too much to drink.

Lota sighed. 'I never imagined I could be so happy!' she said softly. 'How stupid I have been refusing to come here with Papá these past years! But you come every year with your family, don't you, Benito?'

The boy nodded, content to hear Carlota express her happiness in his company. Excited by the feel of her soft little hand in his, he felt fiercely protective, and would happily have killed any man who accosted her. He knew he might have to wait another year before he could once again walk beside her like this, as an equal, and carefully he avoided the thought that he might be far away from Andalucía by then – as indeed might she. Her parents, she had once told him, were always talking of sending her to England to the convent which her sister attended. His heart went cold each time he permitted himself to think of such a possibility.

'Come!' he said softly. 'I shall take you to see *la Virgen*. She is the most beautiful lady in all the world.'

He guided her carefully through the singing, carousing throng of people to the door of the little chapel.

As they entered, Lota noticed how stark it was in its simplicity, the room with its sandy floor bare, the only furnishings a few wooden benches and a single confessional box. In front of the iron altar railings, candles had been lit, and behind, on a dais, reposed the statue of the Virgin.

As Benito lit a candle, Lota moved slowly forward past the kneeling figures of other pilgrims and knelt at the altar. Her eyes were drawn to the face of the statue. It was not really beautiful, she thought, her breath catching in her throat, and yet there was a strange loveliness about the young, serene countenance. At last she understood why the White Dove was so greatly revered that thousands of people came year after year to visit her. Benito came to kneel beside Lota and pointed silently at a mark on the pale, sweet face. For a moment, Carlota thought it was a tear on the Virgin's cheek before she realized its true significance – it was a single drop of dew.

She held tightly to Benito's hand as, followed by the maid, they emerged from the candle-lit chapel into the street. She felt transfigured as she had done only once before, on the day of her confirmation. A group of young men and women on the other side of the street called out greetings and invited them to share their wine. Benito returned their greeting but shook his head when Lota suggested they might join the party.

'It is time I took you back to your house,' he said, realizing, as she did not, that the revellers had been drinking for many hours. He knew, too, that it was not unlikely that a young high-spirited señorito riding past them might scoop up his precious charge onto his horse and disappear with her into the darkness.

Before leaving her in her governess's care, he took each of her hands in his and stood gazing deeply into her eyes. 'If I know you will come to the Rocío next year,' he said urgently, 'it will not matter so much that I cannot see you very often in between. *Will you come, Carlota?*'

The look in his dark eyes seemed to Lota to penetrate her heart like an arrow, and she cried softly: 'No matter what, I'll come on the *romería* next June. I promise, Benito. And you must promise, too. But maybe you will be far away in another province and . . .'

'No matter where I am, I shall return in time for the *romería,*' he vowed. 'But you, Carlota – suppose you have been sent to England and . . .'

It was her turn to interrupt. 'I give you my word,' she said quietly.

The intensity of their expressions softened into smiles. Slowly Benito raised her hands to his lips and, oblivious to the maid hovering sympathetically in the shadows, kissed each hand in turn, passionately and reverently.

Her heart pounding, Lota finally drew them from his grasp. 'I must go!' she whispered. 'We will see each other tomorrow.'

He nodded and made no attempt to detain her as she turned and went into the house. That night he lay in the open not far from where Lota too, lay awake. Each dozed fitfully until dawn broke – a blazing hot Whit Sunday.

After High Mass in the open air, which many of the pilgrims, including Don Jaime, attended on horseback, the day was given to religious devotions. In the cool of the evening, Don Jaime attended the fraternal dinner of his brotherhood. They dined in the open air, table cloths spread under the trees, eating and drinking from the leather bottles being handed round full of Bollullos wine. The meal over, the brotherhood set out for the chapel where the candlelit rosary would be recited.

Aware of the unbridled revelries which inevitably would follow the ceremony, Don Jaime had refused his young daughter the permission she sought to go out walking once more with Benito. More amused than worried by the obvious rapport between the two youngsters, and aware that he was soon to enjoy yet another night carousing and making love to his mistress, he relented sufficiently to permit them to sit together on the veranda of the house – Josefa, nodding in a chair not far away, acting as chaperon.

But Miss Smart was far from happy about the developing relationship. Carlota's face was too revealing and, not a half hour after Don Jaime had ridden off into the night, she ordered the girl indoors.

'You are keeping poor Josefa and me from our beds at this late hour!' she complained, knowing that the appeal would touch Lota's heart and thus achieve her aim to separate the young couple.

Just before dawn, Don Jaime returned to wash, change his clothes and make his way with his family to take his appointed place in the chapel where Mass was said before the long-awaited emergence of the Virgin. Outside the crowd shouted, jostling one another to get nearer to the chapel doors and surging forward in a wild rush when at last the sacred statue appeared. A magnificent gold, silver and white canopy covering her head, the White Dove was carried on the heavy platform by forty or more strong men from Almonte towards the village square, followed by a thousand spectators. From time to time, a cripple or a beggar would push forward to touch the effigy, and all round there echoed cries of '*Viva la Virgen!*' and '*Viva la Blanca Paloma!*'

Miss Smart and *los chicos* stared at the scene from the veranda of their house. As the statue was carried along the scorching Real, Our Lady's float seemed to be sailing on a tempestuous sea. The noise of the clapping, the weeping, the prayers and shouts of '*Olé, olé, olé*' was deafening as the effigy was carried shoulder-high from one brotherhood to another.

It was almost four hours before finally the Virgin was returned to the altar of the chapel where her feet could rest once more on the ancient, hollow treetrunk beneath which the shepherd had originally found her. Stunned by the noise, the dust, the very fervour of the pilgrims, Lota stepped back from the hot sunshine into the shadows, covering her ears with her hands. Even then she could still hear thousands of voices shouting 'Olé, olé, olé', and felt the crowd's emotion as part of herself.

Despite her longing to be with Benito, she nevertheless slept in the jolting wagon for a large part of the journey home. She knew that Benito was riding alongside; could hear his voice in answer to her father's deeper tones, and knew that she did not have to be close to him physically to feel so in her heart. He had promised once more as they left the Rocío that, come what may, he would be there again next year; and she had done likewise.

It had been a kind of betrothal, she thought sleepily. It was as if, by exchanging their pledges at the shrine of the White Dove, the Lady of Miracles had given a far greater meaning to their promises, and transformed them into sacred vows which nothing but death itself could break.

CHAPTER ELEVEN

September 1922

As the taxi passed Victoria Station and turned into a side street, Joscelin stole a glance at Cassy. For once, she looked pale and serious as she stared down at her clasped hands. Beside her, Lota was even paler. There were huge dark rings beneath her eyes and she looked quite absurdly young. In Tía Pamela's borrowed cloche hat and beige coat frock, she appeared exactly what she was – a fifteen-year-old dressed in a grown-up's finery.

Joscelin turned hurriedly away from the disturbing sight of the girl's unhappy face, and stared out of the window. Noting the drabness of the back street down which the taxi was now crawling, her apprehension grew. Until this morning, Cassy had been so full of bright confidence that Joscelin was able to stifle her own misgivings; but now her throat went dry as her long-held suspicion that Cassy's plan was a mistake became a certainty. Unfortunately, it was the only one they had been able to devise to assist poor Lota to escape the consequences of her folly.

Following Lota's first visit to the Rocío the previous year, she and Benito had been separated whilst the boy was serving his apprenticeship. They had been reunited during this year's June pilgrimage, and no one had suspected that Lota might be so overcome by her love for Benito that she would allow herself to be seduced by him. At least, that was how Cassy put it, although Lota had confessed to Joscelin that it was *she* who had seduced *him*.

Benito, she swore on her sacred oath, would not even have

dared to kiss her had she disallowed it. She had wanted him to love her; she had chosen this way to make him understand that she loved him and hoped to marry him, and she blamed only herself when, two months later, she realized that she was almost certainly going to have a baby – God's punishment for her sin.

Too afraid to confess her fears to her mother, she had turned to Cassy for help on the evening of her sister's return home for the summer holiday. Cassy had been in turn disbelieving, then shocked, then angry, but had nevertheless set herself the task of trying to find a way to solve Lota's problem.

At least Cassy had been successful in keeping the truth from Doña Ursula, Joscelin reflected. Cassy had telephoned her from Spain and let her into the secret. Joscelin was instructed to ask her parents to invite both girls to spend the last few weeks of the summer holiday with her in England, and two weeks ago she and her parents had driven down to Southampton in Mr Howard's new Morris Cowley to meet them off the P & O liner from Gibraltar.

As soon as possible, Cassy had visited an old school friend, Beryl, with whose help she had developed the plan to 'rescue' her sister, and upon which they were now embarked.

The taxi ground to a halt and, sliding open the glass window dividing him from his fares, the driver called over his shoulder: 'You sure this is the place you want, miss?'

Lota did not look up, but Cassy and Joscelin stared out of the side window at the seedy-looking hotel outside which the taxi had stopped. Its paint was peeling and in front of it stood a large dustbin without a lid. A cat, as dirty and non-descript as the grey stone face of the building, shot out from behind the bin and dived down the crumbling steps into the basement.

'*Of course* it's the place we want!' Cassy said firmly.

As Cassy paid the driver, Joscelin busied herself helping Lota from the taxi cab. Lota's pregnancy was no longer in doubt, and it was this certainty which had prompted them to go ahead with the second part of Cassy's plan – for Lota to have something called 'an abortion'.

'It's really just sort of forcing a miscarriage,' Cassy had told them vaguely, 'so there's absolutely nothing to worry about. Mamá's had three miscarriages and was only laid up for a week each time. Beryl says it's quite simple – so long as you have the money to pay the right doctor to do it.'

Beryl, older than Cassy, had left the Convent two years previously. Her mother was a well-known actress who had married into the aristocracy – and unlike other parents who never discussed sex with their young daughters, Beryl's mother happily passed on to her offspring the knowledge she had acquired. She had even, at Beryl's request, supplied her daughter with the address of a man who would oblige her pregnant friend. Neither Joscelin nor Lota knew his name and Cassy had been evasive, telling them emphatically that 'secrecy' was a part of 'the deal' since the dangers to everyone, including Beryl, were extreme if anyone discovered what they were up to. As for the man, he could be sent to *prison!*

Cassy had waved aside Joscelin's fears that it all sounded too risky. 'Honestly, there's nothing to worry about, Lota,' Cassy had insisted. 'As for you, Joss, I thought you wanted to help! You said you'd do anything you could, but now you do nothing but cast doubts about the safety of it. *Of course* it's safe – Beryl said so!'

But now Cassy, too, looked worried as Joscelin pulled on the hotel's rusty iron bell handle. The door opened and a grey-haired woman in carpet slippers scrutinized them with sharp, beady eyes.

'I'm Miss Smithson,' Cassy said, her voice bravely attempting to sound authoritative as she gave their assumed surname. 'I booked a room by telephone yesterday.'

The woman nodded. 'I thought you was! Payment in advance, dearie. That's the rule, and you might as well know there'll be no refund if you don't stay the night!'

Joscelin looked at the claw-like hand outstretched towards

them and shivered. Beside her, she felt Lota trembling as Cassy withdrew five shillings and a sixpenny piece from her purse.

'But of course we'll be staying the night!' she said sharply. 'Why should we book the room if we didn't want accommodation?'

The landlady took the proffered payment with a shrug, as she realized her mistake in assuming that the young girls standing in the front hall were 'three more of the usual'.

'We would like to go to our room immediately. My sister is not very well and we're expecting a visit from her doctor,' Joscelin said, trying to make her voice sound matter-of-fact as she repeated the lines Cassy had made her rehearse.

The landlady shrugged. 'There's no porter here,' she informed them wryly. 'You'll have to carry up that suitcase yourselves. Room 18, second floor, first on the right!' Pulling her shawl closer round her shoulders, she shuffled back to her sitting room in the basement.

Joscelin put the portmanteau down on the grubby eiderdown of the big brass double bed in No. 18 and stared round the shabby room with distaste.

'It doesn't look very clean!' she said doubtfully.

Cassy turned back the bedcovers and with a look of disgust on her face she cried out: 'Joss – look! I don't think these sheets have been properly laundered!'

Lota joined them by the bedside and all three girls stared at the grimy bedclothes and shuddered.

'Will I have to lie in there?' Lota asked in a small, horrified voice.

For a moment, Joscelin did not reply. She felt a sudden fierce hatred for Cassy. She should not have persuaded them to come here! It was *her* plan – even to choosing this fifthrate, horrible, dirty hotel. It was unfair of Cassy to include her. Lota was not her responsibility.

'Joscelin!'

Lota's voice, close to panic, brought Joscelin's thoughts back to the immediate problem of the filthy sheets. No, Lota could not lie there! She glanced at her watch and saw that there were still two hours to pass before the man came.

Cassy had turned her back on the bed and walked over to the window, as if to indicate by her action that she had no further wish to be involved. Someone must do something about the sheets, Joscelin thought. It was all very well for Cassy to insist that there was no danger in what was to be done to poor Lota. She had read in the big blue medical dictionary in her father's bookcase that women could contract something called 'puerperal fever' after a miscarriage; and she had read the dictionary's frightening caution – *'treatment is too often utterly in vain . . .'* Cassy had seemed to ignore the dangers, but now, Joscelin knew instinctively, she was every bit as frightened as herself.

The knowledge had a strange effect on Joscelin. It was as if Cassy's weakness lent her strength. Someone, after all, had to look after Lota . . .

'You wait here with Cassy,' she said, hoping her voice sounded calmer than she felt. 'There's a shop in Buckingham Palace Road called Gorringe's which can't be far away. I can buy new sheets there. They won't be linen because we can't afford it, but at least they'll be clean . . .'

Lota looked doubtfully at Cassy and wished that she would go for the sheets and leave Joss with her.

She must endure this ordeal for Benito's sake, Lota told herself, as indeed Casilda had told her a hundred times already. What would he think if he knew what was to happen to her? Casilda had made her promise that she would say nothing to him of her pregnancy or of the reason for her visit to England. She agreed to this, knowing that Benito would never allow her to risk her life in order to get rid of their child. Worst of all, she did not want to get rid of it. Casilda did not seem to consider the baby as a living human being. Joscelin understood better – at least, Lota thought she did – for she was unfailingly sympathetic and patient. Although she was not a Catholic, she even appeared to understand Lota's fears of God's vengeance upon her for the Mortal Sin she was about to commit.

'You can confess it afterwards,' Cassy had said casually, 'so stop worrying. Besides, unless you want to risk telling Mamá the truth, you've *got* to get rid of it. Joss will come with us to help look after you. You know I faint at the sight of blood – but she's always calm and level-headed. Beryl said there's really nothing to it; lots of girls have it done!'

Joscelin was feeling very far from calm or level-headed as she made her way back to the squalid little hotel. As she opened the front door with the key the landlady had lent her, she was aware of the horrid reek of cooking vegetables mixed with the oily smell of the damp linoleum that served to carpet the hallway.

Lota was sitting in a chair, shivering partly from cold and partly from nervous anxiety. She attempted to smile but tears filled her eyes. Cassy looked relieved as she greeted Joscelin, taking the parcel of sheets from her.

'Let's light the gas fire,' Joscelin said in an attempt to cheer everyone's spirits. 'I should have thought of it before.' She fumbled in her purse for a coin and slipped the penny into the meter. There was a quiet plopping noise and the gas flamed, turning slowly from blue to a pale golden glow.

With a smile, she turned to Lota. 'That's better, isn't it!' she said. 'Let's change the bedclothes now.'

Without realizing it, Joscelin had taken charge. She persuaded Cassy to help her to remake the bed – a task Lota had clearly never before had to perform, Joscelin thought wryly.

Was it possible, Joscelin asked herself, that Lota had considered the way she might have to live were she married to the penniless Benito? She glanced at her watch. Only ten minutes before the man would arrive. In Cassy's purse, now lying on the end of the bed, was the money they must give him – in advance, Beryl had warned Cassy – and they must not give their real names. Total mutual anonymity was an essential part of the arrangement. It was even possible, Beryl had said, that the man might come in disguise.

The theatricality of the assignment struck Joscelin anew. It seemed as if the three of them were characters in a play. Act 1 Scene 1 had already begun! The curtain had gone up and here they were, alone in this horrible room waiting for a stranger to come and force poor little Lota's body into mis- carrying her baby. But Joscelin knew they were not play-acting. This was reality and she must not give way to the panic that was now knotting the pit of her stomach.

She tried to concentrate her thoughts on someone other than Lota; and the memory of her mother's happy, trusting face came into her mind. As she had kissed them all goodbye after lunch, she had called out to them: 'Have a nice time, children, and give my fondest regards to dear Lady Costain . . .'

Joscelin hated the lies she had been obliged to tell her mother – that they were meeting Lady Costain at Lyons Tea Shop at Marble Arch and that they would be returning with her to spend the night at Rutland Gate. Without any cause for suspicion, Mrs Howard had helped the two visitors to pack, made sure they had money for their bus fares and waved them on their way.

Joscelin could not imagine her mother's reactions were they to have told her the truth. She would simply not have believed that Lota had 'fallen into disgrace', and was hoping at this very moment to have the baby 'removed'. Misled by Lota's air of fragility and her shyness, Mrs Howard treated her as if she were still a little girl.

Lota, her small figure huddled into the green wicker armchair by the gas fire, did look nearer thirteen than fifteen, Joscelin thought. Although she herself was only a year older, she was a full six inches taller. And in contrast to Cassy, who was usually so completely self-assured and extroverted, Lota gave the impression of helplessness and innocence.

Joscelin's reflections were interrupted by the sound of

footsteps on the landing outside their room. She held her breath, waiting for and dreading the inevitable knock on the door. Behind her, she heard Cassy gasp.

They all jumped to their feet as the knock came, followed by the recognizable Cockney voice of their landlady: 'It's yer doctor, Miss Smithson!'

Joscelin bit her lip as she attempted to steady the hurried beat of her heart. She tried to ignore Lota's terrified face as she went to unlock the bedroom door. Cassy seemed rooted to the ground, her eyes as frightened as her sister's.

The calmness of her voice surprised Joscelin as she said: 'Good evening, doctor! I'm sorry to call you out so late. My sister was taken ill on the train.'

His muttered reply was inaudible. He stepped into the room, a portmanteau grasped in one large, hairy hand, his gloves in the other. Without curiosity, the landlady disappeared down the stairs and Joscelin closed and relocked the door.

'This is the patient then?' the man asked, nodding towards Lota, who was now standing by the bed, her face a white, terrified mask. He removed his shabby black homburg and turned back to Joscelin. 'You have my fee?'

Cassy stepped forward and, as he held out his hand in a blatant gesture that made no attempt to hide his greed, she reached for her purse and withdrew three crisp white five-pound notes.

Their visitor placed them carefully in his wallet and nodded towards Lota. 'Get undressed, young lady,' he said brusquely, '. . . and get into bed. The quicker this is over the better.' To Joscelin's bewilderment he suddenly removed his moustache, then his beard and, most horrifying of all, his hair, revealing a shiny bald pate.

'Can't be too careful, can we?' he muttered, grinning first at Cassy, then at Joscelin, in a conspiratorial manner that revolted her.

'*All* my clothes?' Lota asked in a whisper.

The man shrugged. 'Below the waist,' he answered in that

same clipped manner. 'Don't want to get those pretty things messed up, do we? You've brought towels?' As Joscelin produced them, he looked more closely at Lota who, with her back towards him, was now divesting herself of her petticoat.

'Bit young, isn't she?' he asked Joscelin doubtfully. 'I was told she was seventeen.'

'She's older than she looks,' Joscelin said quickly, unsure whether she would be pleased or sorry were this horrible man suddenly to back out of the assignment. But his qualms at Lota's youth were only momentary. He was staring at the young girl as she struggled out of her clothes. Joscelin went quickly to place herself between them in an effort to provide Lota with a little privacy. Perhaps such niceties were ridiculous in the light of what must now be done, she thought as she helped Lota into the bed.

The room was still cold despite the faint warmth coming from the gas fire, and Lota was shivering violently. Cassy had returned to her stance by the window as if to disassociate herself from the events now taking place.

The man edged past Joscelin and, without preamble, dragged the bedclothes down, revealing Lota's naked white legs and stomach. His voice was rough-edged as he said brusquely: 'All you girls make out you're not far gone. No point lying to me, young lady. When did you get yourself in this mess?'

'She isn't sure!' Joscelin broke in, aware that Lota was beyond speech.

'More's the pity. Let's have a look then . . .' His hand began to prod Lota's stomach and, with a barely subdued gasp, Joscelin observed that his fingernails were far from clean. The sight of those probing hands on the girl's shivering body was an obscenity and Joscelin's courage began to fail. She turned quickly away at the sound of that matter-of-fact, impatient male voice commanding Lota to part her legs. The young girl was now crying openly, and as Joscelin held out her hand Lota grasped it so tightly that her fingernails indented Joscelin's skin.

The man probed further into Lota's body and, as she

cried out in pain, he straightened up and looked sharply at Joscelin.

'She should have had this done before!' he said flatly. He gave a sigh of exasperation. 'All the same, you girls! Either too stupid or too innocent to know what's what – yet willing to take the risks.'

Joscelin's mouth tightened as her fear gave way to anger. 'You haven't been paid to stand here moralizing,' she said in as autocratic a voice as she could muster.

To her surprise, the man ignored her reproach. 'This could be dangerous,' he said bluntly, 'but I suppose you know that.' He nodded towards Lota. 'She's willing to take the chance?'

'What chance?' Joscelin asked, her self-confidence undermined by fear. 'Are you trying to tell us there is a serious risk if . . . if you bring about a miscarriage?'

The man looked even more exasperated. 'I'm not *trying* to say it, Miss Smithson. I *am* saying it. If things went wrong . . .' He left the sentence in mid-air, shaking his head dubiously. 'I don't like it – I don't like it at all. I should have been told how far gone the girl is . . .'

Joscelin felt physically sick. One look at the sobbing girl in the bed increased her awareness that the responsibility for going ahead with this horrible business lay with Cassy – she was the eldest! But Cassy was mute and she herself was hopelessly unqualified to make such a decision. She knew nothing about childbirth, let alone miscarriages. Supposing Lota were to die?

Disregarding the hesitant 'doctor', she knelt down by the bed and took Lota's face between her hands. 'Look at me,' she said gently. 'Don't be frightened. You don't have to go through with this if you don't want to. We'll find some other way . . . we'll arrange something somehow, won't we, Cassy?'

Lota's eyes, drenched with tears, opened wide and stared into Joscelin's. 'I'm so afraid . . .' she murmured. 'He . . . he hurt me . . .' she added as more tears spilled down her cheeks. 'Casilda said I must be brave – for Benito's sake . . . but . . .'

Whilst they had been conversing, the man stood silently weighing up the dangers to himself if he went ahead with the abortion. He was far from easy about performing the operation. There were always dangers – but this time they were manifold. For a start, all three girls were clearly younger than they pretended . . . minors with guardians, parents, who might force the facts from them. The older girl seemed dependable – but the silent, foreign-looking one and his potential patient were not to be trusted. The girl in the bed was hysterical already – and he'd done little more than probe around inside her. He felt a flash of warning not to pursue this particular episode – although he could do with the money.

'Better make up your minds, young ladies,' he said curtly. 'Don't say I haven't warned you . . . not that I can give you your money back. Time, you see . . . taken a good deal of my time already getting here. Tell you what, I'll give you the half back if we call it a day and that's more than a fair deal. Here . . .' He bent down to withdraw the notes he had stuffed into his wallet and held one out to Cassy. She looked at it in horror.

'Take it, Cassy!' Joscelin whispered, knowing that they must do so, despite her inner longing to tell the man he could keep his money – keep it all if he wanted – so long as he did not again put those large, unclean hands into Lota's body.

Her mind was suddenly made up. She crossed the room to Cassy's side. 'We can't put Lota's life at risk,' she said quietly. 'We must think of something else. Maybe your aunt will know what to do – and Lota doesn't *have* to tell Lady Costain who the father is. We're too young to decide what's best, Cassy, don't you see that?'

Cassy looked at her helplessly. 'Beryl should have warned me!' she said petulantly.

'Well, she didn't!' Joscelin replied sharply. 'And unless Lota herself wants to risk her life, I'm not going to be a party to it. It's better for her to be disgraced than to *die*, Cassy. You *must* see that.'

She went back to the bedside. 'I'm going to send the doctor

away Lota,' she said gently. 'You don't want him to do anything, do you?'

'Oh, Joscelin, please no!' Lota cried. 'Send him away. I don't want him near me . . .' She broke into a torrent of Spanish Joscelin could not understand.

'You'd better leave!' she told the waiting man, forcing herself to take the note from him. 'My sister has changed her mind.'

It was by no means the first time one of his patients had had eleventh-hour misgivings, and the man bore no animosity for the lost half of his fee. The amount he was keeping more than compensated him for the hour it had taken him to get to Victoria, and one of the reasons he'd stayed free of trouble with the law was because he only obliged a patient when he knew for a certainty that he could depend upon their total reticence. Not that either one of these young ladies knew his name or address – but they'd seen him without his disguise and they *could* recognize him if ever he did end up in court and his picture was in the newspaper. But the younger girl was too far gone for his liking. He was well out of it.

Within five minutes, Joscelin was opening the front door for him and he was hurrying down the gas-lit street towards Victoria Station, where he knew he could get an omnibus to take him back to his lodgings.

Despite her relief at his departure, Joscelin's mood was far from composed. Her fears for Lota's safety had led her to imply that an alternative to the operation could be found – and she had absolutely no idea what possible alternative there was.

But as she re-entered the bedroom, this concern was dwarfed by a far greater one. Lota was now writhing beneath the bedclothes. Cassy was pacing the room in panic.

'I have such a pain!' Lota whispered. 'His hands hurt me so much when . . . when he felt inside. Oh, Joss . . . I think I may be bleeding. The sheets . . . *Madre de Dios, ay de mí!*'

Joscelin felt sick with apprehension. Was that rough probing inside Lota sufficient to start a miscarriage? If only she knew more about such things! Why, oh why, wasn't Cassy saying something – doing something!

'Don't concern yourself about the sheets Lota,' she said aloud, hoping her voice sounded a great deal calmer than she felt. 'They belong to us, remember? And if you are bleeding, we can tear them up for pads.'

But when she drew back the bedclothes, Joscelin's attempts at calmness gave way to horror as she saw the bright red stains. For all she knew, Lota might bleed to death.

Cassy, who had also seen the blood, was retching into the china washbowl in a corner of the room. Quite suddenly, Joscelin realized that, no matter what the penalties of discovery were, this was one occasion where a grown-up must be involved. Better that Lota *and* the boy who had brought this trouble on her should both be punished, even disgraced, than that Lota should die.

'We must get you dressed,' she said gently but firmly. 'I'm going to call a taxi cab and we'll take you to your Aunt Pamela's. We can stay the night there . . . your aunt will know what to do.'

Lota's mouth quivered. 'Please don't tell Tía Pamela, Joss. She will tell Mamá and Papá and then . . .'

'We'll just say you're unwell . . .' Joscelin broke in as Lota's voice began to rise hysterically. 'Lots of girls have a bad time with the curse and we can say it's that.'

Privately she had made up her mind that she would tell Lady Costain the truth. But the first task was to get Lota to the comparative safety – and cleanliness – of Rutland Gate.

A quarter of an hour later, as she hailed a passing taxi cab, she was aware that their landlady was observing their hurried departure through the parted net curtains of her basement sitting room. It was as if they were criminals making a surreptitious getaway, Joscelin thought shamefacedly, for she knew this was not so far from the truth.

It was partly with relief that the three girls learned from Lady Costain's butler that Her Ladyship was out, but that he

would inform Miss Dawkins of their arrival. The elderly woman
who had once been Isobel's and Barbara's governess was now
Lady Costain's sewing woman. She had already retired for the
night, she explained as she came hurrying into the hall.
Apologizing for her attire, she informed the three girls that
Lady Costain was not expected back until late. Startled by
the girls' unexpected, unchaperoned appearance, she looked
questioningly at Cassy and Joscelin and then at Carlota's tear-
streaked face and untidy hair. She tut-tutted, her false teeth
clattering as she did so.

'We were returning to my home in Surbiton, Miss Dawkins,'
Joscelin said quickly. 'But Lota felt very poorly and we thought
it best to bring her here. I am sure Lady Costain would be
pleased to let us stay the night. We missed our bus, you see,
and it's getting late for us to be out on our own.'

'Of course, my dear, Her Ladyship would certainly not
want the poor child to be travelling unwell. The Blue Room
is all prepared – I was using it as a sewing room this very
afternoon – so the fire was lit and it will be warmer than
the other guest rooms. Off you go, and I'll tell one of the
maids to bring you up some hot cocoa. You all look perished.
I hope you're not sickening for something. Should you telephone your parents, dear, and let them know why you aren't
back? They'll be worrying, I don't doubt, at this time of
night!'

Joscelin blushed guiltily, knowing that her mother was not
expecting her home since she had been told that they would
be staying the night with Cassy's aunt.

'Yes, thank you, I'll telephone now. Please go back to bed,
Miss Dawkins. Cassy and I will look after Lota. I'm so sorry
we disturbed you.'

Her anxiety for Lota intensified as she helped her into bed.
Had the 'doctor's' internal examination in some way harmed
her – or the baby? Lota, she recalled, had cried out that he
was hurting her . . . and she was still bleeding. She had ceased
crying and lay quietly against the pillows, shivering despite

the warmth of the room. She seemed apathetic – almost as if she had resigned herself to whatever fate awaited her.

Cassy took Joscelin's arm and drew her to the far side of the room where Lota could not hear her.

'What if Tía Pamela guesses it's something worse than the curse? I'm frightened, Joss. I'll be the one who gets blamed and they'll send me back to Spain.' She looked at Joscelin appealingly. 'Don't you understand how ghastly it would be? Alan promised he'd come down early from Strathinver so we could see each other before he goes back to Oxford. If I'm sent home, I'll never see him and . . .'

'For heaven's sake, stop!' Joscelin interrupted fiercely. 'Don't you realize Lota could be *dying*? If something has gone wrong, we've simply *got* to tell your aunt. Even if you do get punished, you'll see Alan again eventually.'

Cassy was not unaware of the censure in Joscelin's voice, and had the grace to look shamefaced as she watched her walk back to the bed where her sister was lying.

Joscelin sat by Lota's side watching the clock on the mantelpiece. The hands seemed to crawl round the dial, each hour seeming twice as long as they went from eleven to midnight and finally to one. There was now no one to share her vigil, for Cassy had fallen asleep in an armchair. She tried to think of anything but the shabby hotel room and the coarse, shifty man probing poor little Lota's exposed body. But her mind seemed only to retrieve unhappy memories which were far from reassuring – in particular Doña Ursula's severe, autocratic voice and critical eyes. No wonder Cassy and Lota were so frightened at the thought of her knowing the truth! Now, as she tried not to imagine the reactions of Lota's mother if she knew of her daughter's association with Benito, her horror at her own involvement struck her with renewed trepidation. What would *her* mother and father say!

Joscelin bit her lip, ashamed of herself as she realized that she was thinking of her future rather than of Lota's, for whom the repercussions could only spell total disaster.

The sound of voices on the stairs woke Cassy and roused Joscelin from her chair. With a gasp of relief that now she could share the responsibility with someone else, she flung open the bedroom door and came face to face with Cassy's aunt.

Lady Costain stared in surprise at Joscelin's white, distraught face.

'It's Joscelin, isn't it? Agnes told me you and Cassy and little Lota were staying the night. Why aren't you in bed? Is something wrong?'

Without warning Cassy burst into tears. Joscelin opened her mouth but no words came from her throat. Lota buried her face deeper into her pillow. The smile left Lady Costain's face and her customary vague manner gave way to a look of concern. The dishevelled state of Joscelin's hair and clothes was most unusual in a child who somehow always managed to look neat and feminine. A wave of anxiety now penetrated the warm, happy glow induced in her by champagne, the dancing and the gaiety of her fellow party-goers.

'Agnes, you can go to bed,' she said. 'I'll manage by myself tonight.' She walked over to Cassy and put an arm around her shoulders.

'Tell me what is upsetting you, my dear,' she said, looking anxiously into the girl's tearful face. 'Whatever it is, it can't be *that* bad . . .'

'But it is – it is!' Joscelin whispered, suddenly finding her voice as her instinct told her that this extraordinary relation of Cassy's was at heart a sympathetic person and not nearly as stupid as her vague manner led people to believe. 'It's poor Lota . . .'

'Is she ill?' Lady Costain asked. As Joscelin nodded, she beckoned to her and to Cassy to follow her down the corridor to her bedroom. She seated herself at her dressing table and began with studied casualness to remove her jewellery from around her neck and wrists.

'Sit down, both of you – there, on my bed. Now, one of you tell me what can be so wrong with Lota that it distresses you to talk about it. Did some nasty man accost her in the street? Is that it?'

'No, no, it was nothing like that!' Joscelin burst out, unaware that she was wringing her hands. 'Cassy, will you *please* tell your aunt the truth? Honestly, it isn't a question of sneaking. We've just *got* to tell someone!'

Lady Costain regarded her niece's unhappy face, her own eyes puzzled. It was not like Cassy, of all the children, to be tongue-tied. One was usually trying to stop her chatter.

'Joscelin, dear, since Casilda has lost her voice, will *you* please give me an explanation. *What* is wrong with Lota and *why* are you up so late? This is most unlike you, dear. I always think of you as being so sensible. Cassy, will you please find a handkerchief and stop sniffing. You can rest assured, both of you, that I shall not betray any confidences. Has little Lota had too much to drink? Is that it?'

Joscelin felt the tension leave her body as, again, instinct told her that she could trust this youthful aunt of Cassy's – so different in every way from the daunting Doña Ursula.

She pressed her hands deeper into the satin coverlet of the big bed and blurted out: 'Lota's going to have a baby, Lady Costain, and Cassy and I have been trying to help her get rid of it and now she's bleeding badly and . . .'

A deep sob from Cassy interrupted her as the older girl jumped off the bed and flung herself at her aunt's knees. 'We weren't going to tell anyone,' she wept. 'But now we've got to because Joss thinks the man may have hurt Lota and . . . oh, Tía Pamela, please, *please* say you don't think Lota's going to die!'

Shocked beyond words, Lady Costain looked from her hysterical niece to Joscelin. The expression in the girl's eyes confirmed her worst fears, for unlike the hysterical Casilda, Joscelin looked all too sane.

'I don't know, Cassy,' she said quietly, rising quickly to her feet. 'Let's go and take a look at Lota – and then . . . then we'll just have to see.'

But Cassy would not go back to the sick room. It was Joscelin who accompanied Lady Costain and who had finally to relate the events which had led up to this horrifying night and the terrible outcome of Cassy's plan.

CHAPTER TWELVE

September 1922–July 1923

In the week following upon Joscelin's confession, Pamela was at her wits' end trying to find a solution to what appeared to be an insoluble problem. It was no easy time for the kindly woman upon whose shoulders so much responsibility now lay. Bitterly she reflected that it was her sister, Ursula, who should be involved in the task of protecting Carlota. But she understood only too well why Cassy and Joscelin had taken matters into their own hands, appalled though she was by their naïve and desperately dangerous attempts to rescue Lota from her predicament. Since she herself had not the courage to telephone Ursula, how could she blame her nieces for their failure to confide in their mother? She knew only too well how rigidly Ursula adhered to her doctrines; how unrelenting she could be with those who transgressed.

Pamela knew that before making any decisions regarding Lota's future, she must attend to the girl's physical well-being. She sent at once for her gynaecologist, Sir Gerald Arbuthnot. Whilst awaiting his arrival, she decided to invent a ruptured appendix as a reason for his presence in the household so late at night. Most of her staff could be counted upon not to gossip, but there was too much at stake to take any chances. Although her physician was unable to conceal his abhorrence of all back-street abortionists, he was sympathetic and immensely practical in his attentions to Carlota. As soon as he was assured that the girl had ceased to haemorrhage, he removed her to his private nursing home, supporting Lady Costain's story of a ruptured appendix.

With the immediate danger averted, Lady Costain was beset by further anxieties. Cassy and Joscelin were involved in the conspiracy to protect Lota and she realized that, were they to return to Surbiton, inevitably both would be required to tell further lies to the Howards. She took it upon herself, therefore, to inform Joscelin's parents that, since it was so close to the start of the new term, she would keep the two girls at Rutland Gate where they would be so much nearer to hand to visit the unfortunate Lota. It was a feeble enough excuse, but the Howards did not question it.

It was a great relief to Joscelin, who hated the deceit, and for once she and Cassy were happy to return to school, since it removed them from the tensions in Rutland Gate. Cassy seemed to recover more easily than she could, Joscelin thought on the last night of the holidays when Lady Costain came to their room and told them that they must not worry about Carlota, whose life was not in danger. She had not lost her baby, and Sir Gerald had suggested an infallible method of avoiding any future disgrace. As soon as it was born, Lota's baby was to be adopted. Sir Gerald himself would arrange matters, and eventually Lota would be able to resume her life at home as if nothing had happened.

Lady Costain did not add that Lota herself was resisting this sensible solution; that at times she was insisting hysterically that she wanted to keep her baby whatever the disgrace.

'So you have nothing to worry about, my dears,' she said, kissing Cassy and Joscelin in turn, 'and you will best please me by forgetting about Lota and concentrating on your school work like good girls.'

As Paget drove them back to the Convent, Pamela breathed a sigh of relief. She knew how indiscreet Cassy could be, and an unguarded word in the wrong ear could bring total disaster upon them all – not least if Ursula ever discovered the truth. As Sir Gerald had pointed out, Lota was a minor and her parents' responsibility. Lady Costain was taking a big risk assuming guardianship without their authorization. Whilst it was perfectly easy for Lady Costain to pull the wool over her husband's eyes, Alan guessed that his mother had far greater worries on her mind than a mere appendectomy. He invited her confidence, and for the first time in her life Lady Costain appreciated that her son was no longer a boy but a sensible young man upon whom she could rely. Moreover, she needed a dependable ally. She arranged therefore for Alan, instead of Paget, to drive her down to the Kent coast to inspect the home of a couple recommended by Sir Gerald who, for a fee, would take care of Lota until her baby was due.

Having installed her there, she visited Lota once a fortnight, taking the train once Alan had returned to Oxford. Although the girl was now in good health, her misery was all too apparent, and not even the gifts Lady Costain took with her could divert Lota from her pleas to be allowed to keep her baby. It distressed her kindly aunt to see the flow of tears that always came when it was time for her to leave.

During the Christmas holidays, with Alan acting once more as chauffeur, Lady Costain took Joscelin with her on these visits, hoping that more youthful company might cheer her niece. Cassy, who had returned to Spain, was given the task of reassuring her parents that her sister's prolonged 'convalescence' by the sea was really necessary.

It was Joscelin who finally succeeded in reconciling Lota to the fact that she must surrender her baby when the time came. She pointed out that only one person in a thousand would have taken the personal risk that Lady Costain was still taking to save Lota from disgrace; and furthermore, that even if Lota's baby was not offered for adoption, *she* would never be permitted to keep it since she was not yet sixteen.

The one bright star that Christmas was the news that Sir Gerald had found a childless American couple who were desperately anxious to have the baby, and were prepared to remain in England until March when the birth was due. Unable to have children themselves, they were young, wealthy and could give the child every advantage.

For Joscelin, too, there was a bright star that Christmas holiday. On Boxing Day, Alan came with his mother to pay a surprise visit to the Howards. It was the first time either of them had ever been to Whitegates. They brought belated Christmas presents and explained that they had stopped off on their way to a party at the Piermonts in order that Lady Costain could ask Joscelin's father if she could share a Season with Cassy in June.

Joscelin would happily have declined this invitation but Mrs Howard was in transports of delight at the prospect, and when Cassy returned for the start of the spring term she stated categorically that if Joscelin refused to be presented she would do likewise.

'Anyway, Joss, you've just *got* to let Tía Pamela give you a Season. It's her way of thanking you for saving Lota's life,' Cassy insisted. 'I heard her telling Alan that Sir Gerald had said Lota had come close to a terrible death from septicaemia – whatever that is!'

At last Lady Costain felt she could relax. Ursula wrote saying that she was once more with child and had therefore given up her intention to visit Lota during her 'convalescence' – a possibility that had thrown Pamela into momentary panic. It occurred to her that the advent of another baby in the Montero home could have a disastrous effect on the girl's state of mind. She appreciated how bitter Lota might feel, knowing that her mother, who already had eight children, could keep her new baby, whereas Lota would be obliged to surrender her infant. Lady Costain was afraid that the child might break down and betray the whole conspiracy if she returned home after her confinement. In February, therefore, shortly before the baby was due, Lady Costain arranged for her daughter, Barbara, to invite Carlota to spend a year with her in Italy. It would in part be educational, she wrote to Don Jaime, since Lota could learn the language, but also Barbara would welcome her cousin's assistance with little Ernesto, who was now a year old. Barbara was expecting another child and

Lota could gain useful experience in learning to run a large household.

Don Jaime raised no objections to the proposal and his wife was pleased to have Carlota's welfare in other hands. The girl's shyness and reticence irritated her mother, who hoped that the past six months in England might have altered her daughter's insular outlook, and that another year abroad would be of further benefit.

Three weeks after the birth of a little boy, Lota was dispatched to Milan in the care of a Universal Aunt. The baby was handed over to its adoring new parents and Lady Costain was at last able to breathe a sigh of relief and devote her energies to arranging Cassy's and Joscelin's Season.

For Cassy, her appearance at Court was wildly exciting. For Joscelin, fearing that she would trip over her train, mismanage her curtsey or make some other gaucherie, it proved very much the ordeal she had anticipated. But she did not regret it. The large framed photograph in the lounge at Whitegates was her mother's prized possession. Proudly Mrs Howard showed 'our Joscelin' in her Court dress to every visitor. Even the milkman was shown it.

For her mother's sake Joscelin did her utmost to enjoy the Season, and the fact that she did not derive the same pleasure from all the parties and entertainments as Cassy was entirely her own fault, she decided. She felt guilty when she found herself praying for the end of the summer when she could realize her dream and begin her training at the Slade School of Art.

Only Alan seemed to understand her increasing boredom and weariness with the endless round of parties. Each dance, he remarked as the summer wore on, was a replica of the one the night before, only the venue changing. He was sick of making conversation to stupid partners with nothing more interesting to discuss than yesterday's social events. He was, he said, longing for August when they would go up to Strathinver and he could be out in the fresh air on the moors, away from 'all this razzmatazz'! In the meanwhile, since his mother expected him to do the débutante round, he never had enough time to work.

As the Season drew to an end, there was little doubt that Cassy would be given the title of Deb of the Year. Radiant, beautiful, she was never without a partner nor an invitation, in which she always insisted upon Joscelin's inclusion. She still maintained that Alan was her 'true love' and that she was utterly determined to make him propose before the Season ended; but this did not prevent her from flirting with every attractive, eligible young man in her orbit. Not least, she flirted outrageously with her most ardent admirer, James Deighton.

Not unlike Alan in looks, the young Viscount was very different in character. Amusing, extroverted and immensely self-assured even at the age of twenty, he had acquired quite a reputation for being a playboy. Joscelin gleaned from Cassy that his father, the Earl of Ladbury, was very wealthy. Jimmy, the eldest son and heir, was considered to be the year's most eligible bachelor.

Joscelin was uncomfortably aware that most of their fellow débutantes were expecting the Season to end with an announcement of Cassy's engagement to the youthful Lord Deighton. Many an evening was ruined for her by the sight of Alan's unhappy expression as he watched Cassy whirling past in a dance, smiling up at Jimmy as if he were the most important person in the world.

Alan did his utmost to conceal his jealousy. Like all the other young men in Cassy's orbit, he had fallen under her spell. He was disturbed by his physical longings for her, although he never doubted that she herself was innocent of her ability to arouse the most primitive of passions in any man she met. Ashamed that his lustful feelings somehow demeaned her, he hid his emotions behind a façade of cousinly teasing. If, during a dance, she moved too close, he forced a smile and told her she was creasing his shirtfront. When she curled up beside him on the sofa on one of their rare evenings alone with his mother and father at Rutland Gate, he fabricated an excuse to get up and cross the room, then reseated himself far away from the heavy temptation of her inviting little body.

Although it was true that his adorable Cassy was totally uninhibited in displaying her affection for him, she was equally demonstrative with anyone she liked; and she flirted with all her admirers – including Deighton.

The thought crossed Alan's mind that Jimmy Deighton would be an excellent match for Cassy. A contemporary of Eduardo's with whom he had been at Downside, he was a frequent visitor at Rutland Gate. Reluctantly, Alan was forced to admit that the younger man's charm was unfeigned, and that, in a superficial way, he was likeable enough. Moreover, Deighton was a Catholic, which would matter very much to Cassy's parents, if not to her.

When Alan was not obliged to participate in the jollifications of the Season, he attempted to suppress his feelings in his work. He was thus engaged on the afternoon preceding the big ball his mother was giving as a finale to the girls' Season. He retired to the seclusion of the library, where the sound of preparations for the party could not reach him and where he was permitted to smoke his pipe. With his father at his club, Alan expected to remain undisturbed for several hours. He was soon deep into a book entitled *Wild Spain* from which he was making notes, and he did not hear the door opening nor the soft sound of Cassy's feet crossing the thick carpet.

Startled, he jumped as she put a hand on his shoulder. 'I thought you and Joss were supposed to be resting!' he said accusingly.

Cassy stood staring down at him, a mischievous glint in her eyes and a hint of laughter curving her full red lips. She was wearing a simple, short-sleeved muslin summer frock, its whiteness enhancing the honey-golden colour of her arms. Her scent, disturbingly familiar, permeated the room, overriding the smell of his pipe smoke and his father's cigars. He felt a sudden desperate urge to take her in his arms and crush that moist, tempting mouth; feel the rounded softness of her close against him.

Cassy's gaze did not waver and, for one moment, Alan wondered if, for all her innocence, she somehow guessed how violently her proximity was tormenting him. There was a look in her eyes which prompted him to believe that she knew very well the effect she was having. But the moment was quickly gone.

'Gibson told me you were in here, Alan. I'm so fearfully bored, and there are hours to go before the dance.' Cassy glanced down at the table, strewn with Alan's books and papers, and flicked the lid of his inkwell shut with a snap. 'Talk to me, Alan!' she said, moving a step closer to him so that she brushed his knees. As he put down his pipe and was about to rise, she perched herself on the arm of his chair so that he was virtually a prisoner.

'I'm beginning to think you are deliberately avoiding me!' She pouted and caught her forefinger between her white teeth. 'Have I done something to annoy you? And don't pretend you aren't cross with me. You only asked me for *one* dance last night!'

Alan attempted to laugh. 'What utter nonsense, Cassy! Why should I be cross? As to not dancing with you, it was pretty obvious you had plenty of partners to fill your programme. I was superfluous to your requirements.'

Cassy's eyes flashed and she tossed her head. 'Ah, I *knew* that's what it was – you're jealous! It's because I had the last waltz with Jimmy, isn't it?'

Alan drew a deep breath and in as calm a voice as he could muster, he said quietly: 'You can dance with whomever you please, Cassy, and that includes the last waltz – although I do recall you once saying to me that you would always keep it for me.'

Cassy leaned a little closer and he felt her hand ruffling his hair as she said in a low, husky voice: 'You're a silly, grumpy old bear, Alan, but shall I tell you something? I'm glad you're jealous of Jimmy. It shows you do care a little bit about me! I've wondered and wondered why you won't admit it. Jimmy says he thinks I'm fascinating and beautiful, but *you* never say anything nice.' The corners of her mouth drew downward, and for one horrifying moment Alan thought she was about to burst into tears. Her voice sounded tremulous as she added wistfully: 'You're so cruel to me, Alan, when you know perfectly well how much I love you.'

The declaration hung in the air between them, and Alan discovered himself in a situation he had been seeking to avoid. He had been in love with Cassy now for over a year, but there were too many reasons why he could not reveal it – not least his doubts as to Cassy's feelings for him. This barrier was now gone but many more remained. Cassy had only just come out and apart from *her* youth, he himself was still an undergraduate and had only last year come of age. He had no income of his own and, despite the generous allowance he received from his father, it would be at least three or four years before he was in a position to support a wife. He would, therefore, need his parents' approval were he to marry so young, and although his mother seemed fond of Cassy, his father made little pretence of hiding his antipathy to her. Alan was certain this was a reflection of a general dislike of all Roman Catholics (in company with foreigners and Jews), since he himself was convinced that everyone must love Cassy.

Her soft, husky voice with its faint Spanish inflection hung in the air between them. She loved him. *She really and truly loved him*! He could still not believe it. That she had once had a schoolgirl crush on him was quite another matter and he had taken his mother's gentle teasing as his due, believing, as she did, that Cassy would grow out of it. But this summer everything had been so different. He was forever within reach and sound of her laughter; within sight of her bright, vivacious face smiling at him across the dining room table as she appealed to him to escort her and Joscelin to a party, to the races, to

Henley. Of her own volition she had filled his days and his heart, yet she had seemed so smitten with Jimmy Deighton, who always managed to accompany them and be close by her side. Now he knew her intention had been to make him jealous and thus force him to declare himself.

He stood up abruptly and pulled her into his arms. 'For God's sake, Cassy, don't you realize that I'm in love with you? I've been trying to hide it because I thought you were keen on Deighton. I love you more than anything or anyone in the whole world!' As his mouth came down on hers, Cassy melted against him, pressing herself closer and closer. She returned his kisses passionately. The unexpected violence of her response startled Alan sufficiently for him to regain control of himself.

'My darling, dearest *darling* Cassy,' he said as he drew carefully away from her, 'we must keep calm. Even if *you* don't mind, *I* care about your reputation. What on earth would old Gibson think if he saw us? Forgive me, I shouldn't have kissed you like that. I'm a brute!'

Cassy gave a low, happy laugh. 'Don't be silly, Alan, there's nothing to forgive. I *wanted* you to kiss me. I want you to kiss me again. Who cares about my silly reputation?'

'I do!' Alan said firmly as she took a step towards him. 'It's not as if we're engaged, Cassy, and . . .'

She flung herself back into his arms. 'But I *want* to be engaged. If you really love me, you should want it too. You *said* you loved me . . .' She looked at him accusingly, daring him to deny it. She was so uncontrolled, so child-like in her simple honesty, Alan thought, as his emotions changed and gave way to a feeling of overwhelming tenderness. He reached up and brushed a shining strand of dark hair away from her forehead.

'I do love you, and if it were possible I'd marry you tomorrow. But don't you see, Cassy, our parents would never agree. I couldn't support you on the allowance Father gives me, and your father has every right to expect your future husband to keep you in a proper manner.'

'But we don't have to get *married*,' Cassy argued. 'We can be engaged. I don't mind how long I have to wait, honestly I don't.'

Deeply touched, Alan had not the heart to point out to her the obvious deterrents to their union. He did not want Cassy to think him afraid to speak to his parents, and yet instinct warned him that his father would veto even an engagement. Meanwhile, he wanted to keep that bright, glowing face as happy and adoring as it was at this moment. He took one of her hands in his and touched the ring finger of her left hand.

'I'll speak to the Pater tomorrow, Cassy. If we can get his approval, then I will approach your father. Uncle Jaime and I have always got on well, although your mother . . .' He broke off, preferring not to think of these hurdles, and was grateful that Cassy, too, was obviously not considering them.

She stood on tiptoe and kissed him ardently on the lips. 'I am so happy! Darling Alan, isn't life absolutely divine! What a stunning end to my Season. Oh, I'm so happy, so utterly, utterly *afortunada*.' She swung away from him and danced across the room, pausing as she opened the door to blow him a kiss.

'I'm going to tell Joss,' she announced, 'and don't look so worried, Alan, I know it's got to be a secret until you've spoken to Tío Angus, but Joss is different and I've just got to tell *someone*.'

She was gone before he could stop her. Slowly he sat down at the table and stared with unseeing eyes at his papers which only half an hour before had seemed so important. He wished desperately that he could feel 'utterly happy' like Cassy, but the truth was he felt only a strange, inexplicable unease.

Cassy raced up the stairs and found Joscelin resting on the bed in their room. She flung herself down on the adjoining bed and lay there spreadeagled, her hands behind her head.

'You'll never guess, Joss, and I'm not going to wait whilst you try. Alan is going to lunch with Tío Angus at his club tomorrow and ask if we can get engaged!' Cassy's voice was breathless with excitement. 'If he agrees – and he's just got to,

Joss – then Alan'll talk to Papá when he comes over here next week. I suppose Tío Angus will object – me being one of his hated Papists! But Alan's twenty-one so he doesn't have to obey anyone any more and can do as he pleases. Of course, Tío Angus might cut him off without the proverbial penny, but as Alan's his only son I don't think he will, do you, Joss? And I'm sure Tía Pamela will be on our side. All she'll care about is that Alan is happy.'

Joscelin had been half asleep when Cassy burst into the room. The endless round of entertainments and late-night parties which had gone on since their presentation in June had left her exhausted, and she needed the rest before Lady Costain's ball tonight. Sleep, however, was now out of the question as she looked at Cassy's radiant face.

Cassy showed no sign of fatigue as she said breathlessly: 'Of course, we won't get married for ages! Anyway not until Alan comes down from Oxford. He still thinks I am too young to know my own mind, but I absolutely adore him and I nearly went through the floor when he kissed me.'

Of course she was happy, Joscelin thought. Not only was she clearly the most popular of all the débutantes, but now she had finally achieved her dearest wish.

'Alan would have proposed ages ago, but he thought I preferred Jimmy,' Cassy explained.

Joscelin frowned. 'Well, you do let Jimmy fill in a lot of dances on your programme!' she commented. 'No wonder Alan was jealous.'

Cassy leaned on one elbow, her dark eyes impatient as she looked towards Joscelin's bed. 'But that's just what I wanted Alan to be, you old stupid!' she said. 'Anyway, Jimmy's a divine dancer – and he's jolly good fun. Alan can be so serious, Joss – you know what he's like about his work. Anyone would think his silly book was a matter of life and death!'

'If Lord Costain did cut him off without a penny, maybe his book *would* be a matter of life and death!' Joscelin said wryly.

In a way, she could understand why Cassy found Jimmy Deighton amusing. His eligibility was certainly not in doubt and, according to Lady Costain, the mothers of other débutantes were none too pleased that the handsome Jimmy seemed to have set his sights on Cassy. Unaware, as was Lady Costain, that Cassy wanted to marry Alan, everyone suspected that her Season might well end with an engagement to young Viscount Deighton.

'People are bound to say you led Jimmy up the garden path,' Joscelin remarked. 'You can't deny you've been egging him on.'

Cassy picked up her pyjama case and tossed it at Joscelin with a laugh. 'Who cares what people say? Besides, Jimmy's terribly popular and there'll be dozens of other girls after him. I'm surprised *you're* not interested, Joss, although perhaps he isn't really your type . . .' she added vaguely.

'Nor I his!' Joscelin acknowledged. For a start, she had grown yet another inch this past year but without developing curves. Cassy kept telling her that boyish figures were *fashionable*, yet she was proud of her own full breasts and made certain that whatever dress she wore showed them to full advantage.

She told Joscelin that she had seen Jimmy staring at her bosom and once he had touched her nipples accidentally with his arm – a contact which had, she confessed, both embarrassed and excited her. 'It made me tingle all over!' she had confided in her uninhibited way.

But it was not only her figure which had convinced Joscelin she herself was unattractive to young men. She seemed unable to flirt, and found the effort of making light-hearted conversation exhausting and even welcomed Eduardo's company, since he did not seem to care whether she spoke or not. He had become her shadow and was always hovering somewhere at her elbow with an invitation to dance if she was without a partner.

As if aware of Joscelin's thoughts, Cassy said: 'I'm sure

you're going to get a proposal too, Joss, from Eduardo. He asked me last night if I thought you would consider becoming a Catholic, and looked frightfully down in the dumps when I said I doubted it. Of course, Mamá would never allow him to marry a Protestant – and there'll be a terrible rumpus about *me* marrying *Alan*. We'll probably have to elope, and I may even be excommunicated. Papá will be against it, too. I shall tell him that, if he'll let me get engaged, I'll probably be able to convert Alan in time for us to be married properly.'

'But supposing Alan doesn't want to be converted . . .' Joscelin said doubtfully.

'I don't think Alan minds much about religion. I suppose you wouldn't change your mind and accept Eduardo if he does propose, Joss? It would be simply ripping if we were sisters-in-law!'

'Not even to become your sister!' Joscelin said, smiling. 'You know I'm not in love with him, nor ever could be!'

But she could not tell Cassy the reason why she could *never* love poor Eduardo; that her heart belonged irrevocably to Alan. Although he had been unfailingly kind to her throughout the summer, and spent a good deal of time talking to her when Cassy was otherwise occupied, she had never pretended to herself that his interest was in the least personal.

On one occasion, he had remarked: 'Cassy seems to think you should marry Eduardo, but somehow I don't think he's quite your type, is he? Anyway, I hope you don't rush off and get married too quickly. Don't forget I'm counting on you to illustrate my book!'

He had been smiling, and Joscelin had not allowed herself even to imagine that he was serious. But her stomach had turned over, as it always did when Alan praised her, and she had made some silly pretext to leave the room before her emotions could betray her. She was immensely grateful that Cassy had never once suspected how she felt.

'Isn't life absolutely wonderful, Joss?' Cassy broke in on her thoughts. 'If only our Season would never end! But we still have the hunt balls and the house parties to look forward to when we get back from Scotland. Thank goodness your parents are letting you come up to Strathinver with us. Aren't you excited, Joss? Mamá has insisted Eduardo goes home for the rest of the summer, so *he'll* miss all the fun.'

Joscelin *was* looking forward to the month in the Costains' Scottish castle – for one thing, Alan had promised to take her to meet his Uncle Fergus – but for the present, she could not share Cassy's happiness or her excitement. There was still tonight's ball to be lived through; Eduardo's hot, gloved hand on her back; the duty dance with Alan, whose eyes would be searching the ballroom for Cassy.

'It will soon be time to get dressed,' Cassy said relentlessly. 'Are you going to wear your new violet taffeta, Joss? I'm going to wear the red chiffon. It's Alan's favourite and I don't care if everyone *has* seen it before; the flounces flare out when I dance and show my knees.' She giggled as she pointed one toe up in the air. 'Doesn't Alan look absolutely divine in tails? Even Eduardo looks passable in them.'

Two hours later, they joined Lord and Lady Costain in the ballroom where they were waiting to receive their guests. As soon as the dancing started, Cassy was surrounded by a circle of young men anxious to put their names on her programme. Jimmy Deighton was among them, and Joscelin saw Cassy glancing surreptitiously at Alan as he stood watching her on the edge of the group. His face was expressionless and, with a toss of her head, Cassy smiled brilliantly at Alan's rival and disappeared onto the dance floor with him.

Alan came over to Joscelin. 'May I claim a waltz, Joss?' he asked with a smile. 'You dance it so well!'

Mutely, Joscelin handed him her programme. At least, she thought, she no longer blushed except on the rarest occasions, and Alan could have no suspicion of the way her heart doubled its beat at his compliment.

'I see your most ardent admirer approaching,' he said in a low voice as he handed her back her programme. 'I'll make

myself scarce before Eduardo can complain that I am monopolizing you. See you later, Joss.'

If only Alan *did* try to monopolize her! Joscelin thought
as, with a deep sigh, she allowed Eduardo to lead her onto
the floor. He seemed even more tongue-tied than usual and,
in an attempt to be kind, Joscelin tried her hardest to be nice
to him. She quickly realized her mistake, for immediately he
broke into a stammering torrent of words. He must, he said,
speak to her – *alone*. Early next week he was returning to
Spain and could not be sure when he would see her again . . .

With a sinking heart, Joscelin recalled Cassy's warning that
Eduardo was thinking of proposing to her. She had not taken
it seriously, but now she could think of no other reason for
poor Eduardo's nervous trembling.

'Perhaps a bit later on . . . after the supper dance . . .' she
said vaguely. 'We could sit out the lancers. I always seem to
get the directions muddled up and feel an awful fool when I
go wrong!' She knew that she was rambling on for no better
reason than to prevent Eduardo talking. Mercifully the dance
ended and, murmuring some excuse, she hurried away from
his soulful gaze.

As she approached the entrance to the ballroom, Lady
Costain came sailing towards her. Recognizing Joscelin, she
beckoned to her and said: 'Dear child, how pretty you look!
How fortunate that I should find you at this moment. I've
lost my cigarette holder and all the servants seem madly busy.
I'm almost certain I left it on the sofa table in the library . . .
yes, I'm sure I did. Would you be very kind, my dear, and see
if you can find it for me?'

Joscelin nodded, happy to perform any task for her.

It did not occur to Joscelin to knock on the library door
and she was startled to find Lord Costain sitting reading the
evening paper, a glass of port on the table beside him.

In all the years that Joscelin had been a visitor at Rutland
Gate, she had not spoken more than a few sentences to Cassy's
peppery uncle. Like everyone else, she was slightly frightened

of him, for his tempers were fierce and unpredictable. She now stammered out an apology for interrupting him and explained her mission.

'Never mind!' he barked out. 'Come over here, girl, where I can see you.' As Joscelin approached, he peered at her over the top of his pince-nez. 'Umph, pretty girl, aren't you? But no match for young Casilda. Mustn't mind my bluntness. Sit down. Joscelin isn't it?'

With no ready excuse for refusing, Joscelin sat down on the chair beside him.

'Father's a bank manager, isn't he?' The old man chuckled and, without waiting for a reply, said: 'People think I don't know what goes on in this family, but I know a lot more than they imagine. You, thank heaven, are a bit more sensible. Got your head screwed on. Not like the women in my family. Take my girls. Both married to bloody foreigners. M'wife wanted them off her hands, but mark my words, girl, it won't be long before there's another war. They said the last one was going to be the end of it . . . but it won't. Know anything about politics? Suppose you're too young!'

Joscelin found her voice. 'I am not entirely uninformed, Lord Costain,' she said primly. 'My father says I should be conversant with world affairs.'

'Quite right, quite right!' muttered Joscelin's host, and paused for a moment to relight his cigar. 'Did y'father tell you there's going to be a strike before long? More hunger marches too, I dare say, since that fellow Baldwin can't solve the unemployment problem. He's about as ineffectual as the League of Nations! Fat lot of good *that's* proving. No stability, political or financial.'

He broke off to sip his port, and then jabbed a finger inconsequentially at his folded newspaper as if to point out a particular item. 'Dare say your father's aware of the mess Europe's in. Great Scott, look at Italy! Fascist fellow Mussolini making himself Premier and promising to put the country on its feet. Calmly walks into Corfu and annexes it without the slightest

regard for the League of Nations. God help Barbara living in
Italy under that Fascist upstart! M'daughter Isobel's even worse
off, I should imagine, married to a Hun!'

'My father said there has been the most appalling poverty
in Germany ever since the mark collapsed,' Joscelin said tentatively, and, glad of a chance to prove to this irascible old man
that she was not entirely ignorant, she added: 'He said it was
quite wrong for England to go on presenting her bill for war
reparations when it's obvious Germany cannot pay her dues.'

Lord Costain's face relaxed briefly into something resembling a smile. 'Quite right, although *I've* no sympathy for the
Huns. Shouldn't have started the war, should they? Read an
article last week by some journalist or other; mentioned a
revolutionary chap called Hitler; said he'd formed a clique
with some other rabble rousers – Goering, I think one was
called, and a fellow named Hess. Rotters are stirring up trouble
in Munich. Of course, Isobel's living in Wurttemberg. Things
aren't so bad there, but her husband's bothered about the
Communists. You've only to look at Soviet Russia to see how
quickly Communism has spread since the revolution. Be
happening in Germany before long, mark my words.'

As he paused for breath, Joscelin once again found courage
to speak. 'The newspapers say that Lenin is very ill and likely
to die and no one seems certain who will succeed him.'

'Communist fellow, Stalin!' Lord Costain retorted. 'Or
Trotsky . . . either one won't bring the Soviets into the League
of Nations . . .'

Quite suddenly he reached out and patted Joscelin's arm.
'Shouldn't be bothering a pretty head like yours with politics,'
he said, contradicting his earlier statement. 'Wouldn't give a
damn m'self – pardon my language – if it weren't for Alan.
Only son I've got, d'you see. Wouldn't want him turned into
cannon fodder if there was another war. Now run along, girl.
You'll find m'wife's cigarette holder on the table beside you.
Filthy habit, smoking – don't start it. Now go and enjoy
yourself – if you can with that din going on. If that's American

jazz, it's a pity they didn't keep it their side of the Atlantic. Now away with you!'

Joscelin picked up the cigarette holder and, with a polite goodbye to Lord Costain, she hurried back towards the ball-room. She was astonished not only by the old man's apparent eagerness to talk to her but by the fact that she herself had not once been bored. He was not in the very least what she had always thought him – a bad-tempered, uncaring old man! Taciturn he might be, but underneath that brusque exterior he was concerned not only for his country, but for his family, his daughters' futures – and Alan's. For that alone she would never again dislike him.

Lost in thought as she entered the ballroom, she collided with someone standing by the open doors. It was only a passing knock, but sufficient to jolt the glass in the stranger's hand, and the contents spilled down the trouser legs of his immacu-late tails. Aghast at her clumsiness, Joscelin stammered out an apology while her victim mopped at the dripping wine with a silk handkerchief. He looked up at her anxious face with a sympathetic smile.

'Such misfortunes are more often my lot than I suspect them to be yours,' he said in heavily accented English. 'I have noticed you on several occasions, Signorina, and you move with much grace.'

Joscelin looked into a pair of dark, smiling eyes and felt instantly less embarrassed. She even essayed a smile. 'I really am sorry,' she said. 'It's nice of you to be so nice about it . . .'

The eyes were laughing now with genuine amusement. 'So useful this English word "nice"! May I introduce myself, Signorina? My name is Marco da Cortona. I come from Italy.'

Joscelin took the proffered hand, noting that his was cool and firm as she said: 'I'm Joscelin Howard. I really am sorry, Signor da Cortona. I was looking for Lady Costain.'

'Then I can help you find her, as I have just seen her pass by on the dance floor,' her companion said easily. 'May I have the pleasure, Miss Howard?'

The band was playing a selection from the popular Jerome Kern musical *Sally* and Joscelin's partner danced effortlessly. He was not, she thought, what Cassy would have described as 'a deb's delight' – but she found him an exceedingly pleasant companion. As soon as she had returned the cigarette holder to Lady Costain, he appropriated her for the supper interval and found a place for them to sit on the wide staircase leading into the ballroom. There, as Joscelin toyed with the rich food, she was able to observe her partner. He was, she decided, about thirty years old or perhaps a little younger. He was not unlike a youthful Don Jaime, olive-skinned with black hair and eyes. He, too, was stockily built and not much taller than herself. He had a diamond ring on one finger and his clothes were perfectly tailored. His manners were those of a mature man who was absolutely at ease with women.

'I shall not invite you to tell me about yourself,' he said with light-hearted candour, 'since I have already made inquiries from young Patricio who answered my curiosity concerning you. However, I feel it only fair that you should know a little about me. I am a friend of del Valbo, Barbara's husband. I called on Lady Costain this morning and she very kindly invited me to this function. For your further information, I am what you might call in your idiomatic language "a wealthy playboy" – that is to say I am fortunate enough not to be obliged to work for my living, but may live for no better reason than to enjoy myself. I am an incorrigible flirt and therefore not to be trusted by innocent young ladies like yourself. So now you cannot ever say in the future that I did not warn you!'

Joscelin found herself laughing. 'At least you are honest, Signor da Cortona. I will consider myself warned, although I cannot see that there will be occasions in the future when I might need to recall your warning. The Season is nearly over and I shall shortly be going away on holiday. In the autumn I begin my studies at the Slade School of Art and I shall not be attending any more parties such as this.'

Marco da Cortona smiled. 'Nor, indeed, shall I, Miss Howard. But we shall meet again very soon, I promise you.'

Joscelin was now quite at her ease. As her escort beckoned to a passing waiter to refill their glasses, she said: 'I shall soon begin to believe that you are everything you told me – an Italian "playboy" who is an incorrigible flirt.'

'But a sincere one,' he replied as he touched his champagne goblet to hers. 'To *una signorina molto simpatica*. You see, I meant what I said. We shall meet again, much sooner perhaps than you think!'

'You sound very certain about it,' Joscelin replied, 'but I shall be leaving London next week. Lady Costain has kindly invited me to go to Scotland with the family for the month of August.'

There was a smile of amusement in the dark eyes regarding her. 'And I too, have been invited!' he told her. 'When Patricio told me you would be in the house party, I made myself very charming to dear Lady Costain and hinted that I had never yet had the pleasure of shooting grouse, which I had always longed to do. Not quite true, I admit, but the ploy succeeded.'

Despite herself, Joscelin laughed. She was by no means convinced that this agreeable companion was serious; in fact she suspected that he was teasing her – flirting with her, Cassy would have said.

But there was no doubt that he really was going to Scotland, for Eduardo now came hurrying over to them and, having claimed his next dance with Joscelin, he said stiffly: 'Good evening, da Cortona. My brother told me he had run into you at the buffet and that you are going to Strathinver next week.'

Marco smiled pleasantly. 'Your delightful aunt has invited me to join the shooting party,' he said. 'You will be returning to Spain to celebrate your coming of age, I am told, so I will not enjoy the pleasure of your company.'

Eduardo glowered at the older man who had monopolized Joscelin for the best part of an hour. He resented Marco's maturity and self-confidence, and now that he knew the Italian was going to be in Scotland with Joscelin he was hot with jealousy. Yet he had quite liked da Cortona when he had met him in Florence the previous year at the christening of his cousin Barbara's son, Ernesto, to whom he and Marco were godfathers. Wanting Joscelin to himself, Eduardo quickly made his adieux to Marco and helped her to her feet.

Avoiding the ballroom, and with one hand firmly clasping her elbow, he escorted her into the conservatory and halted by a tall potted palm. With an obvious stiffening of his shoulders, he turned to face her.

'I . . . I wanted to talk to you, Joscelin . . . alone!' he said urgently. 'As you know, I'm going home next week and it may be ages before I see you again.' His face took on a look of desperation. 'I know it's wrong to talk like this . . . I mean, I should speak to your father . . . my parents . . . but Casilda said I'd be making an ass of myself asking their permission to propose to you when it's perfectly obvious you . . . you don't return my feelings!'

He gritted his teeth and fingered his spectacles as he stared anywhere but at Joscelin's face. 'I suppose there isn't a chance that Casilda's wrong? That you *might* care just a little bit for me, Joscelin? I'm dreadfully in love with you!'

The words were out at last, and Joscelin felt both relief and pity. It seemed so silly of Eduardo to lay himself open to rejection when he must have known she did not return his love. She said gently: 'I'm sure you can't really be in love with me, Eduardo . . . I mean, I know you think it's true, but honestly it wouldn't work, would it? Your parents wouldn't like it one bit if you married a non-Catholic girl and . . . and I couldn't leave my parents. I'm an only child and they'd be heartbroken if I went to live abroad. And besides . . .' she added helplessly, 'I'm really much too young even to think about getting married. I want to complete my course at art school and . . . and I'm fearfully sorry, Eduardo, honestly I am, but I wouldn't want to marry anyone,' she finished lamely.

'So there's no hope!' Eduardo sighed. With a smile that was

almost a grimace, he said apologetically: 'I'm afraid Casilda was right and I have made an ass of myself.'

As if on cue, the band struck up the opening bars of 'Limehouse Blues' and he added with a look of relief: 'I expect you're booked for this dance, Joscelin. Shall we go back to the ballroom?'

His pride, Joscelin thought, was helping him cope with his disappointment. Silently, she accompanied him back into the ballroom where, mercifully, Patri came hurrying towards her. 'My dance, Joss!' he said jovially, and with a quick glance at his brother's face he led her onto the floor, his eyes sympathetic. 'Don't tell me – poor old Eduardo has been *despachado*! Well, don't look so guilty, Joss. We all warned him he was barking up the wrong tree. Tell you what, why don't you marry me? I'd make a splendid husband – or anyway, I will do in a few years' time. Got to finish school first, drat it!'

As he guided her round the floor, Joscelin felt a rush of affection for him. His hazel eyes were dancing with laughter and despite his youth, he looked surprisingly handsome and manly in his white tie and tails.

'Oh, Patri!' she said. 'I wish you *were* older. I'm really very very fond of you – almost as fond of you as I am of Cassy!' Patricio's gaze followed Joscelin's and rested briefly on his sister's radiant face as she swayed dreamily by in his cousin Alan's arms. Looking down once more into Joscelin's grey eyes, he said with his teasing smile: 'Of course you adore me, dearest Joss – everyone does! But I'll wager my best cricket bat and a guinea or two that there's someone you love far more than me or Casilda!'

Only as he saw the betraying colour rush into Joscelin's cheeks did he realize, with a perceptiveness belying his years, that his harmless teasing had been all too close to the truth. But it was too late by then to wish the words unsaid.

PART TWO

1923–1934

LOVE

... I am a golden knot
Binding together the loose years.
I sparkle and run
Like ice in the moonlight, like frost in the sun
And when you have found me, then life has begun ...

'Romance'
by Lady Margaret Sackville

CHAPTER THIRTEEN

August 1923–April 1926

Cassy's banishment from England two days after the ball was a heartbreaking blow to Alan. He was informed that she would not be permitted to return for at least two years, during which time he would not be made welcome in Sevilla by his Spanish relatives. Both sides of the family were united in this decision, for not only was Lord Costain bitterly opposed to the engagement, but Cassy's father was equally determined to keep the young lovers apart. No amount of pleading from Cassy could change Don Jaime's mind, and Alan was brought to heel by his father's threat to cut off his allowance if he attempted to see her.

'We are not even permitted to write to each other!' Alan told Joss unhappily when he called to see her at Whitegates a few days after Cassy's tearful departure to Spain. 'I shall have to rely on you for news of her, Joss.'

But Cassy, who had never yet observed any rule that displeased her, quickly established Joscelin as a go-between, and although Joscelin sometimes felt guilty in her capacity as postman, she never failed to forward their letters to each other.

In the autumn she started at the Slade School of Art and this made up in part for the loss of her friend. Moreover, her parents had reluctantly agreed to her moving into a flat in a mews off Queen's Gate.

'But she's still so young!' Peggy Howard wailed to her husband. 'And she'll be living on her own – goodness knows what might happen to her!'

'Joscelin likes being on her own,' he said gently, 'and I think we can trust her to manage her independence sensibly. She has earned it.'

Joscelin settled happily into her new home, where she entertained her own small circle of friends, none of whom belonged to the 'smart set'. Like herself, they were students at the Slade, and art was their main topic of conversation. Although in the year following she received several invitations to parties from débutantes she had met during her Season, she declined them all. Her life was otherwise occupied.

Soon after she had moved in, Alan called to see her. The pleasure of his unexpected visit was marred by the fact that he had come to say goodbye. Having finished at Oxford, he was leaving on an expedition to Alaska. It would be eighteen months before she would see him again, and it seemed to Joscelin when he left as if all her connections with the Costain family had been severed.

One Saturday morning, as she was about to leave to visit her parents, she found Marco da Cortona on her doorstep. He had learned her new address from Lady Costain. He insisted upon taking her to lunch, rejecting all excuses why she could not accept.

'You shall telephone your parents from the restaurant and explain why you will be a little late,' he said masterfully. When Joscelin pointed out that they had no telephone at Whitegates, he overruled this difficulty, saying that they would stop at the nearest post office and send a telegram.

Joscelin was embarrassed by the fact that she had no clothes suitable for the expensive venue he had chosen. But her companion seemed impervious to her attire, telling her over a pre-lunch cocktail that he found her even more beautiful than before.

Although Joscelin did not take the Italian's flattery seriously, she found his compliments satisfying to her ego. She forgot her customary shyness and began to enjoy her lunch.

He told her that Alan's father had invited him up to Strathinver for the shooting, and said easily: 'I was quite heartbroken that our meeting in Scotland came to so unfortunate an end last summer. I had been so much looking forward to it. I gather the pretty little Casilda was sent home in disgrace and that young Costain has gone abroad. I thought her an amusing, lively girl. You must tell me how you two met.'

The lunch lasted far longer than Joscelin had expected and Marco insisted she should travel to Surbiton in a taxi. As he assisted her into the back he took her hand in his and kissed it continental-style, then turned it over and pressed a kiss into her palm.

'I see you still blush just as charmingly as ever,' he said with a smile. 'By the way, Joscelin, I quite forgot to tell you that I do not leave for Scotland until Tuesday, so on Monday night I shall take you out to dinner.'

He closed the cab door, paid the driver and ordered him on his way before Joscelin could think up a reason to refuse his invitation.

True to his word, Marco took her to cocktails and dinner at the Ritz. She enjoyed the evening until the moment when he suddenly asked her to marry him. Thinking about it later that night, Joscelin was unsure whether he had meant his proposal seriously. He had made it so casually, smiling as he spoke, that she doubted whether he really did want to marry her. The whole idea seemed too improbable. It was only the third time they had met. She had, of course, refused him, for although she liked him and was attracted to him, she was not in love with him. Nor could she see any reason why he should possibly think he was in love with her. He had taken her rejection philosophically, dismissing it with a smile and the comment: 'I shall ask you again when the time is right!'

But that time could never come, Joscelin told herself. Marco's feelings might be questionable, but she had no doubt about her own. She knew that no evening spent with him could ever compare with the joy she felt when one of Alan's rare postcards plopped into her letter box. Although she recognized that their sole purpose was to give her the next address

to which she could forward Cassy's letters, at least she knew
where he was.

She no longer tried to deny to herself that she loved Alan
wholeheartedly. The strength of that emotion left no room for
any other love and endured throughout the long year that
followed. Marco called briefly to see her at Christmas, and a
beautiful bouquet of flowers arrived from him on her birthday
in February. But he did not visit her that summer, and by
September she was caught up once more in her tuition at the
Slade and would have forgotten Marco but for his postcards.
They arrived far more frequently than Alan's, from all over
the world – each one ending with the words: 'I wish you could
be with me, *cara mia.*'

She was beginning to look forward to these affectionate
communications when Alan suddenly returned to England. He
arrived at the flat without warning at the end of February, and
from then on called to see her with increasing regularity.

She was well aware that his pleasure in her company was
impersonal and twofold. He was eager to see her drawings
and paintings, which even her tutor had praised; but first and
foremost he wanted to talk about Cassy. He worried endlessly
about the future. Had he the right to come between Cassy
and her religion, even if she did not take it seriously? Was he
being pig-headed, sticking to the principle that it would be
wrong for him to adopt a religion in which he had no faith?
Would Cassy tire eventually of waiting and marry some other
fellow – Deighton, for example, who had been to Spain to
visit her? His mother, he told Joscelin, offered no support and
his father showed no sign of withdrawing his opposition to
the marriage.

Those hours spent in Alan's company were for Joscelin a
mixture of pleasure and pain. She wondered anxiously whether
she should show him Cassy's most recent letter to her. She
decided against doing so, knowing that Cassy's ecstatic references to the 'fun' she was having with Jimmy Deighton and
Monty Piermont, who were staying with her, would distress

Alan. The two young men had called on the Monteros whilst on a driving holiday, and had been invited to spend a fortnight with the family in Sevilla. According to Cassy, Doña Ursula was encouraging Jimmy to stay on for a third week. 'As you know, Joss, he's an RC so Mamá thinks he's marvellous,' Cassy had written, 'and I heard her telling Papá that he would make an excellent match for me.' She had gone on to say that of course she still loved Alan, but Jimmy was 'terribly amusing and a dreadful flirt' and she couldn't help liking him.

Joscelin's reluctance to pass on these comments to Alan was irrelevant, for Cassy had mentioned Jimmy's visit in her last letter to Alan. His envy of Deighton was tempered by Cassy's comment that she might be able to use her parents' approval of her friendship with Jimmy to persuade them to allow her back to England. 'I think they'd give their blessing if Jimmy proposed,' she wrote, 'so I'm letting them think I'm keen on him . . .'

As Joscelin's love for Alan deepened each time he visited her, she tried harder to bury it, afraid lest it should surface in his presence. Alan sometimes asked her why she had no boyfriends, and it was therefore a relief when without warning Marco da Cortona turned up once more. As before, he took her out to dinner, and once again he proposed. He looked at Joscelin curiously when she told him she did not love him, but made no comment and the following morning arrived at her flat with a gigantic bouquet of red roses and asked her to spend the day with him. He took her to the Sitwell recital at the Chenil Gallery and on to Boulestin's for dinner where he proposed for the third time.

On this occasion he added thoughtfully: 'Or is there someone else you have lost your heart to, my beautiful Joscelin?'

Partly from honesty, but also in the hope of discouraging any further proposals, she nodded, hoping that he would not demand to know who it was she loved. Surprisingly he did not question her, but disappeared from her life as abruptly as he had re-entered it.

Joscelin had started to work closely with Alan drawing the illustrations for his book. Suddenly in the middle of March he received news that put all thoughts of work out of his mind. He turned up at her flat looking like a boy who had just been given his first bicycle.

He caught Joscelin by the waist and whirled her round the small studio, sending her easel flying. Breathless, he collapsed onto the sofa saying: 'Cassy's coming to London. Isn't it ripping? My mother had a long telephone call from Uncle Jaime last night. It went on for ages as she had to go and consult my father, but finally everyone has agreed. She's coming to stay with us!'

He leaned forward, clasping his hands between his knees, his eyes bright with excitement. 'My mother's view is that, since Cassy's now twenty-one, she's of an age to be responsible for herself.' He grinned cheerfully. 'To tell you the truth, Joss, I have my doubts as to whether Cassy will *ever* be of an age to take care of herself! But if I have my way, it won't be long now before *I* will be able to look after her. No one is going to come between us this time. I'm going to marry her, and if the Pater cuts me off, I shall earn money to support her.' Unable to sit still he paced round the room. 'My grandfather left money for me in a trust which becomes mine in September, so we shan't starve. I simply can't remember when I was last so happy! By the sound of it, that clever ruse of Cassy's – pretending she's considering Deighton for a husband – seems to have worked. We must go along with the pretence until September. Then if the Pater puts his foot down, I'll simply tell him I'm going to marry Cassy, and that will be that.'

Alan was still too full of his good news to relax. He walked over to Joscelin's easel, righted it absent-mindedly and turned to look at her. 'I've just remembered, Joss, the Piermonts have invited me down for the second weekend in April. Monty's planning a treasure hunt, and I know I can get him to invite Cassy. You too, Joss – and don't shake your head like that! Cassy's sure to want you there, and come to that, so do I.'

Joscelin tried to steady her heartbeat as finally he paused by her chair and gave her that familiar lopsided smile.

'You've been a wonderful friend, Joss!' he said. 'I don't know how I would have survived this separation if I hadn't been able to confide in you. And we've both depended on you for forwarding our letters – even if Cassy's have been somewhat few and far between! But that doesn't matter now. Only another week, and she'll be here.'

Joscelin wished she could share Alan's happiness, but she was afraid that somehow he would be hurt again. It was clear that he expected Cassy to be unchanged, but she could not believe this would be the case. She knew how greatly she herself had altered in the past two years. She had grown up, become independent, knew exactly where the future was leading her. Alan's publisher had seen some of the illustrations she had done for his book on wildlife, and had offered her freelance work illustrating children's books when she left the Slade. This had added to her growing self-confidence and she considered herself mature in her outlook. Surely, she thought, two years must have had an effect upon Cassy, too. Perhaps she would not be as eager as Alan to rush into marriage.

But Cassy sounded exactly the same when, within hours of her arrival at Rutland Gate, she rushed round with Alan to Joscelin's flat and promptly swept aside all Joscelin's excuses why she could not join the Piermonts' house party.

Her cheeks as bright as her pink tweed Lanvin suit, she hugged Joscelin, laughing as she said: 'But of course you're coming. We'll pick you up at teatime on Friday.' Smiling apologetically, she added: 'We can't stay. Tía Pamela has friends coming for cocktails and we promised to be back.' She kissed Joscelin on both cheeks and linked her arm through Alan's. 'Must rush. See you Friday!' she called over her shoulder as they hurried down the steep staircase, leaving only the heady fragrance of her scent to remind Joscelin that she had actually seen Cassy again.

It was as if the past two years had never happened, Joscelin

thought three days later as Alan drove them down to Shamley
Green. She had forgotten how funny and lovable Cassy could
be. It seemed as if they were in their childhood once more,
Best Friends, as Cassy would have it, and the long separation
of no import to either of them.

'Do you remember the last time we were here?' Cassy
remarked as they were shown into one of the guest rooms of
the Piermonts' mansion. 'I think we had this very room. I'd
almost forgotten that ghastly day when I nearly drowned! We
dripped all over this carpet!'

She chattered on whilst a maid unpacked their suitcases.
When the girl had finished, Cassy waved her away.

'Now at last we can talk *privately*,' she said with a smile
as she started to undress. 'I hardly know where to begin!'
Joscelin removed her frock and, retrieving Cassy's from the
floor, she hung them both in the wardrobe. Putting on her
dressing-gown, she sat on the edge of one of the beds and
watched Cassy, perched on a stool in front of the chintz-
curtained dressing-table, dabbing powder on her pert retroussé
nose. Seeing that rounded, perfectly formed body dressed only
in pink silk cami-knickers made Joscelin long for her sketchpad.

'I simply can't tell you how utterly heavenly it is to be back
in England,' Cassy was saying as she licked a forefinger and
smoothed her thick, dark eyebrows into arched curves. 'I don't
think I could have stood another week watching Mamá
drooling over my baby sister, Amalia. Everyone spoils her.
Papá says she looks just like I did at that age, but Eduardo
says she's prettier! Not that I set much store by Eduardo's
taste – Mercedes is as plain as a donkey, and I think he married
her on the rebound from you, Joss – although she does have
money, and surprisingly she adores him.'

Cassy paused whilst she leaned forward to outline her
mouth with a scarlet lipstick. 'You can borrow this, Joss, if
you haven't got one. You know you could look quite stunning
if you bothered.'

Joscelin laughed, happy to be in her friend's company again.

As she took off her dressing-gown and drew her lace-collared velveteen frock over her cropped fair hair, Cassy said inconsequentially: 'I'd almost forgotten how frightfully good-looking Alan is – and he's terribly grown up! I'd forgotten too, how serious he always is. Compared to Jimmy he's awfully straitlaced.' She frowned. 'Do you know, Joss, Alan was quite shocked when I went to his room last night, and actually sent me back to bed like a naughty child. I bet Jimmy wouldn't have done that!'

Joscelin felt a sudden chill of anxiety. 'You do still want to marry Alan, don't you, Cassy?' she asked.

'Of course I do,' Cassy replied without hesitation. 'You can have much more fun if you're married. At least, in England you can – Tía Pamela goes out nearly every night. Spanish wives have to stay at home and wait for their husbands to return when it suits them. That's why I shall marry an Englishman. Haven't you found someone *you* want to marry, Joss? You want to get married, don't you?'

Joscelin nodded, embarrassed by the question. 'But not for a while, Cassy. I haven't finished at the Slade and I'm determined to get my diploma before I do anything else.'

Cassy grinned. 'Is that why you keep the handsome Marco at arm's length?' she asked. 'And don't look so sheepish! Alan told me all about your faithful admirer. He ran into him just after he got back from Canada and Marco kept asking questions about you. He's frightfully eligible, Joss, and I gather he described you as "mysterious and fascinating". Nobody's ever called *me* mysterious!'

'Honestly, Cassy, you are quite potty! Marco's just the type of man to pay compliments without in the least meaning them. As to his being "faithful", I know very well I'm not the only girl in his life. There was a picture of him in the *Tatler* the other day with a remarkably pretty woman – the Contessa di Something-or-other. I've no doubt whatever that he only proposes to me to make me blush, and he'd have fifty fits if I accepted! Of course he isn't serious, and nor am I.'

'Alan said he *was* interested in you, Joss,' Cassy argued. 'I expect those other females he takes out are just to make you jealous. Men do that sort of thing, you know, just the same as girls do. Which reminds me, Joss, I need your help this evening.' There was a glint in her eyes which Joscelin recognized from the past. It meant Cassy was up to mischief. But she was unprepared for the words which followed.

'Jimmy telephoned me last night. He'd heard from Monty that I would be here, and he says that we're all going to be paired off for the treasure hunt. Anyway, I've promised to go in his car. Naturally, Alan's expecting I'll be with *him*, so when Jimmy announces that he's taking me, *you've* got to say that you'd like to go in Alan's car.'

Joscelin picked up the silver-backed mirror and, with unnecessary concentration, applied Cassy's lipstick. Her heart was pounding and she needed these few minutes to regain control of herself.

When she could trust her voice, she said quietly: 'Surely there's no need to make Alan jealous, Cassy? He's as much in love with you as anyone could be. He was like a man reprieved from the gallows when he heard you were coming back to London. He wants to marry you, Cassy.'

Cassy stood up, tossing her head and frowning. 'Of course he *says* he does, but if he loved me all that much he'd have come to Spain and taken me away with him. When Tío Angus and Papá made all that fuss, he just gave in without a fight. I don't call *that* love.'

'Cassy, that isn't fair!' Joscelin was stung to retort. 'You were only eighteen and Alan was still at Oxford – and besides, he understood your father's concern about you being excommunicated if you married a Protestant.'

Cassy pouted. 'Then he should have agreed to be converted!' she said airily. 'After all, Joss, he wouldn't have to *stay* a Catholic, would he? He could take the vows and then lapse – lots of people do!'

Their conversation was interrupted by the entrance of the

maid. Cocktails were being served, she informed them and Lady Piermont was expecting them downstairs.

The maid helped Cassy into her green georgette dress and fastened the long jade beads around her neck. Cassy pushed two gold slave bangles up above one elbow and, tucking a flowered chiffon scarf through them, she linked her arm in Joscelin's. She was smiling brightly as they made their way down to the drawing room.

There were thirty other guests already assembled. Some of them were friends of Monty's parents, but the majority were of his generation. With a friendly smile, the young man came hurrying across the room to greet them.

'There you are at last! Alan warned us you'd be gossiping – but you're well worth waiting for! You both look stunning, if I may say so!'

His eyes were on Cassy; but she was glancing over Monty's shoulder, watching Jimmy Deighton as he made his way over to them.

It was the first time Joscelin had seen Jimmy since Lady Costain's end-of-season ball. He had changed very little since then, she thought as he stood talking to them. He was smiling down at Cassy as he teased her good-naturedly.

'Well, well! So our hothouse orchid has finally been tempted away from Spain! It's good to see you, Cassy.' He smiled at Joscelin, politely including her in the conversation. 'Last saw the beautiful señorita shouting her head off at a bullfight, Miss Howard!' he said. 'Never saw anything so bloodthirsty in all my life!'

Cassy laughed, enjoying his banter. 'You know *you* enjoyed the *corrida* every bit as much as I did, Jimmy,' she said with mock reproach. 'It seems ages since you were in Sevilla. We had great fun, didn't we?'

A manservant edged forward with a tray of cocktails and, although Joscelin did not much care for these concoctions, she took one in order not to look odd man out. Sipping the drink, her eyes searched the crowded room for Alan's figure.

As always, her heart missed a beat when she caught sight of him talking to their hostess.

With a self-assurance that her independent life had taught her, she made her way over to them.

'Good evening, Lady Piermont!' she said. 'I'm Joscelin Howard, Casilda Montero's friend, and I'd like to thank you for including me in your house party at such short notice.'

Lady Piermont nodded pleasantly. 'Of course, I remember you, Miss Howard. You came one summer to watch Monty and Alan batting for our cricket team. I recall how astonished I was, Alan, that your dear mother should have allowed two such young girls to arrive without a chaperon! We were most amused when the truth emerged and quite admired your daring. What naughty girls you were!'

Alan grinned at Joscelin. 'They both consider themselves grown up now, Lady Piermont, but I am far from sure they have outgrown their "naughtiness".'

'Dear Casilda, Monty quite lost his heart to her the year she was presented. But then all you young men were competing, were you not?' Lady Piermont patted Alan's arm playfully with her fan. 'I'm afraid Monty has stolen a march on you, dear boy. He has insisted upon sitting next to Casilda at dinner. However, I know that you and Miss Howard are well acquainted and will have plenty to talk about.'

As their hostess moved off to greet a newly arrived guest, Alan took Joscelin's arm and said: 'Glad we'll be sitting together, Joss. I've thought of a new opening chapter for my book and I want your opinion.'

She was grateful that he did not seem to mind being paired off with her instead of Cassy during dinner. Perhaps it was only important to him that he should be with her for the treasure hunt. She wished fervently that Cassy had not devised her plan to ride with Jimmy Deighton.

When finally Cassy drove off with Jimmy in his Lagonda, Alan made no attempt to hide his disappointment. 'I just don't understand,' he told Joscelin miserably as he helped her into his Bentley. 'One might almost think she *wants* to hurt me!' He started the car and, with a sudden change of mood, roared off down the long gravel drive: 'Well, I'm not going to let Cassy spoil our fun. Open the envelope, Joss, and let's see what we have to find. You and I are going to be first back. We'll put Deighton's nose out of joint when we scoop first prize!'

There were twelve people in six cars now heading for Shamley Green churchyard, where they hoped to find the first object – a beribboned twig from the big yew tree standing by the lychgate. Only certain branches had been tied with tiny red bows, and torches were required to identify them.

There was no sign of the Lagonda as they parked in front of the old church, and Alan's spirits began to revive as the hunt continued.

'I've been an idiot,' he said cheerfully as they drove off in search of the second object. 'Cassy and I agreed to throw people off the scent until I come into my inheritance. Her choosing to pair off with Deighton was a good idea, and I should have realized what she was up to.'

Joscelin remained silent. If Alan had discussed marriage with Cassy, she could see no reason why Cassy should feel a need to make him jealous.

They were obliged to drive quite far afield to collect a beer mat from a pub in a village three miles away. Twenty minutes later, they were scrambling along the barbed wire perimeter of a field in search of a strand of sheep's wool. Soon afterwards, Alan was removing his socks and shoes in order to wade into the swampy edge of the village pond to retrieve a duck's egg.

'We're doing splendidly!' he told Joscelin with a smile as he dried his muddy feet with his handkerchief.

The last item to be collected was one of Monty's lead soldiers. As they drove back towards the house, Joscelin felt strangely happy. Alan really seemed to be enjoying the treasure hunt and was boyishly delighted that they could see no other cars in the driveway.

'The quickest way to the nursery is by the back stairs,' he said as he helped her out of the car.

The 'treasures' tucked carefully into a box beneath her arm, Joscelin followed Alan up the servants' staircase to the third floor. Alan knew just where to look for Monty's soldiers. No more than a few minutes passed before they were reporting their return to Sir Charles Piermont. He was awaiting the treasure seekers in the billiard room and confirmed that Alan and Joscelin were the first to arrive back. A retired brigadier, he checked their list with military precision, and informed them they had won the first prize.

'A congratulatory drink is in order, I think.' He turned to the footman nearby. 'Tell Benson to bring in the champagne, on the double, James!'

'I'll just nip upstairs and tidy myself, sir, if you don't mind,' Alan said. 'I got a trifle muddy raiding the village pond!'

During Alan's absence, three more couples returned.

'M'wife's rustled up some little prizes,' Sir Charles announced when the last pair arrived. 'Now where's that young man got to, Miss Howard? Anyone seen Costain? And where's young Deighton?'

And where, thought Joscelin with a sudden shiver of apprehension, was Cassy?

At that moment, Alan reappeared. His face was deathly pale as he walked over to her side and said in a taut whisper: 'I'm leaving as soon as I can, Joss. Sorry to spoil the fun, but I *must* get away.'

'What is it? What's happened?' Joscelin whispered back. 'Nothing's happened to Cassy, has it?'

The flash of fire in Alan's eyes frightened her. He seemed to be both shocked and angry. Whatever it was that had upset him, it must be serious to oblige him to leave a weekend house party so abruptly.

Immovable in his intent, as soon as the prizegiving was over Alan asked his hostess if he might use the telephone. His father had not been well, he said vaguely, and he had promised

FROST IN THE SUN

his mother he would speak to her before he went to bed in
case she needed him.

In the meanwhile, Cassy had reappeared with Jimmy. At
the first opportunity, Joscelin went over to ask her if she
had any idea what had disturbed Alan. Cassy was almost
as pale as Alan, and looked as if she might have been crying.
By her side, Jimmy was fidgeting with his bow tie, unnaturally
silent.

'Go away, Jimmy. I want to talk to Joss – *alone!*' Cassy
said to him in a low but violent tone.

Looking thoroughly sheepish, Jimmy walked off and Cassy
drew Joscelin to a quiet corner of the room.

'Something utterly *ghastly* has just happened!' she whispered, her nails digging into Joscelin's arm. 'You've simply got
to help me, Joss.' Her voice rose hysterically and quietened
only as Joscelin said, 'Sshh! Cassy!' knowing with a sickening
certainty that, whatever Cassy had to confess, it was not for
other ears.

'It's Alan, isn't it?' she prompted.

The beautiful eyes regarding her filled with tears. Joscelin
thought Cassy was going to start crying.

'If you don't tell me, I'm going,' she said sharply.

'*Dios me ayude!* It wasn't my fault, I swear it. It . . . it just
happened. And then Alan came in . . . and he saw us! Oh
God, Joss, what am I going to do?'

Fear increased Joscelin's anger. 'What "*just happened*"?' she
asked sharply. '*What did Alan see?*'

Bit by bit, the truth emerged. It seemed that Jimmy and
Cassy had decided not to bother with the treasure hunt. They
had stopped the car in a wood and started kissing. That was
all she meant to do, Cassy kept repeating. But Jimmy thought
it would be a lot warmer and more comfortable if they drove
back to the house by the tradesmen's drive, parked the car
behind the stables and went up to his bedroom. He was in
the east wing in a big double room which he was sharing with
Alan. Knowing that Alan could not possibly return from the

treasure hunt for at least an hour, Cassy had let herself be persuaded to go and lie on the bed with Jimmy.

'He got terribly worked up!' Cassy said, an edge of excitement in her voice as she related the details Joscelin had no wish to hear. 'He started to caress me . . . I can't tell you what it was like, Joss . . . a sort of magic. I didn't want to stop him, the kissing and the touching and everything. I suppose I knew it was wrong . . . but I meant to stop him before anything awful happened . . . then suddenly I didn't want to stop and . . . and I let him. I let him do it, Joss . . . *everything*!'

Joscelin tried not to see the picture Cassy was painting so vividly. But the confession begun, Cassy was beyond suppression.

'After it was over, Jimmy got in a bit of a panic – he hadn't realized I was a virgin. He said we'd have to get married as soon as possible because he hadn't done anything to make sure it was safe, but that it didn't really matter because he loved me and wanted to marry me. We were getting dressed when . . . when suddenly the door opened and Alan came in. Of course, he jumped to the worst possible conclusion. Joss, he didn't say a word – just looked at me as if he hated me! I tried to tell him we were just necking – but I know he thinks I don't love him, but I do, and I don't want to marry Jimmy. You've got to help me convince Alan, Joss. He'll believe you if *you* tell him that although I flirt with other men, I don't . . . don't let them make love to me.'

'But, Cassy, you *did*! You let Jimmy . . . you said so!'

Cassy's eyes widened. 'But I didn't *mean* to, Joss. It just happened. It all sort of got out of control.'

'No wonder Alan's in such a state!' Joscelin said in a small, tight voice. 'I'm going to find him. It isn't safe for him to drive in that mood. I'll go with him. At least I can stop him doing anything dangerous.'

Cassy gripped her arm, her face brightening. 'You'll talk to him, won't you, Joss? You've just got to make him understand.

I couldn't bear it if he stopped loving me. If he wants, I'll never see Jimmy again. I promise, Joss . . .'

Joscelin pulled away from Cassy's grasp. She must find Alan before it was too late.

He was standing in the entrance hall bidding his hostess goodbye whilst a servant carried his luggage out to the car. Uncaring of Lady Piermont's opinion, Joscelin hurried over to him.

'If you will wait just five minutes, Alan, I'll return to London with you. Your mother may need my help!'

It was the lamest of excuses, since Lady Costain had a houseful of servants to carry out any possible requirements she might have. But Lady Piermont did not question it and, although Alan protested that there was absolutely no necessity for Joscelin to spoil her weekend, Lady Piermont supported her.

'You know how foggy it can be round London at this time of the year, Alan, and four eyes are better than two. Never mind! You must both come down again this summer. Run along now and pack. I'll send Robert up for your suitcase, my dear.'

Ten minutes later, Joscelin followed Alan out to the car. He drove in silence, winding his way through Shamley Green to the main road. When he did speak, it was almost angrily.

'There was really no point whatever you forgoing a perfectly good house party just because I chose to leave, Joscelin!'

Since there was no answer to this, Joscelin said obliquely: 'Lady Piermont was right about driving conditions. It's quite misty now.'

Making no reply, Alan turned onto the London road and put his foot down hard on the accelerator. He was not really driving dangerously but the speedometer rose to near its maximum of seventy miles an hour. They were little more than ten miles from Shamley Green when the steady purr of the engine changed suddenly to a throaty roar. Their speed slowed noticeably and fumes came from beneath the bonnet.

'Hell and damnation!' Alan swore as he slowed to a halt. 'Sounds like a manifold gasket. Clearly not my night,' He climbed out and lifted the bonnet. Despite his warm coat, he looked both cold and dispirited. He came round to Joscelin's side of the car.

'We might be able to limp a few miles further, but we'll never make it to London. Sorry, Joss, you shouldn't have come with me.'

'Well, *I'm* not sorry!' Joscelin said. 'There's sure to be a pub or a hotel somewhere along the road. We haven't passed one for ages. We can stay the night and have the car fixed in the morning.'

'There's the Miller's Arms outside Ripley, if we can get there,' Alan said. 'They'll be shut, but I dare say we can rouse the landlord.'

Backfiring intermittently, they crawled forward until the inn came into sight.

'Thank God for small mercies!' Alan said as he got out of the car and threw a handful of small pebbles at the only lighted window to be seen. A moment later, a head appeared. Hearing of their plight, the landlord came down at once to unlock the door. He could, he said pleasantly, give them a room apiece for the night, but first they must have a glass of brandy.

'You look perished, the pair of you!' he said.

Joscelin only sipped the spirit but Alan allowed the good-natured landlord to refill his glass. They were by now seated in the empty saloon bar close to the big fire which their host had managed to revive.

'Tell you what, sir,' the landlord said as he poured a third glass of brandy for Alan, 'as you're nice and cosy here, I'll nip off to bed and leave you to help yourselves! No need for you to hurry.'

'Top-hole!' Alan said instantly. He was feeling a good deal better, and the shock of seeing his beloved Cassy in a state of near-nudity with Deighton was gradually lessening under the influence of the brandy.

The landlord handed them their room keys and departed, leaving them alone. Alan leaned back in his chair, stretching out his long legs.

'Good idea, you coming along, Joss,' he said companionably. 'Would have been a bit lonely on my own . . . hellishly depressed, don't you see. I still can't believe it . . . not my Cassy!'

He was a little tipsy, Joscelin thought – enough to make him talkative – and this was probably just the release he needed.

'You shouldn't jump to any conclusions, Alan,' she said quietly. 'I know Cassy loves you. She's dreadfully upset . . .'

Alan's face darkened. 'Don't you understand, Joss, it's all over now. I could never marry a girl who could behave like that. Why, Joss? That's what I don't understand, *why*?'

'Girls have feelings too, Alan,' Joscelin said tentatively. 'I know Cassy didn't mean things to get out of hand. You've got to remember she's been on a very tight rein these past few years. It's much worse for girls in Spain than it is here – they don't have the same freedom. *You* know how strict Doña Ursula is.'

For a moment, Alan did not comment. Then he said in a bewildered voice: 'Two nights ago, she came to my bedroom. We were both so tremendously happy to be together again. Mother had gone out to a party and my father was in Scotland, so we had the house to ourselves. We sat on the sofa more or less in each other's arms, and of course we were kissing. She was so sweet, Joss, I can't tell you! Well, about midnight Mother came back and we told her we were as much in love as ever and she promised to sound the Pater out – see if he was still totally opposed to the idea of my marrying Cassy. After all, we're old enough to make up our own minds. But naturally I'd rather get married with the old man's approval. Anyway, Mother was jolly decent about it and then we all turned in. Half an hour later, Cassy came along to my room . . . just to talk, she said. She sat on the end of the bed looking quite stunningly beautiful. She was wearing a dressing-gown but somehow it came open and . . . and I wanted her so much, I thought I'd die!'

He had forgotten who she was, Joscelin thought; or else the brandy had dulled his sensibilities and the realization that he ought not to be talking to an unmarried girl about such things.

He was staring down into his glass as he continued: 'I sent her back to her bedroom. Maybe I should have let her stay. But I respected her! Have I been incredibly naïve? *Perhaps she wanted me to make love to her?*'

It was a question Joscelin could not answer. Cassy had always played with fire . . .

Alan seemed not to notice her silence. He said bitterly: '*You* wouldn't go to a chap's bedroom in your nightclothes unless you trusted him absolutely not to take advantage. Or am I being hopelessly old-fashioned? Maybe I am! I've met some pretty liberal-minded girls since I came back from Canada.' He sighed. 'Perhaps even the nice girls nowadays feel it's all right to sleep with a chap before marriage. Perhaps *you* do, Joss. How the deuce is a fellow to know?'

Despite herself, Joscelin smiled. He sounded so like a confused little boy. 'At least I can speak for myself, if it's any help,' she said. 'I haven't . . . and I wouldn't . . . at least, not unless I was very much in love. Even then I'd be frightened. I suppose fear would hold me back whether I wanted to or not.'

It seemed an extraordinary conversation for them to be having, Joscelin thought. But then the whole evening had been bizarre. Now it was past one in the morning and Alan looked exhausted. She did not think it could be good for him to drink any more.

'I suggest we turn in, Alan,' she said. 'We can talk in the morning.'

He emptied his glass and stood up unsteadily, muttering: 'Sorry, old thing! Selfish of me to keep you up . . . Forgive me!'

Their rooms were adjoining and, as Alan put Joscelin's case by her door, he said suddenly: 'Reckon I fell in love with the wrong girl, Joss. Should have picked you, not Cassy. You used to be such a plain little thing . . . like a skinny little stork. But you've grown into a very attractive girl. Did you know that?' He reached out and touched her cheek, then without warning, he bent his head and kissed her on the mouth. It was not a friendly kiss, but a fierce, hungry one.

Joscelin closed her eyes, allowing the maelstrom of emotions to overwhelm her. *She loved him!* She had loved him all her life and this might be the only time he ever kissed her as he was kissing her now. Cassy had forfeited Alan's loyalty by her own thoughtless actions; forfeited *her* loyalty too. As Alan's arms tightened around her, she surrendered herself to the sensations he was arousing.

She was brought back to earth by Alan's voice as, quite suddenly, he drew his mouth away from hers.

'Sorry, Joss! Shouldn't have done that. Lost control for a moment. Forgive me. See you in the morning, eh?'

Still apologizing, he opened her door and put her case inside, and then, smiling contritely, he disappeared into his own room. Joscelin closed her door and stood perfectly still, her heart thudding. Through the thin partition that separated the two rooms, she could hear Alan's movements – the thud of each shoe as it fell to the floor; the creak of the springs as he fell into bed. Was he very drunk, she wondered, or just slightly befuddled? Had he known what he was saying when he had called her attractive? Had he wanted more than just kisses?

All the strength had gone out of Joscelin's legs and she sat down on her bed, trembling. Her cheeks were hot, her hands cold – but her body felt on fire. There had been too much talk about making love. And it was not just Alan's hunger that she was aware of. She wanted him to go on kissing her; wanted far more than that . . .

Joscelin undressed and put on her pyjamas. The silky material was cold against her skin. Standing in front of the wardrobe mirror, she began to brush her hair. The movement lifted her breasts beneath the smooth satin of her pyjama top and she noticed how sharply her nipples were defined. Laying down the brush, she placed her hands on her breasts and felt an ache of longing sweep through her. It was not her hands but Alan's she needed; his touch; his kisses. He had aroused in her a desperate need that she had never felt before. She knew that she did not want to climb into her cold, empty bed. She wanted to go next door and climb in beside Alan; put her arms around him; comfort him.

A long sigh escaped from her lips as she turned away from the mirror. Her thoughts frightened her for they dominated her mind, her reason.

'You wouldn't go to a chap's bedroom in your nightclothes, not unless . . .' Alan's voice; Alan's words; and her reply: *'Not unless I was very much in love . . .'*

But she did love him – with all her heart, with her very being. It did not matter that it was Cassy he really wanted.

She was unaware how long she stood there, staring uncertainly at the wall which separated her from Alan. It was only when she heard some distant clock strike three that her mind was suddenly made up. Cassy was not the only one who could be impulsive. She, Joselin, was twenty-one years old and free to make her own decisions.

Her courage faltered as she quietly opened Alan's door. The room was in darkness and she could see only a vague shape beneath the feather eiderdown.

Standing hesitantly in the doorway, she heard his voice: 'Who's that? What do you want?'

There was no going back, Joscelin thought.

She approached the bed and saw the faint glimmer of Alan's face as he turned to look at her. Had he been asleep? Had she woken him? She felt his hand reach out and touch her thigh.

'You!' he whispered. 'It's you!'

With a swift, rough impatience, he sat up and encircled her

waist with his hands. Her body trembled violently as he drew her towards him. He was whispering endearments; hurried, incoherent words tumbling from him as he moulded her shivering body against his own. She felt as if every nerve she possessed had suddenly sprung to life, aching for his touch, and, as if aware of it, Alan's mouth found hers. His hands caressed her, evoking a passion equal to his own.

Once only was the rising crescendo of emotion within her momentarily arrested, as she thought she heard his voice murmuring Cassy's name. But she closed her mind to it. It was her, Joscelin, he held in his arms; her he wanted and nothing else in the world mattered. She would give him peace; she would give him the love he craved; she would give him herself . . .

It was over very quickly. For Joscelin a moment of intense pain was followed by a mounting excitement so extreme that it would have overwhelmed any last-minute regrets. *But she did not regret it.* As Alan's grip relaxed and his movements ceased, the faint feeling of incompleteness that swept over her was countermanded by her mental satisfaction. Alan had loved her, albeit briefly. She would never forget this night. She didn't care that she was no longer a virgin. At least now she knew what it was to be made love to by a man.

But in the release of tension, Alan had sobered, appalled at what he had done.

'God, I'm sorry!' he said, leaning on one elbow and bending down to look into her eyes. 'I feel an absolute rotter, Joss. You must really hate me and I don't blame you. I can't think how . . .'

'But it was what I wanted!' Joscelin interrupted quietly. 'I knew what I was doing when I came to your room, Alan. I know you are still in love with Cassy; that nothing has changed. I . . . I wanted the first time to be with someone I liked, respected . . .'

Alan was still staring at her and she looked away, pulling the edges of her pyjama top together in a belated gesture of modesty.

'There's no need to look so guilty, Alan. Even you must admit that I wasn't even invited here. For all I know, you may not have wanted to . . . to . . .'

His face relaxed into a sudden smile of tenderness. 'Don't be such a little idiot, Joss. How could any man not *want to* . . . as you put it. You're a very desirable girl and if I wasn't . . . didn't . . .' He broke off and tried again. 'If it wasn't for Cassy . . . but you know that. I'm in one hell of a muddle, Joss, I just don't know any more what I feel. I suppose in a way, your being here like this has made me understand that, given the opportunity, the mood, the right person, it's terribly easy to get carried away. Perhaps I ought not to blame Cassy too much, but I just can't bear to think of her lying in Deighton's arms!'

Joscelin tried not to let go of the happiness she had been feeling; but hearing Alan's voice talking of Cassy whilst she herself lay beside him was more than she could bear. She climbed out of bed and stood looking down at him.

'Let's just forget this ever happened, Alan,' she said, astonishing herself by the casualness of her tone. 'The whole night has been a bit strange, hasn't it? In the morning, we'll get the car fixed and drive back to London. I think you should have a talk to Cassy; find out her point of view and then decide how you feel.' As Alan made as if to get out of bed, she added quickly: 'I can see myself back to my room. It's all those carrots my mother made me eat as a child. She swears they help you to see in the dark!'

She knew she sounded indescribably silly, but she needed to talk herself through this departure. She bent and kissed him on the forehead. 'Go back to sleep!' she said softly. 'Sorry I disturbed you!'

And in a way she *was* sorry, she thought as she climbed shivering into her own cold bed in the adjoining room, for she knew that she had sealed her future isolation . . . that she could never marry anyone else. From now on, Alan's ghost would be between her and any man who made love to her.

Even to think of sharing those same intimacies with someone else was horrifying. She belonged to Alan, but he belonged to Cassy and she must never forget it.

But as sleep finally overtook her, her last thought was that, however barren her future, given the same circumstances she would do the same thing all over again.

CHAPTER FOURTEEN

April–May 1926

Joscelin woke early on Monday morning, aroused by the noise of the milkman's pony and trap making its way up the mews. Feeling hopelessly keyed up, she made herself a cup of tea and wandered into the studio. On her easel stood the half-finished charcoal drawing of a sea otter. One of its eyes, she thought critically, was not quite right . . . she must change it; but the hand holding her half-empty teacup was trembling and she knew she would no more be able to work today than she had been yesterday.

Her thoughts returned to the weekend. Alan had mended his car and had driven her back to London before lunch. Neither had made reference to the night before and their conversation had been stilted and carefully directed towards 'safe' topics.

When he dropped her off in the mews, she had heard him drive away with a feeling of desolation which had remained with her all afternoon. Unable to work, she had tried to lose herself in *The Forsyte Saga*, and finally sheer exhaustion had lulled her to sleep.

But now there was another day to be lived through and a further two weeks before art school reopened after the Easter holiday.

Oh, Alan! she thought wretchedly. Where are you? What are you doing? Sleeping? Dressing? Shaving? Or was he longing for the sight of the errant Cassy just as she, Joscelin, was pining for the sight of him?

Restlessly, Joscelin wandered back into the bedroom and

sat down at her dressing table. Leaning forward, she stared at her reflection in the mirror. Her thin face, eyes deeply shadowed, stared back at her. Did she look different? she wondered. Surely there must be some visible sign of the change from virgin to woman! Would her mother – or Cassy, perhaps – see any tiny alteration that would betray her? She looked the same – yet she knew she would never be able to return to that happy schoolgirl innocence. She had only to think of Alan's body entwined with hers to become aware of an ache of longing.

Hot tears stung the backs of her eyes. Determined not to give way to self-pity, she fought against the urge to weep in sorrow for the hopelessness of her love. The whole episode would have been so much easier to bear, had it not brought to an end the wonderful, easy companionship she and Alan had shared. The uncomplicated, friendly hours spent talking about his book and his adventures in Alaska had been highlights of her life this past year. She could not expect them to continue now, since he must be quite as embarrassed by what had transpired as was she herself! Now there was nothing to look forward to.

Willpower was what she needed, Joscelin decided as she washed, tidied her hair and pulled one of her painting smocks over her head. Engrossed at last at her easel, she did not notice the sound of a car halting outside her front door. There was always a lot of traffic in the mews and she became aware that she had a visitor only when the doorbell rang.

Hurrying to the window, she stared down to the cobbled street below and her heart jolted suffocatingly. Alan's Bentley was parked outside.

Her body turned hot, then cold, as panic overwhelmed her. *She couldn't face him!* But as she saw him turn back towards the car, she flew downstairs and flung open the door. Alan turned as she called to him and smiled – his ordinary, familiar smile, she thought, as she watched him reach into the back of the car and lift up a bulky package.

'Thank goodness you're here, Joss,' he said. 'Presumed you'd gone out when you didn't answer the bell. I thought you might be able to help.' He held out the bundle she had mistaken for a box and laughed. 'Don't look so horrified – it's a pup – only a few weeks old, I'd say. I found it in a dustbin, poor little devil. Makes you sick, doesn't it? The vet wanted to put it out of its misery but maybe we can save it, Joss. It's only a mongrel, of course.'

Her embarrassment forgotten, Joscelin reached out and took the puppy from Alan's hands. He had wrapped it in his scarf, but despite this, it was shivering.

'Hot milk!' she said briefly. 'Although I'm not too sure if it's old enough to lap.'

Alan followed her upstairs. 'I once saw Uncle Fergus feeding a badger cub with a finger from an old chamois-leather glove!'

'I've got some kid gloves, which would be the next best thing,' Joscelin said. 'Hold it whilst I heat some milk!'

For twenty minutes they knelt by the gas fire, trying to persuade the puppy to feed. When at last it began to suck, they looked at one another triumphantly.

'You really are a good sport, Joss!' Alan said, smiling at her. 'I knew the moment I found the pup you'd be the person to help. My mother would have had fifty fits. The only alternative was to take it away with me.'

Joscelin looked up, her breath catching in her throat. 'Take it with you, Alan – but where?'

Alan sighed. 'I'm off to Scotland. Leaving after lunch, as a matter of fact.'

'To Scotland!' Joscelin echoed stupidly. 'To visit your father?'

'No, as it happens. I thought I'd spend a week or two living rough with Uncle Fergus. Thought it might do me good . . .' He stood up and walked over to the window. 'The fact is, I can't face Cassy at the moment. I need time to think – and I couldn't do that with her living at Rutland Gate. Am I being an awful funk, Joss?'

He turned back to face her but now it was Joscelin who

looked away, busying herself with the small bundle on her lap. 'You've got to do what you think best,' she said. 'Cassy will be dreadfully upset. I know she loves you, Alan. I'm sure the . . . the nonsense with Jimmy was just a silly idea to make you jealous.'

Alan's face darkened. 'Well, she certainly succeeded. But that's not the point now, is it? It's a question of whether or not I still love Cassy, and I'm far from sure I do.'

'You must still love her,' Joscelin said quietly. 'If you didn't, you wouldn't be so hurt.'

Alan grimaced. 'Maybe it's just my pride that is hurt, Joss. Anyway, I'm feeling jolly low and pretty confused. Life as nature intended – as lived by dear old Uncle Fergus – will restore my equilibrium. I've told my mother I'm going on a walking holiday – partly true, as I don't doubt we'll tramp for miles over the moors. I don't want anyone to know where I am. The problem is, I don't think the pup is strong enough to survive such a long drive.'

Joscelin put the puppy, now fast asleep, on a cushion near the fire. 'I'll look after it until you get back, Alan. With a bit of luck it might live. But shouldn't we give it a name?'

Alan's gaze went to the small bundle and he smiled. 'First time I saw it, I thought it looked just like Sir Charles Piermont – it's that little tufted military moustache! I suppose we could call it Brigadier after Sir Charles! Or Brig, for short? Whatever you want, Joss. You know, I hate to think that someone chucked that puppy into a bin like so much rubbish!'

'Perhaps it was a poor person who couldn't afford to buy food for it,' Joscelin suggested. 'My father says there are an awful lot of people like the miners on starvation wages. He thinks they will strike if the government subsidy isn't renewed.'

Alan nodded, and said doubtfully: 'I suppose our sort have been cushioned from hardship, and we don't know enough about conditions in industry. Certainly, no one should be allowed to starve, but we can't let the trade unions dictate their terms, Joss. Let's hope your father is mistaken and the miners will see sense.'

Joscelin sighed. 'Perhaps it isn't easy to see sense if you are almost starving,' she said.

She felt a sudden guilt, knowing that she did not really care about the miners. There was a limit to the amount of misery a heart could hold, and hers was already filled to the brim by the knowledge that, in a few minutes, Alan would be gone.

'You're not put out, Joss, because I landed the Brigadier on you?' his voice broke in on her thoughts. 'Perhaps it was a bit presumptuous. Sure you don't mind?'

'Of course not. I'll take the best care I can of him,' she said, feeling suddenly happier. The little dog's life was important to Alan, and he had entrusted it to her.

'In that case, I'll push off,' Alan said, stooping to pat the coarse brown and white hair of the puppy's head.

He grinned disarmingly and helped Joscelin to her feet. 'I wish I had a sister like you, Joss,' he said suddenly. 'You're a splendid person and I really do admire you. Best friend I've got, I reckon!'

He bent and kissed her on the cheek – a brother's embrace, Joscelin thought, remembering the very different kisses which, it seemed, *he* had forgotten. But at least they were friends again – best friends, Alan had said. With that crumb of comfort – and the Brigadier – she must be content.

She spent the rest of the afternoon between caring for the pathetic little animal and her easel. The puppy made endless puddles and was obviously going to involve a great deal of her time, she thought, but already it had begun to take a hold on her heart.

She had just completed its fifth feed when a taxi cab pulled up outside her door. She was not sure whether to be pleased or sorry when she opened it to find Cassy standing there.

'Alan's gone!' she announced dramatically as she drew off her gloves and flung them onto the sofa. 'What am I going to do, Joss?'

She paced up and down as she related how Jimmy had driven her back to London, only to be informed by her aunt that Alan had departed on a walking tour.

'Tía Pamela didn't know how long he would be gone. He's run away, Joss. I just know he has. He doesn't want to see me!'

Joscelin went over to the fireplace and knelt down to stroke the sleeping puppy. There was little doubt that Cassy was genuinely distressed, she thought. She decided to keep as near as possible to the truth.

'Alan was here this morning, Cassy,' she said. 'Look, he brought the Brigadier for me to take care of . . .' She smiled as she heard Cassy's gasp of horror.

'Not a cat, Joss. You know I can't stand them!'

'No, it's a puppy. Alan found it in a dustbin. Cassy, do stop fidgeting. There's really nothing you can do. You must realize Alan is terribly upset. I did try to convince him that nothing had actually happened between you and Jimmy, but I don't think he believed me.'

Tears filled Cassy's eyes as she collapsed onto the sofa. 'It's all gone wrong!' she wailed. 'I like Jimmy, but I don't love him the way I love Alan. Didn't you tell him, Joss – that I really *do* love him? You promised you would.'

Despite the gravity of the situation, Joscelin nearly smiled. It was so like Cassy to see only her own point of view. Even now she had not really appreciated how horrified Alan had been to find her in a bedroom, undressed, with another man. Because she had not intended anything to take place, Cassy assumed she was guiltless. But she could have said 'no'. Jimmy was not the type of young man who would have seduced her against her will. On her own admission she had wanted it, just as Joscelin had wanted Alan to make love to her. They were both guilty. They had both been equally irresponsible.

'I can't even *write* to him!' Cassy was saying. 'What am I to *do*, Joss?'

'There's nothing you can do except wait for him to come

back,' Joscelin said. She paused uncertainly. 'Cassy, don't answer this without thinking about it seriously – do you *really* want to marry Alan? In many ways, Jimmy seems far better suited to you.'

Cassy's face turned pink with indignation. 'How can you suggest such a thing, Joss! I thought you understood. Jimmy's fun and I like him, but I *love* Alan. You know I do! But when I went to his bedroom the night I arrived in England he didn't even kiss me. I don't think he even noticed when I let my dressing-gown fall open. He just told me it was time I went back to my own room.'

'Oh, Cassy, that was because he loved you – not because he didn't want you!' Joscelin said, her heart aching with the memory of Alan's behaviour with *her*. 'Don't you see, he wanted to protect you.'

Cassy pouted. 'You just don't want to see my point of view, Joss. Anyway, why should he try to "protect" me? We'd agreed that we'd get married no matter what our parents said. He said we should never have been prevented from marrying when we first wanted to get engaged, and that if he'd been older he would never have given in. It was all arranged . . . and then . . .'

She stood up and walked away from Joscelin, pausing by the easel which she fingered with restless hands. 'It was really Alan's fault that I gave in to Jimmy. If Alan had made love to me when I wanted him to, I'd never, ever have let Jimmy touch me. Now he's punishing me! It isn't fair!'

Tears were now streaming down her face and, with a sigh, Joscelin went to put her arms round her. She felt a hundred years older than this sobbing girl who seemed to be treating love like some kind of nursery game.

'Don't cry, Cassy,' she said. 'Just give Alan time. When he returns, you will be able to convince him that you do really love him. He'll want to believe you. He's every bit as unhappy now as you are.'

Cassy's tears ceased flowing. 'I knew I'd feel better if I

talked to you, Joss. You're always so sensible, although . . .'
she added with a sparkle returning to her eyes, '. . . I don't
think it's frightfully sensible taking that thing.' She wrinkled
her nose as she pointed to the puppy. 'Look, it's puddled all
over the floor! I should get rid of it.'

Cassy, Joscelin thought as she went to find a cloth, had the
most astonishing ability to send her emotions rocketing from
pity to anger, to love, and even to total alienation. She could
feel envy and admiration. What she could never feel was
indifference.

With a typical change of mood, Cassy relaxed and stared
around her curiously whilst Joscelin made some tea. 'It's a
funny little apartment, isn't it!' she commented. 'Quite tiny!
However do you manage, Joss? All the same, I quite envy you
having a place all of your own. Isn't there even a room for
your maid?'

'I don't have one!' Joscelin said laughing. 'Unlike you, Cassy,
I can do most things for myself. I love it here!'

Cassy drew out a tortoiseshell case from her purse and lit
a cigarette. Joscelin was reminded suddenly of Lady Costain.
'I haven't seen your aunt for ages,' she said. 'How is she?'

'Madly busy, as always,' Cassy answered. 'You know how
social she is. A divinely good-looking American called just as
I was leaving, to take her to the theatre. He was quite old,
but of course Tía Pamela must be forty-something by now.
Not that she looks it. Mamá looks *years* older. I suppose that's
having all those children. My new sister is awful, Joss. I've
come to the conclusion I just don't like children and do you
realize I may soon be *an aunt* – I just can't bear it! – but
Eduardo and Mercedes actually want a big family. I wouldn't
be surprised if Mercedes is already *encinta*!' She seemed to
have forgotten Alan, and chattered on: 'You'll never guess
what our Patri has been up to, Joss; Mamá is *está furiosa* but
Papá says Patri is far too young to be serious and he'll soon
get over it.'

'Get over what?' Joscelin demanded.

'He's fallen in love with a German Jewish girl called Rebekka Schwarz. She's at the same university as him in Munich. Actually, she's a Catholic, because her father is, but her mother is Jewish and Mamá is quite losing her rag about it. Her father is in banking and has offered Patri a job, and he says he may stay in Germany and become a banker. I can't see Patri banking, can you, Joss? Cousin Isobel wrote to Papá and said the Schwarzes were a very nice family and friends of the von Lessens. Do you know, Isobel's boy, Heinrich, is five years old? Doesn't it make you feel positively *ancient!*'

'No, it doesn't!' Joscelin said, smiling. 'If you write to Patri, Cassy, please give him my fond love. I often thought how much I'd have liked him for my brother. I'm glad he's enjoying himself in Germany. My father said things are much better there now than they were after the war.'

'Oh, I never pay any attention to politics,' Cassy said yawning. 'Papá and Cristobal bored me to tears last Christmas talking about our war in Morocco. It was quite a relief when Cris went back to Rome. He's spending a year there with Papá's sister – to learn the language. He's crazy about Italy. Can you wonder I was bored? So was Lota, but she was pretty boring too! All she could do was talk about Benito. He is due to take his *alternativa* this spring and she was expecting him back in Sevilla.'

'Yes, I know,' Joscelin said. 'She writes to me. Her last letter said that she had made up her mind to take the veil if she is not allowed to marry Benito once he becomes a matador. But she dare not even suggest such a marriage to your father until Benito has made a name for himself.'

Shrugging off her sister's dilemma, Cassy's mind switched to *los chicos*. 'You'd never recognize them, Joss. They're growing up so fast!' she said. 'Papá has changed his mind about having them educated in England and the boys are to go to university in Madrid. Luis is nearly sixteen, Joss – can you believe it?' Her eyes suddenly clouded. 'Oh, I wish Alan was here now,' she said wistfully. 'It's perfectly mean of him to dash off like that when I've only just got back to England.'

She sounded so dejected that Joscelin said: 'Look, Cassy, I'll give the Brigadier a last feed and then we'll go to *Ben-Hur*.'

Cassy jumped up and hugged her. 'It's gorgeous being back with you, darling Joss!' she said. 'I can't think how I survived so long without you.'

She continued to chatter inconsequentially until they reached the cinema and she became absorbed in the film. Joscelin did not enjoy it as much, for she was worried about the puppy. It had come to no harm, however, and during the next two weeks it slowly gained strength. It was totally dependent upon her, and she was determined that by the time Alan returned from Scotland its survival would be assured.

But Alan did not return and Cassy became at first worried, then angry. She accepted several invitations from Jimmy, telling Joscelin that 'it serves Alan right'! She ignored Joscelin's point that, since Alan knew nothing of Cassy's activities, she was not getting her own back on him as she seemed to suppose.

Jimmy talked of little else but the strike which he was in no doubt would soon take place. His father, who lived at Arlingham Hall in Leicestershire, owned one of the mines in the area. If trouble broke out, Jimmy was to return home at once and 'do his bit'.

On the following Monday morning the government declared a state of emergency, as the country awoke to the realization that the threatened strike had finally started. Factories were idle and transport was crippled. The navy was called in to man the power stations. Since there were no buses, Joscelin had to cancel a proposed visit to her parents. For once she did not welcome her solitude, and was really pleased when Cassy arrived the next morning in a state of tremendous excitement.

'Jimmy wants me to go home with him this afternoon, Joss. He says I can help him drive a train. Tía Pamela is going to man the telephone switchboard at the *Daily Express*.' She laughed excitedly. 'Can you imagine the confusion? Jimmy says you can come with us. You will, won't you? Monty's coming too.'

Joscelin was in two minds. She would like to help, but felt that staying with Jimmy's family would be disloyal to Alan.

'If I come to Leicestershire, what about the Brigadier?' she asked tentatively.

'Oh, we'll take him with us – Jimmy won't mind!' Cassy said airily. 'Do come, Joss. Whatever would you do here in London all alone?'

Joscelin allowed herself to be persuaded. By the time Cassy returned she was packed and ready to climb in beside Monty in the back seat of Jimmy's Lagonda, the Brigadier tucked cosily into a big cardboard box at her feet. Jimmy drove expertly through the strange assortment of traffic which cluttered the roads, avoiding the many horse-drawn vehicles which had been resuscitated for the emergency. Before long they were out on the open road heading towards Stamford.

Joscelin had supposed that Jimmy's father would be like Lord Costain – elderly and vinegary. But this was far from being the case. The jovial gentleman who greeted them had the same ebullience as his son and welcomed his guests as if they were old friends. There was no Countess, Jimmy's mother having died many years previously.

After dinner, the Earl requested that the men repair at once with the ladies to the billiard room, where there was to be a meeting to finalize his plans for the following day. He refused to give details until everyone had arrived and the doors could be closed to ensure secrecy.

Slowly the room filled with visitors. Joscelin became too confused to remember individual names. Several had been at Cambridge with Jimmy; one or two were Downside school friends, and the others were sons of the local landowners.

The Earl removed the sheet covering the billiard table and all eyes turned curiously to the model he had made with ingenious use of his sons' clockwork train set and lead soldiers. In a cigar box lay some small pieces of coal.

'Now then,' he said, pointing with a billiard cue at the box. 'That's Nunhead mine – miners are locked out, of course. My men are guarding it and we're not expecting trouble. But there's coal to be moved and that's going to be your responsibility, Gilmore. You'll have young Piermont here as stoker, and my two boys as guards. You'll take the trucks from here . . .' he jabbed at the heap of coal, guiding it along the single line of railway track. 'That's Bagworth and Ellistown Junction,' he said. 'Nothing much there other than the two villages. That's where the coal will be loaded onto the goods train coming up these double tracks running between Leicester and Burton-on-Trent. Now here's the focal point! Tomorrow morning at ten minutes past eleven, a goods train will be coming from Burton and will halt at the Junction to pick up our coal. Trouble is, we think the miners have got wind of our plan. If they get into cahoots with the railway strikers, there could be a nasty confrontation. That's where you come in, James, and the rest of you. Bertie and I will take over the signal box. You are to guard the points and Piermont's trucks when they arrive. You'll be armed, of course; but no shots to be fired except in the air; just enough noise to scare them off. Anyone got any questions?'

Cassy had. 'I'd like to know, sir, where Joss and I fit in. We've come up here to help and we're willing to do anything. Joss can drive and I can fire a gun – a twenty-bore, that is.'

'Can't have the ladies mixed up in this,' the Earl said emphatically. 'Could be dangerous.'

'But there must be *something* we can do!' Cassy persisted.

Jimmy put his arm around her shoulders. 'Surely they could be useful, sir? They could take the Lagonda down to the Junction, park it out of sight but be near enough for us to rustle them up if one of us needed a nurse, or something!'

To Joscelin's surprise, the Earl nodded. 'Don't see why not,' he said, 'so long as they lie doggo.'

Joscelin caught Cassy's arm and whispered: 'I've only just learned to drive my father's Morris. I don't think I could possibly drive Jimmy's Lagonda . . .'

'Of course you can! Keep quiet, Joss, or we'll miss all the fun.'

When they retired to bed, Cassy was too excited to sleep. It was the Cassy of their schooldays, Joscelin thought, involved in some mischievous escapade that had an element of danger. She, too, was excited, but she could not forget the background to the strike. The miners were being offered a raw deal. If the strike went on for any length of time, many would be starving. The men were being misled by their Communist leaders, her father had said. They had been promised better wages which the mine owners had not the least intention of giving them. The fight would be bitter, possibly dangerous, and absolutely disastrous for them.

Tomorrow's escapade was being treated as if it were a game, Joscelin decided, an alternative to polo, cricket, the races.

Although Jimmy's father had planned his campaign with meticulous care, 'the enemy', as he called the miners, had somehow been informed. When he and his youngest son, Bertie, reached the signal box next morning, it was already occupied by six burly railwaymen. Since they faced two loaded shotguns, the men allowed themselves to be tied up with a submissiveness which was so unnatural that the Earl was suspicious.

'Now then,' he said. 'You know who I am, and you know I can have all of you arrested for unlawfully occupying railway property. But I suspect that you've been led into this against your better judgement. In the circumstances, I might be prepared to put in a word for you. But I want the truth. Out with it! What are you doing here? What's your game?'

It was several minutes before the Earl was successful in bullying the strikers into admitting that a counterplot had been hatched by the miners to foil the coal delivery. The six men in the signal box were to have halted the 11.10 and forced it to return to Leicester. Meanwhile, the miners were out in force, blocking the track leading from the Nunhead mine so that the coal trucks could not get through.

But no amount of cajoling or threatening could coerce the

men into telling the Earl where the blockade would be placed. Leaving Bertie to guard the prisoners, the Earl hurried away to find Cassy and Joscelin.

Scarlet in the face and puffing from his exertions, he shouted to them to get off as quickly as they could to alert Monty and his two guards.

'Follow the road running beside the line to Nunhead,' he gasped, 'but on no account are you to stop if you see the men laying their blockade. Get past them any way you can. Halt as soon as you see Piermont's train and blow your horn. *You've got to make him stop – understand*? I'm going back to pick up Jimmy and some of the others stationed at the points. We'll need help getting the branch line cleared. Get a move on!'

'Do hurry!' Cassy squealed as Joscelin attempted to reverse. 'Poor Monty could be killed!'

She sounded more excited than worried, Joscelin thought as she struggled to find bottom gear. She herself was anxious. Suppose they had a puncture? Suppose the men laying the blockade saw them and attacked them and prevented them reaching Monty in time to warn him of the danger? The weight of responsibility consumed her and she drove as fast as she dared along the bumpy cart track. They were halfway to the mine which was some nine miles distant when suddenly Cassy shouted: 'There they are, Joss – the blockaders! Quick, before they see us!'

Gritting her teeth, Joscelin pressed her foot hard on the accelerator. The car lurched, jumped forward and swerved violently as it hit a pothole. From the corner of her eye, she could see the mass of figures on the railway line below them in a cutting.

'They've seen us!' Cassy shouted as several of the men started to climb the embankment. 'Oh, do be quick, Joss!'

But at that moment a farmer, leading two carthorses, turned out of a gate into the lane. Instinctively, Joscelin's foot jammed down on the brake pedal and Cassy shot forward, hitting her head on the windscreen. In her effort to keep the car under

some sort of control, Joscelin forgot to change gear. The engine
stalled and they came to a skidding halt a few yards from the
farmer.

Cassy was screaming, but louder than her voice was the
screech of train brakes as Monty's engine rounded a curve in
the track and the blockade came into his view.

From that moment things happened so quickly that, later,
Joscelin was unsure of the true sequence of events. The goods
engine ploughed into the blockade and toppled sideways,
dragging the foremost coal truck with it. At the same time
three cars halted behind the Lagonda and, with Jimmy leading,
twenty men charged down the embankment to do battle with
the strikers. Whilst the farmer stood gawping in astonishment
at this extraordinary spectacle, Cassy stopped screaming,
opened her door and stood at the top of the embankment
shouting encouragement to the young men as they charged
into battle. Aching in every limb, Joscelin went to stand beside
her.

'Look, Joss, how brave they are! There's one man down
– two, no three? *Olé! Olé*! Joss, look! We're winning!'

But Joscelin's gaze was distracted by the movement of
something beneath the engine from which a cloud of steam
was escaping. Her heart jolted. 'It's Monty!' she gasped. 'He
must be hurt. Quick, Cassy, get the first aid box. It's on the
back seat!'

Suddenly, the sound of a gunshot split the air, followed by
silence as the shouting ceased abruptly. A second shot was
fired and then, one by one, the men moved at a slow, sullen
pace into a single group. Jimmy had taken command. He
forced them to form a gang to right the engine, which was
leaning perilously against one side of the embankment. There
were thirty strikers and at least twenty of Jimmy's friends.
Between them, first the engine was tipped back into position
and then, with less difficulty, the truck. Piece by piece, the coal
was thrown back into it. By now, Monty had been pulled clear
and Cassy was bandaging his cuts whilst Joscelin went to the

aid of those injured in the fight. Some of the strikers refused her assistance, looking stubbornly away from her sympathetic eyes, resentful and disappointed by the turn of events.

The belated arrival of the Earl in his car brought everyone to attention. He looked in the best of spirits as he called down to Jimmy: 'Get a move on, old chap. The 11.10's waiting at the junction. Quarter past already. Never mind the rest of that coal. Get along as quick as you can.'

Grinning, Jimmy called back: 'Trying to get up steam, sir. Won't be long now!'

The Earl walked over to Joscelin. 'See you didn't make it here in time to warn Piermont,' he commented. 'Didn't think you would. Worth a try, though. No harm done – we're going to get the coal through, eh? Objective achieved!' he added with obvious satisfaction.

Three of Jimmy's friends had been hurt, and the Earl detailed Joscelin to drive them back to Arlingham Hall. Cassy remained with Jimmy.

Luncheon was a very late affair when finally the Earl's 'troops' returned from their morning's work. A cold buffet was laid out in the dining room and, when the pangs of hunger had been assuaged, they drifted into the drawing room where, their host told them, he wished to make a speech. He was awaiting only the arrival of Jimmy and Cassy, who had returned later than any of the others and were still lunching. Jimmy, one young man informed Joscelin, had risen to the occasion magnificently and had driven the goods engine safely to the Junction.

When Jimmy and Cassy finally joined the gathering, Joscelin noted with surprise that the couple were holding hands. Cassy's eyes were sparkling. Jimmy went over to his father and murmured something in his ear, whereupon the Earl clapped his son on the shoulder, his face beaming.

'Well, troops!' he said, as he stood up to face them all, 'it's been a first-class campaign, and I want to congratulate you all. We succeeded in our undertaking and I'm deuced proud of the lot of you. And that includes the two charming young ladies in our midst.' He nodded at Joscelin and then at Cassy.

The Earl paused whilst a burst of clapping filled the room. 'Now I have something else to tell you,' he said portentously. 'My son James has decided to settle down at last. Subject to her parents' approval of the match, I am delighted to welcome into the family his future bride, Miss Casilda Montero. Couldn't have picked a prettier girl myself. Congratulations to the pair of you!'

Under cover of the crescendo of clapping, Monty said to Joscelin: 'Good grief, Deighton's stolen a march on us all! Wondered why he was late for lunch. Must have popped the question on the way back from Bagworth. By Jove, this is going to put Costain's nose out of joint. Glad I won't be the one who has to break the news to him. I wonder who will?'

Not I, thought Joscelin. In a thousand years and with a firing squad in front of her, she would not be the one who broke Alan's heart.

CHAPTER FIFTEEN

May–December 1926

A week after the strike ended, on the eve of her departure to Spain, Cassy turned up at Joscelin's flat alone. Since their engagement Jimmy had been her shadow, and their brief visits to the mews had precluded any possibility of private conversation between the two girls. But now Cassy was obviously in the mood to talk and, as Joscelin prepared a light supper for them both, she curled up on the sofa, her expression for once lacking the excitement that had been uppermost ever since her engagement to Jimmy. Her recall to Sevilla had followed a telephone conversation with her father, during which he had requested that Jimmy should accompany her to Spain so that their future marriage could be discussed. As Cassy had supposed, her parents had welcomed the proposed union.

If there were any flaw at all in Cassy's happiness, it was that Alan had still not returned to London.

'Not that I care!' Cassy said now as she lit a cigarette and blew smoke in the direction of the Brigadier, who was trying to nibble the toe of her shoe. 'Why should I, Joss, when it's perfectly obvious he doesn't love me? I shall be far happier with my darling Jimmy.' She glanced at the large sapphire and diamond ring on her finger and the excitement returned to her face. 'Isn't it beautiful, Joss? It belonged to Lady Ladbury. Lord Ladbury says I am to have all her jewellery when Jimmy and I are married. And Joss, guess what he's giving us for a wedding present – an aeroplane! A Gipsy Moth. And Jimmy's going to learn to fly just as soon as we get back from our honeymoon, and he says I can learn too, if I want!'

'It sounds as if you're going to be very happy,' Joscelin said as she carried two supper trays into the studio.

Cassy frowned. 'But *you* sound as if you don't really believe it!' she countered. 'I suppose everything did happen frightfully quickly.' She paused briefly to swallow a few mouthfuls of food before she pushed her plate to one side. 'I'm much too *emocionante* to eat!' she declared. 'This time tomorrow Jimmy and I will be on the boat.'

She chattered on whilst Joscelin removed their trays. 'I suppose none of this would have happened if I hadn't let Jimmy do what he did at the treasure hunt. I know you think it was awful of me, Joss, but Jimmy says that was when he made up his mind to marry me.' She lit another cigarette and regarded Joscelin through a cloud of blue smoke. 'It seems as if "it" matters an awful lot to him,' she said thoughtfully. 'Doing it, I mean. He gets terribly excited. But to tell you the truth, Joss, I think making love is a bit disappointing. I'm not saying I don't like it but . . . well, no one can possibly say the thing men have is beautiful! I got quite a shock the first time I saw Jimmy's – but then I suppose you've seen lots of naked men at your art classes, haven't you?'

Without waiting for Joscelin's reply, she continued: 'Of course, I knew more or less what happened but honestly, Joss, it all seems a bit pointless, really – and messy. I suppose I'll get used to it. We've done it several times now. There doesn't seem much sense in refusing to let him since we're going to be married. I know I'm not a virgin any more, but I really don't *feel* any different!'

'Perhaps you will after you're married,' Joscelin said without conviction. She was disturbed by Cassy's intimate confidences. For one thing, Cassy believed her totally innocent – a virgin – whereas she was in no position to criticize her. For another, she hadn't thought it 'pointless', as Cassy put it, and for a few brief minutes she had 'floated into another world'. Was it because she loved Alan, *really loved him*?

'Cassy, are you sure you are truly in love with Jimmy?' she asked tentatively.

Cassy's astonishment was not feigned. 'But of course I am! We have the most fantastic fun together!' Her eyes brightened. 'Jimmy says I don't have to have babies if I don't want to. He's the eldest son and so he'll have to produce an heir one day, but not for ages and ages, and anyway he's got five brothers, so Lord Ladbury doesn't have to worry about the title. Jimmy's terribly rich and he absolutely adores me. I shall have everything in the world I want and he says you aren't to worry about the cost of travelling to Spain for my wedding. And don't look like that . . . I won't get married at all if you don't come. I want you there more than anyone in the world.'

'Oh, Cassy!' Joscelin said helplessly. 'You don't really *need* me.'

'But I do!' Cassy cried, hugging her. 'You're my Best Friend, and I just couldn't stand the thought of doing anything *important* without you.'

Joscelin laughed. 'Well, you'll have to change your ideas, Cassy, once you are married to Jimmy. He'll be the one you want to share everything with.'

Cassy shrugged. 'I suppose you're right, but he doesn't know me the way you do, Joss. I can say anything to you; and you know all about my wicked past and Alan and everything.' She grimaced. 'Jimmy doesn't like me to talk about Alan. On the way back from the fight I told him I'd been in love with Alan for years and years and he got quite angry. He said I belonged to him and no one else, and he wanted to know if I'd ever done it with Alan, but of course I hadn't. He cheered up and kissed me and asked me to marry him and I said yes.'

Cassy only mentioned Alan once more – to say that she intended inviting him to the wedding . . . 'though I dare say he won't come!' She seemed to have no idea how profoundly she had hurt him. When finally he returned to London a week after Cassy's departure to Spain, he arrived at Joscelin's flat in so highly charged an emotional state that he did not even notice the Brigadier.

'I have made up my mind, Joss. I'm going to Thailand or Borneo or some such place where cruel little flirts like Cassy don't exist! How could she, Joss? How *could* she?' He would become a recluse like his Uncle Fergus, he stormed, and commune with animals rather than human beings who could not be trusted.

But his mood quickly gave way to a different one, and he confided in Joscelin that he was not going to give Cassy the satisfaction of knowing how deeply she had hurt him. His pride now uppermost, he threw himself whole-heartedly into the Season, always in the company of a group of friends which included several pretty, eligible girls. He took Joscelin to the summer exhibition at the Royal Academy and sometimes to the opera or the theatre. But they were not happy occasions, for sooner or later he talked despairingly of his feelings for Cassy – Joscelin, as she well knew, being the only person to whom he could unburden himself. He was remarkably lacking in bitterness towards Jimmy Deighton, who, he admitted, was 'a harmless fellow' and could not be blamed for falling in love with Cassy. As the weeks passed, he even went so far as to admit that he thought the couple were well suited, although he was still not reconciled to what he called Cassy's betrayal.

July gave way to August – and far away in Spain, the elaborate plans for Cassy's wedding in December were progressing.

'We have received our invitations this morning,' Alan said, his voice surprisingly matter-of-fact as he and Joscelin walked the Brigadier round Kensington Gardens one hot summer evening. 'Mother's going to accept but my father won't. I don't think he ever much liked poor Cassy, and Spain, of course, will be full of "bloody foreigners"! We will travel out together, shall we, Joss!'

Joscelin stared up at him in astonishment. 'Then you *are* going!'

Alan shrugged. 'Why not? I'd like to see young Patri again – and both Barbara and Isobel will be there with their kids. I've not been much of an uncle to them. Somehow I haven't been able to raise any enthusiasm for visiting either Germany or Italy.' He smiled. 'Besides, I might as well show the family that I've got over Cassy – a bit of pride, don't you know!'

Joscelin called the little dog to heel, partly to discipline it but also to give herself time to think. Did Alan really mean what he said – that he had ceased to love Cassy?

As if answering her thoughts, he added: 'I had a letter from Cassy last week. She asked me to forgive her and said she'd always love me but in a different way to the way she loves Jimmy. I came to the conclusion, Joss, that she hasn't the faintest idea what love is and that if the truth be known, she doesn't love either of us! I'm not angry with her any more. I even find myself hoping that she will be happy. I've better things to do than waste my life mourning my loss. I've started work in earnest on my book. When we get back to the flat, I want to talk to you about the next two chapters. Can you spare the time, Joss?'

She would make the time, Joscelin thought, as she nodded casually, bending her head to fasten the Brigadier's lead so that Alan would not see the bright pink of her cheeks. He could have no idea how immensely happy his words made her, proving as they did that he was beginning to get over his bitterness. Moreover, she would have his company during the wedding celebrations, and not least, she told herself as Alan linked his arm in hers and led her from the park, their old friendship had been firmly re-established and she had the coming winter to look forward to, sharing his interest in his book.

On 3 December, Cassy and Jimmy were married in the Parroquia de San Isidoro in Sevilla. The church was filled to capacity with guests, a great many of them friends and relatives of the Ladbury family who had made the journey from England. Joscelin, who was staying with the family, met Alan's sisters again for the first time in seven years. Neither Isobel nor Barbara had changed much, although both looked matronly. Their two little boys, Heinrich and Ernesto, were pages carrying Cassy's long train. Her thirteen-year-old sister Carmen was the only bridal attendant.

Lady Costain stood in the front of the church watching Cassy take her place beside her bridegroom and smiled happily at the group of women and girls gathered around them – her sister Ursula, Lota and Joscelin, little Amalia held firmly by Miss Smart, and the Monteros' and Deightons' female friends. For once, Ursula was not in black but was wearing a blue velvet coat. She was frowning slightly, her gaze on Don Jaime who stood on the bridegroom's right, the collar of his morning coat lying not quite flat. He was, Lady Costain knew, suffering from a severe hangover.

At the back of the church, Cassy's and Jimmy's brothers and all the other male guests were chatting quietly together, for the most part paying scant attention to the ceremony taking place at the altar. Amongst them stood Ursula's eldest son, Eduardo. Such an unattractive young man, Lady Costain thought. The younger brother, Patricio, was quite the opposite – and so like her darling Alan to look at. No wonder the dark-haired German girl was so madly in love with him! At the family party the night before, Patri had announced his intention of becoming engaged to Rebekka.

Ursula looked none too pleased by her son's choice, she thought now. But the child came from a good family high up in banking circles in Bavaria and Pamela herself would not have objected to such a daughter-in-law.

How long, she wondered, before Alan chose a wife for himself? There were a great many girls in England who would be only too willing to marry him. But he never seemed to take a special interest in one particular girl, and with a sigh Pamela decided that he was still harbouring his adolescent love for Cassy. This marriage to Jimmy Deighton might prove a blessing, for it would put her naughty little niece beyond his reach once and for all.

'Doesn't Cassy look perfectly beautiful?' Joscelin whispered as the young couple turned to go to the vestry. 'I do hope she'll be happy!'

Lady Costain's sarcasm was unintentional as she replied: 'My dear girl, Casilda has chosen a husband who will dote upon her every whim. Of course she'll be happy!'

As she gathered up her gloves and handbag ready to follow the other relatives into the vestry for the signing of the register, she glanced at the young girl beside her. How colourless Joscelin looked in that navy blue coat and hat – more like an overgrown schoolgirl than a former debutante twenty-one years of age. If only the child would make more of herself, she thought with genuine regret. If she went on the way she was, only bothering her head about other people, she was going to be left on the shelf!

The wedding reception took place in the Hotel Madrid – a lavish affair laid on by Don Jaime without regard to cost.

Patri wound his way through the milling throng of guests to Joscelin's side. 'Our Casilda seems to be enjoying her Big Day,' he said with a grin. 'I think Papá is delighted to have her safely married at long last!'

Seeing Patri again more than compensated Joscelin for having to participate in such an occasion. She had almost forgotten how fond of him she was. He had grown several inches these past three years and was exceedingly good-looking. His smile was always close at hand, and he treated Joscelin like a favourite sister, his manner teasing but affectionate.

Serious for once, he led her to a quiet corner of the room. 'I want to ask you, Joss, how you like my Rebekka? Papá has really taken to her and *los chicos* adore her. We're going to be married as soon as we both get our degrees. Rebekka's frightfully clever, you know. She's reading English and Spanish.'

'I like her very much, Patri,' Joscelin said. The girl had a sparkling personality that was endearing, and she obviously worshipped Patri.

'That will be three of them off my hands!' Don Jaime had

said jovially on the night before Cassy's wedding, when Patri's forthcoming engagement had been mentioned at the dinner table. 'Your turn next, Lota . . .'

Carlota had pretended not to hear the remark and adeptly struck up a conversation with Isobel's husband, Rupert, who was sitting on her left. Observing her from the opposite side of the table, Joscelin had noted how she had changed from the unhappy sixteen-year-old she had last seen on Victoria Station. There was a subtle difference in the way Lota held herself, and although she still limped, she made no attempt to hide shyly behind a cloud of fair hair, but stood erect, almost proudly, *almost* – Joss decided – defiantly.

Now, surprisingly, she even seemed to be enjoying the reception and was smiling happily. Since she and Joscelin were sharing their bedroom with Carmen and Amalia, they had no opportunity to talk privately until the day before Joscelin was sailing back to England. They were able to go out for a walk alone together under the orange trees in the square and Joscelin at last discovered the reason for the change in Lota.

'Unlike Casilda, I have been steadfast in my first love,' Lota confided, her eyes glowing. 'In fact, Joss, I shall never have a second love. Benito is back in Sevilla and we met twice out at the Hacienda – and he, too, has been totally faithful.'

At long last, she said happily, Benito believed that there might be a future for them. He was now a fully fledged *novillero* and beginning to be noticed by the aficionados. Not even the fact that he would be away for the whole of the bullfighting season, travelling with his manager, could destroy her confidence in him, or her happiness. She still pined for the loss of her baby, of whose existence Benito remained ignorant; but she was content to pass the days amusing little Amalia, thus easing her own thwarted maternal instincts.

'I'll never forget how good you were to me, Joss,' she said. 'I have even thought sometimes that you saved my life that dreadful day. And darling Tía Pamela – how kind she was, although I hated her then for taking my baby away. I think of him often, Joss. I pray all the time for his happiness. But Benito and I will have another baby one day. In the meanwhile, I shall shortly have one to cuddle. Mercedes is due to have her first child quite soon, and since she and Eduardo live so near to us I shall see the infant as often as I wish.'

Although Joscelin was ostensibly Cassy's best friend, she was aware that in a great many ways she was closer to Lota, their natures far more similar. Perhaps she and Cassy had become friends simply because they were opposites, she reflected, wishing that she could love Cassy as blindly as she had in their schooldays. But now she could see the flaws, although she tried not to do so, and it was difficult at times not to hate her for the cruelty of her behaviour towards Alan.

Rightly or wrongly, the deed was now done and Cassy was Jimmy's wife.

'You and your husband made such a handsome couple, Lady Deighton,' Cassy's companion drawled in her North American accent. A coy smile creased her plump cheeks as playfully she tapped Cassy's wrist. 'A little bird told me you were on your honeymoon,' she whispered. 'So romantic!'

Cassy wished the woman would stop talking. She was middle-aged, dull and a snob, she reflected, with nothing remarkable about her except the magnificent sapphire necklace and earrings she was wearing. A fellow guest at the Captain's table had informed her during dinner that the good lady's husband was a millionaire. Cassy had been unimpressed, but after dinner when the American husband had asked the Captain if he might play the piano in the music room, she had quickly become interested. He had, it seemed, made his fortune composing background music for a number of Hollywood films, and for the past hour he had kept them all wonderfully entertained as he played the latest jazz hits in the most professional way. At the request of one of the other first-class passengers, someone would be arriving at any moment to roll back the carpet so they could dance, and Cassy could not wait to join in the fun.

But Jimmy had other ideas. 'It's almost midnight, old thing,' he said, tucking his arm through hers. 'Been a long day, what? I think we should turn in!'

Cassy was on the point of protest when the woman beside her said: 'You must both be quite exhausted!' Even Jimmy looked embarrassed as she added *sotto voce*: 'And you, dear boy, will be wanting your beautiful bride all to yourself!'

Cassy's mouth tightened as Jimmy took the opportunity to say their goodnights and lead her out of the room.

'Thank goodness she's disembarking at Istanbul!' she said. 'She's the most dreadful bore, Jimmy. I wanted to listen to the music but she kept on and on about all the places we're going to which *she* has seen before. Rhodes, Corfu, Venice, Sicily – she's "done" the lot, whatever that means.'

'Then I rescued you just in time!' Jimmy said cheerfully as he guided her past the lounge and card room towards the first-class cabins. 'And the old girl was quite right, darling, I do want you to myself. Do you realize we haven't had a single minute alone all day? Even when we got to our cabin, your maid was there unpacking for you; and then when we changed for dinner, Polly was helping and I couldn't even kiss you!'

Cassy laughed. 'Polly wouldn't have minded, silly! You'll just have to get used to her being around. I couldn't possibly manage without her.'

Jimmy grimaced. 'You've not kept her up tonight, have you, old girl?'

'Well, of course I have,' Cassy rejoined. 'She never goes to bed until she's finished seeing to me.'

'Well, of course, darling, but dash it all . . . it *is* our wedding night . . .'

Cassy sighed. Perhaps she should have realized that Jimmy was bound to be impatient to do it . . . and now that they were married, they'd be able to do it properly for the first time. She'd simply forgotten about it in the excitement of coming on board and watching Polly, her English maid, unpack her beautiful new trousseau. Then there'd been the further excitement of unpacking Jimmy's wedding present to her – the perfectly gorgeous Ladbury diamonds which had belonged to his mother; and then dinner at the Captain's table . . .

'I'll get rid of her as quickly as I can!' she said, returning the pressure of Jimmy's hand.

His handsome face was instantly smiling again. 'Right-ho, darling! I'll take a stroll on deck – if it isn't too windy. See you in a jiffy, eh?'

As they halted outside their cabin door, he kissed her eagerly on the mouth and Cassy felt a stir of excitement deep down in the pit of her stomach. Doing it would be quite different now they were married, she thought, as she opened the cabin door. So far there had been only a few thoroughly uncomfortable scrambles – in the back of Jimmy's Lagonda; in the tiny telephone cupboard in the hall at Rutland Gate; and, of course, that time on the bed in the Piermonts' spare room when Alan had walked in and . . . but she wasn't going to remember how awful she had felt afterwards – not now, on her wedding night.

As Polly undressed her and drew the beautiful French satin nightgown over Cassy's head, her feeling of excitement intensified. Lots of her married girlfriends had told her that making love was absolute bliss. Until now, she had found it all rather pointless – and disappointing. She had described it to darling Joss as similar to being asked by a favourite partner to dance and the music stopping just as you got to the dance floor! Joss seemed to think it might only be perfect if one was really in love – and now, of course, she *was* in love with Jimmy. Not only was he divinely good-looking but he was always cheerful, and happy to do anything she wanted. If she had really wanted to stay on this evening and dance, Jimmy would have agreed rather than see her upset. Dear, kind Jimmy! His pyjamas lay neatly folded on the twin bed adjoining hers. The poor darling had been dreadfully disappointed because they had not been given a double bed – but he had already booked the honeymoon suite at Shepherd's Hotel in Cairo where they would be staying for two days' sightseeing after they docked at Alexandria.

'Will there be anything else, miss? I mean madam?' Polly asked with a barely concealed giggle. 'I can't get used to you being married, Miss Cassy.'

'Well, it's time you did!' Cassy said not unkindly. 'And try to remember, Polly, in front of other people you have to call me Your Ladyship. I just wish it didn't sound so old!'

She dismissed the maid and waited with growing impatience for Jimmy to return from his nocturnal promenade. Would he be filled with passion when he saw her in her new nightgown? The silk was so delicate that both her nipples showed through the material. Tonight they seemed especially large and protuberant.

Jimmy came hurrying into the room, his fair hair tousled, his cheeks pink, and with barely a glance at her he burst out eagerly: 'There's quite a gale blowing up on deck. Good thing we're both good sailors! One of the ship's officers took me up to see the wireless room. It's quite topping – you can telephone America if you want. We'll give your father a ring tomorrow, what d'you think, old girl?'

Disappointed that he had not noticed her appearance, Cassy scowled. 'I wish you wouldn't call me that,' she said. 'It makes me feel positively ancient.'

The glow on Jimmy's handsome young face gave way to a look of concern as he stared at his bride. 'I say, I'm dreadfully sorry, old thing. I mean to say, you do look terribly young – and absolutely stunning . . .' his voice thickened, 'and utterly ravishing. Gosh, you're beautiful, Cassy. I'm deuced lucky to be married to you.'

He sat down on the edge of the bed and, putting his arms round her, he hugged her. 'Was a time I was dashed scared you'd chose Costain instead of me. You do love me, don't you, darling?'

Cassy snuggled against him. He smelt of salt sea air and his slim, strong young body was warm, comforting and strangely exciting. 'Of course I do, silly!' she said. She lifted her face and he kissed her, his hold tightening as he did so. As he drew his mouth away, she saw his eyes travelling slowly over her, lingering unguardedly on her bosom. She did not draw back when his hand reached out and grasped one of her breasts. He held it firmly – as if he were about to bowl a cricket ball – too firmly.

'You're hurting me, Jimmy,' she whispered.

He took his hand away at once, his blue eyes apologetic. 'Sorry, old girl! It's fearfully easy for a chap to get too rough . . . forget women are such delicate little things. Forgive me, darling?'

Cassy did not want an apology. She had wanted . . . what was it she wanted? She turned her head into the pillow as Jimmy began hurriedly to divest himself of his clothing. Surely he didn't mean to undress *altogether* in front of her, she thought, with a sense of real shock as she recalled the Convent days when the nuns had declared it an act of utmost immodesty even to look at one's own body!

She stole a glance from the side of her eyes and saw Jimmy's back. He was in his vest and knee-length drawers, his black evening socks held up by black elastic sock suspenders. She was torn between laughter at the ridiculous sight he presented and dismay at the change from the glamorous, impeccably turned out young man who had escorted her in to dinner. Unaware of her gaze, he was humming a cheerful imitation of Ted Lewis singing, 'Hey Diddle Diddle . . .'

Again, Cassy felt a surge of irritation. Jimmy might at least have chosen a romantic song – 'Deep in My Heart', for example, from that wonderful show she and Alan and Joss had seen in London six months ago.

But as Jimmy removed his underclothes and turned towards the bed to reach for his pyjamas, she felt renewed excitement. Were it not for the fact that she feared he would think her forward, she would like to put her hands on those slim masculine hips; to draw him down to her; to touch that strange-looking male part of him which was unfamiliar and dangerously interesting. There was a yearning need in the very pit of her stomach which she had only felt once or twice before. It had happened on one occasion when Jimmy had brushed her nipples accidentally with his arm, she thought as he disappeared into the bathroom. Her impatience grew as she awaited his return. Maybe tonight the feeling would come back. After all, Cassy reminded herself, she was now Jimmy's wife and so they could do just as they pleased; touch and feel and kiss and . . .

Jimmy came back from the bathroom, his cheeks pink-scrubbed, his breath smelling cleanly of Pepsodent toothpaste. His fair hair had been sleeked back with water. 'All spick and span – or should I say shipshape!' he said, grinning as he climbed into her bed whilst she hastily made room for him. He turned off the lamp on the bedside table and added cheerfully: 'Storm's getting worse. If we don't watch out, we'll be rolled out of bed. Can't say I fancy spending our wedding night on the floor!'

In the pitch darkness, Cassy felt his arm ease its way under her neck and his other arm reached around her waist. His hands felt warm and masterful. Cassy pressed closer against him.

'Don't let's talk,' she whispered. 'I want you to kiss me, Jimmy.'

He responded instantly and she could hear his breathing quicken before he pressed his mouth hard down on hers. The pressure was painful but lasted only a moment or two before he climbed on top of her. The weight of his body on her chest made it difficult for her lungs to expand. Did he realize he might be about to smother her, she wondered in sudden panic?

But then he raised himself on his knees and she could feel his hands struggling to lift the hem of her nightgown. Sensing his urgency and responding to it, Cassy pushed back the bedclothes and arched her body so that her weight no longer prevented Jimmy from sliding the soft folds of satin up to her waist. With a small cry of pleasure, Jimmy eased himself down between her legs and thrust into her. Cassy's small gasp of protest died on her lips as he began to move back and forth inside her.

As the rhythm quickened, the soreness of his entry was forgotten, swept into oblivion by the whole new world of sensation she was experiencing. Her hands dug into Jimmy's back with a growing intensity of longing. Vaguely she heard herself murmuring endearments.

'I love you, Jimmy. I love you . . . I love you . . .'

Without warning, Jimmy's hold slackened and he withdrew from her. Before Cassy could protest, he sprang out of bed. A moment later she heard him cry out in pain as he stumbled in the darkness against a piece of furniture. She found her voice.

'What on earth are you doing, Jimmy? What's wrong?' Her voice was trembling, but he sounded remarkably normal as he replied: 'Stubbed my toe, silly ass that I am! Won't be a jiffy, darling!'

'Where are you going?' Cassy persisted. She was not so much shocked now as angry.

'Looking for something, old thing . . .' He broke off as he collided with yet another piece of furniture.

Her excitement now thoroughly cooled, Cassy felt only a consuming irritation. 'I'll put the light on!' she suggested, resigning herself to the fact that Jimmy did not intend to return to her until he had found what he wanted.

Now his voice sounded vaguely panic-stricken. 'No need to put the light on!' he gasped. 'I've remembered where I put them . . .'

Cassy now heard the rattle of drawers being opened one after the other. Feeling thoroughly insulted by Jimmy's inexplicable desertion of her, her mouth tightened. The farce had gone on quite long enough, she thought, and clearly Jimmy wasn't going to find what he was looking for whilst the room remained in darkness. Determinedly, she reached out and switched on the light.

Jimmy was standing at the foot of the bed wearing only his pyjama top. He was holding something in one hand and, as the room flooded with light, he tried quickly to conceal it and at the same time to conceal his limp nudity. His face was scarlet as he muttered in a low, agonized voice: 'Put the light out, Cassy, for heaven's sake!'

But Cassy had no such intention. Her curiosity now outweighed any other emotion. What, she wanted to know, was Jimmy trying to hide from her . . . and why? His expression was so like that of a child caught with its hand in the biscuit tin that, despite her sense of outrage, she nearly laughed. She patted the empty space beside her.

'Don't just stand there, Jimmy!' she said. 'Come back to bed. And bring whatever it is with you. I want to see what all the fuss is about!'

For a brief instant Jimmy hesitated, and then he dived back into the bed and with one hand drew the sheet over him. In the other, he clutched the mysterious object.

'Come on, show me!' Cassy demanded.

His face was still scarlet, his voice sheepish as he protested: 'Dash it all, darling, it just isn't the sort of thing girls *should* see!' His fist remained firmly clenched.

'I'm not "girls",' she said. 'I'm your wife and now we're married we shouldn't have secrets from each other. You're being perfectly beastly, Jimmy. It's not fair!'

For the first time since she had known him, Jimmy seemed reluctant to comply with her wishes.

Cassy changed her tactics. She snuggled down beside him and kissed his cheek. '*Please* show me, Jimmy. I'll be dreadfully hurt if you don't!'

He responded at once, an apologetic grin on his face as he said: 'But you'll think I'm such an awful mug, darling! I mean, you've every right to lose your rag. I should have put one of these in the bedside drawer so it would be handy . . . but you looked so adorable when I came in and saw you sitting there in bed that I just couldn't wait to hold you, and

I honestly never thought about it until . . . well, until I realized I needed it.'

Cassy listened to this outburst with total incomprehension. She strove to keep the irritation from her voice as she said slowly and carefully: 'You still haven't told me what "these" are. *If you'd only show me,* Jimmy, you wouldn't have to tell me since you seem to find it so difficult to talk about.'

'Gosh, Cassy, you don't understand!' Jimmy said. 'Besides, you wouldn't know what it was even if I did show you. And don't be angry, old thing. If you'll only turn out the light, I'll try to explain.'

Resigned now to the fact that her husband wasn't going to let her see what he was holding, but aware that she could search next day amongst his belongings and find it for herself, Cassy turned off the light. She could feel Jimmy moving restlessly beside her as he struggled for words and, with difficulty, she curbed her impatience.

'It's something I have to put on . . . to stop you having babies!' His voiced sounded more normal now, although still tinged with embarrassment. 'A friend at Cambridge put me wise to them. He said I'd need them one day – I reckon that day has come. Of course, it's against the rules . . . I mean against the rules for Catholics, but the only other ways simply aren't safe. You've always been so adamant about not having babies right away, I thought you wouldn't mind, old girl! I mean, I'll be the one who'll have to confess . . . and that's why it would be best for you not to know anything about it . . . why I didn't want to tell you.'

Cassy let out her breath. She was intrigued and relieved and not in the least bit concerned about the religious aspect of the matter. Above all, she was curious. But she sensed that this was not the moment to press Jimmy for a more detailed explanation.

Her mood softened, and she turned once more to kiss him. 'Put it on now, Jimmy!' she murmured. 'I don't care what it is, I want us to do it!'

Beside her, Jimmy lay unmoving. 'Dashed sorry, old thing, but I can't . . . I mean, not right now. Perhaps in a little while . . . damn thing's gone down you see – all the bother . . . pretty useless I'm afraid.'

But Cassy, unaware of his incapability, was not interested in postponing the event. Furiously angry, she turned her back on her impotent bridegroom and struggled against the tears of disappointment and frustration that now threatened. The silence lengthened, broken only by the steady throb of the ship's engines. This was supposed to be her wedding night, she thought miserably, and somehow it had all gone wrong. For weeks now, she and Jimmy had been counting the days to the start of their honeymoon and the exciting cruise round the Mediterranean. All her friends had been green with envy and said it sounded 'wildly romantic'. 'It'll be such *fun*!' everyone had promised. But this part of the honeymoon wasn't proving any fun at all, she thought bitterly, tears stinging her eyes.

Jimmy's hand reached tentatively for hers. 'You're such a stunning girl, Cassy,' he murmured. 'I still can't believe we're really married. I felt no end of a swell when I introduced you to the Captain tonight as my wife! All the other chaps envied me and I felt deuced proud of you, old thing. There isn't a girl on board who can hold a candle to you – or in the world, come to that!'

Cassy's mood softened. Compliments always pleased her, and ever since their engagement Jimmy had done everything he could to make her happy. There would be plenty of other times to do it, and in a way she ought to be feeling grateful to Jimmy for remembering about her not wanting a baby; and for being willing to break the rules and commit a sin by using whatever-it-was. In the morning, she thought sleepily, she would look in the drawer and discover the secret. But now, suddenly, the exhaustion of the long day overcame her and, still holding Jimmy's hand, she fell asleep.

Cassy was not sure how long she had slept when she

awoke with a start to find Jimmy once more on top of her. The cabin was still in total darkness, and for a moment she was unable to remember where she was. But Jimmy's demands were unmistakable and, as her body sprang to life, she encouraged him to enter her. This time, she thought as excitement stirred in her, Jimmy would be prepared and there would be no sudden withdrawal.

Barely had the thought passed through her mind than he rolled away from her and she heard the drawer of the bedside table rattle as he drew it open. For several minutes she heard nothing but his hurried breathing as he struggled with the mysterious object which, she now guessed, was as unfamiliar to him as to her. But with a small cry of triumph he flung himself once more on top of her.

It was over so quickly that Cassy felt only a deep sense of outrage. It had been no more enjoyable, after all, than on those two other scrambled occasions in the car and the telephone cupboard. Moreover, she felt sore and uncomfortable and she was about to get cramp in one of her calves. More than anything in the world, she wanted him to get off her. But now he was covering her face with kisses and telling her she was the most adorable, wonderful, perfect wife and promising that they would live happily together for the rest of their lives.

It was with a great sense of relief that Cassy finally heard him disappearing into the bathroom and, a few minutes later, returning to his own bed. Afraid lest a word from her might encourage him to start the ritual all over again, Cassy stayed silent.

'You asleep, old girl?' Jimmy whispered. 'Been a long day . . .'

At least he doesn't snore, Cassy thought as his breathing slowed and she realized that he had instantly fallen asleep. Her mother complained endlessly about Papá's snoring and had warned Cassy it was one of the tribulations of marriage she must be prepared for. What else must she be prepared for, Cassy wondered as she turned restlessly on her pillow? No one had told her how often Jimmy was going to want to do it . . . but she hoped very much it would not be every night. If this was all that marriage had to offer, then how could her girlfriends call making love bliss? As far as she could judge, it was all quite pointless, and the less often she and Jimmy had to do it the better.

When Cassy awoke, Polly was drawing back the curtain and the sun was streaming through the porthole. Jimmy's bed was empty.

'The master said to tell you he wouldn't be long,' Polly said. 'He's ordered breakfast and you're to have it in bed. He said as how he's really going to spoil you, miss – I mean Your Ladyship.'

Cassy yawned, her spirits strangely low as she watched Polly tidying the cabin. She supposed she must have been sleeping deeply since she had not heard Jimmy leave the room . . . but her body seemed to ache with fatigue.

The door burst open and Jimmy strode into the room. He was wearing his white flannels and striped blazer and his arms were filled with a huge basket of flowers.

'Best I could get from the ship's shop!' he said, grinning, as he balanced the basket precariously on the bed. Ignoring Polly's presence, he bent over and kissed Cassy's cheek. 'Morning, darling! And a perfectly spiffing one it is. After breakfast we'll go on deck and watch the ship dock. The purser said we'll be at Alex by 10.30. Gosh, I'm hungry! Where's this breakfast I ordered? Go and see what's happening, Polly, there's a good girl!'

As Polly departed, Jimmy sat down on the edge of the bed and planted a kiss on Cassy's head. He was beaming happily. 'How's your appetite, darling?' he inquired. 'I'm as hungry as a horse. I've ordered scrambled eggs for both of us.' Unaware of Cassy's horrified stare, he added shyly: 'And a bottle of champers – to celebrate – well, getting married and all that!' He cleared his throat and laughed. 'Get used to it soon, I dare say. Just can't tell you how happy I am, darling! Now when we get to Cairo, I'll take you shopping – I want to buy you something very special. You admired that American woman's sapphires last night so we're going to find some for you just like them. Ah, good, here's the steward with our grub!'

Cassy watched her new young husband tucking eagerly into a huge plateful of scrambled eggs. To please him, she toyed with her own, as she reflected that, whatever her disappointment, there was no doubting that Jimmy had been entirely satisfied by the previous night's activities. This morning he was as happy as she had ever seen him and obviously anxious to prove his love for her. Flowers – champagne for breakfast – the promise of a necklace . . . if these were to be her rewards for making him happy, then she would just have to put up with the boring part of marriage, she decided. Doubtless she'd get used to it in time and at least she could be certain she would not end up pregnant. Besides, there was always the chance she might learn to enjoy it and, if not, that Jimmy would get bored doing it. It could all have been far, far worse and it was best to forget all about it now and enjoy the new day.

'Happy, darling?' Jimmy asked through a mouthful of toast and marmalade.

Cassy was surprised to realize that her depression had vanished. 'Yes, of course!' she answered, and did not think to question her reply.

CHAPTER SIXTEEN

December 1926–September 1927

Perhaps, given time, Alan would get over his loss, Joscelin told herself as she returned to England to spend a quiet Christmas with her parents. They had been taking care of the Brigadier whilst she was in Spain and both had become devoted to the mongrel who had grown into a sturdy adolescent, full of mischief but always anxious to please.

'Can't even leave my pipe by my chair,' Mr Howard complained in mock anger, 'but the little bounder picks it up and brings it to me whether I want it or not.'

Quite often, as the cold winter months gave way to spring, Alan would join Joscelin in long, companionable walks in Kensington Gardens. But in May he found a new interest which originated with, of all people, Marco da Cortona. The Italian turned up unexpectedly in London to invite Joscelin to accompany him to the Eve of Derby ball at the Albert Hall. The American aviator, Charles Lindbergh, was to be the guest of honour, Marco informed her and having watched his arrival in France after his epic flight across the Atlantic, Marco was determined to make his acquaintance. Unfortunately, the date of the ball coincided with an invitation from Alan to go to see the new revue *Lido Lady* at the Gaiety Theatre.

'This you can enjoy on another night,' Marco said pleasantly to Alan, who had been going through his manuscript with Joscelin when the Italian called to see her. 'I am more than happy to include you too, Costain, in my invitation. Are you interested in aviation?'

'I most certainly am!' Alan said with enthusiasm. 'It's very good of you. I'd love to go along – that is, if Joss is agreeable. We could take in the revue next week, Joss. What do you say?'

'My only comment is that I have nothing suitable to wear!' Joscelin said.

Alan would brook no such excuse, insisting that his mother would be pleased to lend her a pretty frock.

Lady Costain was delighted to help, and in her usual generous way gave Joscelin three beautiful dresses. The following night, as Joscelin entered the Albert Hall with two of the Season's most eligible bachelors in attendance, she felt an unaccustomed self-confidence. She was conscious of the many envious glances – and curious ones – cast in her direction by the other women present. Yet she was not entirely at her ease, knowing that Marco was quietly observing her.

She knew that, beneath the banter, he really did find her attractive. But she was not attracted to him in the way he wanted and both knew it.

Tonight she feared that Marco might guess why she would never respond as he wished; that he was astute enough to see through the façade of casual friendship she always assumed towards Alan. Marco made no comment during the evening of the ball, but he insisted upon taking her to lunch next day and broached the very subject she had hoped to avoid.

'I perceive that my pursuit of you at the present moment is ill-timed,' he said in his gentle, teasing manner. 'Ah, Joscelin, how utterly charming you look when you blush! And do not spoil that beauty with a scowl. I do not mean to be impertinent. I wish only for honesty between us. You think yourself in love with young Costain, do you not?'

'I cannot see what my feelings for Alan have to do with you, Marco,' Joscelin prevaricated.

'They have everything to do with me,' Marco insisted. 'I am very much in love with you and therefore I must know if you are in the right frame of mind to fall in love with me!'

Despite herself, Joscelin smiled. 'You're talking a lot of

nonsense, Marco. I truly believe you are only interested in me because I have not succumbed to your charms. I am therefore a novelty to you.'

'You are indeed a novelty, my lovely Joscelin, because you are not like other girls. You want more from love than most – and I suspect you have far more to give. But at the moment, you imagine yourself in love with this agreeable young Englishman who is too blind to see what is beneath his nose. Am I not right in recalling that he was hoping to marry your friend, the fascinating Miss Montero?'

Since there seemed little point in being evasive, Joscelin said: 'That's quite true. But Cassy is now married to Jimmy Deighton. He and Alan are quite good friends. Alan and I dined with them last week at their house in Eaton Terrace and there was no awkwardness. We all got on splendidly together, and I'm sure Alan meant it when he said he was no longer in love with Cassy; but I don't delude myself that he will one day fall in love with me. I'm not the type of girl who interests him. We have a good relationship – like brother and sister – and I value it far too much ever to let my feelings intervene. Alan has no idea how I feel about him.'

Marco made no further comment until after the waiter had served the first course. Then he said: 'It is not good to – how do you say in English – bottle up your emotions. You need to love – and be loved, Joscelin. If you truly believe that Costain will not turn to you for comfort, then *you* should think quite seriously about turning to *me* . . . and do not smile, I am quite serious! I could teach you things about yourself that you are far too innocent even to suspect. Think about it, Joscelin, and when the time is right let me prove to you that there is far more to life than you realize and that it is not good for you to live on dreams alone.'

His subsequent proposal was, Joscelin knew, perfunctory. Clearly he expected her refusal, and accepted it with a smile as he helped her into a taxi.

'As I said earlier, *carissima*, the time is not yet. But it *will*

come and I shall see you again quite soon. *Ti amo*, Joscelin
– and that is not a joke!'

Joscelin might have forgotten him as quickly as she had after
other such lightning visits but for the fact that he passed on
some of his enthusiasm for flying to Alan. He came round to
the studio three days after the ball.

'I've bought an aeroplane!' he announced, 'a Gipsy Moth,
and next week I'm having my first lesson at the London
Aeroplane Club in the Edgware Road. You can come with
me if you want. The instructor said that if I showed any sort
of promise as an aviator, I could learn to fly in eight hours.
You shall be my first passenger – if you dare! Anyway, if that
fellow Marco can flip around Europe solo, I reckon I can, too.
Do you think I'm quite mad?'

Taking it for granted that she did not, he continued: 'It's a
beautiful little biplane. I thought I'd call her *The Brigadier*
although I suppose she ought to have a girl's name.' He grinned,
unaware of the effect of his smile on Joscelin as he paced up
and down the studio. 'Perhaps I'll call her *Joss*. She can do a
hundred miles an hour – just imagine! – although the chap
who sold her to me says she cruises at eighty. She'll go up to
twenty thousand feet and cover three hundred miles plus on
a full tank.'

It was more than a year, she thought, since she had seen him
so happy, and she hesitated for a moment before telling
him that Cassy had been to see her two days previously with
the news that Jimmy, too, now had a Gipsy Moth – his father's
wedding present – and that he had already enrolled as a member
of the Club.

'It's red and silver, Alan, so it must be identical to yours.'

But she need not have worried about Alan's reactions. He
said casually: 'By Jove, what a coincidence! Now it will be a
race to see which of us gets his licence first.'

So began a summer of sunny afternoons spent almost
entirely at the clubhouse where Joscelin and Cassy lounged on
deckchairs watching the little aeroplanes taking off and

landing. Jimmy talked Cassy into having a lesson, but after one attempt she confessed that she could no more learn to fly than to drive a motor car.

Much as Joscelin would have loved to try her hand as a pilot, she could ill afford the cost of lessons and was too proud to allow Alan to pay for her. She therefore pretended that she would rather watch than take part.

It was only a matter of weeks before both young men obtained their 'A' licences. Linked by their common interest, they had become good friends. No one, Joscelin thought, could dislike Jimmy. He had the sunniest of dispositions. That there was little beneath this surface of bonhomie somehow seemed unimportant, certainly to Cassy who did not herself care to think too deeply into a subject. Sometimes she would sulk if Jimmy did not immediately allow her to have her own way, but he could always laugh her out of such moods and, in any event, he was only too happy to indulge his young bride's every whim.

When first they started to go regularly to the Club as a foursome, Joscelin was worried by Cassy's seemingly irresistible need to flirt with Alan. She had a way of looking up at him through her thick, sweeping lashes that was undeniably provocative. If one of the deckchairs beside her was vacant, she would beckon Alan to occupy it even if Jimmy was without a seat. Yet not only did Jimmy seem unmoved by her efforts to attract Alan's attention, but Alan, too, seemed impervious to them. He adopted a casual attitude towards her, very much that of an indulgent elder brother.

By the end of the summer, Joscelin was caught up in the exhilaration of soaring up into the clouds with only the wind and the blue sky and the sight of Alan's helmeted head for company. For the most part, she was Alan's passenger and Cassy was piloted by Jimmy. Occasionally they would change places, but although the instructor had indicated that Alan was the better pilot of the two, Jimmy was the more daring and Cassy was thrilled by his attempts at aerobatics. It was a new excitement that Jimmy was only too happy to provide. Danger enthralled her and, she said proudly, Jimmy was as fearless as she. Sometimes she taunted Alan with being too cautious. It had become almost a once-weekly habit for the four of them to fly up to Desford, near Leicester, to lunch with Jimmy's father and fly back after tea. But Alan always refused to make such trips unless he was convinced that the weather was unlikely to deteriorate.

'I know Cassy thinks I'm stuffy!' he said to Joscelin. 'But it's not the same as driving a car – you can't pull in to the side of the road if you hit fog! And neither Jimmy nor I are *experienced* pilots.'

But as the novelty of being airborne wore thin, Cassy became bored with what she called 'short flips'. One late September afternoon, having listened to a pilot talking about the King's Cup Air Race, she suggested a race between Jimmy and Alan across the Channel to Paris and back. Jimmy was instantly enthusiastic.

'Ripping idea!' he said. 'Tell you what, Alan, we'll chip in fifty pounds apiece as a stake. Loser has to stand dinner for the four of us when we get back to London. How about it, old chap?'

'I'm on!' Alan agreed. 'But we don't take the girls along.'

Cassy's face reddened and her dark eyes flashed. '*Cómo que no?*' she flared. 'Of course we're going! Why on earth shouldn't we?'

'The girls will enjoy it, old man,' Jimmy said placatingly. 'Much more fun if we take them along.'

Joscelin could see that Alan's acquiescence was half-hearted. As he drove her home in his Bentley, she questioned him. 'Surely it's an everyday thing now to cross the Channel?' she said. 'Why don't you want us to go with you, Alan?'

His eyes were thoughtful. 'The devil of it is, Joss, I can't give you a reason – at least, not a rational one. I have this odd feeling that something *could* go wrong. Supposing one of us had to come down in the sea. *You* wouldn't panic, but

Cassy might. She can't swim and she hates the water.' He shrugged and then suddenly smiled: 'Maybe I am being a bit of an ass. I don't think I ever told you about it, but when I was with Uncle Fergus last year he had a premonition, at least I suppose that's what you'd call it. He had taken me out for the day to see a golden eagle's eyrie. It was a perfect afternoon. We were climbing up a steepish hillside when suddenly he pushed me against the rock face. A few seconds later there was a terrifying fall of rock where I had been standing. I swear there was no warning of that landslide – no noise, no reason for it. Later that evening I asked him how he knew it would happen, and he just shrugged and said: "I felt it!" I wondered whether, being so close to nature, he'd heard or seen something that I'd missed. But then, just before we turned in for the night, he said: "Never ignore a warning, boy – no matter what anyone says!"'

Alan seemed to be lost in his own thoughts until he turned into the mews and parked the car outside the studio. Then he said to Joscelin: 'I suppose he *could* have what they call second sight, Joss, and I'm wondering if I've inherited the faculty!'

His laugh made light of what Joscelin realized was a genuine concern, but he made no further mention of racing the two Moths until the morning of the race itself. The two little red and silver biplanes were ready on the runway when Jimmy and Alan emerged from the control room.

Alan's face was unsmiling, his mouth set in a rigid line. 'Weather forecast is not too good, I'm afraid,' he said quietly. 'They think it best to postpone the trip.'

'But it can't be bad weather!' Cassy cried. 'It's a perfectly beautiful day. Jimmy, you *can't* let Alan talk you out of it. There isn't a single cloud in the sky.'

Jimmy looked skyward into what appeared to be perfect flying conditions. 'Fellow only said it *might* be tricky on the return trip!' he said doubtfully.

'But we can't be sure,' Alan argued. 'So why take a risk? We can just as easily race tomorrow or next week.'

'No, we can't!' Cassy said scowling. 'Jimmy and I are off

to New York soon and we won't be back until November, when the weather really will be bad.'

She looked as if she was about to burst into tears. Jimmy put an arm around her shoulders and glanced at Alan questioningly. 'Surely we can nip over to Le Bourget and then check on the weather before we nip back here? It's certainly fine at the moment.'

Alan stared at the ground, obviously uneasy. To add to his uncertainty, aeroplanes were buzzing round the sunny airfield without a cloud in sight.

Cassy released Jimmy's arm and went to stand in front of Alan. 'If it really was risky, they'd not allow you to take off, would they? Can't we go, Alan, *please?*' she pleaded.

Joscelin saw the muscles of Alan's jaw tighten. She heard, too, the reluctant softening of his tone as he stared into Cassy's beseeching eyes. Don't weaken, Alan! she thought, but the words remained unspoken and she heard his voice, quiet but determined. 'Very well, we'll have the race – but without you two girls on board. I'm sorry, Cassy, but that's all there is to it. We go on our own – or not at all.'

The tears of disappointment in Cassy's eyes spilled over.

'Tell you what, old girl,' Jimmy said, obviously discomfited by her tears, 'if we find the weather won't hold up for the trip back from France, you and Joscelin can get the boat train over and join us there. We'll all have a couple of days in "gay Paree". How about that?'

It was a compromise Cassy was forced to accept although she did so with bad grace, ignoring Alan completely and sulking until the two pilots were ready to take off. At the last minute she clung to Jimmy's arm, showering him with kisses and begging him to take care. It was an exhibition put on for Alan's sake, Joscelin thought as the two little aeroplanes disappeared in the direction of Croydon on the first and shortest leg of their journey.

No sooner were they out of sight than Cassy's mood changed and she herded Joscelin into the clubhouse for a cocktail.

'Alan can be such an old stick-in-the-mud, can't he?' she said airily. 'I'm sure I made the right choice marrying Jimmy. We're terribly happy together.' The time passed quickly as they ate lunch and afterwards sat outside in the sunshine awaiting Jimmy's promised telephone call from Le Bourget. Shortly after two o'clock, it came. The weather, it seemed, was far from good over the Channel. The airfield controller had left the decision whether or not to fly back to the pilots' discretion. Alan was remaining in France, but Jimmy had made up his mind to return and expected to be back by half past five.

'Looks as if Alan has funked it,' Cassy said crossly as she relayed the news to Joscelin. 'He's forfeited the race, of course, although Jimmy said Alan had landed five minutes ahead of him and stood the best chance of winning. I do think Alan's a bad sport, don't you, Joss?'

Joscelin made no reply. Cassy's reference to Alan's 'funking it' had brought sharply back to her mind Alan's story of his Uncle Fergus. He too had been called a coward. As if it were a tangible thing, fear crept up her spine, and despite the warmth of the September sun she shivered.

'Please God, don't let Alan change his mind,' she prayed silently.

She looked at Cassy's bright, carefree face and tried desperately to believe that she had no real cause for her fear. Allowing herself to be drawn into the group of young men now gathered around Cassy in the clubhouse, she settled down to await Jimmy's return. Although one or two addressed Joscelin politely, it was really Cassy who claimed their attention as she laughed at their jokes and returned their cheerful banter. It was easy to understand her popularity, Joscelin thought. Even in her present mood she herself was affected by the atmosphere Cassy created when she was happy.

But suddenly Cassy looked anxiously at her wristwatch and, detaching herself from the man at her side, she moved closer to Joscelin. In a hushed voice she said: 'Did you hear that pilot, Joss? He said it was getting very misty on the coast. He's just flown in from Shoreham.'

'Yes, I heard,' Joscelin said quietly. 'But it's only five o'clock. Jimmy said he wouldn't be here until half past. I'm sure there's no need to worry.'

Cassy frowned. 'But I don't understand it. Alan said it might be *cloudy* but he didn't mention *fog*.' She glanced out of the window and bit her lip. 'You can't see the sun any more,' she muttered. 'It's quite hazy.'

More pilots came into the room. From their conversation it became obvious that there would be no more flying that day. Cassy, who would normally have responded to their greetings, ignored them.

'If anything happens,' she said in a low, fierce tone, 'it will be my fault. I was the one who urged Jimmy to go against Alan's judgement.'

Haltingly, she confessed she had wanted the excitement of knowing that the two young men who mattered most to her were competing against one another.

Joscelin forced herself to put an arm around Cassy's shoulders. 'I'm sure Jimmy will be here safe and sound in a minute or two,' she said as tears filled Cassy's eyes. 'Any moment now, Jimmy is going to walk through that door and you're going to feel very silly!'

A brief smile lit Cassy's face, but a moment later she was frowning and said: 'Why aren't I more like you? You always think about other people and I only think about myself. I sometimes wonder why you even like me, Joss!'

This time Joscelin smiled. 'You really are talking a lot of poppycock. As to why I like you – it's because you're beautiful and fun and enjoy life. You make the world come alive for everyone.'

Such a compliment coming from Joscelin instantly restored Cassy's self-confidence. 'All the same, I'm not nearly such a *nice* person as you. And I'm sure Alan hates me,' she murmured.

Joscelin smiled again. 'You know that isn't true. You just want to hear me say it!'

Cassy pouted. 'Well, he certainly doesn't love me any more.

I still love him. I suppose I always will. Of course I adore Jimmy but somehow it's different. I sort of look up to Alan.'

'You mean you respect him,' Joscelin said quietly. 'That's because Alan is stronger than you – you couldn't make him do something he felt was wrong. No one could.'

Cassy drew a deep sigh. 'I suppose you think Jimmy is weak, because he gives in to me. Oh, don't let's talk about things like that, Joss. What time is it? It can't really be half past five!'

'I'll go and talk to whoever is in charge,' Joscelin said, standing up. 'Maybe someone can find out if Jimmy has landed at Shoreham. If the weather is bad, that would be nearer than this airfield.'

But she knew Jimmy would have telephoned if he had landed.

By the time Joscelin returned, a group of young men had again gathered around Cassy. On this occasion there was no light-hearted banter and on their faces were expressions of unconcealed anxiety.

'Lady Deighton has been telling us about her husband's flight plan,' one of the pilots said to Joscelin. 'We've told her not to worry, but I don't like the look of it. Weather's closing in fast.'

Word spread quickly round the Club. An official came over and said it had been arranged for Croydon to switch on the lights; if Jimmy was trying to find a landmark, hopefully he would see them if he had overshot Shoreham. Someone else came to tell them a small aeroplane had been heard circling overhead. Despite the chill of the damp, misty evening, Cassy ran coatless onto the veranda whilst mechanics hurried out onto the airfield with torches. Joscelin went to stand beside her. There was scarcely a sound as everyone strained their ears skywards.

Then someone shouted: 'I can hear it! I can hear an engine. Listen!'

Now Cassy, too, could hear it and she gripped Joscelin's

arm. She was shivering violently. 'It's Jimmy – I know it is!' she cried. '*Ay, gracias a Dios!*'

The sound of the engine faded and, whilst everyone stood holding their breath, someone said: 'There it is again. It's coming back. He's seen the lights!'

'Joss, how can you be so calm?' Cassy cried almost angrily as her eyes strained for the sight of the little scarlet aeroplane. But before Joscelin could reply there was a chorus of gasps as the engine spluttered, coughed, spluttered again and then died.

'There he is!' A hand pointed to a tiny speck just visible through the mist. In complete silence, it came racing towards them.

It's going too fast! Joscelin thought, only half aware of Cassy's nails digging into her arm. It's out of control!

Suddenly it touched down, bounced into the air again and hit the ground a second time, lurching sideways. As the wing tip touched the ground, the Moth slewed round, careering towards the perimeter fence. Everyone started to run towards it. Cassy would have gone too, but Joscelin held her back.

'They don't need us, Cassy. We'd be in the way.'

There was a sickening crack of wooden wing struts as the biplane hit the fence posts, but no sudden flash of fire. Either the aeroplane had run out of fuel, Joscelin thought, or the pilot had cut off the fuel supply to the engine. Cassy covered her eyes with her hands.

'I think he's all right,' Joscelin said. 'They've pulled him out and he's on his feet. Look, Cassy . . . Jimmy's all right!'

But it was not Jimmy who came limping towards them. The man in the helmet and goggles was taller, thinner. It was Alan.

Without stopping to think, Joscelin started running. Her court shoes hampered her progress and she kicked them off. There was only one thought in her mind. This was Alan walking towards her, limping, hurt – Alan, Alan, *Alan.*

Gasping, she continued to run until she was only a foot or two away. He had taken off his goggles and she could now see the thin trickle of blood running down his face. There was a long, ugly gash in the sleeve of his flying suit and thick black oil besmattered him from head to foot.

'Are you all right?' she asked stupidly and stood staring at him like a halfwit. As she watched, the corners of his mouth curved in the slow smile that never failed to turn her legs to water. Oh, Alan, I love you, I love you, she thought as she heard her voice saying in a perfectly normal tone: 'We've been very worried . . .'

Alan looked across her shoulder towards the clubhouse. 'Is Cassy still here?' he asked. 'I'm afraid the news is not good, Joss.' He was no longer smiling as he said: 'Looks as if Jimmy's down in the drink. I saw him lose height just before we reached the coast – trying to see land, I imagine. I went down after him but visibility was as bad as it could be. I thought I heard him hit the water but I couldn't be sure. I hung around as long as I dared, searching. But the weather was getting worse and I decided I'd best make for Shoreham and alert the coast-guards – but I missed the field. Thought *I* was lost then, but thank God there was a break in the cloud just as I was going over London. Must have missed Croydon, too. But I got my bearings and knew my way here. Then the engine cut. Must get in quickly now and report the position I think Deighton went down. Wish I could be certain . . . Warn Cassy, will you, whilst I make my report?'

He was staggering slightly as he attempted to hurry forwards.

'Steady, old chap!' said one of the men. 'No point rushing it.'

Joscelin could not withhold the question that now burst from her lips. 'I thought you weren't going to fly back from Le Bourget,' she said. 'What made you risk it, Alan, when you knew it wasn't safe?'

He shrugged his shoulders, wincing slightly as he did so. 'Had a feeling Deighton mightn't make it. Thought I'd be able to help.'

Joscelin turned to walk back to Cassy. Maybe there was

still hope for Jimmy. Perhaps the coastguards would find him. Perhaps he had not gone down into the sea, but had landed safely at another airfield. Perhaps . . .

But even as she produced these possibilities to the sobbing Cassy, she knew in her heart that they would never see Jimmy again.

CHAPTER SEVENTEEN

October 1927–March 1928

Cassy could not remember a time in her life when she had felt so unhappy. The years she had been obliged to spend at home during her enforced separation from Alan had been boring, the more so because first her grandmother and then six months later her grandfather had died, and she had been in mourning. But they were years not entirely devoid of pleasure and certainly not actively unhappy.

Now, at the age of twenty-three, she was a widow and in mourning yet again – this time for poor darling Jimmy. The wreckage of his aeroplane had been washed up on the beach five days after the race, but his body had not been found until a week later. The funeral was held in the little Catholic church near Arlingham Hall. She had thought her heart was breaking when the priest spoke sadly of the loss of so young and promising a life.

Somehow, with Joss's help and the support of the Earl and Jimmy's brothers, she had lived through the day. No one had blamed her – but that was a contributory reason for her unhappiness, she told Joscelin.

'Not even Jimmy's father said one unkind word to me. I feel so *guilty*, Joss!'

Joscelin, as always, had managed to calm her. No one knew that Cassy had persuaded the young men to race. Besides, it was an accident.

Lord Ladbury tried to persuade her to stay on at Arlingham Hall, but she could not bear the sight of the sad faces of the family. Tía Pamela offered her a refuge at Rutland Gate but

Alan was there – a constant reminder of that horrifying afternoon.

'I shall go home to Eaton Terrace,' she told Joscelin, 'but only if you'll come with me. I can't face it without you.'

Joscelin had packed a suitcase, collected the Brigadier and moved into the empty house. She telephoned the Monteros to explain that Cassy did not feel well enough to go home as they suggested, nor wished her parents to come to London.

'Your father is desperately worried about you,' Joscelin said at the end of one of these telephone calls. 'He thinks you're ill, Cassy. You must pull yourself together and talk to him tomorrow night.'

Cassy shivered as she drew back from the window and let the curtains fall into place. The room was brightly lit, and as Joscelin rattled the poker in the grate a shower of sparks shot up the chimney.

'That's better!' Cassy said, going to sit on the white hearthrug beside Joscelin. 'I wish we could put the gramophone on. It's so quiet! It would only shock the servants, I suppose. But *you* understand, don't you? I'm sure Jimmy wouldn't like the house this way. I hate being in mourning.' She glanced at Joscelin. 'It's so hard to believe it's such a short while since it all happened. It seems like years . . . and yet when the door opens, I still expect to see my poor darling Jimmy come in. I never realized death could be so . . . so awful! I can't believe he's never coming back.'

Tears filled her eyes and Joscelin put her arms round her and held her as she sobbed.

'It'll be easier to bear in time,' she said. 'You may not be able to imagine it now, but in a year or two this will all seem like a nightmare. You're only twenty-three, Cassy. Life has to go on.'

Cassy drew away from Joscelin's embrace, her whole being suffused with an intolerable sense of guilt. Joss was so kind, so sympathetic, so understanding – and yet she did not really understand at all. How could she when she assumed, as did everyone else, that Cassy's heart was broken? Most of her feelings of guilt stemmed from the fact that she knew very well her heart was *not* broken. Her grief was genuine enough, and she simply could not bear to think of Jimmy's body floating in the sea! But now that the first shock had worn off, she was feeling the familiar restless urge to get on with her life; to do something; anything . . .

'I can't stand the idea of living in this house on my own,' she said. 'Can't you give up the studio and come and live here with me, Joss? You could have a studio and paint all day if you wanted.' Her eyes brightened. 'Or we could travel together. We could make the trip to New York which Jimmy and I had planned . . . it seems silly to waste the tickets, and anyway Jimmy wouldn't want me to sit here all alone being miserable, would he?'

Joscelin sighed. 'Oh, Cassy, darling, I do understand how miserable you are – but my coming to live here with you wouldn't work. When you are feeling better you'll want to invite lots of friends here, and as soon as you're out of mourning you'll be giving parties and I'd get no work done at all. I've just got to earn my living, and there's Alan's book . . . I'm late already with some of the illustrations.'

'Why does money spoil everything?' Cassy said crossly. 'But you'll stay as long as I need you, won't you, Joss?' she persisted.

Joscelin's answer was interrupted by the entrance of the butler, who informed Cassy that Lady Costain was on the telephone. Cassy hurried away to take the call, and returned looking a great deal happier.

'She and Alan are coming round to dine with us,' she told Joscelin. 'Darling Tía Pamela – she guessed I'd be feeling low . . .' Kneeling down once more beside Joscelin, she said confidentially: 'Elizabeth Madeley rang me up yesterday, and guess what she told me, Joss – about Tía Pamela. She's been seen all over the place with that American industrialist

– Walter Someone-or-other. Liz said he's married and has a wife in the States, but that it's common knowledge he and Tía Pamela are having an affair.'

She had Joscelin's full attention now. 'If it's true – and that is a big "if", Cassy – then it's absolutely none of our business and I hope you told Liz Madeley to mind hers. I wish you hadn't told me,' she said. 'We've got to face your aunt at dinner tonight and I shall feel thoroughly embarrassed.'

She would have to face Alan too. Part of her longed to see him – but she knew it would be a strain not to look too happy if he paid her a chance compliment, not to hang too obviously on his every word.

'I suppose I can't wear my green georgette!' Cassy was saying. 'At least my new black frock from Chanel is really chic. You, lucky thing, don't have to wear black.'

'But I shall,' Joscelin said quietly. 'I am mourning Jimmy's death too, Cassy – even though I was only a friend.'

But Cassy did not wish to be reminded of Jimmy. 'I suppose if you won't come to America, I may as well go home for a little while. It's so cold and dreary here in the winter. At least it would be warmer in Sevilla.'

She repeated the remark during dinner, adding soulfully: 'Only there's no one to go with me. Joss says she's too busy.'

Lady Costain laid down her knife and fork and turned to her son. 'Why, darling, that would fit in wonderfully with your plans!'

Alan, she explained, had only that morning told her that he wanted to go to the Serra da Estrella in Portugal to study the wolves there. 'You could escort Cassy to Sevilla, Alan,' she suggested.

'I had planned to leave for Portugal in two weeks' time,' Alan said, 'but if that's not too soon, Cassy, I'll happily take you to Gibraltar.'

'Oh, Alan, that would be divine,' Cassy cried. 'I can't face the winter in London all by myself.' Her voice became husky. 'Joss is helping me answer the condolence letters and Jimmy's accountant says I shall have more papers to sign. But I could be ready in a fortnight.'

Joscelin, seated opposite Alan, could see the unguarded expression that swept over his face – a gentle, protective look. With a sudden chill of apprehension, she realized that Cassy was free again – free to marry Alan in the future – if that was what they both wanted. Even after her marriage to Jimmy, Cassy had maintained that she still loved Alan. It might have been the perfect solution had Joscelin not known them both so well; known that they were hopelessly unsuited.

Glancing at Lady Costain, she wondered if Alan's mother must be sharing her thoughts, for her expression was one of anxiety. Was she regretting her impulsive suggestion that Alan should accompany Cassy to Spain?

Alan said: 'I wish I could spare the time to go with you to Sevilla, Cassy, but I'm meeting up with a chap who's taking me to see a particular species of wolf in the mountains bordering the wine-growing country of the Alto Douro.'

As he outlined their plans he had forgotten Cassy momentarily, Joscelin thought, but for once Cassy seemed content to stay silent. She was formulating her own plans, Joscelin discovered after Alan and Lady Costain had departed.

'Do you realize I'll have four whole days on board to persuade Alan to forget about his silly old Portuguese wolves?' she told Joscelin excitedly. 'I'm sure I can make him come home with me.'

But to Cassy's bitter disappointment, Alan was not to be deflected. He was considerate to her throughout the voyage, but his manner bordered on the formal and he made it clear to her that he had been deeply shocked by Jimmy's death, and expected her to be more grief-stricken than she sometimes appeared.

For the first few days after her arrival home, Cassy's spirits were lifted by the degree of attention she received. Even her mamá showed sympathy and attempted to indulge her by ordering her favourite dishes and helping her to choose some new clothes. But the sympathizing began to get on her nerves as she was obliged to receive calls from all the family friends who wanted to offer condolences. Equally irritating was her mother's constant urging that she should seek the consolation of her religion through Padre Alfonso.

But perhaps it was Lota most of all who caused her to wish she had never left London and the more congenial company of her darling Joss. Lota seemed to take it for granted that Cassy would want to lead the rest of her life alone. Her young sister, Cassy thought, was convinced that there could only be one true love in a girl's life, and that true love endured even beyond death! Lota was deeply shocked when, by Christmas, Cassy admitted that she had to study Jimmy's photograph to remember exactly how he had looked.

'After all, Lota, I didn't know him for very long, did I?' she said defensively. 'He was only really a part of my life for a few months. It's different for you and your precious Benito. You've known him all your life, so of course you wouldn't forget him, although I still can't understand how you can imagine you're in love with him.'

The flush of her sister's cheeks warned her that she had said the wrong thing. Fiercely Lota argued that she did not 'imagine' herself in love. 'We're going to get married,' she added in a determined voice. 'Since you were last here, Benito has become famous. Papá is very proud of him. He makes his debut here in March. There will be posters of him all over the city. He is going to dedicate his second bull to me and I shall be the proudest girl at the *corrida*. Afterwards, he will drive Francisco Lopez here to talk to Papá about our future.'

Momentarily Cassy was diverted from her own affairs as she regarded her younger sister in dismay. 'But Lota, you cannot be expecting that Papá will allow your betrothal to . . . to the son of his *mayoral*!'

The colour flared once more in Carlota's face. 'Papá knows what kind of man Benito is. I have heard him say that he knows no one of greater courage. He boasts of him to his friends.'

'Lota, brave as he may be, Benito cannot be suitable as a husband for a daughter of the Marqués de Fernandez de la Riva. You *must* know Papá and Mamá would never permit such a marriage.'

Lota's chin lifted. 'Then I shall run away with him,' she said simply. 'I have told Benito that I will do so. He makes enough money now to support us both. There is no longer any doubt that he will become very rich. It will be for Papá to choose whether he gives us his blessing or whether I must marry against his wishes. If we cannot find a priest to marry us in Spain, then Benito says he will take me to Mexico. He has already been offered fights there, but he has so far refused such invitations because it would take him too far away from me.'

Cassy was impressed by Carlota's self-assurance, and even excited by the thought of the bombshell the young matador intended to drop on the family in a few months' time.

Half regretting that she would not be at home to witness the outcome, she decided to return to England soon after Christmas. She wrote to Joscelin telling her to expect her back in London by mid-January; but no sooner had she posted the letter than one arrived from Patricio saying that he and Rebekka would be coming to Sevilla at the end of the month to discuss their wedding. Cassy decided to wait to see her favourite brother.

Patricio and his fiancée arrived unexpectedly in a large Bugatti driven by a bearded man whose clothing identified him as a foreigner.

'Papá, this is Milton Fleming,' Patri introduced his companion. 'He was good enough to offer Rebekka and me a lift in his car from Málaga, and I have invited him to stay the night as he has no hotel booking in Sevilla.'

Cassy, who was standing beside her mother awaiting introduction, eyed the stranger with interest. He was a large man, taller even than Patricio and a good deal broader. He was, she thought, many years older, too – almost middle-aged. His eyes were a brilliant cornflower-blue, his complexion tanned. His beard, like his hair, was dark brown.

'Mr Fleming is a writer,' Patri explained as he lifted the five-year-old Amalia into his arms. 'He's gathering material for a book on bullfighting, Papá, and I have promised to take him out to the Hacienda to see the best fighting bulls in Spain!'

He hugged Casilda and expressed his sympathy at her bereavement. 'I'm frightfully sorry, old thing,' he said, sounding very English as he addressed her in that language. 'I only met Deighton once but liked him a lot. Casilda, meet Mr Milton Fleming!'

Cassy felt a stir of excitement as she looked into the cool, blue gaze of the visitor's eyes. He's sizing me up, she thought. He thinks I'm attractive!

But the American had already turned his glance to Lota and she could not see him looking again in her direction until it was time for dinner.

'It is my intention to rent a small house here for perhaps six months,' he informed Doña Ursula as they seated themselves at the table. 'I would like to observe your Holy Week and perhaps make the pilgrimage to the Rocío. But mainly, I am concerned with the bullfights. I am a great aficionado, and some would say I am by way of being an authority upon the subject.'

'Then you may have heard of the matador, Benito Lopez,' Carlota said shyly. 'He is Papá's protégé. He grew up in our Hacienda at Alauquén.'

The American nodded. 'I saw Lopez fight a few weeks ago in Barcelona. Most impressive.'

'It is unusual to hear of a foreigner writing books about our national sport,' Don Jaime said. 'May I inquire what first aroused your interest, Mr Fleming?'

The visitor gave a slight shrug of his broad shoulders. 'My father owned a large cattle ranch in Texas. I was reading up the subject of bull breeding at college when the origins of the fighting bulls first came to my attention.'

As the meal progressed, Cassy was irritated by the fact that not once did the visitor address her, although he seemed perfectly at ease in the unfamiliar company, and his manners were impeccable. His hands, she noted, were large, and square but he was not clumsy. He ate with his fork, American-style.

Cassy struck up an animated conversation with Patri's fiancée. She allowed her eyes to brighten with interest when Rebekka spoke of the beautiful lace wedding dress she was to wear, and from the corner of her eye watched the American to see if he was aware of her, but although his head turned once or twice in her direction, he did not allow his gaze to linger.

I suppose it is because I'm in mourning, she thought resentfully, for never yet since her coming-out dance had a man failed to acknowledge with his eyes that she was beautiful.

'You must be our guest for as many days as you wish,' she heard her father say. 'It may take you a day or two to select a house you like.'

'Whatever happens, I've promised Mr Fleming we will take him out to the Hacienda,' Patri said. 'More than anything else, he wishes to see your bulls, Papá.'

In reply to polite inquiries from Don Jaime, the American explained that it was not only the skills involved in bullfighting, but the fascination of violent death which interested him.

'In our country millions of people never experience this fascination. I hope one day to write a novel that will paint a true picture of death. Do I sound presumptuous?'

'*No, en absoluto!*' Don Jaime replied, but Cassy knew from the tone of his voice that her father failed to understand why all foreigners should be so preoccupied with this aspect of bullfighting. But Cassy understood, for although she disliked the sight of blood, perversely she felt a unique excitement akin to exaltation each time she witnessed the death of a bull.

She was unaware that her cheeks were glowing and her eyes sparkling, until she saw the stranger staring at her in a way that left her in no doubt that he had guessed her emotions and considered them unseemly. So be it! she thought. Why should she care if he thought her indelicate! His opinion meant nothing to her.

Nevertheless, she was profoundly disappointed when her father stated that he would prefer the ladies to retire, and she was obliged to spend the remainder of the evening in her mother's and Rebekka's company. With difficulty, she pretended an interest in the younger girl's announcement that her father had bought a beautiful house for her and Patri in Munich.

Cassy excused herself and went to bed. Everyone seemed to expect her to be prostrated by poor Jimmy's death, but she simply could not cry all day and night. Joss would understand, she thought. She would go back to England as soon as she had seen a little more of her favourite brother. Maybe Alan would have returned from Portugal and life would be fun again . . .

It was not of Alan but of the American stranger she dreamed that night – a menacing figure walking towards her across an empty bullring whilst she sat, filled with apprehension, knowing that if he came near enough to touch her she would be tossed into the air as if by the sharp, cruel points of a bull's horns. Agonizingly she waited to run, yet was glued to her seat until, against her will, she found herself floating from her hard, wooden bench closer and closer until the bushy brown beard was but an inch from her face.

She awoke screaming in the darkness and heard Lota's gentle voice beside her saying: 'Poor Casilda, don't be frightened. You were only dreaming! Jimmy is with God now and he would not want you to suffer so. Go back to sleep! I'll stay with you until you do.'

Cassy's nightmare was only half-remembered next morning when she re-encountered Milton Fleming in the dining room at breakfast. He rose politely as she entered but almost immediately he reopened his conversation with Patri. He paid her no further attention as she toyed with the freshly baked hot rolls and seemed interested only in her father's plan to spend the following day at the Hacienda.

Cassy looked eagerly at Don Jaime. 'May I go with you, Papá?' she inquired. 'A day in the country would benefit me. I have not been sleeping well.'

Don Jaime hesitated. Lota, who had now taken her place at the table, intervened: 'Casilda had a terrible nightmare last night, Papá. It would do her good. Can we not all go together? I'm sure Rebekka would enjoy it too.'

Cassy went quickly round to her father's place at the head of the table and, winding her arms around his neck, she pressed her cheek against his. 'Oh, Papá, please say yes!' she pleaded. 'I could go into our little chapel there and light candles for Jimmy. He would like that.'

Across the table, she saw Milton Fleming staring at her, a quizzical smile narrowing his eyes. Cassy had the feeling that he was mocking her; that he no more believed she wished to light candles for Jimmy than that she could fly to the moon! Her father patted her hand.

'Very well, *niña*! You shall do so whilst the rest of us ride round the estate. Lota is right, you do look pale. You shall sit quietly in the garden and rest.'

'But Papá, I wanted . . .' Cassy broke off, angrily aware that she had overplayed her hand. She was further irritated by the expression on the American's face as she returned to her chair.

The rest of the day was devoid of action or excitement, for Patri went with Milton Fleming to inquire about houses available for rental and they did not return until evening. At dinner, despite Cassy's attempt to appear interested in the accommodation he had settled upon, the American replied only in monosyllables and she was left once again with the impression that he had not the slightest interest in her. She decided quite definitely that she did not like him and told Lota so. Lota was disinclined to discuss their visitor.

'He will be moving into his own house before the end of the week,' she said practically, 'so he will not be here to get on your nerves, Casilda!'

He was not so much 'on her nerves' as a sharp thorn in her awareness, Cassy thought next day as she drove out with Rebekka, Lota and the two men to the Hacienda. At the last minute, Don Jaime had been called away on business and Patri was in charge of the party. With none of the older generation present, the atmosphere was relaxed, although Patri was in agreement with his father's directive that Casilda should observe the conventions and remain behind whilst he showed their guest the bulls.

Impatient for their return, Cassy made her obligatory visit to the little chapel where she did, indeed, light candles for Jimmy and say a prayer for him.

The servants who lived permanently at the Hacienda had prepared a luncheon which was served in the patio where the slight breeze was cut off by the surrounding walls and the sun was warm enough for them to enjoy until it was time for the siesta.

'I'm not sleepy,' Cassy announced. 'I shall stay here and write to Joss.'

The American looked at her over the top of his wineglass. 'Then may I please stay here in the garden with you, Doña Casilda? I, too, wish to write. I have notes to make on all I have seen this morning. Would that be in order, Patricio? I don't wish to flout any of your conventions.'

'It might be best if I send one of the servants to sit here with you,' Patri replied.

Thus Cassy found herself virtually alone with their guest, for the old servant, Pia, spoke no word of English, and in no time at all was fast asleep on the chair she had placed some short distance away from her young mistress.

'Well now!' said the American with a sideways glance at Casilda. 'I don't wish to be impertinent, but I have been intensely curious. You don't seem to fit into the picture. For a start, I have the feeling that you actually resent all the sympathy that is being foisted upon you. Would I be wrong?'

'Perhaps not, but you certainly are being impertinent,' Cassy said tartly. 'However, since we're apparently being honest with each other, may *I* ask *you* if I would be wrong in assuming that you don't much like me? I would certainly like to know *why!*'

Milton Fleming gave a short, deep-throated laugh. 'On the contrary, Doña Casilda, I find you quite fascinating. Why, I ask myself, is this beautiful Spanish girl not decimated by the death of a young husband who, from all accounts, was handsome, charming and utterly devoted to her? I suspect your grief goes no deeper than the surface.'

'Then you suspect quite wrongly,' Cassy said furiously. 'Jimmy's death was a terrible, terrible blow to me . . .'

Suddenly, the misery of the past three months overwhelmed her and tears spilled down her cheeks. She cried softly, the desolation too much to bear alone. She sensed the man watching her.

'I don't need your pity!' she said defiantly, wiping away her tears with the back of her hand like a small child. 'If you really want to know, the whole ghastly thing was my fault!'

Haltingly, she told him the story of that dreadful September day; of the harrowing week whilst they waited for news that Jimmy's body or wreckage from his aeroplane had been washed ashore. Her tears were falling again as she described the moment when her husband's body had been placed in the family vault.

'That explains a great deal,' her companion said quietly, handing her a handkerchief. 'Well, my dear, guilt is a very uneasy bedfellow and, having now acknowledged it, you would do best to forget it. All of us have moments in our lives that we do not care to remember. But we are not gods – we are human, and you, of all people, are very, very human.'

Casilda managed a half-smile. 'You even make your compliments sound disparaging,' she said. 'Tell me, Mr Fleming, don't you like women?'

His eyes narrowed as if he needed time to consider his reply. Then he said: 'On the contrary, I recognize my need of them. Women are an unfortunate but necessary interruption to those activities I wish to follow and which I can best do alone. I therefore try to avoid women – especially beautiful ones.'

Cassy felt suddenly happier. 'You are avoiding me?' she asked directly.

'My dear child, you are unavoidable! However, you are in mourning and one does not trifle with the carnal pleasures of life in such circumstances.'

Cassy's mouth tightened. 'I don't care for the word "trifle", nor indeed do I understand why you should speak of "carnal" pleasures. What has that to do with our conversation?'

'Let's not waste time in pretence,' he said. 'Were I to have met you in different circumstances, I should be starting an affair with you. You have a very beautiful body beneath those widow's weeds.'

'You are insulting!' Cassy cried, but without conviction. She was both repelled and fascinated by this man's bluntness. Quite truthfully, she added: 'And besides, I am not interested in "affairs", nor ever have been. Since you seem to approve of honesty I can tell you *honestly* that I have never much cared for *that* sort of thing.'

He laughed. 'You are younger than I thought,' he said. 'One day, honey, you are going to discover the true delights of those carnal pleasures. But not with me! I have no time for children!'

Cassy's eyes were stormy. 'Call me a child if you wish,' she said haughtily. 'You think yourself superior because you are a man and older than I am. But perhaps it has not occurred to you, since you appear to be very conceited, that a girl of my age would choose a younger man than you, were she to consider an affair. I have no interest whatever in *you*. As I said to Lota this morning, I shall be pleased when you have moved to your own house and left ours in peace.'

Milton smiled. 'You must come and visit me in my new

abode,' he said. 'With your parents, of course. It is a very nice house; I have been granted a six months' tenancy. I shall be around for some time yet.'

'Well, I shall not!' Cassy said sharply. 'I am leaving for England within a week or two.'

'That is regrettable, but perhaps wise,' the American said casually, as if he did not care one way or the other, and then abruptly he excused himself, saying he wished to take some snapshots.

'I'll be back shortly,' he told Cassy, but he did not reappear until the siesta was at an end and Patri, Rebekka and Lota came to join her in the garden.

'The man has no manners whatever,' she wrote to Joss. 'I shall certainly not stay here in Sevilla now that I know he is going to be around . . .'

But despite her threat to return to London, Cassy put off booking her passage, encouraging Lota to believe that she was only staying in order to lend her moral support when Benito approached their father next month.

Neither she nor Lota knew that Don Jaime had already discussed with his *mayoral* the impossibility of any liaison between their offspring. Francisco Lopez was in complete agreement that his son could have no pretensions to Señorita Carlota's hand and had promised so to inform his son.

Unaware that the die had already been cast, Lota continued to dream.

As the day of the Corrida Benefica approached, she became increasingly nervous.

'Papá has always listened to you,' she said, hugging Cassy. 'I'm so grateful to you for staying. Oh, Casilda, if there's ever anything I can do for you . . .'

'Well, there is,' Cassy said as the two girls prepared for bed. 'I want to go to the *corrida* with you. I've just got to think of some way to get there and I may need your help.'

Lota looked deeply shocked. 'But Casilda, you know you can't go – you're in mourning! Papá would never allow it.'

Cassy's mouth tightened. 'You don't have to remind me, Lota,' she said crossly. 'We'd be outcasts in society and the servants would all die of shame and so on . . . But I shall find a way. Perhaps I can persuade the American to take me.'

Lota looked even more shocked. 'But Mr Fleming will be with Papá in his *palco*. Patri and I will be in the box also, and . . .'

'Of course I cannot go with the family, silly!' Cassy broke in. 'But since Mr Fleming professes to be an expert, I imagine he is aware that he will see far more from a ringside seat than from a *palco*. Tomorrow I shall ask him to take me . . .'

It was a forlorn hope, Cassy knew. Since their afternoon together at the Hacienda, they had met on a number of occasions when he had come to the house, and once Mamá had taken her to see his new home. But he had paid her no more attention than he afforded her mother or Lota. During their conversation at El Campanario, he had admitted that he thought her beautiful but despite this, he was still disinclined to further their acquaintance.

'He is invited to luncheon tomorrow, Lota. If he arrives early, as he did last time, I want you to suggest that we take a walk in the gardens of the Alcazar. It must be you who suggests the walk, and you who invites him to join us. I have to talk to him. I've got to persuade him to take me to the fight. You *know* I have always loved the *corridas* and this one is special, you must agree, since I have never seen Benito perform either as a *novillero* or a fully fledged matador. I want to see for myself if he is as brilliant as you say.'

Lota's face relaxed and her voice softened as she said: 'Benito is quite marvellous, Casilda. You will see! As for Mr Fleming, I will do my best – but I don't know if Mamá would permit him to accompany us on a walk even if he agrees!'

But surprisingly, Doña Ursula raised no objection, perhaps because Patri and Rebekka said they, too, would enjoy a stroll. It was not difficult, therefore, for Lota to engage her brother and his fiancée in conversation and increase her pace sufficiently for Cassy to lag behind with the American.

Somewhat to her annoyance, Milton Fleming's first words were blunt. With a hint of amusement, he said: 'Do I smell a rat? I fancy you and your charming little sister have engineered that you and I should be out of earshot!'

Cassy's chin lifted defiantly. 'You are very perceptive, Mr Fleming, but since you ask, yes, I do want to speak to you alone. I want to go to the bullfight next week. My parents would never permit it and the scandal if I were recognized by anyone would be . . . well, irreparable. But I am determined not to miss the fight, and if you will not take me I shall find some other way to go.'

The American did not look particularly surprised. He regarded her thoughtfully. 'And how do you plan that I should take you?' he inquired. 'In disguise? I imagine a beautiful girl like you would find it hard to remain unrecognized. Your family are well known.'

Cassy bit her lip. 'I could wear a blonde wig, dark glasses,' she said breathlessly, 'and if anyone spoke to us, you could introduce me as an American.'

She hurried on to explain that he could easily excuse himself from attending the fight with her father. Many people preferred the *barrera* seats . . . even Papá sometimes chose to sit close to the ring.

His glance was sardonic. 'What makes you think I might be willing to tell lies on your behalf, Doña Casilda. Is there a bargain, I wonder? Your favours in return for my help?'

Cassy flushed. 'Mr Fleming, if you are suggesting that I let you make love to me . . .'

His deep laugh interrupted her. 'My dear girl, I am suggesting no such thing. I thought that *you* were. I see now that my part in your scheme is simply intended as a gesture of goodwill – the response of any man appealed to by a beautiful but singularly spoilt female who is accustomed to getting her own way!'

'Very well, please forget that I asked for your help,' Cassy said haughtily. 'I had not expected that you would be so – so provincial!'

He made no attempt to argue the matter, but after a slight pause said: 'Nevertheless, I am interested to discover how far your scheming has taken you. How, for instance, do you escape the eagle eye of your family, even supposing that I were to agree to your crazy idea?'

Cassy's hopes soared. 'Lota will help me. She can tell Mamá I have a headache and wish to be undisturbed, and then distract the attention of any servants who might be about whilst I slip out of the house. Or if that were impossible, I could say I intended visiting Mercedes. Lota would accompany me there, and when she departed home I could put a shawl over my head and walk to your house.'

'I see! And all this cloak-and-dagger nonsense just so that you can go to a bullfight?'

She could, she suggested, draw his attention to the finer points he might otherwise miss.

'And if you were unmasked, Casilda, what then? My good name as well as yours would be forever defiled!'

'You're mocking me,' Cassy said angrily. 'If you are too frightened to risk it, then say so.'

The blue eyes were expressionless as he gazed into hers. 'I am not convinced it is the bullfight alone that inspires such daring. Would it be closer to the truth to say that it is the challenge of getting your own way in spite of the odds against you? Well, never let it be said that I am scared. I will get you a blonde wig and some suitable clothes. My former wife used to tell me I had excellent taste. The rest is up to you. You realize, don't you, that my part in this minor crime will leave you indebted to me?'

Cassy caught her breath. Was he serious? What exactly did he mean by 'indebted'? It would be much easier if she could guess his real intentions towards her – if indeed he had any. But she was not going to waste time worrying about *his* motives.

Her last thought before she slept that night was that if Mr Fleming thought to frighten her by threats of her indebtedness, then it only went to show how little he knew her. She was not afraid of him. He meant nothing in her life other than as a means to an end.

CHAPTER EIGHTEEN

March 1928

Life, thought Joscelin, seemed unnaturally quiet without Cassy or Alan. Although engrossed in her work, there were times when she would have given a great deal to see them, and she never walked the Brigadier in the park without missing Alan, who was deeply attached to the boisterous mongrel. She visited her parents, wrote letters to Cassy and watched the post for the longed-for card from Alan. Only one had arrived from Portugal, saying that he was about to start his journey to the Alto Douro, since when there had been silence.

February gave way to a bitterly cold March. Heavy snowfalls were followed by sharp frosts, and the grass in Hyde Park was covered with a glistening white carpet, a novelty which sent the Brigadier into transports of astonished delight. Despite the cold, Joscelin tried to walk him at least once a day. One Sunday afternoon as she waited to cross Kensington Gore, a large, cream-coloured car drew to a halt directly in front of her and Joscelin recognized the Costains' Daimler.

As Paget opened the nearside door, Lady Costain waved and called out to her: 'Joscelin, my dear child, I thought it was you! You look perished. Whatever are you doing out in this weather?' Without waiting for a reply, she patted the seat beside her. 'Do you have a minute or two to spare? Paget, put that animal in the front with you. Come and sit here, Joscelin.' She drew back the heavy fur travelling rug wrapped cosily around her knees. Joscelin handed over the soaking Brigadier to a reluctant Paget and settled herself on the soft white upholstery, hoping that her coat would not leave damp patches.

Through the glass dividing window, Joscelin noted with dismay the Brigadier determinedly making himself comfortable on the seat beside the chauffeur. Paget was equally determinedly attempting to coax him back onto the floor.

Lady Costain picked up the speaking tube. 'Stop fussing, Paget!' she called down it, and added: 'Drive round the park whilst I talk to Miss Howard!'

'I was going to write to you, my dear,' Lady Costain said as Paget turned into the park. 'I'm going away, you see.' She turned her head to glance at Joscelin and added inconsequentially: 'What lovely eyes you have, child! You should make more of yourself. Yes, I'm going away next week – to America. I'm not telling a soul, of course, but when I saw you just now it suddenly occurred to me that you are the one person who ought to know; the only one I can trust.'

Joscelin felt totally bewildered.

'Walter is such a dear man,' Lady Costain continued. 'I know I shall be happy with him – and he assures me I shall adore the United States. Of course, I shall hate being so far away from Alan and the girls, but it isn't so far these days, is it? Only five days on one of the big liners. And Walter says it won't be long before we shall be able to go by aeroplane!'

Joscelin felt a moment of shock. The visit to America no longer sounded like a holiday but a permanent move.

Lady Costain sighed. 'I suppose people will be fearfully shocked. But my husband is far too engrossed in his own affairs to miss me – although the scandal will be a blow to his pride. Not that he has ever paid much attention to society gossip – and my darling Alan is far too good-looking and eligible to be dropped. It isn't as if he or the girls need a mother any more, and they can all come and visit us. Walter says they can all stay as long as they wish. You must come too, my dear. And poor little Cassy.'

She reached out a hand and placed it gently on Joscelin's arm. 'I suppose others will think me selfish and even cruel, abandoning my husband and children. You are very young – but I have the feeling that you will not condemn me too harshly. Will you try to help Alan understand why I'm going away? It isn't easy, you know, for women of my age to face a future devoid of love and companionship and Walter adores me. I shall never again be lonely, do you see?'

'You – *lonely*?' Joscelin cried disbelievingly. 'No one has more friends than you, Lady Costain. Everyone loves you . . .'

'No, my dear, they do not. They enjoy my parties and know that I will be an asset at theirs. The life I am leading has no greater significance than tinsel on a Christmas tree. It glitters for a little while, but becomes ever more tarnished with the passing of the years. I hope to find real happiness with Walter.'

Impulsively, Joscelin took Lady Costain's hands in hers and pressed them warmly. 'Alan will want you to be happy. I'll do everything I can to ensure his understanding.'

'Dear child,' Lady Costain murmured. 'There is one final matter.' She leaned back against the soft-cushioned upholstery. 'It is strange, is it not, how everything we do in our lives spreads beyond our expectations? Do you know that I met Walter through Carlota? He is godfather to the American woman who adopted Lota's baby boy. When this young woman heard that Walter was coming to London, she asked him if he would call to see me so that he could tell me how much she and her husband love the child, how handsome and happy he is.'

She gave a deep sigh. 'It is hard to believe that he is almost five years old. Walter has left it to me to decide whether to pass on to Lota this information. I have been quite unable to decide what is best, but now that I am on the point of leaving England I can delay no longer. What is *your* opinion, Joscelin? Do you think it would distress Carlota to hear about her baby?'

Joscelin tried to think clearly. Her first reaction was that Lota would be happy to know that her baby was thriving. But then the same doubts as had obviously beset Lady Costain entered her mind. Five years was a long time; Lota had mentioned her baby less and less over the years; she would want to know *who* had provided the information; whether it was possible for her to see the child – and all this when she was on the point of asking her parents' permission to marry Benito. To be reminded of her child, of whom Benito was still ignorant, could only add to her worries.

'I can see by your face that you are not in favour of the idea,' Lady Costain said. 'Walter, too, feels it would be wrong.'

'I think she might find it very disturbing if the past were resuscitated now,' Joscelin agreed.

Lady Costain nodded her head. 'You are a sensible girl, Joscelin, and I value your opinion. Now, child, will you wish me well?'

It was with genuine affection and a great deal of emotion that Joscelin and Lady Costain finally parted outside her flat.

As she and the Brigadier dried themselves in front of the gas fire, she found herself remembering her many visits to Rutland Gate and how kind Alan's mother had always been to her. It was she who had been mainly responsible for helping Joscelin to mature in a world far better suited to her than was her own home background in Surbiton. Moreover, she and Lady Costain were linked inextricably by their shared love for Alan; by their complicity in protecting Lota; by their mutual fondness for Cassy.

What was Cassy up to, Joscelin wondered when no further letter arrived. She had sounded so bitterly unhappy in her last letter.

Cassy, had Joscelin but known it, was very far from unhappy as she, Lota and her English maid, Polly, drove in the carriage in the direction of Mercedes' house. Cassy was laughing as she looked at Lota's anxious face.

'For goodness sake, what have *you* to worry about?' she said. 'As far as you're concerned, you and Polly dropped me here. Where I go subsequently is my affair, and you cannot be blamed for it.'

'But you will be careful!' Lota pleaded as Cassy got out of the carriage.

'Of course I will, silly goose!' Cassy said impatiently. 'And Polly, be sure to go straight back to my room, and tell anyone who asks to see me that I have locked myself in and am not to be disturbed.'

The girl grinned, delighted to be a party to her young mistress's adventure, her rôle in which would undoubtedly be generously rewarded.

As the carriage vanished round the corner of the street Cassy hurried off in the opposite direction. With a veil pulled over her face, she was not afraid that she would be recognized. It took but ten minutes to reach the door of Milton's house. To her surprise, he opened it himself.

'I've dismissed all the servants for the day,' he greeted her as she walked across the patio. 'Do come in!'

He watched her step out of the bright sunshine into the dark hall, noting her flushed face with amusement.

'I admit, I doubted whether you'd keep your cool when it came to the point of playing hookey!' he said in his slow drawl. 'All the same, I've kept my side of the bargain in case you did. Your clothes are in the guest room over there.' He pointed to an open door.

Regarding him from the corner of her eye, Cassy thought he looked very relaxed – and somewhat supercilious. Antagonism rose in her and, wordless, she marched through into the bedroom and stared down at the clothes laid out for her approval. She gasped. The apricot silk dress with its matching coat was beautiful and probably French, she thought. Beside them lay a blonde wig and a pair of heavy-rimmed dark glasses.

With a renewed feeling of excitement, she began hurriedly to undress. Let Mr Milton Fleming patronize her if he pleased – she did not care! Only as her dress slipped to the floor and she stood there in her petticoat did she realize that, in her hurry, she had left the door open. Turning to look over her shoulder, she saw that the American was in the adjoining room reading a newspaper, and that although he could easily have observed her, he was not doing so.

Aware that time was slipping away, Cassy quickly donned the new dress. The pleated chiffon panel, filling the deep, V-necked décolletage, lay delicately on her breasts. The handkerchief-pointed hemline hung gracefully to her knees. The frock fitted as if it had been made for her, and she smiled delightedly as she twisted and turned in front of the mirror. The delicate colour glowed in the half-light of the shuttered room. As she quickly adjusted the wig, her smile deepened. She looked quite, quite altered! No one would ever recognize her.

She turned and walked through the doorway.

'Well, would you know me?' she asked. 'It's perfect, Mr Fleming.'

He looked up and rose to his feet. 'Very stunning, m'lady. But the frock would look even better were it fastened.'

He moved behind her and she felt his hands on her shoulders. A shiver of fear ran down her spine. Was his touch accidental?

'You have a beautiful skin, pale gold, like honey,' he said and deftly hooked the neck fastening. 'And now, my dear, we should be off.'

For the first time Cassy noted how elegantly he was dressed, in a grey lounge suit, perfectly tailored, with a red spotted bow tie.

He picked up a panama hat and hung a pair of binoculars around his neck, the hint of a smile playing about his mouth as he led her out into the hot, dusty street.

'Shall we walk?' he inquired. 'The bullring is not far away.'

His arm linked protectively in hers, they made their way towards the Plaza de Toros. The crowds became ever more dense as they neared the great iron gates of the bullring. The American had difficulty in forcing a passage through to the third row seats on the shady side of the arena. They were pushed and shoved, but good-naturedly, the excitement of the festive crowd almost a tangible thing.

Milton handed Cassy a leather cushion he rented from an usher and she settled herself on the stone bench.

'Now tell me what is going on below us that we cannot see from here,' he said. 'Is it true that the picadors are stuffing their horses' ears with newspaper as well as covering their eyes?'

'Naturally!' Cassy answered with a shrug. 'The less the horses are frightened the easier the picadors' chances of placing their *picas* well.' She pointed to the barrier encircling the sandy arena. 'See, they have taken the pink and yellow capes and spread them on the *barrera*. The names of the men who will use them are in black on the yellow side. And there in the rack near the *toril* – the pens where the bulls are waiting – are the *picas*. They have sharp steel points which have been smeared with vaseline. And there are the *banderillas* hanging on that wire, with cork tips to guard the points.'

The man beside her grimaced. 'And it is with these pretty tasseled spears that the muscle in the bull's neck is weakened until he can no longer hold his head high, thereby making the *coup de grâce* possible for the matador.'

Cassy frowned, sensing a note of criticism in his comment. 'Well, of course! I thought you were an aficionado, Mr Fleming; that you enjoyed the fights?'

'Oh, I do! There are some aspects of it, however, which trouble me – the inevitability of the bull's death, for instance.'

Cassy shrugged. 'Sometimes it is the matador who dies, which he will surely risk if the bull's head is not lowered sufficiently for him to place his sword correctly . . .'

She broke off to clutch her companion's arm. 'Look, there is Papá – and Patri and our little Lota – in that box over there.'

'I doubt very much that they would recognize you, even if they notice me,' the American reassured her. As the bandleader raised his baton, trumpets flared and the tempo of a pasodoble filled the arena. The huge crowd applauded when the three matadors began their parade around the ring behind the two *alguacilillos* – the traditionally costumed mounted officials of the bullring.

'Look, there is Benito – Benito Lopez!' Cassy cried, 'the one in purple and gold. Doesn't he look handsome?' She broke off to lean further forward, the better to see the *banderilleros* in their flaming colours as they circled the arena.

The matadors bowed to the President, whose entry had signalled the start of the bullfight. Their sword-handlers were standing in the *callejón*, the covered sandy corridor behind the *barrera* which encircled the arena. They now gave the three matadors their working capes in exchange for the ornate ones in which they had paraded.

People near enough to do so shouted their good wishes: '*Suerte, Coriano! Suerte, Benito! Olé, Francisco!*'

The waiting men smiled back and expressed their thanks.

The *alguacilillos* galloped across the arena, received permission from the President to release the first bull from the pen where it was held in readiness. One of the two men now gave the symbolic key to the keeper of the gate before galloping out of the ring. Above the Plaza de Toros, the sun burned fiercely down from a blue sky. The heavy metal bolt on the gate of the bull pen slid open. Cassy caught her breath as one of her father's magnificent beasts charged into the ring and then stopped to sniff the hot sand. It charged forward a second time, stopped again and raised its head, horns held high, to meet the challenge of its new surroundings.

'Magnificent!' murmured Milton Fleming.

Suddenly there was a blare from the trumpets and a loud drum roll. The two mounted picadors entered the arena, circling it on their horses. El Coriano stepped from behind the barrier and regarded the bull, sizing up the animal. Without haste, he caped it into position.

The bull's attention was now on the picadors facing him. It charged towards one of the horses. As it closed in, the picador stabbed his lance into the huge swelling muscles of its neck, pushing the bull to his right in the direction of the matador. A second time, El Coriano lured the animal into position; a second time it charged the picador's horse and received yet another *pica*. But on the third charge the picador failed to find his target; the bull's horns tore into the horse's side, throwing it to the ground and pinning the picador beneath it. The horse writhed in pain and fear and breathing heavily, the bull backed away and charged again. As the horns found their target a second time, the horse was raised from the ground, freeing the picador beneath.

The matador and *banderilleros* ran forward with their capes to distract the bull from the fallen man. The bull now turned to attack one of the *banderilleros*, but the man raced quickly behind the barrier, which echoed with a dull thud as the horns struck the heavy wooden planks. A second *banderillero* stepped forward, waving his pink and yellow cape. The bull's concentration was centred on the cape. Once more it charged and again the *banderillero* was forced to retreat, the horns only just missing his body as he ran for cover. The crowd yelled their approval. Meanwhile, the injured picador had risen to his feet, but the badly gored horse had to be dragged from the ring.

The first act of the drama was resumed and the second picador placed the last of the three obligatory lances in the neck of the now infuriated and suspicious bull. The animal swerved as the *pica* was withdrawn from its neck. The trumpet blared, signalling the commencement of the second act of the fight.

El Coriano's two *banderilleros* now stepped forward, their capes discarded as they offered their unprotected bodies to the bull. Pitting their speed and dexterity against that of the bull which, as they evaded its charge, could only turn in its own length, the men placed their pairs of barbed *banderillas* high on the *morrillo*, the hump of muscle on the frustrated animal's neck. The last, on El Coriano's orders, was positioned in the centre of the *morrillo*.

The trumpets sounded for the third and last act. El Coriano stepped from behind the barrier and walked slowly towards the bull, holding out his cape. Without haste he chose where he wished to halt and, feet together, gathered in his scarlet cape, then swirled it to incite his adversary.

'So now the matador's work begins!' Milton said, turning briefly to look at Cassy's face as she leaned forward, her eyes concentrated totally upon the man and beast in the arena. The bull attacked, and as the cape unfurled in front of its eyes, El Coriano guided it past his body in a wide circle. There was little danger to the matador and the crowd remained silent. But then El Coriano hid the cape from the bull's sight so that it twisted and turned in its search for the colourful cloth, and finally stood still in bewilderment. Then it charged. El Coriano extended his right leg, opened the cape and brought the bull close against his body in an arc from right to left. The crowd roared its approval. He performed three more such passes and then, as the bull stood still watching him, he turned his back on it and walked towards the edge of the ring.

'He is master of the bull now,' Cassy said. '*El toro* is weakening!' Her eyes were fastened on the great black beast. Its flanks dripped blood into the sand and its breathing was heavy and laboured. 'But make no mistake,' she added, 'he is still very dangerous!'

Milton Fleming nodded, knowing that it was time to kill the bull; but the matador, proud of his performance and aware of the adulation of the crowd, decided to make further passes.

Cassy gasped. 'He will lose his balance! He should stop now and kill him . . . look, he's losing control of the bull!'

The trumpet sounded, warning the matador that he had run out of the time allotted for the kill.

Fleming held his breath – as indeed did every aficionado present. Moments later, as Cassy had anticipated, the bull's horn caught El Coriano's thigh and the matador was flung onto the sand. As the animal plunged its horns into the fallen man a second time, Benito Lopez ran forward and killed it with a single thrust of his sword.

The American turned once more to look at Cassy, who was shouting as the gored matador was helped out of the arena, and the dead bull was dragged away. Milton could think of no other woman he knew who could enjoy such a barbaric ritual.

Suddenly Cassy grasped his arm as the crowd roared a welcome to the second bull now thundering into the ring.

'This one is Benito's,' she told him as it charged across the sand. '*Olé*, Benito, *Olé!*'

The young matador, Milton observed, was popular with the crowd. Not only was Lopez handsome but his movements were immensely artistic. He directed his bull with a controlled power and confidence. There was a look of arrogance and pride on his face as, holding the *muleta* in his left hand, he steered the animal by the movements of his scarlet cloth. Methodically, instinctively, he regulated the rhythm between himself and the bull; then, standing erect, alone in the ring, he chose his moment to kill. No longer in doubt as to its enemy, the bull attacked, its horns lowered. Benito extended his arm, guiding the thundering beast to the right as he sank his sword between the massive shoulders.

The bull staggered, sinking slowly to its knees. The crowd rose, shouting and applauding in tribute both to the matador and to the brave death of the animal. The men led in the team of mules, attached a rope to the dead bull's horns and dragged it from the arena, whilst on the president's orders the *algua-cilillos* held out to Benito an ear cut from the bull he had killed so perfectly.

Cassy turned a flushed, excited face to her companion. 'Benito must present this one to the President,' she said, 'but with the next he will honour my sister. He intends to dedicate his second bull to her. Did you know he was Papá's protégé?'

She broke off, aware suddenly that she was still holding Milton Fleming's arm. Through the linen sleeve of his jacket she could feel the firm muscle of his forearm. She hurriedly withdrew her grasp.

Irritated by the confusion of her feelings, Cassy told herself that it was absurd to be embarrassed by a gesture that was not especially intimate. Yet she heard her voice chattering inconsequentially about the third and youngest matador who would fight that afternoon, as if trying to cover up a faux pas. Her physical awareness of her companion was unsettling; it surprised her, for she liked the American no better now than on the day she had first set eyes on him. Was it possible to be attracted to a man one thought *unattractive*, she wondered. She might be less confused if he did not stare at her in so calculating a manner – as if trying to read her deepest thoughts.

His look was faintly patronizing – as if he considered her a silly girl whose whim he was prepared to satisfy for his own amusement rather than hers. At least he had kept his side of the agreement and provided her with a perfect disguise. If he had considered the dangers of her being recognized, then clearly he didn't care about them. It was *her* reputation, not his, at stake. They must leave before the last of the six bulls was killed – be away before the crowds milled out into the streets. Milton had agreed to drive her back, allowing her to slip into her house through the garden door which Polly would ensure was unlocked.

It was foolhardy – and *very* risky, Cassy thought with a twinge of apprehension. Yet was it not this very flouting of the rules that made the escapade so attractive? This and the fact that she had wanted to see how far she could push the tall, enigmatic foreigner to do as she wished.

She was, she thought with surprise, a little afraid of Mr Milton Fleming. He was too male, too superior, too old, and she had had no experience of older men.

Most irritating of all, Cassy decided, was his silence. Not once did he attempt to make small talk when he escorted her back to his house before the start of the sixth and last fight of the day.

'May one inquire what weighty thoughts are passing through your mind?' she asked sarcastically as they re-entered his home.

His expression was indecipherable: 'You must forgive my bad manners. I was contemplating the difficulty of returning you undetected! It would be a pity to have got away with this escapade so far and then find ourselves discovered at the last hurdle.'

'I suppose I should thank you again for taking me to the *corrida*,' Cassy said grudgingly as he unlocked the gate and waited for her to walk past him into the cool, shaded patio. 'As you told me so pointedly, I *am* indebted to you.'

'We will discuss that some other time,' he replied briefly, and pointing to the bedroom door he added: 'I suggest you change at once. I'll bring you something cool to drink.'

Cassy nodded, her throat suddenly dry as the thought raced across her mind that he intended to come into the bedroom . . . using the offer of a drink to invade her privacy. Her chin lifted and she marched into the bedroom and firmly closed the door. As it slammed shut, she thought that he must certainly have heard it and guessed its meaning.

Slowly she removed the smart silk coat and frock. She was standing in her petticoat when, without knocking, Milton Fleming entered the room. Cassy swung round, ready to defend herself from his advances; but he was not even looking at her as carefully, he put the glass of wine on a table, and left as silently as he had arrived.

Cassy sank down on the edge of the bed, a blush of embarrassment spreading through her body. She had been on the point of telling him to get out; of accusing him of taking unfair advantage of her. But it was quite obvious that he had had no such intent.

Ashamed of her mistake, she hurriedly changed back into her mourning clothes.

When finally she presented herself, he was again sitting in his armchair reading a newspaper. He looked up at her and gave a slow, lazy smile. 'So! The widow is once more wearing her weeds!' He rose to his feet. 'They don't suit you as well as the clothes I bought you. I shall keep those, I think, as a memento of a most interesting day.'

Cassy crossed the space between them and stood looking down at him. 'You have been very kind, Mr Fleming. I enjoyed the *corrida*.'

His thick eyebrows raised. 'I saw you did!'

Sensing a criticism, Cassy's eyes flashed. 'Didn't *you* find it exciting?' she challenged.

He nodded, his eyes unsmiling. 'Fascinating, cruel, beautiful, relentless and *enormously* exciting,' he acknowledged. 'However, if we remain here talking we shall be meeting your papá on your doorstep!'

As he took hold of her elbow to lead her out to his waiting Bugatti, Cassy drew in her breath, sharply aware of the pressure of his ungloved hand on her arm. The excitement of the bullfight was beginning to wane as the American concentrated upon weaving his way through the crowds now spilling out into the streets. Crouched in the back seat, her black veil concealing her face, Cassy began to experience growing resentment at having to sneak back into her own home like a housemaid who had played truant. She was a married woman, twenty-three years old, and should be allowed to go where she pleased. Now, instead of taking part in the celebrations following the bullfight, she must spend a dull evening at home. She wished that Mr Fleming could be invited to dinner so that she could ask him how he had enjoyed the fights, pretending that she had not been there with him, sharing the secret . . . But suddenly she remembered that it was tonight Benito's father would be coming to see Papá, and a stranger would not be welcome.

Ten minutes later, mistress and maid sauntered casually back into the house to be greeted by Doña Ursula.

'There you are, Casilda! I hear you have recovered from your indisposition. Dinner will be later than usual – Lota tells me Papá is expecting visitors after the fight, although he said nothing to me about them! Be dressed in time to receive them with me, will you, please?'

Cassy hurried upstairs to the bedroom she was sharing with her sister. Lota flung herself into Cassy's arms.

'*Gracias a Dios*, you are safely back!' she cried. 'I've been so worried! I don't know what to wear tonight. Will I be permitted to be present at Papá's meeting with Benito's father? I must look my prettiest – but I don't want anything too white . . . too bridal, lest Papá thinks I have taken his approval for granted. Oh, Casilda, wasn't Benito *magnifico*? He has never fought so well! I am proud of him! Everyone stared at me when he dedicated his bull to me and Papá actually smiled and was pleased, I could see he was! Casilda, do you think . . .?'

Cassy released Lota's hold upon her. 'I hate dashing your hopes, Lota,' she said bluntly, 'but you know very well I've never believed Papá or Mamá will agree to such a marriage. If Papá refuses his permission, accept his ruling without a fuss and then, when the time is right, elope with your precious Benito if you must – though I think you'd be crazy to do so!'

Lota's violet eyes were luminous with emotion. 'I mean to marry him, Casilda! But Benito has fights booked for the rest of the season. He would not be free to go to Mexico until November. I don't think I could survive so long a wait . . .'

Cassy shrugged her shoulders. 'Then come back to England with me,' she said. 'I'm alone now in my house, so it would be lovely to have you. Don't forget I'm rich enough now to buy your passage to Mexico *and* pay for a nice trousseau. We can go shopping and buy whatever you want. The lawyer said Jimmy never made a will, and so everything he owned belongs to me. Lota, are you listening?'

But her sister had heard the commotion downstairs as her father returned from the Plaza de Toros in company with Patri and several of his friends. Close behind him, twisting his black hat nervously between his work-roughened, walnut-brown hands, stood Don Jaime's *mayoral*, Benito's father.

Catching sight of him, Don Jaime embraced him. 'Have you come here to boast of your son's performance?' he asked jovially. '*Magnifico!* The boy's fulfilled every expectation. You must be a very proud and happy man, Francisco Lopez.'

There was no answering smile on the man's face. His head hung low and he looked anything but proud.

Don Jaime frowned. 'Something is wrong? What is it, *hombre?*'

Francisco Lopez's head, was bowed. Reluctantly, he raised his eyes to Don Jaime's. 'My problem is my son, my Benito,' he said in a rush of words. 'He has gone a little crazy in the head – *está loco!*'

Don Jaime patted his *mayoral* on the shoulder. He was smiling once more. But the look of apprehension remained on his visitor's face. 'The excitement of his success has been too much for him,' Lopez stammered. 'I cannot understand it. After you and I had last spoken about the matter, I explained everything to him and he seemed to accept it without argument. It is true, now that I think back, that he made no promises to obey me. But he is a good son. He respects his father and you too, Don Jaime. I have come to you because I don't know what to do.'

'To do about what?' Don Jaime asked. 'I am beginning to think it is you who has gone a little crazy, Francisco. Come to my study and have *una copa*. It will calm you. I too, need a drink.'

From the top of the staircase Lota and Cassy heard the door of their father's study close, shutting out the sound of the men's voices. Lota's face was deathly pale as she dug her fingernails into Cassy's arm.

'Why wasn't Benito with his father? He's not afraid to speak for himself. What has gone wrong?'

'Maybe old Lopez ordered him to keep out of the way!' Cassy said.

Such consideration as Don Jaime chose to give his *mayoral's* problem was short-lived. Within a few minutes the door of the study opened and Francisco Lopez appeared, Don Jaime's arm about his shoulders.

'Then we are agreed!' he was saying as he led his *mayoral* towards the front door. 'Your son may be a fine matador, Francisco Lopez, but the Monteros do not marry *toreros*. *Vaya!* I do not blame you. I blame Benito and my daughter. The young ones of today disgrace us all. Be firm with him, *hombre*, and you may tell your son that I have forbidden him to see or speak to Carlota again.'

As Benito's father disappeared into the street, Lota ran down the stairs and confronted Don Jaime, tears streaming down her cheeks as she pleaded with her father to reverse his judgement.

He regarded her more with pity than with anger, and as Cassy came to stand beside her sister, he said: 'Perhaps you can put some sense into Lota's head, *niña*. Surely the child can see that I could not possibly allow such a marriage? Benito is a good boy, and I don't doubt he will make a good husband. *But marry my daughter he shall not!*'

Cassy put her arm around Lota's shoulders and helped her upstairs. Shutting the bedroom door behind them, she turned to the younger girl. 'For goodness sake stop crying, Lota! It's not the end of the world. If you still intend to ruin your life, you will just have to marry without Papá's permission. Now blow your nose and dry your eyes and think instead of what you will need to pack when you come to England with me. That will keep your mind off Benito. As to letting him know your plans, Polly can deliver a letter whilst he is still here in Sevilla. You'd best get one written right away.'

The tears drying on her cheeks, Lota attempted a half-hearted smile as she listened to Cassy's practical suggestions. 'Suppose Papá tries to stop me going back to England with you?'

Cassy drew a deep sigh. 'Why should he? He'll be pleased

you are going far away from Benito. Do stop worrying, Lota. Everything is possible if you want it badly enough. You've just got to be determined, the way I was about going to the fight today.'

'Oh, Casilda, I forgot to ask you about it,' Lota cried. 'Did anybody recognize you?'

'No, I was too well disguised. Mr Fleming's choice of clothes was exceptionally good. But I don't like him, Lota. I have the feeling I can't trust him. He's the sort who might rape you if you gave him half a chance!' She laughed as she saw the horrified look on Lota's face. 'Oh, forget it, you silly goose. I wasn't being serious.'

Indeed she was not, she told herself sharply, for Milton Fleming had had every possible opportunity to rape her if such was his intent. Far from it; he had not even tried to kiss her. His indifference was close to being insulting, and his remarks were often far too intimate and personal for her liking.

He was conceited, self-opinionated and boorish, she told Lota, adding quite untruthfully: 'And it is to be hoped that I shall never have to set eyes on him again.'

CHAPTER NINETEEN

March–April 1929

'So, my beautiful Joscelin, time stands still in your little apartment, I think. That is both pleasing and disturbing!'

Joscelin glanced over her shoulder at the elegantly dressed man lounging very much at ease in her only armchair, and turned quickly back to her easel. She had been at work when Marco arrived on one of his surprise visits, and he had insisted that she complete her task so that he need not feel guilty for interrupting her.

But the half-smiling contemplation of his dark eyes embarrassed her. With a sigh she laid down her brush and palette, abandoning her work as she knelt down and patted the Brigadier's head, watching his long tail thump the floor at her touch.

'He has grown,' Marco remarked. He looked incongruous sitting there. The epitome of a fashionable Italian, he seemed impervious to the clutter littering her flat as he tried gently to discourage the inquisitive attentions of the Brigadier with the toe of his crocodile-skin shoe.

'Why don't you relax on that large sofa of yours and give me your attention? I have a great deal to talk to you about,' he said.

'You sound like my father!' Joscelin smiled as she sat down. 'Have I done something wrong, Marco?'

He smiled back at her, his teeth white beneath his black moustache. There were laughter lines at the corners of his eyes and mouth.

'I am not here to reprove you for any misdeed,' he was

saying with pretended solemnity. 'On the contrary, if there is reproof at all, it is for lack of misdeed. I cannot allow you to let life pass you by in this manner, *angelo mio!*'

'Really, Marco, you are talking nonsense,' Joscelin laughed. 'These past six months I've been so busy I have not had time to think!'

It was a moment or two before Marco replied. Then he said suddenly: 'I dined with Casilda last night!' He was watching Joscelin's face as she looked quickly at him and away again. 'That surprises you, does it not?'

Joscelin was surprised – but she had no intention of revealing it; nor even that she was a little jealous. Marco was, after all, *her* faithful admirer, insofar as he could be called faithful! At Patri's wedding last summer he had remained at Joscelin's side throughout the festivities. He had even proposed for – was it the fourth time? During the dancing he had held her far too close. 'You excite me as no other woman does,' he had said in a voice that left her in no doubt as to its sincerity. But for Alan, Joscelin had thought, she might have succumbed to the romantic atmosphere of the wedding. Alan had claimed her for what she called his 'duty dance', and for a few brief moments it was as if she was once more in his arms in that hard cold bed in the inn at Ripley.

With an effort, Joscelin brought her thoughts back to the present. Marco was saying: 'I learned much of interest from young Casilda – not least that, among many others, Costain is once more at her feet . . .' He drew out a small leather case and, with a glance at Joscelin for her permission, lit a slim cigar. He gave no sign that he had noticed the bright spots of colour in her cheeks as he continued: 'I understand there is an unofficial engagement, but that Casilda is not yet ready to settle down again to matrimony. It seems she is greatly enjoying her widowhood now that she is out of mourning. However, she left me in no doubt that she will eventually marry Costain.'

Joscelin cleared her throat. 'It has not been an easy time for either of them,' she said. 'Alan felt his mother's departure very deeply . . . and he was anxious that none of the scandal should touch Cassy's good name.'

Marco shrugged his shoulders deprecatingly. 'I doubt our lovely Lady Deighton would worry about society gossip,' he said. 'Doña Ursula, of course, will never recover from the shock! Between you and me, Joscelin, I find it hard to believe that she is mother to Casilda. However greatly that woman deplored Lady Costain's elopement, she must have suffered an even bigger shock when her daughter eloped with that young matador! Casilda told me last night that Carlota has been cast out of the Montero family for evermore. Poor child! One can but hope she will find happiness with the boy. His background, I gather, is most unsuitable.'

'Lota has been in love with Benito Lopez for years,' Joscelin said quietly. 'It's my belief they will be perfectly happy now at last they are together.'

'Ah, *amore!*' Marco sighed. 'It can bring joy – and yet it can bring heartbreak too, no?' He stared pointedly at Joscelin. 'I do not think love has brought *you* much happiness, *cara mia*. That is the purpose of my visit today – to tell you the time is now right for you to begin your life. Do not scowl at me like that – it spoils your beauty! Even at the risk of offending you, I shall now speak openly. I know you have been in love with Alan Costain for many years. But equally I know that he, poor fellow, is ensnared by the lovely Casilda.'

The colour flared in Joscelin's cheeks. Hotly, she said: 'I don't know what right you have to discuss my private feelings!'

Marco put down his cigar and leaned forward, laying his hands lightly on Joscelin's arms. 'I claim no rights – other than those of a true friend; of a man who finds you fascinating, beautiful and who can see, as Costain does not, how much more is hidden beneath the surface. You are half a woman, Joscelin. You do not yet know yourself.' His voice was gentle, 'I am not asking you for your love – only for a chance to show you to yourself. It disappoints me that you will not marry me – although I understand why you won't. It disappoints me that you will not allow me to become your lover – but that, too, I understand. Nevertheless, I am asking you to give me one, two, three months of your life, that is all. I want you to come to Florence with me.'

Too astonished now to be angry, Joscelin said: 'I think you're quite mad, Marco! I am not unhappy. I have my work and . . .'

'And you are twenty-four years old and know nothing – *nothing* of life!' Marco interrupted. 'You will never know what it is to live until you have fulfilled yourself as a woman. It is not enough to be an artist – excellent one though you are. Which reminds me, I have a present for you.'

He withdrew a parcel from the cushion behind his back. 'I lunched with your publisher, George Matheson, yesterday. When I told him I would be seeing you, he asked me to give you this.'

It was an advance copy of Alan's book. Slowly turning the pristine pages, Joscelin felt tears spring to her eyes. Here, at last, was the fruit of their joint labours – the reward for the years of hard work Alan had put into the text; for the hours of painstaking effort she had spent to do it justice with her paintings.

Marco's expression was enigmatic as he watched her face. 'I know you might have preferred to be given the book by Costain,' he said gently. 'But I wanted the chance to explain that on the strength of this talent, I have a job to offer you in Florence. May I explain?'

Marco outlined his proposition. George Matheson was a friend of his father, who also was a publisher. Proofs of Alan's book had been sent to Signor da Cortona with a view to the sale of translation rights. Marco's father had drawn his son's attention to the illustrations, which pictured not only the wild animals to which Alan referred but also their natural habitat. Signor da Cortona was in the process of amassing data for a special book he wished to print for his wife's sixtieth birthday.

She was a fanatical garden lover and the book was to contain not only the history of the beautiful Villa dei Uccelli in which the family had lived for centuries, but every tiny detail of the garden, in particular the *giardino segreto*.

'All the big houses in Florence have or used to have a secret garden,' Marco explained. 'It is where special herbs and flowers can be grown – sometimes also a trysting place for lovers, or just a place where little children can play in safety. It is my father's idea that every plant in my mother's *giardino segreto* should be painted. Both my father and I think you can do this for us.'

Joscelin's eyes were shining. 'I'd love to!' she said. 'What a beautiful idea! But Marco . . .' her face clouded momentarily '. . . it would take ages and I'd have to find out all the Italian names and . . .'

'One, two, three months – what does time matter? You will be our guest. And once again, I must ask you not to scowl, Joscelin. I give you my word that . . . how do you say it in English? . . . that there are no ropes attached.'

'No *strings* attached!' Joscelin said, her face relaxing into a smile. 'But Marco, that doesn't seem fair . . .'

'I have told you, I am expecting nothing from you but your company. I shall have the greatest pleasure in showing you my city, Firenze. I shall have pleasure in opening your eyes to many beautiful things – perhaps even to your own beauty. *Perchè non prova*, Joscelin? Nothing is to be lost by trying.'

Joscelin let out her breath. Three months in Italy – in Florence, where she could see the great works of art, the architecture, the famous masterpieces of da Vinci, Michelangelo, Botticelli. Florence . . .

'Marco, I'd love to go for many reasons. But . . .'

He smiled, and reaching into his breast pocket he withdrew a white envelope which he put on the table in front of her. 'There are the rail tickets,' he said, 'for two people for the week after next. Have courage, Joscelin! Come with me and I promise that you will not regret it.'

'The Brigadier . . .' Joscelin murmured, but she knew the dog was only an excuse. Her mother and father would care for him. No, it was Alan and only Alan who kept her from accepting this miraculous invitation without further hesitation. She knew he was not happy. For a while after he returned from Portugal he had been too concerned about Lady Costain's elopement to think of much else. Lord Costain had retreated to Strathinver – just as his wife had forecast – and Alan had gone to Scotland to see him, only to return in distress. His father had taken the same attitude to his erring wife as he had done to his brother; her name, like that of Uncle Fergus, was never again to be mentioned. Alan doubted his father would ever return to Rutland Gate.

'It has hit him hard, Joss,' he had said. 'I think in his way, he loved her. I just hope the Mater is happy . . .'

Shortly after Patri's wedding, Alan had gone to the States to see for himself if his mother was content with her new life. He had seemed far happier on his return, for although Walter Hamilton had not fulfilled his promise to divorce his wife he had installed Lady Costain in a luxurious penthouse apartment off Park Avenue and spent the greater part of his time with her.

'He adores her,' Alan confided. 'She looks years younger and she tells me Walter spoils her as the Pater never did. She told me I was to take you to New York to visit her some time. She's very fond of you, Joss.'

There was no similar invitation to Cassy – or if there had been, Alan made no mention of it. Cassy was now out of mourning and her house at Eaton Terrace had become one of the hubs of society. She was intent upon making up for that 'lost' year when she had been unable to enjoy life as she wished. She filled her house with guests and entertained on the most lavish scale. Alan, living on his own at Rutland Gate, was always on the fringe of her circle, her 'unofficial' host, her escort. He had temporarily abandoned work on his second book, and as far as Joscelin could ascertain was involved in the whirl of gaiety in which Cassy now steeped herself. The occasional rows he had with Cassy were solely because she refused for the time being to marry him. Although Alan never spoke of his relationship with Cassy when he was alone with Joscelin, Cassy, as always, confided every detail. It was useless for Joscelin to protest that she did not want to know the private aspects of Cassy's life.

'But I *want* to talk about it, Joss,' Cassy had insisted. 'I know you think I'm not treating Alan very well, so you ought to know that I'm letting him make love to me. It took me ages to persuade him – he was so old-fashioned and kept saying we *must* get married first! Anyway, it keeps him happy because he knows I don't do it with anyone else although . . .' she had giggled, '. . . lots of men want me to. I do sort of belong to Alan, only I don't want to be his wife yet. Sometimes I go to Rutland Gate and sometimes he stays at my house. Have *you* done it yet, Joss?'

Only once, Joscelin had thought. There had been no one since Alan . . . no one to hold her, caress her . . .

'You are trembling, *cara mia*!'

Marco's voice brought her back to the present. His hands imprisoned hers, strong and strangely comforting. Was it possible that some time in the future she might let this man make love to her? Could she bear other arms than Alan's around her? Other lips kissing hers?

'He who hesitates is lost!' Marco said gently, persuasively. 'Come to Italy with me, Joscelin. I promise you will not regret it . . . and see, here . . .' he withdrew from the envelope a third piece of paper . . . 'Your rail ticket home!' His eyes crinkled into laughter. 'That's yours to keep, Joscelin, in case I forget my promise not to seduce you.'

Suddenly, Joscelin laughed. 'Oh, Marco, you are a fool!' she said. 'And I can assure you that I'm not in the least afraid of you!'

Marco stood up. 'Then you should be! I am the wicked playboy, remember? And you are the most intriguing girl I have ever met. It is small wonder I am so crazy about you! To think that I, Marco da Cortona, should be reduced to cajoling a female to going away with me who will not even allow me to kiss her! *Mamma mia*! What have I come to!'

Not only was he kind – immensely so – but he was tremendously flattering, Joscelin thought. And he was an attractive man. Cassy would think her mad to keep him at arm's length. Were it not for Alan . . .

With a quick, indrawn breath, Joscelin stepped forward and, before she could change her mind, she leaned towards him and kissed Marco's cheek.

'That's to thank you,' she said shyly. 'I shall try my very best to do justice to your mother's book; but, Marco, I have no clothes suitable for . . .'

Marco recaptured her hands, holding them tightly in his own as he interrupted her.

'Always the same excuse! You will not need clothes, my lovely Joscelin. It will be one of the pleasures I personally shall receive from our arrangement that you permit me to buy you suitable garments in Florence. And I do not mean those shapeless painting smocks you wear! Like your friend Casilda, I have too much money. If you allow it, I shall dress you as *I* please, so that I shall enjoy looking at you.'

'Then I am to be a kept woman?' Joscelin asked with a smile.

'Not exactly! You will be my own private work of art – something I am bringing to life because I know the result will be beautiful, and I appreciate lovely things. I, for once, shall be the painter and you the finished portrait.'

Now Joscelin laughed, 'But I could never be beautiful, Marco, and you know it. That there is plenty of room for improvement I don't for one moment doubt. But *beautiful* . . .'

'We shall see!' Marco said pleasantly. 'Now, I shall take you out to lunch to celebrate.'

Only then did Joscelin remember the book lying on the table in front of her – the book she and Alan had worked so hard to achieve. It was with him she should be having a celebration lunch. But perhaps he had not yet received a copy? Whatever happened, she must not feel bitter. She had always known for as long as she could remember that she was no more to Alan than a fond sister and colleague. She should try to forget his very existence, and she could begin by enjoying her lunch with her amusing, kind and thoughtful companion.

'Give me five minutes, Marco,' she said, 'and I'll be ready.'

It was as if a new life had already begun.

With a sense of unreality, Joscelin stood beside Marco in the new sacristy in the Medicean Chapel. It was her first day in Florence and Marco had sensed her urgent desire to see at least some of the treasures of the city. With the same solicitude for her wishes and comfort as he had shown on the long rail journey from London, he had announced to his parents before breakfast that he planned a day's sightseeing in Florence itself before showing her the beauties of their home, the Villa dei Uccelli.

Joscelin stared up at the two princes of the Renaissance in the cool, grey-blue and white interior of the sacristy. Proudly aloft in one of the narrow niches over the Medici tombs, Lorenzo the Magnificent sat in contemplation of Dusk and Dawn. In the other, Giuliano, with a baton between massive hands lying across his marvellously sculpted knees, had his small, patrician head averted from both Night and Day.

Marco smiled as he stood staring, not at the sculptures but at Joscelin's rapt face. 'For me, the night is for sleep – and for love, of course!'

Joscelin laughed and said with mock reproof: 'Marco, you have a one-track mind!'

He returned her smile and linked his arm in hers. 'Come, let us go to the Accademia and worship at the statue of David.'

Marco was the perfect host, Joscelin decided, the perfect companion to show her Florence and all its treasures. She liked his family, too. His father, Alfredo da Cortona, was a shorter, grey-haired version of Marco, friendly and highly intellectual. His mother, a chic, attractive woman in her late fifties, had welcomed Joscelin with an easy grace.

It was obvious to Joscelin that Marco was their favourite son. His elder brother, Roberto, was a studious, portly man already showing signs of middle age. He was deeply involved with his father in the publishing business and lived at the Villa dei Uccelli with his parents, his wife Valeria and his four young children.

Valeria was attractive in a dark, Latin way. Like her mother-in-law, she was beautifully dressed and coiffured and very much an influential member of Italian society. According to Marco, she lived a life not dissimilar to that of Lady Costain, her engagement diary filled with cocktail parties, soirées, visits to the theatre and opera and, in the daytime, appointments with her dressmaker or hairdresser.

One morning, a week after Joscelin's arrival, Valeria approached her on the terrace after breakfast. 'I thought I might find you here,' she said, glancing over Joscelin's shoulder to look at the half-finished pencil sketch on her lap.

'The view is so perfect from here,' Joscelin replied, staring across the garden basking in the spring sunshine. From the wide terrace Joscelin could see the stone wall enclosing the *giardino segreto*, its entrance guarded by two stone griffons, each atop a pillar. She had already sketched the proud expressions on their faces, and had made Signora da Cortona laugh when she had suggested that the mythical animals were daring her to trespass in her private garden.

'Marco said this was to be a holiday for you,' Valeria said now. 'He has suggested I should take you with me to the *parrucchiere* – the hairdresser. Would you care to accompany me? He told me it was to be a birthday treat from him.'

Why the fib? Joscelin wondered; but to please Marco, she agreed to do as he had suggested.

'You have very pretty hair,' Valeria said as they drove to

Florence. 'I envy you your fairness. But the cut is not exactly fashionable and I think you will be pleased with what Ugo does with it. He is by far the best *parrucchiere* in Florence.'

'Marco must have seen all the sights so many times already,' Joscelin remarked as they reached the outskirts of the city. 'He's very kind to act as my guide.'

Valeria shot her an amused glance. 'My dear girl, he is obviously head over heels in love with you. The whole family is agog. You are such a change from Marco's usual choice of female companion. You don't mind that I say this?'

Joscelin shook her head. 'Of course not – but I don't think it's true that Marco's in love with me. Besides, he knows I don't feel that way about him.'

Valeria sighed. 'Poor Marco! But for once it will be good for him not to make his usual easy conquest. Perhaps that is partly why you fascinate him!'

It was the start of a new friendship for Joscelin, for although she was at least ten years younger than the Italian woman, Valeria appeared to enjoy her company and to share Marco's interest in what she called Joscelin's transformation.

A delighted Ugo trimmed her long hair tight into the nape of her neck, leaving soft curls over her forehead. The effect was both classic and feminine.

'*La signorina* has perfect nose and forehead,' said the approving *parrucchiere*. '*Affascinante!*'

'He says you are ravishing!' Valeria translated with a laugh as she led Joscelin out of the salon. 'And I agree with him. Now I will take you to my favourite Florentine fashion house. They have models from the Fortuny collection and it would be my pleasure to choose for you something quite new and different. Will you allow me – for your birthday, of course?'

'It is beginning to feel as if it really is my birthday,' Joscelin said, admitting to Valeria that the pretence was Marco's way of concealing her own lack of money.

'Your honesty is as charming as your enthusiasm for every-thing!' Valeria said as the chauffeur drove them along the

Via della Scala. 'My mother-in-law was enchanted because you told her your bedroom was like a palace and a museum rolled into one.'

Joscelin nodded. 'It's true! Such beautiful furniture . . . and the ceiling like a Tiepolo painting. And I would expect to find such lovely pieces of furniture in one of the museums Marco has taken me to. It must be quite wonderful for you to live there.'

The older woman shrugged. 'I suppose one takes it all for granted. That is why we are all so happy to have you staying with us, Joscelin. You make us see with fresh eyes . . . and there is no doubt you do have an eye for beauty.'

But it was Valeria whose eye detected the perfect choice of clothes for Joscelin: a deeply pleated skirt and a loose crêpe de Chine blouse to wear under a simple collarless jacket; and a fantastically expensive wine-coloured evening gown which Joscelin felt unable to accept.

But Valeria insisted; 'Marco's mamma is giving a reception tomorrow and you must have something appropriate to wear. I was not supposed to tell you it is in your honour, Joscelin!'

With the same kindly determination Valeria sought out matching shoes, gloves, a pochette and a delicate chiffon scarf which, she told Joscelin, she must wear wound round her throat with the ends thrown back over her shoulders.

'As for jewellery,' she announced on the journey back to the Villa dei Uccelli, 'I shall lend you something of mine.'

But next morning, as Joscelin sat painting in the *giardino segreto*, Marco suddenly appeared behind her. He put a hand over her eyes and deposited something in her lap. 'It is a small birthday present to accompany your new evening frock!'

She turned to look up at his smiling face, her own serious as she said: 'Marco, you know very well it is not my birthday – and I cannot accept . . .'

'I have gone to a great deal of trouble to find the right colour,' he said persuasively. 'Valeria gave me a little piece of fabric to match, and it has taken me most of the morning to find something of such little value that you cannot refuse to accept it from me. The stones are only garnets! But the colour, I think, is just right.'

Joscelin held up the necklace and saw at once that the colour was perfect. But as to its value . . . 'Marco, it's lovely, but . . .'

'But it is not your birthday and you cannot take it from me!' he finished for her. He seated himself beside her on the marble bench and, looking directly into her eyes, he said: 'I know it is not your birthday, *cara mia* – but is it not as good as any other day to start to live? You have existed before, it is true, but have you really *lived*? Today I think you are alive . . . happy . . . a little excited, too, at the prospect of wearing your new gown.' He smiled. 'Valeria tells me you look beautiful in it, but it lacks this final touch. I beg you take the necklace, Joscelin – to please Valeria if you do not wish to please me.'

'But I do, Marco!' Joscelin cried impulsively. 'You are so kind – your whole family. I feel I am living in a dream – this beautiful house, Florence, the sun, the flowers, the colours . . .'

'And you are happy!' Marco said quietly. 'I no longer see that wistful look. Do you know, my Joscelin, that you have the most beautiful eyes I have ever seen?'

Joscelin smiled. 'I would like to believe your outrageous compliments, Marco, but honestly, I can't. Nevertheless, I thank you for all the nice things you say and, indeed, for this . . .' She held up the necklace. 'I will do as you suggest and pretend just for today that it really is my birthday, but it would be unfair of me to allow this little game of "let's pretend" to go too far. I may feel like Cinderella at tonight's reception, but I am not searching for a Prince Charming.'

Marco took her hand and raised it to his lips.

'*La speranza è sorella della disperazione!*' he said smiling. 'An Italian proverb, Joscelin, which states that hope is the sister of despair. Whilst your words would have me despair, I am at liberty to hope.'

Joscelin laughed. 'You are incorrigible, Marco, but I am

truly very fond of you. Cassy always said I was no good at flirting and I'm afraid it's true, but I do enjoy it when you flirt with me. You make me feel – special!'

'Then I have all the more reason for *la speranza*!' Marco said lightly. 'And now I shall leave you to continue your work in peace.'

Perhaps this was a kind of birthday, Joscelin thought. Tonight, in her fabulous new frock, she would come of age – become a chic, sophisticated, amusing, interesting woman, and maybe . . . just maybe . . . beautiful.

Valeria came to her bedroom whilst she was putting the finishing touches to her hair. She stood surveying Joscelin's reflection in the mirror and then said: '*Perfetto*, Joscelin. *Molto bella!*'

The bodice of the dark satin fell in a shimmering sheath from tiny narrow shoulder-straps to Joscelin's hips. There it was caught to one side by a chiffon sash of the same wine red, below which the skirt billowed out in a cascade of colour. Marco's garnets glowed at her throat and her hair shone in the soft bedroom light as she turned to look anxiously at Valeria.

'Marco was right – you *are* beautiful!' Valeria said. 'It isn't just the dress or your hair, you are feeling different, are you not?'

Joscelin smiled. 'I *am* excited,' she admitted. 'But I'm worried too, Valeria. I have never had a reception entirely in my honour. Suppose I let your mother-in-law down? I speak so little Italian and . . .'

'You are going to be a great success, I promise,' Valeria interrupted. 'Men will be at your feet and the women will be curious and envious. Now put a little mascara on your lashes. It helps to make your eyes look even bigger. And just a little brush of colour on your cheeks . . .'

Joscelin felt memory stirring in her; Cassy telling her to borrow her lipstick, Cassy saying: 'You could be really pretty if you tried!' Well, she had tried tonight and, if Valeria was to be believed, she had succeeded. Would Marco think so?

'Joscelin, did you not hear me? It's getting late. We should go downstairs now. Here – your gloves.'

There was no sign of Marco as the Signor and Signora da Cartona stood with Roberto to receive their guests. Each new arrival was presented formally to Joscelin. There were so many that she soon gave up trying to remember all their names. This, she thought, was proving almost as much of an ordeal as being presented at Court!

One woman, tall and elegant, in a blue and gold lamé dress, stared at Joscelin after their introduction. She had a small, grey-haired man at her side – Conte dell someone, Joscelin recalled – who presumably was her husband. The Contessa was Valeria's age – a contemporary of Marco's. Joscelin wondered why the stranger was continuing to stare almost rudely at her. Suddenly she knew. From the big *salotto* in which an orchestra waited to entertain the guests, Marco appeared. The smile with which she was about to greet him only half reached her lips as he stopped in front of the Contessa and kissed her outstretched hand.

Beside her, Valeria whispered: 'The Contessa Brigida dell'Anselmo was Marco's mistress for years. She hoped he'd marry her but had to make do with poor Conte dell'Anselmo instead! My mother-in-law hates her, but she had to invite her because her husband is one of my father's best customers. He collects rare books.'

Joscelin only just had time to digest this piece of gossip before Marco approached her.

'You must forgive me for failing to be at your side this past ten minutes, Joscelin. The Fraschini broke down on the way from Firenze and neither Frederigo nor I could get it started again.' He kissed her hand, then his mother on both cheeks, and smiled at Valeria and his father. 'I think most of our guests must be here, Mamma. Is it permitted to absent ourselves? I would like a glass of champagne!'

The Signora da Cortona looked at him fondly, patted his cheek with her fan and told him he might take Joscelin away. 'And don't monopolize her,' she said with mock severity.

Marco put his hand gently behind Joscelin's elbow and led her towards a less crowded part of the *salotto*. 'Now at last I can tell you that you are unquestionably the most beautiful woman here tonight,' he said. 'You surpass all my expectations, Joscelin.'

'You're exaggerating as always, Marco,' Joscelin replied, unable to keep a slight edge from her voice. 'I would not expect to compete with the Contessa dell'Anselmo. She is truly lovely.'

'Oh, Brigida!' Marco said, taking two glasses of champagne from a passing waiter. 'Yes, I suppose she is. But it is skin-deep, I do assure you. She is both devious and dangerous, although she looks like a Madonna.' He gave Joscelin a searching glance. 'May I inquire why this interest in Brigida?'

Suddenly light-hearted again, Joscelin laughed, 'Oh, just something Valeria told me . . .' she said with deliberate vagueness.

'You have not been working too hard today?' Marco asked, leading her to a sofa where the noise of the orchestra did not intrude.

'I *was* working – if you can call anything work that I do in your mother's delightful garden,' Joscelin replied truthfully. 'It is so peaceful there, Marco. But it is not easy to put on paper – the light is always changing and the colours change too. I think there's magic there!'

Marco smiled. 'As children we believed Mamma's story that it was there the angels played their harps! Many times I stood at my bedroom window looking down in the moonlight, hoping to see one, but I was always disappointed. Perhaps tonight you will come there with me, Joscelin – then I shall realize my childhood dream.'

Joscelin felt momentarily uncomfortable, yet she was not untouched. 'I will draw a picture for you, Marco – a little boy staring down into the *giardino segreto*, and angels sitting round the fountain in the moonlight.'

'And where shall I find you in this picture?' he asked softly.

'Oh, I shall be standing, a stranger looking in, wanting to be part of the magic, but hesitating to take that one step forward.'

She had not meant to speak so revealingly, but the words were impulsive and, once said, she saw their symbolism. For twenty-four years of her life she had stood on the outside, looking in, afraid to take that vital step for fear . . . for fear of being hurt? Yet no one had ever hurt her – at least, not consciously. Moreover, she *had* once risked that dangerous step forward on the night she had gone to Alan's room.

'I will not permit it,' Marco said suddenly, sharply, beside her. 'You are looking sad, *cara mia*, and this is an evening for rejoicing. What must I do to make you smile? Tell you that I am hopelessly crazy about you? That always makes you laugh!'

'Oh, Marco!' Joscelin protested, smiling despite herself. 'Honestly, I wouldn't think it funny if you really were. Anyway, I *am* happy.'

Marco sighed. 'I suppose we shall have to forgo this tête-à-tête until later and circulate. Come, Joscelin, we shall go and say the right things to all our friends. Then, hopefully, we shall eat and afterwards dance. I cannot wait to hold you in my arms. The mere thought excites me!'

Later that night, after the sumptuous cold buffet had been cleared away and dancing had begun in the *salotto grande* to a small jazz band, Joscelin saw Marco dancing with the lovely Contessa Brigida. They were performing the charleston – a modern dance Joscelin had never mastered – and were doing so with remarkable agility.

Other couples halted to watch and Roberto, who had been sitting out the dance with Joscelin, said grudgingly: 'One has to admit that Brigida knows all the steps – and the actions, although it surprises me that my parents permit such dances in our home.'

Joscelin's eyes followed Marco's agile figure as he matched his partner's gyrations. Brigida's face was flushed and Marco was smiling as she twirled a long row of beads in a provocative way. Joscelin felt a sudden stab of irritation, but she was not sure if it were caused by the seductive glances of the Italian woman, by Marco or by her own attitude. It was all very well to sit there pretending to herself that she did not wish to learn the charleston. The truth was she was envious of people like Brigida dell'Anselmo who could be so happily extrovert in public, so uncaring of what others thought.

A waiter passed by with a tray of glasses and, although aware that she had already had enough to drink, she accepted the champagne Roberto held out to her. Perhaps she needed to get a little tipsy; lose some of her inhibitions. Marco must think her so dull, so boring when he had women like the voluptuous Brigida dell'Anselmo to amuse him.

Joscelin emptied her glass and felt a curious giddiness which changed her mood. Her critical outlook gave way to one of nonchalance. Why should she care what others thought? Did? Why should she care what she herself did? One had only to live in a place like Florence, steeped in the antiquities of the past, to realize how fleeting was the lifespan of a human being compared with the enduring qualities of the great works of art.

'*Scusi*, Roberto, I wish to have this dance with Joscelin!'

Marco had suddenly appeared beside them. The music had changed, she realized, as he put down her empty glass and propelled her towards the dance floor. The band was now playing a soft, romantic tango.

'And don't tell me you cannot tango,' Marco pre-empted her as he put his arm around her waist. 'Just relax, *cara mia*, and allow your body to follow mine.'

He danced beautifully, perfectly in time to the music and Joscelin found no difficulty in responding to the haunting tempo. Marco's arm held her tightly against him, his cheek only a breath away from hers. Sometimes their thighs touched and the pressure of his hand on hers intensified. She was aware of the warmth of his body; of the faint smell of cigar smoke on his lapel; aware, too, of the total masculinity of this man, and his desire for her.

For a fraction of a second she stiffened, every instinct alert to the fact that, although they were dancing in public, Marco was making love to her, with his eyes, with his body . . .

'Joscelin!' he whispered, the calling of her name both a question and a caress. '*Ti amo, ti amo!*'

So he loved her – or thought that he did! As for herself, all she knew was that she wanted him to hold her even closer. She could feel his thigh pressed against hers and her own legs trembling. A strange kind of fluidity spread through her so that she felt herself melting against him, almost leaning on him for support.

Their hurried breathing seemed to become synchronised and she heard Marco's voice, deep, tenderly teasing as he murmured: 'You are blushing, my adorable Joscelin . . . my beautiful girl! *Non sia così timida.* You must not be shy with me.'

The champagne, the music, Marco's voice . . . all were clouding her thoughts. 'You promised you would not try to seduce me. Remember, Marco? No ropes attached, you said!'

But her reprimand did not even convince her, and she heard Marco's soft laugh.

'I am not trying, *amore mio*. Hopefully, I *am* seducing you. But not, I think, against your will?'

Joscelin did not answer his question but, seeing her eyes close, feeling her soft silky hair against his cheek, Marco smiled. He knew then that it was only a matter of time before they would make love.

CHAPTER TWENTY

April 1929

'For goodness sake, Polly, stop fussing. Anyone would think
you'd never been abroad before!'

Cassy's temper was sharper than she had intended, but
despite the casual air she wished to assume, she was nervous.
Her maid's unspoken disapproval of this adventure added to
her unease. Not that she cared one whit what Polly thought,
she told herself as she watched the bellhop bring her luggage
into her suite at the Hotel George V, and reached in her purse
for a tip. She had been mistaken ever to confide in Polly, but
she had needed a confidante . . . and with Joscelin irritatingly
absent in Florence she had impulsively shown her maid the
letter from Milton Fleming.

'The American gentleman who took you to the bullfight in
Spain!' Polly remembered instantly. That little episode had
been one of the rare occasions when the girl was eager to
participate in one of Cassy's unconventional escapades! Cassy
did not understand the distinctions Polly now made between
her conceptions of 'right' and 'wrong'. Why should it be wrong
to go to Paris to meet Milton?

'After all, Polly, it's only a flirtation, for heaven's sake! All
he suggests is dinner and a night at the Comédie Française,
and I'm bored to tears with London.' But she had failed to
convince Polly that she was prepared to travel all the way
to Paris just for dinner and an evening at the theatre with a
man she did not like!

Now, as the girl began to unpack, Cassy walked restlessly
to the window and stared down into the Champs Elysées. She

was crazy to come here, she told herself. It was over a year since she had last seen the American. How impudent of him to assume that she would cancel whatever engagements she had and take the trouble to come to Paris for a 'date' with him – as he put it! His invitation had read: 'I saw a picture of you in *The Tatler* last week and it reminded me of our last encounter. I shall be in Paris on an assignment on 27th, 28th, 29th and if it would amuse you to join me there, I shall be more than happy to entertain you. Please telegraph me . . .' He had given an address in Geneva, and in a postscript to his letter added that he would be staying at the George V.

Her first reaction had been one of anger at his presumptions; her second had been curiosity. *Why* did he want to see her again?

She had told Alan she was going to spend the weekend with Jimmy's father in Leicestershire, and now here she was in Paris. In an hour's time, Milton Fleming was meeting her in the foyer before taking her to lunch.

'I'll wear the Molyneux dress and jacket, Polly,' she said. 'And for heaven's sake stop frowning! All I'm going to do is lunch with a friend.'

'Yes, Milady!'

Noticing that the frown was still there, Cassy said sharply: 'I'm beginning to wish I'd left you at home, Polly.'

The girl made a half-hearted attempt to look more cheerful, but she was devoted to young Mr Costain and could not think why her mistress was delaying marriage to him when he was obviously wanting to do things 'right'. Polly disapproved of Cassy staying all night when she visited at Rutland Gate; and she objected to the winks and nudges of the downstairs staff whenever Mr Costain stayed overnight at Eaton Terrace. It wasn't fair to Mr Costain. There'd been enough talk about his mother and *her* goings on. Polly was silent as she helped her mistress to change her clothes.

Cassy, too, had little to say. She was feeling surprisingly nervous – yet there was an element of excitement, too. The

American was very much outside her sphere of experience. Were he in his twenties like Alan or Monty, she would know exactly how to conduct herself. But he was forty – maybe older – and a foreigner, and her memory of him was of a ruthless, self-assured man to whom women were no mystery. Perhaps, she thought, this was why she had been tempted to meet him. At least she looked stunning enough to turn any man's head, she decided, surveying her reflection with satisfaction. Her new Molyneux dress and jacket were made of lime-coloured panne velvet, and the jacket was trimmed with monkey fur at the elbows and around its sloping hem.

She recognized Milton instantly as she left the lift and walked out into the foyer. There was no mistaking the dark brown hair and beard; the sheer size of the man. There was a smile on his face as he stepped forward to greet her.

'You surprise me with your punctuality,' he said, as if they had last met only the day before. 'I had expected to wait a lot longer.' He tucked his arm through hers. 'Shall we go through to the bar?'

Cassy was annoyed. She had not noted the time, and it occurred to her that he must be thinking her very eager to see him again – the last impression she wished to give.

'Until midday yesterday, I thought I would have to send you a telegram to say I couldn't come to Paris after all,' she said as he led her to a quiet table in a corner of the room. 'I had visitors staying who . . .'

'But you came – and that's what is important,' he broke in as if he had no interest in any difficulties she might have had to get there. 'If I may say so, honey, that photograph in *The Tatler* did not do you justice. You have grown into a singularly beautiful woman.'

Cassy shrugged, unsure whether to be pleased with the compliment or annoyed by its implications. 'I have not "grown into" anything!' she retorted. 'It's only a year since we last met, you know.'

He smiled lazily. 'Ah, but a year as a merry widow can

cause many changes,' he said. 'According to the tabloids you are now "One of London's most popular and beautiful young society hostesses". Obviously you have been enjoying your freedom and making the most of it, Casilda.'

He stopped a waiter and ordered cocktails with easy authority.

Cassy took out her long amber holder and immediately her companion offered her a cigarette and lit it. She became aware of the half-amused smile on his face. Her chin lifted. 'You said in your letter that you were on an assignment,' she said. 'What is that supposed to mean?'

He shrugged. 'I'd forgotten that you did not know; I'm now a foreign correspondent for *The Globe*. I'm covering the French elections. When I finished my book boredom set in. I thought life as a journalist might add a little excitement. What I'd really like is to be a war correspondent, but I need a war to start somewhere to realize that particular dream.'

'*War!* That's all men seem to think about!' Cassy said scornfully. 'That and politics.'

'Then let us talk about you,' Milton Fleming said easily. 'I sure am pleased to be sitting here with you, and asking myself if that charming little mole I recall was on your left shoulder or your right.'

To her annoyance, Cassy blushed. 'I suppose you were acting Peeping Tom when I changed my clothes at your house in Sevilla. You had no right . . .'

'Come now, Cassy, I had every right. On that occasion I was being the audience and you were putting on an act for me . . . don't try to deny it, my dear. I've said this to you before – there must be no pretence between us. You can pull the wool over the eyes of the other men in your life, but you would be wasting your time trying it on me. There is a very strong bond between us. We both know what we want and we go out and get it. Well, honey, I want you; and I'm pretty sure you want me.'

Cassy gasped, but quickly recovered her composure. 'Then

I fear you will be disappointed. I don't have the slightest intention of allowing you to make love to me. For one thing, I don't find you attractive and for another, I think lovemaking is thoroughly overrated.'

Her companion seemed not in the least shocked by her bluntness. 'As to the first half of your statement, I frankly don't believe it,' he said calmly. 'If you had not felt attracted to me you would not have come to Paris. As to not enjoying the act of love, that is simply because you have not so far tried it with the right partner. Young men are usually inexperienced. To enjoy a woman, one must know how to please her, how to give *her* enjoyment. It is a fallacy that the female sex cannot get pleasure from sexual encounters.'

Cassy knew that she ought to put an end to this outrageous conversation immediately, but he had excited her interest. Was it true that young men were bad lovers because they were ignorant? *Would* it be different with someone who was older, experienced? With *this* man?

'If you have finished your drink, I suggest we go and have lunch,' he said quietly, his change of subject so abrupt she felt strangely frustrated; but she allowed him to lead her to the dining room.

Throughout the meal he talked impersonally, inquiring about her family and listening whilst she told him of Tía Pamela's elopement.

'A woman of courage!' he commented, refilling Cassy's wineglass. 'It is to be hoped that your aunt's lover has a tight grip on his resources. America is rushing headlong into a financial depression and I suspect that a great many people may get their fingers burned. But perhaps your aunt has private means.'

Once again, Cassy was shocked. A gentleman should not mention money in a lady's presence. Was he always so unconventional?

Her companion broke in on her thoughts. 'I have tickets for the Comédie Française for tonight. Afterwards, if it would amuse you, I will take you to the Folies-Bergère; I imagine your education has not so far included such a place? But in the meanwhile, we must not waste such time as we have together making idle conversation. I have a suite on the fourth floor. I suggest we now take coffee there.'

'In your suite?' Cassy echoed stupidly – and immediately regretted her remark. She was not some silly girl afraid to go to a man's rooms.

He was smiling.

'By all means, if that's what you wish,' she said nonchalantly.

She had the uncomfortable feeling that he was not deceived by her feigned indifference, but he said nothing as he signed the bill and led her to the iron-grilled lift in the foyer.

Milton Fleming's suite on the floor above hers was almost identical to her own, elegantly furnished and comfortable. The door into the big double-bedded room was ajar and Milton nodded casually in its direction, saying: 'The *salle de bain* is adjoining, honey.'

As Cassy went silently through to the bathroom to powder her nose and remove her hat, she found herself thinking that, whilst this was the first time she had ever gone to a man's room in mid-afternoon, it was certainly not the first time Milton had invited a woman to such a *tête-à-tête*. She hoped her nervousness was not too obvious and was pleased to see that her cheeks were flushed, and the colour was becoming. Although she was far from sure she *liked* him, she had to admit that she found him attractive and would not mind one little bit were he to kiss her . . .

He stood up as she walked back into the *salón*. There was no smile on his face as he approached her. Cassy's heart missed several beats as, silently, he took her in his arms. His kiss was long, searching and at the same time passionately demanding. It left her breathless and gasping. Wild thoughts raced through her mind. Never had Jimmy or Alan kissed her in such a way;

never before had her heart raced so uncontrollably; never had a kiss left her so confused. She wanted him to release her, and yet when he did so, she wanted instantly for him to kiss her again. Her heart was pounding and she felt an unfamiliar trembling in her legs. She stood, her lips parted, her breath coming in little gasps, watching his eyes travel slowly, sensuously, over her body. His glance was like a caress.

'Milton, please . . .' she stammered, her voice sounding faint and tremulous. 'I don't want . . . I didn't mean to give you the impression that I was willing . . . really, I *mean* it, Milton. I don't want . . .'

His expression was immensely self-assured as, in his slow drawl, he broke in: 'Ah, but you *do* want, my Casilda. And after I have satisfied that need, you will admit that this is why you accepted my invitation. You want me to make love to you as surely as I want to do so.'

It was a statement, not a question, and he lifted her effortlessly into his arms and carried her into the bedroom. As she fell back on the bed, he bent over her and slowly, without haste or urgency, kissed her again. This time his hands began with the same unhurried movements to caress her body. They lingered on her breasts, feeling their outline through the soft fabric of her frock.

Cassy struggled with the conflicting sensations he aroused as his tongue searched her mouth, and his fingers stroked her nipples. They seemed to have swollen into life, developing a need of their own to feel the soft touch of his fingertips.

Milton straightened up and, as he stood staring down at her, his shadow came between her and the sunlight. 'Stay there!' he ordered. 'I'll draw the curtains.'

I ought to go now, before it's too late, Cassy thought. But her body felt languid, hot, feverish and without the power of movement. She was not even certain if her legs would support her. I've had too much wine, she told herself, her head turning towards the bathroom door through which the American was now disappearing.

When Milton returned to the bedside a few moments later he was wearing only a thin silk dressing-gown, tied loosely at the waist. His expression as he looked down at her was unfathomable. He sat on the edge of the bed and began casually and methodically to undress her. Cassy was overcome with embarrassment. At home with Jimmy she had tried always to undress in private with Polly to assist her, and to be in her night attire when he had come to her room. Here now was this unfamiliar stranger unhooking her brassiere as if he were accustomed to divesting a female of her underwear. But as his hands cupped her bared breasts, she forgot her embarrassment and quickly wrapped her arms around his neck, drawing his mouth down to hers.

Her body arched towards him. Somehow, between kisses and caresses, he divested her of all her clothes, and she lay naked beneath his gaze. She felt a fierce, unfamiliar pride in her body; in the golden sheen of her skin; the firm fullness of her breasts; the curve of her hips and stomach. Suddenly, she wanted this man to be totally overcome by her beauty, so inflamed by her desirability that he lost all control. She wanted him to beg her for release from his torment. He, like all her other admirers, must become her slave . . .

But Cassy's imagined scenario was not to be enacted as she wished. Although Milton's breathing had quickened and there was a look in his eyes which she recognized as one of intense desire, he remained completely in control of himself – *and of her*. He continued his caresses and now he began to kiss her, not on the mouth, but on all the secret erotic areas of her body as if he knew perfectly well what would most excite her. Her body strained towards him, towards that butterfly touch which tantalized, aroused, but never satisfied her longing.

'Oh, please, please . . .' she heard her voice crying out as if it did not belong to her. 'Please, Milton, *please* . . .'

She could not have said how long it was before at last he knelt above her. He forced one leg between her knees, separating them, exposing yet even more of her body to his eyes.

His dressing-gown was discarded and she found herself staring at his nude, male form in horrified fascination. His chest, stomach and legs were lightly covered in brown hair . . . and she hated hirsute men, she thought wildly. She hated, too, the sight of his unconcealed erection surrounded by the same dark brown hair. It looked immensely large, immensely threatening; and yet she could see her hand . . . it had to be hers . . . moving against her will towards him, reaching out to touch, to hold. How white her fingers looked, curled round it! How horrible a thing it was – as if it had a life of its own!

She closed her eyes against it but she could not let go. As she felt his urgent hands between her thighs, involuntarily her grip tightened and she felt herself trying to draw this pulsating, heavy male body closer.

She became aware of a burning need in her lower abdomen. Momentarily he ceased his tantalizing caresses and she cried aloud in frustration; but then, as his tongue stroked her fiercely jutting nipples, she heard herself moaning in pleasure. She could not be certain of the exact moment he went into her. Her fingers dug into his back, urging him deeper, deeper until there seemed no divisions between them. The rhythm of his movements quickened, intensified, but he allowed his own tumultuous conclusion only when he had heard Cassy's wild cry of pleasure as, for the first time in her life, she experienced total fulfilment as a woman.

It was several moments before he withdrew, rolling over on his side and reaching for a packet of cigarettes. He blew a cloud of smoke into the air, and looked lazily at Cassy's flushed face.

'Okay, honey?' he inquired casually.

It was not what she had expected him to say. She had been waiting to be told how wonderful she was; how beautiful; how exciting.

Hurriedly she pulled the sheet up to her chin, covering their nudity, unable to believe that she had exposed herself so shamelessly. Her body felt limp and exhausted, yet the memory of the thrill she had experienced stirred somewhere deep inside her, reawakening desire. It had all been over too quickly, she thought. She wanted to be lost once more in that unbelievable transcendent sensation.

As if he, too, was remembering, the man beside her said softly: 'It will be better still next time! I see I have a lot to teach you, Casilda.'

Suddenly Cassy felt deeply angry. He was patronizing her again when he should be adoring her. Her mouth turned down at the corners. 'There may not be a "next time",' she said. 'It depends how I feel. I may not be in the mood and . . .'

His face broadened into a smile but he was serious as he interrupted her: 'I've told you before, Casilda, don't pretend with me. I know you enjoyed it. Women do try to fake pleasure on occasions but I am not interested in such niceties. And not even you could pretend the satisfaction you felt just now. Was that the first time you felt pleasure?'

Cassy's emotions were in turmoil. She was a little frightened by the knowledge of this man, who knew her so slightly, yet seemed to know her so well; frightened by the thought that he, not she, was in control. But there was, too, a certain amount of relief in being with a man who understood her needs . . . needs she had never really been aware of before. Harder to accept was the knowledge that he was also right in his belief that she would want him to make love to her again. If he were now to lean over and touch her . . .

Cassy's mouth tightened. She reached for his dressing-gown, and hurriedly pushed her arms into the sleeves.

'My maid will be wondering where I am,' she said in a small, cold voice. 'I must get dressed at once and go back to my room.'

Milton lay back against the pillows, one arm behind his head, and drew on his cigarette. 'That suits me, honey. I have several letters to write. I'll meet you for cocktails in the bar at around six.'

Having expected him to try to detain her, Cassy was far

from pleased by his reaction. She got out of bed and marched towards the bathroom in the over-long dressing-gown, collecting her discarded clothes on the way. She was furiously angry. This rude, ill-mannered man was not even going to get up to open the door for her! He was not even pretending that he regretted her decision to leave him so precipitately.

As she fought to fasten the tiny buttons at the back of her frock, her hands trembled and her indignation mounted. Perhaps, she thought, she would not keep their date for the Comédie Française; not meet him at the bar. She might even catch the night ferry back to England! There were other men in the world beside Milton Fleming.

Cassy did not need to see the many opera glasses pointing in her direction, nor to notice the interested glances of the men as she took her place beside Milton in their box at the Comédie Française, to be certain of the effect she was creating. Partly to give herself confidence, but secretly in the hope that she would impress her escort, she had chosen her most elaborate evening gown, a Paquin model in white satin, low-backed and dipping to a petal-pointed hem. A white fox fur wrap was draped casually over the creamy gold of her bared shoulders. Round her throat were the Ladbury diamonds, and a *ferronnière* decorated her dark, shining hair, which had been washed and waved that evening by the hotel coiffeur. Whilst being pampered and cosseted by the suave young man who had attended her, her angry mood had changed. She had allowed herself to dwell on the more satisfying aspects of that extraordinary hour of intimacy spent with her new lover.

Momentarily honest with herself, she admitted that the element of danger had lent the occasion an added excitement. Under the hair dryer, she had closed her eyes and allowed herself to consider how intensely satisfying it would be to have this man at her feet. It would be victory, indeed! Some of the most powerful men in history had been slaves to women, and she could envisage Milton becoming increasingly dependent upon her favours once she learned what it was about herself that fascinated him.

After the opera, he took her to supper. Although seemingly amused by her bright, inconsequential chatter, he made no attempt to touch her, nor did he mention the afternoon. It was as if they had never been lovers and she felt a return of her irritation with him. He was the one who had said *she* should not pretend, and yet he was choosing to act as if nothing at all had happened to change their relationship! She was not even certain that he would invite her to his room when they returned to the hotel. She had instructed Polly not to wait up for her and not to bring breakfast in the morning until she rang for it. Now it looked as if such precautions were irrelevant.

In the taxi taking them back to the George V, she became acutely conscious of Milton's thigh pressing against her own. He seemed unaware of the contact, and she tried to slow her hurried breathing as her nerve ends sprang to life. She could feel her breasts throbbing and a wet warmth in her groin. She wanted him as she had never before wanted a man, but would rather die than let him know it. When they reached the foyer she would tell him she was tired, and . . .

'I ordered a bottle of champagne to be put in my room. I thought we'd share a nightcap, my dear!'

His voice – that slow, lazy drawl – assaulted her ears. Before she could refute the suggestion, he spoke again. 'And then to bed, I think. I've been wanting to make love to you this past hour.'

At last she found her voice. 'Do you always take people for granted, Milton? I would have expected a man of your age and experience to show a little more finesse!'

Annoyingly, he laughed. What was there about that soft, derisory laughter that seemed to hit her in the very pit of her stomach?

'I pride myself that I know when finesse is desirable and

when it is unnecessary. You have only to look at your own face, honey, to see that you are more than ready for what I have to give you. Desire, my dear, is not easily concealed.'

Idly, casually, he lent over and touched one of her breasts. There was no way in which Cassy could control the little gasp that burst from her lips. Involuntarily she leaned closer to him. Again without haste, he kissed her.

A sudden wave of hatred mingled with a fierce hunger surged through her. She clenched her teeth against his probing tongue, and when he tried again to force his way in she bit down upon his lower lip. With a slight shrug, he drew back and dabbed at his mouth with a silk handkerchief.

'So the tigress has been aroused!' he said nonchalantly. 'I can expect a little more participation tonight.'

He caught the hand she had raised to hit him, and turning the palm uppermost, ran the tip of his tongue from the base to one fingertip, then drew her hand down to his lap. Her cheeks scarlet with embarrassment at the shamelessness of his action, Cassy could nevertheless feel the hardness of him and struggled against the desire to grip him. Only the halting of the cab outside their hotel saved her from giving in to her need. As if nothing untoward had been happening, Milton paid the driver and helped her out of the taxi. The uniformed doorman hurried towards them with a welcoming *'Bonsoir, M'sieur, M'dame!'* and ushered them through the revolving doors into the brightly lit foyer.

Now, Cassy thought, was the moment when she must make it clear she was going to her own room. She pushed past Milton, who had already asked the *concierge* for his key, and demanded her own.

Placing his hand beneath her elbow, Milton led her towards the lift.

'I presume you do prefer the privacy of my room to yours,' he said as the bellboy drew back the iron gate. 'Since you were thoughtless enough to bring your maid, we don't really have an alternative, do we? But you won't want to be seen leaving my rooms after breakfast in that pretty gown, so be sure to bring with you something to wear in the morning. I'll see you *chez moi* in a few minutes, my dear. Oh, and Casilda – bring your own dressing-gown, will you? Mine now smells of your scent. I'd prefer you did not wear it again!'

Cassy sat down on her bed, wishing she had not dismissed Polly. If the girl were there, she could not go off to Milton Fleming's room, however much she was tempted to do so. She drew a deep breath.

Restlessly, she got off the bed and went to her dressing-table. Her cheeks were aflame. Her lips were trembling. Remembering how savagely she had bitten him, she hoped now that she had hurt him. He was hateful – and crude. Love was supposed to be romantic, poetic, beautiful.

Slowly, Cassy drew down the shoulder-straps of her frock and allowed the bodice to slide down to her waist. Unclasping the diamond necklace, she felt her hands, surprisingly cool, around her neck. Involuntarily, her eyes closed as she remembered Milton kissing her, his lips travelling from her earlobe down to the hollows at the base of her throat and then slowly, tantalizingly, down to her breasts.

Her arms clenched together in her lap, and for a moment she rocked to and fro, huddled over them as the yearning hollow inside her throbbed with an unbearable longing. If she did not now go to Milton's rooms he would be angry, and might never want to see her again; then she would never again feel that indescribable sensation he had evoked. Would any man ever again make love to her in such a way? Would she ever want a lover as totally as she wanted this man?

Just once more, she whispered. If this time it isn't so magical, so beautiful, it will be easy to refuse him next time . . .

When Cassy woke next morning, all pretence, all self-deception was gone. As she ran her hand lovingly over Milton Fleming's beard, she confessed how nearly she had decided not to come to his suite; how angry she had been with him for taking her for granted.

'I wasn't sure it would happen to me again. Yet I suppose I must have known somehow . . .' She smiled as she leaned over to kiss him. 'What I didn't know was that there would be something more. You've taught me so much, Milton. I had no idea that men and women could give each other such pleasure! That it could ever mean anything to me . . .'

'But *I* knew!' he broke in. 'The moment I set eyes on you I guessed that you had remained unawakened. I thought then how much I would enjoy being the man to put a match to the fuse.'

Cassy smiled, content to lie lazily beside her lover exchanging such confidences. She pouted. 'But you ignored me that day . . . in your house. I think I wanted you to make love to me then, or at least to try!'

He shrugged. 'The time was not right, honey. Besides, I don't get much pleasure from adolescent snatches of passion. One cannot hurry lovemaking and expect it to be fully rewarding.'

Cassy frowned. 'That sounds so . . . so preconceived!' she protested. 'I suppose you've made love to hundreds of women, and that's the way you've learned how to do it.'

Again, he shrugged. 'I don't deny it. I am ten years older than you, Casilda, and I have made the most of my opportunities. I don't consider it unreasonable.'

Cassy sighed. 'Not *unreasonable*, but not very romantic! What happened between us last night . . .' her voice faltered, became uncertain, '. . . and this morning . . . it was special for you too, wasn't it, Milton? You haven't done . . . those things with other women, have you? They haven't kissed you as I did . . . where I did . . .?'

She was blushing but he seemed not to notice it. Nor did he answer her questions.

'I'm going to order breakfast for us. *Café au lait? Croissants?*'

He lifted the telephone by the bed and, without waiting for her reply, asked for room service. She *was* hungry, Cassy thought, but only for more love. She was a little shocked by her own insatiability, even more by her intense enjoyment of everything her lover had done to her; everything he had instructed her to do to him. His body as well as her own were new discoveries, and although there were parts which were sore and uncomfortable, she knew only too well that if he reached out and touched her, she would be ready for him again.

Was this, she wondered, what it meant to be in love? If so, she had never been in love with Jimmy, nor indeed with Alan. She had not with either felt this trembling need to touch, to be close. Even now, she wished Milton would come back to bed and demonstrate in some way that he was a little in love with her. But he had gone to the bathroom and she could hear the water running.

By the time he emerged, the floor waiter had deposited breakfast in the adjoining salon.

'The coffee will be getting cold,' Milton said as he came by in his dressing-gown.

Obediently, Cassy climbed out of bed. She felt uncomfortable – and unhappy. The euphoria that had gripped her since she had woken had now given way to depression. Something was wrong – but she was not sure what. It had to do with Milton's behaviour, so very different out of bed than in it! Perhaps, he would show his feelings later.

But his manner remained unchanged. When he took her to Longchamp, to the opera and then on to the Folies-Bergère, he was well-mannered and an amusing companion; but, unlike when they were in bed, quite indifferent to her emotions.

On their last night together, she asked him hesitantly if he was feeling sad at the thought of their separation next day.

He agreed that he would most likely miss her, but his smile was distant.

The last morning, pride kept Cassy from begging him to take her to Geneva with him. She lay in his bed, watching him pack, and tears of disappointment and frustration filled her eyes. Even now, at this eleventh hour, he was giving no sign that he cared about her, she thought unhappily.

Seeing her tears, he came over and sat down on the edge
of the bed. She noticed angrily that there was a half smile
narrowing those extraordinary blue eyes of his.

As if he were the parent and she the child, he said quietly:
'No scenes, honey! No man likes an emotional farewell. We've
had a swell time together. I think you will admit that you got
everything you came for . . . maybe a bit more, eh? Now it's
over – anyway for the time being. We'll meet up again, honey,
you can be sure of it. But I told you a year ago that I didn't
intend to become involved with any woman. And that includes
you.'

'But I never thought . . .'

He put a finger beneath her chin and lifted it, so that she
was looking into his face. 'Okay, so you'd like it to go on.
But for once in your sweet little life you are not going to be
able to have what you want, Casilda. I'm a selfish, self-centred
bastard and no woman – not even one as pretty as you – is
going to change my way of life. I'm sorry, honey – but that's
how it is.'

Cassy's tears dried on her cheeks. A little of the old fire
returned and her eyes flashed as she said: 'Don't you care
about me at all? Aren't you even going to ask me what I shall
do with *my* life? Perhaps you won't be quite so happy if I tell
you that this could be the last time we meet as . . . as lovers.
I'm sort of half engaged to Alan Costain. I've told him I'll
marry him. And when I do, I won't be free to meet you like
this. Alan's in love with me and . . .'

He stood up abruptly, his mouth hardening. 'Don't be a
little fool, Casilda. You're no more in love with this chap than
you are with me. You should stop playing these childish games.
I seem to recall that Costain is still in his twenties. It's none
of my business, honey, but if you are going to marry again,
what you need is a man, not a boy; someone who can satisfy
you in bed. If I've done nothing else for you, I've shown you
the woman you really are. Find yourself a man, Casilda, if it's
marriage you want – but don't expect *me* to fit the bill. I'm

a bachelor born and I'll die one. Any time it's convenient, I'll be happy to be your lover – but that's all, honey. Understand?'

She was for once in her life too angry for words; too angry and too hurt. Even now she could not quite believe that, after all they had been to each other, he could be walking out of her life as if she meant no more to him than one of those women who did it for money.

'Go on then, get out!' she said, finally finding her voice. 'If you think I care what you intend to do with your life, you're very much mistaken. As to seeing you again, I hope I never do.'

Picking up the telephone, he rang down for a porter to collect his luggage. Then only did he look at her.

'Sure am happy to be able to fulfil your last wishes, honey,' he said. 'But next time you order someone to "get out" in that aristocratic little voice of yours, try and make sure that you are not ordering them out of their own room!'

Leaving the bags where they stood, he picked up his hat and gloves and, without looking at her again, he closed the door between them. Cassy turned her face into the pillow and wept.

CHAPTER TWENTY-ONE

April–July 1929

'Can you hear me all right, Joss? It's Alan. Your mother asked me to telephone you . . . Are you there?'

The line crackled and Alan's voice became indistinct, fading one moment and then sounding as if he were next door. Joscelin felt a variety of emotions. Her heart had doubled its beat when Valeria had told her a Mr Costain was calling on a person-to-person basis from London. Whilst she waited to be connected, her mind whirled. Could Alan be about to announce his engagement to Cassy? Or was it the book? But no, he had said *her mother* had asked him to ring . . .

'*Can you hear me, Joss? It's Alan . . .*'

Totally unexpected tears stung Joscelin's eyes. She had had barely four hours' sleep. Last night's dancing had ended in the early hours of this morning, and when Marco had taken her into the moonlit *giardino segreto* and kissed her after the last guests had departed, she had been astonishingly happy. As she felt her body responding hungrily to his kisses, she had known they would soon be lovers. He had promised to take her next day to his palazzo near Siena where they would be alone but for the servants. The centuries-old palace, situated high on a hilltop, was a place made for love, he assured her. Resolutely, she had put Alan from her mind and fallen asleep, remembering the feel of Marco's lips on hers. Now, hearing Alan's voice, distorted although it was across such a distance, she knew instantly that he was the only man in the world she could ever love; that were she to give herself to Marco, it would be a betrayal.

'Yes, I can hear you, Alan!' How ordinary, how unemotional she sounded! Yet the palms of her hands were wet with sweat.

'Listen to me, Joss, I'm ringing because I think you should come home. Your father isn't too well and your mother is rather fussed. She told me not to ask you to break your holiday, but I think she does need you. Joss, can you hear what I'm saying?'

She shivered, her body suddenly chilled by a fearful apprehension. 'What's wrong with Daddy?' she asked abruptly. 'If it's serious, I want to know.'

He did not hesitate. Quietly, he answered her question: 'I think it *could* be serious. We don't know yet exactly what is wrong but your mother told me your GP was referring him to a specialist. I hope you will think I've done right, but I got in touch with the very best man for this sort of thing, and I've asked him to take on your father's case.'

'What "*sort of thing*"?' Joscelin's anxiety deepened.

For a moment, the line went dead. After what seemed to Joscelin to be an eternity, they were reconnected. 'Nobody is sure yet, Joss. The consultant is going to investigate. It's just that your father is in pain and they want to find out what's causing it. Now don't panic – everything is under control. Mr Howard is being moved to St George's and I've told your mother she is to come and stay here at Rutland Gate. You too, Joss, if you come home . . .'

'I'll be there,' Joss said sharply. 'Tell Mummy not to worry – and Alan, thank you for everything you're doing. I'm very grateful.'

'Don't be an ass, we're second Best Friends, remember? Let me know when to expect you and I'll meet your train . . .'

The line went dead and Marco appeared at her side. '*Buon giorno, cara mia!*' he said softly. 'The telephone call was not bad news, I trust?'

Joscelin bit her lip. 'I'm afraid it is – my father is ill. I've got to go home, Marco. I'm sorry . . .'

'After last night, I know you would not leave me unless it

was necessary. You will come back when this emergency is over – no?' He added tenderly: 'Do not concern yourself about me, Joscelin. As soon as you are packed, I will drive you to Milan. In the meanwhile, I will see what fast trains are available to take you back to England.'

He managed to secure a sleeper for her on the Simplon-Orient Express. Not only could she board the train at Milan and enjoy a good night's rest, but she would not be required to disembark until the train reached Calais. She could expect to be in London by teatime the next day.

On the drive to Milan, he did his utmost to distract her attention with his inconsequential talk, and when finally he helped her on to the train Joscelin was filled with gratitude. Solicitous to the end, his last words were a promise to put a call through to Alan to advise him of her time of arrival.

As the boat train drew into Victoria Station, Joscelin saw Alan's tall figure hurrying along the crowded platform towards her. She closed her eyes as he enveloped her in a bear hug, and for just a moment allowed herself to cling to him.

He tucked her arm beneath his and said: 'I almost didn't recognize you, Joss. I like your new outfit. Dashed smart. But let's get your luggage and I'll bring you up to date with the news as we drive home. Your mother is at the hospital.'

The pleasure Joscelin felt at seeing him receded. At least, she reassured herself, Alan would not have smiled when he greeted her if anything terrible had happened. But what *was* wrong with her father?

As he guided the Bentley skilfully round Buckingham Palace and into Birdcage Walk, Alan did his best to enlighten her. 'I spoke to Mr Petersfield the consultant last night. There is some kind of blockage which is the cause of your father's pain, and which would explain the somewhat alarming loss of weight. Mr Howard is eating well enough – but he can't always keep his food down. Petersfield was not prepared to be specific as yet, but he mentioned a possible tumour. I didn't tell your mother. I saw Mr Howard this morning and he asked me to keep her in the dark as long as possible – if it does prove serious, I mean.'

Joscelin's cheeks paled. 'But you think it is, Alan?' she asked quietly.

'I honestly don't know, but it could be. I don't think Petersfield would otherwise have had your father moved into a private room up here at St George's. Mrs Howard has been worrying about paying for it all, but I told her a bit of a fib and said the insurance would cover it. And I don't want any more arguments from you, Joss, about letting me foot the bills. I owe you a great deal. I thought it would be easier for you and your mother to be based at Rutland Gate,' he was saying. 'It's right on hand for visiting St George's, and Mrs Howard likes to spend every possible minute with your father. I've brought the Brigadier back, too. He'll be pleased to see you!'

He had thought of everything, Joscelin realized as he halted the car outside Rutland Gate. He had even put Paget and the Daimler at her mother's disposal.

'Thought you'd want to tidy up before you go to see your father,' Alan said as he lifted her suitcase out of the dickey. Joscelin was conscious of tears filling her eyes. She tried to thank him, but the words choked in her throat. Fortunately the Brigadier had heard the car and, as Gibson opened the front door, the dog came bounding towards them. In the confusion caused by his welcome Joscelin's handbag went flying, and by the time she had retrieved the contents she was once more in control of herself.

'I'll take the old boy to the park whilst you're visiting your father,' Alan said. 'Down, you ugly brute! Who'd have thought he'd ever grow to this size, eh, Joss?'

But the dog's rapturous welcome, Alan, even his kindness, were all forgotten when one of the nurses ushered her into her father's room. Peggy Howard sat in a chair to one side of her husband's bed, a piece of crochet work lying idle in her lap. Clifford Howard was asleep, his gaunt face barely recognizable to Joscelin as her mother put a finger to her lips before giving a parody of a smile. Her cheeks and eyes were puffy, and it was obvious that she had been crying.

Joscelin approached the high hospital bed, desolation sweeping over her. No one had told her that her father was dying, yet one glance at him convinced her that this was the case. Alan should have warned her, she thought, longing to throw herself into her father's arms.

As the nurse closed the door behind her, his eyes opened. They stared up at Joscelin as if he were trying to bring her into focus. Then suddenly, he smiled. 'Hullo, Poppet!' he said, his voice sounding perfectly normal. 'Alan said you'd be here this afternoon. Got fed up with the Eyeties, I gather!'

As Joscelin bent over to hug him, she offered up a silent prayer of thanks to Alan for thinking up this white lie. Her father would have known at once how seriously ill he was if he'd thought she had come back to England especially to see him. She forced herself to smile.

'Florence was beautiful, Daddy, but there's a limit to the amount of sightseeing even an ardent art-lover like me can enjoy,' she said lightly.

'And your young man, da Cortona – didn't he come up to scratch?' The gentle, teasing voice touched her almost to tears.

'Marco's really very nice,' she said, the smile now fixed on her face. 'But you know what the Italians are, Daddy – dreadful flirts! I got tired of fending him off!'

A smile touched Clifford Howard's mouth. 'Do you good, Poppet,' he said. 'As a matter of fact, I think the trip *has* done you good. You're looking different . . . very smart. Didn't I always tell you, Peggy, that our duckling would one day grow into a swan?'

Joscelin smiled and he continued: 'Before I forget, you must thank young Costain for me, Poppet. I don't know how your mother would have managed without him. You know what she's like – flying into a panic if I so much as sneeze. Dyspepsia's a common enough complaint in chaps of my age. Can be uncomfortable at times, but with the quacks giving me something to ease the old heartburn, I'm right as rain.'

'Now Clifford, you know very well they aren't quacks,' Mrs Howard said. 'And I do worry, Joscelin,' she added. 'No one will tell me when they're going to let your father come home. Mr Petersfield said he still had more tests to do. I want *you* to talk to him, Joscelin. The sooner we get Daddy home, the happier I'll be.'

Joscelin was unable to ignore the expression on her father's face as he kept his eyes fastened upon her. She could see an appeal in them as clearly as if he had asked her outright for her collusion.

'Of course I'll speak to the specialist, Mummy, but it's sensible for Daddy to stay here until they discover what is causing his indigestion. They'll do X-rays and barium feeds, and all that sort of thing takes time. Besides, it won't do him any harm to have a holiday from that wretched old bank of his. How long since you took more than a week off, Daddy? I don't suppose you can even remember.'

Suddenly Joscelin noticed a tightening of the muscles of her father's jaw and she felt his pain as if it were her own.

'I dare say it's time for Daddy's medicine,' she said intuitively, concealing her own sense of panic. 'Why don't you come home with me, Mummy? I haven't even unpacked yet and I haven't seen you for ages.'

Later that night, after her mother had retired, Joscelin sat alone with Alan, the Brigadier stretched out at their feet.

'Daddy wanted my mother out of the room, Alan, I know he did. He looked so grateful when I persuaded her to come back with me. That can only mean he was in pain – severe pain. Mummy might drive other people crazy with her chatter, but normally *he* never minds.'

Alan frowned, then said quietly: 'Petersfield telephoned me at teatime. I'm afraid there is a tumour, Joss. He asked me to warn you that an operation might not be possible. I'm frightfully sorry.'

Alan grasped her hands. They were shaking.

'Darling Joss, please don't give way. You're to be brave for both of them.'

Tears trickled slowly down Joscelin's face. 'I never thought of my parents dying,' she murmured. 'Daddy's only in his fifties. He and I . . .'

'I know, Joss, I know!' Alan broke in. 'But those years have been very happy ones.'

Joscelin bit her lip and said desperately: 'But how will I tell Mummy? What's going to become of her?'

But Clifford Howard had already considered his wife's future. He succeeded in having his daughter to himself one afternoon of the following week, and came straight to the point. 'I know this isn't easy for you, Poppet, but circumstances make it impossible for me to spare you, and I must tell you of the plan I have for your mother. Now I want you to be brave . . . and very calm. I know I can depend on you, Poppet. Mr Petersfield has told me that I haven't a lot more time, so we must face the fact for your mother's sake.'

Quickly, Joscelin covered his hands with hers. 'I'll go home and take care of Mummy. You've nothing to worry about. I will always look after her and . . .'

'No, Poppet, don't say any more. That isn't what I want. You have a life of your own to lead and a career to follow. Now listen to me, darling. You've heard your mother talking about Aunt Nellie, and you've seen the photographs your aunt has sent from time to time from Canada. She's widowed now and has a nice house and garden, and *that*'s the place for your mother. Nellie will look after her . . . and Peggy will cope with life much better if she doesn't have too much to remind her of the past. I've written to your aunt and I've no doubt what her reply will be.'

He paused, plainly fatigued by the effort of so much talking.

'There won't be a fortune for your mother, but I'm happy to say I'll be leaving her well provided for. There's my life insurance and of course, my bank pension . . . I'll be leaving you a bit – enough for a small income which will guarantee the rent of your flat. Perkins and Partners have my will and it should be all quite straightforward . . . except for the business of persuading your mother. I'm afraid she won't want to go, Poppet.'

Once more he paused. 'Now this is where I need your help, darling,' Clifford said gravely. 'You've got to be very firm with your mother – insist that Whitegates *must* be sold. You may even have to tell a few fibs – say that there isn't the money to maintain it, if you like; that although you'd visit her as often as possible, you couldn't give up your career and go to live with her. She must be made to leave. I know her so well. She needs someone to fuss over . . . and she needs someone like Nellie to look after her. Nellie is a practical woman, but kind too – and your mother admires her.'

Joscelin let her head fall forward and no longer tried to stem her tears. 'You know I'll do anything . . . anything in the world that I can. I don't care about Whitegates; I don't care about anything except . . .'

'I know, darling, but we all of us have to come to terms with death sooner or later. It isn't the end, you know. I'm quite convinced of that.'

He sounded at peace with himself and, more than anything in the world, it was what she wanted for him; this, and to believe his conviction that there would be no permanent parting from him.

'I consider myself a lucky man,' he said suddenly. 'Lucky to have married the woman I did; lucky to have such a daughter.'

Joscelin was once again threatened by tears and fought against them. Glancing at her father, she saw that he was almost asleep. She held his hand, waiting for his eyelids to close, but he had one more thing to say to her and he struggled against the effects of the drug he had been given.

'You'll know when you've met your true love, Poppet – just as I did when I met your mother. Don't ever settle for second-best. Love is a very precious thing.'

They were the last words he ever spoke to her. For two more days, he drifted in and out of a coma, kept mercifully from feeling the worst pain of the tumour. The fact that her mother went completely to pieces kept Joscelin from being swept into a dark void of grief. Alan was constantly at her side and he guided her through the unbearable day of the funeral. It was he who sent off the cable to Aunt Nellie; who forced her to listen whilst old Perkins read out her father's will.

Cassy returned from Munich where, following her meeting in Paris with Milton, she had gone to visit Patri and Rebekka. She turned up at Rutland Gate and, surprisingly, was able to lift Peggy Howard from the tearful apathy into which she had fallen after the funeral. It was Cassy who thought of trivial diversions, such as taking the unhappy woman to have her hair washed and waved; to Liberty's to choose material for some new curtains for Eaton Terrace. Moreover, Cassy was able to persuade her to consider going to live with her sister in Toronto.

But it was not Cassy's nature to pursue any course of action for long, and finally, bored by the widow's continual bouts of weeping, she went less frequently to Rutland Gate as she picked up the threads of her social life. She still called round, but more to try to persuade Alan to accompany her on whatever outing she had planned than to comfort the bereaved woman or the silent Joscelin.

Alan insisted that both Joscelin and her mother remain his guests at Rutland Gate, but as Joscelin recovered slowly from the shock of her father's death, she knew it was time to face Whitegates with her mother. True to her father's wish, she had already inferred that the little house would have to be sold, and she was now able to keep her mother partially diverted by the need to sort out the contents. Most of the furniture would be auctioned. It was the personal belongings of her parents which caused Joscelin the greatest heartache, for everywhere, inevitably, there were mementoes of their former life together.

Unable to bear her mother's tearful reminiscences, Joscelin

said recklessly that Mrs Howard must pack everything she wanted to keep into a big cabin trunk and take it with her to Toronto. 'You and Aunt Nellie can sort it all out when you feel up to it,' she said firmly.

Somehow, everything was finally ready to go. Prospective buyers came to view the house and Joscelin showed them round.

One after another, cables arrived from Aunt Nellie. Mrs Howard tut-tutted at the extravagance of such a method of communication, but was as impressed by it as by her sister's obvious desire for her company.

'It's what Daddy wanted you to do!' Joscelin reiterated whenever her mother wavered, protesting that she did not want to leave Whitegates – or Joscelin.

At last the house was sold, and Joscelin and her mother returned to Rutland Gate to await the sailing date of the liner that would take the tearful Mrs Howard to her new life. Alan drove them down to Southampton and lavishly tipped one of the stewards to look after her on the five-day journey. He filled her cabin with flowers, and turned the parting into a celebration by ordering a bottle of champagne for them to share before the boat sailed.

'A toast to your new life in Canada!' he said, his arm around Mrs Howard's shoulders.

He forced a second, then a third glass into her hand until finally she was smiling as she remarked to Joscelin with a little giggle: 'I'm getting quite tiddly! I am really!'

'All the more reason to have a nice rest after we've gone,' Alan said.

Taking her cue from Alan, Joscelin suggested her mother lie back on the bunk and give her feet a rest.

'I *am* a little sleepy,' Peggy Howard admitted. 'It's that naughty young man over there pouring me too much bubbly.'

'Don't worry if you do nod off, Mrs Howard,' Alan said. 'The steward has promised to wake you when it's time for dinner.'

She was almost asleep when Joscelin bent down to kiss her goodbye.

Somehow Joscelin managed to keep back the tears which had threatened all day, and it was only on the drive back to London that she finally gave way to them. Alan gave her his handkerchief and told her to enjoy a good cry.

He stopped the car and waited until Joscelin had herself under control. Then he said: 'I'll be going up to Strathinver to see my father and Uncle Fergus at the end of the month. Why don't you come up with me, Joss? You've never been there, and I think you'd love it. There'd be masses for you to draw and paint and I have the feeling you'd hit it off with Uncle Fergus. What about it? Think how the Brigadier would love the moors! And the Pater would be pleased to see you. I've been trying to talk Cassy into coming, but she says she may possibly go to Italy. Barbara has just had her third baby and there's to be yet another family gathering, which I'm ashamed to say I am shirking. But maybe if Cassy knows you are coming to Strathinver, she'll change her plans.'

Was that why he had invited her? Joscelin wondered. But if he was so anxious to be with Cassy, he could go with her to his sister's.

'How are things between you two?' she asked hesitantly. 'It seems ages since I had a chance to talk to Cassy on her own. She's always rushing off somewhere!'

Alan laughed ruefully. 'Don't I know it! Her energy is quite astonishing. But if I suggest a quiet evening on our own, she gets restless. I've come to the conclusion that it may take longer than I thought for her to feel ready to settle down . . . not that I've said I want to start a family right away, or anything like that. When we're married, she'll still be free to enjoy herself however she pleases, and we could travel together. I want to go out to New York in the autumn to see my mother, and I thought Cassy might like to go on to Mexico – a sort of honeymoon trip – and see Lota. Cassy says Lopez is really making a name for himself out there and that Lota writes the happiest of letters.'

'I'm so pleased for her,' Joscelin said. 'She does write to me – but not as often as she did before her marriage. She has better things to do with her time now.'

'My mother always maintained Lota owed her life to you,' he said. 'I hope *you* are going to find happiness one day, Joss. When Cassy told me you'd gone off suddenly to Florence last March, I wondered if perhaps da Cortona . . .'

'No, it was a business arrangement,' Joscelin interrupted quickly. 'I'm very fond of Marco, but I'm afraid both you and Cassy will have to reconcile yourselves to the fact that I'm a modern young woman – a career girl, and don't wish to get married.'

She had promised to dine with Alan at Rutland Gate before he drove her back to her flat. Cassy was to be there too, and as they neared London Joscelin was grateful that she could delay for a while longer the loneliness she knew she had to face. She would take the Brigadier home with her, of course, and be glad of his company, but she knew that, with no conversation to distract her, her real grief for her father would be certain to overwhelm her.

But there was not, after all, to be even the consolation of the big, shaggy dog for company. They were greeted by Alan's butler, with the shocking news that the veterinary surgeon had just left, taking the Brigadier's body with him. Half an hour ago, he had been run over by a car and killed instantly.

'Good God, Gibson, how *could* it have happened?' Alan demanded furiously. 'He's not allowed out. I gave instructions that he was never to go out of this house without his lead.'

The butler stood staring at him, his mouth agape. Alan's voice sharpened still further.

'Who was responsible? Answer me, Gibson!'

'Oh, sir . . . Mr Alan . . . it was Miss Cassy – Her Ladyship, I mean. She had a telephone call to go somewhere and I offered to send for Paget but she said she'd take a taxi-cab. She hurried out, sir, and the dog heard her going and rushed after her. I don't think she saw him. I ran after him but I was too late . . . the car was coming round the corner at the end of the square. I don't think Miss Cassy knew what had happened. She'd stopped a cab further along, you see . . . I really am *very* sorry, sir, miss.'

Alan held out his arms and Joscelin laid her face against his jacket. As if from a distance, she heard his voice.

'Get some brandy, Gibson. And when Miss Cassy comes back, I'd rather you didn't tell her how it happened. Whatever it was that sent her rushing off in such a thoughtless hurry must have been some kind of emergency. I just hope *she's* all right!'

'I can't say what it was, sir. It was a Mr Fleming who telephoned. Miss Cassy was white as a sheet when she went. I'll get the brandy, sir, right away.'

'Never heard of the fellow,' Alan said as he led Joscelin gently into the sitting room and sat her in a chair. 'God, I'm sorry, Joss – on top of everything else, too. Poor Cassy will feel terrible if she finds out it was her fault. We must keep it from her. Obviously, it *was* an emergency. I just wish I knew what this fellow Fleming wanted!'

Always the recipient of Cassy's confidences, Joscelin had heard all about Paris and the American. She did not need to speculate as to the reason for Cassy's pell-mell departure. She already knew.

CHAPTER TWENTY-TWO

July–September 1929

Alan and Joscelin dined alone, although neither could eat much. By unspoken consent, neither mentioned the Brigadier. Cassy had telephoned shortly before dinner, apologizing for her absence and giving the excuse that Mr Fleming was a family friend who had arrived in London unexpectedly and whom she felt obliged to entertain.

'She could have invited him to join us,' Alan said. 'But it's typical of Cassy. She never stops to think until it's too late!'

Inevitably, his words invoked the unbearable picture of Cassy running thoughtlessly into the street, the Brigadier bounding behind her. With a look at Joscelin's face, Alan changed the conversation.

Cassy never knew that she was responsible for the dog's death. She was genuinely distressed on Joscelin's behalf and wanted to rush out next day and buy her another puppy.

Not long after Joscelin had returned to her flat, she went round to spend an afternoon there. Curled up on the old horsehair sofa, she chattered whilst Joscelin stood at her easel, painting.

'I know you don't approve of me having an affair,' she said, watching Joscelin's expression in an attempt to gauge her reaction. 'But you simply don't know how utterly fascinating Milton can be, Joss.' She gave a deep sigh. 'It's hard to explain, but I can't seem to keep away from him. He does such fantastic things to me. I know you object to me going into details, but you'd understand if it were *you* he was making love to. I suppose you'll be pleased if I tell you I may not see him again.'

She sighed again.

'He just refuses to make any promises,' she said. 'We have these fantastic times together and then he vanishes. First it was in Paris – and then here in London when he telephoned me out of the blue. For all I know, it could be years before he turns up again.'

Joscelin paused to open a new tube of paint, her eyes thoughtful. 'It sounds to me as if your Mr Fleming knows exactly what he's doing,' she said. 'By making himself so elusive, he remains a novelty to you, Cassy. He isn't going to play your game and wants you to play his. I can't think why you bother about him, especially if you don't even like him. Besides, what about Alan?'

'What about him?' Cassy said, pouting. 'I've told him a dozen times I'll marry him when I'm ready to settle down. I suppose you think I ought to go up to Scotland with him next month instead of going to Deauville.'

'I don't think you *ought* to, Cassy – I just don't understand why you don't *want* to,' Joscelin commented, laying down her palette.

'Scotland is just hundreds of miles of barren moors and dreary old lochs,' Cassy retorted flatly, 'and Strathinver Castle is huge and draughty. I hate Tío Angus and I know he doesn't like me, and it just never stops raining!'

Despite herself, Joscelin smiled. 'Alan says it'll still be sunny and warm in September, and as it's the shooting season the house will probably be full of friends.'

'Well, the van Vreedens want me to go to Deauville,' Cassy said. 'They have a villa there and a yacht and they're going to take me to the casino. Why don't you come too, Joss? I'm sure the van Vreedens wouldn't mind one bit if I asked them to invite you.'

'Have you told Alan?' Joscelin asked, not troubling to decline Cassy's suggestion. 'I think he's half expecting you to go with him.'

Cassy grinned. 'Now don't go on at me, Joss. I *will* tell him soon – but he's bound to get upset. He's so fearfully jealous. I just daren't think what he'd do if he found out about Milton. It's strange, isn't it, but Milton isn't the least bit jealous of Alan.'

Joscelin hurriedly turned the conversation and not long afterwards Cassy departed, leaving, as always, a cloud of her favourite scent in the air to linger long after she had gone.

Was she a prig? Joscelin asked herself. If Cassy chose to have affairs, so too did lots of other women. Might she herself not have succumbed to Marco's charms if fate had not brought her back to England? Now it was too late to go back to Florence. Marco had written that he was coming over to England. 'If you will permit me – and perhaps even if you will not – I shall come and visit you, *cara mia*,' he ended his letter. 'We shall lunch together and you shall tell me when you will return to Florence.'

But the pleasure of a few friendly lunches with Marco could not compare with the prospect of spending three whole weeks in Scotland with Alan. She wrote by return of post to tell Marco that she was going to the Highlands with the Costain family on the dates in question, leaving him to draw what conclusions he might from her admission that she did not intend altering her plans.

Alan was unable to conceal his deep disappointment when Cassy told him she was going to Normandy with her friends. He tried to convince himself that she was not being unreasonable in preferring Deauville to Scotland, and throughout the long drive to Strathinver he tried to convince Joscelin too.

'Cassy is so full of life, so eager for activity. I can see that she needs diversions,' he rationalized when they stopped for the night at Carlisle. 'She isn't self-sufficient like you, Joss. You enjoy solitude, and have your work to stimulate you. Cassy needs friends around her, entertainment. I fear it *is* awfully dull at Strathinver . . . if you aren't interested in wildlife, that is, and beautiful scenery, or . . .' he added with a rueful grin, '. . . taking a gun out on the moors. I dare say there will be a rumpus from the Pater when I refuse to go shooting with him. I've never been able to make him understand that I don't like killing things any more. It was Uncle Fergus who made me see things differently. I suspect my father knows it was his influence, but since Uncle Fergus's name mustn't be mentioned, he can hardly accuse him of subverting me!'

It was six years since Joscelin had last seen Lord Costain. Now, although his hair was snow-white, his eyes were the same piercing blue and regarded her through his pince-nez as he came out onto the stone terrace fronting Strathinver Castle to welcome them. 'Tea's ready!' he grunted. 'Dare say you're both hungry. Cook's made some scones.'

He nodded briefly at Joscelin, prodded Alan with his shooting stick and turned to lead the way indoors.

Despite the warmth of her coat, Joscelin shivered as she followed her host inside. The vast Gothic hall was panelled in dark brown oak and decorated by rows of antlers, foxes' masks and glass cases containing stuffed fish. She was glad to see a log fire blazing at one end of the large drawing room. Shabby armchairs were grouped round the granite fireplace, above which was a huge oil painting of a gory Highland battle scene, its detail obscured by years of wood smoke. Lord Costain's black labrador ambled over to the skin rug by the fireplace and stretched itself full-length in front of the fire. The pungent smell soon emanating from the animal's coat reminded Joscelin of the Brigadier, and tears stung her eyelids.

'Sit down, sit down, the pair of you!' Lord Costain said, tipping a pile of newspapers and magazines off the sofa with his stick. 'Looking well, Alan, m'boy. As for you, young lady, grown up a bit since I last saw you. Sorry about your father – Alan told me. But we'll soon put some colour into those cheeks – best air in the world up here in the Highlands.'

Alan caught Joscelin's eye and smiled.

As much to please him as Lord Costain, she tried to do justice to the tea that was now brought into the room.

Fortunately, the dog ambled over to sit at her feet, and Joscelin was able surreptitiously to dispose of some of the delicious but unwanted cakes and scones. She was suddenly overwhelmingly tired, her eyes stinging, whether from the smoky air in the room or from the effects of the six hundred-mile drive, she was not sure.

Noticing her poorly disguised yawn, Alan stood up. 'It's bed for you, my girl,' he said. 'I shall dine alone with the Pater tonight and I'll get one of the servants to bring you a supper tray.'

Half an hour later, Joscelin was ready to climb into the mahogany four-poster which awaited her so invitingly. A maid had put a stone water bottle between the linen sheets, unpacked her suitcases and brought her hot water to wash in. She had instructed the girl not to draw the brocade curtains, and she stood now at the windows watching the sun setting over the purple moor. But for the dark silhouettes of the pine trees of a distant forest, the soft rise and fall of the sweeping moorland seemed to stretch into eternity. She knew that there, beneath the great red-gold orb of the sun, lay the ragged coastline where the Atlantic poured into Lochinver. Alan had promised to take her to sketch the sea birds and seals. On the drive up from London he had talked of a dozen such wonderful pleasures in store for her, not the least being a visit to his Uncle Fergus.

Joscelin climbed into bed and lay back against the frilled pillow case. She wondered sleepily whether the luxurious bedroom furnishings were relics of Lady Costain's days, contrasting as they did with the shabby, masculine, disordered state of the rooms below. Lady Costain would never have allowed it!

The next evening, as she changed into a long dress for dinner, Joscelin watched the setting sun from her windows. She was beginning to understand the sense of peace and serenity Alan said it gave him. Cassy found it dull and was depressed by the lack of flamboyance in these Highland people and their surroundings. Perhaps she, too, might find it depressing in the winter when the rain swept ceaselessly from leaden skies. But Joscelin had fallen in love with the Highlands, and her feeling of kinship deepened during the next few days when Alan took her to see some of his favourite haunts.

Lord Costain did not accompany them on these trips. He had been invited to a neighbour's grouse shoot together with half a dozen visiting friends from London. Because the old man seemed anxious for Joscelin to see for herself what fine sport could be had, Alan, to please his father, drove her over one morning to their neighbour's moor. Joscelin hated to see the slaughter of the little dark brown birds, and was not sorry when Alan suggested they drive home to Strathinver for lunch.

From then on he took her only to the glens and lochs, and one afternoon to see a golden eagle soaring above the five-hundred-feet-high granite ridges. Never without her drawing pad, Joscelin slowed their progress as she stopped repeatedly to make sketches. Alan would sit quietly smoking his pipe whilst she drew the delicate ferns edging a burn, or a waterfall cascading into a stream, rainbow-hued in the sunlight. To Joscelin's delight they saw an otter, a grey-brown streak as it dived into the river from a mossy bank. One sunny afternoon Alan pointed out a kestrel, a mountain buzzard and a pair of grey-brown ptarmigan. 'The Pater would shoot these if he saw them – they are quite a delicacy!' he told her with a wry grin.

He planned to take her next day through the forest to meet his uncle. Unfortunately Lord Angus's labrador, Bess, fell ill and Alan felt he should shoulder the responsibility for the dog since his father was still a guest at his neighbour's shoot.

'The Pater has had the dog for goodness knows how many years,' he told Joscelin as they waited for the veterinary surgeon to drive over from Inchnadamph. 'Bess has always been his favourite. She's obviously in pain.'

Joscelin helped to make the dog as comfortable as possible in front of the fire. The labrador did look ill and she could imagine Lord Costain's feelings if his dog should die.

The veterinary surgeon seemed puzzled by the labrador's condition.

'She's caught a wee chill,' he said finally. 'I'll gie ye a tonic, and if she's no' better in a day or two, ye kin call me agin.'

Alan called off the plan to visit his uncle, spending the afternoon quietly with the dog whilst Joscelin wrote a long letter to her mother. Bess seemed a little better by teatime, and Alan relaxed.

'Maybe McNaught is right and it's just a chill,' he said. He stretched his arms above his head and smiled at Joscelin.

'We haven't had our daily dose of exercise, have we?' he said. 'What about a night excursion for a change, Joss? I don't suppose you've ever seen a badger's sett, have you? I happen to know there's one on the edge of the forest. We could go along and watch the brocks – if you'd care to.'

Joscelin needed no second bidding. Wearing stout shoes and a warm coat, she followed Alan over the moors towards the dark line of trees.

'It's best to be here well before dusk,' Alan said, his voice dropping to a whisper as they drew closer to the trees. 'Badgers are shy animals and won't come out if they sense danger.' He licked one finger and held it up to test the direction of the wind, then selected a large pine tree against which they could conceal themselves. 'Mustn't let old Brock see our silhouettes against the skyline,' he explained, 'and as the wind is blowing towards us here, he won't get our scent.'

He had brought an old mackintosh on which to sit, and as Joscelin settled herself as quietly as she could against the treetrunk he squatted down beside her, one arm around her shoulders.

'Now for the tiresome bit – waiting!' he whispered, unaware of Joscelin's racing heart as he moved even closer to her. 'It could be an hour or more before he decides it's dark enough to put his nose out. I'm expecting there to be a sow too, and four or five cubs. They'll be pretty big by now and the parents will be teaching them how to hunt.' He chuckled as he added:

'At least we won't have to wait all night. Uncle Fergus says if badgers aren't out by ten o'clock, you can reckon not to see them!'

Gradually Joscelin's breathing slowed and she allowed her head to lean against Alan's shoulder. She knew their proximity was no more than accidental. Nevertheless she felt supremely happy, knowing that there was nowhere in the world she would rather be; no one she would rather be with.

Occasionally, Alan slapped at a midge or mosquito. Once he put his hand quickly over Joscelin's mouth to still the sound as she gasped at the sudden screech of an owl. 'Nothing to be scared of out here,' he whispered against her ear.

The touch of his lips against her earlobe sent a shiver down Joscelin's spine and Alan, mistaking its cause, pulled her collar closer about her throat.

'Sure you're not too cold?' he asked solicitously as the twilight deepened and dusk fell. He seemed satisfied when she shook her head. He tucked her hand in his, saying: 'You're a jolly good sport, Joss, and a hell of a lot more sensible than I am. If I don't stop talking, we never will see old Brock.'

Joscelin had sincerely believed she would not mind if the badgers never appeared, but when Alan suddenly nudged her and she felt his body stiffen, her own tensed in anticipation.

'There! See?' he whispered, pointing to the steep, earth-covered bank where the several cave-like entrances to the sett could only just be discerned.

The boar appeared first, a tangle of dried grass caught comically on his silver-backed head. He lifted one paw and sniffed the air, scenting for danger. After a few minutes, satisfied that it was safe, he disappeared into the sett and reappeared a moment later followed by the sow and several large, boisterous cubs.

Joscelin watched enraptured as the young badgers tumbled about and played like puppies on the earth bank. The parents seemed in no hurry to take their offspring on their nocturnal foray for food.

Suddenly Joscelin heard a twig snap behind her, and as she turned to see what had made the noise a terrifyingly dark shape loomed out of the shadows. Alan, too, had seen it and only just succeeded in stilling the cry of fear that had risen to Joscelin's lips.

'Uncle Fergus!' he breathed.

Stealthily the man moved closer and squatted down behind them. The boar stopped his vigorous scratching and paused, his suspicions aroused. Then he stretched himself and slid down the bank, followed immediately by his family. They disappeared into the undergrowth.

'They'll not be back 'til the break of dawn!' The man's voice was deep.

'This is Joscelin, Uncle – Joscelin Howard,' Alan said. 'We were coming over to see you today, but Father's dog was ill and we had to wait for the vet. Joscelin's the artist who illustrated my book.'

There was no answer – only a grunt; but now that her eyes had become better accustomed to the darkness, Joscelin could see what she thought was a smile on the man's face.

'It's getting cold,' Alan said, helping Joscelin to her feet. 'We'll come over and see you tomorrow if Bess is better.'

There was still no word from Fergus Costain, but he seemed to be in no hurry to leave and walked with them across the moors. As they approached the stone walls bordering the home farm fields, he grunted once more and left them as suddenly as he had appeared.

Alan chuckled and linked his arm through Joscelin's. 'You don't realize it, but you've been greatly honoured,' he said. 'Uncle Fergus usually runs a mile if he sees a stranger.'

The labrador seemed little better on their return to the castle, barely raising her head to glance at them, and her condition had deteriorated by the time Alan's father returned home next evening. He bent over her and patted her head, his movements almost as stiff as the dog's. Her tail thumped a welcome but she did not try to get to her feet.

Lord Costain's voice was gruff as he said: 'Go and ring that fool McNaught, Alan. He's to be up here first thing tomorrow . . . or better still, tonight!'

But the vet was out on some inaccessible farm and was unlikely to be back before dawn. Lord Costain greeted the news tetchily, and it was some time before Alan and Joscelin were able to persuade him to go to bed. When Joscelin came down to breakfast the following morning, he was already pacing the floor of the drawing room with growing impatience.

'Is she no better?' Joscelin asked anxiously.

Alan came to stand in the doorway beside her.

'That idiot McNaught saw her early this morning,' Lord Costain grunted. 'Didn't see any point in waking you. Damned fool said there was nothing he could do. Internal trouble. Incompetent jackass! Said I should let him put her down.'

The huskiness in the old man's tone left Joscelin in little doubt that the old man was unable to face the prospect of losing the labrador who had been his constant companion for the last twelve years. It was all too easy for her to imagine how he must be feeling when she recalled that she had only had the Brigadier for three years, and yet nothing had filled the gap his death had left in her life.

Her eyes went back to Bess. Alan's Uncle Fergus! *He* was the person to whom all the local people took their sick animals; who had his own natural remedies concocted from herbs and plants . . .

Her checks flushed, Joscelin said impulsively: 'Lord Costain, couldn't you take Bess to Uncle Fergus? Maybe *he* would know what was wrong and . . .'

She broke off as she realized that she had raised a forbidden subject. For the first time in a long while she blushed as she saw the look of concern on Alan's face and noted the tightening of his father's jaw. How could she have been so stupid as to have forgotten that Fergus did not even exist as far as Lord Costain was concerned!

Alan said quietly: 'Joss is right, Father. If anyone can save

Bess, it's Uncle Fergus. We planned to go and see him this afternoon. Why don't you come with us? You could bring Bess in the governess cart. This might be the one chance of saving her.'

Joscelin saw the muscles working in Lord Costain's face but could only guess at the emotions tormenting him. He sat down shakily in one of the armchairs, staring down at the dog. It was a full two minutes before he spoke, and then he did little more than grunt an assent. She let out her breath, heard Alan do the same and knew that he had been as tense as herself.

In a tone that was deliberately casual, Alan said: 'I'll tell Lockhart to have the governess cart at the front door around three o'clock. You'll have had your cat-nap by then, Father. I've some business to do with Uncle Fergus, so I'll go over ahead of you both and let him know you're coming.'

Lord Costain rose stiffly to his feet and stumped out of the room.

The moment the door closed behind him, Alan turned to Joscelin, a look of excitement in his eyes. 'I can scarcely believe it! Thanks to you, we may get the two of them together – after all these years. The poor old Pater must be desperate! Now it's up to me to make sure Uncle Fergus doesn't skedaddle off into the woods to avoid seeing him!'

'Surely he wouldn't do that, Alan – not if there is an animal needing his help?'

'No, you're right!' He turned to look at the dog. 'We must pray Uncle Fergus can do the trick,' he said thoughtfully. 'If Bess dies . . .'

'Don't think about that,' Joscelin broke in. 'But, Alan, isn't it odd that your father never suggested we should take Bess on our own? *He* doesn't have to go. Nor did he suggest you asked your uncle to come here to the house.'

'Uncle Fergus would never do that – and Father knows it. Besides, by openly acknowledging Uncle Fergus's existence he will be making a kind of apology for the way he treated him all those years ago – or at least offering the hand of friendship.' He sighed. 'My father has always been narrow-minded – there's only one way of doing things and that's his way. He doesn't understand people who are different, and it's possible he expects Uncle Fergus to react now as he himself would react were he the one to have been disowned! I can tell you this much, Joss – my uncle may not be anxious to see the Pater, but he has never hated him. If anything, he feels sorry for him.'

Immediately after lunch Alan departed, making a last-minute appeal to Joscelin not to allow his father an opportunity to back out of their plans. But promptly as the grandfather clock in the hall struck three, she heard Lord Costain's voice in the hall, irritably asking the butler why Lockhart was late.

'Begging your pardon, M'Lord, but Lockhart is waiting in the drive. He's put plenty of straw in the back so the puir old dog won't feel the bumps. I'll tell Miss Howard you're ready to leave, sir. Lockhart and I can carry Bess between us.'

Lord Costain made no attempt at conversation on the way to Fergus's cottage, although once or twice he looked anxiously at Bess's outstretched body and grunted. Alan was waiting for them, chopping logs outside the tumbledown white stone cottage. Beside him, piling the logs into a handcart, was his uncle. Seeing him properly for the first time, Joscelin realized that he really did look like Cassy's 'Wild Man of the Woods'. His red beard was bushy and unclipped and fell to his massive, hairy chest. His thick mane of hair had turned grey although it, like his beard, was uncut, reaching down to his shoulders.

He looked up from his work as Lockhart halted the governess cart, glanced briefly at Joscelin and then, as if he had seen his brother only the day before, he nodded to him. 'Good day to you, Angus!' he said, as if conversation were quite normal to him. 'Where's this dog of yours, eh?'

With no visible sign of emotion Lord Costain pointed with his walking stick.

'In the back, man. Watch how you handle her. She's touchy with strangers!'

Fergus ambled over to the cart and, reaching in a long hairy arm, stroked Bess's head. Then without a word, he lifted her up in his arms and strode with her into his cottage, laying her on a truckle bed.

Lockhart helped Joscelin and his master down from the cart, and Lord Costain went to join Alan at the door. He was too shocked by what he saw to conceal his horror as he stared round the derelict cottage and its few contents. Obviously his brother's abode had startled Lord Costain far more than the sight of the man himself, Joscelin thought. Two chickens were scratching contentedly on the earth floor. A young partridge with a damaged wing was crouched on one of the two rickety chairs drawn up to a rough wood table. On the other side of the room a wild cat, nursing a kitten, spat furiously at the strangers in the doorway. Fergus's broad shoulders hid Bess's body from view.

Lord Costain backed out into the sunshine and sat down heavily on an oak bench propped against the cottage wall. Lockhart removed himself to a respectful distance, and Alan came over to sit beside his father. Joscelin seated herself nearby on an upturned chicken coop.

'Bloody shambles!' the old man muttered in a shaken tone. 'Won't do, Alan! Won't do at all!'

'It's the way he likes it, Father. He wouldn't want to live in a house like ours.'

Lord Costain hurrumphed, his lips pursed as he drew a pipe out of his coat pocket and started absent-mindedly to fill it.

'Bloody cold in the winter,' he murmured, 'and damp, I don't doubt. Where's the privy?'

Alan grinned, pointing to a rough shelter some twenty feet or so from the cottage. It was no more than a cupboard-sized shed put together from pieces of sawn treetrunks and roofed with a few broken slates.

'He gets his water from that pool over there,' he said. 'It's good, Father. Would you like to taste it? Uncle Fergus says it's the purest, softest water in the Highlands.'

'Water, indeed! You know I never drink the stuff. Now what's Fergus up to in there, eh?' He looked anxiously over his shoulder before turning back to relight his pipe.

'I can't hear Bess complaining,' Alan said gently. 'Uncle Fergus must be the only stranger she's not growled at since she became as crotchety as you in her old age.'

His father grunted.

'Journey too much for her, I dare say!' he replied, adding with renewed anxiety: 'What the devil's he doing to her, eh?'

It was another five minutes before Fergus appeared in the doorway.

'Can't promise anything . . .' he said abruptly. 'Best leave her here. Do what I can, Angus!'

Lord Costain half rose from his seat and then sank back, his face distorted by conflicting emotions. Joscelin was in no doubt that he was averse to leaving his beloved dog behind.

He muttered something about the possibility of her fretting. 'Not as if she knows you, what?'

Fergus nodded as if to imply that he understood his brother's anxiety, and, wordless, indicated with his head that Lord Costain should look inside the cottage. Alan rose quickly and helped his father to his feet. As they went indoors, the injured partridge scuttled out past their legs into the sunshine. Bess was lying contentedly on the end of the truckle bed. Her tail thumped a welcome as she recognized her master, but she made no attempt to get off the bed. Lord Costain stooped to pat the dog's head. She licked his hand but still made no attempt to follow him as he moved away.

'She seems to have settled in, Father,' Alan said quietly. 'I think you should leave her with him.'

'You keep your opinions to yourself, m'boy!' his father said sharply.

Aware that the rebuke was merely to cover his emotion,

Alan left him alone. It was several minutes before the old man
came out and faced his brother. 'What the devil's wrong with
her?' he demanded.

Fergus scratched his cheek and squinted his eyes as if to
focus upon some distant point of interest on the horizon. 'Bit
of a lump where there ought not to be one,' he answered, his
tone expressionless.

'*Will she get better?*'

To everyone's surprise, not least Lord Costain's, his brother
suddenly walked over and put a hand on his shoulder. He
looked down directly into his eyes. 'Can't promise, Angus. Do
my best!' he said quietly.

For a moment their eyes held, then Lord Costain carefully
tapped out his pipe on the edge of the wooden bench. He
replaced it in his pocket and, leaning on his stick, rose
awkwardly to his feet. Once again, his eyes met his brother's.
'Suppose it's too much to expect you to come up to the house
to report on her progress,' he said gruffly. 'Have to come down
m'self in a day or so, by the look of it. Confounded nuisance!
Too old now for rattling round in a bloody cart. Lockhart,
where the devil are you? Expect me to wait all day? Bring
that contraption over here, man!'

He climbed up into the cart with Alan and Lockhart assisting
him, then turned to his brother. 'You look well enough, Fergus,'
he told him. 'I'll say that for you; but all the same, this place
is a bloody shambles. Wouldn't surprise me if Bess comes
home riddled with fleas. Damned disgrace! In you get, Joscelin,
and get a move on, Lockhart. I haven't got all day. Lazy
blighter!'

He did not turn his head again as the horse responded to
the touch of Lockhart's whip and broke into a gentle trot
down the track. Soon the cottage disappeared from sight, and
only then did the stiffness of Lord Costain's shoulders relax
as he leaned back against the padded cushion of the seat.

'Can't go on living in that squalor,' he said, continuing a
train of thought. 'Dammit, the fellow's a Costain. God knows,

Strathinver Castle is big enough for all of us. Too big for me, when all's said and done. Alan must get the man to tidy himself up – cut his hair. Looks like one of our bloody Highland cattle! Scare the wits out of you if you ran into him in the dark!'

Joscelin smiled, partly at the simile but also remembering how frightened she had been when she had seen Uncle Fergus at the badgers' sett. But then her face became serious as she said gently: 'I'm not sure if Uncle Fergus would want to live at Strathinver, Lord Costain. Alan said he likes living wild. He's not lonely, you know. The animals are his friends. He's happy the way he is.'

Lord Costain turned to look at her. 'Fellow must need a *few* comforts. Not a young man any more. Deuced cold there in the winter, I dare say. Fellow's off his head, of course. Bound to be eccentric if you're off your head.'

That evening, after his father had retired to bed, Alan sat in a chair in front of the fire, Joscelin on the floor bent over her sketchpad. His thoughts elsewhere, Alan absent-mindedly entwined his fingers in the soft, silky strands of her hair. Unaware of the effect his touch had upon her, he said:

'The old boy won't admit it, Joscelin, but secretly he's as pleased as punch to be reconciled with Uncle Fergus – if you can call it reconciled. All these years the Pater has pretended he didn't know I was visiting my uncle, and tonight he tore strips off me because I hadn't reported the state of the cottage years ago! Of course, we'll have to be careful about letting him interfere too much in Uncle Fergus's way of life. The last thing *he* will want is workmen crawling all over the place disturbing the wildlife. Putting in a privy where the old dairy house used to be is not a bad idea of Father's, though. Perhaps I can suggest a search for wild cats up in the mountains to get Uncle Fergus off the premises. But we'll have to wait until Bess recovers.'

'You think she will get better?' Joscelin asked.

Alan sighed. 'I don't know. After you and Father left, he

told me it was touch and go. He seems to know of some herb or other which might do the trick. He was off to the woods to see if he could find what he wanted when I left. Bess seemed happy enough. Strange, isn't it, Joss? You'd think the old dog had known Uncle Fergus all her life the way she settled down.'

'Your father was quite impressed by it.'

Alan smiled, saying lightly: 'If you must hog the fire, sit here in front of me. You can use my legs for a back rest.'

Uneasily, Joscelin did as he asked. He laid his hands on her shoulders. 'I don't think the poor old Pater has ever really got over my mother leaving him. Most people thought he didn't really care one way or another – except for the blow to his pride. But in his own way, I think he loved her. He just can't show affection.'

Joscelin nodded. 'Do you think your mother will ever come back, Alan? It's not as if they are divorced.'

'I doubt it!' Alan said. 'She and my father were ill-suited in almost every way. I think there's got to be more than love in a successful marriage. There has to be friendship, too.'

He sighed. 'You know, Joss, I'm beginning to think Cassy and I are total opposites. I'll be twenty-eight next month and I've reached the age where I feel there has to be more to life than just rushing around amusing myself. There are times when it all seems so pointless. I can't seem to handle her the right way. Sometimes I think I get on her nerves, and other times I think I ought to steam-roller her into marriage! When she came back from Isobel's, she really seemed to be getting keen on the idea . . . but just as I began to feel I'd won, off she goes to Deauville as if she doesn't care whether we're together or not.'

He sounded so hurt, Joscelin longed to comfort him. 'You know Cassy says it's always too cold for her up here!' she said with an attempt at jocularity.

Alan's grin was half-hearted. 'No, the real reason is that there aren't enough dances and parties now that my mother isn't here to organize them; added to which Cassy doesn't get on with my father.'

'Cassy just needs more time to grow up, that's all,' Joscelin said wryly.

But Cassy was growing up a great deal faster than Joscelin was aware of. She had discovered that Milton Fleming was in Cowes and persuaded her hostess, Mrs van Vreeden, to invite him to join the house party in Deauville. He stayed only a week, but during that time they were always together, either in company or alone – and in bed. Alternating with the ecstatic moments of pleasure, Cassy knew moments of despair. Milton showed no more sign of being in love with her at Deauville than he had done in Paris or in London.

'Passion, honey! That's what we share,' he kept reminding her. 'You and I match – but *only* in bed. Stop pretending you're in love with me!'

Alternately tearful and angry, Cassy ceased to care whether she was in love or not. She wanted this man. No sooner was she satiated than the mere sight of him across the room could start that burning need once more. In her more vindictive moods, she threatened never to see him again; but such threats left him unmoved.

'That would be your loss, honey – there are plenty of other dames who can satisfy me!'

She didn't believe him. During their love-making he was fiercely demanding, as ardent as she was. He had taught her what pleased and excited him, and she knew how to tempt him almost beyond endurance. She could play his game . . . but only up to a point, and then her surrender was inevitable. Always, in the end, she surrendered – because her need was greater than his. *And he knew it.*

But although he readily admitted that he had not before come across a woman like her, he would never commit himself to the next meeting. 'Who knows where I'll be next month? We'll meet up some time, honey!'

Cassy went round to the flat as soon as she learned that Joscelin had returned from Scotland. She was not interested to hear that Alan's Uncle Fergus had saved Bess's life. All she wanted to talk about was Christmas. 'I know it's not for another three months, but I want to make plans. I've decided to give a ball – I'm going to call it a Snow Ball. Everyone will have to wear something white and wintry. I'm writing to Patri to see if he and Rebekka will come over, and we'll ask Monty and his fiancée and . . . and I shall have a dress especially made. I'll be a snow queen and Alan says he'll go as a snowman and . . .'

Cassy was like a child, Joscelin thought after she had left – a radiant, glowing child. Yet to look at, she was all woman. She seemed to have matured physically in the last year. But there was a new restlessness about her, too. Joscelin detected a certain petulance in her voice which convinced her that, despite her denials, Cassy was unhappy. She wondered if the American were still hovering somewhere on the perimeter of Cassy's life, but if he were, for once Cassy did not confide in her.

Milton Fleming was in London. His newspaper had sent him to cover the story of the arrest of the brilliant young financier, Clarence Hatry, who had been struggling to save his group of companies. Now he was in Brixton Prison, charged with conspiring to obtain over two hundred thousand pounds by false pretences. Hoping that Cassy might be able to put him in touch with someone who could arrange for him to interview Hatry, Milton telephoned her.

Although Cassy knew no one who could assist him, it was a heaven-sent chance to meet Milton – one that she had been praying for. So desperate was she to meet him that she arrived at the Savoy half an hour early and went directly to his suite. Milton was not yet dressed, and opened the door to her wearing only his silk dressing-gown. He looked at Cassy and smiled his approval.

'*Buenas tardes*, Milton!' she said. 'May I come in?'

She threw the fur-trimmed black velvet cape she was carrying onto the nearest chair and turned to face him.

He grinned as he ushered her into the room, eying her close-fitting dress. 'Since you are early, honey, may I suggest you remove that finery, pretty as it is, and we will not then waste the hour I have to give you before my dinner date.'

He took a few steps towards her, but for the first time in their association Cassy did not run into his open arms. She backed away, her face pale beneath its light dusting of rouge.

'No, Milton, I don't want to. I have to talk to you – seriously. I've been trying to locate you for over a week, but no one knew where I could find you. Milton – *something perfectly terrible has happened.*'

He walked over to the side table and unhurriedly poured two cocktails from a shaker. His face was expressionless as he said: 'So, Costain has finally found out about me? Is that it?'

Cassy shook her head.

The American handed her one of the two glasses, his eyes now thoughtful. 'Financial troubles?'

'No, Milton, *no!*' Cassy's voice was almost shrill, a note of panic not far from the surface.

'Whatever it is, you might as well sit down.' he said, walking over to the sofa. When she made no move to follow him, his eyes narrowed. 'Out with it, Casilda. I told you on the telephone, I'm dining with Sir Peter Henry and I don't intend to be late. He says he may be able to get me into Brixton and . . .'

In a small, tight voice she said: 'Milton, I'm going to have a baby. Are you listening? I'm going to have a baby . . . and it's yours!'

She saw his mouth tighten fractionally, but his hand was steady as he took an olive from a dish on the table behind him and calmly put it in his mouth. His eyes searched her face. 'You're sure?' he asked curtly. 'About being pregnant, I mean?'

Cassy nodded as tears filled her eyes.

Milton's face remained expressionless as he gazed into his glass. 'Are you sure it's mine?' he asked smoothly. 'Why not Costain's?'

Cassy's face registered her shock. 'But it isn't! I conceived in August . . . Alan was in Scotland and you and I . . .'

With a little cry, she crossed the room and knelt at his feet. 'Milton, it's yours, I know it. At first I was terribly upset, but then I remembered how wonderful things always are between us and I know we could be happy if we were married; and I'd get a nanny to look after the baby and . . .'

'No nanny! No baby!' the American drawled. 'Sorry, honey, but that's not for me. No baby – and certainly, *no marriage.*'

Cassy looked up at him disbelievingly. 'But, Milton, we've *got* to get married. I can't just have a baby without . . . without . . .'

'Then get rid of it,' he said harshly. 'I'm sorry, my dear, but that's the end of it as far as I'm concerned. Count me out. If you need money, I'll provide it.'

'I can't just "get rid of it"!' she cried. 'You don't understand. I was there when my . . . when a friend nearly had an abortion and it was terrible, she nearly died and . . . and I *couldn't*, Milton.'

'I'm not going to marry you, Casilda. Now get up and have that drink – you need it. And stop crying or I'll have to turn you out of my room. I can't stand hysterical women.'

His cold, calm voice stilled the hysteria which he had correctly divined was threatening. She got to her feet, stumbled into the chair he indicated, and stared disbelievingly at his impassive face. 'You can't mean this, Milton. I know you've never pretended you loved me but it *is* your baby. You've just *got* to do what's right . . . it's only fair!'

'Casilda, I am not one of your aristocratic buddies who can be counted on to do the gentlemanly thing and make an honest woman of you. If you want to have the child, that's your business. I'm sorry, my dear, but that's the end of the matter as far as I'm concerned. Now, if you'll excuse me, I must go and get dressed or I shall be late.'

Cassy jumped to her feet as he rose from the sofa. 'But what about me? What's going to happen to me?' she asked. 'I can't have a baby if I'm not married . . . *it's got to have a father* . . .'

He paused, his fingers curled round the handle of the door, his eyes travelling the length of her body. 'Better find one then, Casilda. I don't doubt there are half a dozen would-be husbands waiting in the wings. You don't need me. Get that fellow Costain to father your brat.'

It was several seconds before the shock receded and a white-hot anger consumed Cassy. She picked up the nearest object to her – the cocktail shaker – and threw it at him with all her force. But by the time it had crossed the room Milton Fleming had closed the door behind him, and with a crash the missile intended for him shattered into a thousand glittering pieces. They lay like a light covering of frost on the carpet.

Cassy stared down at them unseeingly. Only pride kept her from crossing the room, beating her fists on the closed door and pleading with him to change his mind. She hated him now as fiercely as she had once wanted him, and more violently than she had ever hated anyone in her life.

CHAPTER TWENTY-THREE

November 1929–June 1930

Although it was not yet dark, the houses across Eaton Square were hidden from Joscelin's view by a blanket of fog.

Memory stabbed at Joscelin's mind, the scene outside Cassy's bedroom window recalling another foggy twilight two years ago almost to the day. On that occasion she had come to comfort Cassy after Jimmy had died, but now it was not the loss of a beloved husband for whom Cassy was grieving but the disappearance of her American lover at the same time as Alan had gone to America.

Alan, it seemed, had left a fortnight ago to be with his mother – 'because of some silly stock market crisis,' Cassy had said – and left her all alone. She was so utterly depressed; she was even thinking of ending her life. '*You simply must come and stay with me, Joss. I need you desperately . . .*'

Cassy did indeed look unhappy, propped up in bed, her small figure encased in a swansdown bedjacket, her hair tied with a matching ribbon. Her eyes were red-rimmed and an occasional tear trickled down her cheeks as she stared forlornly at Joscelin's back.

'I wish you wouldn't stand over there!' she said. 'Draw the curtains, Joss, and come and sit by me. It looks so gloomy and I have to talk to you.'

Obediently Joscelin shut out the view and walked reluctantly to the bedside. Even before she had answered Cassy's call for help, she had known that she would not want to hear what Cassy had to tell her. The intimacies Cassy shared with her lover were personal to them.

'I know you are upset,' she said gently, 'but maybe it will all turn out for the best, Cassy. You said you didn't even like Mr Fleming!'

Cassy's eyes flashed. 'I hate him, Joss! But you don't understand . . . I haven't told you yet what happened . . .'

'Cassy, I don't want to hear!' Joscelin broke in.

'But you've *got* to hear, Joss – all of it, I mean,' Cassy persisted. 'I can't just forget about Milton . . . and I shall never, *ever* be happy again!'

The dramatic declaration was so typical of Cassy that Joscelin smiled. 'Of course you'll be happy again. Alan will be back soon and you know how much *he* loves you. He was only going to New York for a few days.'

'There is a major crisis going on,' Alan had told Joscelin when he'd had called to say goodbye to her. '*The Times* yesterday said they thought it was over, but I'm going to see for myself. I have to make sure the Mater is all right. Poor old Hamilton's been dreadfully hard hit!'

With a sigh, Joscelin turned her thoughts back to Cassy. The rift with Milton Fleming scarcely warranted her retiring to bed *ill*; yet she did look pale and wan.

'You *are* feeling all right – apart from being miserable?' she asked tentatively.

Cassy's eyes narrowed. She drew in her breath as if to draw in the courage to speak. 'I'm pregnant, Joss!' she said finally. 'It's Milton's baby and he won't marry me. And I'm not all right. Most of the time I feel so sick, I think I'm going to die!'

Tears filled her eyes as she stared anxiously at Joscelin's face. 'I knew you'd be terribly shocked, Joss,' she whispered. 'But I just had to tell someone. It was Milton's *duty* to marry me – any decent man would at least have offered . . . but Joss, he just told me it was *my* problem – as if it had nothing whatever to do with him! He's despicable – loathsome!'

For once, Joscelin felt no pity, no sympathy – only dismay and a growing abhorrence. Memories of Lota swam into her mind and she shivered.

As if she had divined Joscelin's thoughts, Cassy said tearfully: 'I can't have an abortion, Joss – I just can't. I'd be too frightened after what happened to Lota – Tía Pamela said she might have died. So you see, I haven't any choice but to marry Alan . . . quickly . . . and I didn't *want* to get married yet. I'm not ready to settle down and . . . and . . . oh, Joss, I don't *want* a baby.'

Joscelin felt a hard cold lump form in the pit of her stomach. She stared at Cassy, her face aghast. 'But you can't marry Alan now you're carrying another man's child!'

Cassy's mouth drew down in a sullen pout and she looked away from Joscelin's horrified gaze, saying: 'You don't think I'm going to *tell* Alan, do you, Joss? He'd be horrified just to know I'd been doing it with someone else. He thinks I only do it with him . . . and that's why my plan will work. Don't you see, Joss? It has to be his so long as he never knows there was anyone else.'

'Cassy, no!' With an angry gesture, Joscelin forced Cassy's head around so that she was obliged to look at her. 'You can't do that to Alan,' she said. 'It would be the worst kind of cheating. You can't mean it. You know how anxious he is to have children – yours and *his*. And have you thought what would happen if it was a boy? Alan's eldest son will inherit the title, the estate . . . and . . . Cassy, you *can't*. I simply won't allow it.'

'Don't be angry with me, Joss,' Cassy pleaded. 'I don't *want* to deceive Alan – but what else *can* I do? I can't have an illegitimate baby – I'd be absolutely ruined. It's the only way out.'

'I don't believe it!' Joss cried. 'There has to be another solution. You could have it adopted, Cassy . . . yes, it could be adopted at birth like Lota's baby. I'd help you hide away until it was born. We could . . .'

'No, Joss, I've thought about that too, but it wouldn't work. I can't just disappear for six or seven months. Alan would want to know where I was and all my friends would ask, too.'

Joscelin bit her lip as she strived to keep her voice calm. 'What about going to Lota – to Mexico?' she suggested.

Cassy's mood was changing and her tears dried. 'I can't – Lota and Benito are returning to Spain. She's pregnant, too, and they're hoping the baby will soften Papá's heart, especially now Benito is becoming so famous. Besides, Joss, you know perfectly well Alan would want to visit me wherever I hid myself. Anyway, I can't see why you should think it so terribly unfair to him. He's madly in love with me and he'll be divinely happy just knowing I'm finally willing to marry him. And I'll make it up to him by being the very best of wives . . .'

Joscelin could find no words to express her reactions. Cassy, she thought, was an irresponsible child. She believed Alan wanted only one thing from his wife. The kind of companionship and love Alan needed was beyond Cassy's understanding, her experience. She had learned next to nothing during her brief, shallow relationship with Jimmy, and still less from her passionate encounters with her American lover.

'Oh, Cassy you just *can't*!' Joscelin whispered at last, too distraught now to be angry.

Cassy tossed her head. 'Well, I'm going to. I've thought it all out. As soon as Alan gets back from America I shall persuade him to marry me by special licence.' She drew a deep sigh. 'Everyone will think it was just like me to rush off and have a secret wedding, and they'll think it great fun. I'll still be able to have my Snow Ball in December and it'll be weeks before I start getting big, so no one will suspect anything. Lots of people have premature babies. Mercedes's last one was a seven-month baby and I'll remind Alan about that when I have mine. So do stop worrying, Joss! It's not as if anyone else knows about Milton – only you, and you're the one person in the world I can trust. You'll be a godmother, of course and . . .'

'Cassy, be quiet!' Joscelin's voice cut into Cassy's monologue. 'Understand this once and for all. I won't have anything to do with this plan. I *know* it's wrong. I won't help you palm this baby off on Alan. I mean it, Cassy.'

For twenty minutes Cassy wept, argued and pleaded until finally the implacability of Joscelin's silence halted her. Joscelin stood up. 'I know you think I'm being hard, Cassy,' she said quietly. 'I'm sorry. I realize how frightened you must be feeling. But it's a matter of principle. As far as I am concerned, I don't want to discuss this ever again – not *ever*, although I shall go on being your friend.'

Cassy lay back against the pillows, her eyes thoughtful. 'I wasn't asking you to *do* anything, Joss – just to understand. You make such a fuss about telling a few fibs, when everyone knows it's often better to tell a couple of little white lies when the truth would only be hurtful. And I do love Alan, although I know you don't believe it. But I do, Joss – and I don't want to hurt him and he'd positively die if he knew anything about Milton . . .'

'Rationalize it any way you can, Cassy. I've said all I'm going to say. Now I'm going downstairs to listen to the six o'clock news on the wireless.'

As she closed the bedroom door behind her, she knew with a horrified certainty that Cassy would not change her mind. Her only hope lay in the possibility that Alan would object to a secret, clandestine marriage; that he would want everyone to be there to see him wed his beautiful bride.

But deep in her heart, she knew that Alan would take Cassy at any price.

'You should not look so surprised to see me, *cara mia*!'

Marco's voice was gently teasing as he edged Joscelin to a quieter corner of the crowded drawing room at Rutland Gate. 'Believe me, I had no difficulty in engineering an invitation to this little celebration.'

He found two empty chairs and held Joscelin's champagne glass whilst she seated herself, still too astonished to find her voice. Cassy had not told her Marco would be coming to the infant Douglas's christening.

His dark eyes were bright with amusement as he explained his presence on what was really a private family occasion.

'I never fail to read the announcements in *The Times*,' he told her, 'in order to keep my finger on the pulse of society, you understand. It would be unfortunate, for instance, were I to invite a young lady to the theatre and discover she had acquired a husband since I had last entertained her.' He smiled as he added: 'Good, I have removed that sad look I saw on your face during the christening of your little godson.'

How nearly she had not become the baby's godmother, Joscelin thought, remembering the perplexed look on Alan's face each time she had found some excuse to refuse the honour. He had remained adamant. If Joscelin would not agree to be godmother to his little son, he would postpone the christening until she did! The two godfathers, Patri and Monty, were happy to take on the responsibility. He simply could not understand why she should decline.

'*Por Dios*, Joss, say you will,' Cassy had pleaded. 'Can't you see that Alan will start to suspect something if you don't? Isobel has already pointed out that it's highly unusual for a seven-month baby to weigh almost eight pounds at birth!'

Despite her admonitions to Cassy that she would have no part in the deception, Joscelin had had no alternative but to appear thrilled by their spur-of-the-moment wedding; and when Cassy had announced she was pregnant, Joscelin was obliged to listen to Alan's protestations of delight too.

Now, across the room, Joscelin could see Alan, his arm lovingly around Cassy's shoulders as she displayed the baby to her father. Despite Don Jaime's initial objections to his daughter's elopement, he had been unwilling to cut her out of his life. The more furiously his wife and Padre Alfonso had vilified Cassy, the more excuses he found for his favourite child. Although it distressed him that she was now 'living in sin', he had written to say he would come to England for the christening of his grandchild.

'Joscelin!' Marco's voice brought her thoughts back to her

present surroundings. 'I have not come all this way to see you still so disturbed,' he said quietly but firmly. 'Costain is married to Casilda, and they have a child to complete the magic circle. You, *cara mia*, cannot waste your life standing on the edge of that circle.'

His words, so exactly reflecting the desolation of her own feelings, unnerved her. They were too close to the truth. She had already determined that, once little Douglas had been christened, she would go away – far away where she need never see the pride and pleasure on Alan's face as he looked at the son who was not his.

'I'm taking you away,' Marco said – so casually that he might have been suggesting taking her out to dinner. 'We are booked on the Simplon-Orient Express on Tuesday week. We shall travel to Italy together.'

Joscelin lifted her head and met his resolute gaze. The words of protest died on her lips. Handsome though Marco was, she did not love him – *but she did need him*. He was offering her a way out; an escape from Cassy's demands on her friendship; from Alan's presence. Marco was right – now that Alan and Cassy were finally married there was no place for her in their lives and it was time she started to live for herself.

'You will come with me,' Marco said quietly, as if he were stating a matter of fact, 'and this time, Joscelin, I make no promises.' Suddenly, he smiled. 'I confess to you quite openly that this time it *is* my intention to seduce you, although I shall not insist upon it immediately. Do you know, *cara mia*, that you have grown even more beautiful this past year? But you are too thin. I shall have to choose your meals very carefully – lots of rich *pasticcini*!'

Joscelin was still searching for a reply when Cassy came hurrying over to them. She beamed at Marco. 'Wasn't I good not to give away our secret?' She tucked her arm in Joscelin's. 'Were you surprised to see him, Joss darling? Now I know who will be your partner at Henley next week. Alan and I have taken a house there, Marco, for the regatta and Joscelin has been refusing to go, but you will now, won't you, Joss? And you, Marco.'

'I am so sorry to disappoint you, Casilda,' Marco said, 'but Joscelin is coming back with me to Italy. It's a resumption of the visit that had to be postponed last year. You do understand, don't you?'

'How perfectly divine for you, Joss!' Cassy said, kissing her warmly on both cheeks. 'I must go and tell Alan. When will you be leaving?'

'On Tuesday,' Marco answered for her, as if it had all been agreed. It was then Joscelin knew there would be no turning back.

Throughout the journey, she allowed Marco to take complete command. He had announced that they would not be going to the Villa dei Uccelli but directly to the Palazzo Petrucci, near Siena.

It crossed Joscelin's mind that, whatever was to happen between her and Marco, her reputation was to remain unscathed. She wondered if he had thought of this before deciding to take her to his country home. He seemed to have thought of everything else necessary for her well-being.

She was grateful that he did not try to touch her, holding her hand or arm only for as long as it was necessary to assist her. Not once did he try to kiss her. Only his flow of compliments indicated that he found her attractive . . . and this comforted rather than distressed her.

It was not until four days after her arrival at the Palazzo Petrucci that Joscelin realized she had been through some kind of nervous breakdown, and that Marco had sensed her need for total freedom from emotional tension. The days passed lazily, sometimes spent sitting quietly with Marco in the shady loggia enjoying the beautiful panorama of the Sienese countryside; sometimes spent walking side by side in the sun-baked gardens. Sometimes he left her alone with her sketchpad, saying he had matters to attend to.

One afternoon Joscelin said to Marco: 'Have you ever

thought how lucky you are? If I were you, I could never bear to leave this house. Everywhere I look, there is beauty.'

'It makes me happy to know that you are so happy here,' he said, his voice deepening.

She turned to face him, her eyes dropping as she saw the passionate intensity of his gaze. She felt ridiculously shy. 'I am so very grateful to you, Marco, for bringing me here,' she faltered. 'Already I feel . . . different, more relaxed. But I do feel guilty, too. I have been such dull company and . . . .'

'There is plenty of time, Joscelin,' he interrupted quietly. 'No limits have been set on the number of days we shall spend together. It is important never to hurry that which needs no haste. It pleases me very much to hear that you are feeling happier.' He rested his hand against the nape of her neck, the gesture casual yet strangely intimate. 'Tomorrow I have planned a little outing for you, *carissima*. I shall drive you down to Siena and show you the Campo, the big square where next month the famous Palio horse race will take place. Siena is nearly as beautiful as Florence, and many of our greatest artists have lived there. Its history goes so far back in time it has become legendary.'

The beauties of the old walled town of Siena surpassed all Joscelin's expectations and Marco's promises. She was exhausted and yet wildly stimulated by the end of a long day's sightseeing.

Looking at her flushed, excited face, Marco suggested they should round off the day by dining at a hillside restaurant instead of returning to the palazzo. 'To celebrate your return to life!' he explained enigmatically.

It was quite late when they finished and darkness had fallen when he suggested he should drive her to see a nearby lake which, he told her, was most spectacular in the moonlight.

It was a hot, sultry night, and Marco took down the hood of the Fraschini so that Joscelin could get a better view of the large expanse of silvery water. Dark silhouettes of cypress trees bordered the edges of the lake, and across the water Joscelin could see the twinkling lights of little lakeside villages. A great swathe of moonlight formed a path across the mirror-like surface. Above the incessant chirping of the cicadas she could hear the gentle lapping of the ripples of water. High above their heads was a roof of stars, and the moon hung like a pale yellow orb in the eastern night sky.

Quietly, without warning, Marco drew Joscelin into his arms and kissed her. It was a soft, exploratory kiss, not tentative but without haste, as if he were unwilling to frighten her; as if he were well aware of the confusion of her emotions. One part of her wished to respond . . . yet she could think only of Alan, Cassy's husband now, whom she had no right to love. But her heart was crying out for his, not Marco's kisses.

'*Carissima*!' Marco murmured as he gently stroked her hair. 'I have been content until today to see the happiness returning to your face; but now I hope to see a look that tells me I am not just a friend, but a man – one who attracts you.'

Joscelin bit her lip. 'Marco, I like you very, *very* much,' she said, 'and I do find you attractive, both as a person and as a man. Because of that, I can't cheat by pretending I'm falling in love with you. I think it would be easy if things were different, but however hard I try, I don't seem to be able to make myself "fall out of love" with . . . with . . .'

'Costain?' he filled the name in for her. 'He is not for you, Joscelin, and you know it. So let me help you to forget him. I can, if you will trust me. I am in love with you and I wish one day to marry you. I would wish to marry you now, immediately, if I thought only for myself. But I understand that it is too soon to expect you to return my love. I know also that you are too honest a person to pretend. So I am happy for the time being to accept from you only what you can freely give. I believe love will come in time.'

If she did allow Marco to become her lover, *would* it help her to forget Alan? Joscelin asked herself. Was it possible that for all these years she had been nurturing a romantic dream? Marco was reality. He loved her . . . and he had been unbelievably patient in his pursuit of her. He found her desirable and, if she were honest, she could not deny that her body, if not her heart, responded to him. Perhaps, as he suggested, she could learn in time to love him.

'Marco . . .' she said hesitantly, 'it doesn't seem fair . . . I mean, all the giving would be on your side. You seem so sure that I could respond, but I could disappoint you. I . . .'

He silenced her with another long kiss, but this time there was passion as well as tenderness in it. When he released her, he said: 'My darling Joscelin, I know you are twenty-five years old and that you consider yourself both independent and self-reliant. But you are a child where love is concerned. I shall take you home now and you must believe that I know what is right for us both. Trust me, *cara mia*, and we shall be happy. You will see.'

When they reached the Palazzo Petrucci, as if it were his custom he followed her into her bedroom.

Joscelin had had time on the drive home to regret her weakness; and panic was now overwhelming her. She would look silly, so naïve, if she turned now and told him she had changed her mind; that she couldn't go through with it!

Marco came to stand behind her. He placed his hands on her shoulders.

'*Ti amo*, Joscelin,' he said softly. 'Don't be afraid!'

'I'm sorry, Marco. I'm not used to . . . to doing this kind of thing!'

He kissed the top of her head and said lightly: 'That is not something for which you need apologize, *cara mia*. It pleases me very much that I might be the first.'

The colour rushed into Joscelin's checks. 'Not exactly . . .' she faltered. 'There was once . . . once when . . .'

'You do not have to tell me about it,' he broke in as he turned her round to face him and put his arms around her waist. 'From your face, I see that the occasion is not a happy memory. But *we* shall be happy tonight, you and I. Trust me!' he said again.

Slowly, he unloosed the silken sheath of her dress and it slid downwards. Joscelin closed her eyes. She could feel his kisses where the shoulder straps had been, and suddenly she felt as if this were all quite unreal; that she herself was an onlooker, watching the half-naked woman standing silent, trembling, whilst her companion continued to undress her. This, she thought, was not happening to her, but to some stranger who resembled her.

'You must think only of love!' Marco said. 'Love is beautiful, *carissima*, and *you* are beautiful!'

His words made her suddenly aware of her nakedness, and in an agony of shyness she pressed herself against him and buried her face in his shoulder. His arms tightened about her and she felt his soft kisses against her neck and throat.

Effortlessly he lifted her and carried her to the bed, laying her down against the soft white pillows. For a moment he stood silent, looking at her. Then he smiled. 'Wait there for me. I won't be long!'

He returned a few moments later wearing a dressing-gown. He sat down on the edge of the bed and, sensing Joscelin's nervousness, he said with a smile: 'Do you like my robe, Joscelin? I believe Noel Coward has made these very fashionable!' He took one of her hands and gently kissed the palm. 'All the same, I am pleased *you* are not wearing one. You are perfect just as you are!' His expression was tender as he added: 'Alas, I cannot see in the moonlight if I have made you blush. You are the only girl I know who blushes so easily – and so charmingly!'

Somewhere deep in her consciousness, Joscelin realized that he was deliberately giving her time to relax, and that he had no intention of forcing her into something she might regret. She wondered if he had any idea how vulnerable she felt – and how confused. At one moment, he was the familiar friend of the past week – thoughtful, adoring and immensely kind; and a second later, when she dared to look at him, he was a threatening stranger who wanted to take possession of her body.

Her eyes closed, shutting out Marco's face but not his presence. She felt herself gathered against him; felt his hands gentle but demanding on her body, in which, unexpectedly, an insistent trembling had begun. It deepened slowly and became a compulsive longing she could not suppress.

Marco was now lying beside her as naked as she. She could hear his voice murmuring endearments in his own language, but could only sense their meaning. Her body acquired a will of its own as it responded to his caresses. His lips were against her throat, her ears, on the nape of her neck as she strained against him, aware of her own softness, his hard maleness and her burning need.

Suddenly he was inside her. She felt herself rise and fall in rhythm with him, and knew that all sensation began and would end with the measured thrusting of his movements. She heard herself cry out her need. Only then did he release control of his own passion, sweeping her with him to an ecstasy she had never imagined.

As their hurried movements slowed, Joscelin felt his lips on hers.

'*Amore mio!*' he whispered. 'Tell me that I have made you happy!'

Tears sprang to her eyes – her sadness irrational, for she *was* happy and fulfilled in a way she had never imagined possible. She brushed the tears away, and taking one of Marco's hands, clasped it passionately to her heart. 'I never imagined it could be so wonderful,' she murmured truthfully.

He kissed her again and then pulled the covers over them, enfolding her in his arms and drawing her head onto his shoulder.

'Sleep now, *carissima!*' he said. 'We will talk in the morning. Now it is very late. I want you to fall asleep in my arms.'

Obediently she closed her eyes, feeling once more that deep lethargy which demanded she stop trying to rationalize her emotions, and leave herself in the care of this man who seemed to know her far better than she knew herself.

Birdsong assailed Joscelin's sleeping ears next morning. Beside her Marco stirred. '*Carissima!*' his sleepy voice demanded her attention. '*Buon giorno, amore mio!*'

'Good morning,' she ventured, feeling absurdly shy.

'You have slept like a lady in love!' The teasing tone made it suddenly possible for her to meet his eyes. He reached out one hand and stroked her hair.

'If you did not sleep in contentment, then I have failed at my first attempt to make you fall in love with me.'

Joscelin smiled, her embarrassment gone. 'I slept very well, Marco, but surely to be content is not necessarily to be in love. Is it so important? Can't we be happy as . . . as we are?' she asked, suddenly serious.

'It is important because I am in love with you. I cannot make love to a woman unless I know she cares for me, and then always I am a little in love myself.'

Joscelin said truthfully: 'I should like *very much* to fall in love with you, Marco, but . . .'

'It is not a decision you have to make now,' he interrupted firmly. Moving gently but decisively, he drew her down to lie within the circle of his arm. Very softly, he kissed one bare shoulder and then her mouth. After several more kisses, Joscelin realized that her body was once more responding of its own accord and that she wanted Marco to make love to her again.

It was not until several days later that Joscelin admitted that she seemed insatiable. Marco aroused her to an intensity of passion she had not known she possessed. She had become a stranger to herself, and even noticed a difference in her appearance on which Marco commented.

'Every day you become more beautiful!' he said and, staring at her reflection in the mirror, Joscelin could see that it was in part true. Her face had filled out; her body too, its curves more noticeable as she put on weight. Marco persuaded her to let her hair grow, and at his suggestion she now wore it parted in the middle and curling forward over her ears because he liked it that way. And it suited her. She allowed him to buy her new

clothes, softer, more feminine, more becoming than those she
would have chosen for herself.

She wanted very much to please him; to make him as happy
as he made her – and, to her surprise, she was far more often
happy than sad. When he was not making love to her, Marco
drove her in his Fraschini round the surrounding countryside
and for walks along the lakeside, stopping to eat at little
restaurants or cafés where he held her hand and made love
to her with his eyes.

England and the past began to recede further from Joscelin's
thoughts, although the occasional letter from Cassy brought
back painful memories.

> Alan and I went to *Bitter Sweet* at His Majesty's. You'd
> have loved, it, Joss . . .
>
> Will you believe Alan wanted to know when he could
> order a kilt for Douglas . . . Costain plaid, of course. He's
> crazy about the baby, so you needn't worry . . .
>
> I never say no to Alan, but I always think of Milton and
> what he did and I get so bored. Are you doing it with
> Marco? Is he a good lover? I wish you were here to talk
> to . . .

This letter reinforced Joscelin's relief at being exactly where
she was. She could not have borne to hear Cassy talk of the
intimate life she shared with Alan.

After a particularly exhilarating day in Siena at the Palio
horse race Marco finally drove Joscelin home. He looked at
her flushed, excited face as he took her into the bedroom and
grasped both her hands tightly in his own.

'You are happy, *carissima*, are you not? You have enjoyed
today?'

She wound her arms round his neck. 'You know I have,
Marco – and I am *very* happy. I never imagined I could feel
so content.'

For once, there was no smile in Marco's dark eyes. He was

staring at her intently. 'Could you be happy here with me *always*?' he asked. 'You must know that I love you. I want to marry you, Joscelin. I want you to be my wife.'

Joscelin drew in her breath. Deep down she had known that Marco was on the point of proposing. She tried to marshal her thoughts. Did she really love him . . . or just the happiness he gave her? The future would be so easy were she to marry Marco, have children, paint, let life drift by as it had these past few weeks. She need never see Alan again, she could forget she had ever dreamed of a different love.

Marco put one finger beneath her chin and forced her to look at him. 'Do not give me your answer unless you are going to say "yes",' he said, 'but I wanted you to know that for me this is not just an affair. I want you to be my wife. *Ti amo*, Joscelin.'

Tears filled Joscelin's eyes. 'Oh, Marco, I'm not sure if I know any longer what love is. I do know that I am *very* fond of you; that I have never been happier, that I find you very attractive. But is that enough, Marco? It could be just gratitude I feel. You have given me so much . . .'

He drew her against him and kissed her, at first gently but with growing passion. 'We won't discuss it further tonight,' he said as he began to remove her dress. 'It is enough that you want me. Tell me again that you do!'

Joscelin needed no second bidding, for this at least involved no self-questioning. As she surrendered herself to him, she abandoned her thoughts too – all but the one burning question: whether this after all was love.

CHAPTER TWENTY-FOUR

July 1930

On 3 July, Cassy saw Milton Fleming again. They were both guests at the wedding of Maureen Guinness to Lord Ava at St Margaret's, Westminster. Amongst the vast throng of people, Cassy's former lover did not see her – for which she was grateful. The pounding of her heart and the trembling of her legs were warning enough that, despite her marriage and the birth of her child, she was not yet immune to the fascination this man had for her. She needed time to collect herself; to be certain whether she wished even to acknowledge him; but throughout the reception she was never in any real doubt that, although she hated him as she had never before hated anyone in her life, she *must* see him again.

Skilfully manoeuvring herself from one society hostess to another, she learned at whose house he would be dining that night and shamelessly wheedled an invitation for herself, using Alan's absence in Scotland as an explanation for her having no previous entertainment arranged.

As the hour approached for Polly to begin dressing her, Cassy's restlessness increased. As her maid laid out her evening clothes on the bed, she unfairly chastised her for being late. Polly knew better than to argue when her mistress was in one of her moods – and it was clear that madam was upset about something. Polly imagined the cause of her edginess was anxiety about the baby.

'I dare say Nurse has no cause to be in such a pucker about Master Douglas!' she volunteered, hoping to soothe Cassy as she searched for her shoes.

'Stop chattering, Polly, and run my bath,' Cassy said sharply. She did not wish to be reminded that Nurse had been fussing all day about the baby's health. She had mentioned it when Cassy was getting ready for the wedding, going on and on about his colour and his temperature. Cassy had visited the nursery just before leaving the house, and although she thought the baby did look a little flushed, he seemed otherwise in perfect health.

'I'll phone the doctor when I get back if Baby's any worse,' she had promised. She resented the implied criticism of herself for paying so little attention to the child, visiting the nursery only twice a day and remaining as short a time as possible. But each time she looked at the infant, the cornflower blue of his eyes staring up at her reminded her painfully and unpleasantly of Milton Fleming.

Understandably enough, Alan could not understand her aversion to the baby any more than did Nurse, thus adding frustration to Cassy's irritation with them both and her lingering feelings of guilt.

Returning from the wedding reception, Cassy had wanted only to go to her room where she could rest and think about what she would say to Milton when she met him at dinner. She would be cutting; let him see that he had not ruined her life; that she had managed perfectly well without him. But, of course, it was not entirely true. Each time Alan made love to her she gritted her teeth and closed her eyes, the longing for her lover tormenting her as she lay in the darkness remembering what *he* had done to her . . .

No sooner did Cassy reach her bedroom than Nurse had demanded to see her. 'I really think we should have the doctor immediately, madam. Baby took his two o'clock bottle but I don't like the look of him.'

'Very well, Nurse, I'll telephone Dr Scott,' Cassy had conceded in order to be rid of her. 'But you'll have to see the doctor. I'm going out tonight and I must have a rest first.'

Cassy had tried to telephone the doctor but his number had

been engaged, and with so much else on her mind she had forgotten until after her rest when Polly's remark reminded her. Now she glanced anxiously at her watch. It was getting late but, she thought, doctors were paid to make calls at whatever time they were needed. She would telephone again the moment she was dressed.

An hour later, Cassy stood in front of her mirror surveying her reflection, then she looked at the little clock beside her bed and hurriedly grabbed her gloves and pochette. She had intended to make a late arrival, an entrance – but *not* as late as this. As Polly followed her onto the landing, Nurse came hurrying downstairs to confront her. She said accusingly: 'Doctor's still not been, madam. Do you think we should telephone again?'

Cassy bit her lip, guilt instantly dousing her excitement. 'I'll do so immediately, Nurse,' she said. 'It really is very lax of Dr Scott to keep us waiting.'

At the foot of the stairs, she found the doctor's number and asked the operator to connect her. Impatiently, she waited to be put through.

'I'm sorry, caller, the number is engaged. Will you hold the line?'

Cassy hesitated, glancing at her little diamond wristwatch. 'No, don't worry operator. I'll try again later.'

She would telephone from her hostess's house, Cassy thought as she donned her wrap and hurried across the hall to the front door. Lady Minton lived only a short distance away in Sloane Street . . . and a few more minutes could not possibly matter.

But Cassy was not the only guest to arrive late at Lady Minton's house. As the butler opened the door to Cassy she heard Milton Fleming's drawl:

'Well, if it's not the beautiful Lady Deighton . . . correction, Mrs Costain! I'd know that posterior anywhere. So we meet again, Casilda.' As if he were her escort, he tucked his arm through hers and led her indoors.

Somehow Cassy managed to smile at the maid waiting to conduct her upstairs to the room where she could leave her wrap; somehow she managed to say 'Good evening' in a level tone of voice to a fellow guest arriving late like herself; somehow she found the strength to walk back downstairs; to deny the raging, tormenting temptation to throw all caution to the wind and run down the curving staircase and into Milton's arms.

So complete was her concentration upon her effort to control herself that she forgot everything but the need to maintain her dignity. She forgot, too, the telephone call she had determined to make for her child.

'Oh, Cassy, darling, *please* stop crying!'

Alan sighed as she twisted out of his arms. He was at his wits' end to know how to cope with her. The doctor had forecast that time would be the best cure . . . other than having another baby as quickly as possible. But when Alan had tentatively implied this, Cassy screamed at him as if he had suggested something terrible.

He looked at his wife's drooping shoulders as she went to the window and stood staring down into the street. Since the tragedy, she sometimes stood there for half an hour at a time, refusing to speak to him. He reminded himself that she was still very shocked, that it was only a fortnight since, following a convulsion, poor little Douglas had died.

When Alan had arrived at the house twenty-four hours later he was hard put to discover what had actually happened that dreadful night. Both Cassy and Nurse were hysterical, Nurse gabbling that she had been anxious all day that the baby was ill, but that Cassy wouldn't telephone the doctor. Cassy swore she *had* done so, saying that Nurse was trying to put the blame for the little boy's death onto her. She had insisted upon the poor woman's instant dismissal.

For Cassy's sake Alan tried to hide his own grief from her. But he found it difficult to mention the baby or the inevitable funeral arrangements without a break in his voice, and his attempts at self-control seemed only to aggravate Cassy's private torment. Between bouts of crying, she rounded on him.

'You blame me, don't you, Alan? You think it was my fault. Well, I did everything I could . . . *everything*. How was I to know that silly woman was not just fussing about nothing? You know how she was with the baby . . . fuss, fuss, fuss all the time!'

She paced round the drawing room, the colour in her cheeks heightening as she parodied the nurse's voice.

'"*He was hiccoughing all morning, madam!*" "*The poor little mite was sick this afternoon, madam!*" "*I think we'd best call the doctor, madam. Baby has a nasty red spot on his tummy!*"' Cassy glared at Alan. 'How was I to know it was serious this time? And anyway, I *did* telephone the doctor and it wasn't *my* fault the number was engaged or that he was out when I finally got through to his surgery . . .'

Alan crossed the room and tried to put his arms around her. He wanted to comfort her; to be close to her so that they could share their grief.

Cassy backed away from him. 'Leave me alone!' she cried. 'I know you hate me. Why don't you just say so and be done with it!'

Alan's arms dropped to his sides. 'Cassy darling, you don't know what you're saying,' he said gently. 'I love you very much. And the very last thing I feel like is blaming you for what happened. You know very well that it was an unfortunate, terrible accident. No one was at fault, Cassy. Please, darling, don't cry like that.'

She ought to have her mother here to comfort her, he thought, knowing at once that the idea was ridiculous. Aunt Ursula had refused to accept the marriage and had not written to Cassy when the baby had been born. His own mother would have known how to deal with Cassy, but when Walter had been bankrupted by the Wall Street crash his wife had left him, and he and Alan's mother were trying to remake their lives together in New York. The Mater had taken a job as saleslady for a cosmetic firm, and could not afford the time to come over to England.

There was only himself to offer comfort, Alan thought wretchedly, and he was proving incapable. Unless . . .

'I'm going to telephone Joss and ask her to come and stay with us,' he said on impulse. 'You'd like that, darling, wouldn't you?'

Cassy's face brightened. 'Oh, Alan, yes, I do want Joss! She'll understand how I feel. You must tell her how much I need her.'

Not trusting himself to speak, Alan walked slowly out of the room. Cassy did not mean to be cruel, but it hurt him dreadfully to know that she felt her best friend could comfort her, understand her, whereas he could not.

It was over an hour before the operator was able to put through a trunk call to the Palazzo Petrucci, and then, since Joscelin was not expected back until the evening, leave a message for her to telephone him as soon as she could.

It was the following morning before Alan heard from her. The line connecting them was surprisingly good, and her gasp of horror as he outlined his terrible news was clearly audible. He cut short her condolences, for her sympathy was more than he could bear at this moment.

'I'm frantic with worry about Cassy,' he told her. 'She seems to think it was her fault. She needs you desperately and I do, too. Perhaps *you* can bring a little sanity back to this house. I don't want to spoil your holiday . . .'

Holiday! Joscelin's stay had ceased to be any such thing. She had told Marco that she would remain in Italy with him until such time as she felt absolutely sure that she wished to marry him. Each day since he had formally proposed to her, she had felt more certain that a marriage between them might work. Marco was a perfect lover. He understood her. He was tolerant, kind, an amusing and interesting companion. She really *liked* him . . . and only very occasionally, usually when she was on the point of falling asleep, had the memory of Alan returned to haunt her.

'. . . not if it interferes with your plans!' Alan's voice brought her back to the immediacy of the problem. He sounded almost embarrassed.

'Can I ring you again and let you know?' Joscelin broke in. 'I'll talk to Marco. I'm so *very* sorry, Alan.'

For a long while after the call had been disconnected, Joscelin stood motionless as she tried to rationalize her feelings. She did not *want* to go, to leave this sunny haven where she was surrounded by love and beauty; where life seemed so tranquil and easy. Even less did she want to listen to Cassy's protestations of guilt.

Her guilt was probably retrospective, Joscelin thought, as she stood in the big, empty hallway. Cassy was superstitious enough to believe that, because she had once wished the baby out of existence, her wish had now come true. Poor Cassy! Perhaps she thought this was God's vengeance on her for marrying outside her religion and for pretending the baby was Alan's.

No, Joscelin thought uneasily. She was not going to spoil her idyll for Cassy, however unhappy she was. But Alan had sounded so desperate, so lost! Having seen his delight in his little boy before she left England, Joscelin could imagine his sorrow. He had said *he*, too, needed her.

As she returned to the loggia where Marco was sitting, Joscelin's uncertainty increased. Marco was smiling as he rose to kiss her before drawing her down onto the marble bench beside him. How could she find the courage to tell him that for the second time in their lives she was going to let him down?

But Marco knew she had been telephoning Alan and her anxious face left him in no doubt that the matter must be serious. He prised the facts from her, his face darkening as he began to understand. It was Alan Costain who was taking her away from him . . . the man he had hoped was forgotten; the man Joscelin had loved for so long.

'Costain has no right to ask you to sort out *his* troubles!' he protested violently. 'Are you not supposed to have a life of your own, Joscelin?'

Joscelin understood his anger; that if she were to leave him now for Alan's sake, he could be in no further doubt that her affection for him took second place.

'Don't go, *carissima!*' Marco said in a low, fierce voice. He took both her hands and looked deep into her eyes. 'Can't you see what is happening? If you go back, it will not be long before you start believing again that you are in love with Costain. Even were you to forget all that we have shared, what future is there for you in loving a married man? And you were beginning to forget him, Joscelin. You have come close enough to loving me. Has all this meant so little to you that you can throw it aside because *his* wife is unhappy? Why *you*, Joscelin? Let someone else console them!'

His words were convincing, his appeal not to be ignored. But as Joscelin stared back at him it was as if these last few magical weeks were a dream, and Marco was a stranger. She could almost sense an invisible barrier rising up between them. This man had been her lover, yet she felt herself wanting to withdraw her hands from his grasp; to step back from him.

'I don't *want* to go!' she said helplessly. 'Oh, Marco!'

High overhead in the brilliant blue sky, a tiny aeroplane was tracing fluffy white vapour trails. The golden face of the tower glowed in the sunlight, swifts weaving their way with unerring precision to and from their nests in the stonework. The pungent smell of roses and carnations permeated the air. A terrible sense of desolation swept over her. She knew that if she left Marco now, it would be all over between them.

He drew her to her feet and kissed her passionately in a way that only an hour ago would have evoked her instant response. But now she could see Alan's face. Perhaps if he had not said he needed her . . . but the words had been spoken and she could not ignore them . . . whatever the cost to herself or to Marco.

'I'm sorry, Marco, I'm so very sorry!' she whispered. 'But I have to go.'

He held her for a moment longer, a look of great sadness in his eyes before he turned away, saying, 'Then I'll drive you to Milan. You had better go and pack your things, *carissima.*'

She knew then that she would be unlikely ever to hear that particular endearment again.

People like Cassy, Joscelin thought, as the mannequin postured in front of them in yet another Worth creation, did not have nervous breakdowns. Those belonged to people who bottled up their emotions, whereas Cassy openly expressed her every mood. For the moment she was happy, choosing garments to wear at Cowes the following week. The previously arranged visit to Henley regatta had, of course, been cancelled and Cassy looked upon Monty Piermont's invitation to join his house party at Cowes as a compensation.

Alan, Cassy confided, was adamantly refusing to accept the invitation. Despite this, she was certain he would change his mind at the last minute in order not to disappoint her, and she was determined to have her wardrobe fully prepared.

Now she was listening eagerly to the vendeuse telling her that the widely flared trousers of the shantung beach pyjamas were 'the very latest thing'. Next year, the saleswoman was saying, every woman would be wearing them, and madam would be setting the fashion at Cowes. Madam must try them on.

Cassy turned to Joscelin, her eyes shining.

'Aren't they fun, Joss? You must have a pair, too, and don't say you can't afford them . . . I *want* to treat you. It gives me a chance to show how grateful I am.' She lowered her voice as she added. 'Thanks to you, I've stopped feeling so guilty about the poor baby. Besides,' she added mischievously, 'I'm going to need your help this evening to persuade Alan to change his mind about the regatta!'

This past week, Joscelin had come close to hating Cassy. Once Joscelin had convinced her that her forgetfulness was forgivable since she had not realized how ill the infant had been, Cassy had stopped crying and reverted to her normal bright self, her inexhaustible energy driving her to pursue activities that met with Alan's disapproval. He felt it was far too soon after the death of the child for Cassy to be rejoining their social circle.

'Well, I'm not going into mourning the way I did after Jimmy died! You said you wanted me to be happy . . . but you don't seem to like it when I am!'

Looking thoroughly distressed, Alan had appealed to Joscelin for her advice. 'I simply don't understand Cassy's attitude,' he said helplessly. 'Surely she can't feel like being jolly? I know she's trying to cover up her unhappiness – but people wouldn't know that. They'd be shocked if they saw us out on the town enjoying ourselves!'

'It's the only way Cassy knows to help her forget the tragedy,' Joscelin had replied, her heart aching at the sight of Alan's miserable face. 'I expect she is suffering every bit as much as you . . . only she can't show it.'

Now, as Cassy busied herself trying on yet another outfit, Joscelin knew that she had not been honest with Alan. Cassy had never wanted the baby and she was not grieving for it.

Cassy was struggling back into her clothes. 'Let's go and have tea at Fortnum's. Alan can hardly object to *that*!' she added with a bitter edge to her voice.

That evening Cassy said with pretended casualness: 'It would be so perfect if I could wear some of my new clothes somewhere *special*, Alan. I've been thinking all day, ever since I tried on those stunning beach pyjamas, wouldn't they be absolutely right for the regatta?' Her voice quickened as she felt Alan stiffen. 'Of course, I know we wouldn't be joining in any of the cocktail parties and that sort of thing. We'd just sit quietly and watch the boats or go for walks and . . .'

'No, Cassy!' Alan's tone was unusually sharp. 'It's simply not suitable in the circumstances. You must see that. It's only three weeks since . . .'

Cassy jumped to her feet, knocking over her coffee as she did so. Her cheeks were flaming and her eyes were flashing. 'You don't want me to be happy!' she cried. 'You don't care how miserable I am! All you can talk about is what's suitable. All you really care about is what people would think. Well, I *don't* care!'

'If you'll excuse me, I'm off to bed,' Joscelin said, rising to her feet. But Cassy was not going to allow her to leave. She ran to her and caught her arms.

'Why don't you tell Alan how utterly selfish he's being!' she cried. 'He's just trying to punish me!'

Joscelin tried to release herself from Cassy's grasp, her eyes going involuntarily to Alan's unhappy face. Now he, too, was on his feet.

'Cassy, you don't know what you're saying. I realize that you are disappointed, but do *please* try to understand. I am *not* trying to punish you. I don't even care what people think of us. But it simply isn't on, darling. If you're honest, you'll admit we wouldn't be able to sit quietly and go for walks the way you're suggesting. You'd want to join in everything – and Cassy, I couldn't – not even for you.'

Joscelin's heart ached for him as she sensed his feeling of impotence.

'It's probably my fault for not making it clearer to you how I felt when the boy died,' he said quietly. 'It's not the sort of thing I find easy to talk about. It hit me harder than you realized, Cassy, and no matter how much I tried, I couldn't face parties just yet. I can't forget that easily.'

Cassy twisted away from Joscelin, releasing her restraining arms as she took a step towards Alan. Her eyes were dark with anger as she stormed at him. 'That's all you think about . . . the baby . . . the baby . . . the baby! I'm sick to death of you shutting yourself up in your study moping hour after hour. Well, I'm not going to be second-best. For the last time, Alan, are you or aren't you going to take me to Cowes?'

With a sick dread in the pit of her stomach, Joscelin stepped forward, but Cassy pushed her aside. 'Cassy, no!' Joscelin cried sharply. 'Calm down. *Think what you're saying.* Cowes doesn't matter . . . not really. *Cassy . . .*'

Cassy's chin lifted. 'Leave me alone!' she shouted. 'Answer me, Alan, are you going to take me? Yes or no?'

His voice almost inaudible, Alan said: 'I'm sorry, Cassy, but the answer is no. I think we should show some respect for our child.'

Joscelin closed her eyes. As if echoing down a long tunnel, she heard Cassy's voice: '*Our* child, Alan, *ours*! Well, perhaps you'll change your mind when I tell you he was *my* child, certainly – but he was never, ever yours!'

CHAPTER TWENTY-FIVE

July–August 1933

'So I've finally tracked you down!'

Patri's hazel eyes were bright with pleasure as he stood in the doorway of Joscelin's studio and surveyed the tall figure of his cousin, Alan, spreadeagled on the carpet in front of the unlit fire.

Joscelin put down her paintbrush and, with a cry of pleasure, hurried into his arms.

'Patri! What a lovely surprise! Why didn't you let us know you were coming?'

Alan was now on his feet, smiling as he put an arm affectionately round his cousin's shoulders and led him to the sofa.

Patri grinned.

'I came over from Germany last night on a spur-of-the-moment business trip. Rebekka had a miscarriage recently – it would have been our third child – so she wasn't well enough to come with me. I'll be here a few days, Alan, and hoped I might beg a bed from you?'

'Superfluous question!' Alan commented. 'You have two children, Patri? I only knew about little Carlos. Why didn't someone write and tell me about the other!'

'Because most of the time, none of us knew where to write!' Joscelin said, laughing. 'And I could hardly put "Somewhere in Africa" on the envelope. Patri and Rebekka had a little girl two years ago.'

'Well, congratulations, old man!' Alan said, the tiniest of inflections in his voice causing Joscelin to glance surreptitiously at him. It was the first hint she had had since his return to

England last Christmas that he still felt bitter about the baby. He had never referred to the subject after that dreadful evening when Cassy had blurted out the truth. Nor, so Cassy told her, had he ever inquired who was the father of the child. A fortnight after her confession, he had departed to Africa – almost three years ago today, Joscelin thought now as Alan sat beside Patri on the sofa and lit his pipe. Cassy had left a week later to stay with her friends, the van Vreedens, who had rented a villa in the South of France. Since then, she had put in fleeting appearances in London between further visits to Paris, New York, Venice, Cairo, Switzerland. She did not hide the fact that, whenever it was possible for her to do so, her travels took her to the part of the world where she knew Milton Fleming would be.

Nevertheless, when Alan finally returned to London last Christmas, Cassy too came home, and as far as Joscelin and their friends were aware, the marriage was patched up. For once Cassy did not come round to Joscelin's flat to pour out her confidences, for which Joscelin was grateful. Her sympathies lay with Alan. As far as she knew, Cassy's life was now a continuous round of social activity, and these past few months it was Alan, not Cassy, who was her frequent visitor, using her studio flat as a home from home. He was fired with enthusiasm for his new book and spent hours discussing the illustrations with her. Neither one mentioned Cassy or the past except in the most general of terms.

'. . . difficult to think of you as the father of a five-year-old!' Alan was saying as Patri produced some snapshots of his wife and family. 'One forgets how old we're all growing. In a couple of months' time I'll be thirty-two – an old man! And that makes you twenty-seven, Patri, or is it twenty-eight?'

'Twenty-seven!' Joscelin broke in. 'He's nine months younger than I.'

Patri grinned. 'You don't look your age, Joss. You get prettier each time I see you, don't you agree, Alan?'

Alan nodded and then smiled. 'As a matter of fact I do, but

Joscelin won't thank you for the compliment, Patri. You'll make her blush!'

Joscelin laughed, enjoying their teasing. 'Ran into an old flame of yours last summer,' Patri said, 'Marco da Cortona. Got himself married to an Italian contessa. Rebekka and I were invited to the wedding but we couldn't go. Dare say you saw the announcement in *The Times*.'

Joscelin had not done so and the news came as a shock. But she pretended it was no surprise and quickly left the room on the excuse that she would make them all a cup of tea.

Although it was now over three years since her affair with Marco, she had often wondered whether she had ruined her life by refusing the chance of becoming his wife. At such moments she believed they might have been happy together, and there were many more when she lay alone in bed, wishing he were there beside her.

But now she knew that Marco's marriage was more a blow to her pride than to her heart. She had managed to fill her life with her work, and was even beginning to make a name for herself as an illustrator. Money was no longer a problem and she could afford to indulge in her liking for really good clothes, and for paintings. She had a growing collection of works by lesser-known artists which particularly pleased her. These, together with some of her own paintings, now vied with each other for room on her studio walls. Occasionally she sold one of her own canvases but, although she had been offered a high price for it, she had refused to part with her sepia sketch of Marco's Palazzo Petrucchi. Perhaps she would feel less sentimental about it now she knew he was married, she reflected.

Joscelin returned with the tea-tray to hear Patri describing life in Germany now that the National Socialist leader, Adolf Hitler, had become Chancellor.

'Things were bad enough even before January,' he was saying to Alan. 'Anti-Semitism has been growing quite alarmingly, much as it did in Poland and Romania after the war.

Of course, Hitler has been exploiting conditions in Germany. He makes promises he cannot hope to fulfil.'

Alan looked at Patricio with interest. 'We all read about the Reichstag fire in February. A lot of the newspapers refuted the idea that the National Socialists were behind it.'

Patri's young face suddenly looked grave. 'Few people outside Germany seem to realize what *is* going on,' he said. 'It's common knowledge, of course, that professional people are no longer permitted to practise if they are Jews. It's the same for all intellectuals of Jewish origin, or anyone who openly opposes Hitler's ideas. Those who can do so are trying to get their money out of the country via the foreign embassies, and Herr Schwarz and I are doing our best to help. Thousands have already left Germany and gone to the United States or elsewhere. We've managed to get out some of Rebekka's relatives, the Stolbergs, but her mother won't leave without her husband. He isn't Jewish, of course, and he's one of the few people who can help the Stolbergs and Jewish families like them.'

'Is Rebekka in any danger?' Joscelin asked. 'Surely no one would harm her, the wife of a Spanish citizen?'

Patricio frowned. 'I'm worried,' he admitted. 'I'd like to take her and the children back to Sevilla, but Rebekka won't leave her mother. Frau Schwarz's brother was one of the professors who was flung out of the university in May. And it isn't just the Jewish people who are in danger. Anyone opposed to the party and prepared to say so risks being sent to a concentration camp. That's how serious it is!'

Alan stretched his long legs in front of him. 'These so-called stormtroopers, the SA – what are they really like, Patri?'

Patricio's mouth hardened. 'The truth doesn't make very pleasant listening, I'm afraid. I'll quote you a couple of lines from one of the most popular National Socialist songs: "When Jewish blood spurts from under the knife; / Things will be twice as good as before." It's quite inconceivable when you think of some of the people these words presumably apply to

– Arthur Schnabel, Germany's most revered pianist; Bruno Walter, the conductor; Einstein, the physicist – men of that ilk! And two months ago the Party ordered the mass burning of banned books in the square outside the Berlin opera house – lorry-loads of them, including works by Goethe. Imagine the English banning and burning Shakespeare's works because of his religious beliefs.'

'It's incomprehensible,' Alan agreed.

'Burning thousands upon thousands of books is bad enough,' Patri said bitterly, 'but what concerns me far more is the systematic torture – physical horrors – being inflicted on innocent people. They actually have torture chambers where their "suspects" are beaten with steel rods and rubber truncheons and whips, and their faces and bodies are kicked to a pulp. We know it's true because it has happened to friends of the Stolbergs. Some are killed . . . and others have been so badly injured they were glad to die. The Communists are as often victims as the Jews. Women, too, suffer the same appalling treatment. The police are powerless to help.'

As Patri fell silent, Joscelin said quietly: 'Surely Rebekka and the children *must* be made to leave? It is too great a risk to stay there, Patri. For you, too, if you are helping people to leave the country illegally.'

He drew a deep sigh. 'I know! But Rebekka feels that, once we have gone, her mother's side of the family will be at far greater risk. For the present, Herr Schwarz's position at the bank is secure and he is probably the only man we know with sufficient influence to help the Stolberg family. He is a wealthy man, and with these corrupt people he can often use bribes to get the rules bent. But for how long? If this tidal wave of anti-Jewish feeling grows, *how long* before they realize Herr Schwarz is married to a Jewess and they dispossess him of his banking organization, perhaps take *him* in for questioning?'

'I'd no idea things were so bad,' Alan said, patting Patri's shoulder sympathetically. 'If there's any way at all I can help, you must let me know.'

'Will do!' Patri said, his expression becoming cheerful once more as he questioned Alan about his explorations in Africa. As Alan's eager description of the rare white rhino came to an end, he grinned. 'Wish I could have been out there with you. Sounds fun!'

'Me too,' Joscelin said. 'But Alan's promised to take me next time he goes abroad, haven't you?'

Patri smiled at her. 'You're a strange girl, Joss. I believe you're a born naturalist like Alan.'

Joscelin laughed. 'Alan taught me how to appreciate nature when we went to Scotland,' she said. 'Uncle Fergus showed us birds and animals we would never have spotted on our own. We walked miles and miles and I wore out a pair of brogues completely.'

Patri grinned. 'You and Casilda must be about as opposite as the two poles,' he said. 'While you wear out your walking shoes, she wears out her dancing shoes. Don't you like socializing, Joss? I know Alan thinks that sort of thing a waste of time, but for a girl . . . well, you should be out having a good time.'

'I *am* having a good time,' Joscelin argued. 'I'm doing what I like doing. Cocktail parties and tea dances aren't my line, Patri – and never were. As for dancing, I only enjoy doing the pasodoble with you!'

They continued their banter until Alan put down his pipe and announced that he was taking them both out to dinner.

It was one of the happiest evenings Joss could recall in a long time. Patri was great fun to be with, his laughter spontaneous as he flirted with her in the old, familiar way. Although quiet, Alan's mood was cheerful enough and he was even laughing as he and Patri dropped her at her flat before returning to Rutland Gate.

'A nightcap, I think,' he said as he went into the drawing room.

The heat of the July day had cooled and the big room was a pleasant place to relax in as they sat down, glasses in hand.

'I'd forgotten what good company Joss is,' Patri said yawning. 'She has a wonderful sense of humour even though she's so quiet.'

Alan nodded. 'She's intelligent, too. One doesn't usually think of women as friends, yet she and I have had a marvellous platonic friendship most of our lives.'

Patri grinned. 'A *platonic* relationship? With someone as attractive as Joss? She's grown into an amazingly pretty woman, don't you agree?'

Alan sighed, running one hand through his hair thoughtfully. 'I suppose she has! I'd forgotten what a mouse-like little kid she used to be in the old days. She's been one hell of a good friend to me, and of course a colleague too. She's remarkably talented.'

Patri nodded. 'One wonders why she has never married. When I last talked to Casilda, she seemed to think Joss would end up marrying da Cortona. But obviously that's all off now. Seems a pity she hasn't found herself a husband. She'd make a damned good wife to some fellow.' He glanced at Alan and added: 'There was a time when I thought *you* might have married her. You remember that two-year break when our parents barred you from seeing Casilda? She fell for that chap Deighton; and when I heard they were engaged, I told Rebekka you'd probably marry Joss now Casilda was out of the running. At the time, we both agreed you'd be frightfully well suited, whereas you and Casilda had practically nothing in common. Still, love doesn't always take account of suitability, I suppose.'

For a moment or two, Alan did not speak. Then he said lightly: 'I'd no idea you had grown so profound in your old age, Patri! Fatherhood has obviously matured you! Meanwhile, how about another drink?'

They talked for a further half hour – mostly about Patri's mother, who had not been well recently, and about Spain.

'A great many changes have taken place and, according to Papá, life is far more difficult for big landowners. The working classes have been given grandiose ideas as to their rights, but the government is finding it far from easy to keep their promises to improve matters.

'Law and order has gone by the board,' Patri continued, 'I suppose because the restraining influence of the Church ceased when the Republic showed itself to be anti-clerical. They encouraged the working classes to think their enemy was the Church. Did you know the people burned over a hundred churches and convents a couple of years ago? It happened all over Spain, even in Sevilla. It was madness! It turned those Catholics and clergy who had supported the government into rabid anti-Republicans. Papá is hoping the Conservatives will regain power in the November elections. They want to restore the monarchy.'

'Having been in the depths of South Africa until recently, I'm out of touch,' Alan commented.

Patri shrugged. 'Ignorance is bliss, old chap! Nothing good has happened in Spain. I would give a great deal to have a chance of a talk with Carlota's Benito, now that's he's so well-off and can live almost as well as my father. He must reflect both points of view. The fact of the matter is, the poor are almost as badly off as ever.'

His mother, he went on to say, had been horrified by the desecration of Catholic property and had lost a lot of her cool detachment. Her nerves were in a bad way and his father was concerned about her health. She spent most of her time either praying with Padre Alfonso or lying in a darkened room complaining of severe stomach pains for which the doctors could find no cause.

He yawned sleepily. 'Casilda really ought to go and visit poor Mamá.'

Later, lying alone in the darkness, Alan reviewed his conversation with Patricio and realized that his cousin had for the most part avoided all but the most casual of references to

Cassy. Only once had he raised the topic of their marriage. It had surprised and disturbed Alan when Patri had remarked that he and Cassy had little in common. In a way, he had always known it, but supposed that they complemented each other, he providing a steadying influence, whilst Cassy . . .

Wearily Alan passed the back of his hand over his forehead. It was still singularly painful to him to recall how immorally she had behaved. It was impossible now to believe that she had ever loved him. Nevertheless their marriage existed, and although Cassy had pointed out that in the eyes of the Church it did not, there remained the question of a legal divorce. The subject had not been discussed since that terrible night when she had confessed the truth about the baby.

'You can do what you like. I don't care!' Cassy had wept when he had told her he considered their marriage was at an end. The following day, when he felt a little calmer and suggested a trial separation to give them both time to think things over whilst he was in Africa, Cassy had cheered up at once.

With an astonishing naïvety she had said: 'By the time you get back, Alan, maybe you will have forgiven me and we can start all over again. We can forget this ever happened . . .'

Perhaps *she* could forget, Alan thought now, but he wondered if he would ever be able to do so. In a strange way he did still care about her, and by the time they had both returned home the previous Christmas a great deal of his bitterness had subsided. Cassy behaved towards him as if there had been no long separation, no cause for the rift, kissing him and chattering excitedly as she made plans for the festivities.

But, despite her obvious desirability, Alan could not bring himself to go to her bedroom, and Cassy had made no demur when he continued to sleep in his dressing room.

Inevitably they had been invited to parties, dances, hunt balls – and had entertained and gone about as any other married couple. The subject of divorce was not raised, and when Cassy had gone off to Switzerland for a ski-ing holiday in the New Year he had for a short while missed her bright chatter and busy presence in the large house. But gradually he had become immersed in his new book, his visits to Joss's studio occuring more and more frequently.

Alan turned restlessly on his pillow. Patri's personal comments about Joss's appearance had disturbed his familiar image of her. Now, suddenly, he found himself seeing her not just as a friend but as an attractive woman. His memory stirred, evoking an image of Joss standing by his bed in the inn at Ripley, an apparition who had come to comfort him; give him peace. He could recall the feel of her soft body in his arms . . .

Alan sat up and turned on the bedside lamp. He was filled with anger towards Patri for putting such thoughts into his head. He and Joss were friends, no more, and he was not going to have that straightforward relationship disturbed!

He lit a cigarette and blew the smoke into the air above his head. His mind was racing and he did not care for the crossroads his thoughts were leading him to. Joss, beautiful and kind, but still unmarried; Joss leaving da Cortona when he, Alan, had asked for her help; Joss crying on his shoulder when the Brigadier had been killed; drawing comfort from him when her father died. And the two of them at Strathinver working as one to bring his father and Uncle Fergus together. Joss had become a part of his family, Alan thought, his discomfort returning, caring about his father, his Uncle Fergus, Cassy, and *most of all himself*.

Stubbing out his cigarette, Alan knew he could no longer hold at bay the fear that Joss might be in love with him. If it were true, it meant that she had denied herself a normal happy married life and a family because of him – a fact which aroused a terrible feeling of guilt. He should have looked beyond his own need of her and seen what was happening; he should never have encouraged their close working association; he should never have taken her with him that summer to Strathinver; he should never have asked her to return from Italy when the baby died.

Alan switched off the light, but the darkness brought only the unhappy certainty that without Joss his days would have been immeasurably the poorer; that it was she who had provided all the elements in his life that Cassy could not.

He no longer loved Cassy. Their rapprochement had been superficial and he had never been seriously tempted to make their reconciliation complete. Now, were he to divorce her, he would be free to remake his life, to begin again. Perhaps Patri was right, he thought as sleep finally drew him into unconsciousness – he should never have married Cassy. He should have married Joss instead.

Joscelin moved so abruptly that one of the boulders at her feet was dislodged. It rolled over the edge of the cliff and fell in an eerie silence until it hit the rocks below with a reverberating crash.

Beside her, Alan repeated the question which had so startled her. 'You must answer me, Joss. If Cassy will divorce me, *will you marry me?*'

Slowly, Joscelin turned to look at him. He appeared perfectly calm, and it was obvious that this was no question delivered on sudden impulse. 'It isn't fair!' she said angrily. 'You bring me up to Scotland for a holiday, behave as if everything were perfectly normal . . . and then without warning, you . . .'

She broke off as Alan smiled, and closed her eyes against the sight of his mouth curving at the corners in a way that had always devastated her. She felt his hand on her arm. 'I wanted to take you by surprise,' he said softly. 'It seemed the only way I could discover if there is any real possibility that you might care about me . . . really care, I mean.'

'Oh, Alan!' She gazed at him openly now. 'Of *course* I do. I never thought I would say this but . . . I love you. If you were free, my answer would be yes, of course I would marry you. But you're Cassy's husband – and Cassy is my best friend. No matter how badly she has behaved, I owe her so much more than you may realize. I couldn't ruin her life.'

The smile on Alan's face was replaced by a look of bitterness. 'You honestly think it would ruin Cassy's life if she were divorced from me? You are deluding yourself, Joss. She doesn't love me. Not once when she was home for Christmas – or since – has she asked me to help put our marriage on a proper footing again. She behaves as if nothing has happened and seems perfectly happy with an "in-name-only" arrangement. It wouldn't surprise me one bit to learn that she has been unfaithful again. She isn't interested in marriage, or in me; and certainly not in motherhood. Quite simply, Joss, she doesn't love me – and you must know it as well as I.'

Joscelin sighed. 'I don't think that's altogether the point. Cassy *needs* you – and whatever she has done to hurt you, she *is* your wife.'

'Needs me!' Alan echoed bitterly. 'For what? As a lover? To support her? To entertain her? No, Joss, she is completely independent and all I supply is the protection of my name. And it isn't enough!'

Joscelin gently withdrew her arm from Alan's grasp. 'I believe you still love Cassy,' she said finally. 'I know she hurt you terribly, but only because she couldn't think of any other way to protect herself. It was *you* she turned to. As for her present behaviour, she is reacting to you. She knows you haven't forgiven her and she is too proud to beg . . .'

'I'm not going to listen to you defending her,' Alan broke in. 'You've done so all your life and it's high time you thought of yourself first for once. You admitted just now that you loved me. And whether you believe it or not, I'm in love with you. *I want to marry you.* Cassy can take care of herself.'

Joscelin resisted the impulse to touch him. 'No, she can't, Alan – and you know it. But apart from that, I don't believe you are in love with me, although I'm flattered you should think so.' She gave a wry smile. 'I shall never forget that you said it, or that you believe we could be happy together. I think we could, too – but not in these circumstances, Alan.'

Alan's eyes were stormy. He stood up and pulled Joscelin

to her feet. The wind from the sea was blowing her hair across her face and carefully Alan reached out his hands, sweeping back the silky, fair strands and cupping the back of her head. Slowly he drew her towards him and then, in one fierce, determined movement, pressed his mouth down on hers.

Involuntarily, Joscelin's arms reached up to draw him closer still. She ceased to rationalize her thoughts, knowing that at long, long last, she was where she most wanted to be. She returned his kisses, her body pressed against his in a growing need for something far more than a touching of their lips.

'I love you, Joss, *I love you!*' Alan murmured huskily as he drew her down to the grass and began kissing her eyes, her neck, the hollow at the base of her throat. 'I want you so much. Joss, Joss . . .'

Now one hand was cupping her breast, the other tight around her waist. For a fleeting moment she thought of her nights with Marco but in the same instant knew that he had never been able to evoke in her such a yearning desire to surrender herself; to become part of another person.

'I love you, Alan!' she whispered. 'I've always loved you . . .'

Strangely, her words had the effect of calming him. He kissed her again, but this time with great tenderness. Then he lay, his arms still around her, staring into her eyes.

'I want you to be happy, my darling,' he said. 'I want only what *you* want. I know I have just taken advantage of a moment of weakness. I didn't give you a chance to defend yourself. I don't know what is going to happen in the future, but right now I'm going to take you home. You know how much I want you . . . but if we're to become lovers, it has to be because *you* want it, too. It is for you to decide.'

Joscelin nodded, willing the fire in her blood to subside so that she could think and talk as calmly as Alan. But he, too, was breathing deeply and she knew it would take but a tiny spark to reignite the fire between them. If she were to kiss him now . . . but she would not. Even if Alan did not remember Cassy, Joscelin knew that she must.

Joscelin thought of the letter she had received from Cassy shortly after Patri had gone back to Germany. She was in Rome where, she had written, she had 'run into' Milton Fleming. He was gathering information for a series of articles about the blacksmith's son, Mussolini, who for the last ten years had held total power in Italy. Cassy appeared to be impressed by Il Duce, the powerful and popular Italian dictator.

Joscelin herself was only mildly curious about the Fascists' rise to power. She was more concerned by the implication that Cassy was continuing her affair with Milton Fleming, yet gave no indication that she wished to be divorced from Alan. Even from Rome she had asked Joscelin to use what influence she had to persuade Alan to 'stop being so angry with me' so they could 'make it up'.

That evening, as Joscelin dressed for dinner, she tried desperately to clear her mind. Only one fact was indisputable – that she loved Alan. But did Cassy love him – in her own way? Clearly she wanted to re-establish her marriage. And did Alan really, in his heart of hearts, love Cassy? He had tacitly agreed that the marriage was still in force by living under the same roof with her this past Christmas.

Yet Alan wanted *her*. And she, Joscelin, wanted him. He had left the decision as to whether they might become lovers to her, and she was not prepared for the responsibility. Alan was the man to whom she had lost her virginity, and since then she had had an affair with Marco. It would be ridiculous, therefore, to worry about the moral issues of an affair with Alan. As to the possibility of her eventual marriage to him, it was not even relevant at this moment. What was relevant was Alan's existent marriage to Cassy.

As Joscelin joined Alan and his father in the drawing room, both men rose to their feet and Lord Costain said:

'Sit down, sit down! Been waiting to hear how you enjoyed your day at the Point of Stoer.'

Joscelin was grateful that Alan's back was towards her and he could not see the blush on her cheeks as the memory of them lying entwined on the clifftop came unbidden into her mind.

'It was a wonderful day,' she said quickly. 'And just as you promised, we saw a whole school of dolphins. I never realized they jumped so far out of the water. Alan told me they leaped their own length.'

'Saw a basking shark there once,' Lord Costain remarked. 'Lots of seals, of course, and a killer whale or two.' He gazed down into his whisky tumbler and added thoughtfully: 'Fergus and I found a young one once beached in Clashnessie Bay when we were lads. Lost its bearings, I suppose, or got washed up on a high tide. Fergus spent the whole afternoon pouring buckets of water over it, silly young fool. Funny thing . . . hadn't thought about it from that day to this. Must have been damn near sixty years ago!'

'Ask Uncle Fergus if he remembers it when you see him on Thursday,' Alan suggested. Seeing the puzzled expression on Joscelin's face, he smiled. 'The Pater usually goes down to the croft every Thursday afternoon,' he explained. 'The habit began when Uncle Fergus was looking after Bess . . .'

'Kept the dog far too long,' his father interrupted testily. 'Six confounded weeks. Got fond of her himself – that was the trouble. Didn't want to part with her.'

'You know very well that wasn't the reason!' Alan laughed. 'He just wanted to make sure Bess was perfectly fit, and I don't blame him. If she had had a relapse, he would never have heard the end of it!'

Lord Costain's reply was forestalled by the sudden movement of his dog, a half grown labrador puppy.

'Damned fool animal!' he exploded as the glass ashtray crashed to the floor, scattering the ashes on the carpet. 'Down, sir. Down, damn you!' As the dog cowered at his feet, he gave a deep sigh. 'Wouldn't have got Bess doing a bloody silly thing like that. Get rid of it soon if it can't learn to behave.'

'He's still a puppy!' Alan protested.

But his father was not listening. He was fondling the dog's

head. 'Burnt his nose!' he said. 'Perhaps that'll teach him a lesson.' He reached over to the biscuit barrel on the table by his chair and threw the dog a Bath Oliver. The puppy forgot his injury and thumped his tail approvingly.

'Shares my taste for 'em!' Lord Costain said to Joscelin.

Alan caught Joscelin's eye, and she was hard put to conceal her laughter. Alan's father was such a fraud, she thought. He concealed a heart not so very far short of being as soft as his brother's.

Later that night, Alan took Joscelin for a stroll round the castle grounds. The warm air was alive with midges and the soft rustle of nocturnal animals emerging to find food.

He reached for Joscelin's hand. 'You're right, of course – I am far from certain I ever did really love Cassy. I was desperately attracted to her, I admit – but that's not necessarily love, is it? How does one distinguish between the physical and the mental?'

For a long moment, Joscelin was silent. Then she said: 'Perhaps when it's the real thing, one doesn't have to distinguish – they go together. I think you *did* love Cassy, Alan. I think you still do, even if it isn't in quite the same way. I can understand why. She has always been fascinating, so eager for life. Oh, I know she can hurt people – but she doesn't mean to. In a way she's like a child, impulsive, selfish too, maybe, but generous to a fault. She doesn't only give *things* – she gives *herself* whole-heartedly. During all those years at the Convent Cassy took me under her wing and never once deserted me. She has never consciously done me any harm. That's why I . . . why I'm so uncertain about us, Alan.'

'Cassy's damned lucky to have you for a friend!' Alan said, his voice tinged with bitterness. 'It isn't so easy for me. I thought I'd never get over it when she married Deighton. I'd just about come to terms with that when the poor fellow was killed. Then when we got married and the baby arrived, I thought I was the luckiest, happiest man who had ever lived. I was so pleased . . . so proud . . . Dammit, Joss, Cassy may be my wife still, but she has forfeited all claim to my loyalty! Even you must see that!'

The pain in his voice was almost more than Joscelin could bear. She realized it was the first time he had been able to bring himself to speak of the baby, and it was a good thing that he could finally do so. Bitterness could only fester whilst it lay concealed, and was destructive.

As they returned to the castle, Alan paused and drew her into his arms. 'I need you, Joss,' he murmured. 'God, how I need you!'

Perhaps if he had said he loved her, his words would not have touched the same chord in her heart. Nothing mattered but the acknowledgement of his need. Whether he truly loved her was immaterial, and the future, some far-distant question mark which did not have to be answered now. She needed him, too. She was twenty-eight years old and it was three years since she had known a man's love. Now the only man in the world she had ever loved was asking her to give herself to him, unaware that every nerve in her body was crying for him.

'Go to bed, Alan,' she whispered. 'I'll come to you there.'

He was waiting for her, sitting on the edge of his bed smoking a cigarette when Joscelin tiptoed into his room. He had turned out the lamps, but the curtains were drawn back and moonlight streamed through the casements as he hurried towards her. For a moment, as he stood staring down at her, she felt absurdly shy. Then suddenly, as he reached out and touched her, her nervousness vanished. With a little cry, she flung herself into his arms.

'My love, my love!' he said between kisses. 'I was afraid you would change your mind . . . Joscelin . . . oh, my darling . . .'

He carried her to the bed and helped her out of her dressing-gown. But it was Joscelin who, unprompted, drew off her nightgown. She heard Alan's gasp as she did so and was aware of the moonlight turning her bare skin to silver. Within seconds he too was naked and, staring at him unashamedly, Joscelin thought she had never seen anything more beautiful than his strong, male body. Then he was kneeling, his face pressed to her breasts, his hands burning hot against her stomach, her thighs.

She felt a surge of gratitude to Marco, for he had given her the confidence now to lie here beneath Alan's gaze, proud of her body, unashamed to respond with equal passion to Alan's demands.

Alan made love to her tenderly but with a fierce, hungry passion, and she closed her eyes as at long last she felt him sliding into her with deep rhythmic thrusts. Her fingers dug into his shoulders as she sought to take him deeper and deeper into her. They were moving as one, a whirlwind of sensations carrying them both faster and faster to the very top of the mountain; then down slowly into a sea of delight; a sense of perfect peace.

When finally Joscelin became aware of the cool night air on her damp face and shoulders, Alan at the same instant withdrew from her saying: 'You'll catch cold, my darling. Let me cover you up.'

He drew up the sheet and, as he swung his long legs over the side of the bed, he leaned over and kissed her. 'I want you to know, Joss, that nothing so wonderful, so completely perfect, has ever happened before in my life. I love you *very* much.'

He kissed her again before going to close the windows. When he returned, he slipped into bed beside her and gathered her into his arms.

'I've been such a fool,' he said. 'It's taken me thirty years to discover what I want out of life. All that time, I've just drifted along allowing things to happen instead of taking the reins into my own hands. Now I know what I want. I want you, Joss. I think I've always wanted you but was just too stupid to realize it!'

With half her mind, Joscelin knew that she should not allow him to say such things; but her heart craved to hear them and for this night at least, she thought, she would be weak. Tomorrow they could discuss the future, Cassy, the impossibility of their relationship becoming permanent. But not now – now she asked nothing more than to lie beside him, his arms around her, his voice murmuring endearments in her ear.

CHAPTER TWENTY-SIX

August–November 1934

'Milton, don't you love me at all?' Cassy was close to tears as she watched the big, husky American reach for his third *croissant*. She herself could never eat breakfast after a night of lovemaking, but she always got out of bed, put on her negligée and sat with Milton at the breakfast table set up in their suite, for no better reason than to stay physically close to him. His apartness the morning after a night of intimacy never failed to hurt her. It was as if he was deliberately declaring his independence.

'Sometimes I think you don't care about me one little bit!' she said petulantly.

'Sure I do, honey!' Milton said casually. 'How many more times do I have to tell you, there isn't another woman in the world I'd rather sleep with. You're special, honey.'

His words did little to comfort her. She had been following him round the world now for five years – and she reflected bitterly that nothing had changed in their relationship since that first weekend in Paris. He admitted she was 'special' but never, ever that he loved her. He was cruelly blunt about that, too.

'Nor are you in love with me, Casilda. You just need what I can give you – and believe me, honey, I'm not giving up my freedom just to keep you satisfied in bed.'

For once Cassy was silent as Milton picked up his morning edition of the *New York Herald* and immersed himself in the news. Pity for herself and a violent irritation with him vied with the inevitable need to go back to bed and lose herself once more in the world of sensual delight he alone could provide. But she knew from past experience that, once up and dressed, Milton had mentally detached himself, and his concentration would be upon the day's activities and not upon her. He had now made a considerable name for himself in journalism and he was shortly to do a series of articles about Adolf Hitler.

He refused to commit himself as to when he might return from Germany and would say only that he planned to go back to the States after the assignment.

'You've been in Paris a fortnight. Isn't it about time you showed your face to that husband of yours?'

Cassy's mouth tightened. 'Alan doesn't control my life,' she said angrily. 'Anyway, I think he's got a mistress. He certainly isn't interested these days in *that* side of our married life.'

Milton's dark eyebrows raised and there was a glint of amusement in his blue eyes as he said: 'That's his loss, my dear. He's unlikely to find himself a better lay than you!'

Cassy's eyes flashed. 'You're despicable, Milton Fleming. You reduce everything to its lowest level. You don't know what it is to be in love. Alan loved me. He really did love me.'

Milton shrugged his shoulders. 'That's your business, honey. Frankly, if I'd been in his shoes I'd have divorced you years ago. You were a little fool ever to tell him the kid wasn't his. You should go back to your husband and start building some kind of life for yourself before it's too late. And now *I* shall be late if I don't get a move on. I've an appointment at the German Embassy in half an hour. If you haven't packed your bags and gone home, I may see you for dinner tonight.'

I won't stay here all alone waiting for him, Cassy swore softly as he left the room. She was bored with buying dresses and hats in the Champs Elysées; bored with sessions at the hairdressers and beauty parlours; bored with long hours of her own company.

She reached out her hand to pick up the telephone. There was a sudden knock on the door and one of the hotel pages handed her a telegram. It was from Joscelin – the only person who knew where she was staying. The message was brief, stating that Eduardo had telephoned to say that their mother was very ill and wished to be reconciled with Cassy before she died.

Cassy had known for over a year that her mother was ill . . . but the news of her approaching death was nevertheless a shock. She had never been very close to her, and the rift that opened up between them when she had married Alan in a registry office was of little concern to Cassy other than that she had not been allowed to go home to Sevilla. Her father had visited her in London whenever he was in England, and remained as devoted as ever. He would be very distressed if she did not answer her mother's request to see her now.

Her mind made up, Cassy rang for the chambermaid to come and help her pack.

By the time Cassy arrived in Sevilla, it was too late for the reconciliation with her mother to take place. The Marquesa de Fernandez de la Riva had already received the sacrament of extreme unction and was now unconscious. Horrified by the sight of her mother's emaciated face, Cassy sat by the bedside with her father and brothers and the weeping Lota. Three hours later, the Marquesa died and Padre Alfonso said the office for the dead.

Despite Cassy's lack of any real affection for her mother, she wept, the solemnity of the religion she had all but abandoned taking a renewed hold upon her. When her father led them all into the library, she clung tightly to his hand, as much to comfort herself as him.

The heat of the August day was stifling and she could feel the perspiration running down her back between her shoulder blades.

Unbidden, the thought went through Cassy's head that her mother had lacked all consideration for others in choosing to die in mid-summer, when all but those who had urgent business to see to would be enjoying their holidays by the sea.

The door opened and a maid brought in a fresh supply of *tila*, the lime tea soothing their nerves as they waited for the arrival of the two Sisters of Charity who would come and lay out the body.

At her request the Marquesa was clothed in a nun's habit, a suggestion made by Padre Alfonso which had not entirely met with Don Jaime's approval. However, he had conceded to his wife's last wishes, hiding from her his relief that after the funeral Padre Alfonso would be retiring to the nearby home for elderly priests and the household would be free of his unctuous presence.

For once, Don Jaime seemed willing to hand over the responsibility for his household to his eldest son. Eduardo sent to the Funeraria El Ocaso for a mahogany and bronze coffin and arranged for the main ground-floor *salón* of the house to be set up as a chapel. The walls were hung with tapestries and coverings of gauze and black velvet. Four large candles in tall, silver candlesticks were placed round the catafalque.

Despite the gravity of the situation, Patricio had been unable to leave Germany. Eduardo detailed Cristobal to notify the press.

'I should have advised you sooner that the end was near, Casilda,' Don Jaime said sadly as they withdrew from the bustle around them to the privacy of his study. 'Your mamá wished you to know she had forgiven you. It was her intention to ask you to give up your marriage to Alan and return to the sanctity of the Church.'

'I'm afraid religion does not play a great part in my life,' Cassy said, 'but if it comforts you, Papá, I no longer "live in sin" with Alan. We share a roof but not a bed.'

Don Jaime looked at her sharply, but Cassy avoided meeting his eyes. 'We drifted apart after the baby died,' she said evasively. 'It just happened, and now we go our own ways.'

Don Jaime would have questioned her further but for the

arrival of the governess, wishing to know if she should try to find dark clothing for Amalia to wear.

Don Jaime nodded, adding to Cassy: 'You had best find Carlota and telephone the dressmaker.'

Cassy went upstairs to her old bedroom where her sister was now temporarily installed. Lota had her own house in Sevilla where she lived with Benito and their two children, but she had been staying at the family house during the last few days of her mother's illness. She was sitting in a chair by the window weeping.

Lota had changed quite a lot this past six years, Cassy thought. Her face had filled out and there was now a matronly look about her, possibly because she was once more pregnant.

'I'm sure it isn't good for you to sit there crying. It won't bring Mamá back, and anyway you really weren't very close to her!'

Lota looked shocked. 'She was our mother!' she protested, nevertheless drying her eyes. 'And you don't understand, Casilda, you weren't here. Mamá changed a lot during her illness. She finally agreed to receive Benito, and she was quite taken with little Franciso and the baby.'

Cassy drew out her cigarette case and lit a cigarette. 'It's difficult for me to believe my little sister is now the mother of two!' she said, adding with a smile, 'soon to be three, Papá tells me. Are you happy, Lota? Do you still love your precious Benito as much as ever?'

Lota's eyes shone. 'I must be the happiest woman who ever lived!' she cried. 'You know Benito is now famous all over the world. People think it an honour to know him – even Papá boasts about his son-in-law! And he is the perfect husband and father. I can't wait to show the children to you, Casilda!'

Cassy sighed. 'Don't expect too much of me, Lota. You know I'm not very fond of *los niños*. But I shall be interested to meet Benito again. I suppose he is much more sophisticated than he used to be. But how do you manage, Lota . . . with your in-laws, I mean? It can't be easy . . .'

Lota smiled. 'There is no problem,' she said. 'We go to visit them whenever Benito comes home from a season of fights. Benito bought them a house and his mother no longer has to take in sewing. Francisco Lopez does not need to work either, but he has stayed with Papá as his *mayoral*. He likes it the way it always was. It suits Papá, too, because he says Benito's father is the best worker he has ever had. Of course, Papá is very good to his employees and pays them far higher wages than his friends are willing to do. He must be the only land-owner in Spain who is not having trouble with his workers.'

Unconsciously she placed her hand over her stomach, the smile leaving her face as she said softly: 'I was so sad for you when your baby died.'

Cassy stubbed out her cigarette, her mouth tightening. 'It's all in the past, Carlota. I don't want to talk about it.'

Lota looked at her anxiously. 'The pain will pass,' she said. 'I know because I no longer grieve for my "lost" baby. I think of him often, but I do so now without suffering.'

Cassy stood up. 'I really don't want to talk about it, Lota. Tell me about Cris. I haven't had time to speak to him yet.'

Once again, Lota's eyes filled with tears. 'He has changed, Casilda. I feel I hardly know him now. He told Papá that he never intends to return to Spain. He has lived so long now in Italy with Tía Maria–Concepción that I think he is more Italian than Spanish! He can talk of little else but Mussolini, and would not listen to Papá's opinions about Il Duce. Papá, of course, is a royalist and he believes it will not be long before the Italian king is obliged to go into exile in the same way as our own King Alfonso. Papá cannot come to terms with the fact that our country is now a republic, and he is very worried about the situation here.'

Cassy frowned. 'Don't you start talking politics to me, Lota. You know how they bore me. Tell me about Amalia. She has grown so tall I hardly recognized her.'

Lota gave a wry smile. 'She's rather out of favour with Papá at the moment. She has become very holy all of a sudden. She says she wants to be a nun and Papá has forbidden her to speak of it. Poor Mamá was encouraging Amalia in the idea, but I myself don't think she has the temperament. She's too like you, Casilda – or should I say like you were when you were her age!'

'Naughty!' Cassy said, and the two sisters laughed.

The funeral, held in the Iglesia Parroquial de San Isodoro, was a sombre affair, very different, Cassy thought, from the simple family service when Jimmy had died. Violinists and cellists accompanied the choir, who sang Fauré's Requiem. Cassy and Lota sat with the women on the right of the church, the men on the left.

It was two hours before finally the coffin was carried out to the solemn sound of Bach's G minor Fantasia and Fugue.

'I simply can't stand much more of this,' Cassy told her sister when at last the long day ended and they could retire to bed. 'I know I owe Mamá respect but what use is all this now, Lota? I shall send myself a telegram saying I am needed at home.' She put her arms affectionately round Lota's shoulders and smiled. 'Don't worry, I'll come and see Benito and the children before I go – I promise.'

They talked for a while longer, about Patricio who, Lota said, was running unknown risks by remaining in Germany; about Rupert von Lessen who had arrived just in time for the funeral to represent Cousin Isobel; about Tía Pamela.

'Papá offered to send Tía Pamela the money for the fare from New York because she could not afford it,' Lota explained. 'But she told Papá she could not be absent from her work to make so long a journey.'

Cassy frowned. 'But Alan gives Tía Pamela an allowance. I can't believe she lacks enough money for a boat ticket!'

Lota sighed. 'Papá says she and Mr Hamilton are very poor. Mr Hamilton cannot get work and Tía Pamela supports them both on the little she earns. I believe the allowance she receives from Cousin Alan pays the rent of their apartment, which they could otherwise not afford.'

'I'll talk to Alan about it when I go home,' Cassy said. 'Maybe I can help. Alan says I'm so rich I couldn't begin to spend all I have, however hard I tried!'

Lota's face glowed. 'Oh, Casilda, that would be kind!' she said, beaming with pleasure. 'Tía Pamela was so wonderful to me when . . . when I was in trouble.'

'Did you ever tell Benito – about the baby?' Cassy asked curiously.

'No, I didn't. I often thought about it – but what good would it do? Sometimes when I look at little Francisco and the baby, I think about the other little boy and pray to *La Virgen* to keep him safe and happy.'

Cassy learned the following day that Rupert was leaving for Germany at the end of the week. Her heart missed a beat. Milton would be there – perhaps for as long as a month, he had told her. He planned first to go to Berlin and then to Munich, Adolf Hitler's National Socialist headquarters. If she were to go and stay with Patricio and Rebekka . . .

Isobel, her husband informed Cassy, would be delighted to receive a visit from her cousin. He himself would be pleased if she accompanied him on the long train journey.

The night before their departure, Don Jaime called Cassy into his study. His face looked drawn and tired.

'There is something I would like you to attend to for me,' he said. 'Rupert has told me that Patricio and his family are at risk. I wish you to find out just how serious the situation is, and when you get back to England you are to telephone me. Will you do this? I would have gone to Germany myself but for your mother's illness – and now I cannot go.'

With her promise to her father firmly in her mind, Cassy settled down to enjoy the long train ride. She found Rupert a dull companion but the time passed quickly in a harmless but amusing flirtation with a young Frenchman.

Cassy planned to stay only one night with the von Lessens, but surprisingly Isobel begged her to stay longer.

'I need your advice!' she said urgently, soon after Cassy

had arrived. She had come to Cassy's bedroom as she was changing for dinner. 'I can't explain now, Casilda, there isn't time, and you must say nothing at dinner tonight in front of Rupert and my son. But I must talk to you tomorrow when we can be alone.'

Curiosity outweighed Cassy's desire to get to Munich as quickly as she could. Poor Cousin Isobel was clearly distressed. She looked far older than her thirty-five years.

The situation became somewhat clearer to her at dinner, when for the first time she met Isobel's son, Heinrich. Now thirteen years old, the boy was their only child. He had the Costains' fair hair and blue eyes and was tall for his age. He was handsome enough but his surly manner and frequent scowls detracted from his good looks. He appeared as the dinner gong sounded, wearing black shorts and a khaki shirt with a swastika embroidered on the left sleeve and a triangular scarf knotted under the collar.

The atmosphere at dinner was so tense that Cassy felt obliged to try to lighten it. She set out to charm Isobel's young son and succeeded. The scowl on his face gave way to a look of suppressed excitement as he replied eagerly to her questions.

'I am one of the Deutsches Jungvolk,' he told her. 'Next year, when I am fourteen, I shall be a member of the Hitler Jugend.' He showed her the black triangle above the embroidered swastika on his sleeve. 'This shows the name of my *Gau*, my region,' he explained. He pointed proudly to his black leather belt and white, knee-length socks. 'Do you not agree that my uniform is very smart? I have a brown Käppi – Mütti calls it a forage cap – and I am hoping very soon to earn my dagger. Then I shall have a silver badge on my right arm.'

'It seems very similar to the English Boy Scout uniform,' Cassy commented.

Heinrich stiffened. 'We are much superior. We go on exercises like real soldiers. We must obey all orders instantly. Those who do not are punished or even expelled, but if you are good, like me, it can help you to do well at school and later get into university.' Momentarily, his scowl returned as he added: 'My parents wish me to go to school in Britain next term. I do not wish to leave Germany, to attend a place of education run by a man our Führer has dismissed from our country. If it should become known that I am a pupil there I could not become a Hitler Jugen.'

'That is nonsense, Heinrich,' Isobel said sharply. 'You cannot be held to blame for what your parents decide is best for you. Now let us have no more of this at table. Tell me, Casilda, have you heard from my mother lately?'

There was no further discussion that evening, but as Cassy retired for the night she was of the opinion that Isobel, rather than her husband, was the cause of their son's obvious state of rebellion. She could understand the boy's feelings about being sent to a British public school when he was clearly so happy in his present environment. But she changed her mind very quickly next morning when Isobel took her into the garden, and in a voice bordering upon hysteria expounded her fears.

'I would have written to Alan, but Rupert was afraid of the consequences if our letters fell into the wrong hands. No one is permitted to speak against National Socialism. To do so is to risk questioning, torture, even deportation to one of the concentration camps that have been set up for dissenters.'

Her laugh was bitter as she saw the disbelief on Cassy's face. 'I am not exaggerating, Casilda. You have no idea how bad things are. There is no justice any more. The Party controls everything and will allow no one to stand in its way. Everyone must support the Party, and if they do not they suffer.'

She paused to take out a handkerchief which she rolled into a little ball and passed nervously from one hand to the other.

'Rupert has had to join the Party, although secretly he abhors Adolf Hitler and his policies. The Nazis are evil thugs and murderers. But there is nothing anyone can do now to stop them.'

'Could you not come to live in England?' Cassy asked.

Isobel shook her head. 'It's not possible! Aunt Luisa is alone now and she needs Rupert to run the vineyards. All the von Lessen wealth is tied up in the production of wine. No, we cannot leave, and so long as we pretend outwardly to acknowledge Hitler, we are safe enough. It is Heinrich I must save!'

'Heinrich!' Cassy echoed. 'But he seems so happy here!'

Isobel pressed her handkerchief to her mouth. 'Don't you understand, Casilda? That's the problem. Hitler is his idol, National Socialism his creed. His bedroom walls are covered with posters, photographs, emblems. Nothing is without a swastika! In the schools they are teaching the children the National Socialist doctrines. They ban lessons or books that might challenge such theories, and fill the children's minds with false idealism. They appeal to their sentiment with special songs, with their smart uniforms, with the idea of a superior German youth that is purely Aryan. At the age of thirteen, Heinrich is convinced that the Jews and Communists are responsible for all Germany's troubles and has been taught to dismiss as subversive all the great Jewish intellectuals.'

'So you are sending Heinrich to Britain,' Cassy said.

Isobel nodded. 'Gordonstoun is a new school in Scotland. The headmaster is progressive in his ideas and, having been ousted from Germany, he will understand that Heinrich has been indoctrinated and know how best to deal with him. Patri arranged this for us when he was last in England.'

Cassy now understood in part Isobel's anxiety to send her son away from Germany. But remembering the fervour in the boy's eyes when he talked of his involvement in the Hitler Youth movement, she said: 'But when Heinrich returns here for the holidays . . .?'

Isobel's laugh was without humour as she interrupted: 'I don't intend that he shall come home. That is why I need your help, Casilda. If you and Alan cannot have him in the holidays, then I need you to speak to the headmaster for me. I want him to keep Heinrich there. Or perhaps he can go to his cousins in Sevilla. If things are better next year, then maybe . . .'

She broke off, obviously not believing matters would improve. 'Rupert agrees with what I'm doing but he dare not say so openly. Awful though this might sound, we cannot trust our own son. If Heinrich felt it his duty to report his father or even accidentally to repeat one of Rupert's anti-Nazi remarks, we could all be endangered.'

Casilda was shocked, and inclined to believe that Isobel was exaggerating the situation. But that afternoon Isobel took her to Heinrich's bedroom. Apart from the Nazi decorations covering the walls, on Heinrich's desk lay an exercise book in which he had been copying from a Nazi song book. Isobel picked it up and translated two of the lines: 'The red blood, beat them to a pulp!/Stormtroopers are on the march – clear the way!'

'Who in their right mind could put such thoughts in the heads of children?' Isobel said. 'I don't care for the Communists, but that's horrible!'

As they made their way back downstairs, she said: 'Tonight we have Gerhardt Strasser dining with us. He is from the Ministry of the Interior and has recently been appointed Ministerial Adviser and Expert for Racial Research. Rupert and he were friendly in their university days and they met by chance in Munich. Rupert had no idea when he invited the man to dinner that the Herr Doktor had been a supporter of the National Socialist party for years. In their student days, I think Dr Strasser was impressed by Rupert's aristocratic background, and cultivated his friendship for this reason. He had the nerve to invite himself again. I wanted to find an excuse to put him off, but Rupert thought it unwise, especially as Heinrich was thrilled to have such an important Party member under our roof. At least *you* will be here tonight to help entertain the man, for I shall be hard put to be civil to him.'

Cassy, however, had no such difficulty. In his early forties, fat, balding and with the self-importance so often to be found in men of short stature, Gerhardt Strasser was bowled over by the von Lessens' Spanish cousin. It amused Cassy to encourage his inept attempts to flirt with her. It eased the atmosphere for Isobel, delighted Heinrich and left Rupert much to his own company.

When Isobel and Cassy retired to the drawing room, Isobel's face was almost as red as her hair. 'Casilda, how could you allow it?' she gasped. 'I saw him touch your hand beneath the tablecloth and you weren't even angry. Besides, the man has a terrible reputation. He's dangerous!'

Cassy laughed as she lit a cigarette. 'I see no reason to be afraid of him,' she said. 'He's just a silly little man who thinks he's important. Besides, he can be useful. He heard I was going by train to Munich tomorrow and has offered to drive me there. Apparently he has a ministerial car and a driver at his command.'

Isobel collapsed into a chair. 'The way you were smiling at him, I thought you *liked* him!' she exclaimed. 'Nevertheless, Casilda, you must be careful with men like that. He may strike you as silly, but he carries a great deal of power here in Bavaria.'

'All the more reason he should approve of me,' Cassy retorted mischievously. 'He'll feel indebted to you and Rupert for introducing us. If you like, I'll let him take me out to dinner one night!'

'Be careful, Casilda!' Isobel said again. 'You must not forget that your brother, Patricio, is married to a half-Jewish girl. Dr Strasser can't harm you – but he *could* harm Rebekka.'

Cassy shrugged. 'I think you have let things get a little out of proportion, Isobel.'

'Let me quote you the latest National Socialist proposal which they intend to make law,' Isobel replied quietly. 'Every person who is of foreign racial blood to the extent of one-half Jewish is judged a "foreigner". Such "foreigners" can no longer describe themselves as Germans. Marriages between Germans and "foreigners" are prohibited, and relationships between them punishable by penal servitude. "Foreigners" will rank with drunks, drug-takers, criminals, gipsies and prostitutes. A German girl becoming friendly with a "foreigner" will be branded with the initials JH – "*Juden-Hure*", which means "Jewish prostitute". I think I have made my point.'

'I think you have, too,' Cassy agreed uneasily, remembering her father's anxiety about Patri and his family. 'Don't worry, Isobel, I'll be careful. But from all you have told me, I'm not sorry I allowed myself to have a little fun with our fat Herr Doktor. Now I shall really try to make him fall a little in love with me. Who knows – he could be useful not only to you and Rupert, but to Patri and Rebekka, too.'

Now that Cassy knew there was more than a hint of danger in what she was planning to do, she began to enjoy herself. Careful always to keep the man at arm's length during the car ride to Munich, she made herself as tantalizingly attractive as she could. When he deposited her outside Patricio's house, she promised to telephone him and let him know which night she would be free to dine with him.

Patri's face as he came into the hall to greet her was completely devoid of its usual cheerful grin. 'Do you realize who that was?' he exclaimed. 'What in heaven's name were you doing with a man like that?'

'Calm down!' Cassy said, hugging him. 'I'll tell you all about it, but first I want to see Rebekka and *los chicos*. It's at least five years since I saw Carlos!'

Dr Strasser was forgotten whilst greetings were exchanged. But when Rebekka took the children back to their nursery Patri drew Cassy down onto the sofa and demanded an explanation.

Whilst Cassy spoke, he remained silent. Only his fingers tapping on the polished surface of the table beside him indicated his excitement.

'He's quite crazy about me!' Cassy ended her story with a smile. 'Of course, what he really wants to do is take me to bed. I know it and he knows it – but I told him I was looking for a man who really and truly loved me because, sadly, my husband did not! I think he was conceited enough to think he could be the man I'm searching for!'

Patri's face broke into an excited smile. 'I suppose I shouldn't be surprised at all this – coming as it does from you, Casilda! You can't possibly know, of course, but this could be an incredible stroke of luck. I'll tell you why.'

Twenty minutes passed before he came to the end of his story. He told Cassy how he and Rebekka's father had been assisting Jews to get out of the country, mostly by huge bribes in the right quarters. But now Jews could no longer get passports and their situation had worsened. An elderly uncle of Rebekka's was actually in hiding in their house, together with a nineteen-year-old Jewish girl who had been working for him. Both had been tortured – and the girl raped by the stormtroopers.

'They will have to be got out of the country secretly,' Patri said. 'But there are many others, Casilda, for whom we are still trying to obtain passports. It is difficult and dangerous, but Rebekka and I feel we must do what we can.'

He took his sister's hands in his. 'You could help us, Casilda,' he said urgently. 'Strasser has influence. A word from him to the passport officials that someone is "racially pure" will carry great weight. I could give you names and you could tell Strasser they were friends of yours – pretend you were at school in Germany for a while in your youth, and that they are old school fellows. It would be silly to try to pretend that they were *not* Jews, because he will know that they are. Make light of it – tell him he can spare one or two amongst so many. At worst he will refuse. And he cannot harm *you*. You are a Spanish and British citizen, and Germany is doing everything it can to blind the rest of the world to what is happening here. You could use that too, Casilda – tell him you have many influential friends in London in the newspaper world, and that you would be happy to point out when you go back home that it is nonsense to suggest that Jews are being kept prisoners here.'

Cassy's eyes shone. 'But what about Rebekka's uncle and the girl you are hiding?'

'We'll think of something!' Patri said. 'It's too risky keeping them here much longer. Rebekka is reasonably certain that the servants won't talk – but you cannot trust anyone these days. We have dispensed with all but two because of this. That is why Rebekka is without a nanny for *los chicos*. It is good for her to be fully occupied. She has less time to worry!'

He broke off to look at Casilda speculatively. 'I know Cousin Isobel is violently opposed to Hitler. Do you think if we could get our two fugitives to Württemberg, she might find a way to get them across Lake Constance into Switzerland . . .?'

'It would be difficult with Heinrich at home,' Cassy admitted. 'But he goes to school in Britain in a few weeks' time. I think she might help, but Rupert may not allow her to do so.'

'Then Cousin Isobel would have to keep it from him,' Patricio said. 'I will go and see her. If I can persuade her to assist us, we would have the escape route we need so badly.'

He put his arms round Cassy and hugged her, his eyes uneasy as he said: 'I've no right to involve you, Casilda. I am involved because of Rebekka, but you have no part in this nightmare.'

Cassy laughed. 'But I shall *enjoy* the adventure, little brother. Don't worry. I can take care of myself.'

For the next half hour they talked of their recent bereavement, Cassy describing the funeral and its aftermath. Although saddened by the event, Patricio had not been close to his mother.

'Mamá had time only for Eduardo,' he said. 'I think he, and more recently Amalia, were the only two of her children she really cared about. As for Papá – well, I cannot believe his heart is broken, as mine would be if I were to lose my beloved Rebekka.'

They spoke once more of the danger Rebekka was in, and Patricio admitted that he was praying her grandfather would be willing to leave Germany and go to live with relatives in America, thus freeing Rebekka to go with Patricio to Spain.

'They are a very close-knit family,' he explained. 'Both Frau Schwarz and her husband have tried to convince Rebekka she should put our children first, but she insists they are safe because they are only a quarter Jewish; and for the time being, only half-Jews are classed as "foreigners".'

'I will do what I can,' Cassy promised. 'I shall telephone Dr Strasser and tell him I will lunch with him tomorrow.'

Cassy's motives were not altogether altruistic. Although in the main she genuinely desired to help Patri, she wanted to find out if Milton was in Munich and, by the sound of it, Dr Strasser might be able to locate his whereabouts more easily than she could.

So began a series of rendezvous with the amorous Nazi minister. Cassy quickly assessed that it was not only her physical attraction which appealed to him. The Führer himself had recently taken into his circle a young English aristocrat called Unity Mitford. She was often to be seen with him at meetings and rallies. Cassy's admirer was by now aware that she had connections with the Earl of Ladbury, was the daughter of a Spanish marquis and married to the son of an English lord. He was impressed by her background, which he assumed to be even more exalted than that of Adolf Hitler's young friend. Cassy let him know, too, that she was immensely rich.

There was no doubt that, by the end of her first week in Munich, she could twist Gerhardt Strasser round her little finger. Her main problem lay in keeping him at arm's length. She found him physically repulsive, and even the feel of his hot, sweaty palm was almost more than she could bear. When he tried one evening to kiss her, she quickly turned her cheek and constantly reiterated that she dared not be unfaithful to her husband.

The love-sick Nazi did everything he could to please her.

He put a car and a driver at her disposal. He discovered Milton Fleming's whereabouts, deceived by her story that she was so impressed with the new National Socialist regime that she hoped to be able to influence the American journalist to write well of the Party. But Milton was on the point of leaving Munich, and as Cassy could think of no excuse to give Patri for staying a night away from their house, she was able to spend only two brief hours with Milton at his hotel. As usual, she failed to persuade him to stay longer – or to postpone his return to Berlin.

When she told him of her involvement with Dr Strasser, he glanced at her curiously. 'If you are looking on this as a new game to play, Casilda,' he said, 'I must warn you that it is an extremely dangerous one. These Nazis are a ruthless lot, and if you're not very careful you could lead your precious Dr Strasser straight to the Stolbergs. My advice to you is to go home, honey. Stop meddling in matters way above your pretty little head.'

Infuriated by his patronizing attitude, Cassy doubled the number of her meetings with Herr Doktor. Following Patri's instructions, she made her first request for his assistance.

'If you really want to please me so much, Gerhardt,' she said over dinner one night, 'there *is* a little matter you might look into for me.'

She launched into her story of a German school friend, her voice deliberately casual, her hand remaining in his far longer than was her custom. 'Poor Miriam is terribly anxious to go to America – she has relatives there who can help her to go on the stage. She was always stage-mad even in our schooldays. But she doesn't seem to be able to get a passport. She says it's because she's half-Jewish, but that's ridiculous, isn't it, Gerhardt? Surely you don't want to keep Jews here in Germany? I understand why your party considers them racially impure, but Miriam is just a girl and quite harmless. I'd like to help her if I could. But perhaps it's beyond your power to intervene, Gerhardt?'

He took the bait with an ease which surprised her. 'Of course I have the power to arrange such things!' he said self-importantly. He ran his hand up her bare arm and added coyly: 'If I help your little school friend, *Liebchen*, how will you thank me?' His voice thickened and his hot breath covered her face as he leant towards her.

'I'd have to think about that, Gerhardt!' she said playfully. 'Perhaps I shall allow you to take me to that lake, Tegernsee, you told me about. We could spend the day together. I would have to think of a good excuse to give my brother. He would not like me to go on a picnic alone with a man. He understands how passion can lead a woman from the path of virtue. It is so easy to be tempted when one's husband is not there,' she ended with a sigh.

By the end of September Cassy had been instrumental in obtaining passports for three people, including Rebekka's cousin, Miriam, who was now on her way to America. But Patri was becoming worried. He knew Dr Strasser would not be fobbed off by Cassy much longer. Once he realized she had no intention of allowing any real intimacies, he might turn nasty. If he were to start looking too deeply into her family connections here in Munich and in Wurttemberg, Patri's plans to establish an escape route via Isobel would be jeopardized. Far worse, Rebekka's relationship with the Stolbergs might come to light.

'You've been wonderful,' he told Cassy, 'but I think you should go home now. Tell Strasser your husband is threatening to come out here to see what you are up to. Say you'll come back as soon as you can – to see *him*. We can keep the connection going this end – maybe even enlist his help ourselves. He must think it strange we have not yet invited him to dine with us.'

Cassy grinned. 'On the contrary, Patri. I told him you had suggested it was high time you made his acquaintance, but that I myself thought it unwise. I told him you were very perceptive, and might quickly guess from the way he and I look at each other that it is a little more than friendship between us.' She laughed. 'Gerhardt was delighted and warned me to be careful not to mention him too often to you!'

But Cassy could not deny that she was finding it increasingly difficult to refuse her German admirer closer intimacies, and although she had been finding it quite amusing to lead him on, now the game was beginning to pall. Moreover, Patri's suggestion that she should go home was reinforced coincidentally by an unexpected telephone call from Milton. He was back in Munich for two days, after which he was going on to Paris, he told her. If she wished, she could go with him.

Cassy was agog with excitement, although she pretended she needed time to consider his invitation.

'It would be nice to have someone to escort me on the journey,' she told her brother casually. 'All the same, Patri, I wish I could help with those two downstairs before I leave. Maybe Mr Fleming will travel by car and he and I could smuggle them out!'

Her remark had not been made seriously but Patri took it up at once. Perhaps her precious Nazi would provide her with papers to ease their way over the border? Was Fleming to be trusted?

Milton's reluctance to become involved was short-lived. He had seen and heard enough during his explorations in Germany to realize what was happening.

Cassy introduced Milton to her brother. A suitable car was purchased, and whilst Cassy dined with Strasser, Milton and Patri removed the spare wheel and enlarged the boot. Even then, there was barely enough space for two people, but it was a risk they had to take, Patri said. Suffocation was a kinder death than they could expect in a concentration camp.

A heartbroken Dr Strasser sat in the back of his car and wept on Cassy's bosom. She stroked his bald head and told him it was perhaps all for the best that she was leaving; that her resistance was low and she had been thinking of late how wonderful it would be to go away for a weekend with him.

She had to leave before she was overcome by the temptation to be unfaithful to her husband.

'But I must have you – just once!' he begged. 'Come home with me now, *Liebling*! I am crazy with love for you!'

'I *dare* not go with you, Gerhardt,' Cassy said, trying to stifle her laughter. 'My brother has insisted that I return by midnight at the very latest.'

She allowed him to fondle her breasts whilst she pretended anxiety about the long drive to Paris.

'My brother tells me one is continually stopped by the storm-troopers. Of course, they are only doing their duty – but it takes so much time, especially at the frontier . . .'

Loath to miss an opportunity to boast, the Herr Doktor insisted that he could arrange papers to ensure that their journey would be unhindered. As he did so, his hand went from her breast to her thigh. Cassy allowed it to remain there for a few moments and then said: 'Perhaps tomorrow night, Gerhardt. I will see if I can convince my brother that a girlfriend would like me to spend my last night in Germany with her. And then . . .' She broke off, returning his hand firmly to his lap as she smiled at him. 'Let's have dinner together tomorrow, Gerhardt. You can bring me the papers, and afterwards, perhaps I shall be able to go with you to your apartment.'

The following evening Strasser greeted her with a great deal of hand kissing and, almost before they were seated at the table, he pressed an envelope in her hand.

'There you are, *Liebchen*, no one will now interfere with your journey.'

Cassy squeezed his hand. 'Oh, Gerhardt, you are divine!' she said. 'I just wish it were you who was driving me to Paris tomorrow and not that self-opinionated American! I think German men are *so* much more attractive than Americans. You are so considerate!'

She chattered on, giving him no chance to ask the question burning on his lips – was she going back to his apartment after the meal? But finally over coffee, he managed to do so.

Cassy contrived to look crestfallen as she explained that her brother would not hear of her spending her last night away from him. 'Try to understand, Gerhardt!' she pleaded. 'I am as disappointed as you!'

He made no attempt to hide his frustration, and for once there was no adoring smile on his face.

'I am beginning to think you have been toying with my affections,' he said accusingly. 'You permitted me to believe that you had become fond of me. I suspect that you have been making very much the fool of me.'

Cassy remembered both Patri's and Milton's warnings that men like Strasser could be dangerous when thwarted, and she felt a chill of fear as she looked into the man's steely eyes.

'Oh, Gerhardt, you mustn't be cross with me!' she said. 'I do care for you . . . very much. But I dare not go home with you.'

He hesitated but, wanting to believe her, he put his pride before his instinct.

'Then let us go for a little drive in my car,' he said firmly.

Dismissing the driver, he himself steered the car down innumerable back streets until finally he parked it at the end of a deserted, unlit cul-de-sac. Disregarding the usual preliminary kisses, he took her arm and conducted her into the back seat.

Tonight, Cassy realized, her would-be lover was a great deal more determined and persistent than he had been previously. The only way she could keep his eager hands from searching their way up her skirt was by reaching out to touch him. Closing her eyes against the sight of his perspiring face, she gritted her teeth and began to stroke him in the way Milton had taught her. Knowing exactly what she must do, she pretended to be overwhelmed by passion and demanded he put his arms around her, thus successfully removing his hands from her thighs. Sickened by his proximity, she nevertheless forced herself to continue.

It was over very quickly and he collapsed on top of her, panting and muttering endearments. She gave him a moment or two to recover before edging as far away from him as she dared.

'You must take me home now, Gerhardt!' she urged him. 'I wish I could stay longer with you. But at least I have been able to prove how much you mean to me, have I not? Now *you* must prove you really care about me. Please, Gerhardt! Take me home.'

Now that he was recovering his composure, the man decided that there was little point in remaining where they were. In one way, he was disappointed. For weeks he had dreamed of seeing the beautiful Spanish girl naked on his bed, begging him to make love to her. On the other hand, he had been surprised and gratified that she had found one way to satisfy him. He was a little shocked that she had behaved so brazenly, but told himself that he had no previous experience of foreign girls, and that this one *had* twice been married.

'You will come back to Germany?' he asked as he drove her home. 'I must see you again, *Liebchen*. Tonight I . . .'

'But of course I will,' Cassy broke in hurriedly. All she wanted now was to be as far away from him as possible. 'My husband cannot object to my visiting my relations from time to time. I will come back as soon as I can!'

After one long farewell kiss, Cassy was safely back inside the house where Patri awaited her. She waved the precious safe conduct papers at him.

'I've got them, Patri!' she said triumphantly. 'You can telephone Milton now and say that it's all on for tomorrow. Don't you think I'm clever?'

Cassy saw tears in Patri's eyes as he hugged her.

'Not only clever,' he said huskily, 'but very brave!'

Milton paid her the same compliment when finally they reached Paris with their two Jewish escapees safe and unharmed. Rebekka's uncle was having difficulty with his breathing, but they left him in a hospital with the girl and adequate funds.

Milton took Cassy to the Hotel George V. This time, he had reserved rooms for her adjoining his own.

'You really have surprised me, honey,' he said after they had made love. 'But perhaps I should have known you capable of great courage. Danger excites you. I noticed it in Sevilla when you played hookey in order to go to the bullfight with me. The excitement you feel is your reward, isn't it? I don't suppose you really care about those unfortunate Jews. But you must have been scared, especially when we were stopped at the frontier. We took a dreadful risk. Tell me, was it worth it?'

Cassy nodded, unable to explain that her real reward lay in the fact that, quite without meaning to, she had somehow earned Milton's grudging respect.

'You must be there to greet her, Alan!' Joscelin said quietly. She picked up the last letter she had received from Cassy, written the day after her mother's funeral. 'She sounds utterly miserable. She's going to need you and we can't possibly go to Strathinver now.'

Alan's arm tightened around her. 'Will you always go on worrying about Cassy's feelings? My darling, you know quite well she came close to disliking Aunt Ursula. I see no reason to suppose she'll need me.'

'Alan, we promised each other we'd never let Cassy suffer if we became lovers, remember?' Joscelin said quietly.

Alan sighed. 'I know! But I don't think Cassy will be suffering – and I've been so looking forward to going up to Strathinver. Joss, aren't you ever going to change your mind? Let me ask Cassy for a divorce. I want to marry you. I love you, dammit. I want to be with you all the time. I hate this clandestine nonsense – hiding away here in your flat as if we were doing something shameful.'

Joscelin's face paled. 'We *are* doing something shameful,' she argued. 'We're committing adultery every time we make love, and nothing Cassy has done in the past justifies that. I love you with my heart and my soul. It's because I feel as I do that I know we'd lose the happiness we now have if we demanded more *at Cassy's expense*. You say she doesn't need you, but I think she does. How do you think I would feel if she accused me of stealing you from her?'

Alan's face was flushed with a rare anger as he stopped his pacing to stare at her. 'You make me sound like one of Cassy's possessions. I don't *belong* to her.'

Joscelin's voice was ominously quiet. 'Alan, you do. You're her husband.'

'Then I shall stop being her husband,' Alan retorted. 'What possible reason is there for continuing a marriage like ours?'

Joscelin was silent. She was finding it increasingly difficult to explain her feelings. The more time they spent together and the deeper they fell in love, the harder it became. Only very occasionally did Alan seem to feel guilty – and she could understand his view that Cassy had treated him unforgivably. But Cassy had never done *her* any harm. On the contrary, for as long as she lived she would always feel indebted to her. Alan saw only his own point of view.

Wisely Joscelin stopped arguing with him. Divorce was a subject they could no longer discuss. She held out her arms, knowing that she could bring him at least temporary happiness with her love.

It was a week before she saw him again. He came racing up the stairs to the studio, bumped his head as always on the lintel of the door, and swept her into his arms.

'I've marvellous news, darling. Cassy telephoned half an hour ago. She's going to stay with Patri and Rebekka – probably for several weeks. That means we can go up to Strathinver together as we'd planned. You can still get away, can't you, darling?'

'Give me time to deliver these illustrations to Matheson and I'll be ready to go!' she told him.

Their holiday in Strathinver was perfect. It was the nearest she would ever come to having a honeymoon, Joscelin told herself, since, unlike Alan, she could see no real hope for their future. They were together every minute of every day and for the best part of the nights, Alan insisting upon returning to his own bedroom before dawn to safeguard her reputation. Privately, Joscelin did not think anyone was deceived. If Lord Costain disapproved, he gave no sign of it and, though terse as always, his manner towards Joscelin was affectionate.

But Uncle Fergus – usually so sparing of words – astonished them with a blunt statement revealing they had not deceived him by their pretence at mere friendship.

'Should get yourselves married,' he said one afternoon as he and Alan put the finishing touches to a new bird table they were erecting outside the croft. He pointed to a pair of wood pigeons cooing at each other on the roof of his cottage. 'They're like swans – mate for life,' he muttered. 'Belong together – like you two.'

Their holiday came to an end and they returned to London in mid-September; Cassy could not ignore the fact that Alan was far from happy. The closeness of their holiday only highlighted their separateness in London. He was finding it increasingly difficult to work when she wasn't in the room with him, he told her. He dreaded the moments when he had to return to Rutland Gate. Cassy was still away in Germany where, according to her postcards, she was having 'a very exciting time'. It crossed Joscelin's mind that Cassy's lover must be with her to keep her away so long.

'Perhaps you are willing to go on like this indefinitely,' Alan said one evening as they lay in front of the studio fire. The October evenings were becoming cold and Joscelin was aware of winter approaching. It had, she thought, a certain symbolism. Last month Alan had had his thirty-third birthday, and in another year she herself would be thirty! They were wasting their youth.

She pressed herself closer against Alan's warm body, trying to draw comfort from his proximity.

'Even if you are willing to go on, I am not!' Alan said quietly, shocking her into a sitting position. 'I'm sorry, darling. But whoever the fool was who said it was "fun" or "exciting" to have a love affair, didn't know what he was talking about. I *love* you, Joss. I hate going to dinners, the theatre without you. When one of the chaps at my club asks about my wife, I think of *you*! I want to be with you all the time. I want you to be the mother of my children. I want a home, Joss, a family, but most of all, *I want you*!'

He sounded so despairing that Joscelin could not bear it. She threw herself back into his arms and kissed him passionately. 'I want you too, Alan. And I want our children. I love you so much I sometimes feel I'll die from it!'

'Then *let me talk to Cassy*,' Alan said fiercely. 'Let me ask her for a divorce. Has it never occurred to you that she wouldn't even mind if we parted? She lives her life without me. She doesn't need me.'

Perhaps Alan was right, Joscelin thought. They *could* be sacrificing their happiness unnecessarily. Cassy might shrug her shoulders and say, 'but of course. How silly of you both not to tell me before!'

'Very well,' she said softly. 'If Cassy really doesn't mind . . .'

She got no further, for Alan was covering her face with kisses, and in the contagion of his joy she felt a great wave of happiness sweep over her, obscuring her doubts and leaving her for the first time free of any vestige of guilt.

For the ensuing fortnight they waited impatiently for Cassy's return, although, now that the decision was made, they each achieved a certain contented equanimity. Cassy telephoned from Paris to say that she would be staying on there for a special party but would be back by the weekend.

'Haven't I told you Cassy doesn't need me around in her life to enjoy herself?' Alan said to Joscelin. 'She wasn't in the least interested in what I had been doing – or you, come to that. All she could talk about was this spectacular "do" being put on by that millionairess, Barbara Hutton.' He laughed happily. 'Cassy's such a child, isn't she? I thought I hated her . . . but of course I don't. We'll make her understand how much we love each other. She'll set me free.'

It was not, however, to be Cassy who set Alan free, but Alan who was to obtain Cassy's release on 15 November from a prison in Paris. The telephone call he received from a French lawyer was explicit. Cassy had been driving a car full of young people from a party at the Ritz Hotel to the Arc de Triomphe soon after four o'clock in the morning. There had been an accident. A man in the other car had been killed. Cassy had had so much to drink that she was unable to give a clear explanation of what had happened. She was being kept in custody and later that day – unless Alan could prevent it – she would be formally charged with manslaughter.

CHAPTER TWENTY-SEVEN

November–December 1934

'Oh, Joss! I can't tell you how horrible it was! Half the time I couldn't understand a word they said to me – and when the lawyer told me I would have to spend the rest of the night in the police cell, I thought I would die!'

Joscelin was shocked by the sight Cassy presented. Her dark hair was in disorder, her long evening gown torn and muddy. There was a big black bruise beneath one eye and she was very pale.

'I've asked the hotel to send up a doctor,' Alan said. 'She's very shocked!'

'I'll put Cassy to bed,' Joscelin said.

Cassy burst into tears. 'It's all my fault!' she wept. '*Lo siento mucho*! I'm so sorry! *Lo siento*!' she repeated.

'Try not to think about it,' Alan said quietly. 'It was an accident – the lawyer said so. He was certain you won't have to go to prison.'

'I couldn't bear it,' Cassy whispered. '*I couldn't bear it*!'

'Well, it isn't going to happen,' Joscelin said firmly. 'Now I'm going to run a hot bath for you, Cassy. Alan, go and get some sleep.'

Alan nodded, his face white with weariness. He was still trying to reconcile himself to the fact that Cassy had actually killed someone and was now awaiting charges for *homicide par imprudence* – which, so he now understood, was akin to manslaughter. He had had no difficulty in obtaining her release on bail, although the sum had been substantial. According to the French lawyer, there would be a further charge for driving

without a licence. For her to have been driving at all was sheer
lunacy.

For the moment, he preferred not to think of the consequences.
Anger had warred with pity when he had seen the state Cassy
was in at the police station. Unlike Joscelin, Cassy was inclined
to go to pieces in an emergency, and when she had flung herself
into his arms she had been close to hysteria. Now he felt an
immense sense of gratitude towards Joscelin. She had insisted
upon coming to Paris with him and had taken charge of Cassy
and calmed her as he knew he could not have done.

It could be three or four months before Cassy's case would
be heard. The *juge d'instruction* had set the terms of her bail
and insisted she remain in the country until her indictment.

There was little doubt that Cassy's sentence would include
a term of imprisonment as well as a heavy fine – but the
lawyer was reassuring on this point: the sentence of imprisonment would in all probability be suspended, which meant that
unless Cassy was involved in further trouble, she would not
have to serve her sentence.

As Joscelin helped Cassy into bed, the same thought was
running through her mind as through Alan's – Cassy's lifestyle
would have to change radically if she were not to run any
risk in the foreseeable future. She was going to need a steadying
influence – Alan's . . . and Joscelin could see only one solution
that would protect Cassy from her wild nature. She needed
her husband to take care of her.

Tears filled Joscelin's eyes as she faced the unbearable fact
that it was no longer possible for Alan to ask Cassy to divorce
him. Cassy had the right to his protection, and Alan was far
too honourable a man to walk out on his responsibilities.
There was no alternative, Joscelin thought. He must be free
to pick up the threads of his marriage and try to find happiness. She would wait a few days in case there was anything
else she could do to help, *then she must leave*. Patri and
Rebekka had been pressing her to visit them, she would accept
their invitation.

Through her tears, she could see Cassy's bruised face and her heart filled with pity. She looked so helpless, so beaten! It would be some time before she recovered from the shock of what she had done. Perhaps she would never be quite the same carefree, happy person again. Poor Cassy! she thought, feeling a sudden overwhelming pity for her, for Alan and, not least of all, for herself too.

It was clear from the number of people jostling one another on the platform that the Arlberg-Orient Express was going to be crowded. The *wagons lits* were fully booked and Alan had had difficulty in reserving one of the first-class sleeper cabins for Joscelin.

'I've rechecked the time of your arrival in Munich,' he said as he tipped the porter and also the steward who would be looking after her on the overnight journey. 'You should be there by teatime tomorrow.' He glanced at his watch and then at Joscelin's white face.

'We've a quarter of an hour before the train leaves,' he said. 'Shall we go back onto the platform – or will you be too cold, my darling?'

A bitter north wind was tunnelling down the platform, tossing empty cigarette cartons and paper litter onto the railway lines. The Gare de l'Est was a cold, miserable place to be this late November night. He tucked her arm beneath his and walked her away from the crowds, stopping near a pillar where only the occasional shrill hissing of an engine letting off steam could interrupt their conversation.

'Joss, darling, *must* you go? You're running away, aren't you?' he said, his voice tense as he stared down at her. 'But you don't have to. I give you my word I won't try to see you. Please change your mind – *don't go!*'

Joscelin gripped her hands tightly inside her fur muff. She was close to tears. There were still fifteen minutes to be lived through before the train left. Part of her was longing for these farewells to be over; for Alan to go; but equally, she clung to the precious last few moments when she could be with him. There had been so little chance to talk alone these past ten days. Now there was hardly any time left for explanations.

'It'll be easier for both of us,' she said, feeling she could bear anything but the look on Alan's face. 'I know you wouldn't break your word, Alan, but Cassy would think it strange if I never came to Rutland Gate, and I don't know if I could behave as if nothing had happened between us each time she came to the studio to see me. She *would* come – and she'd talk about you and . . . Alan, I *have* to go. You know I do!'

For a moment he was silent. Then he said roughly: 'I'll be so damned frightened for you, Joss. Even allowing for Cassy's exaggerations, Patri's situation sounds appallingly dangerous. Promise me you won't do anything risky – like Cassy!' Alan said, grasping Joscelin's gloved hands in his.

She attempted a smile. 'I shall be perfectly safe. I have an English passport and however horrible the National Socialists may be, they cannot harm me personally. You mustn't worry! I won't do anything silly.'

'I just can't bear the thought of you going away. I shall miss you dreadfully!'

His words brought the tears rushing to her eyes. She struggled against them but as Alan put his arms round her, they poured down her cheeks.

'I shall think of you every moment of the day – and night,' he said huskily. 'I'll take care of Cassy as best I can, but I'll never stop loving you, needing you.'

'Alan, you must try and help me,' Joss said brokenly. 'Don't look at me like that . . . please!'

A jet of steam escaping from the big engine silenced his reply. With a last despairing gesture, Joscelin reached up and kissed him before tearing herself out of his arms and running towards her carriage, praying he would not follow her. Knowing she would be unable to bear the sight of him standing forlornly on the platform as the train drew out of the station, she stood in the passageway until it did so. Only then did she go to her sleeper. The curtains had not yet been drawn across the window and all she could see was the last waving figure on the platform disappearing from sight. Like an automaton Joscelin drew the curtains, unpacked her night things, washed her face, cleaned her teeth. Turning out the main light, she climbed between the sheets and discovered that she was shivering violently despite the heating from the hot water pipes.

As the train raced through the dark night, rattling and swaying on its noisy journey, Joscelin told herself that although she could no longer show her love for Alan she could still help him – by keeping out of his life . . . and of Cassy's too. If Patri and Rebekka did not need her, then she might break into her savings and go to Canada to visit her mother. At all costs she must not return to England.

Patri, however, left her in no doubt on her arrival at Munich the following afternoon that her visit was heaven-sent.

'Rebekka has been quite ill, Joss, and with good reason. Her grandfather has disappeared. Together with a number of his colleagues, Herr Stolberg was arrested – "for his own protection", the police said, but now he has vanished. We fear the worst, and Frau Schwarz, Rebekka's mother, is on the point of collapse. Herr Stolberg knew we were hiding his brother – it was whilst Casilda was staying with us – and if he were to reveal this under torture . . .'

For the first time since she had left Paris, Joscelin completely forgot her own unhappiness. 'I had no idea things were so bad,' she said as Patri turned the car into Poschingerstrasse.

He drew up outside his front door. His voice was deepened by anxiety as he said quietly: 'If the stormtroopers come to our house to question Rebekka about her uncle, she will naturally deny we helped him to escape, but there is Carlos. He is too young to understand what is happening – yet old enough to talk. Rebekka and I have been discussing the advisability of sending him to Isobel now that Heinrich has gone to England. Carlos will be safer there. Now that you have arrived, and could perhaps take care of the baby, Rebekka can drive Carlos to Württemberg.'

He gave her an apologetic smile as he led her into the house. 'Enough of my problems – let me take your coat and hat. We have no servants now – it is too dangerous, for reasons I will explain later. We have also withdrawn from any kind of social life other than that involving me at the bank. No one comes here and my poor Rebekka is often very lonely. She can't wait to see you.'

His smile faded as Rebekka came hurrying down the stairs and threw herself into his arms. 'I am so glad you are safely back!' she wept. 'I have been so frightened. Twice I have seen cars driving up and down past the house, and men in uniform were staring out of the windows. I am so afraid, Patri. I tried to telephone Mütti but there was no reply. Suppose they have taken her in for questioning?'

Gradually Patri calmed her down and they went into the living room where a fire blazed a cheerful welcome. As Joscelin sat down, Patri's little boy, Carlos, climbed onto her lap, his small face serious as he listened to his mother's anxious voice. Joscelin was shocked that any child should have to live in such fear. But as Rebekka calmed down in the presence of her husband, her explanations of the reason for her state of nerves only added to Joscelin's growing horror.

'Even murder is excused, and Patri and I have had first-hand accounts of many "legal" killings. The bankers and rich merchants have not been attacked as yet,' she added, 'even though many are Jewish. It is the workers, the traders and professional men who have been suffering the most. Julius Streicher is a fanatic and everyone knows it is only a matter of time before he achieves his aim – the complete extermination of our race.'

Patri nodded. 'Outwardly, this country might seem to have benefited from Hitler's management. But he only maintains the degree of power he needs by having around him men who are prepared to be as ruthless as he – men who are either too stupid, too greedy or too ambitious to question the morality of what is happening.'

A look of consternation on his face, Patri added: 'I can only apologize for my shocking lack of manners. You have not even had a cup of coffee and here I am talking about our problems. You must excuse me, Joss, on the grounds that these problems are not exactly little ones. Rebekka, *cariña*, take Joscelin to her room and allow her to rest if she wishes.'

'No, I'm fine, Patri!' Joscelin said, glancing anxiously at Rebekka's pale little face. 'Let's stay and talk. It's such a long time since I last saw you.'

Rebekka must have lost over a stone in weight, Joscelin thought, since she had last seen her in Sevilla eight years ago. Carlos also looked underweight.

'Patri said you were thinking of taking Carlos to Isobel,' she said, stroking the little boy's dark curls. 'I will be happy to look after the baby whilst you are gone – providing you leave me instructions for her routine. I haven't much experience of babies, I'm afraid.'

Patri smiled. 'Would you believe that I am almost as efficient as Rebekka?' he asked. 'Like it or not, I have had to learn how to look after my children. I wish I could be the one to drive Carlos to Isobel's – but I have to keep an important appointment tomorrow. I am meeting Casilda's Nazi "friend", Strasser.'

Still speaking in English, which little Carlos could not understand, he said: 'Casilda will have told you that she assisted two of our refugees to get to Paris. Since then, we have taken in three others, two of whom Isobel has managed to get to Switzerland. Now we await news from her that she can arrange facilities for the one we still have here.'

Deeply concerned for them, Joscelin slept fitfully that night. When morning came, she set about helping Rebekka with the children.

If Carlos had caught at her heartstrings, even more so did the baby, Ruth. Now sixteen months old, the child had the same enormous dark eyes as her mother and Patri's laughing mouth and friendly nature. She toddled after Joscelin wherever she went.

'I've written out her daily schedule for you,' Rebekka said as they washed the dishes together. 'She has obviously taken to you, so I hope you won't have any trouble with her.'

She looked much more relaxed as she prepared Carlos for the long drive to Württemberg. Isobel, she explained, had two young Swiss girls working for her who would take care of the little boy. The remainder of the staff were old family retainers who were violently anti-Hitler and could be depended upon not to repeat any comment the child might let slip about the stranger in the house. She drew an anxious sigh. 'If only we could discover what has happened to Grossvater. It is terrible of me, but I pray that he is dead – then my parents will feel free to leave Germany with Patri and me. Patri intends to request holiday visas for us all – a family visit to Spain, he will say. Then no one will suspect we are leaving for ever.'

Unexpectedly, Rebekka hugged Joscelin. 'I know it's silly, but I feel so much safer whilst you are staying with us,' she said. 'You are certain you don't mind being left alone with the baby, Joscelin? Patri will only be out for a few hours after lunch.' She clung to Patri as he kissed her and his little son goodbye. It was almost as if they feared they might never see each other again, Joscelin thought.

As she prepared lunch for Patri and the baby, Patri spoke of his Jewish refugee. It was safer that she should neither know his name nor where he was hidden, he told her quietly. It was always possible that some Nazi official might ask her questions, since he was certain he and Rebekka were under suspicion.

'I don't understand why the German people tolerate this awful regime,' Joscelin commented as she put Ruth into her high chair.

Patri frowned. 'Not long ago there were six million un-employed,' he explained, 'but because of the massive rearmament programme most of them now have jobs producing guns, ships for the German navy, aeroplanes, tanks – all in defiance of the Versailles Treaty, of course. My father-in-law is certain Hitler's ultimate aim is war.'

He hurried away as soon as he had finished lunch for an appointment with Cassy's Dr Strasser, who had been pressing him for some time for news of her.

After Joscelin had cleared away the meal, she put the baby in her cot upstairs for a nap, freeing herself to wash her hair, which she felt must be black with smuts from the train smoke, then went downstairs to dry it in front of the fire in the living room.

The baby had not yet woken when Joscelin heard the sound of cars pulling up in front of the house. Unprepared for visitors, she tied her half-dried hair in a scarf and hurried to open the door.

On the doorstep stood six armed storm-troopers. They pushed her back into the hallway and surrounded her, one brandishing his revolver in her face as he kicked the door shut. Two others caught her roughly by the arms.

'*Frau Montero? Komm mit! Schnell!*'

Horrified, Joscelin tried to wrench her arms free. She had not understood their commands, but realized that they thought she was Rebekka; moreover the word '*Komm*' indicated that she was expected to go with them. But where? Why? She realized this was no friendly visit. She recognized the word '*Jude*' as the leader of the group spat abusively in her face.

I am in no danger, she told herself. I have only to fetch my passport and show them that I am English and they will leave me alone . . .

But even as the thought flashed across her mind, so too did the possible consequence. If they knew she was *not* Rebekka, they might search the house for her. They would find the baby . . . and, far worse, the hidden Jew in the house. On the other hand, if she were to go with them there was at least a chance Patri would be home in time to remove the fugitive before the men realized their mistake and came back for the real Frau Montero.

Two of her 'visitors' had pushed past her. One quite openly put Patri's silver cigar cutter into his pocket. The other picked up a child's chalk lying on Patri's desk and was now desecrating the wall with huge letters saying 'JUDE'. At least Patri would guess what had happened, Joscelin thought, as without further ado, she was dragged roughly out of the house. She felt a sharp pain in her ankle as one of the men kicked her and then she was pushed into the back seat of the foremost car.

I mustn't speak, Joscelin thought. If I say anything at all, they might realize I am English.

The cars drew up outside the National Socialist Headquarters in Mozartstrasse. There she was bundled into a room where a number of other people were seated. As the stormtroopers entered, all but one man sprang to their feet, held out their right arms and shouted: '*Heil Hitler!*'

To Joscelin's disbelief, the man who had not given the Nazi greeting was immediately attacked by two of the stormtroopers, one of whom delivered a number of lashes with a dog whip. After several more lashes the recipient gave the Nazi salute. Horrified, Joscelin wondered if these men were, like herself, awaiting interrogation.

Suddenly, the stormtroopers left the room. The man beside Joscelin whispered something in German, but she could not understand what he was saying. Opposite them a door opened. Yet another prisoner joined them, staggering into the waiting room, his right eye full of blood.

Now very frightened indeed, Joscelin was sustained only by the thought that the longer she remained here, the better the chance of Patri getting home before she was taken back. After several minutes, two of the stormtroopers came in and removed one of the prisoners, dragging him through the door by which she had entered. The man beside Joscelin crossed himself, and pointed to the floor. From his whispered comment, she deduced that the *Kommunist* had been taken down to the

Keller. She understood from his gestures that the prisoner was about to be beaten. He did not come back.

On the wall facing Joscelin, the minute hand of a clock ticked its way slowly past the hour. Her fear was beginning slowly to subside. At any time, she had only to open her mouth and declare herself to be a British citizen for them to release her. But her calm was shortlived. The door opened again, a stormtrooper grabbed her roughly by the arm and pushed her through into the inner room.

At a table covered by a large swastika banner sat an SS officer. Joscelin recognized the black uniform which Patri had pointed out as he had driven her home from the railway station. The officer sat with his back to the window, the blinds half drawn so that his face was in shadow. Hers, on the other hand, was exposed to the glare of a table lamp.

His voice was dangerously quiet as he bombarded Joscelin with questions, none of which she could understand and which, in any event, she had no intention of answering. But when, after he had finally fallen silent, she still made no reply, one of the stormtroopers standing behind her dealt her a painful blow on the side of her face. The second stormtrooper came round to stand beside her, a steel rod in his hand and a look of sadistic anticipation on his face. Joscelin did not need to speak the language to know what was in store for her if she continued to remain silent.

Her interrogator began again. She understood the name of Herr Stolberg, the words *Jude* and *Keller*. Once again, she summoned up the courage to say nothing, but this time she was knocked to the floor and kicked. She felt an excruciating pain as unceremoniously she was shoved roughly back in the chair.

There was little doubt now that she was to be forced by whatever means to give answers to the questions her interrogator was asking. Painfully, she lifted her arm and removed her headscarf. Then she said quietly:

'My name is Joscelin Howard. I am a British subject and I have a British passport. I demand an apology for the shocking manner in which I am being treated. I think you understand what I am saying. I shall report you to the British consul.'

The SS officer was disconcerted. Joscelin's tone of authority confused him, and yet he could not be certain if she was bluffing. He leaned towards her and peered at her more closely, addressing her once more in German.

'I don't understand your language,' Joscelin interrupted, 'any better than I understand your disgraceful behaviour. If you wish to speak to me, do so in English.'

The man barked out an order to one of the stormtroopers, who left the room; then he turned back to Joscelin. 'I think not English. You are German citizen. *Sie sind Frau Montero, nicht wahr?*'

'Not Frau Montero, Fräulein Howard!' Joscelin said forcibly. 'I have a British passport. If your men had asked me to identify myself, you would have saved yourself a great deal of trouble.'

The stormtrooper who had left the room now returned with a photograph which he handed to the SS officer. It was obvious to Joscelin that it must be a snapshot of Rebekka for he stood up at once and bowed, an expression of dismay replacing the former arrogance.

'Excuses please, Fräulein,' he said. 'My men is very stupid. For the passport in house should ask before you are coming here. Deutschland are treating all the Engländer very well. I ask that this error you will forgive.'

Overcome by a mixture of relief and fear, Joscelin discovered that her hands were trembling. Gripping them together, she forced herself to employ further delaying tactics. She could not be certain that Patri had returned home, and now that this man knew she was not Rebekka, Patri's wife was terribly at risk.

'It is not enough for you to apologize, officer,' she said coldly. 'Your men have injured my ankle and I have a broken rib. I shall report this very serious matter to your superiors. In the meanwhile, I demand a doctor immediately.'

The man regarded her with a growing sense of anxiety. If

she did carry out her threat to report him he could be in very serious trouble. At the same time, he himself had been acting upon instructions to bring in Frau Montero for questioning. The information the authorities had so far received was insufficient to allow the search of a house belonging to the influential young Spanish banker.

Recently, however, interrogation of an elderly Jew by the name of Stolberg had brought to light the fact that Frau Rebekka Montero was his granddaughter and half Jewish. The old man had died before they could extract further information from him. He would be excused violence executed on a half Jewess, he told himself now, but *not* upon an English visitor to the country.

'I arrange for a doctor immediately to come,' he said. 'I regret most sincerely what happened has. The men who have this mistake made, shall be most severely punished. You are the guest of Herr and Frau Montero, Fräulein Howard?'

'Obviously!' Joscelin said, coldly sarcastic. 'Otherwise I would scarcely be staying in their home, would I? As to your treatment of me, I am sure you will understand that on reflection I do not wish to be attended by one of your doctors. Please arrange for a taxi to take me back to my friends' house.'

'*Gnädiges Fräulein*, I assure you . . .'

'You have no right to detain me,' Joscelin broke in sharply. 'And if it was your intention to have me driven home by those thugs of yours, please forget it. I will take a taxi. Now will you telephone for one at once, or must I get in touch with the British consul?' The very last thing she wanted, Joscelin thought, was for a car full of stormtroopers to escort her to Poschingerstrasse where Patri might be in the process of removing the fugitive from the house.

He made one further attempt to persuade her to await the arrival of their own doctor, but despite the acuteness of her pain, Joscelin banged her fist on the table. 'You have dragged me to this place without any justification whatever. You kept me waiting in that room out there as if I was a criminal, and then you allowed me to be beaten by your underlings. As if that were not enough, you are now refusing my request to be taken home in a taxi. I don't think this will look well for you when I make my report.'

But as the officer reached for the telephone, the door opened and Patri came hurrying in. He was followed closely by a bald, bespectacled man who was obviously recognized by her SS interrogator, as he immediately jumped to his feet and gave the Nazi salute.

'Dr Strasser!' he said after the inevitable exchange of *Heil Hitlers*. 'You do me an honour! I was just about to telephone for a taxi to take this young lady home . . .'

He had lapsed into German. Joscelin felt Patri's arm around her. She could not subdue a cry of pain as he hugged her. His face was white with anxiety. 'Thank God I've found you. Are you all right, Joss?' he whispered.

She attempted a smile. 'Don't look so worried . . . I'm fine now you're here.'

'But your face!' Patri said in a horrified voice. He turned angrily to his companion. For a few moments the three men conversed rapidly in German and, suddenly exhausted, Joscelin collapsed into a chair. She was shivering violently as delayed shock set in. She did not register the fact that she had heard Dr Strasser's name before and thought only that, if Patri was here, his refugee must be out of the house and the danger to Rebekka and himself averted.

It was a further quarter of an hour before finally they were driven home in Dr Strasser's official car.

'You will understand that I cannot invite you in,' Patri said to him as he helped Joscelin out of the front seat. 'I must telephone the doctor for Fräulein Howard immediately. Thank you for your assistance, Dr Strasser. I must write and tell my sister how *very* helpful you have been.'

When the German had made his adieu, Patri took Joscelin into the house and led her to the sofa. He built up the fire and put a warm rug over her knees. Joscelin felt close to tears as he went out to the hall to telephone the doctor. He returned within minutes to sit down beside her.

'Our doctor is a pleasant fellow,' he told her reassuringly. 'He abhors the Nazis as much as we do. He's one of the few men left in the country who will treat a Communist or a Jew! Now, Joss – if you feel up to it, tell me exactly what happened. I gathered that somehow you had been mistaken for Rebekka, but why didn't you show those brutes your passport? Then they would never have abducted you!'

Joscelin nodded. 'I realized that, but I was afraid if I told them Rebekka was not here, they might search the house. I wasn't being brave, Patri. I simply didn't know what they would do to me. Now I know, I'm glad Rebekka wasn't in my place. I knew I could end the "interrogation" at any time. She would have been so much more vulnerable.'

'It was very brave of you, Joss,' Patri said simply. 'When I arrived home, one of my neighbours told me the stormtroopers had been here and taken a woman away with them. I knew Rebekka could not possibly have made the round trip to Württemberg so quickly.' He paused to put more coal on the fire. Then he said:

'My one idea was to find you as quickly as possible, so I telephoned Dr Strasser and asked him for his assistance. He promised to try to locate your whereabouts. Meanwhile, I asked my father-in-law to get the refugee out of the house as I feared we might later be searched. Ruth was taken in by my neighbour, and then Dr Strasser arrived in his car to drive me to the Nazi headquarters. The fact that you were Cassy's best friend stood us all in good stead!'

Patri did not add that he was desperately concerned for Joscelin. She was a living witness to a mistake the Nazis would do anything to hide. If she stayed in Munich, an 'accident' might occur which would prevent her giving evidence of their barbaric behaviour. Clearly someone at headquarters was now aware of Rebekka's connections with the Stolberg family and henceforth they would be under the closest scrutiny. Even Dr

Strasser could no longer be counted on as a 'friend'. He had turned quite pale when the SS officer had mentioned that Rebekka was half Jewish. Given a little more time, he might connect Casilda's requests for passports for her 'Jewish school-friends' with a more sinister attempt to help the Stolberg family as a whole.

When the doctor arrived, Patri risked a telephone call to his cousin, Isobel. He returned to the living room in time to thank the doctor and show him out.

Alone with Joscelin, he said urgently: 'Could you manage a car journey, Joss – a longish one? Frankly, I think we've got to get out of here quickly. Isobel has offered to put us up at the Schloss. My plan is to leave as soon as Rebekka returns. When I collect Ruth from my neighbours, I shall tell them that I am taking you all on a skiing holiday. Then if anyone comes looking for us, they will not suspect. Isobel says there are German patrol boats on this side of the lake, but if we can get hold of a fast boat and go by night we should have a good chance of avoiding detection. The crossing from Langenargen to Romanshorn in Switzerland is just over ten miles.'

'You mean – leave Germany altogether?' Joscelin asked. 'But what about Rebekka . . . her mother . . .'

Patri's face looked almost old as he said quietly: 'I must put Rebekka and the children first. Perhaps it was wrong of me not to do so long before this. I will give Rebekka time to telephone her mother and grandmother and invite them to come with us. If they will not, then we must leave without them . . . providing *you* are well enough to travel, Joss.'

'Of course I am,' Joscelin said quickly, although her legs were trembling and she felt a little sick. 'The doctor gave me some painkillers, and he has strapped up my ribs so well that I can't do myself any damage. I'll be all right. What of the Jewish man you were hiding?'

'My father-in-law will conceal him until he can be taken to Isobel. Herr Schwarz is a practical man, and when I told him what had happened here this afternoon he appreciated that he might no longer be able to protect Rebekka's mother by his name and standing, still less so her grandmother. Naturally Herr Schwarz does not wish to be parted from his wife, but although he too would like to leave Germany, his sudden absence would be noticed and we would all be at far greater risk if he came with us.'

Patri walked over to his desk to withdraw his passport. 'Our first hurdle is persuading Frau Schwarz and her mother to come with us. My father-in-law will let it be known that he intends to join us on holiday after he has attended to some business in Geneva. Of course, once there he will not return to Germany. For some time now we have both been secreting money in Switzerland, and he seems certain that he and his wife will be allowed into the United States.'

So this was not a sudden plan, Joscelin realized. It had been carefully thought out; only the reluctance of Frau Schwarz to leave her elderly parents behind had held up the family exodus.

Would the elderly grandmother be able to stand up to what sounded like an arduous car journey? Patri's original plan to go by train with official visas for Spain was no longer practical, he explained. Trains these days were held up frequently by searches for escaping Jews. They could be arrested at any checkpoint and detained for questioning.

'I shall put two sets of skis on top of the car,' Patri said, 'and we will depart in the direction of Garmisch-Partenkirchen. The Nazis may *think* themselves clever, but it is possible to outwit them if you can think a jump ahead of their reasoning.'

The painkillers the doctor had given her must have contained some kind of soporific for, despite the urgency of the situation, Joscelin dozed off in her chair by the fire. She was woken by the sound of Rebekka's and Patri's voices in the hall and by the cries of the baby. Forgetting her injuries, she jumped to her feet and gasped as the pain jabbed at her consciousness. Rebekka came into the room carrying the crying child.

'Could you possibly nurse her, Joscelin, whilst I go and

pack? Patri is going now to fetch Mütti and, we hope, my grandmother.'

She handed the little girl to Joscelin, who sat down again and took the baby on her lap.

'Patri has told me what happened,' she said, her voice husky with emotion. 'I am so very sorry that you suffered for me, and I shall always be grateful – always!'

Joscelin did her best to sound matter-of-fact as she said: 'You're not to give it another thought, Rebekka. Off you go and pack. Little Ruth will be all right with me, won't you, darling?'

It was easier to soothe the child than Rebekka's mother and grandmother when they arrived at the house with Patri. Both were in tears, and although Joscelin could understand very little of what they said, she repeatedly heard the name of Herr Stolberg. Rebekka had finally convinced her grandmother that the poor man was almost certainly dead.

It was nearly ten o'clock before the car was packed with their few belongings and the skis strapped onto the roof rack. It was a wise precaution, Patri reiterated as they drove away, for he could see lights in their neighbours' windows and the silhouette of a figure watching them as they turned out of the gateway onto the road.

It was a long, exhausting journey, made worse by flurries of snow which turned into a veritable snowstorm as they neared the mountains overlooking Walchensee.

As the car rattled and occasionally skidded on the snow-covered roads, Joscelin found herself longing for Alan. Patri looked so much like him that it caught at her heartstrings. Now her resistance was at its lowest ebb and she knew that were Alan, by some miracle, to be waiting for her at Isobel's she would not have the courage to leave him ever again.

When at last Patri brought the car to a halt in the interior courtyard of the Schloss, only Isobel and one of her trusted servants hurried out to help them. Rupert, she explained, was staying overnight with friends in Langenargen where he hoped to be able to borrow or hire a boat for them in which to make the crossing to Romanshorn. Although the ferry still crossed from Friedrichshafen it was, of course, as strictly guarded as any frontier post, for ten miles across the water lay Switzerland – and freedom.

It was eight years since Joscelin had last seen Isobel. Although she was fatter than she had been and her carroty hair streaked with grey, she was otherwise unchanged. She marshalled the bedraggled group into a small salon where a log fire blazed. On a table stood coffee, brandy and food. A tureen of soup was steaming on a trivet over the fire. Isobel had even thought of heating milk for the baby.

Joscelin was too tired to eat but Patri fell on the food hungrily and, between mouthfuls, he gave Isobel an account of the events leading up to their decision to leave Munich so hurriedly.

'I was afraid to say too much on the telephone,' he told Isobel. 'I would never forgive myself if I were responsible for you and Rupert receiving the kind of interrogation Joscelin had today.'

'I imagine you're regretting your decision to visit Patricio and Rebekka,' Isobel said to Joscelin with a wry smile. 'I had a letter from Alan this morning telling me that I might see you. He gave me a censored version, I imagine, of what that irresponsible wife of his had been up to in Paris. I'm sorry for Alan. It's time that girl settled down.'

It was a thought that lingered in Joscelin's mind long after she had retired to the comfortable room provided for her. But total exhaustion, combined with two further painkillers, finally sent her to sleep.

It was mid-afternoon when she awoke. Rebekka was standing by her bedside with a tray.

'Isobel thought you might like a nice English cup of tea,' she said. 'You have missed lunch, I'm afraid, but there are sandwiches and pastries if you are hungry. Dinner will be served very early this evening so that we can leave at seven.'

Joscelin sat up in bed, every limb in her body aching. 'Leave? You mean we are crossing the lake tonight? So soon?'

Rebekka sat down on the edge of the bed. 'Patri feels

that the longer we stay here with Isobel, the greater the danger for the von Lessens. Rupert has bought a boat from one of his friends further up the lake. Tomorrow morning they will report it "stolen". Patri has orders to take a crowbar so that it looks like a genuine theft.'

It was snowing once more as, shortly after seven, Isobel and Rupert helped Patri and his family into the car.

'The snow may be a nuisance now,' Patri said as they drove along the lakeside towards Langenargen, 'but it will benefit us as we cross Lake Constance. The German patrol boats are far less likely to spot us in this weather!'

In fact the weather worsened, and if any German boats were patrolling the refugees neither saw nor heard one. Patri managed with difficulty to navigate the ten miles across the lake to the Swiss town of Romanshorn, where he reported to the police station. Because Frau Schwarz and Frau Stolberg had no passports, they were detained for some time whilst discussions took place on the telephone. But the Swiss authorities were sympathetic. Since Patri, Rebekka and Joscelin held valid passports, they were all allowed to book rooms for the night in a local hotel and to proceed by train the following morning across Switzerland to Geneva.

Exactly forty-eight hours after leaving Munich, they walked into the lobby of the Hotel Beau Rivage.

Patri went over to the reception desk to sign the register for his family of six. When he returned with a porter and the keys to their rooms, he grinned at Joscelin. 'Casilda has been trying to telephone you, Joss. Heaven knows how she discovered you were coming here. The call is being put through again in an hour's time, so I told Reception you would take it in your room. We'll see you at dinner.'

He enveloped her suddenly in a careful bear hug. 'We've made it! We've done it, Joss!' he said triumphantly. 'I feel a hundred years younger!'

'Well, I feel like soaking in a hot bath!' Joscelin said with a smile. But the strapping round her ribs would make this impossible, she thought as she went to her room, nor dared she risk missing Cassy's telephone call. Her nerves felt raw. She could think of no reason why Cassy should need to speak to her. And *how* had she discovered that they were in Geneva and staying at the Beau Rivage?

She was still trying to puzzle out the answer when the telephone by her bed rang.

'Mademoiselle Howard? I have a call for you from Paris. Hold the line, please.'

The palms of her hands were sweating as she waited whilst various French voices strove to make the connections.

'You are through now. Mademoiselle Howard is on the line.'

But it was not Cassy who spoke. Unbelievably, it was Alan.

'Joscelin, is that you? Operator, I can't hear anything.'

'Yes, it's me, Alan, it's me!' Joscelin shouted – then, drawing a deep breath, she lowered her voice. 'Can you hear me?'

'As if you were in the next room, Joss. Are you all right? Cassy's been trying to get you for hours. Now she has gone down to the cocktail bar for a farewell drink with Uncle Jaime. I suppose she forgot to cancel the call. Are you still there, Joss?'

She sat down on the side of the bed, hugging the telephone receiver to her ear. At any moment, she thought, I shall wake up and find I've been dreaming. She was talking to Alan, listening to Alan's voice.

'I'm fine! I just didn't expect to hear you. I was told Cassy had telephoned earlier,' she said shakily.

'I never expected to talk to you either. Cassy insisted on making the call in the first place . . . said she hadn't thanked you properly for holding her hand here in Paris.'

'How did she know I was here?' Joscelin asked, wanting nothing more than to hear the sound of his voice.

'She tried to ring Patricio but could get no reply. This morning she managed to get Herr Schwarz at his bank and he told her the family had gone off on a skiing holiday. That seemed very strange when you'd only just arrived. Herr Schwarz suggested Cassy telephoned Isobel, of all people, and added that *you* would be in Geneva. Frankly, I was worried . . . why only you? It didn't make sense.'

'Your three minutes is up, sir. Do you wish a further three minutes?' the operator intervened.

'Of course – don't interrupt me again,' Alan said sharply. 'This will probably be a long call.'

'And an expensive one!' Joscelin said, trying to sound light-hearted. 'There's no need to worry, Alan. I'm not alone. Patricio and the family are here too. I'll explain.'

Briefly she outlined what had occurred, leaving out any mention of her injuries. 'So you see, neither Herr Schwarz nor Isobel would have dared say over the telephone where the others were in case anyone was listening in. But we're all safe now.'

'Oh, darling, thank God you're all right!'

The endearment brought tears to Joscelin's eyes. For a moment, she could not speak. Then she said: 'Is Cassy all right? How are things, Alan?'

His voice sounded suddenly stiff, guarded. 'We're both fine. Cassy's doing everything she can to make amends for all the trouble she's caused. We're planning a trip to Cairo this winter. Joss, what are *you* going to do now?'

'I'm going back to Spain with Patri and Rebekka,' Joscelin replied. 'I shall help with the children. I'll be fine, Alan.'

The ensuing silence hung between them until finally it was broken by Alan. 'I miss you terribly! I know I promised I'd never try to get in touch . . . this call wasn't my idea. But dammit, Joss, I can't ring off without saying it. I love you. I'll always love you. Not a minute of the day or night passes that I fail to think of you. Life seems so damn pointless without you. Joss, can you hear me?'

Tears spilled down Joscelin's cheeks. 'Please, Alan, don't say any more. I know how you feel – it's the same for me – but we'll get used to it in time . . .'

She broke off, partly because she was crying, but partly

because she knew her words lacked any real conviction. She would never get used to a world without him . . . and if this call proved anything, it was that the break had to be complete, as final as death itself.

'Joss, are you still there? Dammit, I can't hear you . . .' There was the sound of the receiver clicking several times before Joscelin heard his voice again. 'Operator, there's something wrong with this line . . . I've been cut off.'

There was a moment's silence before the girl's voice said patiently: 'You're still connected, sir. Perhaps the party on the other end has cleared?'

'But of course she hasn't hung up on me!' His voice sounded angry, out of control. 'We were in the middle of . . . Joss? Are you there? Can you hear what I'm saying?'

'Only just!'

Not only was there crackling on the line but Joscelin could hear French voices drowning Alan's. She gripped the receiver to her ear, as if somehow this futile gesture could bring him back. Quite suddenly, she heard him as clearly as if he were in the same room. He sounded desperate.

'. . . big hotel, for God's sake; the switchboard must have cut her off. Are you certain we are still connected?' The relief of hearing his voice undermined her resolve.

'Alan, I can hear you,' she shouted. 'Alan? Can you hear me? I love you. I'll always love you, always, *always*. You mustn't worry about me, I'm . . .'

There was a buzzing in her ear and the line went dead. A moment later, she heard the soft French accent of the hotel operator.

'We have been cut off, Mademoiselle. If you replace your receiver, I will call you again when the line has been reconnected.'

For a long time, Joscelin sat waiting. She could think only of her last words to Alan. Had he heard them? It seemed the most important thing in the world that he knew she loved him. But as the time passed and the bedside telephone remained silent, she knew that, even if he had heard her, it was not enough. She needed to hear him . . . just once more. Please God, let the telephone ring! she prayed. But it did not do so.

Unable to bear the tension, she lifted the receiver. The girl on the switchboard answered.

'There was a call for me a little while ago – from Paris,' Joscelin said. 'We were disconnected. Are you sure they're not trying to get through to me again? I'm here in my room . . . number 105,' she added unnecessarily. 'It's very important.'

'*Oui*, Mademoiselle! But the party in Paris has cancelled the call. If you wish, I can try to reach the party for you. Have you the telephone number?'

No, I haven't, Joscelin thought as despair gripped her. Alan had thought better of ringing her back . . . and she understood only too well why. Exchanging declarations of love could serve no purpose other than to weaken their resolve to put a final end to their affair. And even their short conversation had weakened her. If Alan were to speak to her now, she knew she would not have the strength of mind to deny her need of him. He would know it – just as he knew and understood everything else about her.

'You wish me to obtain the number for you, Mademoiselle?'

'No, no thank you!' Joscelin said, struggling against the tears constricting her throat. 'It doesn't matter. I'll try another time.'

Returning the receiver to its cradle, she lay down on the bed and pressed her face into the pillow. But as her tears soaked the pillowcase, they brought no accompanying relief, for she knew that it *did* matter – and that if there was to be any chance of happiness for Alan in the future, there must never be 'another time'.

PART THREE

1936–1939

WAR

. . . Therefore be bold,
Of my hand take hold,
And swing in the track of my garment's fold!
Cling to me, follow me, set your heart free;
I am all that can never be,
A song, a spell, a key of gold,
Which can unlock the heart and the sea . . .

'Romance'
by Lady Margaret Sackville

CHAPTER TWENTY-EIGHT

July 1936

'You will have to speak more slowly – *más despacio!*' Joscelin said as she struggled to understand the Spanish nursemaid, Manuela.

With an expression that was part fear and part excitement, the girl dragged Joscelin to the window that looked eastward from the sardine village of Torremolinos towards Málaga. Grey columns of smoke were rising into the sky above the town. Manuela was once again in full flow, and for the hundredth time Joscelin wished that she could understand the language better.

'Come with me, Manuela,' she said carefully. 'We will find Señora Montero.'

Rebekka was sitting with Miss Smart on the sandy beach, keeping an eye on the children. Amalia and eight-year-old Carlos were paddling in the gentle wash of incoming waves. Ruth was happily engaged with a bucket and spade, 'making a pudding' she had informed them. The only other people to be seen on the endless stretch of sand were the usual group of fishermen's children who always came to stare at the foreigners with smiling curiosity.

Soon it would be too hot to sit on the beach and the family would be obliged to seek the cool of the hotel. In a few days' time, Don Jaime and Patricio would rejoin them, but for the present they had returned to Sevilla to attend to some urgent business.

'I simply cannot understand what Manuela is saying!' Joscelin told Rebekka. 'There's obviously a big fire of some kind in Málaga and she wants to tell me about it.'

Arms flying, the excited maid broke into a fresh torrent of words. The curiosity on Rebekka's face was replaced by a look of anxiety as she turned to Joscelin, frowning.

'According to Manuela, the revolution has started! She says she heard the latest news this morning from the women in the village and they had heard it from someone who was in Málaga. She insists there is fighting in the city; that bullets are flying in all directions and men are driving around in lorries and cars, armed to the teeth! She says they are burning the houses of Fascists. She seems to think they might come here and we shall all be killed in our beds because we, being "rich", will be thought to be Fascists.'

'We must go back to Sevilla immediately,' Miss Smart declared, gathering up the children's rope-soled sandals and beach towels. 'When Don Jaime told me last week of the murder of the statesman Calvo Sotelo, he warned me there'd be trouble. We should never have remained in this isolated place without a man to protect us!'

'But Patri said that Sotelo's assassination was in reprisal for the murder of an army officer and unlikely to lead to a military rebellion,' Rebekka told the governess soothingly. 'He said the government has arrested the culprits and it will all blow over.'

Despite Rebekka's reassurances, Joscelin was far from easy. She found it difficult to understand Spanish politics, but from what Don Jaime and Patricio had explained she knew the country was far from peaceful. Since she had come to Spain with Rebekka two years ago there had been constant changes of prime ministers, uprisings by landless peasants, strikes by low-paid workers and sporadic outbreaks of violence. Everyone seemed to be violently anti something.

She had noted that Patricio had become increasingly anxious about the political situation. He had remarked cynically to Joscelin that he and Rebekka had seen the results of Fascist dictatorship in Germany and had lived through the brutal extremes of nationalism, and now he feared the results of a Fascist-dominated Spain.

'I think Miss Smart is right – we should return to Sevilla.' Rebekka broke in on Joscelin's thoughts. 'We have only the chauffeur to protect us if there's any trouble and Alberto is neither young nor strong. We must think of the children . . .'

At this juncture, Manuela burst into tears and ran across the sand to gather Ruth into her arms, hugging her protectively.

'We will go back to Sevilla,' Rebekka said again. 'But we cannot possibly leave today. The drive will take at least six hours, and since it will be too hot to cross the plains this afternoon we cannot begin our journey until evening. Nothing will persuade me to go in the dark. We have no idea what is going on elsewhere, and for all we know there could be trouble en route! We'll pack everything today and leave before dawn tomorrow.'

'Don't you think I should make some inquiries at the hotel first?' Joscelin suggested. 'For all we know, Manuela may be exaggerating the danger. I'll go and have a word with the owners whilst you give the children their lunch.'

She hurried towards the narrow crumbling path leading up the steep cliff face. Today there were no residents to be seen other than one guest sitting on the verandah with the English couple who ran the hotel. They confirmed Manuela's accounts of the seriousness of the situation. All the other guests were already on their way to Gibraltar. They had received word that British destroyers were standing by to take off the English tourists and the expatriates who had settled on this southern coast of Spain.

The owners themselves had decided to remain where they were. The hotel was their livelihood and they had no home in England to return to. They refused to believe that the Spanish people, whom they had always found so friendly, would harm them. They agreed, however, that since Rebekka and Joscelin had small children in their charge they would not be justified in taking any risks. Convinced now that the trouble was really serious, Joscelin returned to their rooms to help with the packing.

Throughout the day, Manuela appeared at intervals with fresh rumours and gossip she had gleaned from the village. An Englishman had been shot travelling in his car to Gibraltar; red banners were hanging from the buildings still standing in Málaga; the town was in ruins.

'If only a small part of what the girl says is true, we have cause to be frightened,' Rebekka said as she took the children to the now deserted hotel dining room for lunch. 'If Patri and his father have heard what is happening in Málaga they will be worried. Maybe they are on their way here to protect us.'

Joscelin was unable to sleep during the siesta that afternoon. The heat was oppressive and she could not be certain if the rumbling noises she heard from time to time were caused by guns or thunder. Fear, she thought as she tried to find a cool patch on her pillow, was contagious. Rebekka had reverted to the nervous state she had been in when she had first escaped from Germany.

Because she and Joscelin were both foreigners in another country they had grown close. But as Rebekka slowly recovered from her unhappy experiences, her dependence became centred once again on Patricio, and she herself had played a very small part in Rebekka's life. The children, on the other hand, were wonderfully rewarding, for they adored Joscelin, and Carlos was her shadow. They were like her own children, the children she would now never have.

She tried not to think of the future. Here in Spain, day-to-day existence was bearable because it seldom brought memories of Alan and the love they had once shared. She could never be truly happy without him, but at least she was not unhappy nor plagued by the temptation to see him – as she would have been living in England.

Despite Rebekka's anxiety, Joscelin announced that she was going to walk down to the village as she sometimes did in the cooler air of the early evening. Reassuring both Rebekka and Miss Smart that she would return immediately if she met the slightest sign of trouble, she set off. The village, she discovered with relief, looked utterly normal, peaceful and dormant at the end of the siesta. The small herd of goats which the owner brought each day to the hotel to be milked at the door were grazing by the roadside. Nothing disturbed the peace of Torremolinos at seven o'clock in the evening. Only the smoke hanging in the air over Málaga gave credence to the certainty that all was not peaceful there.

Amalia greeted her on her return with an unusual show of emotion, hugging and kissing her as if she had been absent for a week.

'I was so frightened for you!' she said, close to tears. Amalia had not fully recovered from the 1931 demonstrations, when the terrorists had burned the churches and one of her favourite nuns had died. At the age of thirteen she was almost a young woman and, although her adolescence exaggerated her moodiness, she was stunningly pretty and so like her eldest sister as to bring back haunting memories to Joscelin of the carefree years of companionship she had once shared with Cassy.

Cassy wrote often, her untidy handwriting scrawling across the thin airmail paper unaware of the heartbreak each one would cause her 'dearest friend'. She and Alan were reunited. The dreadful horror of the car accident was a thing of the past. Alan had agreed that she could travel abroad on her own during the winter. 'It means I can see Milton sometimes but I have to be careful,' she wrote. 'Alan has never guessed. I shall come and visit you all next Easter, I promise . . .' Or next summer, or Christmas, or for Holy Week . . . But she never came.

Whilst Joscelin soothed Amalia's fears as best she could, her thoughts turned to Alan, as they so often did against her will. She knew she would always be lonely for him. At least she had the company of Cassy's family living here in Spain. Carmen, now twenty-three, was expecting her first baby; Luis and Mariano still attended the university in Madrid, despite their father's anxiety about the student uprisings against the government. Both young men had heated political arguments with their father, reflecting as they did their contemporaries' ideology of a new Spain. But Don Jaime was devoted to his two youngest sons, who were happy to conform to the norms of the Marqués de Fernandez de la Riva's social circle. They were currently on holiday with their eldest brother Eduardo and his family at Punta Umbria.

Amalia clung to Joscelin's hand as they walked across to the hotel for their evening meal. She ate little, the subdued atmosphere in the empty dining room increasing her nervousness. The girl became even more agitated when they were met by Alberto in the courtyard as they returned to their rooms. The town was in chaos, he told them. He had been lucky to get petrol for the car and had paid twice as much as he should have done for the concession.

The children were put to bed early since they must rise before dawn. Fortunately the sea air and heat had made them sleepy, but neither Joscelin nor Rebekka could do more than doze that night.

'I am so frightened!' Rebekka admitted. 'Running for safety brings back terrible memories of those last months in Germany. I thought we should be so safe here in Spain.'

'I'm sure it will be peaceful in Sevilla,' Joscelin said without conviction. 'You know the Spanish temperament, Rebekka – they flare up suddenly, but it always blows over. Don Jaime refutes any idea of a real revolution. Stop worrying!'

The streets were empty as shortly before dawn the chauffeur guided the big Hispano-Suiza around the outskirts of Málaga, but there was ample evidence that Manuela's descriptions of violence the previous day were all too true. Fires were visible in the darkness, the flames rising up against the night sky. Houses, burned to shells, were still smouldering.

As they wound their way slowly round the hairpin bends snaking up into the hills north of Málaga, the first rays of sunshine revealed the magnificent views of the surrounding sierras sweeping down to the coast. Safely on the open road to Antequera, they saw the first signs of life as they passed isolated homesteads – a man leading a mule from a ramshackle farm building; a woman milking a goat outside her house.

At Antequera, the alleyways swarmed with people beginning their day's work. A single café was open, where the family stopped for a breakfast of still warm bread, cheese and honey. Alberto found a two-day-old, dog-eared copy of *El Popular*.

When they resumed their journey along the main road from Antequera to Sevilla, he informed them that there had been a military rebellion in Morocco but that the government was 'master of the situation' and nobody in Spain had taken part in the plot.

Before they reached Sevilla, it became obvious to them that the disturbances had not been confined to Málaga. Through the open windows of the car they could hear the sound of heavy gunfire. A pall of smoke rose from the districts of Triana and St Julian. Groups of men stood gossiping to one another outside their houses. Nearly all the shops were closed and shuttered, and numerous large portraits of General Queipo de Llano were plastered on walls. The civil guard, heavily armed, were much in evidence.

It was now ten o'clock and the sun burned fiercely down on the roof of the car. The heat inside was intense, for they were all agreed that with so many armed soldiers about they must close the windows. But as they neared the centre of the city, they were stopped several times by uniformed soldiers and civil guards. They let the family continue unmolested, cautioning them to remain indoors once they reached their house as the city was not yet fully under General Queipo de Llano's command.

'We are fighting now to take the airport,' one of the soldiers told them. 'We shall soon have the rabble under control. They have no arms. *Arriba España!*'

'But this is civil war!' Miss Smart cried, her face horrified. 'May the good Lord preserve us! We shall all be murdered in our beds!'

Joscelin pretended a calm she did not feel as Alberto turned into the Plaza San Isidoro. The Monteros' house and all the other houses were heavily shuttered, but she knew that this could be the usual summer precaution against the heat. On an adjoining rooftop a maid was hanging out washing as if this was any other Monday.

Miss Smart recovered her equilibrium the moment one of the servants opened the door to them. 'The children are exhausted!' she said to Rebekka. 'I shall put them to bed. And you, Amalia, must go and lie down. You can read a book if you wish. But wash your hands and face first.'

'The Señor Marqués and Don Patricio have important visitors,' José said as he took two of the suitcases from Alberto. 'The Señor Marqués has instructed me that they are not to be disturbed.'

'Then we will not do so,' Joscelin said firmly, sensing Rebekka's urge to rush into the *salón* to the safety of her husband's arms.

It was over an hour before Don Jaime's visitors departed. By then Joscelin and Rebekka had washed and changed into clean cotton frocks. The air in the house was stifling and there was a frightening smell of smoke from the fires in the city. Occasionally, they could hear the sound of heavy guns from the Triana district across the river.

As Patricio took his wife in his arms, Rebekka burst into tears. 'We were afraid for the children,' she sobbed. 'We thought we would be safe in Sevilla, but it seems even worse here than in Málaga.'

Don Jaime looked tired and worried as he said quietly: 'We heard on the wireless that the government has decided after all to give arms to the trade unions. Until now, the people have had no weapons with which to oppose the army takeover. Now, I fear, there could be a counter-attack. The workers naturally oppose military authority.'

Patri's face looked grim as he said forcefully: 'And with every justification, Papá. Armed rebellion is no substitute for an elected government. Mark my words, Hitler is somewhere behind this uprising as well as Mussolini. As Don Federico said just now, it would suit their purpose to have a Fascist Spain.'

José came into the *salón* with freshly made coffee and lemonade. When he had served the drinks, Don Jaime said: 'Naturally you are biased against your hated *fascistas*, Patri, but I can assure you they pose far less threat to our class than do the *comunistas* and *anarquistas*. I for one have no wish to have my lands and wealth taken forcibly from me; nor be murdered merely because I oppose their aims. And do not forget that this is a Catholic country and the restoration of the Church is possible under the *fascistas*.'

Patri looked as if she were about to argue, but Joscelin intervened. 'Are we safe here, Don Jaime?' she inquired. 'I understand the army is in control of the city.'

Don Jaime nodded. 'They took command with remarkable ease and not a little cunning!' he added.

'As we drove through the city, we saw no signs of fighting,' Joscelin said.

'There were men in the Giralda – sharpshooters – but very few had arms whereas the army was soon able to set up their machine guns,' Don Jaime explained. 'Today, there is heavy fighting to gain control of the districts. The army has captured the airport and I have just learned that General Franco will shortly be arriving by aeroplane to supervise matters. But now the government has changed its mind and agreed that arms should be distributed to the people, so we cannot be certain what will happen. There is trouble all over the country, it seems. I think you and the children should go to the Hacienda. You will be safe there. I can be sure my workers won't harm any member of my family.'

'But how can you be so sure, Papá? You have not been out there for several days.'

'Lota would have got word to us if there had been trouble in Alauquén,' Don Jaime answered calmly.

'You will both come with us?' Rebekka asked anxiously.

Patri nodded. 'We will join you tomorrow,' he said. 'We have another meeting in the morning and I shall stay here tonight with Papá. Now you should go and rest, *cariña*. You look very tired and there will be much to do when you arrive.'

Despite the tensions of the past two days, now that she was back with Patri Rebekka managed to sleep during the siesta. But Joscelin could only doze. After they had eaten, Patri announced that he had decided to accompany them to the Hacienda just to be sure all was peaceful there. Then he would drive back to Sevilla with Alberto.

'What news of Eduardo's family and the boys?' Joscelin asked as Manuela and Miss Smart repacked their suitcases.

Don Jaime frowned. 'As far as I am aware they are still at Punta Umbria. I believe Huelva is with the government and there has been no army coup, so hopefully they are not in danger.'

The village of Alauquén was bathed in moonlight as they drove through it and there was no sign of life.

'Papá was right, you will be quite safe at the Hacienda,' Patri said as Alberto turned up the dusty track towards El Campanario. 'The workers here respect the family.'

Miss Smart did not share his opinion. After the children were in bed, she took Joscelin to one side and said: 'There is no knowing what these savages will do! Oh, I'm not saying a word against Spanish people like the dear Marqués and his family; or, indeed, their friends. They are decent, well-educated people. But the peasants are *illiterate*! And they hardly ever wash!'

Despite her growing fatigue, Joscelin smiled. 'It is not their fault, Miss Smart,' she argued gently. 'Most have had no schooling – they are too poor. As to washing, you must know that every drop of water has to be fetched from the village wells. Maybe one day someone will provide them with running water and then they will wash themselves as often as you do!'

But she could see the governess was not convinced, and marvelled that Miss Smart could have lived some thirty years in a country without a better understanding of the people.

Their children might be dirty, but they were loved. Babies might sit bare-bottomed in the dusty alleys outside their homes, but no one saw harm in this. Miss Smart still carried in her heart her Victorian ideas of respectability.

Poor Miss Smart! Joscelin thought as she climbed into bed. It was really time for her to retire. But her only living relative in England had died two years ago and, if the truth be told, Miss Smart had nowhere to retire to. The advent of Rebekka and her children had enabled her to retain her position of importance in Don Jaime's household, Joscelin thought as she drifted into sleep.

She woke suddenly, her heart pounding, to the sound of voices – a man's deep tones and then the higher ones of Angélica, the elderly Spanish cook.

Joscelin pulled on her dressing-gown and hurried towards the front door. A man stood there shaking Angélica by the shoulders. She had her apron over her head and was crying hysterically.

'Dáta prisa! Dáta prisa!' the man was shouting at her.

Seeing Joscelin, he turned towards her and gabbled incoherently in his Andaluz dialect. She understood only that he was begging them to hurry up – but for what purpose she did not know. The gardener, Domingo, appeared from the servants' quarters. Once again, the man burst into a storm of words, his arm now pointing frequently in the direction of Alauquén. Joscelin realized from the look of anxiety on Domingo's face that something serious was happening. Rebekka and Miss Smart joined them, and now at last someone was able to translate the torrent of words.

'He has come to warn us,' Rebekka said in a small, frightened voice. 'There is a group of men on their way here. They are not from Alauquén and he thinks they may have come from Déya nearby. He says they are bad men – very drunk, and they have weapons. He is one of Papá's labourers. He says Don Jaime has been good to his family and he felt it a matter of honour to warn the servants at the Hacienda.'

'Of course, he was unaware that *we* were here,' Rebekka said shakily. 'Now he is afraid for us, too. He says we should hide. He came on his mule and the mob is on foot so we have a little time to conceal ourselves. What are we going to do, Joss? I'm so frightened!'

'We can hide in the little tower above the olive press,' Joscelin said soothingly. 'The servants will not betray us. They can go to the fields and hide there – Manuela too. At worst the mob will loot the house. You must warn the children, Miss Smart, to be very quiet. No one will know we are here if we make no sound.'

But if they were to set fire to the Hacienda, she thought as Rebekka turned away to give orders to the servants, they could not be in a worse place than the tower! There was only one narrow staircase leading up to it and no other means of escape. But there was nowhere else they could go. The children could not run fast enough to reach the comparative safety of the fields.

Within ten minutes the children and the three women were installed in the tower. Already they could hear shouting and the sound of the big bell clanging discordantly over the arched entrance in the wall surrounding the Hacienda. Someone had found a ladder and climbed the wall, to shouts of encouragement from his comrades below. The dogs in the stables set up a furious barking. Through the slats of the window shutters Joscelin could see at least twenty men in the bright moonlight as they swarmed up the ladder and into the main patio. She could see no guns, but all were armed with hoes, pitchforks or wooden staves. One flourished a sickle which flashed in the moonlight as he brandished it above his head.

She turned to caution the children to remain quiet. Rebekka was crouched in one corner of the room, Carlos and Ruth huddled white-faced in the protective circle of her arms. Amalia was sobbing whilst Miss Smart whispered nervous instructions to the young girl to pull herself together.

The men were now moving towards the house. One was

urging the others forward, shouting as he battered against the heavily barred door with an axe. Joscelin held her breath as one or two of the ruffians hesitated, but as the door burst open they needed no further encouragement and followed their leader indoors, disappearing from view.

The silence that ensued was almost more frightening than the noise that had preceded it. It was several minutes before the shouting broke out once more, this time from within the house. There was the sound of breaking glass, the crash of something heavy falling and then the leader appeared in the patio. In one hand he brandished a bottle, in the other one of Doña Ursula's most treasured possessions – a small, seventeenth-century statue of La Virgen.

He hurled it against the stone base of the fountain and it disintegrated into fragments. The pattern of the next ten minutes had been established. Paintings, ornaments, furniture were brought out of the house and brutally smashed. The men had now carried out the barrels of specially blended sherry Don Jaime had sent to him from Jerez. They were drinking indiscriminately – either from the barrels or from bottles of wine and brandy, whichever lay nearest to hand. Ignorant of the worth of the objects they destroyed, they kept only what they recognized as important – silver, saucepans, food, clothing.

It did not occur to them to set fire to the buildings. Their aggressive instincts seemed satisfied by stealing or smashing the contents. Some of the men were by now almost too drunk to stand upright.

Joscelin saw their leader pointing to the chapel, could hear him shouting as he strode towards the door: 'Death to the rich! Death to the priests!'

Within minutes, it was plundered.

But the urge to destroy was fast waning, and an orgy of drinking and singing now took place in the patio as more barrels were brought out from the house. Only the leader seemed unaffected by the amount of alcohol and the euphoria which engulfed the mob. As the first streak of green slit the night sky, he urged the men to their feet. Slowly, they began to make their way out of the courtyard laden down with their loot. A strange hush descended on the deserted Hacienda.

Joscelin discovered that she was clenching her fists. Slowly, she uncurled her fingers and took several deep breaths.

'I think they have gone,' she whispered.

Miss Smart walked over to her side. 'Savages!' she muttered as she surveyed the appalling pile of debris in the courtyard below. Then she said firmly: 'I shall go down and investigate!'

'I don't think you should, Miss Smart!' Joscelin said quickly. 'I think we should stay here until Don Jaime and Patricio arrive.'

The governess removed Joscelin's restraining hand. 'No, dear, that may not be until midday, and I for one do not intend to remain cooped up here all morning.'

'Then wait just a little while longer,' Joscelin said uneasily.

Miss Smart grimaced. 'That will not be possible. Nature, I fear, takes no account of the behaviour of a band of brigands. It is necessary for me to relieve myself without delay!'

Joscelin nearly smiled but, realizing the poor woman's discomfort, cautioned her once more to take care. Wearily, she sat down beside Rebekka. 'Don Jaime seemed so certain his workers would remain loyal to him,' she exclaimed quietly. 'I can't imagine what he is going to say when he arrives. He will be heartbroken. But *why*, Rebekka? He has never harmed anybody.'

'Perhaps these men hate Papá simply because he is rich and they are poor!'

They fell into an uneasy silence. Joscelin struggled against the overwhelming desire to sleep. It was over twenty-four hours since they had left Torremolinos. Her eyes were hot and dry and, although she struggled to keep them open, she was unable to stay awake.

Downstairs in the courtyard outside the kitchen door Miss Smart gave way to the needs of nature. She felt unable to reach the tiny cupboard of a room at the far end of the house which contained the only lavatory. Having no torch or candle, she had stumbled over the debris in the kitchen and, with no further time to spare, was relieving herself in the dark little yard.

She would have been more embarrassed than afraid had she been aware that two pairs of eyes were watching her as she squatted awkwardly, her white cotton bloomers round her ankles. She was in the process of readjusting her underclothes when one of the two drunken voyeurs crept into the yard and flung himself upon her. Her fall knocked the breath from her body and she had no chance to cry out before he had placed his huge, dirty hand over her mouth. He was joined by his companion and between them they carried the struggling woman into the byre.

One of her assailants flung her down onto the soft straw and quickly straddled her. She was aware of the stench of his unwashed body, the smell of liquor on his hot breath. Most of all, she was aware of his weight and his rough hands lifting her skirt, tearing off her underclothes. A filthy piece of rag was stuffed into her mouth as the hand that covered it lifted. Then her skirt was flung over her head.

Her first thought was that she was about to be killed. It was several seconds before she realized that she was about to be raped. She was not so much afraid as appalled at the indignity that was being forced upon her.

Blinded by her skirt and petticoat, she could see nothing, but now she heard voices speaking in the rough Andaluz dialect she had never been able to understand. She had been aware that there were two men. Now she feared there might be more. The one above her was gasping, the other calling out encouragements and shouts of '*Olé!*'

Hands were dragging her legs apart and then she felt an alien object forcing itself into her with fierce thrusts. The pain was so intense it wiped all fear from her consciousness. It seemed to spread upwards through her body to her chest, becoming one single arrow of agony piercing her heart. It did not ease, even when the weight above her slackened. The slight relief afforded by the return of her ability to breathe was only short-lived. As one man withdrew, the second fell upon her.

She was aware of pain once more between her legs and her own powerlessness to protect herself. A strange pattern of thought replaced her first horrified understanding of what was happening. Now she could divorce herself from the bestiality; the humiliation of what was being inflicted on her, *her* – Mabel Violet Smart, a respectable English spinster in her late sixties. Now she clung to one thought only – she must survive this ordeal for Amalia's sake. Since Doña Ursula's death, the child had depended upon her. She must survive . . . survive . . .

Miss Smart lost consciousness at the moment Benito Lopez rode into the courtyard. His horse, lathered from the hasty journey from Alauquén to the Hacienda, was breathing heavily as the rider dismounted and untied the rope attached to his saddle. The man at the end of the rope fell to his knees. Benito's expression was merciless as he jerked the captive to his feet and led him over to the bougainvillaea tree where he tethered him as if he were a goat.

'Now we shall see what mischief you have committed, Jorge Ortega!' Benito said, his voice deceptively calm. As the man began to speak, he hit him across the face with his crop. 'You will regret this night's work!' he continued quietly, as with growing dismay he surveyed the debris in the patio. 'As to your "right" to revenge yourself – I spit on it. Don Jaime is a good man, as everyone knows. If you were dismissed, the quarrel lay between you and Don Jaime; yet you stirred up trouble in your village amongst others who had no grudge. Now they too will be punished.'

Benito had been in La Linea for a bullfight, returning home late in the evening. He was aroused from a deep sleep by a man shouting outside his window. A former employee of Don Jaime's had set off some hours previously to loot the Marqués's Hacienda, taking with him a band of anarchists who were spoiling for a fight.

Benito calmed his wife as best he could, dressed, saddled his horse and set out to protect his father-in-law's property. Despite Carlota's anxiety, he felt well able to deal with the situation alone. There was not a peasant in the whole of Spain who did not revere the name of Benito Lopez. He was one of the few among them who had realized all their dreams when he became one of the world's great matadors. Whatever revolutionary idea Jorge Ortega may have put into their heads, it would need but a word from him, the famous Lopez, to send them scuttling back to their homes.

But a mile from the Hacienda, Benito knew he was too late. The looters, laden with spoils, were almost too drunk to carry what they had stolen. It took but a few questions to learn what had happened, and seeing there was no point in taking them with him to the Hacienda he had roped their ringleader, who was by no means as drunk as his followers. In turn truculent, aggressive and violent, Jorge Ortega proclaimed the justice of his actions. But he soon lost his voice as Benito pulled him along behind his horse at the end of the rope towards the Hacienda.

Benito was about to enter the house when a noise to his left made him turn swiftly. Two men were staggering from one of the stables, grinning as they waved and shouted their greetings to the prisoner.

'Hola! Jorge, we thought you had gone home. What are you doing, eh? Watering the tree?'

At the same moment Benito saw a figure running towards him. It was Joscelin.

'Thank God you are here, Benito!' she gasped as she reached his side. She pointed to the window in the tower. 'Rebekka and the children are up there. We were warned the men were coming and we hid. Amalia and Miss Smart are there too . . . at least, Miss Smart was with us but . . .'

She broke off, realizing for the first time that Miss Smart had never reappeared. How long had she herself been asleep? The sound of Benito's horse had woken her. How long had

Miss Smart been absent? Where *was* Miss Smart? With a growing sense of unease, Joscelin looked up at the sky. It was a delicate flamingo pink as the sun rose above the line of hills on the horizon.

Benito took her arm to steady her. She was trembling violently.

'You are not harmed?' he asked anxiously.

'No, no, we are all right,' Joscelin said hurriedly. 'I don't think the men knew we were here. But Miss Smart left us and hasn't come back.' She glanced at the man tied to the tree and then at the two men who were edging towards the door in the patio wall. 'Who are they?' she asked. 'We thought they had all left hours ago. If Miss Smart had known they were here . . .'

Benito let go her arm and walked purposefully towards the two fugitives. One broke into a run but Benito drew his revolver and fired over the man's head. He dropped instantly to his knees, his hands held out in supplication as if begging for mercy. His companion ran back to Benito and started to talk, too rapidly for Joscelin to comprehend. As she watched she saw, as if in slow motion, Benito's arm lift. His gun glistened in the slanting sunlight.

He couldn't possibly be intending to shoot them! But Benito's movements continued, with the same unfaltering precision as he sighted along the barrel. Suddenly the morning air was shattered by the sound of the gun firing, first one bullet, then another. The men crumpled, falling to the ground where they lay, two grotesque, dishevelled heaps of ragged clothing. Somewhere a dog recommenced its barking.

Josecelin looked from the men to Benito. 'You . . . you *killed* them!' she gasped.

A grim smile curved Benito's lips. 'What alternative had I?' he parried. 'They are pigs, *bestias*! They have dishonoured their race.'

'Dishonoured? But . . .'

The protest died on her lips as Benito turned on his heel

and strode towards the stable from which the men had appeared. Joscelin followed him. She was standing in the doorway as he knelt down by Miss Smart and gently lowered her skirts to cover her nakedness. But before he did so Joscelin saw the blood, and the sudden understanding of what must have occurred shocked her so deeply that for a moment she could not move. Then she ran forward and took the governess's head onto her lap. Miss Smart's eyes were closed but she was still breathing.

'Oh, thank God!' Joscelin whispered. 'She's still alive, Benito!'

His eyes met Joscelin's, his face a mask of anger as he said violently: 'I am ashamed of my countrymen. For the first time in my life I am ashamed to call myself a Spaniard.'

Joscelin stroked Miss Smart's face and tried pointlessly to smooth back the strands of damp grey hair. Miss Smart's eyelids flickered and a sound came from between her lips. The black button eyes which *los chicos*, when very young, had so cruelly called 'currants' opened suddenly and fastened upon Joscelin. Slowly, her blue-veined hand reached up and touched Joscelin's hair.

'So pretty!' she murmured. 'But very untidy, Carlota!' Her quavering voice steadied, became firmer. 'It really won't do, child. Whatever will your mother say? Now go and give it a good brush before lunch. Manuela can plait it for you . . .' Her voice wavered and then she said perfectly clearly: 'Tell Casilda to be sure to clean her nails!'

Then her body jerked in a dreadful spasm. Her hand moved to her heart and her face contorted with a look of intense pain before her body relaxed.

'*Madre de Dios!*' Benito muttered, crossing himself. '*Está muerta!*'

'Dead? *But she can't be* . . .' Joscelin cried frantically. 'People don't die from being raped!'

Benito's dark eyes were full of pity. 'It is the heart, Joscelin,' he said quietly. 'It beats no more. But fear not, I shall avenge her. The two who defiled her are dead, and now I shall kill the real culprit.'

His mouth tightening, he rose to his feet and strode past her into the patio. Following him in a state of shock, Joscelin paused as Benito walked towards the man secured to the tree. His voice sounded perfectly normal as he said quietly: 'Jorge Ortega, you have one minute to make your peace with God!'

By the frantic gestures of the desperate Jorge, Joscelin understood that the man was pleading for his life, insisting that he had not been one of Miss Smart's attackers. Benito's expression remained implacable.

'Not one of the men you brought here last night would have come of his own accord!' he interrupted, his voice like steel. 'You, Jorge, incited them to come. It is your fault they became drunk, *your* fault they forgot the difference between good and evil, *your* fault they killed this harmless old English lady who has spent her life caring for Spanish children. Ask God to forgive you, Jorge Ortega, for I never will.'

At last, Joscelin found the strength to run forward; to lay her hand on Benito's arm. 'It wasn't he who killed her!' she gasped. 'Don't shoot him, Benito. At least he has a right to a trial.'

Benito's chin lifted and his back straightened. He looked suddenly immensely proud, handsome, invincible. He looked as he might look in a *corrida* when he knew the time had come for him to kill his bull.

'I too am a Spaniard,' he said to Joscelin. 'And this man has brought about my dishonour.'

With the same unhurried gesture as she had seen before, he lifted his arm, took careful aim and fired.

CHAPTER TWENTY-NINE

November–December 1936

Joscelin stood staring at him across the length of the *salón*, and for a few unbearable moments both her voice and her legs were paralysed. The sharp edge of her sketchpad was cutting into her palm where she was gripping it. Her other hand still clung to the door handle. Somehow, she thought, she must go forward . . . say something . . . smile.

Alan! Alan! You look older, thinner . . . don't stare at me like that. Nothing has changed. I mustn't show how I feel. Help me . . .

It was Cassy who broke the unbearable silence – could it really have lasted only a few seconds? – as she ran to embrace Joscelin.

'Darling, whatever have you been up to? You should have been here to welcome us. We've been waiting hours!' She flung her arms around Joscelin and kissed her, Spanish-fashion, on both cheeks. Her dark eyes were sparkling as she imprisoned Joscelin's hand and dragged her into the room. 'You look stunning, Joss, doesn't she, Alan? I always knew you were going to be really beautiful. Oh, it's wonderful to see you! I missed you quite terribly, didn't I, Alan?'

His hazel-green eyes were smiling as he said softly: 'Hullo, Joss. It's good to see you!'

There are lines around your eyes that were not there before. Oh, Alan . . .

'You're looking well, Alan!' To her relief her voice sounded quite normal. 'I'm sorry I wasn't here to welcome you. I was sketching in the Casa de Pilatos and had no idea it was so late. You had no trouble driving from Cádiz?'

'Apart from seeing a few army vehicles and soldiers, there was no sign of *anything*!' Cassy said. 'Despite what Papá has been telling us, I simply don't believe we're in the middle of a war! We were expecting bullets flying everywhere!'

'We are all going to be involved sooner or later,' Patri said forcibly. 'Cristobal is already fighting with the Falangists, and Mariano and Luis were called up and are with the Nationalist army. If Papá has his way, the *fascistas* will win this war and we shall have a dictatorship here in Spain. I'll do anything to prevent that happening.'

Don Jaime held up his hand. 'That's enough, Patricio. We haven't seen Alan and Casilda for two years, and I won't have their home-coming spoilt by arguments.'

Cassy went to stand by his chair and, leaning down, kissed her father's head. 'Dearest Papá, the only thing I care about is that you're well again. It's such a wonderful surprise to find you up and about. Was it *very* painful? When Lota wrote and told us how ill you were, Alan and I were terrified you might die!'

Her father smiled and patted her cheek. 'To tell you the truth, *cielo*, I was terrified too. I wouldn't have minded so much dying from an honourable *cornada*. But to be pierced by a cow defending her calf was enough of an indignity, without that confounded septicaemia.'

'Someone once told me that most of the matadors who are gored die from blood poisoning rather than from their injuries,' Alan said.

'Well, I didn't intend to die from anything!' Don Jaime said. 'Thanks to *los médicos* and to my nurse, Helena, I am now recovering very well. You need not have made the journey to see me!'

'As I was trying to explain earlier, Papá, we came as soon as we possibly could,' Cassy said as she seated herself beside him. 'The morning Lota's letter arrived, I tore round to the Spanish Embassy to get permits allowing us into Spain. You've no idea what a fandango *that* turned out to be! I'd almost forgotten how infuriating it is always to be fobbed off with *mañana* – come

back *mañana*. They didn't seem to care that you were dying!'
She laughed. 'And all the time that I was tearing my hair out,
you were being soothed and petted by that pretty nurse. However
did you manage to find Helena? She sounds terribly efficient.'

'She's half English, half Spanish,' Don Jaime explained. 'She
was born in Jerez but trained in London, so she knows her
job. I probably owe my life to her nursing.'

Joscelin caught the swift glance that Patri gave Alan – a
speculative, questioning look. But he remained silent and she was
not to understand its meaning until several weeks later. Amalia
was now monopolizing Alan's attention and Joscelin was able
to study him surreptitiously. He *was* thinner – and very pale. But
his smile as he chatted to his young cousin was unchanged, as
was its effect upon her. She turned hurriedly away, but not before
Alan suddenly looked up and their eyes met – briefly but potently.

He still loves me! she thought, the knowledge piercing her
heart. This meeting is as traumatic for him as it is for me.

She felt indescribably happy, and at the same time unbearably sad. The unselfish side of her wanted his happiness before
her own – there would at least have been some point to their
separation if he had found contentment with Cassy. But she
was human enough to rejoice in his faithfulness to the memory
of the love they had shared.

Poor Cassy! Joscelin turned to look at her friend and saw
immediately that Cassy was far from being in need of her pity.
She looked glowing, radiant and vibrantly beautiful. The pale,
subdued young woman Joscelin had last seen in Paris had
vanished, along with the dependence upon Alan brought about
by the ordeal of awaiting the sentence of the French courts
after her car accident. Cassy was treating Alan as she always
had, as a friend whom she sometimes needed but often forgot.

She should be an enemy, Joscelin thought, but knew that
she could never stop loving her. Cassy was like a charming
child, and when after luncheon she insisted upon coming to
her room to share the siesta, Joscelin was powerless to keep her
at arm's length. Cassy resumed the intimacy of their former

friendship as if they had been parted for two weeks rather than two years.

She snuggled under the duvet at the foot of the bed and, hugging her knees, said gleefully: 'Now at last we can really talk. *Dios,* how much I've missed you, Joss! And you haven't written to me nearly often enough. What happened to that Spanish admirer you wrote about in one of your letters? I should have thought marriage to anyone would be better than wasting your life here looking after Rebekka's children. And you hardly told me anything about poor Miss Smart. *Jesús!* Whoever could have imagined that the poor old thing would be *raped!*'

Joscelin bit her lip. 'I try not to think about it, Cassy. In a way, I blame myself. I fell asleep, and never realized that she had failed to come back. If I had gone to look for her earlier, maybe I could have prevented what happened.'

Cassy shrugged. 'That's ridiculous, Joss, *qué ridiculez.* You'd probably have got raped yourself. But we won't talk about it if you'd rather not. Tell me about Lota. Is she really running an orphanage? I can't imagine Lota running anything, although she always adored children.'

Joscelin smiled. 'You'll see a great difference in your little sister,' she said. 'Marriage, motherhood, the war – they've changed her quite remarkably. When your father was brought back from the Hacienda and they wanted to take him into hospital, it was Lota who organized the nurse and arranged for the best specialist to attend him.'

Cassy sat up and lit a cigarette. 'That doesn't sound a bit like Lota!'

'You'd be surprised, Cassy. She is very practical, very efficient and needs to be. When the refugees first started returning to Sevilla, Benito bought her that big house where the Duque de Prada used to live. As more and more children who had become lost or separated from their parents poured back into the city, she persuaded the nuns to set up the orphanage for them.'

Cassy shrugged. 'The Duque de Prada would have a fit if he knew what had happened to his lovely house!'

Joscelin smiled. 'As a matter of fact, I believe he was happy to sell it. He was finding it too difficult to manage his estate and his only son was killed relieving the siege of the Alcázar in September. The poor man went off to Rome to join your exiled king.'

Now bored by the trend of the conversation, Cassy sighed. 'I suppose I ought to know more about this war than I do. I think Alan did tell me about the siege, but I wasn't really paying attention. I was in the middle of choosing clothes for my visit to Tía Pamela.'

'Of course, I wasn't *just* going to see darling Tía Pamela,' she continued. 'Milton had promised to show me New York whilst I was out there. We had a perfectly ripping time, Joss! The shops are unbelievable and so is Broadway, and he took me to masses of divine restaurants and nightclubs, and of course I had to see the Statue of Liberty.'

'Tell me about Tía Pamela!' Joscelin suggested, not wishing to hear more of Cassy's unfaithfulness to Alan. 'Is she happy?'

'Amazingly so, considering how poor she is! She absolutely adores Walter, and I must say he *is* rather nice and he's really soppy about her. You'd think they were both too old for all that hand holding and kissing! He still hasn't got a job, but Tía Pamela works all day and Walter actually does the shopping and cooking and things like that, can you believe it? Their apartment is tiny, like a little box. Alan gives his mother an allowance, but she sends it back saying she doesn't need it and he might. Not that he does, because of course I've got masses, enough for both of us. Alan's so silly about money – a bit like Tía Pamela. He won't let me pay for anything unless it's something I want for myself – clothes or my boat ticket or something like that.'

The little frown creasing her forehead deepened. 'You know, Joss, Alan's frightfully nice to me, but sometimes it's an awful *bore* having a husband. I suppose I'm just not the faithful kind, although I *have* been faithful to Milton for years and years. He's my only lover.'

'Oh, Cassy!' Joss murmured half in exasperation. 'Don't you ever feel guilty?'

Cassy grimaced. 'I never think about it. After all, Joss, if Alan doesn't know about it, he can't be upset, can he? Besides, he's not really interested in that sort of thing. Milton thinks he's got a mistress, but I don't – although lots of women do try to flirt with him. He's only really interested in his work, and he spends more time up in Scotland helping with estate business. At least I don't have to go there with him. It's so terribly *boring* there! But don't let's talk about Alan. I want to know about you. Aren't you ever coming back to England? What on earth do you do with yourself here?'

'I see Lota quite often . . .' Joscelin said, relieved at the turn of conversation. 'I draw and paint – and of course I look after Carlos and Ruth now there's no Miss Smart to help Rebekka. Then there's Amalia, whom I chaperon, and I've grown to like the nurse, Helena. She has a boyfriend in England who has just come down from Cambridge. He's thinking of joining the International Brigade. If he does, Helena is going to join the Medical Aid Service if she can and try to get sent somewhere near him.'

Cassy shrugged. 'It seems extraordinary to me that anyone should actually *want* to fight a war. Papá is quite worried about Mariano and Luis, but they're no longer *chicos*, are they? Luis is twenty-five, can you believe it? And baby Mariano almost twenty-two! It makes me feel positively middle-aged just to think about it. And Papá told us before you arrived that little Carmen is expecting her second baby.'

She paused as she pondered whether to express her thoughts. When she did so, it was tentatively, as if she was aware that Joscelin might not approve.

'I suppose it's wrong to be glad that Douglas died, Joss. But I often think about what my life would be like if he had lived. He'd be six years old, and even if I had a nanny a child would be a terrible tie. I'd make an awful mother, I know I would. Do you think I'm horrid, being glad it all happened? After all, it wasn't as if he was Alan's baby anyway.'

As Joscelin's eyes dropped, Cassy's mouth pursed in a pout. 'I know you don't like me to talk about it, but I've got to talk to *someone*. You see, the ghastly thing is I think I might be going to have another! And don't look like that, Joss . . .' she added impatiently as Joscelin gasped. 'I'm not certain yet . . . I've only missed once and anyway, it isn't Milton's, if that's what you're thinking. This time it's Alan's.'

'Does Alan know?' The words escaped Joscelin's lips involuntarily.

Cassy tossed her head. 'Of course not! He'd only fuss, and I couldn't stand him being so *pleased* about it when I can't think of anything more awful. It would be such rotten luck, Joss. We practically never, ever do it, but we were at a party at the Piermonts and they put us in a double bed – we never even share a bedroom at home – and . . .' she suddenly giggled, '. . . we'd both had far too much champagne and for once I felt like it. Now I could kick myself.'

'Cassy, don't talk like that,' Joscelin said sharply. 'Maybe you aren't pregnant, and if you are, can't you be pleased about it – for Alan, I mean? He'd be so happy . . .'

'Well, *I* wouldn't!' Cassy interrupted. 'Anyway, Alan's *never* happy. Can you believe it, Joss, he threw a fit when I said I was coming home to see Papá. He was dead against coming to Spain. He said it might be dangerous going to a country which was in the middle of a civil war, but of course he wouldn't let me travel on my own, and I just couldn't let darling Papá die without seeing him, could I? Now I suppose Alan will think Lota was exaggerating, although you've only got to look at Papá to see how ill he has been.'

Whilst Joscelin and Cassy had been talking in the bedroom, Alan and Patri had also abandoned the siesta and were alone in the now deserted *salón*. Patri's face was tense as he attempted to explain his point of view to his cousin.

'Obviously, I could do nothing whilst Papá has been so ill,' he said in a low voice. 'But he's out of danger now and I simply cannot sit back and ignore what's happening here. I've tried to reason with Papá, but he refuses to believe that General Franco is simply another Mussolini. He insists that Franco's kind of Fascism is different.' He gave Alan a wry grin. 'Papá and his ilk have been bribed into believing that, if Franco wins this war, he will allow Spain to return to the old ways. I truly believe Fascism is the worst creed of the lot. I'm going to do what I can to help the Republicans get rid of Franco and his foreign aides. It appals me to think of crack German troops on Spanish soil.'

Alan was surprised by the new look of maturity he saw on his cousin's face. 'Uncle Jaime said your brothers are all fighting in Franco's army. Surely you couldn't fight against your own flesh and blood, Patri?' he said quietly.

Patri bit his lip. 'Don't imagine I haven't thought how I'd feel if I came face to face with Cris or Luis or Mariano in a battle. But *they* don't realize what an evil Fascism is, Alan. They weren't in Germany, although Cris *was* in Italy and should have seen how ruthless Mussolini is.'

'Won't Rebekka try to stop you becoming involved?' Alan asked. In the brief few hours since his arrival, he had been very much aware of the adoration of Patri's wife for her husband. She sat close beside him, leaning against his shoulder and looking at him in a way that made no attempt to conceal her feelings.

'Rebekka knows how I feel. Rebekka loves me enough to let me do what I feel I must,' Patri said. 'She understands that it's for the sake of our children's future. Can you imagine, Alan, what kind of future that would be if the whole of Europe falls under the Fascist flag? Believe me, Hitler's ambitions are unlimited.'

'My father has said the same thing,' Alan replied thoughtfully. 'But our government doesn't appear to be worried. Personally I agree with you, Patri, although I'm by way of being a bit of a pacifist. At least I always thought I was, but I suppose, if it came to the crunch, I might shoot a man who was trying to harm someone I loved.'

'But that's exactly the point, Alan, don't you see? I could tell you some gruesome stories of atrocities that have already been committed by the Fascists. Papá insists they're all rumours, but a great deal of it is fact. No, Alan – my mind is made up. I've been trying to think of a way of getting into the Republican zone, but first I want to see something of you and Casilda.'

He gave Alan a quick, shy smile. 'I had a crazy idea at lunch that I might be able to persuade you to come with me. I thought I would try to join the Thaelmann Battalion – it's part of the XIIth Brigade of the Internationals.'

It was several moments before Alan spoke. His first reaction was to inform Patri that he had not the slightest desire to become involved in a war. But as Alan's imagination pictured his young cousin going off into the unknown, he felt a strange surge of envy. The past two years had been very far from happy. He and Cassy had no mutual interests, although there were moments of enjoyment – sunny days picnicking on the riverbank at Henley, playing tennis, drinking champagne in their box at Ascot with friends like Monty.

'It's out of the question, Patri,' Alan said finally. 'For one thing, I'd be leaving Cassy all alone. For another, I've a book to finish by next spring. But the real reason, I suppose, is that I honestly don't believe I'd be able to kill anyone, so I'd be pretty useless, wouldn't I?'

Patri laughed. 'You might not want to, but you certainly could!' he said. 'You were once a crack shot, remember?'

'Well, I haven't touched a gun since I carried one for self-protection in Africa,' Alan said, smiling. 'Anyway, old chap, I hope you won't leave for a little while. Cassy wants to stay here for a month at least, and it would be pleasant to have you around.'

Not only pleasant but necessary, Alan thought as each day he found it more and more difficult to maintain the illusion of casual affection for Joscelin. Cassy was always throwing them together. If Alan tried to escape from the confines of the house by saying he was going for a walk, Cassy would say: 'I don't want to walk. Why don't you take Joss with you?' In the evening

Cassy would put a record on the gramophone and say: 'Do you remember how we used to dance in the schoolroom at Rutland Gate? Come on, Patri. Alan can partner Joss . . .'

Joscelin was trying equally hard to avoid him. 'I'm tired, Cassy. Alan can partner Rebekka.'

But Cassy only found some other way to throw them together. 'I don't know what's the matter with you two. You used to be such good friends. Anyone would think you were trying to avoid each other. You haven't quarrelled, have you?'

One afternoon they all went out to see how the redecorating of the Hacienda was progressing, and Alan and Joscelin found themselves making their way alone to the tower room.

At the top of the little stone staircase, Joscelin paused to open the door into the room. Alan came up behind her and, as Joscelin swung round nervously, his arms went out to stop himself falling. Instinctively, he closed them around her waist. Her large grey eyes, wide with anxiety, were gazing into his. He could feel her trembling and he felt suddenly bitter and angry with her for having denied them the life they should be sharing.

'*Dammit, Joss, I love you!*'

She did not turn her face away as his mouth came down on hers. Her lips were warm, soft, welcoming as she responded to his kisses.

'I love you!' he said again.

She looked infinitely sad as she stared back at him. 'I know!' The words were like a sigh, and he was overcome by a feeling of intolerable regret for what might have been.

'I can't stand much more of this, Joss,' he said quietly. 'I love you. Sooner or later I'm going to come right out and say it. I hate this ghastly pretence!'

'I know!' Joscelin repeated. 'It's difficult for me too. I love you so much . . .'

'Then let's stop pretending,' Alan said violently. 'Let me tell Cassy how we feel. We'll go away – anywhere you like. But I don't want to live the rest of my life without you. I need you.'

Tears welled into Joscelin's eyes. She could bear her own

loneliness, but not his – and now fate had once again intervened to keep them apart.

'Alan, listen to me. Cassy hasn't said anything to you because she's hoping it isn't true – but she thinks she might be pregnant. Do you understand what I'm saying? This time it will be your baby, Alan, *yours*.'

The look of shock on his face gave way to disbelief. 'But we haven't . . . we don't. Oh, God, yes! – there was an occasion I'd forgotten. Oh Joss, I don't want to believe it.'

Joscelin bit her lip. 'I don't want to believe it either, Alan. Nor does Cassy. That's why you've simply *got* to want it. You've got to forget about us, Alan. Honestly, you don't have to worry about me. I've learned to live without you. When you've gone back to England, I shall settle down again and . . .'

Alan's arms tightened once more around her. As he laid his face against her hair, his eyes were inexpressibly sad.

'I have learned to *exist* without you, Joss. It isn't living. I'm only really happy when I go up to Strathinver, and then all I do most of the while is mooch around thinking of you, remembering how it was for us, how it could still be if I left Cassy. I knew nothing had changed, or you'd have come back to England. When Cassy said Uncle Jaime was dying and she wanted to visit him, I knew that you and I would be living under the same roof and I tried like hell to dissuade her.'

His unhappy smile wrenched at Joscelin's heart as he added softly: 'I don't know whether to be sad or glad that you still love me. I'm sure of only one thing – that I shall go on loving you until the day I die!'

Suddenly Alan's mind was made up. He could not stay here in Sevilla, living in the same house as Joss. Nor could he pretend to Cassy that he was happy to hear she was finally giving him the child he had so often asked for. He was done with pretending, and his way of escape had been offered him by Patri. He would go; take whatever the fates had to offer in this crazy war. He would be far away from women; from the temptation to be with Joss, love her.

I'll tell Patri tonight, after dinner, he thought. I won't tell Cassy – she'll try to stop me going. Rebekka can tell her after I've gone. She'll be all right here with Uncle Jaime and Joss.

Guiltily he realized that he didn't really care very much what she would do with her life after he had disappeared. The only person he cared about was Joss – and she would unquestionably be happier if he were far away. As to his own happiness – at least his life would have some purpose. He did not necessarily have to kill anyone. He could join the army as an ambulance driver – perhaps help to save lives . . .

Alan and Patri slipped out of the house at dawn a few days later, taking Patri's old Citroen and pushing it round the corner of the Plaza so that no one would wake and see them. Rebekka came into Cassy's bedroom and, with an anxious glance at Joscelin, whom she had asked to accompany her, she handed Cassy a letter.

'It's for you from Alan,' she said nervously. 'He and Patri are trying to join the Republicans. Alan would have told you in person he was leaving, but he was afraid you might try to stop him. Try not to be too upset, Casilda. We've both got to be brave.'

Cassy sprang out of bed and snatched the letter from Rebekka's grasp. Her dark eyes flashed and her hands shook as she paced the room whilst she read. Then she flung the letter to the floor and turned to Joscelin. 'He says he knows I might be pregnant and he's sorry if I feel he's deserting me, but his mind is made up. *Sorry!* I think it's absolutely hateful of him. It's just like him to do something like this without telling me. It's not fair. *It's not fair!*'

Rebekka stared at Cassy in astonishment as she burst into tears. Between sobs, she stormed: 'They might have known I'd have wanted to go with them! Papá said lots of Spanish girls have gone off to war with their men. It isn't fair. I'm to be left here doing nothing and getting bored all by myself, whilst Alan and Patri are having all sorts of adventures. And anyway, *where* have they gone? Alan doesn't say. Do *you* know, Rebekka? I'll go after them. I don't see why I should be left behind . . .'

As deeply shocked as Cassy by the news, Joscelin somehow managed to pull herself together. 'You know they couldn't have taken you with them, Cassy,' she reasoned. 'There's your papá to think of, and anyway you might be having a baby and so . . .'

'Well, *I'm not!*' Cassy interrupted fiercely. 'I got the curse yesterday. I meant to tell you. At least *that*'s something to be thankful for,' she added bitterly, ignoring the look of shock on Rebekka's face. Her tears had dried, and as she sat up she somehow managed to look very beautiful despite the dishevelled state of her hair.

'But what made Alan do it, Joss? He always maintained he was a pacifist. He said no one had a right to take life – and now he's gone off to kill people. It's Patri's fault. He's talked him into it.'

'No, Cassy, that isn't true,' Joscelin said gently. 'No one could *make* Alan do something he didn't want to do. You know that.'

'Then why?' Cassy persisted. 'It's utterly unlike him. He never does things on impulse. When he's going off on one of his trips, he plans for weeks before. Do *you* know, Rebekka? Did Patri tell you anything?'

Rebekka shook her head. 'Patri said that when he'd first suggested Alan might go with him, Alan had refused; but a few days ago he changed his mind. He didn't explain. He just said that if Patri was still determined to go, he wanted to go with him.'

Cassy turned back to Joss. 'Didn't he say anything to you, Joss? Surely you know? I just don't believe he's gone for the fun of it.'

'I don't think it will be "fun", Cassy,' Joss said quietly. 'As to his reasons – well, probably only he knows why.'

And *I* know why, she thought as the truth hit her. Alan had escaped, in the only way open to him. He was too honest a person to live a perpetual lie, and she should have realized it. *She* was the one who should have gone! Only last week, Helena had suggested that they should go back to England together and offer their services to the Medical Aid Committee who were recruiting volunteers for Spain. Joscelin's political preferences were not important, the girl insisted. Men were going to be wounded and nurses were going to be needed. Joscelin would soon learn how to cope. In the old days most of the nuns who nursed were untrained and learned by experience.

'You're wasting your life here, Joscelin,' Helena had said. 'Rebekka can look after her own children. Anyway, think about it.'

It was not until they were alone after breakfast that Rebekka gave Joscelin the second letter Alan had written before he left.

'I think Alan wants you to take care of Cassy,' she said as she put the envelope in Joscelin's hands. 'It's strange how everyone in this family seems to take it for granted that you'll be on hand to help – I do, too. We *all* lean on you, don't we?'

'I've never thought about it,' Joscelin said truthfully. 'But if Alan wants me to take care of Cassy, of course I will – if she'll let me.'

As Rebekka left the room, she tore open the envelope. Alan's letter was very short.

I love you! It will be easier for you without me around. I know that I am doing the right thing. At least I'm certain I shall be fighting for the right cause. I'm hoping you and Uncle Jaime will take care of Cassy, but who will take care of you, my darling, my love? If I die in this silly war, I shall do so wishing that it could have been me. Your Alan.

CHAPTER THIRTY

December 1936–February 1937

Cassy leaned across the table and stared into Milton Fleming's amused blue eyes.

'I just can't believe you're here in Sevilla,' Cassy said delightedly. 'How did you know *I* was here? Why didn't you let me know you were coming? How long are you staying?'

He smiled at her indulgently. Not only was she looking exceptionally attractive, but he found her lack of subterfuge rather touching. Another woman wanting to attract a man might have feigned a more casual welcome. Cassy, however, had come rushing across the room with almost indecent haste and was now making no effort to hide her excitement at seeing him. It was flattering, although he'd known for years now that Cassy could never resist him. Whatever tantrum she cared to throw when he left her after each assignation, whatever threats she made about never seeing him again, she was invariably pleased when he reappeared, as he did when it suited him.

Today she was behaving as if no one else in the room existed . . . and Milton was in need of reassurance. A month ago, in the States, he had tried to date a pretty young model; not only had she laughed at him, but she had pointed out that he was old enough to be her father! The remark had struck home, for he knew he was getting past his prime despite being a well-preserved forty-seven. At least Cassy seemed unconcerned by his age, he consoled himself as he smiled at her.

'Answers to questions: one, I knew you were here, because when I was in London your butler informed me you had been in Sevilla for several weeks – and why. Two, I didn't let you know I was coming partly because communications are almost non-existent, and partly because I myself did not know it until I had orders from my newspaper to cover the landing in Cádiz of the Italian so-called "volunteers". I'm a fully fledged war correspondent these days. And thirdly, as to how long I am staying, it all depends. From what I've gleaned, the Italian troop-landing in Cádiz may be intended as a back-up for the Nationalists in the Málaga area. It can't suit General Franco to have that particular port in Republican hands.'

Cassy sighed, her spirits momentarily deflated by this talk of war. 'I suppose this means you are pro the Nationalists like Papá?' she commented.

The American shrugged. 'I'm not gunning for either side,' he said. 'It just so happens that my paper wanted the war covered from both angles. I was given Franco, and my colleague the Republicans. I wangled the job because I knew Spain pretty well from my travels in earlier years. However, it's not proving as easy to get first-hand stories as I'd hoped. As you know, my Spanish isn't too good and I need an interpreter if I'm to get personal accounts.'

Cassy's red lips pursed into a pout. 'I'm so fed up with this war,' she said. 'It all seems so silly. Alan and Patricio have joined the Republicans. Of course Patri hates the Fascists because of Rebekka, but Alan . . . well, I think he's just gone off for the adventure, and I'll *never* forgive him for not taking me with him.'

Milton's expression revealed his amusement. 'You, honey, are the very last woman a man would consider taking with him to the front line! You don't really expect me to believe you'd have gone with them?'

Cassy's eyes flashed. 'Why on earth not? I'm bored to tears here. Besides, lots of women have joined the men; I'm as good a shot as Patri.'

Milton's face sobered. 'Honey, you don't have any idea what real war is like – the dirt, the awful food, lack of sleep, thirst, the blood and the wounds, the sound of men screaming in agony.' His expression softened as he gazed at her across the table. 'You should see yourself at this moment, Casilda – not a hair out of place. I really don't think you'd be good cannon fodder, honey!'

Partly pleased by his compliment but still not in agreement, Cassy tossed her head. 'I don't see why everyone assumes I'm silly because I happen to look chic. It's not fair – and especially not coming from you. When we got those Jews out of Germany, you said I'd been very brave and "remarkably cool in the face of danger". Those were your words!'

Milton leaned across the table and covered her hand in his. 'Okay, so you were brave, but this is real war, Casilda, and I don't blame your husband for leaving you behind! Besides, I thought you came out here to see your father.'

Cassy nodded. 'Yes, I did. We thought Papá was dying. But he's made a wonderful recovery. I was thinking of going back to England, but now *you're* here . . .'

Her voice was suddenly husky, and abruptly Milton pushed back his chair and stood up. 'We're wasting time!' he said. 'Let's go to my rooms. I want to make love to you.'

Silenced by his directness, Cassy frowned as he drew her to her feet. 'I'll have to be careful, Milton,' she said nervously. 'Everyone in Sevilla knows me.'

Milton's eyebrows rose sardonically. 'Still afraid that husband of yours might find out about us?'

Cassy withdrew her hand angrily. 'No, I'm not! I don't care any more what Alan thinks – not after the way he's gone off. But there's Papá and . . .'

Milton grinned as he interrupted her. 'Okay, we'll be careful. Here's my key. You go up ahead of me. I'll follow in a few minutes.'

As Cassy unlocked Milton's door, she felt the familiar excitement of anticipation and a burning awareness of hunger for his body. It was strange, she reflected, how she could go for months on end without any feeling of desire, yet Milton had only to put his hand over hers to send the blood coursing through her veins. Sometimes his total control of himself – and of her – disturbed her. She would try every feminine wile she could imagine to arouse him to the same pitch of urgency as her own. But he would never relax his control until he was assured she had reached the pinnacle of pleasure, and by then she was beyond caring whether she could dominate him or not.

As Cassy removed her coat and hat, Milton entered the room. Without haste he walked over to her and began gently to caress her. The hot colour flooded her cheeks and he said softly: 'It's been a long while. I always forget how desirable you are. Take that blouse off, Casilda. I want to see your breasts. Do you know that you are the most sensual woman I have ever met?'

Smiling, she began to undress. Moments later she lay naked on Milton's bed, watching him impatiently whilst he, too, undressed. He had put on weight, she thought. There was the beginning of a middle-aged spread round his waist! But, conscious of her eyes on him, Milton drew in his stomach and squared his shoulders as he approached her. As he lay down beside her, she noticed streaks of grey in his beard and that the grizzled hair had begun to recede from his temples. Exactly how old was he, she wondered? He had never told her. But now he was running his warm hands over her nipples and, as they sprang to life, she felt the ache of longing begin.

He kissed her slowly, his tongue searching her mouth. Her eyes closed as her need of him intensified.

'Come into me, *please*, Milton!' she gasped. 'I want you inside me . . . please!'

'Wait!' he commanded, refusing to allow himself to be drawn on top of her. 'I want to enjoy this – all of it . . .'

He pinioned her arms to her sides and allowed his mouth to wander over her, tantalizingly, sensuously. As her legs parted he kissed the inside of her thighs. With a little cry, Cassy tore her hands free and clasped them round his head. He shifted his position and moved upwards so that she felt his weight flattening her breasts. His hands were exploring the secret places which he alone seemed to know.

He began to stroke her purposefully until she cried out

again: 'Please, please, Milton. Oh, *Madre de Dios*, I want you! I need you!'

He took her as a bull might thrust himself into one of her father's cows, Cassy thought irrelevantly, as a shout of exultation burst from her lips. Their two bodies, damp with perspiration, seemed now as one. She could feel him pulsating deep inside her and as she came a second, then a third time, she knew that she would never stop wanting him.

Later, as they lay quiescent side by side, Cassy realized that these brief moments on a bed with Milton were the only times in her life when she was truly alive. The petty excitements that filled her days were pointless parodies of pleasure compared with the ecstasy Milton aroused. Every day, every hour she was not with him was a waste of her life; a waste of herself.

She turned on her side and touched his cheek, knowing from past experience that her appeal would fall on deaf ears and yet unable to prevent herself from asking: 'Can't I stay with you, Milton? It's so good for us. Why won't you let me stay with you? I don't care if you won't marry me. I just want to be with you. I love you!'

For once, he did not laugh. He met her anxious eyes with a look in his own that was almost of regret. 'You know that isn't possible, honey, especially not now. God knows where I'll be next week, next month – it depends where my editor sends me. Besides, I have to be free. I'm no more cut out for marriage than you are and . . .'

Cassy interrupted him. Sitting up in bed, her eyes flashing, she gripped his arms in a sudden explosion of excitement. 'You could take me with you!' she cried. 'You said you needed an interpreter. I can speak and understand some of the provincial dialects; I can speak French and English and I can make myself understood even in Italian. And I know people, Milton – people who are important – so I could get doors open for you through my father's connections. I might even be able to get you an interview with General Franco. Milton, are you listening to me? I just want to be with you, and I wouldn't be a nuisance, I swear. *Let me come with you!'*

Milton sat up and thoughtfully he lit a cigarette. 'It wouldn't work, Casilda. Your father would never permit it, for one thing, and there is no way I could guarantee your safety. War correspondents may be unarmed, but that doesn't prevent them getting killed.'

'Then I won't tell Papá I'm going,' Cassy argued. 'Patri didn't – he just went off without saying a word. Cristobal joined the Falangists and then announced he had done so at dinner one night. Milton, *please*. It would be such fun!'

'That it would *not* be!' Milton said firmly.

But Cassy could see he had not entirely rejected the idea. She resumed her arguments, stressing once again how useful she could be to him.

'I don't deny it,' he said finally. 'But I doubt if you know what you'd be getting yourself into, Casilda. You find me comfortably installed in a first-class hotel and imagine that's where you'd be living if I took you on my travels. But it could be a barn, a pig-sty for all I know. This war isn't like the Great War, with front lines clearly defined. There is no single battle-front. This is a war between a rebel army of insurgents against the people; and even the people are split into factions, who may be united momentarily against the Nationalists but who are liable at any moment to start fighting each other. Civilized behaviour as *you* know it has gone to the four winds.' He drew her down beside him, and with a sudden smile he added: 'You would certainly get raped if we were captured by the wrong side!'

'Oh, don't be so silly!' Cassy said, aware that he was half in earnest. 'You'd be there to defend me, and besides I could take one of Papá's guns. I shoot well enough to defend myself. You're just making excuses because you don't want me with you.'

Milton planted a kiss on top of her head. 'I'll think about it,' he said. 'Will that satisfy you? I wonder how you'd look in trousers? A little broad from the back view, I guess, but tempting none the less.'

He stubbed out his cigarette and, lying back against the pillows, he pulled her on top of him, placing his hands over her buttocks.

'You have the darndest way of attracting me, Casilda. You're the only woman who can make me want her again when I'd thought myself satiated.'

It was the first time he had ever said such a thing to her, and Cassy felt triumphant as she straddled him. She was different from any other woman he knew. Virility was important to men, and maybe if she could make him desire her badly enough he would take her with him. He *must* take her with him. She wanted it more than she had ever wanted anything in her whole life. Not only did she long to be with him, not only did she crave the adventure, but it would serve Alan and Patri right for going off without her.

She wondered how long it would be before Milton made up his mind.

If Joscelin had been shocked by Alan's impulsive decision to go off with Patri, she was doubly shocked now. Cassy had given her no warning of her extraordinary and precipitate departure. Poor Don Jaime, who had not known of Milton Fleming's presence in Sevilla, was even more shocked by Cassy's disappearance than she was. He was concerned not only for Cassy's safety, but for her marriage.

'Whatever would Alan say if he knew she'd gone off with this fellow, unchaperoned and without a thought for her reputation? Women shouldn't be fighting in the first place and Casilda . . . well, I take hope from the fact that she will soon tire of the discomforts and return home. Doubtless she will be back within the week!'

But Cassy did not return either for New Year nor in the first weeks of January. Cristobal came home on a few days' leave and Don Jaime received a hopelessly outdated letter from Luis and Mariano – but no word came from Cassy. Don Jaime looked worried but was obviously becoming resigned to the idea that his favourite daughter was not, after all, going to abandon her adventure as quickly as he had hoped.

Nor was there any news from Patri and Alan.

'Maybe Robert, my boyfriend, could find out where they are,' Helena suggested. 'I think he's in Madrid and that's where I shall try to go, Joscelin. I don't care how bad it is there. If Robert's going to be killed, I want to be with him.'

Joscelin understood Helena's feelings all too well. If Alan was in danger, she wanted to be with him. Now that Cassy had finally gone off with her American lover, Joscelin felt no lingering doubt that she and Alan had been sacrificing their own happiness pointlessly. The future no longer seemed important now that they were caught up in this war. What mattered was the present – and with Alan.

'I wish I could simply catch a train to Madrid!' Helena commented as she began her packing. 'But the Nationalists now hold most of the west of the country and there's nothing else for it but to go back to England first. At least I have a British passport.'

She paused, smiling at Joscelin who was perched on the end of her bed. 'I wish I could persuade you to come with me! You'd be so terribly useful. You'd soon learn the ropes – nursing is mostly a matter of commonsense anyway!'

A feeling of excitement stirred in Joscelin. If Helena could find Robert, *she* might find Alan – and when she did, there would be no more restrictions, no guilt! If they had only one day together, it would be worth any danger, any risks . . .

'I will come with you, Helena,' she said impulsively. 'But first I must tell Don Jaime. At least he will still have Rebekka and Lota to keep an eye on him – you know how he dislikes Mercedes and Eduardo bossing him about! Benito is thinking of joining the Nationalists, and if he does, Lota will come to live here. Don Jaime would like that. Can you wait another day or two, Helena, whilst I burn my boats?'

Helena's face registered surprise. 'You really do mean it, Joscelin? Maybe I should never have suggested it! You could get yourself killed, you know.'

Joscelin smiled. 'Which I wouldn't particularly want,' she said wryly. 'But if that did happen, Helena, at least there's only my mother to mourn my loss.'

And Alan, she thought. He would care. He loved her. It was for her sake he had joined in this stupid war. Now *she* would join *him*. If the fates were kind, they would be reunited; and if not, she might just as well spend the next few months of her life making herself useful.

War, Alan thought as he drew his muddy blanket closer around his shivering body, was very far from reflecting what his imagination had conjured up. For one thing, the enemy was not the Nationalist soldier occasionally visible across the ravine a hundred and fifty yards away – it was the cold. Everyone suffered. Bitter winds penetrated their inadequate clothing, which invariably was soaked by the rain and caked with mud. In the foxhole he shared with Patri, it was fractionally less cold than in the trenches. There was little or no firewood, since most of it had long since been appropriated by the militia troops who had manned these posts earlier in the winter. In an hour's time he must go back on sentry duty, but for the moment he could rest and try to restore the circulation in his frozen body.

Forewarned about the cold, he and Patri had bought trench coats in Valencia, but the men had been given only three greatcoats and these had to be passed from man to man as they went on sentry duty.

Alan glanced at his watch. In half an hour's time Patri would be coming off duty, and he would be obliged to spend what was left of the night in the freezing air keeping the sentries awake. It was hardly likely that they would be attacked by an enemy patrol in this appalling weather, but watch must be kept.

They had been up here in the hills above Alcubierre for over a month. It was two months since he and Patri had set out from Sevilla at dawn to make their way from Nationalist-held territory to Valencia. The government had moved there when Franco's troops had come too near Madrid for comfort, and Patri had a vague notion that someone in authority might know where to direct him to make best use of his ability to speak German. Travelling as English tourists, they had bluffed their way into Republican-held Málaga, Patri driving the car and Alan showing his British passport whenever they were stopped for questioning. Bribes were usually more effective than passports, and although twice their car had nearly been commandeered, they finally reached Valencia without mishap. It was a chance meeting one evening with a corporal that had changed Patri's plans to offer his services to the government. The man had been fighting with the POUM militia on the Aragon front where he had befriended a thirteen-year-old boy. The lad had volunteered with his father, an Andaluz peasant. The father had died in an unfortunate accident when his rusty Mauser had misfired; the bolt had blown out and one of the splinters from the burst cartridge case had pierced his eye, killing him instantly. The freezing weather and lack of sleep had already undermined the boy's health and his father's death had finally broken his spirit. The corporal had brought him to Valencia where the youngster had relatives and he himself was on his way back to the Front.

Alan was horrified to hear that so young a boy should have been permitted to volunteer; and even more so when the corporal told him that, although fifteen was a more usual age, children as young as eleven or twelve had been enlisted by their parents in order to get the ten pesetas a day payment.

'We need all the help we can get,' the corporal had informed them.

Alan and Patri had agreed to go back with the Spaniard to Alcubierre, where, he assured them, their knowledge of guns would be of inestimable value to the cause.

A gunnery instructor was a far more appropriate job for Alan than becoming an ambulance driver, Patri had commented on the journey north to Alcubierre, and would not require him to kill anyone!

Alan smiled as he recalled the totally erroneous picture he and Patri had had of life in the POUM militia. They had imagined a conventional military organization, whereas reality proved this army to be a disorganized, ill-assorted collection of farm labourers and factory workers, with no training other than experience gained at the Front. Military discipline was non-existent. The militia were volunteers and could go home if they wished. Their obedience and loyalty to the Communist party was all that kept them under control.

Equally erroneous was his and Patri's preconceived idea of warfare. Except for an occasional night patrol, the enemy was as preoccupied as themselves in the effort to keep warm. One man had been wounded by a Fascist sniper who had picked him off with a lucky shot whilst he was gathering fuel; such other casualties as had occurred were caused not by the enemy but by a sentry shooting at one of his own men returning from a night patrol, or from the unreliability or misuse of their outdated firearms. Until now, Alan had not been required to fire a single shot. The enemy remained a remote black dot on the hillsides across the valley.

Because of their knowledge of firearms, Alan and Patri had been given officer status. Alan knew he commanded the respect of his men, but it was Patri they adored, mainly because of his ability to joke with them and join in their singing – a pastime they indulged in whenever possible to cheer their spirits.

Joscelin was never far from Alan's thoughts. He longed to write to her, but with Cassy – so he supposed – living under the same roof he could not risk a letter accidentally falling into his wife's hands. Were it not for the possibility of the coming child, he would have forced Joss to realize that her misplaced loyalty was ruining both their lives. Fate, he thought with increasing bitterness, had stepped in with a cruel disregard for his happiness. He should have put an end to his marriage that day Cassy told him she had tricked him into fathering another man's child. Tormented by regrets for what might have been, and by memories of Joscelin, he had counted on his life as a soldier on active duty to preoccupy him totally. But far from doing so, the long nights and the pointless inactivity of their days in the muddy trenches were affording him far too much time to brood.

It came as a great relief to Alan when, in mid-February, the entire division was ordered to join the army besieging Huesca, fifty miles to the north. But the lack of action continued even after they had reached their new positions.

It was obvious that the strategic point was the Jaca road on the far side of Huesca, and their presence was purely to divert Nationalist troops from the area commanded by the Republicans.

Outwardly Patri did his best to remain cheerful, although the prospect of an attack on Huesca seemed as if it would never materialize. Like his men, he longed to be in the midst of the fighting. He did not try, however, to hide from Alan his belief that he was wasting his time and had begun to regret that they had joined the POUM.

On Alan's next visit to his cousin's dugout though, Patri was in the best of spirits. When he had offered his services to the POUM, he had taken care to hide his aristocratic origins lest he was thought to be a spy. He was known simply as Patricio Montero. But now, he told Alan, he had been recognized by an Andaluz militiaman who had worked at the Hacienda as a summer labourer.

'When I knew my true identity had been rumbled,' he explained, 'I thought I'd better make a clean breast of it before someone decided I was a *fascista* and shot me on the spot!'

They ducked instinctively as a shell whined overhead.

'To get back to the good news,' Patri continued after the shell burst somewhere to their rear, 'I went to see our battalion commander and told him who I was and that I had three brothers fighting on the side of the Nationalists. He looked as though he was about to have apoplexy, but after I'd explained about Rebekka he began to understand. He seemed very interested in my ability to speak fluent German. After a couple of glasses of brandy – God knows where he scrounged it from! – he said he'd recommend my transfer to the Batallón de Choque.'

His smile deepened as he saw Alan's look of incomprehension. 'It's a newly formed battalion made up of several hundred German refugees and they'll almost certainly be in action before long. At last I shall be doing something!'

A fortnight later, he sent Alan a note to say his transfer had come through. 'Can't wait to shoot my first Fascist,' he wrote. 'Wish you were coming along too. *Hasta la vista, camarada*!'

Throughout March the weather remained cold, with chill winds sweeping across the plateau. There were violets and wild hyacinths near the ditches bordering the ice-cold stream running down from the sierras. For the first time in weeks, Alan was able to take a bath and rid himself, at least temporarily, of the lice that had plagued all the men. But within days the parasites had returned and, to add to the general discomfort, the men were now running short of tobacco, soap, matches and olive oil – and their uniforms and boots were dropping to pieces. They were, however, better supplied with ammunition insofar as they each had a hundred and fifty rounds instead of fifty.

His father now knew of Alan's whereabouts and had managed to send him several food parcels. Surprisingly, some of these parcels from the Army and Navy Stores actually arrived, though many were stolen. Mail arrived spasmodically, but one important letter from Rebekka did reach Patri.

He sent word to Alan asking him to meet him at La Granja, the military store and cookhouse. They met outside one of the adjoining lime-washed farm buildings.

'Your message said you'd had news from the family,' Alan said as they sat down side by side in the spring sunshine. He handed Patri one of the precious cigars his father had sent him. 'How is everyone?'

Patri looked uncomfortable as he busied himself lighting the cigar. 'Papá is well. Rebekka and the children too . . .' he murmured. 'But I'm afraid the news about Casilda is . . . well, I don't think you're going to be too happy, old chap.'

Alan put a hand on Patri's shoulder.

'Cassy has found out she isn't going to have a child after all? I half expected it, Patri, and to be truthful I don't mind all that much. Cassy didn't want a baby and . . . well, with the war and one thing and another, it's probably just as well.'

He broke off, aware that Patri was staring at him anxiously. 'That's not exactly it, old man,' he said. 'Obviously Casilda isn't pregnant or she wouldn't . . . dammit, Alan, she's gone off into the blue with an American correspondent. Fellow called Fleming. Rebekka said Casilda was going to act as his interpreter. My crazy sister can't have given a thought to her reputation. She is a married woman, *por Dios*! Papá is furious – and worried, too. Nobody knows where she's gone! I'm terribly sorry, old chap.'

Alan's first reaction was one of overpowering anger. He neither knew nor cared how Milton Fleming came to be in Spain, but Cassy had sworn that her affair with the American was over all those years ago after she had confessed that Fleming was the father of her child. He had trusted her; done his damnedest to make a go of their marriage; denied himself the chance of real happiness with Joss – when by the look of it Cassy must have remained in touch with her former lover. He did not believe for one minute that she had gone off to war for political reasons. Could it be that Cassy was in search of adventure? he asked himself as his anger cooled. And in any event, did he really care *what* she was doing or if people believed him cuckolded? What mattered far more than his reputation or hers was Joss . . .

As if divining Alan's train of thought, Patri said: 'Joss has gone too. Seems she left soon after Cassy. She went off with Papá's nurse whose boyfriend is in the International Brigade. Rebekka said Joss wanted to make herself useful as a nurse.

That makes sense – but Casilda . . . I imagine you'll want to ask for leave, so you can go and find her. The way things are here, we don't seem to be achieving much, do we? I suppose our presence *does* keep the Nationalists from advancing up the Jaca road. I just wish we could attack. It's spring and we're still doing nothing!'

To Patri's surprise, Alan gave a wry smile. 'I wouldn't know where to begin searching for Cassy,' he said, 'and I honestly don't think she'd appreciate my laying down the law to her if I did find her. You see, Patri, our marriage hasn't been even remotely like yours and Rebekka's. Cassy goes her own way. I stopped minding years ago. Naturally, I wouldn't want anything awful to happen to her, but if she's helping a war correspondent, I imagine she won't be in the thick of the fighting. No doubt Uncle Jaime will pull strings to have her sent home if he thinks it desirable. I'll worry about our marriage when this miserable war is over.'

Patri sighed and rose to his feet. 'I'll have to be getting along, Alan. I'm sorry to be the bearer of bad news – but I dare say you are right. Casilda always was a law unto herself, and if you aren't too upset there's no reason for me to be. Knowing my sister, I don't suppose she'll stick it out for long – not with these confounded lice crawling all over her!'

As they shook hands, Alan had no idea how soon he was to see his cousin again. A week after their meeting, Patri led his men into an attack on the Nationalist-held fortress of El Manicomio. Despite the fact that the Batallón de Choque was made up of men far better trained than the militia, the commander who led the attack was stupid enough to fling a bomb into the enemy lines forewarning them of the advance, and thus eliminating any chance of a surprise attack. The militiamen were mown down by machine gun fire, and Patri was among the wounded sent to hospital in Lérida.

On the same day as Alan received word of Patri's misfortune, he himself was ordered to move his men down to the stream a few hundred yards from the Nationalist fortified farmhouse, Casa Francisca, their own advance being needed to divert the enemy from the far side of Huesca where the Anarchists were attacking on the Jaca road.

The April night air was bitterly cold. Crouched in a boggy marsh at the water's edge, Alan occasionally heard the noise of the working parties nearby, filling sandbags for the newly dug trenches and parapets.

For the moment, he thought, the Nationalists had no idea they had moved forward into no man's land, but when dawn broke they would certainly see the new positions which were only a few hundred yards from the Casa Francisca.

Alan fingered the rifle beside him. It would be stupid to pretend he was unafraid of possible death; but he was even more afraid of how he would feel knowing he had killed someone else. His men had no such qualms and were eagerly awaiting the chance to get at the enemy. As the night drew to an end, the cookhouse orderlies arrived with buckets of wine laced with brandy, and it was not until dawn that the atmosphere of anticipation suddenly dimmed. Now they could all see the sandbagged windows from which the enemy guns were pointing directly at them.

'*Joder! Me cago en los fascistas!*' the man next to Alan swore crudely. As they hurried into the protection of one of the trenches he began to burrow into the sides in an effort to deepen the shelter.

Without warning, a hail of bullets sang overhead. Here and there Alan saw men falling, but although the crack of each bullet sounded deafeningly close he felt strangely detached. A wounded man was carried past him down the mile-long trench to where they had been told the ambulances would be waiting. The man was conscious, his cries of pain affecting Alan far more deeply than the sound of the bullets. Alan's mood suddenly changed. He was eager now for the order to attack.

But it never came. Instead, he was instructed by wireless message to get his men back from the firing line as soon as dusk fell. As they began to file along the trench, Alan's eye was caught by the movement of a body lying between their trench and one much closer to the Fascist lines.

He was appalled. The forward trench was manned by the JCI, the youth league comprised of children, boys who should have been at their school desks or at home.

'That boy's alive,' he said to his corporal, a swarthy Catalonian mill worker. 'We must get him in.'

'Nothing we can do, *camarada*! The snipers shoot them the moment they move.' He tugged at Alan's arm. 'You can't help him. Maybe he'll reach safety when darkness falls.'

'If those swine haven't picked him off first,' Alan said, pulling his arm from the other man's grasp. 'We can't possibly leave him there!'

He squirmed over the side of the trench and began to worm his way towards the injured boy. Such light as remained was fading, and for a while he was unobserved. Over to the west he could see the red gun flashes and hear the subsequent deafening explosions. It had started to drizzle, and the ground beneath him became a sticky morass which seemed bent on slowing him down. Quite suddenly darkness fell, and he was no longer sure that he was heading in the direction of the wounded boy. He lay perfectly still wondering if the wretched child had died. But then he heard him moaning, calling for his mother, and Alan began to worm his way forward again.

But now his movement must have been detected for he heard the a bullet sing past his head. Instinctively, he pressed deeper into the ground.

The drizzle turned now to lashing rain, beating down on Alan's back and soaking him to the skin. For a few moments longer he lay still, comforted by the fact that no further shots were fired. Gingerly he moved his arm and was met only by silence. But the penetrating blackness of the night made any hope of seeing the wounded boy impossible and he realized that, unless he were to lose all sense of direction, he must risk calling out to him.

'*Camarada! Camarada!*' He waited but there was no answer.

Just as he was beginning to fear the boy might be dead, he heard the sound of quiet sobbing. He hurried forward, the mud sucking at his boots, his water bottle bumping softly against his rifle butt.

At first Alan thought he had been hit by a sniper bullet as he felt a sickening blow in the region of his left shoulder. But a second later it occurred to him that the flash had come from very near him. Instinctively he threw himself to the ground, realizing as he did so that his adversary was the boy he was trying to rescue.

'For God's sake, I'm your friend!' he shouted in English. Then, cursing himself for a fool, he repeated in Spanish: '*Amigo, amigo! Republicano.* POUM!'

A soft cry reached his ears. '*Americano?*'

'No, *Inglés. Teniente Inglés. Amigo!*'

'*Lo siento, camarada!*' In a desolate voice, the boy added that he had thought Alan was a Fascist come to finish him off and that was why he had fired at him. He seemed unaware that he had hit his target.

Alan rose once more to his feet, the pain bringing a gasp from his lips as he did so. As he edged nearer the boy, he found himself smiling at the irony of the situation – three months in the front line and he had been wounded by one of his own militia, and a child at that!

But his smile quickly vanished as he reached the bundle of sodden rags he was risking his life to rescue. Both the boy's legs had been smashed, and as Alan tried to lift him his screams of pain rent the air. How he had dragged himself this far from the forward trench, Alan could not imagine. Cradling the rain-soaked head, he crouched beside the boy wondering what alternatives were open to him. To remain here could benefit neither, and yet to carry him back to safety would cause the child unbearable agony – even supposing that with his own injury he *could* carry him.

The boy solved the problem by slipping into unconsciousness. Ignoring his pain, Alan hoisted the thin body over his uninjured shoulder and began to make his way back in the direction of his own trench. If he could reach it, he could follow it back to the farmhouse where they were to spend the night. Someone there might have morphine; or transport to take them both to one of the field hospitals.

Step by step, slipping dangerously in the wet mud, Alan began the long journey towards his own lines. His burden grew heavier with every yard and he became an automaton – one foot in front of the other – thinking of nothing beyond the next step, and the next, and the next.

He could not be sure whether the boy died at the moment they both fell headlong into the deserted trench, or whether he had died long before. But when the agonizing pain in his injured shoulder subsided sufficiently for him to reach once more for the child, he knew at once that the boy had slipped beyond salvation. He stared at the wide open eyes and felt tears gathering in his own. The child could not have been more than fifteen. There was only the hint of down on his cheeks and Alan noticed inconsequentially a dimple in the chin. The waste of this young life hurt him unbearably, and he could not make himself believe that there was good enough reason for such a sacrifice.

With an effort he pulled himself together and drew the lids down over those innocent open eyes. Picking up his rifle, he turned quickly away from the sight of the young, smashed body, hating to leave the child alone in the rain but knowing that he must get back to his own men. He found himself hoping that his sentries did not shoot at him as he approached them; hoping that his shoulder had not been too badly damaged, because now he wanted to get back in the line as quickly as possible to fight the enemy that could shoot at a child trying to escape.

For the first time in his life, Alan felt an urgent desire to kill.

CHAPTER THIRTY-ONE

April–May 1937

When Alan awoke, it was to find himself in a darkened hospital ward. At one end of the room a buxom girl with black hair sat at a table. She was writing in a notebook, the lamp beside her casting shadows over her face.

He became aware of a throbbing pain in his shoulder which seemed to spread up his neck and into the back of his head and down his spine. As the pain intensified, a moan burst from his lips and, hearing it, the nurse came hurrying over to him. Her large, dark eyes regarded him sympathetically.

'I'll give you some pills to ease the pain,' she said in Spanish. 'Tomorrow you will feel much better.'

Alan tried to marshal his thoughts. He could see other beds, each one occupied. Was this Lérida, he wondered?

'*Si, si, Lérida!*' The nurse nodded as she put one arm around his right shoulder and eased him into a better position to drink from the tin mug she held out to him. She put two white pills on his tongue and he drank thirstily. Surprisingly it was coffee, not water, he noticed as he drifted back to sleep.

He was woken the following morning by a different nurse. This one seemed not to understand the meaning of pain as, with a cheerful smile, she shook him back to consciousness.

'*El desayuno!*' she said, holding out a breakfast tray on which was a bowl of soup, a congealing yellow mass which vaguely resembled an omelette and a large covered platter. Encouragingly she lifted the lid, revealing a number of chunks of meat in a dark, oily gravy. Beside the soup bowl was a thick slice of bread and a glass of wine. '*Desayuno!*' she said again.

Alan regarded his breakfast with disbelief. Could the girl really be expecting him to eat this vast, greasy meal? He glanced at the man in the bed next to him. A large weighted pulley supported one of his arms, which was encased in a kite-like splint. With his left hand, he was ravenously tucking into his meal.

'*No tiene apetito?*' his nurse inquired anxiously.

Aware that he had been neither washed nor shaved nor indeed, been to the bathroom, Alan tried to remember sufficient Spanish to indicate his needs.

But even with these relieved, Alan could not do more than pick at the meal in front of him. All he wanted was to be allowed to go back to sleep, to forget the appalling memories of the previous two days which were flooding back into his mind.

When finally he had stumbled back to the farmhouse, two of his men had struggled through the rain, carrying him on a stretcher to the makeshift hospital in Siétamo. A doctor had given him a shot of morphine and his next memory was of hitting the floor of the ambulance truck and screaming in pain. A man beside him, also thrown from his stretcher by the jolting lorry, clutched at his thigh. Blood was soaking through his bandages. Alan vaguely recalled that the poor wretch was dead when finally they carried him into the hospital at Lérida.

For the next three days, Alan was only semi-conscious. As far as he was aware, the occasional administration of pain-killing drugs was all the treatment he received for his wound, although his bandages were changed at regular intervals, and huge meals he could not eat arrived with equal regularity. The Spaniard in the adjoining bed consumed Alan's unwanted food as well as his own, and pressed some tobacco on him by way of thanks. He seemed unconcerned that the smashed bones clearly visible through the muslin casing over his arm were receiving no medical attention. He explained that none of the wounded would be operated on until they reached the hospital at Tarragona – a state of affairs that worried Alan but which he had not the energy to query. No one seemed to know when they would be moved.

Several more days elapsed before Alan and six of his fellow patients were helped unceremoniously from their beds and herded on a train to Tarragona. Despite the intense pain in his shoulder, he could see that the other men had far worse wounds than his own, and were suffering appallingly as they were jolted on the hard wooden seats. Some were sick, and one young boy with a stomach injury was unable to control his bowels. The stench was all but unbearable.

In desperation Alan tried to imagine himself by the side of a Scottish burn, dipping his face into the crystal-clear water, breathing in the soft, clean air of the moors. For a moment, as he closed his eyes, he could see a tall, slim figure walking towards him; see the breeze gently blowing her fair hair across her face. He felt an ache in his throat as a hospital orderly held out a bottle of water and the vision disappeared. They would be in Tarragona in half an hour, the orderly told him; the hospital there was good; there would be surgeons, many nurses, much comfort and plenty to eat.

But for Alan the biggest bonus was finding Patri sitting beside his bed when he regained consciousness after his operation two days later. Patri's right leg was propped up in a plaster cast on Alan's bedside table. He grinned cheerfully as he saw Alan's eyes open.

'Good to see you back in the land of the living, old chap!' He held out a hand-rolled cigarette. 'I've been saving this for you.' He put it between Alan's lips and lit it for him. 'When my nurse told me there had been an Englishman with a POUM card in the new batch from Lérida, I hoped it might be you. Sorry you're wounded, of course, but damned glad to see you.'

Immensely pleased to see Patri, Alan smiled. 'Sorry it's a Spanish fag. Rebekka did send me some decent ones but they were pinched on my way down from the Front. Expect you had all your gear stolen, too.' Patri grinned.

'I haven't checked, but I do know my wristwatch has

vanished,' Alan said. The effects of the anaesthetic were beginning to wear off and he looked at his cousin with pleasure. 'Good to see you looking so fit, Patri. Leg okay?'

Patri nodded. 'Having the plaster off tomorrow. It was little more than a broken bone and a minor flesh wound.' His forehead creased in a sudden frown. 'Got news for you, Alan – not too good, I'm afraid. Rumour has it the Communists in the government suspect our POUM leaders of being in cahoots with Franco. Quite mad, of course, but I've made up my mind to get out – and so must you.'

He paused to help Alan into a more comfortable sitting position and then continued: 'An American patient came into my ward last week and told me the International Brigade were forming a new battalion, the XXth, down south at Albacete. They're desperately in need of volunteers. I wish you were fit enough to come with me, but the *Médico* said it would be a month or two at least before you could hold a rifle. I'm trying to arrange for you to go to the convalescent hospital near Valdeganga. It's too dangerous for you here, Alan. Everyone knows you're POUM militia, and if there was to be a witch-hunt you can be sure they wouldn't stop to ask questions when a bullet would put a tidy end to speculations as to your political loyalties.'

His smile was distinctly sardonic. 'Fortunately, one of the hospital administrators here is an old chum of Papá's. He has agreed to "lose" our POUM cards – make out new papers saying we're volunteers who got caught up in the fighting on our way to join the International Brigade.' His smile deepened. 'Cost me a few pesetas, I might add, but worth every one of them. Be a bit ironic if we were killed by someone on our own side!'

Seeing the whiteness of his cousin's face, he broke off and rose to his feet. 'I shouldn't have pushed all this at you so soon after your op. I'll be back to see you later after you've had a nap. I want to hear how you got that wound – and I've news from home. See you anon, old fellow. Have a good sleep!'

News from home, Alan thought drowsily. Could that mean news of Joscelin? Of Cassy? It was strange how rarely he thought of his wife. But the pain he felt whenever he thought of Joscelin was as real to him as the throbbing ache in his shoulder. He could not bear the thought of her suffering; cold, hungry – perhaps ill.

He had encountered many Spanish girls in uniform. Some had been wounded, some killed, and he had never been able to reconcile himself to the idea that women should be involved in the brutality of war. Even the nurses were not immune, faced as they were in their daily tasks with sickening wounds and death. Few of the cheerful Spanish nurses came from the protected environments to which girls like Joscelin were accustomed. Untrained volunteers, they did their best, often clumsy, never complaining and apparently immune to the insanitary conditions of the field hospitals.

But for how long, he asked himself constantly, could his Joss survive as a nurse in wartime? He could not bear to think of those sensitive artist's hands roughened and chapped with the constant scouring of bedpans. Remembering how her large grey eyes had filled with tears at the sight of a young vixen caught in one of the gamekeeper's snares, he could not envisage her private agony when she saw the suffering of the soldiers.

When Alan next awoke, Patri was again beside his bed, balancing a writing pad on his plaster cast and chewing on the stub of a pencil.

'Thought I'd drop a line to Rebekka whilst I was waiting for you to wake up,' he said. 'They'll be pleased to hear you're safe and sound. Lota, I gather, says endless prayers and lights candles for us both whenever she isn't coping at the orphanage. Did you know Benito had joined the Falange? Funny to think I've three brothers and now a brother-in-law pledged to kill me if they meet up with me! Rebekka says Papá gets terribly depressed at times, thinking how this war has split the family.'

'No other news?' Alan asked as he reached for the glass of

water by his bed. His voice gave no indication of his desperate craving for news of Joscelin.

Unaware of his cousin's emotion, Patri nodded casually. 'Rebekka said they'd had a postcard from Casilda. She was staying at the Ritz in Madrid – and having a "ripping time". Apparently life there for foreign tourists continues as if there were no war, despite the fact that there's a battle going on less than a mile from the centre of the city. So you don't have to worry about Casilda, Alan. As usual, she's enjoying herself!'

He omitted to say that Cassy's comments had been made in the plural and the 'we', Patri presumed, included the American.

'There's news of Joss and Helena, too,' he went on quickly. 'Joss wrote to Rebekka from London just before they departed for France, hoping to get back into Spain across the Pyrenees. The Medical Aid Committee was organizing everything. Good old Joss – I admire her courage. Rebekka misses her terribly, of course, but she spends more time now helping Lota, and she's keeping an eye on Carmen who had twins just after Christmas. Mariano and Luis got leave for the christening.'

'No news of Cris?' Alan asked.

Patri frowned. 'Not a word! Rebekka said Papá was convinced he would be fighting with the Italians. Lota worries about her twin, but I've never been close to Cris and there's an element of the fanatic about him I don't particularly care for. But at least he's doing something – which is more than you can say for Eduardo. *He* continues to manage the estate for Papá as if the war didn't exist! All he seems to care about is making money. No wonder he backs Franco! I don't think he's in the least concerned about the land, or the people, whereas Papá cares deeply about both.'

A Spanish nurse arrived to give Alan his supper. Patri's blue eyes were twinkling as he told her she was pretty enough to tempt him to thoughts of unfaithfulness to his beloved wife.

'Lieutenant Montero is not only married but he is shortly being discharged from hospital,' Alan said in his halting

Spanish as the girl laughed, clearly enjoying the flirtation. 'It is better therefore that you should give all your attention to me, since I am in greater need of your care than he!'

'*Hola, Inglés!*' called out the man in the adjoining bed. 'It is well known your countrymen are cold-blooded. You should devote your attentions to me, *mi pasionaria*! I may have lost one arm, but I assure you I have lost no important parts.'

Giggling and blushing, the girl put down Alan's tray and retired.

Alan was woken from a deep sleep in the early hours of the morning of his seventh day in the Tarragona hospital. Two male orderlies helped him out of bed and guided him down the ward, along the deserted corridor and out into the crisp pre-dawn air. The effects of the sleeping pill he had been given the night before had not yet worn off, and Alan's legs were trembling as he stared in confusion at the truck standing in the courtyard. His head swam as he was lifted over the tailboard and laid beside another patient on a mattress on the floor. The orderlies disappeared and a man in a white coat came up to him. He was the administrator, he informed Alan as he pushed an envelope into his hand; the friend of Patricio's father. Alan was going to an American convalescent hospital near Tarancón. He had been given the place of an American pilot who had died during the night. It would be up to Alan when he arrived to persuade the authorities there to permit him to remain. Since it was Alan's intention to join the International Brigade, the administrator doubted they would turn away an experienced militiaman. He shook Alan's hand and wished him good luck, apologizing for the fact that he could do no more to ensure Alan's safety.

Almost immediately the truck started and, in the dim light of the interior, Alan stared at the other occupants who were regarding him curiously. Suddenly they all began to speak in English, but with a distinct American accent. They were young, friendly and sympathetic, and were on their way to join the

Lincoln Battalion down south. One young Californian informed Alan they were all volunteers who had been fired by the Republican propaganda in their country.

Eagerly they plied Alan with questions about the fighting, expecting naïvely, that they were about to join a conventional army. They would find out the truth soon enough, he thought as his shoulder started to throb with the movement of the truck. No purpose would be served by disillusioning these eager youngsters at this stage.

As the truck jolted over the endless bumps along the narrow coastal road Alan dozed fitfully. From time to time, when the truck was being refuelled, one of the Americans would offer him a drink from his water bottle or a hunk of bread and a slice of garlic sausage. But the throbbing in his shoulder had spread to his neck and head and he felt too nauseated to eat. It was less than a week since his operation and, although he was grateful to Patri and the man who had enabled him to leave the hospital with the American volunteers, he knew it was too soon for him to be travelling. One of his companions informed him that the journey south, covering over three hundred miles, would take them all of twelve hours at the limited speed they could make over such bad roads.

The Americans were sympathetic to his pain but unable to alleviate it, although they did their best to divert him from awareness of it, falling silent only when Alan closed his eyes in an attempt to seek the oblivion of sleep.

The temperature in the back of the truck rose as the heat of the spring sunshine increased throughout the day. Someone placed a wet cloth on Alan's forehead and he realized that he was burning with fever, which did not lessen even when the cooler air of evening filled the truck. He was barely conscious when, nearing midnight, he was carried into the convalescent hospital outside Saelices. He was aware vaguely of a white-coated doctor bending over him, of a needle in his arm and the feel of soft, clean sheets.

Alan's fever raged for twenty-four hours. Drifting in and

out of consciousness he knew himself unable to distinguish dreams from reality, for he could see Joscelin's face bending over him; hear her voice calling his name. Content to remain in this feverish fantasy, Alan ceased trying to fathom where he was.

When finally the fever abated, he awoke to two assaults on his senses – one the tantalizing smell of coffee, the other a shaft of brilliant sunlight slanting through the screens around his bed and spotlighting the tiny gold hairs on his arms. His hands were folded tidily over a smooth white sheet and under them lay a piece of blue writing paper.

For several moments Alan lay still, savouring the feeling of well-being; taking in the sounds of voices and movements in the ward outside the screens. He became aware of the smell of antiseptics; of a thermometer in a glass beside his bed; of an atmosphere of calm and orderliness. For the first time since winter he was free from the incessant irritation of lice. His pyjamas, his sheets, his body were spotlessly clean.

Slowly memory returned and he groaned softly as he recalled the nightmare journey bringing him to this new, welcome haven. The screen moved and a tall, slim nurse carrying a tray came over to him. Her hair was covered by a white headscarf tied at the nape of her neck. She smiled.

'I'm Sister Marshall!' she said. Her English was American-accented. 'How are you feeling? I'll take your temperature and then you can drink this coffee if you wish. Doctor says you may have some breakfast, too, if you feel like it.' She put a thermometer between Alan's lips. 'You're Lieutenant Alan Costain, aren't you? Nurse Howard has been more than a little anxious about you!' Her eyes twinkled. 'She has scarcely left your bedside, you know, and I had to send her off for some sleep last night despite her protests. She left you a note, and will be along to see you soon. I promised to send word to her the moment you woke up.'

She removed the thermometer from Alan's mouth, nodded approvingly and added: 'Almost normal! Now, Lieutenant, if

I permit Nurse Howard to visit you, you must promise not to allow your temperature to go up or I shall have Dr Phillips after me. Ten minutes only! Nurse Howard is on duty at eleven o'clock.' Her voice softened as she patted Alan's hand. 'She'll be pleased to see you looking so much better.'

Speechless, Alan watched her go. Then slowly, he held up Joscelin's note. 'Just in case I am not with you when you wake,' he read, 'this is to say I love you. The American doctor says you will probably be here for at least six weeks. Isn't it wonderful? Get well quickly, my darling. I'll be with you soon, Joss.'

Tears he could not control filled Alan's eyes. The emotion of pure happiness was overwhelming. For a moment he did not see the little sketch Joscelin had drawn on the reverse side of the paper. It was a tiny caricature of himself, his shoulder heavily bandaged, being tipped upside down into a hospital bed, and a nurse looking remarkably like Joscelin hovering anxiously by his pillow with a huge thermometer.

Suddenly he was ravenously hungry, and when a Spanish orderly came through the screens with a tray of food he accepted it eagerly. The food was good – and the coffee especially so.

He was on the point of drinking a second cup when the screens parted once more and he looked up to see Joscelin standing there, a radiant smile on her face. Her fair hair was tucked into a little white cap; her apron was starched crisply and her long, slim legs were encased in white stockings.

'Nurse Howard reporting for duty, sir!' she said, and bending forward she grasped his hands.

Alan drew her against him, his heart thudding wildly with unbelievable joy. He wanted to tell her he loved her but there was a lump in his throat. Instead he kissed her – her eyes, her forehead and then her lips. The love that flowed between them was almost a tangible thing as they clung together in silence.

Then Joscelin drew away from him. Her eyes filled with tenderness, she whispered: 'Oh, Alan, darling! I've been so worried about you. You were unconscious when they brought you in and the doctors thought your wound might have become infected. I couldn't believe it when Helena came to tell me an English officer had been brought in and that it was *you*. It's like a miracle!'

Alan gripped her hands, his eyes watching every expression on her face. 'It *is* a miracle!' he said. He explained how mere chance had brought him to this particular hospital, taking the place of an American who had died. 'What I don't understand is how *you* come to be here, Joss.'

'Helena found out that her English boyfriend, Robert, was at the International Brigade Headquarters at Albacete. She was determined to get nearer to him, and when she heard this hospital was less than a hundred miles away she managed to get us both transferred. Fortunately for us there'd been a large number of casualties from the fighting at Jarama and they were short-staffed, so they took us on. All the other nurses here are American. Poor Helena hasn't seen Robert yet. After his training at Madrigueras, he was sent further south to Pozoblanco.'

'But that's where Patri was going,' Alan said. 'He left hospital in Tarragona soon after I got there. He's okay – only a broken leg which healed pretty quickly.' He stared at Joscelin's face as if he were trying to memorize every detail.

'You look tired, my dearest,' he said softly. 'But very beautiful!'

Joscelin felt her cheeks redden at his compliment. She said with sudden shyness: 'You wear rose-coloured spectacles where I'm concerned, Alan. I have never been beautiful.'

'You are to me,' Alan said simply. 'I love you, Joss, and I want to marry you. It was all over between Cassy and me the day she went off with Fleming. When this wretched war is over, I shall ask her to divorce me. If there's to be a future for me, I want to spend it with you. *Will* you marry me when I'm free?'

Joscelin nodded. 'I knew when Cassy left Sevilla that I had

been wrong, and blamed myself for all the wasted years when you and I could have been together. But by then you'd gone off with Patri, and I couldn't bear the thought of you being killed without my seeing you again. So I joined up with Helena, although I was sure it would be like looking for a needle in a haystack. I'd no idea how I could possibly find you. I hoped Rebekka would hear from Patri and that I could discover through her where you were. But I don't think she could have got my letter telling her where I was, or else her reply went astray. Finding you here . . . it's still hard to believe!'

Alan reached up to touch a tendril of hair which had escaped her cap. 'I have a feeling I shall need a very prolonged convalescence,' he said. 'The war can take care of itself for a little while. I want to spend every minute I can with you, my dearest. Could you get some leave? I want to be alone with you. I want you all to myself!' He paused, then added in a low intense voice: 'Will you come away with me, Joss?'

She held his hand against her cheek as she nodded. 'If Matron won't give me leave, I'll go AWOL!' she said, smiling tremulously. 'Now I'd better go if I'm not to put Sister's back up. I'll be off duty this evening.'

'I'll wait for you!' Alan said, drawing her head down to his. 'A few more hours after a lifetime of waiting should not be beyond the limit of my patience!'

In the ensuing weeks, neither Alan nor Joscelin made any attempt to hide the fact that they were deeply and passionately in love. They held hands unashamedly whenever they were together, and when Alan was well enough to walk in the April sunshine over the cobblestones of the courtyard his arm was round Joscelin's waist.

By the middle of the month, Alan was strong enough to venture outside the walled perimeter of the hospital grounds. He and Joscelin wandered in the warm sunshine through the fields. They made special trysting places of their own – a cool glade in a wooded copse; a dip in the rocky boulders on the edge of a stream carrying water down from the nearby hills.

Joscelin picked armfuls of wild flowers to brighten the hospital wards, whilst Alan lay half asleep in the sun, watching her with loving eyes.

They tried not to let thoughts of the war mar the idyll of their life and agreed not to talk about it. But at the end of the month rumours were rife in the hospital about a catastrophic aerial bombardment of a town in the north of Spain called Guernica. An American on leave visiting a brother at the hospital insisted that German planes from the Condor Legion had flattened the little town one market day, killing and wounding hundreds of civilians. No one could understand the reason for the attack on a defenceless town which could not possibly be considered a military target. If it had any importance at all, it was its claim to be the symbolic capital of the Basque province.

'General Franco is said to have denied he ordered the attack,' the American told them. 'But I can assure you it happened. A friend of mine went with the British Consul to see the damage, and he said that nine out of ten houses were in ruins and beyond reconstruction. He saw men, women and children wandering through the smouldering streets, searching for the bodies of their relatives. If that is an example of Fascist warfare, then the sooner we rid this country of the brutes the better!'

The following day Alan's convalescent leave began. He borrowed a motorbike from a sympathetic doctor, drove Joscelin in the cool of the evening to the walled city of Cuenca, and managed to obtain a room for them in the unpretentious Hotel Iberia not far from the Gothic cathedral.

As far as Joscelin was concerned, she did not care in the least where they were. Simply to be able to lie beside Alan in the privacy of their own bedroom was sufficient joy for her. His shoulder had healed completely and, although in certain humid conditions the muscles stiffened up and caused him some minor inconvenience, he was perfectly fit. Like herself, he was ecstatically happy and determined that this one week in their lives would make up for all those lost years in the past.

Now totally freed from any feelings of guilt towards Cassy, their lovemaking took on a new dimension. They explored one another's bodies and discovered ways to give each other pleasure without shyness or restraint. It seemed to them that they were the only couple in the world who touched such depths of passion and love, and believed themselves unique in their mental and physical unity. They had no need to tell each other 'I love you', although they did so constantly. Alan had a strong romantic streak which had hitherto lain dormant and he found a dozen ways of expressing his love. Joscelin would find little notes tucked under her breakfast napkin or in a bedroom slipper or tooth glass, saying simply that he adored her. She could not admire something in a shop window without finding it next day, beautifully wrapped, on her dressing table. Most treasured of all these little gifts was an antique gold ring, inside which he had had engraved their entwined initials. He slipped it on her marriage finger and, holding her against his heart, vowed to love her 'until death us do part'.

It was the first time either had allowed the prospect of death to intrude on their happiness. In the early hours of the morning Alan woke from a nightmare, soaked with perspiration. 'I dreamed you were shot by a sniper!' he said, his voice shaking. 'I saw you lying on a hillside . . . oh God, Joss, I wouldn't want to live if you died. This isn't your war. Please go back to England! At least I wouldn't have to worry about you then. Will you go, darling, for my sake?'

For a few moments Joscelin was silent. Then she said: 'You are going back to the fighting, Alan, and as long as you're in Spain I want to be here too. You'll get leave and perhaps we can be together again. Don't ask me to go away! Besides, as a nurse in a hospital I'm not likely to be in any danger.'

Alan's hold upon her tightened. 'What happened at Guernica could happen anywhere,' he said grimly. 'I haven't been able to put the horror out of my mind.'

'We're together now, Alan. Don't let's spoil our last few days worrying about something that might never happen.'

By unspoken agreement they did not mention the future again, but filled their days with love instead of fear; happiness instead of regret.

On their last day, Alan took Joscelin on the motorbike to the Ciudad Encantada. They set off early in the morning in the comparative cool before the sun rose in the sky. He would not tell her why the town was called the Enchanted City, but waited until they arrived for Joscelin to see for herself the extraordinary phenomenon brought about by centuries of atmospheric action on the limestone. It had produced an astonishing illusion of houses, streets, vegetation, flowers and even of people, frozen into the stone. Now Joscelin understood why Alan had insisted she bring paper and pencil. Finding a shady place to sit, he lay contentedly beside her smoking the last of his carefully hoarded tobacco whilst she spent the siesta hour sketching the fantasy before them.

'You really don't mind waiting until I finish this, Alan?' she asked anxiously as time slipped by. 'We won't have a chance to explore the town if we stay here much longer.'

Alan knocked out his pipe and stretched himself full length, his arms behind his head. There was a smile on his face as he said half reproachfully: 'Do you really know me so little that you can ask such a question? I guessed this was how we would spend the day, you silly girl, and how better? I can lie here staring at you to my heart's content without embarrassing you by my scrutiny. I love to watch you when you're really concentrating. The tip of your tongue comes out and you tilt your head on one side – like a bird looking at a worm. Your hip juts out and your back is curved in the most alluring way. I'm sorely tempted to make love to you, and it's a very pleasant sensation, not least because I know that when we get back to the hotel I shall certainly do so.'

His smile broadened as he watched the colour flare in Joscelin's cheeks. 'You've no idea how adorable you are when you blush!' he teased. 'It reminds me of those days when you used to visit us at Rutland Gate. You were such a solemn little girl!'

Joscelin picked up a fallen sheet of paper, screwed it up into a ball and threw it at him. 'You never even noticed me in those days,' she said. 'You've probably forgotten all about it, but I can remember nearly drowning one day on the river near the Piermonts' house, and you weren't the least bit concerned about me. You were frantic with worry about Cassy.'

'I do remember!' Alan said quietly, the smile leaving his face. 'And I don't deny I was head over heels in love with Cassy. But it was a boy's infatuation. It was a very long time before I learned that love and lust are not at all the same thing. I know now that I have never loved anyone but you. You are part of my very being, Joss, and I shall love you always.'

Tears stung Joscelin's eyes, and it was a moment or two before her hand was steady enough to continue her drawing. The moment she had mentioned Cassy's name she had regretted it, but now she was glad she had done so. She had no doubt that Alan was speaking the truth, and with their impending separation she needed to know that he loved her as much as she loved him. She had no fear now that he would ever change his mind in the future and take Cassy back once again – if there was a future for either of them. If only he would go back to England, she would go with him! But she sensed Alan's anxiety to get back to the fighting, and he had not tried to hide from her his feelings about the necessity to do so.

'Our politicians at home are blind to the dangers here,' he had said. 'I believe they are going to regret their policy of non-intervention. We've just got to fight against the Mussolinis and Hitlers here on Spanish soil before we find ourselves fighting on British soil. You understand that, don't you, darling?'

Ideals were all very well, Joscelin thought, but Alan's life was more important to her than anything in the world, and she dared not allow herself to think how easily he might be killed. He had not told her when he would be leaving the hospital to go to Albacete. She knew he intended to try to join the International Brigade as Patri had done, but not *when*.

Deep down, she suspected that this 'honeymoon' was the epilogue to the fairy-tale interlude in their lives, but she could not bear to think about it.

It was not until much later that night, lying exhausted, satiated with love and sleepily relaxed in Alan's arms, that he told her he was returning to the hospital only to pick up his discharge papers; that the following morning he would be on his way to Albacete.

She wept silently whilst he tried to kiss away her tears. He had made all the arrangements before they had left for Cuenca.

'I didn't want anything to spoil our week together,' he explained. 'Don't cry, Joss. I can't bear to think of you unhappy.'

For his sake, she pretended she accepted the inevitable. But after he had fallen asleep she lay staring at his beloved face in the moonlight, wondering if she would ever do so again.

CHAPTER THIRTY-TWO

December 1937–January 1938

'*Dios nos libre!*' Cassy exclaimed as the large Buick suddenly careered violently over a mound of frozen snow and slid to a halt twenty yards further up the road. She peered anxiously at the windscreen where the heavy snowflakes were piling up alarmingly fast, obscuring visibility. She could no longer see the red tail light of the army lorry they had been following, and the snow was rapidly covering the tyre marks.

'Why won't it go?' she asked Milton anxiously as he strove to refire the sluggish engine. The whirring of the starter motor filled the interior of the car.

'Battery's okay,' Milton muttered, frowning. 'I'd better get out and have a look at the engine.'

Resignedly, he pulled up the collar of his heavy astrakhan coat and wound his thick woollen scarf around his head. Cold as it was inside the vehicle, he knew it would be even colder outside. When they had set off from Zaragoza at dawn, the temperature had registered minus eighteen. He had bought a goatskin rug to cover their legs; a feather quilt, extra pairs of gloves and fur-lined boots. He had filled two Thermos flasks with hot coffee and a large knapsack with food – bread, cheese, sausage, fruit and several bars of American chocolate.

He believed himself well provisioned for any contingency they might encounter on the journey to the Nationalist base at Concud just outside Teruel – a drive he estimated would take them some eight hours or more. There were plenty of army vehicles travelling south, and even when an hour or two earlier the snow had started to fall he had not been unduly worried but tucked the Buick behind a large truck and followed the red tail light. That beacon in the now blinding snow had disappeared along with the black strip of tarmacadam, and the road was indistinguishable from the land bordering it.

He glanced at his watch as he walked round to the front of the car. It was close on three o'clock and he had estimated that they would reach Concud by two. In this blizzard, what little light there was on this late December day would almost certainly be gone in another hour. His knowledge of mechanics was limited and he offered up a silent prayer that he would be able to find whatever fault there was quickly.

Wind whipped the snow against his face as he lifted the bonnet. Both he and the truck driver had stopped not ten miles back to refuel, and he checked that the gasoline was getting through to the carburettor. Swearing softly beneath his breath, he glanced swiftly at the battery leads. As he had suspected, they were firmly in place. He looked next at the sparking plug terminals. They too, were secure. His eyes followed the leads from the plugs back to the distributor head and he saw at once what had happened – the cap had been jolted from its clip. With a sigh of relief he put it back in position and snapped the clips firmly over it.

'Try the starter now, Casilda!' he shouted, his voice muted by the wind. As she wound down the window, he shouted again. Sliding into the driver's seat, Cassy pulled the starter knob. Immediately the engine fired.

Grinning happily, Milton called out: 'Put her into reverse and I'll give you a push. Don't try to move her until I'm ready.'

He closed the bonnet and battled his way against the wind to the front of the car.

'Now!' he shouted, putting all his weight behind the thrust. Fountains of snow shot up from the back tyres as, for a moment, the wheels skidded. Then suddenly they gripped, and the big car jolted backwards onto the road.

Milton's moment of triumph was short-lived. As he stepped

forward, his foot slipped and for the first time he saw water – a dark rusty-red, ever-growing pool.

'Oh, my God!' he groaned, staring at it in disbelief. He could see Cassy's joyful face as she called out: '*Magnífico, Milton! Colosal! Estupendo!*'

'Switch off!' he ordered. 'Don't argue, Casilda. Do as I say!' Cassy obeyed him instantly. Puzzled, she watched him lift the bonnet once more. As the fan slowed and halted, he took off his gloves and bent over the engine.

His frozen fingers felt for the leak in the radiator. 'God dammit!' he swore, for sure enough there was a small fracture from which the still-warm, dirty water was seeping in a slow, steady stream. He considered the disaster with growing dismay. Had it been a top or bottom hose, he might have been able to bandage it; patch it – if only temporarily. Had the fracture been in a more accessible place, he might have been able to knock the two edges together . . . but the fracture was right at the bottom of the radiator. There was nothing he could do about it.

Slowly he put his gloves back on, aware of the bitter cold and its implications in the light of this present disaster.

'What's wrong?' Cassy asked as he slipped into the passenger seat, his black coat now white with snow.

'Radiator's burst!' he said quietly, striving to keep the anxiety from his voice. 'We must have hit that bank harder than I'd thought. I'm afraid we're stuck.'

Cassy's eyes widened. 'But why, Milton? The radiator only holds water, doesn't it? And the engine was going fine until you told me to switch it off. Surely . . .'

'No, Casilda, we can't run the engine without water in the radiator,' he interrupted her. 'It keeps the engine cool, you see, and if it isn't cooled it will very quickly seize up.'

'How quickly?' Cassy asked anxiously. 'We can't be more than a few miles from the turning off to Concud. You said we were nearly there . . .'

Milton forced himself to meet her gaze. 'I doubt if we'd get further than two miles at the most – if that.'

Cassy glanced nervously out of the window. The blizzard was getting fiercer and she could no longer see across the road. 'But we can't stay here! We'll freeze to death. I'm nearly frozen now . . .'

Milton reached over to the back seat and pulled the feather quilt round her shoulders. 'I don't suppose we'll be here all that long,' he said. 'With a bit of luck a truck will come along and we can get a ride to Concud.'

He knew that the Nationalists were sending up a huge army of reinforcements. They were to assist the troops who were trying to relieve the besieged garrison and civilians trapped inside the walled city of Teruel. Well briefed in Zaragoza, Milton knew that the Nationalist garrison in Teruel had not expected the Republican attack to pose any major threat; but the appalling weather in mid-December had halted the advance of the supporting troops commanded by General Varela. It was this man Milton was planning to meet. Varela was a glamorous example of one of the many professional soldiers in Franco's army. He had served in the Foreign Legion in the twenties in Morocco, where he had earned his reputation for exceptional bravery.

Beside him, Cassy was pouring coffee from one of the Thermoses into a tin mug. She seemed reassured by his suggestion that a truck would come by before long. But Milton himself no longer believed in the possibility. The windscreen was now completely obliterated by snow and the light was fading fast.

'We'll take a chance and drive as far as we can,' he said suddenly as he drained the mug of coffee. 'Maybe there'll be a house further up the road where we can shelter.'

But although the engine started with surprising ease, a great deal of the water had drained from the radiator and, as he had forecast, they covered barely a mile before the engine seized.

Cassy looked crestfallen. 'I do wish you weren't always right!' she said. 'It's one of the most annoying things about you, Milton Fleming.'

'"*One of . . .*" infers there are many others,' he teased. 'You can always leave me if I irritate you to such an extent!'

Cassy threw her arms around his neck. 'Horrible as you are, even *you* wouldn't want to see me walk out in *that*!' She nodded towards the window and shivered, pressing herself closer against him. 'I'm scared, Milton. We could freeze to death if we stay here all night!'

The same thought had already occurred to him. His mouth tightened. 'We are *not* going to stay here,' he said firmly. 'We passed a farmhouse a hundred yards or so back. There just might be someone living there.'

'But we can't go out in *this*!' Cassy gasped.

'Yes, we can! We've got boots on. The walk will do us good – restore our circulations. Don't argue, Casilda! Wrap that quilt round you and take that full Thermos and the mugs. I'll carry the rug and the knapsack and the spare can of gasoline. Now get a move on, honey!'

He was anxious to find his way back to the farmhouse before nightfall. He sensed Cassy's reluctance to leave the comparative haven of the car, but knew her well enough by now to be able to rely on her complying with his commands. He had only to threaten to send her back to her father in Sevilla to put a speedy end to any objections she might have to his wishes. There had been one or two occasions when he had nearly done so. But the truth of the matter was that Cassy had surprised him by her extraordinary adaptability to conditions that were as foreign to her as a desert to an Eskimo. Accustomed as she had been all her life to luxury, she had frequently been obliged to doss down on beds without sheets; to eat army rations cooked under the most insanitary conditions in field kitchens; to go for days on end without a bath. Dirty, bitten by mosquitoes, her beautiful black hair unwashed, she had scrambled up and down rocky paths uncomplainingly. Nor had she shown the slightest fear when they had come under enemy fire. He had grown accustomed to having her around and, true to her word, she had frequently proved herself invaluable with her linguistic ability. He was genuinely fond of her and, albeit reluctantly, he respected her extraordinary courage.

Cassy now plodded along the road beside Milton like a small mountain bear, the huge padded quilt humped over her head. Each step was slow and laboured, the snow ankle-deep as they dragged their way through it. The wind tore at them, filling their eyes and mouths with snow and all but blinding them. Milton longed to help Cassy as she stumbled forward, but the knapsack and five-gallon jerry-can of petrol were like lead weights at the end of his arms. Each breath hurt, the icy cold contracting their throats as they drew great gasps of air into their lungs. It was impossible to see more than a yard ahead, and Milton feared they might perhaps fail to find either the farmhouse or their way back to the car.

After half an hour he could see that Cassy was weakening. He was on the point of abandoning the jerry-can in order to assist her when a dark shape loomed in front of him. His foot hit something hard and he fell forward over the stone step of a building. Forcing himself upright, and with Cassy now clinging to his arm, he stumbled forward into darkness. A gust of wind sent the wooden door slamming after them, momentarily cutting off the icy blast. Hurriedly Milton drew off his glove and fumbled in his pocket for a box of matches. The first failed to strike but the second flared, offering a glimmer of light.

'There's a torch in the front flap of the knapsack,' he said. 'I'll light another match, but hurry, I don't want to waste them.'

Cassy's fingers were so numb with cold that Milton had lit his fifth match before she could undo the buckle of the pocket flap. As the match burned out, her hand felt the ice-cold casing of the torch. She drew it out, pushed the switch and a white beam of light pierced the wall in front of them.

'God be praised, there's a fireplace,' Milton shouted, grabbing the torch. He swung the beam round the room. 'It's little more than a cowshed!' he commented, 'but it'll do. See if you can find something that will burn with which we can light a fire – paper, straw, anything.'

Cassy bent down and lifted a handful of filthy straw covering the earth floor. Her nose wrinkled. 'It smells disgusting!' she said. 'It's mostly dung, I think!'

Milton shone the torch on it and smiled. 'Goat droppings by the look of it, but it's just what we want, Casilda. Natives use dung cakes for fuel. See if there's any wood anywhere. I'll put some petrol on this muck. Christ, I'm cold!'

The room was little more than twelve feet square. At one end snow was drifting in through a small window aperture and piling up on a ledge beneath it. Cassy used her arm to sweep it away and gave a cry of pleasure. 'It's a table, Milton,' she said. 'And there's a broken stool underneath it.'

Milton struck another match and threw it onto the petrol-soaked straw he had heaped up in the fireplace. He held Cassy back as the spirit exploded. Breaking the legs of the stool over his knee, he threw them onto the now smouldering straw, and within minutes a small fire was burning.

'Switch off the torch,' he ordered. 'We'll conserve the battery. First we'll thaw out and then I'll explore. There must be more than this one room. Now give me your hands!'

He rubbed them gently between his own and then suddenly drew her against him. 'We're going to be okay, honey!' he said reassuringly. 'We've got warmth, food and shelter, and that's all we need for survival.'

The colour was coming back into Cassy's cheeks as the fire blazed. A gust of wind sent a balloon of smoke down the chimney into the room and, coughing, she buried her face against Milton's chest. 'If only it didn't smell so horrible!' she gasped.

Milton laughed. 'It's just straw and goat's urine!' he said. 'I'm going to fasten that door – it's letting in the draught – and we must find something to fill that window space. You stay here by the fire and I'll have a look around, okay? See if you can get that quilt and goatskin rug dry. We'll need them for bedding.'

Their greatest need, he thought as he made his way towards the doorway at the far end of the room, was firewood. If there had been troops here, he knew he would be unlikely to find any. His hopes lay in the fact that the hovel was too small to house more than a few men, although some soldiers had undoubtedly looted the place and taken anything of use or value. Shining his torch around him, he saw that he was standing in a byre that was little more than a lean-to against the back wall of the house. There was a gaping hole in the roof where a shell had landed and through which snow was now falling. But the shell, if such it had been, had brought down with the tiles the rafters which had supported them. A further survey revealed a broken ox yoke and hunched over it a filthy mattress, and three donkey panniers.

The mattress would serve to keep out the draughts which were whistling under the front door, he decided as he dragged it back to the room. The straw littering the earth floor of the byre could be stuffed into the pannier baskets and jammed into the window frame.

'I'll do it,' Cassy offered as he told her of his intention. 'I don't mind handling the horrible stuff if I can wash afterwards.'

'We'll melt some snow,' Milton grinned. 'At least we shan't be short of water! We can heat it over the fire in the tin mugs.'

An hour later they sat side by side on Cassy's quilt in front of the fire which they had fuelled with the broken ox yoke. Having washed their hands as best they could, they were now eating some of the food Milton had stored in the knapsack. He had melted more snow in the tin mugs to water down the coffee in the second Thermos.

'It's probably a pointless precaution,' he explained, 'but we can't be certain for how long we'll be marooned here, and it makes sense to keep some of our provisions in store. How are you feeling, honey? Better?'

Cassy sighed, leaning against his shoulder as she said sleepily: 'Much better, Milton. I'm even getting used to the smell. It's quite fun really, isn't it? Joss simply wouldn't believe her eyes if she could see us. I do so wish she was here!'

Milton took a strand of her hair and curled it absent-mindedly round his forefinger.

'Do you really? Why *should* you want her here?'

Cassy sighed as she stared into the flames. 'I don't know – to share the adventure, I suppose. Besides, I always feel safe when Joss is around – I don't know why.'

Milton frowned. 'You don't feel safe with me?' he asked stiffly.

Cassy turned and kissed him lightly on the mouth. 'But of course I feel safe with you, darling. Don't be so silly! You're a great, strong man. I didn't mean safe in *that* way. It's just that . . . I can't really explain it, Milton. Joss is my friend, my *best* friend, and she would do anything in the world for me. I've never told anybody this before, but she once gave up the man she loved for my sake.'

'And you let her?' Milton asked curiously.

Cassy nodded. 'Yes, I did. I suppose since I've made up my mind I'm never going back to Alan, there's no harm in telling you she's in love with him. I found out ages ago – when I had my car accident in Paris. I overheard Alan telling Joss he loved her and wanted her to agree to his asking me to divorce him. Joss kept saying that I needed him and she wouldn't take her happiness at the expense of mine, or something like that.'

'Go on, Casilda,' Milton prompted as she paused uncertainly.

Cassy took a deep breath. 'At first I was simply too astonished to do anything. It had never crossed my mind that Alan *loved* Joss. And I'd never *ever* imagined Joss loved Alan, although I suppose I should have guessed – she had always hero-worshipped him even as a little girl! Anyway, I thought that later on – when I was safely back in England – I'd talk to Joss, but she went straight to Spain with Patri and then Alan and I sort of settled down again.'

She glanced briefly at Milton's face and continued: 'When

Alan and I arrived in Sevilla last year, I knew by the way they looked at each other that they were still in love, but I was horribly afraid I was pregnant and I didn't want to be left on my own with a baby. I suppose you think I've been terribly selfish, don't you?'

'You don't need me to answer that, honey,' Milton said dryly. 'Your father spoiled you, both your husbands spoiled you, Joscelin spoiled you. I am the only person in your life not to give way to your every whim, and that's why you took a shine to me.'

'It wasn't!' Cassy flared. 'I hated you in the beginning and I still do sometimes. But I love you, too. I want to be with you. I don't care what we do or where we go so long as we're together. You don't believe that, do you?'

Milton's expression was unfathomable as he stared down at her flushed face. 'Perhaps I'm beginning to!' he said slowly. 'A girl like you would have to be out of her mind – or in love – to enjoy being in this dump! Yet you really seem passably happy. You're a strange character – not at all the butterfly I once thought you.'

Cassy grinned, running her fingers through his beard. 'I *am* happy – passably. I'd be happier if you'd make love to me. It would be fun, Milton, here on the floor in front of the fire. We won't be too cold. I won't let you be cold. Milton, *can* we?'

Milton regarded her with amusement. Of all the women he had ever known, he thought, Casilda was the only one who could have such carnal inclinations in so unlikely a venue! She was unquestionably a primitive – and as far as he was concerned, all the more desirable for being so. He felt his body harden as she pressed herself against him. A short while ago, when the chill had left the room, she had removed her fur coat. The skirt of her thick tweed suit had creased into a curve over her rounded buttocks; and as her arms tightened around his neck, he could feel the softness of her breasts straining against the pink angora sweater, outlining their fullness. Her thick black hair was tied back off her forehead, revealing a dark smudge of dirt that seemed to him endearingly childish. Yet the body he held in his arms was all woman.

His hands reached beneath her jersey and he released the fastening of her brassiere. He heard her little gasp of pleasure as his fingers felt for her large, taut nipples. Her black eyes widened and became luminous as he pressed his mouth against her parted lips.

'*Lo hacemos desnudos?*' Cassy asked in a low, husky voice. 'I like it best when we have no clothes on!'

'We'll freeze to death!' Milton muttered, but with sudden urgency he pulled the soft woollen garment over her head and drew her down onto the quilt. With clumsy haste he divested himself of his clothes, and throwing more wood onto the fire he helped Cassy remove her skirt and underwear.

'What are you laughing at?' Cassy asked as, naked, he stood staring down at her.

'Those frilly black panties! I swear to God you must be the only woman who'd wear such crazy garments in a blizzard in the middle of a war!'

'I don't see why I shouldn't look nice just because there's a war going on!' Cassy replied, her hand reaching up to caress his thigh. She smiled secretly. 'Besides, you always say you think I'm most attractive in black!'

'Because it makes you look like a French *poule de luxe*!' Milton replied, 'and it excites me.'

He lay down beside her, pulling her on top of him and watched her body moving rhythmically above him, her soft, golden skin rosy in the firelight. He felt a moment of wonderment at the urgency of his desire for her. He was damn nearly fifty – yet she made him feel like a boy on his first date, afraid he would not be able to control himself long enough to give her pleasure equal to his own.

It was perhaps as well their mutual release came swiftly, for the flames were dying down and both could feel icy draughts chilling their damp bodies as they lay breathing deeply in each other's arms.

'Get dressed, Casilda!' Milton said. 'Put your coat on, too. We'll keep the fire going all night, but the temperature is bound to drop.'

Cassy did as he told her. She knew only too well that, once satisfied, the passionate lover very quickly reverted to being the assertive, self-sufficient individual whose independence left no room for concessions or compromise, least of all where she was concerned. Milton had never once declared that he loved her. Yet he had never failed to respond to her unquenchable need for his lovemaking. It was as if familiarity, far from dulling their mutual delight in each other, had enhanced it tenfold.

When finally Milton had gathered a sufficient stack of wood to last them through the night, he curled himself against her back in front of the fire and pulled the goatskin rug over them.

As his hands cupped her breasts, she asked him for the hundredth time: 'Don't you love me just a little bit, Milton? *Un poco?*'

His usual reply would have been: 'For God's sake, honey, don't start that again . . .', given in an irritable, testy tone of voice precluding any repetition of the question. But now there was an edge of tenderness softening his words as he said drowsily: 'I guess I'm none too sure what love is, honey – the kind of love you're talking about. If I were less honest, I'd tell you I did love you. Then we'd both get some peace and much needed sleep! All I can say with truth is that I care one hell of a lot more about you than I could ever have imagined possible when we joined forces a year ago, and that I'm glad you're here!' She could feel his breath warm against her neck as he gave a wry laugh. 'Hell of a place to be marooned on your own. Let's hope the blizzard has blown itself out by morning and we can find our way back to civilization. Go to sleep now, Casilda. You're going to need all your strength tomorrow to trudge through the snow!'

But the blizzard had not blown itself out by the morning,

and as Milton viewed the white desolation outside and saw the drifts piled up by the wind he felt a shiver of apprehension. They had only a little food left in the knapsack. If they were holed up here for several days they were going to be very, very hungry; for a week and they would be starving. But a far greater danger was the cold. The fire had died down in the night and the temperature in the room was not much above freezing, despite the warmth still emanating from the embers. Moreover, the small stack of wood was seriously depleted, and from yesterday's search he knew there was not a great deal more to burn.

'Go look for an axe or chopper,' he told Cassy. 'There might be one on the floor of the byre. I'll see if I can dislodge more of those rafters.'

What remained of the roof of the lean-to looked perilously close to collapse beneath the additional weight of snow which had fallen in the night. Milton realized as he surveyed the timbers that he would be in danger of being buried alive if he dislodged any one of them. Yet he had to risk it – gambling on the odds where the alternative was certain death from the cold.

Cassy shouted joyfully that she had found what he wanted. 'But it's very rusty, Milton!'

'Go back in the room,' he told her sharply. 'And don't move until I give you the all-clear. There's a possibility the roof will cave in. I'm going to pull on that beam that's hanging down and then make a run for it. Take the hatchet with you.'

She did as he ordered, waiting anxiously after the crash for Milton's shout to tell her he was safe. He came into the room grinning, a flurry of snow preceding him. 'Whole bang shoot collapsed! I'll bring in as many rafters as I can before the snow covers them. God Almighty, it's cold!'

He banged his hands together, trying to restore feeling in his numbed fingers. The sooner they could shut the door against the elements, the quicker they could get some heat back into the room.

His eyebrows, beard and moustache were heavily frosted by the time he had dragged in the last rafter. He was shivering violently and was unable to hold the tin mug of hot water Cassy had heated for him. Shocked by the blueness of his face, she removed the quilt from her own shoulders and wrapped it round him. With a look of grim determination on her face, she picked up the hatchet and tried ineffectually to chip at one of the rafters.

For a moment, Milton watched her impatiently and then he took the axe from her. 'The exercise will help restore my circulation,' he said gruffly.

He worked steadily, groaning at the ache in his fingers as the blood started to course through his veins once more. The rusty axe was blunt and the task arduous; but slowly the pile of wood chips grew, and within the hour the fire was burning brightly again.

Exhausted, Milton collapsed in front of it. 'Hell of a way to spend New Year's Day!' he said. 'January 1st, 1938, Casilda. Must be the first start to a New Year I haven't woken with a hangover!'

Cassy snuggled up beside him. 'Can we have something to eat now, Milton?' she asked as hunger pains gnawed at her stomach.

He shook his head. 'Better wait a bit, honey. We don't know how much longer we're going to be cooped up here. We *must* keep some food in reserve, okay?'

She nodded, the first real feelings of fear seeping into her.

He, too, was trying to hide his growing misgivings. Outside, the snowdrifts were piling up as the thick flakes continued to fall with relentless persistence.

'Anyone would think we were in Alaska!' he remarked to Cassy as they huddled by the fire. 'Until I experienced my first winter in this crazy country of yours, I'd always imagined it to be a land of perpetual sunshine.'

'It won't go on snowing much longer,' Cassy proffered optimistically.

But it did. For four days and nights the blizzard raged.

Hunger and cold undermined her determination not to let Milton see how miserable she was. Their limited supply of food had almost run out; and she knew that if they could not soon get out of their self-appointed prison, they would be too weak to do so even if the weather cleared.

She awoke on the morning of their fifth day of incarceration with a strangely euphoric feeling of lethargy. Vaguely she remembered Milton's warning that they might die if they did not keep themselves active during the day. It was all too easy, he said, to give way to the natural desire to curl up and go to sleep; but that was to invite hypothermia and certain death. But today, she decided, he would not be able to bully her into getting up. She would stay here in the pathetically inadequate warmth of the quilt, no matter how angry he became.

During the night, Milton had used the last of the firewood; the temperature in the room had fallen and was now no higher than that outside. Sleepily, Cassy turned to look at him, and suddenly her eyes opened wide. His hair, beard and eyebrows had turned white in the night! So, too, had the goatskin rug covering them both.

Her eyes searched the room. Everything in it was a bright, sparkling white.

'Milton!' she gasped, shaking him with as much force as she could muster. 'Milton, wake up. Please wake up . . .'

She flung back the coverings and she knew that she was not dreaming. Everything in the room, including the two of them, was coated in frost. And through a gap in the straw-filled panniers which days ago she had stuffed into the aperture of the window, she could see the bright gleam of sunlight.

Milton sat up and stared at Cassy in disbelief. Her hair and eyebrows were frosted like his own.

'It's stopped snowing!' she said. 'The sun is shining . . .'

Struggling to her feet, she plodded in her heavy boots across the white floor and pulled at the straw in the window frame. As the panniers came away, she was bathed in a bright, golden light.

Milton grinned as he went over to stand beside her. The carpet of snow blanketing the landscape was sparkling brilliantly, the sun glancing off the frosted surface of the drifts. The sky was azure blue and sunlight transformed the countryside.

Cassy threw herself into his arms, her eyes filled with tears of relief. 'Isn't it wonderful? We can leave now, can't we, Milton? We're not going to die here after all.' She turned to glance over his shoulder. 'Milton, look!' she gasped.

The empty Thermos stood in the centre of the room like a small white statue. The axe, too, looked as if it was made of white marble. The empty knapsack had been transformed into a hump-backed marble turtle. The room appeared to have been dusted with icing sugar.

Touched by her childish delight, Milton drew her attention to the view from the window. The ghostly remnants of an olive tree held out angular white arms with icicles hanging like long, pointed fingernails from the twisted branches.

Cassy clapped her gloved hands, her face radiant. 'It reminds me of one of Joss's favourite poems – something to do with "ice in the moonlight, frost in the sun . . ." Have you ever seen anything prettier, Milton?' she cried breathlessly.

Now fully awake, Milton understood what had brought about the transformation. The fire had finally died out in the night, and for the first time since they had arrived the temperature had dropped to below freezing. He realized that this must have occurred only shortly before dawn, or they would have frozen to death whilst they slept. Now he, like Cassy, was shivering and his arms felt numb as he tried to bang them against his sides to restore their circulation. Slowly his brain started to assess the new difficulties facing them. To get to the road they would have to plough their way through snow now several feet deep. He was not sure if he, let alone Cassy, had the strength to do so. But somehow he felt incapable of explaining this to her; unwilling to wipe the look of joy from her face.

His concern for her astonished him, for it was like an ache in his throat. She had been so remarkably brave and uncomplaining – this extraordinary, aristocratic Spanish girl whose only reason for being here was that she loved him. He felt strangely humbled, and for the first time he doubted that he had ever been justified in treating her devotion with such casual indifference. In so many ways, he thought, he had misjudged her, underrated her.

Impulsively, he said: 'When we get out of here, Casilda, maybe we'll get down to thinking about our future. I'll have to stick around until the war is over, but afterwards . . .'

Cassy's face was thin and drawn. Her skin was sallow, bereft now of its honey-golden sheen. She looked nearer forty-three than thirty-three, her figure shapeless beneath the bear-like rug. It was possible for the first time to imagine how she would look when she was old. But her eyes sparkled as she stared at him.

'You mean you might take me back to Texas with you after all?' she whispered huskily.

He nodded. 'I'm probably raving mad even to consider it,' he said gruffly. 'But I suppose if we can survive this dump without getting too much on each other's nerves, we ought to be able to cope in a civilized environment. We'll see, honey. I'm not making any promises.'

But for once his tone lacked its customary indifference. It even held an underlying note of tenderness as he added: 'Don't stand there doing nothing. Pass me the hatchet! My hands are numb and I'll need to prise the door open. I'll bet that's bloody well frozen, too!'

Speechless with happiness, Cassy handed Milton the axe and stood back whilst he swung it at the door. It fell outwards and sunlight streamed into the room. Milton held up his hand to shield his eyes from the glare.

'There's something moving over there by the road, Casilda, can you see? And that dark shape – I'm pretty certain it's a truck!' His voice quickened with excitement. 'Some soldiers have found the Buick and guessed we'd be sheltering here. Looks like we're being rescued . . .' He broke off and, shouting as loudly as he could, began frantically to wave.

Cassy stared at the tiny black dots some five hundred metres distant. She saw something bright glinting in the sun and then, unexpectedly, Milton knelt down at her feet. The fraction of a second later she heard a sharp 'crack' and, puzzled, she turned to stare down at Milton. A bright, scarlet pool was forming in the snow where now he lay slumped in a foetal position, his eyes staring at her with a look of intense surprise. He was gasping for breath, his hands clutched over his chest. It was only at that moment Cassy realized he had been shot.

'No!' she screamed, the word echoing in her head as she bent over him. 'Milton, *Milton!*'

He was staring past her in the direction of their 'rescuers'. Her eyes followed his. Republicans? Nationalists? It made no difference – they had shot Milton. They were coming closer and might shoot again.

'No!' she screamed. 'Don't shoot! Don't shoot!'

She felt no fear, only anger as she straightened up and started to stumble through the knee-deep snow. Waving her arms, she shouted in Spanish: '*Es americano! No tiene arma! Es un periodista americano!*'

The soldiers were coming towards her, crouching low. She saw them stop suddenly to aim their guns. How stupid! she thought. Only ignorant fools would shoot before finding out if their target was friend or enemy. The deep snow was impeding her progress, yet she knew that somehow she must stop them before they killed Milton. She shouted, again explaining that Milton was an unarmed American journalist and not their enemy . . . Thank God she could speak their language, she thought, her whole being flooded with relief as she realized that one of them must have heard her and understood. He had lifted his arm and was waving back to her . . .

'*Gracias a Dios!*' she murmured, smiling as the bullet hit

her in the temple, and she fell forward into the soft carpet of snow.

She died instantly, unaware that Milton's life had already ebbed away and that she would not now go to Texas with him after all.

CHAPTER THIRTY-THREE

August 1938

Alan ran his tongue over his parched lips and closed his eyes against the searing heat of the sun, trying to imagine the feel of rain on his burning skin.

All around him his men were lying in crouched positions behind the piles of rocks they had built as their only means of protection from the shelling of the Nationalist guns.

Two thousand feet up into the Sierra Pandols, there were only a few trees beneath which the exhausted XVth Brigade could shelter, and desperately needed water was a good two kilometres away from Alan's company's position. Thirst was their prime concern, and had been for weeks past. The provisioning of the British battalion from headquarters had become immensely difficult and dangerous. Men and mules were under constant attack as they struggled up the goat trail. When the German and Italian aeroplanes circled overhead, the supply columns had only scrubland and the occasional black slate rock beneath which to shelter. Food was as scarce as water and tobacco had long since ceased to be obtainable.

There were moments when the heat, thirst, hunger and the sheer futility of the fighting caused Alan to doubt his own sanity in remaining a part of it. The appalling stench of dead men, their bodies rotting where they lay, was an all too gruesome reminder of the probable death awaiting him in these Spanish hills. But at least the dead were not suffering, and the plight of the wounded concerned him far more deeply. Ambulances could not reach them, and their only hope of survival was to be carried down the mountainside at night. Two of his own company were lying now in the inadequate shade of a withered olive tree, crying endlessly for water.

There was nothing he could do until darkness fell. His water bottle was empty, as were those of every man in the company. When night fell, he would go to fetch water.

The journey would be dangerous, Alan knew. The moon was bright enough to turn the darkness almost to daylight, and he risked being seen by Fascist patrols or snipers. There was the risk, too, of getting lost on this rugged, bleak hillside. The rocks were jagged and Alan's boots were in tatters. Every Spaniard in his company had volunteered to join him. He knew that they trusted him implicitly, with a faith in his invulnerability which was totally unjustified. Because he had survived so long when so many hundreds of the British battalion had been killed, wounded or taken prisoner, he had become a kind of legend, and their faith in his leadership was an added responsibility – the more so since there was so little he could do for their welfare. Their uncomplaining good spirits and their comradeship had endeared the Spanish soldiers to him in a way he would never have thought possible. He was not just their commanding officer, but their friend. The British soldiers, too, were brave and resourceful but tended to with-hold the familiarity of true friendship. They recognized that he was not really one of them and was not a dedicated member of the Communist party as they all were, although the long months of fighting side by side allowed their respect for him to broaden into a genuine comradeship.

Whilst the long, blazing hot afternoon wore on, they were under continuous attack from the air. Four men were killed, two others hit and one of the wounded died. Powerless to move, the company lay mercilessly exposed, sweltering in the intolerable heat in their khaki trousers and open-necked shirts. One or two had tin hats in place of berets or peaked caps, but despite the dangers of the bombardment these were too hot to be kept on, and the men covered their heads only as they saw a stick of bombs falling towards them or heard the scream of an approaching shell.

By nightfall, one of the soldiers who had volunteered to accompany Alan to the riverbed had been killed. Another offered to go in his place, but Alan decided he would go alone. The decision to make the trip himself was based on his belief that he was the man who could best be spared. Two days earlier he had been hit in his left shoulder by a rock thrown up when a shell had burst nearby. The scarred area of his old wound had not hurt too seriously at the time; but now the whole shoulder was black and stiff from the bruising and he was almost incapable of holding his rifle against it. The battalion was hopelessly below strength, and every bit of fire-power would count if they were attacked or ordered forward. Moreover, he knew he was not indispensable as their senior officer. His sergeant, a burly Glaswegian who had been with him since the start of the fighting in July, was more than capable of deputizing for him if he did not return.

'Good luck,' the fellow said, grinning, when, as darkness fell, Alan gathered up the empty water containers in readiness for his departure. He glanced up at the huge full moon and added pointedly: 'You'll aye be needing it, I fear!'

Warmed by the accent, which reminded Alan of home, he patted the man's shoulder. 'Don't worry Dalgleish. Just make certain none of our chaps take pot-shots at me when I'm trying to get back past the sentries.'

For most of the time that he was scrambling down the increasingly steep face of the ravine, the night air was cool and sweet-smelling. But occasionally Alan's nostrils were filled with the nauseous odour of a rotting corpse. For either side to bury their dead was almost an impossibility in this rocky terrain. He tried to ignore the pain in his shoulder on the occasions he lost his footing and fell. He kept his mind on the thought of the water he was hoping to find, and on the wounded men whose lives might depend on the precious liquid he would bring them. Dehydration was proving as fatal in the summer as frostbite had proved last winter – a mutual enemy they shared with the Nationalist troops.

It was a strange kind of war, he thought, where today one's enemy could be yesterday's ally. But for Patri's warnings, he would have returned to the POUM after saying goodbye to Joscelin and might now be dead, or lost in some nameless prison camp along with so many of his former comrades-in-arms. In May, the POUM militia had left the front lines after months of bitter, desperate fighting against the Fascists only to discover themselves branded by the Communists in the government as traitors and enemies to the cause for which they had fought with such willingness and bravery. Patri's machinations with the hospital administrator in Tarragona had resulted in their being enrolled in the International Brigade. Patri had been sent to join the XIIIth Brigade, not the XXth as he had hoped; and Alan himself was attached to the British battalion of the XVth. He had learned of Patri's commission when he had reported to headquarters of the brigades in Albacete, but he had not run into his cousin since.

Suddenly Alan saw a flash, then another from one of the rocks to his left. He threw himself to the ground. For several minutes he lay motionless, knowing the wisdom of playing possum. The strategy succeeded, for suddenly a dark shape appeared from behind the rock and started to move cautiously towards him. Alan was still holding his revolver, and as soon as he was certain that the man was within range he fired. The soldier keeled over like a log and lay still.

A small cloud scurried across the moon, and for a moment Alan could no longer see the body of his enemy. Then the cloud passed and his eye was caught by a glint of silver a few hundred yards below him. He drew a deep sigh of relief – this must be the river.

It was still the best part of an hour before Alan reached the water's edge. Warning himself not to drink too deeply or too hurriedly, he thrust his face into the slow-running stream and took a long draught. It was sluggish, and not far from stagnant, but he didn't care. Nothing had ever tasted so good. He splashed it over his arms, his neck, soaking his shirt and his chest. He was contemplating removing his clothes and bathing when he heard a rock splash into the water a little way upstream.

His heart pounding, Alan inched his way back behind a big stone boulder, his eyes straining towards the riverbank upstream.

The moon had lost none of its brilliance and now Alan could see perfectly clearly, not twenty yards distant, the uniformed figure of a Nationalist army officer. He was bareheaded, his peaked cap tucked into his Sam Browne; but the long boots, the breeches, the battledress-type jacket left no doubt as to the side he fought on.

Alan lay perfectly still. His target could not be missed, and if he fired the man would die; but other Fascist soldiers might be nearby and the sound of his revolver would alert them. He could find himself surrounded.

The officer was stooping, and now Alan could see that he was filling a water bottle. They were like two species of African big game, Alan thought irrelevantly, hunter and hunted sharing the same waterhole in a drought, their enmity momentarily suspended.

But no other soldiers came to join the lone figure, and Alan knew what he must do. He would take the man prisoner and force him at gunpoint to assist with the water-carrying.

Holding his revolver ready, he stood up and said in Spanish: '*Manos arriba!*'

The metal water bottle splashed into the water as the man raised his hands. Cautiously Alan approached. Like himself, the fellow was bearded, but olive-skinned and swarthy.

'Don't shoot me . . . *please don't shoot me . . .*' The voice had an edge of panic in it.

'I've no intention of killing you,' Alan replied in the same language. 'Are you alone? Don't lie or I *will* shoot you.'

To his surprise, the tense expression on the young officer's face had given way to one of total astonishment. He was holding out his hand. '*Dios mío!* I can't believe it! You're Cousin Alan, aren't you? I thought I knew you from somewhere, but of all places in the world to meet you . . . I can't believe it!'

Alan kept his gun levelled at the man's head as he studied him more closely. Suddenly, recognition came. This young officer was Cassy's brother, Mariano, the younger of the two boys. It must be at least nine or ten years since he'd last seen him . . . at Patri's wedding.

Slowly, he lowered his revolver. 'It's a good thing you recognized me, as I doubt if I'd have known you, Mariano,' he said wryly. 'Forgive me for being mistrustful, but have I your word you won't try to shoot me or run off? We may be cousins but we're enemies right now . . . and you're my prisoner.'

'*Por Dios*, Alan, I'm not running anywhere . . . and you mustn't kill me. *I've got to get back to Luis* . . .'

There was an edge of hysteria in Mariano's voice as he grasped Alan's arm and said urgently: 'Luis has been terribly badly wounded. It happened three days ago. I dragged him into a cave out of the sun, hoping I could get help . . .' His voice broke. 'Now I'm afraid it's too late. I think he's dying. I came down to get water. It's impossible in the daytime, because your snipers shoot at anything that moves.'

Alan was silent as he tried to make his tired brain appreciate the implications of Mariano's statement. He had a long way to go before this night ended, but with Mariano to help him he would get water back to his own wounded before daylight. Should he let his cousin take water back to the unfortunate Luis or should he put the welfare of his own men first?

Shocked, he saw tears streaming down Mariano's face.

'You don't understand . . . Luis is in terrible pain. He keeps begging me to shoot him but I can't . . . I want to for his sake . . . *but I can't*. He's my brother and I love him. Oh God, help me! You don't know what it's like, Alan . . . the side of his face . . . and his leg . . .' He covered his eyes with his hands and groaned.

'How far away is the cave?' Alan asked.

Mariano's hands dropped and he stared at Alan with dawning hope. 'You'll come and see him? Maybe you'll know what to do. I can't bear to hear him any longer. For the love of God, Alan, please help me!'

'*How far is the cave?*' Alan asked again firmly, knowing that Mariano was near to breaking point.

'Over there – just a little way up the hill . . . by that big rock.'

It crossed Alan's mind that Mariano might be setting a trap for him; that there could be Fascist soldiers in the cave as well as Luis; that Mariano's story was a pack of lies.

But he rejected the thoughts. His young cousin would have to be an exceptionally good actor to simulate the tears, the desperation in his voice.

'Fill that water bottle and we'll have a look at Luis,' he said, his voice as calm as he could make it. 'Maybe he's not as bad as you think.'

His cousin had not been misleading him as to the nearness of the cave. Within five minutes, Alan could hear the chilling sound of the wounded man's groans.

Mariano scrambled ahead, and as Alan entered the cave he heard his voice, gentle, like a woman's soothing a child, as he said: 'It's all right now, Luis. I've got water for you . . . and Cousin Alan is here to help us. You remember our cousin from England? He's going to help us.'

But Alan had stopped listening, his senses appalled by what he could not only see but smell. One side of Luis's face was little more than a dark red pulp. His nose had disappeared and part of his jaw. He was staring at Mariano in an agonized appeal. Alan felt his guts tighten in horror and pity. But worse even than the sight of that mutilated face was the shock of the injured leg. A swarm of disgusting black flies circled the wound, which had turned gangrenous. Despite Mariano's attempts to bandage it with strips from his shirt, pus oozed through the material. The stench was unbelievably awful and it was all Alan could do to kneel down beside Luis.

As he murmured words of reassurance, he knew without a shadow of a doubt that Luis was dying. He understood now why Mariano had said he should shoot his brother. He himself would not have the slightest hesitation in shooting an animal in such a condition. But the man lying here was a human being . . . Mariano's brother . . . *his* cousin . . .

'What are we going to do?'

Mariano's whispered voice at his ear forced him to make a decision for them both, but his brain seemed unwilling to function. He could not remember when he had last slept or eaten a proper meal, and although the water he had drunk half an hour ago had temporarily revived him, the dehydration of his body seemed to have slowed down all his faculties.

Mariano was leaning over his brother, dripping water into Luis's blood-encrusted mouth from a piece of cloth torn from his shirt. Each time Luis swallowed, he cried out with the pain that even this slight movement caused him. Tears were coursing down Mariano's face as he looked up at Alan in appeal.

'All yesterday, he was begging me to shoot him,' he whispered. 'But I can't, Alan, I can't . . . he's my brother . . .'

Gently, Alan drew his cousin to his feet and led him out of the cave. 'We can't save Luis's life,' he said quietly. 'You know that, don't you?'

Mariano nodded.

'You've got to trust me,' Alan went on. 'I know we're enemies – officially – but I'm giving you my word that the decisions I shall now make will be as fair a compromise as possible in the circumstances. Do you understand what I'm saying?'

Mariano nodded again.

'I want you to go down to the stream, find the water containers I left there and fill them,' Alan said authoritatively. 'Then you must help me carry them back up the hill as far as I consider it safe for you to be. Afterwards you must find your way back to your own lines as best you can.'

Mariano's eyes narrowed and his mouth tightened. 'You want me to abandon Luis?' he asked furiously. 'I will not do it!'

'Listen to me, Mariano,' Alan broke in sharply. '*I* will take care of Luis. Do you understand what I'm saying? There is nothing more *you* can do for him. Luis cannot live much longer, and there is absolutely no way he could survive a journey to hospital even if we could carry him between us. You know what I am saying is the truth. We have no morphine, no drugs to ease his pain. We cannot allow him to go on suffering.'

For one long moment Mariano stared at Alan silently, a look of unbearable anguish on his face. Then he took a step towards the cave and in a voice barely above a whisper, said: 'I will do as you say, but first I must say goodbye to my brother.'

Alan grasped Mariano's arm. 'No! Luis must not know what is to happen. From your face and from the tone of your voice he will guess that it is a final parting – and he will know. I will tell him you have gone to fetch more water. Go now, Mariano. It's best if you go quickly.'

The protest died on Mariano's lips as Luis's pitiful voice reached them.

'*Señor, ten compasión de mí. Santa María, ruega por mí.*'

The words were just distinguishable despite the terrible injuries to his face and jaw, and Alan's fist clenched as his resolve hardened.

'Go now, Mariano! *Now!*' he commanded. 'Take your rifle and your water bottle. You'll need them.'

It did not cross Alan's mind that, armed once more with rifle and ammunition, Mariano might shoot him. He thought only of what must be done. He waited until he could no longer hear the fall of loose rocks dislodged by Mariano's feet as he disappeared down the side of the escarpment; then he re-entered the cave. There was only a faint glimmer of light from the candle stub on the ledge above the wounded man, but it was enough for Alan to see once more that torn face with its gaping nostrils and desecrated flesh; his stomach heaved at the horrifying smell emanating from the gangrenous leg wound.

Alan curbed his revulsion and knelt down at Luis's side.

'I'm going to stop the pain,' he said gently. 'You'll be able to sleep now, Luis. Mariano has gone to fetch more water and he asked me to tell you that he loves you very much. Close your eyes now – I'm going to help you to sleep.'

He knew that Luis had understood. His body, which had been rigid and tense with pain, slowly relaxed and his eyes closed.

Standing up, Alan moved back two or three feet and, as silently as he could, he drew his revolver from its holster. Taking careful aim at a point between Luis's eyes, he fired. There was a deafening reverberation as the sound of the shot echoed round the walls of the cave.

Alan looked down at his hands. They were shaking uncontrollably, and suddenly he was violently sick. With so little food inside him his retching was painful and afforded him no relief. Reluctantly, he forced himself to look at Luis. He knew he could hardly have missed at such a short range, but he had to be sure. He lifted one lifeless hand and felt for the pulse in the wrist. There was no movement – Luis was dead and could suffer no more pain.

He had no feeling of guilt as he murmured a quick prayer, but the sight of Luis's body was unnerving him. He hurried out of the cave, conscious as he did so that he had lost a great deal of valuable time. Even with Mariano's help, it would be dawn before he reached his company – and Mariano could not return safely to his lines in daylight.

He found his cousin sitting forlornly on the riverbank. As Alan approached, he said despairingly: 'I heard the shot, Alan! I have been praying for Luis's soul. There was no one to give him Absolution. He cannot go to Heaven . . .'

As his voice broke, Alan said sharply: 'It is only the Catholic religion which threatens such unjust punishment, Mariano. Your brother was a good man and I don't believe even a Catholic God would deny him an eternal resting place simply because he died before he could be absolved.' He patted Mariano's shoulder and drew him to his feet. 'Come now, old chap, you must pull yourself together. Luis is at peace, and we must go.'

Mariano hesitated only a moment before saying quietly: 'It had to be done, but I had not the courage. Thank you, Cousin Alan . . . and may God forgive us both, for we have committed a mortal sin.'

There was no opportunity for further discussion as both men struggled with their loads up the steep sides of the ravine. Panting and weary to the point of exhaustion, they scrambled upwards, Alan hoping that he was following the right trail. He was nearly asleep on his feet when he heard the sound of voices and knew that they had come near to one of the sentry posts.

Mariano, too, had heard the voices and crouched behind his cousin as Alan turned to whisper: 'This is as far as you're going. I should have sent you back before, but I wasn't thinking straight.' To his right, he could see the rocky summit of the hill where the Nationalists held their position. It was now tipped with a pink glow. 'Get moving!' he ordered with a growing sense of urgency. 'I'll try to cover you as best I can. Good luck, Mariano, and thanks for your help!'

He held out his hand, but without embarrassment Mariano put his arms around him and kissed him on both cheeks.

'It is I who must thank you, Cousin Alan – for Luis, and for my life. *Dios te guarde!*'

'God be with you, too!' Alan whispered back. They smiled at one another as if they were truly comrades in arms, and then Mariano turned and ran as swiftly as he could back down the trail.

Alan picked up his rifle and slipped off the safety catch.

He was aware now of the excruciating ache in his shoulder, aggravated doubtless by the weight of the water containers he had been carrying. Momentarily, Mariano disappeared from view, but a minute or two later he picked up his shadowy figure halfway down to the stream. His cousin was making what use he could of the shelter of the craggy rocks, his progress jerky as he moved from one place of concealment to another. But he was visible to anyone with a keen eye, Alan thought anxiously, praying that his sentries – who must be nearing the end of their night watch – were for once not as vigilant as they should be.

Lack of sleep played havoc with one's vision, he thought as he rubbed his sore eyes and tried once more to pick out Mariano's figure. It was important that he kept his eye on the surrounding hillsides. If a sniper took a pot-shot at Mariano, he must note exactly the man's position and pick him off before he could shoot a second time.

Alan's body grew steadily more tense as he saw Mariano reach the stream. When he had set off – God knows how many hours ago – the stream and gully had been invisible in the darkness, and the fact that he could now see it added to his anxiety. The sun was creeping above the horizon and, although the valley was still in shadow, the top of the Nationalist-held hillside was bathed in early morning light.

With a feeling of dismay, Alan realised Mariano could all too easily be mistaken for a Republican soldier making a crazy single-handed attack.

With an effort, Alan steadied his arm. His nerves were close to breaking point and he could feel the sweat on his body chill in the cool morning air.

From above he could hear the far-from-silent changeover of the sentries. Had they no idea how clearly their voices travelled, or were they like himself, too exhausted even to register the basic need for caution? When men had been kept too long in the lines one could not expect them to retain their normal faculties at peak level. Most of them were incapable of thinking of anything but water, food and sleep, and their survival depended upon their animal instincts for self-preservation.

With an angry thud of his heart, Alan realized that his attention had wandered, and that once again he had lost sight of Mariano. He tried to estimate his rate of climb up the opposite hill. Or was he still quite far down in the shadows? he asked himself with increasing uncertainty.

Far away in the distance, he could hear the whine of an aeroplane and then the crackle of anti-aircraft fire. The new day and its customary battles had begun. Hundreds more men would die – men in his company and young Nationalist soldiers like Mariano and Luis, who believed with as much fervour as the Republicans that *their* cause was the right one. Maybe he himself would die – and but for Joscelin, he would not mind too much going to an eternal sleep . . . His head nodded forward and his arm dropped to his side.

The sound of a single gunshot jolted him back to consciousness. Feverishly his eyes scanned the hillside, and a moment later he picked out Mariano's figure. He was crouching low, in full sunlight now as he slipped and scrambled up the rocky hillface. A second shot rang out, but Alan could not see where it came from. Now he saw Mariano on the ground, a small, still heap, unmoving.

'Dear God, don't let him be dead!' The words caught in Alan's throat as he waited and watched. Had the tiny figure moved, or were his eyes playing tricks? No, it had moved. The boy was still alive. But the barrel of his rifle was glinting in the sun – that evil, cruel, revealing sun – and whoever had shot him had an easy target.

'Is that you, sir?' The voice was that of Sergeant Dalgleish. A moment later Alan saw the man's rifle pointing at him, and above it Dalgleish's rugged face.

'You damned fool!' Alan gasped. 'I might have shot you!'

The man lowered his rifle and grinned. 'I'd have shot *you* long before you saw me, sir,' he said. 'When I heard someone move down below, I guessed it was you. I'd reckoned on you being back about now, and I was afeared one of those idiot militiamen might be trigger-happy.' He paused as he saw Alan standing, unmoving, his eyes on the distant hillside.

'Seen something, sir? Enemy patrol?'

Alan did not reply, for on the very point at which he had given up hope of Mariano's survival he had seen the figure stir. He was moving, albeit slowly . . . upwards . . . disappearing momentarily behind a rock . . . reappearing.

Alan turned to follow Dalgleish back to their positions. He felt sick at heart. Men's hatred of their enemy was fed by every death, every brutality. Dalgleish was a decent fellow who had volunteered to fight for his political beliefs. Doubtless he would grunt with satisfaction if he, Alan, told him he had shot a Fascist officer in a cave by the river. But he would not tell him. What he had done was a horror about which he knew he could never bring himself to speak.

CHAPTER THIRTY-FOUR

September–December 1938

'*Virgen Santa!* What have they done to you, Alan? I hardly recognized you!'

Patri's voice barely masked his fear that this newest arrival at the San Pedro concentration camp was in a bad condition. There was very little light or ventilation in the long room where the prisoners lay on the floor shoulder to shoulder, many of them wounded. Somehow, space had been made for Alan.

With an effort, Alan managed a parody of a smile. 'Nothing serious!' he muttered through lips that were swollen almost out of recognition. 'Beaten up by a guard on the way here . . .'

Patri's gaze travelled quickly over Alan's emaciated body. He was in rags, filthy and alarmingly thin.

'Good to see you anyway, old chap,' he said attempting to hide his anxiety, 'albeit not in this hellhole. When did they capture you?'

'During their counter-attack by the Ebro . . . silly, really . . . I'd got dysentery. When my company was ordered to move off, I was too weak to walk and knew I'd be a hindrance. I was in pretty bad shape and one of the lads stayed with me – saved my life, as a matter of fact. He kept me supplied with water and food of sorts. We were holed up for about three days, and I was just recovering enough strength to move when a forward patrol marched up and took us prisoner. The Italian officer in charge was a decent fellow and detailed a couple of his chaps to carry me down to one of their field hospitals.'

'Glad to hear there *are* some decent *fascistas*!' Patri said drily. 'I got picked up by some bastards at Calaceite in the spring last year and I can tell you, Alan, they all rank as sadists as far as I'm concerned.'

'Last year!' Alan echoed. 'You've been a prisoner all this time?'

Patri nodded. 'It sometimes seems like a lifetime!' he admitted wryly. 'There are six hundred or so of us International Brigaders here. It used to be a convent. Apart from us, it's crammed to the brim with Spanish prisoners – literally thousands of them, poor devils. But we're the ones they're trying to break. They go mad because a lot of us refuse to give the Fascist salute. Some of the chaps can't face the beatings. But we do what we can to keep up morale. Look here, Alan, are you sure you're all right? You look worse than when I saw you in the hospital in Lérida.'

'I'll be fine, Patri. I could do with a drink and a wash, but I don't suppose that's possible.'

Patri grinned. 'This isn't the Savoy, old chap. You might as well know the worst – there are three taps to supply the water for drinking and washing for *all* of us, and each prisoner gets five minutes' access a day – hence the none-too-pleasant odour I don't doubt you've noticed! The lavatories – if you can call them that – are in equally short supply and usually blocked, and the daily à la carte will offer you beans and bread, or bread and beans, depending on your epicurean palate. It must be sufficient to live on since I am still alive and so, too, are the various parasites who have selected me for their host. We've the usual plague of lice; most of us have got or have had dysentery, and you'll be hard put to find a man without at least one skin disease.'

He broke off, realizing that Alan's attention had wandered and that his eyes were searching the room.

'Someone you know here?' he asked.

The frown on Alan's face deepened. 'It's the lad who saved my life I'm looking for – chap called Samuel Cohen. He's half Jewish, and one of the prisoners awaiting interrogation with us told us there were German intelligence officers as well as Spanish and Italian, and advised Sam to keep his origins to himself. But he's only eighteen and not all that bright, and I'm worried about him . . .'

His anxiety was more than the concern of any officer for one of his raw young soldiers; more even than a sense of obligation to the man who had forgone his own chance of freedom to save Alan's life. Alan himself was only half aware of it, but Sam bore a strong resemblance to Luis.

It was less than a month since Alan had put an end to Luis's suffering, and during the delirium that had accompanied the worst of his attack of dysentery he had relived the horror a dozen times. In rational moments he had no regret for what he had done, nor would he have chosen to do any differently had he to face the decision a second time. But he could not forget the incident, and the face of the young Jewish boy was a frequent reminder, often becoming confused in his delirium with that of Luis himself.

Since their capture he had felt no fear for himself but had become obsessive about saving Sam's life. The eighteen-year-old had been in Spain only three months when he was sent to Alan's company as a replacement. A week later they were taken prisoner, and Alan was unhappily aware that the youth had had no time to become hardened to army life, still less to the brutalities of this particular war.

'Stay where you are and rest,' Patri broke in on his thoughts. 'I'll make a few inquiries. Someone on the committee will know if your chap is in one of the other rooms.'

Patri had not the heart to tell Alan about the Gestapo officers who, dressed in civilian clothes to hide their true identity, drove to the prison in a large Mercedes to interrogate the Jewish prisoners. Patri knew for a fact that those German Jewish prisoners who would not sign a paper saying they wished to return to the Fatherland were brutally tortured. All the Germans tried to escape. A great many had disappeared in a so-called prison 'hospital', and Patri had lined up with the other prisoners on far too many occasions to watch the coffins being taken from the 'hospital' to the burial ground. They were not the only victims – but certain ones. The camp doctor did nothing to relieve the suffering of those who had been beaten, or indeed of anyone ill enough to report sick. A large dose of castor oil was his remedy, even for the wounded.

In the few days Patri remained at San Pedro, Alan's physical condition improved fractionally although he was still very weak. But Patri became increasingly concerned about Alan's mental state.

In June, a hundred British prisoners had left San Pedro for Palencia where they were awaiting release following their exchange with Italian regular soldiers who had been captured by the Republic. Unknown to Patri, Don Jaime had been making tireless efforts for the past year to get his son released. When he had heard about the proposed exchange of prisoners he had redoubled his efforts, and after secret negotiations with an influential industrialist in Sevilla for whom he could do a considerable favour, he had finally secured Patri's freedom. A fortnight after Alan's arrival, the prison camp commander told Patri he was to be sent directly to San Sebastián. There he would join the hundred British prisoners who had been moved yet again, pending confirmation of the release of the Italians. He would travel with them over the International Bridge into France and from there to England.

Alan received the news with genuine pleasure. 'I'll miss you, of course, but I'm damned glad for you,' he said, 'and there are several things you can do for me in England, old chap. If I can get hold of some paper, I want to write to Joscelin . . .' He confessed that he was in love with her and intended to ask Cassy for a divorce.

'I more or less guessed it,' Patri said as Alan outlined the circumstances leading up to his decision. 'My only comment is, why didn't you do it years ago? I love my sister, but I've never been blind to her faults. Rebekka and I often asked each other why you put up for so long with a marriage which seemed to have little more to it than sharing the same roof – and as often as not, not even that.'

Grateful for Patri's understanding, Alan went on to give him further commissions – a visit to his father, even if it meant going up to Strathinver to see him – to assure him Alan was all right; a transatlantic telephone call to New York to his mother to give her news.

'And last,' Alan said, his hands clenching at his sides, 'I want you to tell Uncle Jaime something for me. You'll be coming back to Spain, I take it?'

'I'll be back the first chance I get,' Patri said. 'What is it I have to tell Papá?'

Forcing himself to do so, Alan told him about Luis. As he came to the end of his account, he was biting his lips to keep from breaking down. Patri put both arms around him and hugged him, tears falling unchecked from his eyes. 'You did what had to be done – and Papá will understand, although he will be heartbroken, as I am, to hear that little Luis . . .' His voice broke. 'But at least Mariano was alive when you last saw him, and we can hope he'll survive.'

He drew back, wiping his eyes on his shirt-sleeve. 'Don't think about it, Alan. You have nothing at all with which to reproach yourself. On the contrary, you were very courageous. I'd have shirked it, like Mariano, poor chap.'

For a few days after he had made his confession and Patri had been escorted away by two Fascist guards to – hopefully – freedom, Alan felt better. But his dysentery returned, and in this weak state of health he began to fear anew for Sam's life. Fortunately the lad had been located and put in his cell and was undergoing daily interrogations from which he always returned bruised and bleeding.

'They know I am Jewish,' he told Alan desperately, 'although I did as you said and called myself Sam Coburn after I'd destroyed my papers. But sometimes when they're beating me, I don't know what I'm saying. I'm not sure I didn't tell them my real name. They're going to shoot me, aren't they?'

The boy's fear was all the more painful to Alan because he knew there was nothing he could do to help him. The following day, when the guards came to fetch Sam, he demanded to be allowed to go with him, but he was kicked to the ground and threatened with a beating if he continued to make a nuisance of himself.

When the boy returned, Alan did what he could to bathe his face, having saved some of his own precious water supply. Looking down at the bruised and bloody mouth, the dislocated jaw, he was reminded sickeningly once more of Luis. His impotence to save Sam from further torture tormented him, and what little sleep he managed to achieve was disturbed by horrifying nightmares.

When they came next day to fetch the boy, Alan made another futile attempt to intervene on his behalf, as a result of which he himself was taken outside and beaten unconscious.

Several hours passed before he was dragged to his feet and frog-marched to a room he had not been in before. His guard pushed him into a chair, and as Alan's head cleared he became aware of two civilians watching him. One of the two – a short, rotund figure wearing thick-lensed spectacles – stepped forward and peered closely at him. In a thick, guttural voice, he began to question Alan about Sam, his tone quiet but unmistakably menacing.

Alan's head and body ached intolerably from the beating. The dysentery had given him a fever, and his senses were swimming and at any moment, he thought, he would either vomit or faint. But at least his mind was quite clear as to the point of this interrogation. The Gestapo were hoping he would confirm their conviction that Sam was Jewish.

'I am not obliged to give you any information other than my name, rank and number,' Alan replied repeatedly. The man's voice rose and the questions became more personal.

'What is your relationship with this soldier? Does he mean

something special to you? Why do you seek to protect him? Are you a Jew-lover? What are you doing here in Spain? This is not your country . . .'

As the man became increasingly angry with Alan's stubborn silence, his voice rose almost to a scream. It occurred to Alan that these men had the power to kill him. One missing British prisoner amongst so many would not be particularly remarkable. As the interrogation continued, he wondered why they had not already shot Sam and why it was so necessary for them to have proof of the boy's Jewish origins.

They would not get their proof from him, Alan determined, as the Italian guard was ordered to hit him. He did so systematically and so weakened was Alan's physical condition that it was only a few minutes before he slumped in the chair unconscious. He was dragged back to his cell.

From that day on, Alan was subjected to many more such interviews, which always culminated in physical abuse. Vaguely, he was aware that Samuel Cohen was dead. According to his tormentors, the boy had finally confessed that his father was a Jew, thereby signing his own death warrant. The reasons for Alan's continued interrogation escaped him, for the questions no longer concerned the boy. He supposed they were simply trying to break him – to force him to talk. But by retreating from the sound of their voices and the ever-present pain of his body he knew he was inviolate, and after a week he no longer gave even his rank and name. Too weak to be sure of anything beyond the now obsessional need for silence, he spoke to no one, not even to his fellow prisoners who did what little they could to help him. He was led to the water tap, given his food, taken to the lavatory and to the compulsory Masses and parades. As far as was possible, he was protected from the inevitable bullying and pilfering that took place in the crowded prison.

Gradually his ability to retreat into his own world increased. He became unaware of his surroundings, of the drop in temperature as November gave way to December, and even of the fact that his interrogations had ceased. Bitterly cold, emaciated, little more now than a living skeleton, Alan was beyond reading or understanding Patri's letter telling him that help was on the way.

'You are looking very pretty, my dear!' Don Jaime remarked as Joscelin sat down beside him at the dinner table. 'You are far too thin, of course. We shall have to try to feed you up now you are home again.'

Home! In a way, the house here in Sevilla was the only home she had, Joscelin thought. It was almost unbelievable that eighteen years had passed since she had sat down to her first meal in the Montero household. How frightened she had been then of Doña Ursula's implacable face and how embarrassed by Eduardo's awkward attentions!

Joscelin glanced at Don Jaime's eldest son. Eduardo looked middle-aged, his hair receding and his body heavy with excess weight. Obviously as a civilian he had not suffered the same privations as the soldiers. He looked positively gross beside Patri. But then Patri had only recently returned from that horrible concentration camp where the prisoners had been close to starvation; where Alan . . .

Determinedly, she forced her attention back to Don Jaime. Despite his attempt to be jovial at this Christmas dinner, he looked old and drawn, and Joscelin was in no doubt that he was as conscious as she of the missing faces at the table. Of his five children who had been caught up in this senseless war, only one had so far come home, and not even his joy in Patri's return could make up for the absence of his favourite child, Cassy. The room seemed full of memories of her, despite the distracting laughter and excited chatter of the children. Joscelin could all too easily imagine Cassy at her father's side, her arms around his neck pleading with him: 'Papá, can we dance after dinner? Please, dearest Papá!'

At the far end of the table, Mercedes was remonstrating with one of her five children who was eating his roast turkey with his fingers. Rebekka was tucking a napkin into the neck of Ruth's party frock, and Lota was spoon-feeding the youngest of her brood of three.

His voice lowered, Don Jaime said suddenly to Joscelin: 'I have five granddaughters but not one of them can hold a candle to my Casilda. She was such a lovely child!' He drew a long, tremulous sigh. 'Ever since I received that letter from the editor of *The Globe*, I've felt in my bones that I won't ever see her again. She would have come home, wouldn't she, if that Fleming fellow had died?'

His dark eyes looked haunted, and Joscelin searched for words to give him the hope she herself did not believe existed. 'The editor only said he *presumed* Mr Fleming to be dead. The fact that he had not reported back to them since he left Zaragoza for Teruel is not proof of his death. Maybe he and Cassy are in prison, like Alan . . .'

She broke off abruptly, knowing that her voice would betray her own desperate fears for Alan's life. She had forced Patri to tell her the truth, although he had tried to keep the worst of the facts from her. Dear Patri! Only he and Rebekka knew the extent of her private torment, for there seemed little point in informing Don Jaime of Alan's decision to divorce Cassy. With Cris, Mariano and Cassy 'missing' – insofar as there had been no news of them for months now – Don Jaime had quite enough distress to contend with.

But her voice must have betrayed some of her anxiety, for now he said: 'I've been meaning to tell you, *niña*. I had a telephone call last night from a friend who informed me there is hope for another exchange of prisoners – one British for ten Italian. I'm going to do what I can to ensure that Alan is amongst them. Of course we've no idea yet when it will take place . . .'

He broke off as the sound of angry voices from the opposite end of the table interrupted his train of thought. Eduardo and Patri were involved in a furious argument in Spanish, their exchange of words too rapid for Joscelin to understand. But

Don Jaime was under no such disadvantage. Without warning, he pushed back his chair, rose to his feet and crashed his fist down on the tabletop.

The wine glasses shuddered, staining the snow-white tablecloth scarlet. One of the tall, gilded candlesticks toppled and was quickly righted by Rebekka. The tiered arrangement of brightly coloured flowers collapsed and Carmen's little girl began crying. The other children stared at their normally jovial grandfather in anxious astonishment.

'*This is the last time I am going to tell you,*' he thundered, his face crimson. 'I will *not* have the war mentioned once more in this house. Do you understand?'

Eduardo's mouth tightened. 'But Papá . . .'

'Be quiet, boy! *Cállate!* I am not interested in what you've got to say. *Dios mío!* Have I not enough to contend with without having my children at each other's throats?'

His voice softened fractionally as he stabbed his finger in Patri's direction.

'Although I understood your motives when you decided to go off and give your support to the government, and why you, Eduardo, and your brothers chose to support an alternative regime, it cut me to the heart to know that my children were fighting against each other. But we are not the only family who has been divided by our differing politics . . . and we are *still* a family. If you cannot tolerate each other's attitudes whilst you are beneath my roof, then I prefer that you stop coming here. Have you forgotten that it is Christmas Day – the birthday of a man who forgave even those who tormented Him as He died?'

He sat down heavily, as if his anger had drained his body of the strength he needed to support him. But his voice remained firm as he looked once more at his eldest son. 'Ever since Patricio came home, you have never lost an opportunity to deride him. I may not personally agree with his politics, but he acted as he thought right, and that is good enough for me. It is to be hoped that, when we have won this war, we shall not all prove as intolerant as you, Eduardo, or may God have mercy on half the population of our country. Meanwhile, I will remind you that we are mourning the loss of your brother, Luis, and since he died mercifully at the hands of a Republican you should be grateful that men like Patricio and your Cousin Alan were a part of the Popular Army.'

Eduardo was tight-lipped and chose to ignore the consoling hand Mercedes held out to him. Patri, however, rose to his feet and went round to his father's chair. 'Forgive me, Papá!' he said quietly. 'I give you my word I will not dispute the matter with Eduardo further.'

As he returned to his chair and one of the servants came forward to refill his wine glass, Joscelin saw that there were tears in Don Jaime's eyes. Impulsively, she reached out to touch his shoulder. 'Maybe the war will be over soon,' she said softly.

According to the newspapers, thousands of refugees were pouring out of Barcelona and the few remaining Catalonian cities still in Republican hands. Hoping to reach the safety of the camps that had been set up in France, the refugees were dying of hunger, exhaustion and from the bitter cold. Barcelona was expected to fall at the next Nationalist onslaught, so weakened were the defences. Madrid had not yet been taken, but the armies elsewhere were sweeping eastward.

Now that General Franco was in possession of two-thirds of the country, victory for the Nationalists seemed inevitable, and traitor though Joscelin felt to Patri's and Alan's cause, she found herself praying for a quick end to the war. Only then could she feel confident that Alan's release would be assured. The International Brigades had been withdrawn last month by governmental agreement, and all the British, other than those still in prison, had gone home. But for his capture, Alan too would be in England now . . . safe, alive! Don Jaime was doing his utmost to help, but it had taken him over a year to negotiate Patri's release and, judging by Patri's description of Alan's health, Joscelin knew he could not survive this length of time.

When the International Brigades were disbanded, the

doctor in charge of the hospital in Tarancón had suggested she should travel back by train with those patients well enough to leave the country. But so long as Alan was in Spain Joscelin would not leave, and when one of the American nurses had announced that she was going to hitch-hike to Valencia on a supply truck, Joscelin decided to go with her. She had heard that a refugee ship was at Valencia and would be stopping at Gibraltar on its way through the Straits bound for Mexico. On reaching Valencia, she was just in time to obtain a passage. On 1 December she had landed at Gibraltar and, using her British passport, talked her way into obtaining a permit enabling her to visit friends in Sevilla. Two weeks later she had walked unannounced into the Monteros' house, none too sure of the welcome she would receive from Don Jaime.

Sitting beside him now, Joscelin felt a surge of affection for the kindly, hospitable marqués who had welcomed her back as if she were truly one of his family. Her political leanings were of no importance to him. He was happy to see her, he said, and Rebekka in particular would be greatly comforted by the return of her dearest friend. As a Jewess, Rebekka had been living in constant fear of persecution by the racist element amongst the Fascist authorities. Fortunately, she was best known in Sevilla as the Señora Montero, and only a few close friends knew of her Jewish parentage. Nevertheless, she had been obliged to keep a very low profile, going out only when it was absolutely necessary. With Patri in prison, Don Jaime explained, his daughter-in-law had become deeply depressed, but now at long last, with her husband home, she was well again and Joscelin's return would doubtless complete her recovery.

Lota, too, had been overjoyed to see her. She was still in mourning following the death of her beloved Benito, who had been killed in the battle for Bilbao. For three months Lota had shut herself up in the house, so prostrated by grief that she had wished herself dead, she told Joscelin. Then Rebekka brought news of the chaos that was overwhelming the orphanage without Lota to take the necessary administrative decisions. Somehow she had pulled herself together and returned to her self-appointed task. She now worked tirelessly, and it provided a means of escape from the knowledge that she would never see her husband again. The only time Joscelin had seen her face light up with happiness was when Don Jaime informed her that work was about to begin on the school he was financing in one of the poorer districts of Sevilla, and where children from Lota's orphanage would receive an education. Amalia, now fifteen, was trying to persuade her father to allow her to become one of the teachers. The school was one of several projects for which he had donated large sums of money, knowing that this would enhance his standing with the new Fascist regime. He had been well aware that the right gesture to the right man could influence his request for Patri's release. He was currently negotiating a place on the board of one of his companies as an inducement to an ambitious fellow who could influence Alan's release.

Lota had sold the house she had shared with Benito and now lived permanently with her father. He was devoted to her three young children and particularly to her eight-year-old son, whom he took with him whenever he went to the Hacienda. The boy was almost as knowledgeable about bulls as his grandfather, Lota said proudly, and had shown great skill when Don Jaime had allowed him into the bullring at the Hacienda with one of the young calves. It was Lota's compensation that her eldest child had inherited not only his father's talent and ambition, but his looks too.

If Alan dies I have no child of his to live for, Joscelin thought, and her heart ached with regret. She looked at Patri, grinning as he joked with young Carlos but who was nevertheless still haggard and painfully thin; and, reminded of the condition Alan must be in, she was close to despair.

Ruth, who had not forgotten Joscelin after a two-year absence, scrambled onto her lap. Winding her arms around Joscelin's neck, she said: 'Do *you* think I'm pretty, Aunt

Joscelin? Ursula says I'm plain and that no one will *ever* want to marry me!'

Joscelin hugged her, knowing that the child was indeed plain but angry with Eduardo's daughter for her cruelty in saying so.

'There is a story about an ugly duckling who grew up and turned into a swan. I'll tell it to you at bedtime. When I was a little girl, my father told it to me. I was not at all pretty when I was your age, but my father said I must wait like the duckling until I was grown up. One day, when I was much older, someone I loved very much told me I *was* beautiful and asked me to marry him. So I shouldn't worry what Ursula says. I expect you'll get married long before she does!'

The small, serious face broke into a smile. 'I don't like her anyway – she's stupid!' Ruth said, and went to sit on the lap of her grandfather whom she adored.

Would everyone and everything contrive continually to bring Alan back into her thoughts? Joscelin asked herself. Was he thinking of her this Christmas Day? Would they celebrate Christmas in prison, sharing out the Red Cross parcels that had been hoarded for the occasion, as Patri had told her was done the previous year? When dinner was over, she must go to her room and write to Alan's father. The poor old man, now eighty years old, had been devastated by the news of his son's capture. Patri, who had seen Lord Costain in Strathinver, said he was very frail but doggedly determined not to die before he saw Alan again. The old man had inquired after Joscelin, but at the time Patri had had no news to give him other than that he supposed she was still nursing in the hospital at Tarancón. Lord Costain had sent a message in case Patri saw her when he returned to Spain – asking her to visit him when she got back to England. She would like to have seen him; to offer him what comfort she could; but whilst even a vestige of hope remained, she would not leave Spain until she knew Alan was safe.

'Don't lose hope, dearest Joss,' Rebekka said later that night as she came to Joscelin's room to say goodnight. 'There were many times when I cried myself to sleep thinking Patri might be dead. But when I woke in the morning, I realized that I had been silly to cry. If he'd been killed, I would have known it. Something deep inside me would have told me. You'd know, too, if anything awful had happened to Alan.'

Dry-eyed, Joscelin stared back at Rebekka's gentle, sympathetic face as she twisted the ring Alan had given her round and round her finger. The expression in her grey eyes was one of desperation.

'When Alan and I said goodbye after our last leave together, I too, thought that the kind of love existing between us would enable me to know if anything dreadful happened to him. But it's getting worse and worse these last few days. It's as if in one way he's very close to me, and yet at the same time I feel he is slipping away.'

She grasped Rebekka's hands and gripped them as if for strength. 'I want to believe he's all right. I want to believe he's coming back to me. *I have to believe it* – but in my heart of hearts I don't. I love him so very much, Rebekka . . . *so much that I can't face the truth.*'

Joscelin's voice dropped almost to a whisper as finally she expressed her fear. 'The truth is I know I shall never see him again. I know deep down inside me that Alan is already dead.'

CHAPTER THIRTY-FIVE

July–August 1939

'Government's got the wind up at last – and not before time either!' Lord Costain jabbed a forefinger at his copy of *The Times*.

Joscelin laid down her book and looked at the old man seated on the opposite side of the drawing room in Rutland Gate. He was peering at the printed page through a large magnifying glass – yet another sign of his advancing years. Now eighty-one, he was crippled by lumbago, and she had been astonished that he had undertaken the journey to London – a city he disliked at the best of times.

'Chamberlain's a damn fool!' Lord Costain continued. 'That bloody Hun means business. Last year it was Austria he wanted – and got! Now it's Czechoslovakia. Sold them down the river for a peace that's unlikely as a pug pointing a grouse!'

'You think the Prime Minister was wrong to make that pact with Hitler in Munich?' Joscelin asked.

Lord Costain regarded her over the top of his newspaper. 'Can't appease a low-class upstart like Hitler. Damned fellow means to take control of central and eastern Europe, and a piece of paper won't stop him! It'll be Poland next, despite him saying he only wants the corridor to Danzig. Now we've guaranteed Poland's integrity – God knows why! We've never had the slightest concern for her before. Of course there's going to be war! It's just a question of when.'

'Oh, no!' Joscelin murmured involuntarily. 'Not another one! The war in Spain has only been over for four months!'

Lord Costain cleared his throat. 'At least *he* won't be part of it!' he muttered, a hint of satisfaction in his voice belying the look of sadness in his watery blue eyes. 'Must be thankful for small mercies, eh?'

Joscelin's eyes filled with tears as she gazed at the thin, silent figure in the armchair by the window. Alan seemed happiest when he could stare out at the sky – or the trees. He was less restless by the window, sitting with his hands folded quietly in his lap when, as a rule, they would be twitching or one would grip the other so tightly that the knuckles shone white.

She felt a terrible despair. Ever since Alan had been brought back to the Monteros' house in Sevilla there had been so many hopes raised; and as many dashed. At first they had believed that rest, food, peace and the love with which they surrounded him would restore his mind as well as his body to normality. Don Jaime had brought in one doctor after another, each one making his own diagnosis – shell shock; amnesia; brain damage from some hidden fragment of metal or a heavy blow; the mind irreparably broken by the tortures he had undergone. But the X-rays had revealed no physical cause, and the partial improvement of his starved, emaciated body had done nothing to change the waking coma that was his life. His face was always expressionless, his eyes vacant as if he were living in another world; or as if he were dead! Yet Joscelin knew his brain was still alive. There was seldom a night when he did not cry out in his sleep. Sometimes in the day, too, he would suddenly gasp, breathe rapidly as if in a nightmare, his limbs twitching uncontrollably.

It was Don Jaime who had suggested that Joscelin should take Alan home to England. 'There will be no memories for him there of what happened to him in this country,' he said. 'His mother telephoned again yesterday, and she thinks if he can return to his home environment he might improve. She's arranging to take the first passage available to be with him.'

For a few weeks Joscelin had lived on hope – hope that Lady Costain would be able to achieve what she could not.

But Alan had regarded his mother with the same blank stare as he regarded Joscelin when she forced him to look at her; and none of the eminent specialists whom Lady Costain engaged to help him had been able to promise more than a remote chance that he might in time recover his lost faculties.

Time! Joscelin thought bitterly. It was now four long months during which Alan had been given every ounce of care and attention it was possible for a sick man to have, yet there had not been the tiniest hint of improvement. Alan had withdrawn into a world of his own. It nearly broke her heart to look at him – the man she had despaired of ever seeing again; the man who was her whole life. But if her heart was close to breaking, her spirit was not, and she knew that she would never leave him. For as long as her life continued she would stay with him; caring for his physical needs; showing him in the few limited ways she could that she loved him as deeply as ever.

Now, in the heat of this summer's July, Alan's father had travelled down to London to take him back to Scotland.

'Never did think this town was healthy – no decent air to breathe. The boy will do better up north. Do you good, too, young lady. Put a bit of colour in your cheeks.'

Maybe Lord Costain was right, and the peace and tranquillity of his Scottish home would be better for Alan than London, where it was hot and noisy and the air was filled with fumes from cars, buses, smoking chimneys. It offered a last tiny ray of hope – and hope was fast diminishing as day after day Alan continued to live in a world apart. Now that his body was restored to health he could walk again – albeit a slow shuffle. When taken to a basin and given soap, he would wash his hands; given his hairbrush, he would smooth back his hair. Like an automaton, he put food in his mouth, dressed and undressed – but only when urged to do so. The specialist looked upon these minor achievements as hopeful in that Alan was at least responding to suggestion, and his brain could not therefore be irreparably damaged. Memory of some kind survived.

'I hear they're letting women into the Air Force – and the

Royal Navy. Next thing we'll be having *you* in uniform, my girl!'

Lord Costain's eyes twinkled behind his pince-nez, but Joscelin could not share his amusement.

'I can't bear to think about another war,' she said quietly. 'I keep remembering all the wounded I nursed.'

Nor could she bear to be reminded of Cassy, she thought, tears stinging her eyes. Even Don Jaime had accepted that his beloved daughter and Milton Fleming must both be dead; otherwise one or other of them would have got word to him when the war ended. How sad Alan would be if he knew that Cassy had disappeared along with so many others. There *were* benefits to his illness. At least he was protected from knowing how many had not returned from the war – Luis, Benito; poor Monty Piermont; his comrades-in-arms.

Abruptly, Lord Costain changed the topic of conversation. 'Heard that young fool Edward took his wife to dinner at the German Embassy in Paris,' he commented. 'Damn good thing he abdicated. That American female is a bad influence. The boy would have made a rotten king – too weak, that's his trouble. Stanley Baldwin was quite right – the country would never have accepted a divorcee as queen – Queen of England, dammit! Now we shall have to see what sort of king Bertie will make. At least he has that nice young wife Elizabeth to back him up. Good Scottish blood there! A pity the children are both girls. I remember how disappointed I was when Pamela produced two daughters – thought I'd never get an heir! Then along came Alan . . .'

He broke off, his gaze returning to his son. Hurriedly, Joscelin went over to Lord Costain and laid an arm comfortingly around his shoulders. 'He will get better! You mustn't give up hope. I never will!'

The old man cleared his throat and reached up a shaky hand to pat Joscelin's cheek. 'Silly young pup should have married you in the first place – always said so. Bit late now for grandchildren, eh? I'd have liked one or two in my old age.'

Joscelin attempted a smile. 'You've got several grandchildren, Uncle Angus, Barbara's Ernesto and the girls Nicola and Nancy; and there's Isobel's Heinrich . . .'

'Don't you mention that boy to me, my girl. The day he ran away from that school of his I disowned him – cut him out of my will. Isobel and that husband of hers should never have allowed him to go back to Germany. She wrote the other day to say he was doing his damnedest to get into the army. Wants to fight for Hitler's "brave new world".'

'Poor Isobel!' Joscelin said. 'I suppose her loyalties must be horribly divided. Rupert doesn't want to leave Germany and yet she must hate living there. Now that Heinrich's home, she can't even be of help to the wretched Jews. She manages to get letters out occasionally to Patricio and Rebekka.'

The old man did not respond. As so often happened nowadays, he had suddenly nodded off to sleep. With a sigh, Joscelin went back to the window and for a long moment stared down at Alan's face. He seemed to be watching a small group of pigeons on the roof of a house further down the road. Were his eyes focused on the birds, she wondered? Perhaps tomorrow she would take him to Trafalgar Square to see if he reacted to the clouds of pigeons there. But immediately she rejected the idea. There would be too much noise – the roar of the traffic as likely to distress Alan as did any noise, like the slamming of a door; the shrilling of the telephone bell; the hoot of a car horn. Worst of all had been his obvious panic when a summer storm had broken and there had been a series of loud thunderclaps.

'Oh, Alan, my love!' she whispered, kneeling beside him and laying her head on his lap. 'Please come back! Don't you understand how much I need you?'

She would, she thought, exchange all that was left of her life to see his head turn, his eyes meet hers, any sign that he was listening to her and that he understood. But he showed no more recognition of her than he did of old Gibson who came shuffling into the room.

'Teatime already, Gibson?' Joscelin said, rising to her feet.
'It's four o'clock, Miss Joscelin. M'lord doesn't like it served any later.'

'Of course! Gibson, Lord Costain has suggested we take Mr Alan back to Scotland. What do you think? I'm not sure if the journey would be too much for him.'

Gibson's eyes went to Alan's motionless figure. There was a look of great affection – and pity – in them.

'I don't see as how it would do him any harm, Miss Joscelin. It's not as if he's been wounded – or gassed – is it? Not like some as came back from our war . . . physical wrecks. Mr Alan puts me in mind of Mr Fergus. I did hear that he was near as normal nowadays – except for living wild, of course.' He nodded his head several times, lost in thought, and then added: 'War's a nasty business – not fitting for young gentlemen brought up soft, if you know what I mean, miss. Out of their depths mostly. Good manners and decent behaviour don't count for much when you've got to stick a bayonet in the enemy's guts, begging your pardon, miss.'

A smile touched the corners of Joscelin's mouth. Obviously no one had told Gibson that she knew all about war – had seen unimaginable horrors. 'You've remembered Lord Costain's cherry cake,' she said. 'He particularly asked for it. Thank you, Gibson!'

The old butler should long since have retired, Joscelin thought, but who would replace him? There had been only a caretaking staff at Rutland Gate since Alan had gone off to fight in Spain, and most of the servants had found better jobs for themselves in industry. Would this magnificent house ever see a return to its old glory, she wondered? It was difficult to recall the dazzling lights, the flowers, the bustle and sense of life and laughter that were once the soul of this big, empty mansion. She, Lord Costain and Alan were little more than ghosts from the past – like Gibson. Yet *his* memories went even further back than her own – to the war in the Sudan when Uncle Fergus had been a casualty just as Alan was now.

Her hand remained poised above the teacups as her mind registered the half-formulated idea Gibson's reminiscences had awakened. Uncle Fergus! *He* would tell them what to do to help Alan! He might have a herbal remedy that would activate Alan's brain! He had saved old Bess's life when no trained vet could do so, and the lives of countless other animals for which there seemed no hope. He himself had been thought by the doctors to be beyond recovery when he returned from the Sudan. Of all the people in the world, *he* was the one who would understand what had happened to Alan . . . and know how to treat him.

Joscelin gave no outward indication of her excitement as she accompanied Lord Costain and Alan up to Scotland. It was as if she dared not mention this new avenue of hope lest talking about it might somehow lessen the chances of success. But as they crossed the border into Scotland and Lord Costain woke from his doze to view the countryside he loved, she found herself wondering if perhaps he secretly shared her hope; that this was why he had come to London – to take Alan back to his brother.

The thought added to her excitement and brought so much colour to her cheeks that Lord Costain remarked: 'There now, you're looking better already, my girl!'

But Alan was so obviously fatigued by the long journey that there was no question of taking him to see his uncle for at least two days after their arrival at Strathinver. Joscelin went for long walks across the moors trying to work off some of her nervous tension. On the third morning, she told Alan's manservant to have him dressed and ready to go out as soon as he had had his breakfast. Saying nothing to Lord Costain of her intent, she ordered Lockhart to bring round the governess cart.

Despite all her warnings to herself not to expect too much from Alan, Joscelin felt the first tinge of disappointment as Lockhart took them down the rough track towards Lochinver. Alan looked neither to the left nor to the right, and his expression did not change as they drove through the pine forest. She realized she had been ridiculous to suppose that these favourite old haunts of his would evoke some memory, and prepared herself for his failure even to recognize Uncle Fergus.

She herself had no difficulty in recognizing him, although he had aged quite markedly in the past four years. His hair and beard were snow-white, the broad back stooped and hunched as he came out of his croft to meet them. The brilliant blue of his eyes had faded; but the smile of welcome was still there. He nodded at Joscelin, then at Lockhart, and finally stared silently at Alan.

In a sudden rush of words Joscelin began to explain, but he put up a hand to silence her. 'Aye, I know all about it!' he said softly.

With Lockhart's help, they assisted Alan down from the governess cart. Uncle Fergus led the way to the seat outside his front door.

'You don't seem surprised to see us!' Joscelin remarked.

'Had a feeling you'd turn up today!' he said simply. 'Knew Angus had gone to London to bring the boy back here.'

A young hind came out of the shadow of the trees surrounding the clearing and hobbled towards them. One of its delicate back legs was splinted. It walked with difficulty but without fear as it approached Uncle Fergus. He felt in the pocket of his shabby jacket and brought out some carrots which the deer munched unhurriedly, its dark, liquid brown eyes flickering from Joscelin to Alan with half-hearted caution.

'*Can you make Alan better?*' The question stuck in Joscelin's throat and she was obliged to ask it a second time. Now the words came pouring from her, as did her tears, although she was not aware of them.

'It's as if he doesn't want to get well!' she cried. 'As if he doesn't want to go on living! I can't bear it. He just stares and stares but he doesn't see anything. Uncle Fergus, I love him. I want him to be well again. No one seems to know what's wrong, but I think Alan himself *wants* to be like this. It's easier than living and having to remember. *Can* you help him?'

Uncle Fergus drew a torn handkerchief from another of his capacious pockets and handed it to Joscelin. 'He can bide here with me awhile. We'll see!' He turned to look directly into Joscelin's eyes. 'Can't promise – wouldn't be fair. Might never get better!'

'Oh, no!' Uncle Fergus's words were so very much the opposite from what she had hoped to hear. 'Never?' she repeated brokenly.

'Mebbe not! Mebbe you should leave him here with me, and try to forget about him. You've a right to your life. You might never have one – with him!'

Joscelin stared at the old man aghast. 'You mustn't say that. I love him. I don't want a different life without him. Nothing in the world matters but Alan. Even if he doesn't get better, I shall spend the rest of my life with him . . .'

Joscelin reached out and caught hold of Uncle Fergus's hand. She clung to it as if to a lifeline. 'You've got to try!' she said urgently. 'You've got to. Please?'

He nodded, his gaze lingering once more on Alan. He had not moved, and if he had seen the hind he gave no sign of it. His body was motionless, his hands clasped as always in his lap.

'You want Alan to stay here with you?' she asked slowly.

He nodded again. 'Tell Angus I'll take care of him. Poor Angus!'

Yes, Joscelin thought, she had been too busy pitying herself to feel sorry for Alan's father. He must be suffering as much as she – Alan, his only son and his heir.

'I'll come and see him – every day!' she said, knowing that she could not bear this agony in her heart much longer. 'May I, Uncle Fergus?'

For the third time he nodded, rising to his feet when she did and walking with her to the edge of the clearing where Lockhart stood waiting with the pony and cart. Wordless now,

Joscelin climbed into the seat, willing herself not to look at Alan sitting motionless as ever, unaware of and uncaring of the fact that she was leaving.

I won't look at him! she vowed, but as Lockhart touched his whip to the pony's flanks her head turned involuntarily. Now, however, her eyes were blinded by tears. Vaguely, she saw Uncle Fergus seat himself beside Alan. Through a haze she saw him reach out as if to take Alan in his arms. But she could not be sure. The sunshine was bathing them in a golden light, but there were shadows too from the tall pine trees. The scent of pine needles filled the air and suddenly Joscelin was reminded of Spain. Last summer – one short summer ago – she had been in Tarancón wondering if the fighting would ever end; wondering what had happened to Cassy; wondering most of all where Alan was.

She had now accepted that her dearest friend had died somewhere in one of those olive groves; on a hilltop; in a ravine. Beautiful, brave, adventurous Cassy! It hurt to think of her gone for always. It was easier to pretend that she was still somewhere in the world, laughing, flirting, dancing, having 'fun'.

The routine of Joscelin's days now settled into a regular pattern. In the mornings she took Lord Costain for his 'constitutional', as he called his walk round the gardens.

In the afternoon, Joscelin drove herself to the croft. Each time she neared the clearing, her hopes would begin to stir. Perhaps Alan was a little better? Perhaps he had smiled? Spoken one word? Perhaps . . .

But Alan was unchanged. He was always in the same place on the wooden bench, his eyes looking vaguely skywards. Uncle Fergus would be somewhere near at hand, sawing logs, building one of his many nesting boxes that were nailed up on every surrounding tree trunk. As the summer days went by, the splint was taken off the little deer's hind leg and she disappeared back into the forest. A young otter had taken her place, one leg amputated by the steel jaws of a trap. Uncle

Fergus worried about the animal. The stump was not healing as it should. He dressed it twice a day whilst Alan held it. The grasp was instinctive and he never looked at it.

Uncle Fergus wouldn't let Joscelin hope that even this small gesture was a sign of improvement. Whenever she could muster the courage, she would ask him outright if Alan was even a tiny bit better. Each time, he shook his head.

But physically, she realized, Alan had improved. The long hours out of doors in the sunshine had tanned his face to a golden brown. His hair had bleached and now shone with good health. When he moved, his legs seemed stronger. His hands were less skeletal and were brown like his face.

She stayed until evening, leaving only because she knew Lord Costain would miss her company at the dinner table and fret that harm had come to her out on the moors alone. Their conversation was always the same – the old man asking about Alan, Joscelin striving to keep the disappointment from her voice when she informed him there had been no progress.

'Think I'll go and see the boy for m'self tomorrow,' he said at the end of a fortnight. 'See Fergus too. You can tell Lockhart we'll need him tomorrow after lunch.'

Joscelin was glad to have the old man's company. He at least would be someone to talk to on her lonely ride back to the castle with her spirits at their lowest ebb. But she suspected that Lord Costain, like herself, nurtured secret hopes that Alan would get better and would feel the disappointment as keenly as she did when such visits revealed no improvement.

For once, the sky was overcast as Lockhart drove them to the clearing. Summer, Lord Costain commented, was nearly over. There was an autumnal nip in the air.

'Extraordinary how time flies when you get to my age. When Fergus and I were boys, the summer holidays seemed to last for ever! Suppose you'll want to go back to London soon if Alan . . . not much point in staying, I dare say. Though you *can* if you wish. Damned if I don't enjoy your company!'

Joscelin regarded him gratefully. 'I don't want to leave,' she said simply. 'Not even if . . . if Alan doesn't get better. I'm sure that this is the right place for him to be. He always said he loved Scotland better than anywhere else in the world.'

'Did he now?' Lord Costain looked pleased.

'I wonder how Uncle Fergus is getting on with his otter?' Joscelin changed the conversation. 'He was worried about it yesterday. I suppose *you* think it would be better dead!' she added with a smile.

'Wring its neck – confounded scavengers, otters! Poach the salmon and trout a damned sight better than the crofters. Fergus had best not put it back in one of my rivers if it survives!'

But there seemed no likelihood of it doing so. As Lockhart drew up outside the croft, Uncle Fergus remained seated beside Alan, nodding an absent-minded greeting as he nursed the sick animal.

Joscelin went to kneel beside him. 'Is it very ill?' she asked. 'Will it die?'

Again Uncle Fergus nodded. The animal's heartbeat was rapid and it was drawing breath with difficulty. 'Humph! Better let Lockhart put it out of its misery!' Lord Costain said. 'Kindest thing to do, Fergus, old chap, eh?'

For a moment, the men's eyes met and they held each other's gaze. Then Uncle Fergus nodded. He lifted the limp body and held it momentarily against his cheek before placing it in his brother's hands. 'Thank you,' he said. 'Couldn't do it myself!'

As Lord Costain called to Lockhart, Joscelin rose to her feet. In the drama of the moment she had not yet kissed Alan's cheek, as she always did on her arrival. She bent over him and pressed her mouth against his warm skin. As she did so, she tasted salt on her lips, salt that could only have come from his tears.

Her breath caught in her throat. She took a step backwards and stared at him. His eyes were not regarding her but were following Lockhart's back as he disappeared into the shadows of the forest. There was an expression in them of unutterable sadness.

'Oh, Alan darling, don't be unhappy!' she whispered. 'Don't cry, please, I can't bear it! Your father is right – the otter won't suffer any more now. Alan? Alan?'

Tears were streaming down her own cheeks as she stared wordlessly at Uncle Fergus.

'There's no pain with death – only with life,' he murmured. 'Let the boy feel pain. It means he's alive again.'

'But he doesn't know me – he doesn't recognize me!' Joscelin cried. 'Won't he *ever* know me, Uncle Fergus? Oh, Alan, it's me, Joss, and I love you so very much.'

Alan neither looked at her nor reached out a hand to touch her. His eyes had resumed their vacant stare at the sky and it was as if the little otter had neither lived nor died.

But Uncle Fergus was smiling. His voice rang in her head: '*Let the boy feel pain. It means he's alive again.*' Hope sprang from his words, and not least of all because on Alan's cheek there was the lingering trace of a tear.

A compelling historical tale of love and tragedy from bestselling novelist Claire Lorrimer.

Clementine Foster is young, innocent, and wildly in love with Deveril – a man who doesn't even know she exists. When, one golden summer night, she steps in front of his horse, he takes her with all the drunken arrogance of a young aristocrat used to having whatever he wants. The repercussions of doing so are to create bonds of hate, love, and tragedy in both their lives.

Clementine bears a son to Deveril as a result of their reckless night – and, according to the law, he has the right to take the child from her if he so chooses. What he doesn't realise is that Clementine is prepared to fight for her son...whatever the cost.

'Matchless story telling'
Yorkshire Post

'Unashamedly romantic and enjoyable'
Evening Telegraph

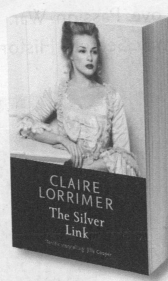

CLAIRE
LORRIMER

The Silver
Link

A sweeping historical tale of family, passion and love from
bestselling novelist Claire Lorrimer.

Until her father's death, Adela Carstairs lives in a secure and
loving home. Then her mother remarries a cruel and hard-
drinking man, and any happiness Adela has left is shattered.
With her younger brother and sister, Adela is forced to flee
her new stepfather's drunken rages. They escape to London
where they seek refuge in the squalor of the back streets.
Addie's desperate hope is that her childhood companions, the
handsome Mallory twins Titus and Barnaby, will find and
rescue them.

Turbulent times lie ahead, and all three siblings find themselves
caught up in the danger and terror of revolutionary France. It is
then that the link between the twins – and Addie's growing love
for one of them – is truly put to the test.

'The perfect holiday read'
Yorkshire Post

Love. Passion. War.
Family. Secrets. History.

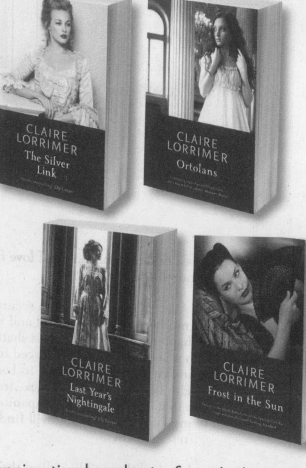

Stunning timeless classics from the bestselling novelist Claire Lorrimer.

Available in paperback and ebook.

HODDER